BLAIZE

BLAIZE

also by Anne Melville

THE LORIMER LINE

ALEXA

BLAIZE

Anne Melville

DOUBLEDAY & COMPANY, INC.
GARDEN CITY, NEW YORK
1981

The characters in this book are entirely fictitious and any resemblance to actual persons living or dead is coincidental.

ISBN: 0-385-14832-1
Library of Congress Catalog Card Number 79-8936

Contents

THE LORIMER LINE

Brinsley
William
John

Matthew — Rascal Mattison — Red

Samuel

Alexander

John Junius m. Georgiana Wells (1800-1879)

Luisa Rent (1852-1886)

Frank Davidson (1885-1906)   Alexa m. Piers Glanville (1857-)

William (1850-1909) m. Sophie Garratt (1853-1913)   Margaret m. Charles Scott (1857-)   Claudine (1859-)   Chelsea (1870-)   Ralph m. Lydia Morton (1860-)

Matthew (1873-)   Beatrice (1877-)   Arthur (1878-)

Robert (1894-)

Jean-Claude (1878-)   Marie (1906-)

Duke (1886-)   Harley (1913-)

Kate (1891-)   Brinsley (1893-)   Mary (1895-1902)   Alexander (1897-1902)   Grant (1905-)

Frisca (1907-)   Lucy (b.&d. 1911)   Pirry (1913-)

(handwritten annotations: Begin the Line, Jennifer, Barbara, John, Bernard, Piers, Pitt, Asha, Rosamund, Ilsa, m.)

BOOK ONE

The Lorimers at War

PART I

WAR

(1914–1918)

1914

1

The darkness of war had spread across Europe, but at Blaize, Lord Glanville's country house on the bank of the Thames, the chandeliers glittered as brightly as though the world for which they had been made could expect to endure forever. Yet the ballroom they illuminated on this October evening was empty, and no sound disturbed the silence of the old house. It was the moment within the eye of a cyclone when the rushing wind suddenly holds its breath in an unnatural calm. The storm was just about to break.

For three days Kate Lorimer had looked on with admiration as the household bustled with activity—preparing for the ball which would celebrate her brother Brinsley's twenty-first birthday at the home of their aunt and uncle, Lord and Lady Glanville. The idea that dancing and dining and drinking and flirting were unsuitable activities for a country at war was not one which was likely to occur to either the hosts or the guests tonight. England was fighting to preserve the values of a civilised society against the clumsy aggressions of a decaying Austrian empire and a brash new German army and navy. Already young men were dying on the battlefields of France. It was necessary that gestures should be made, gestures of gaiety and defiance, to show that a way of life could not so easily be killed.

Amidst all the preparations of the past few days only one small concession had been made to the fact that England was at war. The fragile silk curtains, intended to drape decoratively at the sides of the ballroom windows rather than to cover them, had been stored away. Their replacements were made of a heavier fabric which would prevent any light from being seen outside. It was unlikely that a Zeppelin would waste its explosive load on an isolated country house when the whole city of London, further down the Thames, offered so much more tempting a target. But it seemed sensible to remove even the slightest cause for unease.

Not until midnight would the party supper be served to the guests, so the members of the family who were staying at Blaize had assembled for a light meal earlier in the evening. Most of them now had retired to their rooms for a brief rest or last-minute adjustment of hair or gown. Kate was alone as, dressed for the ball, she wandered through the suddenly silent house. The heavy doors of the banqueting hall were closed. With the secret pleasure of a child opening her Christmas stocking too early, she let herself into the hall so that she could inspect the tables set for the buffet.

The sumptuous display represented the culmination of a month of planning and several days of feverish effort. A patisseur had been brought from London. Out of spun sugar he had fashioned exotic birds and butterflies, creating a feast as much for the eye as for the palate. The wives of Lord Glanville's tenants, tying their aprons and rolling up their sleeves, had augmented the normal kitchen staff in a heroic baking of breads and tarts and hams. A last-minute whipping of cream and the dextrous dressing of cutlets in paper collars had been preceded by two days of steaming endeavour in which the kitchen hobs and ovens were organised with military precision. Lobsters boiled in cauldrons, salmon simmered in fish kettles and suckling pigs turned on spits which, although rarely used, had been maintained in good order for three hundred years.

When it was cold, the food had been arranged on Jacobean banqueting dishes to be glazed and decorated. Sixteenth-century refectory tables were covered with eighteenth-century lace cloths. Waterford glass sparkled with the light reflected off highly polished Queen Anne silver. Starched drawn-thread napkins were piled beside stacks of Waterloo plates, each hand-painted with a different scene from the Duke of Wellington's battles. It was a measure of the secure foundations of Lord Glanville's heritage, as

well as the extent of his wealth, that although it had been necessary to transport a certain amount of china and glass to the country from Glanville House in Park Lane, there had been no need
to hire a single piece.

By now all the preparations were complete. In less than an
hour, as the first carriage or motorcar drew up outside the door,
the inhabitants of Blaize would begin to move in their appointed
tracks like wound-up clockwork figures waiting only for a lever to
be pressed. Lord and Lady Glanville would appear to greet their
guests, footmen would step forward, maids would hurry along
cold back corridors. But now the house was as quiet as though it
were uninhabited. The housekeeper had come from her hall, the
cook from her kitchens, and the butler from his pantry to inspect
the ballroom and the buffet for the last time and, satisfied in
their own spheres, had retreated downstairs again. Blaize was at
peace.

Moving along the table, Kate reached forward to pick out a
cherry from a huge punch bowl and caught sight of her own
reflection in the gleaming silver. Even distorted by the curve of
the vessel, the face it showed her was familiar—freckled and
green-eyed, with wide, strong eyebrows and cheekbones and a generous mouth—but it seemed to be attached to the body of a
stranger. In a way she felt herself at this moment to be as
artificial a creation as the swan which had been made out of me-
ringue or the miniature trees whose fruit, on close inspection,
proved to be not apples but sweetmeats. With the help of her
aunt's maid she had been laced into a corset which constricted
her sturdy waist, and buttoned into a balldress whose shot silk
matched her sea-green eyes. She had refused to wear even the
discreetest cosmetics, but had allowed the maid to pile her long,
thick hair—the tawny colour of a lion's mane, and almost as unmanageable—elaborately high on her head. The strain of maintaining this edifice upright caused her to stand even straighter
than usual.

This effect of stateliness was not one which came naturally to
Kate. She had only recently qualified as a doctor, and her years of
hard work as a medical student had allowed her little time for society entertainments of this kind. In any case, she had no taste

for them as a rule. But she and her brother Brinsley were very
close. She was anxious that he should not be ashamed of his
sister's appearance in this celebration of his birthday.

Kate turned away from her study of the buffet tables, licking
her fingers, and found that she herself had been under observation. Brinsley rose from the window seat of one of the mullioned
windows of the Tudor hall and stepped down to take her hands.

"You really do look absolutely ripping, Kate," he said. "I like
the dress."

"You should have said that before, when Aunt Alexa was listening. It's the one she gave me two years ago for my own
twenty-first. It makes me feel a little like Cinderella—as though
at midnight the clock will chime and all these trappings will
disappear. But I must return the compliment. You look absolutely ripping yourself."

Brinsley was wearing his new second lieutenant's uniform, still
as smartly pressed as when the tailor first delivered it. But he had
made no attempt to sleek down the exuberant curls of his golden
hair in the approved military style, and his eyes sparkled with
high spirits which were equally unsubdued.

"You approve, then?" he asked.

"Oh yes, very smart," said Kate. "How I wish that Mother and
Father could see you. You must have a photograph taken to send
to them. They'll be thinking of you at this moment and wishing
you were with them."

"Could we take a walk?" asked Brinsley abruptly. "Would you
be too cold?"

"I'll fetch a wrap." Kate was strong, and normally unmindful
of the weather. But her balldress was cut low at both back and
front and she guessed she would feel the chill as soon as she
moved away from the blazing log fires of the house.

She took Brinsley's arm as, a few minutes later, they made their
way down the stone steps and strolled towards the river. Had the
war not imposed a need for darkness, their aunt Alexa would certainly have ordered the carriage drive to be illuminated with oil
lamps, the front of the ancient house to be decorated with
coloured lights, and spotlights to be fixed on the roof to pick out
the twisting patterns of the sixteenth-century brick chimneys. As

it was, a full moon provided a romantic substitute for all these. The woodland paths along which Kate and Brinsley wandered were dappled with the moving shadows of the trees, but were lit clearly enough for them to move without hesitation.

For a little while neither of them spoke. Kate guessed that Brinsley, like herself, would be thinking of their parents and of their childhood home in Jamaica. Hope Valley, the village community in which their mother worked as a doctor and their father, a Baptist missionary, as pastor, had been Brinsley's home until he was sent to England for his schooling. Kate had remained longer with her parents in the West Indies, but her wish to become a doctor like her mother had been so strong that when she was eighteen she too had been allowed to go to England to study.

The past five years had been satisfying ones for Kate, but she guessed that her parents must often have been lonely without their two elder children—for two of their other children had died in infancy and the youngest, still living at home, was a cripple. On this evening in particular they would be upset not to have Brinsley with them. Kate knew that her brother, coming down from Oxford in June without distinction but without disgrace, and then enjoying two leisurely months of playing county cricket, had planned to set sail for Jamaica in September, ready to celebrate his coming-of-age in his old home.

Two shots in a Sarajevo street were to change the lives of a whole generation. A birthday party in Jamaica was hardly a significant casualty. Brinsley had shown no interest in politics, and Kate felt sure that the rapid exchange of declarations of war across Europe must have taken him by surprise. Both at school and at university, however, he had been a member of the Officers' Training Corps, so he was one of the first to volunteer and to be commissioned. Now he was awaiting the summons to join his regiment, and it could not be very much longer delayed.

Their walk brought them to the bank of the River Thames. The moon, escaping from the net of the trees, was brighter here, reflecting in the broad band of water which scarcely rippled on this calm night as it swept steadily towards the sea. Peaceful and powerful at the same time, the movement hypnotised them into stillness at first. Then Kate surprised herself by laughing at an incongruous thought. Brinsley's questioning look made it necessary to explain.

"I was thinking, if we were in Hope Valley, we'd both have sat down on the bank of the stream without giving it a second thought."

"When we lived in Hope Valley we were both shabby, all the time," said Brinsley. "No beautiful balldress to be spoiled by mud or grass stains."

"And no elegant uniform." It was true that in Jamaica they had been allowed to run wild. Their mother had cared nothing for her own appearance and felt no need to dress her own children more smartly than those of her patients. In a tropical village, clothes were required for decency but not for either warmth or fashion. "All the same, this birthday would have been a very special day for Mother and Father. They must be disappointed that you're so far away."

"Yes. I'm sorry about that, of course." Brinsley sighed, but almost at once Kate heard the regret in his voice giving way to excitement. "But I don't really feel ready to settle down at home yet. I can't pretend that the prospect of acting as a kind of farm manager for the rest of my life is a very jolly one."

Kate knew what he meant. Their father performed all the spiritual duties which his black congregation required of their pastor; but he was a man of great energy and ability, and early in his pastorate he had been so shocked by the poverty of the villagers that he had organised them into an agricultural labour force. Whipped on by his passionate oratory, they had reclaimed a derelict plantation next to the village, and now the efficient running of the estate had become Ralph Lorimer's chief enthusiasm. Since Brinsley had never shown any bent towards any other profession, it was taken for granted that he would return to help his father manage the plantation. Kate laughed affectionately now at her brother's lack of eagerness.

"What would you rather do instead?" she asked.

"Oh, nothing in particular. Anything that would leave me time to play a little cricket. I shall have to settle down to work sometime, I can see that—and I know I'm lucky to have a family business on offer. All the same, I'm in no hurry to start. A few months of adventure will be just the thing."

Kate glanced across and saw that his eyes were alive with excitement at the prospect. For her own part, she had wanted to be a doctor for as long as she could remember. She had always known that years of hard work would be needed to attain her ambition; and although her mother's generation had borne the brunt of the fight against prejudice and prohibition which had for so long made it impossible for women to become doctors at all, Kate had appreciated that determination as well as study would be required. Her social conscience and serious approach to life made her temperamentally the opposite of her brother, but her affection for him made it easy for her to sympathise with his light-hearted lack of ambition.

All the same, it was difficult not to wonder how "jolly" he would find the next few months. Kate's own vocation was to heal, and she would have been appalled if she had ever found herself expected to take life instead of preserving it. Nor was she absolutely clear why it was so necessary for England to become involved in the war at all. Who were the Serbs, and why should the assassination of an Austrian archduke be of more than local importance? Brinsley had done his best to persuade her that now the war had started it ought to be won quickly; and the best way to win it quickly was to send as many soldiers as possible to fight in France, and with the greatest possible speed. It was certainly obvious to Kate that if the finest young men were required, Brinsley was one of them; but she could not help wondering whether Brinsley himself—although ready and indeed eager to fight—had recognised that at some moment he would have to kill.

The thought worried her, but it was not appropriate to this evening of celebration. Still holding Brinsley's arm, she turned away from the river.

"Time you were on parade at Blaize," she suggested. "They won't be able to start without the guest of honour." They began to walk slowly up the hill towards the house.

"You really do look stunning, Kate." Whatever Brinsley had

been thinking about down by the river, it was clearly not the prospect of killing Germans. "It's a pity I'm not older than you."

"Why?"

"Because a lot of chaps like to marry other chaps' sisters."

"It must be quite difficult to avoid doing so," Kate laughed.

"Oh, come on, you know what I mean. The sisters of their friends. But of course all my friends are too young for you. You and I should have been born the other way round."

"It's kind of you to offer me all your fellow-undergraduates and fellow-cricketers, even if you do promptly snatch the offer back again. But I haven't spent all these years training as a doctor just to give up without making use of my qualifications. I don't intend to marry anyone, whether older or younger."

"There's nothing to say you'd have to stop being a doctor just because you got married," Brinsley protested.

"How many of these friends of yours would allow their wives to work?" Kate asked him. "And how many female doctors do you know who are married?"

"I only know three female doctors altogether," said Brinsley. "One is you, and it's you I'm trying to persuade. One is Mother, and *she's* married."

"Fortunately for our own reputations." Kate was still laughing. "But she's married to a missionary. Missionaries' wives are a special case."

"And there's Aunt Margaret. She was married as well."

"Aunt Margaret is another special case." Kate was silent for a moment, thinking affectionately of their father's elder sister, who had provided a home for Brinsley and herself when they each in turn left Jamaica for England. Dr. Margaret Scott was as dear to both the young Lorimers as their own mother, but no one could pretend that her life had followed the normal pattern of a Victorian woman.

"She didn't marry when she first qualified," Kate pointed out now. "She worked as a doctor until she was in her mid-thirties. And when she did marry, she stopped working."

"That was so that she could have a baby."

"She stopped working," repeated Kate. "The only reason why she went back to being a doctor was because her husband died and she had to support the baby. She wasn't married for more than a few months out of the whole of her life. You can't argue from Aunt Margaret. And if I may say so, it's very *arrogant* of men to think that the only thing in life a woman wants is a husband."

"It may be arrogant, but you have to admit that it's very often true."

"Well, perhaps I can understand it being true of other women, because they can all long to get their hands on a gorgeous creature called Brinsley Lorimer. But since I'm disqualified from that privilege, I hope you'll allow me to get quietly on with my doctoring."

They stepped out of the woodland as they spoke, and paused for a moment to stare in admiration at Blaize. The two wings which had been added to the old house in the reign of William and Mary provided the more comfortable rooms for normal living, but the Tudor structure in the centre of the mansion was the perfect setting for any grand occasion. As soon as it became clear that Brinsley would not be returning to Jamaica for his coming-of-age, Margaret Scott had offered him a party in her small London house; but his other aunt, Alexa, had swept the suggestion aside. She had never behaved as warmly as Margaret to her niece and nephew, but when it came to giving a dance, she would allow no one to consider any alternative to the Glanville country house. At this very moment, as the clock on the stable tower struck the hour for which the guests had been invited, the wide entrance doors were flung open and the carriage approach was flooded with a warm and welcoming light.

"How very thoughtful it was of Aunt Alexa to make sure that the ballroom windows were blacked out!" exclaimed Kate. But there was no trace of anxiety in her laughing voice. In its peaceful country setting, Blaize could surely never be touched by the dangers of war.

"There'll be no Zeppelins tonight," said Brinsley. "It's my birthday, and everyone knows that I was born while Lady Luck was smiling. Only good things can happen on my birthday."

They had been walking arm in arm, but now Kate moved her hand to rest lightly and formally on her brother's arm. They

stepped forward into the light and progressed with dignity up the
stone steps and into the house. But if they had hoped that the
staff would be caught out by the arrival of an apparently over-
punctual pair of guests, they were disappointed. Two lines of
footmen wearing the Glanville livery stood ready to receive them,
and the butler's silver tray awaited the first card which would tell
him whom to announce. From the ballroom, a little way away,
could be heard the last faint scrapings of sound as the orchestra
tuned their instruments. There were a few seconds of silence and
then, as though the ballroom were already crowded instead of
completely deserted, the house was flooded with music as warmly
as with light.

It was time for the ball to begin.

2

Even in portraiture the English nobility was not prepared to
mix with trade. The Tudor long gallery on the highest floor of
Blaize displayed a row of aristocrats with high foreheads and long
noses. They were all descended from one of William the Conqueror's companions at arms, and they were all ancestors of Piers
Glanville, the present holder of the title. But Alexa's father, who
had once owned a shipping company and a bank in Bristol, had
not been invited to join their company.

Instead, the portrait of John Junius Lorimer hung alone in the
screened balcony above one end of the ballroom. The picture
showed an old man, heavily built and dressed in sombre black.
His long hair and beard and profuse side whiskers were white, but
his bushy eyebrows had been painted chestnut. Margaret Scott,
who climbed the steps to the balcony shortly before midnight,
had once had hair as bright as those eyebrows; for, like Alexa, she
was the daughter of John Junius Lorimer. But she was twenty
years older than her half-sister, and now she was fifty-seven, the
colour was fading, and her forehead showed the lines of past sorrow and present responsibility.

In London, Margaret was a professional woman held in high esteem. Like her best friend, Lydia, the mother of Kate and Brinsley, she had been a member of the first generation of women who had succeeded in qualifying as doctors in England, and now she was not only in charge of the gynaecological department of one of the great London teaching hospitals but was also responsible for the welfare of all the female students who trained there. But tonight her role was not that of a doctor but of an aunt and mother. This was a family occasion.

There were chairs in the balcony, but Margaret was a small woman and found that if she sat down she could not see above the solid lower section of the screen. Instead she stood, looking through the lattice at the picturesque scene below. Alexa, tonight's hostess, had been an opera singer in her youth, and when she married Piers Glanville he had encouraged her to convert a tithe barn on his estate into a small opera house. So she had the contacts to turn any party into a production if she chose, and the designer whose more usual responsibility was to create Count Almaviva's house or Don Giovanni's palace on the stage had been given a new challenge for this special occasion. He had transformed the ballroom into a tropical forest, through which the women in their beautiful dresses dipped and swirled like exotic butterflies. Many of the young girls wore white, but Alexa had invited friends of her own generation as well as those on Brinsley's list, and above their rich silks and brocades sparkled the jewels of a wealthy and secure society.

The girls in their debutante season were pretty enough, but it seemed to Margaret that none of them could rival their hostess. Alexa Glanville at the age of thirty-seven was as beautiful as Alexa Lorimer had been at seventeen. Tall and slender, she brought elegance to any gown she wore, and to honour this evening's celebration, her reddish-gold hair was coiled on her head like a crown in which delicate sprays of diamonds glittered, half hidden.

Margaret looked for her son, Robert, and saw that he was partnering Kate. It was surprising how well they were dancing—for Robert did not attend many functions of this kind, while Kate's tall, sturdy body did not suggest that she would be graceful. But she had a musical ear, and Margaret herself had made sure that she had the necessary dancing lessons some years earlier. Certainly the two cousins seemed to be in perfect accord as they circled the floor—although Margaret noticed that Robert looked unusually thoughtful. Perhaps he was needing to concentrate on the steps, for there was no sign of the cheerful grin which had hardly changed since he was a little boy—although the carroty curls which he had inherited from his mother and grandfather had sprung up again from his attempts earlier in the evening to discipline them, and this tousled confusion made him look younger than his twenty years. Margaret felt her heart swelling with pride and love as she watched him. Robert was her only child, born after the death of his father, and her whole happiness was bound up in him.

The wooden treads of the stair to the balcony gave noisy warning that someone was coming to join her. Margaret turned away from the dancers and found that it was one of her many nephews. Arthur Lorimer was the son of Margaret's elder brother, who had died some years before. Although Arthur was a younger son, he had inherited his family's dock and shipping business, because his brother Matthew had abandoned the offices of the Lorimer Line to become an artist. Arthur himself, now in his thirties, found the world of business completely congenial and was never happier than when he was absorbed in his accounts. He lived in the Bristol mansion which had once belonged to John Junius Lorimer and devoted himself to making money. Although his business associates and competitors thought of him as a hard and cold-natured man, he had a strong family feeling, and had welcomed the invitation to join in Brinsley's celebrations.

They chatted now for a few moments, but Arthur's concentration was not on the conversation. "Have you seen Kate?" he asked abruptly. "She gave me the supper dance, but she seems to have disappeared."

"She was dancing with Robert only a moment ago." Margaret turned back to look over the screen, and found that the couple had left the floor, although the orchestra was still playing. "Well, she's hardly likely to go without supper. And she's not the sort of girl who would stand you up."

Arthur nodded his agreement. For a moment he seemed on the point of saying something else; but after looking down once more to check that Kate was not hidden anywhere in the jungle below he changed his mind and went down the steps without speaking.

Always observant, Margaret could not help noticing that he seemed to be under some kind of strain. She wondered, as she had wondered once or twice before, whether he wanted to marry Kate. She had noticed that ever since his cousin's arrival in England he had formed the habit of spending the night at Margaret's house whenever he had to come to London on business, although the return journey to Bristol was not a long one. He was not a man who found it easy to chat to young women or to spare the time from his business to indulge in the formal ritual of courtship. Nor could Margaret ever imagine him falling in love. But the relationship of one cousin with another was a relaxed one, and he had always seemed at ease with Kate.

There was another reason why Arthur—approaching the decision rationally, as he was certain to do—might have seen Kate as a possible wife. She was a doctor. This could make it easier for him to confess to her, as he had earlier done to Margaret herself, the consequences of the attack of mumps which he had suffered at the age of twenty-five. He might also hope that someone dedicated to her profession would be more willing than most ordinary women to embark on a marriage in the knowledge that her husband would never be able to give her children. Not many men allowed their wives to work; but it was a concession Arthur might be prepared to offer as a form of compensation. Whether Kate would allow herself to be bribed into matrimony was another matter.

Margaret tut-tutted to herself. Matchmaking, even when it was only in the imagination, was a temptation which ought to be resisted. The young people were perfectly capable of making their own plans. Of more immediate importance was Arthur's reminder that the next item on the programme would be the supper dance, for which she too was engaged. She turned to go down, and found herself facing the portrait of her father. His piercing eyes reminded her of the many occasions during her childhood when he had demanded an explanation of some misdeed. She had been frightened of him then, but now her chin lifted—not so much defiantly as in triumph. When John Junius Lorimer died, he had left his family ruined and disgraced. If anything was required to prove how hard and how successfully his four children had worked to raise themselves out of that morass of dismay, it was tonight's ball, with its background of wealth and its strong ties of family affection. As she made her way back to the ballroom floor, the war was far from Margaret's thoughts, and she was happy.

3

Kate had been surprised when her cousin Robert interrupted their dance together to ask whether she would talk with him for a few moments. Usually teasing and carefree, he had become unexpectedly serious. They had both spent many holidays at Blaize, and knew their way around the old house. The library was not one of the rooms open to the generality of tonight's guests, so as she followed Robert there Kate guessed that they would not be interrupted.

"I need advice," he said abruptly, closing the door behind him. "I want to join up, like Brinsley. Or at least, I don't know whether I want to, but I think I ought to."

"Robert! You can't do that. It would break Aunt Margaret's heart."

"But everyone else is doing it. Of course no mother is going to *like* it, exactly, but other mothers are letting their sons go."

"Other mothers may have other children, and husbands. Aunt Margaret has no one but you. She'd never have a moment's peace while you were away."

"It would be hard for her, I know it would. But what am I to do, Kate? Have I got to spend the rest of my life wrapped in cotton wool because I'm the only son of a widow? There has to be a moment when I leave home and start living my own life."

"Well, of course," Kate agreed. "And by any normal definition of leading your own life, I'm quite sure that Aunt Margaret would want you to go. But this is different. You must see the difference."

"What I see is that everyone else is going. What am I to say when my friends ask me why I'm still at home? 'I can't leave my mother?' I don't want to hurt her, Kate, but I feel this is my duty. I was hoping you could help."

"If you want help, Uncle Piers is the best person to ask for it." Kate knew that Lord Glanville had been Margaret's closest friend in England for almost twenty years. "But if you're asking me for advice—"

"No." Robert smiled, although it was only an imitation of his usual cheerful grin. "I'm looking for someone whose advice will be to do what I already want to do. I can see you're not the right person. I mustn't make you late for your supper. Who's taking you in?"

Kate consulted the programme which, with its miniature pencil, swung from her wrist, and saw that Arthur had initialled the next dance.

"And he's a punctual man," commented Robert when she told him. He held the door open for her. Kate hesitated, feeling that there must be something more she could say. But although Robert resembled her brother Brinsley in his laughing and apparently carefree attitude to life, there was a difference between the two cousins. Robert's lightheartedness, unlike Brinsley's, was not central to his character, but was the ripple on the surface of a pool of thoughtfulness. He laughed and he teased and he was always ready to play, but at heart he was serious. Brinsley might view with horror the thought of a settled future and a working career, but Robert was already in the middle of training to be a civil engineer. Kate saw that he had spoken the truth when he admitted that he was asking for support rather than advice. It meant, almost certainly, that he had already made up his mind.

Back in the ballroom, Arthur was looking for her with an impatience which contained a hint of anxiety. As Kate smiled, to show that she had not forgotten, she thought how well evening dress became him. Robert was too young and somehow too rugged to look at ease in the shining, stiff-fronted shirt and long tailcoat which were part of the black-and-white uniform worn by all the

civilian men at the ball; while at the other extreme, Lord Glanville, tall and silver-haired, looked distinguished whatever he
wore. But Arthur's clothes changed him entirely for the better. By
day his slightness made him appear insignificant; his face was too
narrow to be handsome and his hair was already beginning to
recede slightly, suggesting that he would be bald one day. Now,
though, he appeared almost elegant.

Or perhaps, thought Kate, it was just that the whole atmosphere of the ball placed the dancers and the surroundings at one
remove from reality. Just as a gauze might be dropped in Alexa's
river-side opera house to blur the edges of the action behind it,
changing it from drama—already far from real life—to fantasy, so
now the romantic setting had transformed all those who enjoyed
it, making all the men seem handsome and all the women beautiful. All except herself, of course—but even she felt herself walking taller, playing her part in the scene.

The doors of the banqueting hall were thrown open and there
were gasps of admiration even from guests accustomed to such
displays of tasteful extravagance. Kate and Arthur, as befitted
members of the family, hung back for a little, accepting a glass of
punch from one of the footmen as they waited. Kate was still
conscious of some kind of tension in Arthur's manner, and
searched for a subject of conversation to break their silence.

A group of Brinsley's friends, who had all volunteered at the
same time as himself, led their partners to the buffet and gave her
the chance to comment.

"How smart they all look in their new uniforms," she said. "Do
you intend to volunteer, Arthur?"

"I'm thirty-six," he said. "Too old to learn to be a soldier. This
is a young man's war. And even if that weren't the case, I can be
more use to the country by remaining at work. We're not being
told very much about the German submarines. I suppose the government is anxious not to alarm the country. But there are certain to be losses at sea. Ships will be sunk, and they must be replaced quickly if the country isn't to starve. The Lorimer Line
has had contracts with the same shipbuilding firm for a great
many years. I bought that firm last week, and I intend to increase
its output at once. I'd hoped to interest Brinsley in the new busi-

ness, as a matter of fact—to keep as much as possible of its profit within the family. Naturally he couldn't do anything until the war is over, but after that I thought he might find a management position in Bristol more exciting than exile to Jamaica. But clearly he has too much to think about at the moment. He wasn't able to give the idea proper attention."

Kate suspected that Brinsley had little interest in business of any kind, and even less aptitude for it. But her brother would have to settle down to some kind of work sooner or later, so she was careful not to spoil an opportunity by putting her thought into words. There was another objection, though. "I imagine my father will want him to take over the work of the plantation eventually," she said.

"It's my impression that your father has already found a capable assistant," said Arthur. "We have a good deal of business correspondence about the bananas which he consigns to my ships. I noticed two years ago that the letters which he signed were written in a different hand. And now his secretary, or whoever it may be, appears to have taken over all the office work. Besides being more efficient in keeping his accounts up to date, he's been quite awkwardly enterprising in looking for alternative markets and ships, which your father would never have done. I was forced to revise my quotations last year." Arthur's thin lips curled in a smile of grudging admiration for the unknown Jamaican who had beaten him in his own field. "It seems to me that if your father needs a manager to succeed him, he already has one."

"Do you know his name?" asked Kate.

"D. Mattison, he signs himself."

"Duke!" exclaimed Kate, smiling with pleasure.

"You know him?"

"Very well. He was our best friend in Jamaica, Brinsley's and mine. He's older than we are—he must be almost twenty-eight by now. He used to play cricket with Brinsley. It's because Duke was such a good bowler that Brinsley became such a good batsman. And he always had a good head for figures. I suggested to Father before I left the island that he ought to take Duke into his office. I'm delighted that he's done so."

"Duke is an unusual name to be christened," said Arthur.

"Not for a Jamaican."

"Are you telling me that he's black?"

"Well, brown, really. Quite a few of the islanders show signs of English blood, and Duke more than most." Kate couldn't help smiling at the expression on her cousin's face. It was difficult to tell whether he was more shocked at the thought that he was doing business with a native or by the need to recognise that moral standards in the colonies had not always been as high as they should. Kate changed the subject quickly before Arthur should express some opinion with which she would be bound to disagree. "Shall we find ourselves a seat for supper?" she suggested.

"There's no hurry," said Arthur, and it was true that the space round the buffet table was crowded. "Will you come into the conservatory with me, Kate? It's very hot in here."

Kate could not control a smile. She had heard from her friends so many accounts of proposals of marriage which had taken place in conservatories that the word had become a joke, as though such an extension of the house existed purely for this purpose, and not for the benefit of the plants which grew there. She was about to tease her partner—for although a few moments earlier she had felt herself enveloped in a romantic atmosphere, it had not touched her emotions—when it occurred to her that Arthur had not spoken in jest. He was displaying all the nervousness of a man planning to put the conservatory to this conventional use.

The idea came as a shock. Kate had been on friendly terms with Arthur ever since she arrived in England to start her medical training, but she had never thought of him as anything more than a cousin, and she did not wish to do so now. Instinctively she took a step backwards, searching for a reason to stay in the crowded hall.

The excuse which presented itself was not one which she would have chosen. While she had been talking to Arthur, Lord Glanville's butler had come into the hall, carrying the silver tray on which he was accustomed to present letters. But no ordinary letter would arrive at this time of night. What Brinsley was reading was a telegram.

His face flushed with excitement. He called to those of his friends who were in uniform and they hurried to read the words

over his shoulder. They spoke briefly to their partners before moving in a little group towards their startled hostess. But Brinsley
called them to a halt.

"One more dance!" he shouted. "Lord Kitchener won't be-
grudge us a last waltz." He dispatched the butler to call back the
orchestra, who were taking their own break for refreshments, and
led the way back into the ballroom. There was an eager chatter of
voices as the other guests left their suppers and followed.

Arthur was saying something, but Kate did not hear the words.
Too abruptly to be believed, the atmosphere of the ball had
changed from a romantic dreaminess to a highly charged drama,
and Kate's blood was cold with a sudden fear. Brinsley, without
doubt, had received his summons to leave for France. His friends,
commissioned at the same time, would in a few moments hurry to
their homes to discover whether similar telegrams were waiting for
them, but Kate's emotions were centred on her brother alone.

"How can he look so excited when he's going into such danger?" she exclaimed, appalled that the family should have admired Brinsley's enthusiasm without stopping to reflect that it
was leading him somewhere where he would have to kill or be
killed.

"How could he go into such danger if he were not excited?"
Arthur countered. His arm was round her waist as though he
feared that she might faint, but Kate was hardly aware of it.

"I can't let him go," she cried, overwhelmed by the nearness of
the parting; but as she tried to hurry into the ballroom, Arthur
tightened his grip.

"You can't hold him," he said. "None of us can. We have no
rights any more. He has to do whatever his country orders. And
when he is happy to obey, it would be unkind of you to do anything but support him."

Kate realised that her cousin was speaking the truth. It was unusual for her to reveal her emotions, but her unhappiness now
made some gesture necessary. She turned into Arthur's waiting
arms, her head pressed against his chest, while she struggled to restrain her tears.

"Brinsley has an aura of good fortune," Arthur said quietly.
"Can't you feel it as you look at him? Some people are lucky,

against all reason, and he's always been one of them. He'll come back. They'll all come back. The war will be over by Christmas." He paused for a moment. "It's natural that you should be upset. Your parents are a long way away. You'll be lonely when Brinsley's gone. We could help each other, Kate. It's lonely for me as well now that Beatrice has decided she must work in London. You're losing a brother: I've already lost a sister. It's ridiculous for one man to live alone with so many servants in a great mansion like Brinsley House. It would make me very happy if you'd agree to share it with me, Kate."

Through the confusion of her anxiety Kate heard the words and—although not immediately—understood them. Appalled by her own weakness, she pulled herself away from Arthur and straightened her shoulders, steadying her body and her emotions at the same time.

"I shouldn't have allowed—I can't—I'm sorry, Arthur."

She seemed unable to communicate and could see that he did not understand what it was that she was failing to say, for his puzzled frown gave place almost immediately to a sympathetic smile.

"I've chosen the wrong time to declare myself," he said understandingly. "How can I expect you to think of anyone but Brinsley at this moment? After he's left we'll talk again."

"Excuse me," said Kate. She knew that she was behaving badly in leaving him so abruptly, but she could not bear to waste any more of the time which she might be spending with her brother. She hurried out of the banqueting hall and into the ballroom, arriving just as the waltz was ending.

"Have you been called to go?" she asked Brinsley.

"Yes, but not till morning," he said reassuringly. "The others will want to push off now so that they can pick up their things and say goodbye to their families. But everything I need is here. There's no reason why I shouldn't dance till dawn. Don't look so upset, Kate."

"But of course I'm upset!" she exclaimed. "It's only a few hours, isn't it, since I said I felt like Cinderella. And now midnight's struck, but it's not my dress that's disappearing. It's—" She was too near to tears to go on.

"It's what?"

"Everything." Her gesture took in the whole of her surroundings; the jungle ballroom and the exotic display of food in the
banqueting hall. "You're all going. And the ball is ending too
soon. It's as though the life we've known, everything about it, is
coming to a close."

"Nonsense," said Brinsley. "Why do you think I'm going, if
not to make sure that everything will be able to go on as before?
And why should the ball stop, when we're still here? Come on,
Kate; keep your chin up. You've never let anything beat you before. Why don't we show them all what we can do?"

He spoke to the leader of the orchestra and then smiled at his
sister as he took her in his arms, allowing her a moment to steady
not only her body but her feelings after such an uncharacteristic
display of emotion. Then they moved smoothly together in a
rhythm which was unfamiliar to many of the guests, for the tango
was still a novelty in England. Doubtless some of the young
debutantes present would have learned the new steps, but in
their eyes Kate knew that she was an oddity, dull and overserious.
They would certainly not expect to see her giving what was almost an exhibition dance. It would be yet another joke on the
part of a young man who allowed nothing to subdue his high
spirits.

It was an odd side-effect of their childhood in Jamaica that
Kate and Brinsley both had a strongly developed sense of rhythm.
Neither of their parents was musical, but the two children
had almost unconsciously absorbed the music in the Jamaican
air. When the members of the Hope Valley congregation sang
Baptist hymns, they transformed them into something powerful
and thrilling. As they worked, they sang other songs, fitting the
rhythms to the tasks; and in the evenings they sang and danced
in a different way—a way disturbing in its intensity. Both the
young Lorimers had learned to feel the throbbing of nonexistent
drums through the stresses of the singers and the movements of
their bodies. The rhythm of the tango was as different from
Jamaican music as Jamaican from English, but Kate and Brinsley
found no difficulty in moving with a graceful precision which
brought applause from the older guests.

For a moment after the music had stopped they stood close together. Neither of them had yet fallen in love, although Brinsley
moved from one flirtation to another: their strongest emotional
attachment was still to each other. Kate knew that this state of
affairs could not survive for much longer, but for the moment she
was bound by ties so tight that part of herself would go to France
with her brother the next day. Brinsley recognised this, and for a
few seconds the gaiety of his smile faded into affectionate seri-
ousness as he looked into her eyes.

"You're not to be frightened for me, Kate," he said. "I shall be
all right. And it's only for a little while. It will all be over by
Christmas."

It was the second time within an hour that Kate had heard
that phrase. She tried to make herself believe it and, with rather
more success, forced herself to smile back into her brother's eyes.

4

In time of war, nothing makes such a fierce frontal assault on
the emotions as military music. The sound of the drums was at
first hardly more than a vibration, an almost imperceptible disturbance of the air, but it was enough to catch the attention of
the excited, shouting, jostling crowds on the departure platform
of Waterloo Station. Within a few seconds the full diapason of a
regimental band could be heard, its bright brassiness piercing the
air and lifting the spirits. Margaret tried to control the excitement which the music induced in her. A feeling of elation
affected not only the soldiers who were waiting to board the train
but also the civilians who had come to see them off. Although she
reminded herself that a mass emotion of this kind was dangerous,
warping the judgement, she was not proof against the contagion of
patriotic pride.

Louder even than the band itself now was the tramp of well-
drilled feet, and Margaret felt her eyes pricking with tears—of
admiration rather than sadness—as a battalion of guardsmen

marched the length of the platform and came to a stamping halt beside the carriages reserved for them at the front of the train.

The civilians cheered them as they passed and the men in uniform—most of them, like Brinsley, volunteer members of the British Expeditionary Force—watched their immaculate professionalism with envy. Then the chatter of farewells was resumed.

Six members of Brinsley's family had come to see him off. Alexa and Piers Glanville, Margaret and Robert and, of course, Kate, had all travelled with him from Blaize. Arthur had said his farewells there and had returned directly to Bristol; but his sister Beatrice had joined the party at the station.

In the years before the war, as it became clear that she would never marry, Beatrice had lived, as convention demanded of a spinster, in her brother's Bristol mansion. Fretting at her uselessness, she had allowed her temper to grow as sharp as her features, and had become the least popular member of the Lorimer family. But since the third day of the war she had been working full time in the London office of the National Union of Women's Suffrage Societies. Over a period of many years she had supported the movement in its efforts to win the vote for women, acting as its local secretary in Bristol. But now the organisation had changed its immediate aim, and was assembling the staff and equipment of medical units to be sent to the Front. Beatrice too had changed as she committed all her time to the cause instead of giving a few hours of voluntary work each week. Her resentment that she was still a spinster had been replaced by confidence in her own new-found efficiency and the knowledge that she was doing a worthwhile job. Almost overnight she had become friendlier and less prickly. Her absence from Brinsley's birthday celebrations had not been because of her admitted dislike of Alexa, but on account of an urgent need to pack up a consignment of drugs for France. Margaret could tell that her eldest niece was genuinely glad of the opportunity to join the family party, and anxious to assure Brinsley of her affection and support.

At the moment, though, it appeared that it was with Margaret herself that Brinsley wished to speak. She felt his hand on her arm as he led her a little way from the others. The platform was crowded, but each family group was intent only on its own leave-taking. Surrounded by strangers, it was possible to speak freely.

There was no time for any preamble. Knowing that he would be leaving at any moment, Brinsley came abruptly to the point.

"We'll be off soon," he said. "Aunt Margaret, you'll keep an eye on Kate for me, won't you?"

"I've never known a young woman better able to look after herself," said Margaret. "What foolishness do you anticipate?"

"She's turned down an offer of marriage from Arthur. I'm certainly not implying that's foolish. Arthur seems to me to be a cold man." Brinsley laughed. "Kate thinks he has his eyes on part of Father's estate as a marriage settlement."

"Then Kate is uncharitable. I agree that Arthur doesn't appear likely to fall passionately in love with anyone, but he's been fond of Kate since she arrived in England. It would fit his nature to choose someone he knows well for a wife, rather than a strange young woman. Anyway, we may agree that Kate has made the right decision."

"But for the right reason? She told me she'd be ashamed to devote herself to the comfort of one man when she should be using her skills to serve hundreds. I wouldn't like her to end up as an old maid like Beatrice."

"One day she'll be swept off her feet by a dashing young prince on a white charger and all her doubts will be forgotten. That's not really what's worrying you, is it, Brinsley?"

"I don't know what's worrying me," he confessed. "But she's planning something. She has that broody look. I'd like to feel that you'd discuss with her any ideas she may be considering."

"Well, of course," Margaret assured him. "You know very well that Kate is almost a daughter to me, just as you are another son. Look after yourself, Brinsley."

It was a foolish remark to make to a young man on his way to a battlefield. For a few seconds Brinsley's smile seemed a little less carefree than usual. As he kissed her goodbye, Margaret could feel the depth of his affection for her. He had never put it into words and he did not do so now, but it was true that for the past eight years their relationship had been almost that of mother and son. While she watched him make his farewells to Beatrice and

Robert and Piers Glanville and Alexa she felt a moment of sympathy for his mother, her dear friend Lydia, who had been
deprived of so many years out of her elder children's lives.

Whistles were blowing. Brinsley had saved his last embrace for
Kate, and for a moment brother and sister clung together as
though they feared that they might never see each other again.
But the prevailing atmosphere was one of excitement, not
sadness. Brinsley leapt onto the train and reappeared almost at
once to smile from a window. Everyone was waving now: the
platform fluttered with handkerchiefs. With a blast from the
steam whistle, the engine began to hiss and puff. Very slowly, so
that Margaret and Kate found it possible for a few seconds to
keep pace with Brinsley as he leaned from the window, the train
began to move. There was a last-minute rush of repeated messages: hands were clasped and reluctantly released. The engine
picked up speed and the band began to play again.

They played "It's a long way to Tipperary." The soldiers leaning from the train sang it lustily and as their voices faded the civilians on the platform took up the chorus. They sang it through
a second time, and a third, still waving at the blank end of the
guard's van as it pulled away along the rails and curved out of
sight.

The soldiers were not, of course, going to Tipperary but to
Ypres. A dead weight of anticlimax stifled the excitement on the
platform as the band ceased to play. The waving handkerchiefs
drooped and were put to a different use, dabbing at eyes unable
any longer to smile. The little group of Lorimers lingered on the
platform, reluctant to disperse—as though the parting need not
be considered final until they as well as Brinsley had left the station. Even Margaret, who had taken time off from her hospital
duties, could not bring herself to move at once. There was only
one farewell which could have wrenched more cruelly at her heart
—if it had been Robert, and not Brinsley, who had just been
carried away. Sometimes she was frightened that such a moment
might come; but then she reminded herself that Robert would
not be twenty-one for another nine months, and surely the war
would be over before then.

Even while she reassured herself, anxiety made her stretch out a hand to Robert for comfort. He took her hand but failed to provide the comfort.

"I want to go as well, Mother," he said.

It was almost the first time in his life that Margaret had seen her mischievous, carrot-haired son looking so serious. She stared at him without at first understanding what he meant.

"Go where?"

"Into the Army. The Royal Engineers. To go on with my engineering training but be of some use to the country at the same time."

The shock was so great that Margaret still could not absorb it. She had prepared herself for the parting with Brinsley, but Robert, surely, was only a boy. Lord Glanville came up to stand beside him.

"Robert discussed this with me at Brinsley's party," he said. "He wanted to be sure that you wouldn't feel yourself alone while he was away. Naturally, I was able to promise that Alexa and I would always be at hand if you needed any kind of support."

You mean, if Robert is killed, thought Margaret, but it was not a thought which could be put into words, though Robert and Piers must already have faced it. She had to struggle against a panic which closed her throat so that for a moment she was unable to speak.

"Well, we must think about it," she said at last, trying to smile; but Robert's serious expression did not change.

"I went to the recruiting office this morning," he said. "It's done."

"Robert, how could you! Without even a word?"

"How could I expect you to debate a decision like that and be forced in the end to say that you agree? It must be easier, surely, for you to accept that it's settled."

"You're not twenty-one yet," she protested. "I could—" She checked herself. Whether or not Robert needed his mother's permission to enlist—and she was not sure what the legal position was—he had made a man's decision and she would never be able to treat him like a child again. They could discuss the decision, and if it proved that Margaret still had the power to annul it, she could try to persuade him to change his mind. What she could not do was simply to say No. She was forced to recognise that every mother must face the moment of realising that her firstborn has grown into an adult with a life of his own. But not many mothers were confronted in that moment with a choice which might be literally one of life or death. Was her whole life to consist of partings from the men she loved? Without making any pretence that she approved or even accepted his decision, she kissed Robert to reassure him of her love.

But the unexpectedness of his news had left her confused, almost dizzy. She heard her name called and turned so sharply that she staggered, needing Robert's arm to steady her.

Kate, who must have left the family group while Robert was breaking his news, was running down the platform towards them, her eyes wide with shock. Margaret held her breath and waited to hear what new horrors this day held in store.

5

Kate had left the family group as Brinsley's train finally disappeared from sight, in order that no one should see how close she was to tears. Sniffing vigorously and rubbing her eyes, she was not at first conscious of her surroundings. When at last she had brought her feelings more or less under control, she was surprised to see a row of ambulances drawing up in the station forecourt. To take her mind off Brinsley, she forced herself to be curious and followed the men who hurried from each vehicle as it came to a halt. They led her to the platform furthest from that on which the band had been playing.

The platform was covered with stretchers, and more were still being unloaded from an ambulance train which must have arrived unobtrusively while everyone's attention was on the departing troop train. Kate stared unbelievingly at the rows of men who lay, too weak or too shell-shocked to move, with grey faces and sunken eyes which stared unblinkingly from black sockets. She began to move amongst them, asking questions and occasionally lifting a blanket to inspect the wound it covered. Then, horrified, she ran as fast as she could to find Margaret.

"Come and see here, Aunt Margaret." She seized her aunt's hand and tugged her towards the other platform while the rest of the family, startled, followed more slowly. For a moment the two women, both doctors, stood side by side, taking in the scene in silence. Then Kate led Margaret over to one of the wounded men with whom she had spoken a little earlier.

"Look at this," she said quietly to Margaret. She raised the blanket which covered his leg. He was still wearing the khaki trousers of his uniform, covered in mud, and his blood-stained puttees: only the boot had been cut away. "It's five days since he was wounded. I asked him. Five days to bring him from the front line to here with only a field dressing. Just look!"

Even in her state of horror Kate had enough tact not to describe what she had recognised. Perhaps the man had not yet realised that he would have to lose a leg. Margaret, staring at the slimy bandage and blackened, gangrenous toes, would not need to be told.

"Where are you taking them?" Margaret asked one of the ambulance men.

"Thirty to Charing Cross Hospital," he said. "The rest'll wait here till we find out where there's room."

The rest of the party came up to join the two women, and Kate repeated her indignant reaction to Lord Glanville. But Margaret gestured them to move away from the stretcher area so that they could talk without being overheard.

"The hospitals must be cleared to make room," she said. "I shall go back at once and stop admissions to my gynaecological ward. Given efficient transport, my patients can perfectly well be cared for in the country. These men need surgeons and skilled nurses, and they need them at once. All the London teaching hospitals ought to make all their beds available to these emergency cases while the crisis lasts."

Kate, who had only recently qualified as a doctor, had none of her aunt's power to take decisions like this. While the members of the older generation discussed what should be done, she stood back in silence.

Margaret had spoken with the authority of a professional woman, and Lord Glanville, even more accustomed to taking decisions at a high level, was considering the situation with equal gravity. Kate knew that he had been personally responsible, fifteen years earlier, for persuading Margaret to leave her country practice and supervise the women students of the hospital of which he was a benefactor and governor. So although he had no medical experience, he was familiar with hospital administration.

"These men are surgical cases, I take it," he said to Margaret. "They'll need operations without delay and surgical nursing for some afterwards—and then what? A less intensive standard of nursing for what could be a considerable period while their wounds heal?"

"If they're lucky, yes," said Margaret. "If they arrive at the operating theatre in time."

"And during this healing period they'll be occupying beds which may be needed by the next trainload of wounded, and the next."

"But this can't go on indefinitely!" exclaimed Alexa—though, like her husband, she kept her voice low. "Obviously there has been a major battle. Something must have been decided by it. And I understood from the newspapers that the war is almost over, that we are on the point of victory."

"The newspapers are telling us what we hope to hear," said Piers. "It was true a few weeks ago that the Germans were in retreat. But when they became too tired to retreat any further they dug trenches to protect themselves for a breathing space and found—as each of the men on this platform has found—that a row of concealed machine guns can be remarkably effective in keeping an army at bay. I suspect that there will be many more injuries of this kind. It seems to me a matter of some urgency that the surgical wards in London should be kept available for acute cases; and that means that convalescent soldiers must be moved out as fast as emergencies move in. No doubt the hospitals are making their own plans. What I have in mind is a specific proposal." He turned towards Alexa. "Your opera house at Blaize is not due to open for its next season until the summer," he suggested. "It would not take too much reorganisation to convert

it into a long ward for men who require rest and some care but
not the most skilled nursing. There would be room in the main
house for the doctors and nurses to stay. It must be your decision,
of course. What do you think?"

"But rehearsals are due to start—" Alexa's first reaction was a
selfish one. Before she could express even a single objection, however, her gaze returned to the rows of stretchers and the men who
lay on them, too weak even to groan. She put a hand apologetically on her husband's arm. "You're quite right, Piers," she
said. "How ought we to arrange it? We should need medical advice if the conversion is to be efficient."

"The best plan would be to attach Blaize to one of the London
hospitals as its country branch," suggested Margaret.

"And since I'm already a governor of yours, there's no need to
waste any time in choosing between them all," said Piers. "I hope
you won't mind if I put forward your name, Margaret, to be medical administrator of the country branch, since we shall all have to
live and work together so closely." He thought for a moment.
"I'll take Alexa back to Park Lane now and then come straight to
the hospital to see what arrangements can be made."

"It's too late!" Kate cried, watching as Piers and Alexa hurried
off. Robert went with them, perhaps still fearing an emotional
outburst from his mother if he stayed. But it seemed that Margaret had for the moment succeeded in pushing her personal distress to the back of her mind.

"To late for these men, perhaps," she agreed. "But Piers's plan
will help others. And all his colleagues in the House of Lords
have large country houses. If a first experimental scheme can be
seen to work successfully—"

"I don't mean that," interrupted Kate. "I mean that it will be
too late for the next batch of wounded as well as for these if they
are always to be sent back to England. How many lives are being
lost by this kind of delay, do you think? The men should be
treated as soon as they are wounded; and that means within a
short distance of the battlefield."

"Well, obviously there must be dressing stations and field
hospitals—" Margaret began; but again Kate interrupted her.

"And obviously there are not enough. Or else they are not adequately equipped. Or else there are not enough doctors. Aunt Margaret, I must go to France as well."

"You may think you see a need, Kate." Beatrice had taken no part in the earlier conversation and she spoke now with the cold edge of sarcasm which came naturally to her voice. But Kate could tell that she had been as deeply affected as any of the others by the contrast between the strong young men who had set off from Waterloo that morning and the broken bodies of those who had returned. "I can promise you, though, that the War Office will not think any emergency great enough to warrant the recruitment of women doctors. In the suffragists' office we have fought this battle twice and lost on each occasion. Since the generals are finding the Germans more difficult to defeat than they had expected, they console themselves by putting women to rout instead."

"What's happened, then?" demanded Kate.

"The French have accepted us. Dr. Louisa Garrett Anderson and Dr. Flora Murray are already in France. They are the leaders of a Women's Hospital Corps which has been entirely paid for by private subscription. And the Scottish Federation has raised enough funds to equip two complete units. The first of them will be leaving for France within the next two weeks, if all goes well."

"I want to go with it," said Kate. She was overwhelmed by the strength of her need to become involved.

"It's fully staffed." Beatrice spoke with a firmness as great as her cousin's. But her brusque comment did not prevent her from looking thoughtfully at Kate as though to estimate how far she had spoken only out of impulse. "But there's still a vacancy in the second unit. We expect that to be ready in January."

"Will you accept me?"

"You haven't had much experience yet," Beatrice pointed out. "But it's not for me to say yes or no. The surgeon who'll be in charge of the unit has already been appointed. You'd have to convince her that you could make yourself useful. I'm expecting her to call at the office this afternoon with the list of equipment she wants me to provide. If you'd like to come at two o'clock—"

"I'll be there," said Kate. "Thank you, Beatrice."

The change in Beatrice did not go so far as to make her smile easily. She nodded at Kate in acceptance of the arrangement and advanced her lips towards Margaret's cheek without actually touching it. Then, businesslike and matter-of-fact, she strode away.

"Don't rush into a decision like this, Kate," Margaret said, putting a hand on her niece's arm as though that would be enough to hold her back. "It's too important to be settled all in a minute. And I promised Brinsley I'd look after you. He's fighting in order that the people he loves shall be safe. He wouldn't want you to put yourself in such danger. Besides, you've seen for yourself how great is the need for doctors here."

"One doctor in France could save the work of ten in London," Kate argued. "Suppose Brinsley were to be wounded, Aunt Margaret. One of the men I spoke to had lain for three days at Boulogne waiting for a ship. No one even changed his dressings. Could you bear to think of something like that happening to Brinsley when I might be able to prevent it? Or if not for him, for some of the others like him." She saw Margaret shiver and guessed that her aunt was imagining not Brinsley but Robert lying on a stretcher in a railway shed. "When you know, absolutely know, that something is the right thing to do, no amount of thinking about it is going to change the rightness. It isn't exactly that I *want* to go, Aunt Margaret. I don't see it as Brinsley does, as a kind of adventure. But the need is there. I have to go. There's no choice."

"I'm frightened, Kate," said Margaret. "It's only a few hours since we were all dancing at Blaize. And now the place is to be filled with wounded men and Brinsley has gone and you and Robert will follow him. Where is it all going to end?"

"God knows. Do you think the Germans are as convinced that God is on their side as we are that he's on ours?"

She tried to make the question sound lighthearted, almost a joke, but in her heart she too was frightened. Everyone in the family—everyone in England—was having to make plans for an emergency which stretched into an indefinite and unpredictable future. Only one thing must be reckoned as certain. The war would not, after all, be over by Christmas.

6

Two days after her interview in Beatrice's office, Kate learned that her offer to serve as one of the two doctors in the next women's medical unit had been accepted. Perhaps her cousin, knowing her to be hard-working and conscientious, had recommended her, or perhaps she owed her success to her youth and strength and energy. Certainly Kate herself was as well aware as anyone else that although she was fully qualified she had not had a great deal of unsupervised experience of dealing with emergencies—and in work of this kind, most of the casualties brought to her were likely to be emergencies.

Since it would be ten weeks before the unit was ready to leave, she took steps to improve her usefulness by volunteering for temporary hospital work. Doctors and surgeons were working round the clock to accept the flood of wounded soldiers sent back from France, and Kate was welcomed as a member of a team which inspected each man as he arrived, supervised the cleaning of wounds, made a detailed observation of the damage, performed the more straightforward operations or those which were necessary to prepare for major surgery, and kept a close watch for a few days afterwards to guard against complications. She worked four twelve-hour duties each week, and this allowed her the opportunity also to play her part in the upheaval which was taking place at Blaize.

On her first visit she found Margaret already installed there. Lord Glanville had wasted no time in making his property available and pressing both the hospital governors and the Army to accept his sister-in-law as its commandant. Alexa had cleared a corner room in the east wing to act as an office, and by the time Kate arrived it had already taken on the appearance of an operations room at the front line. Plans of the various buildings on the estate were pinned to the wall and every piece of furniture was covered with papers listing equipment required or actions to be taken. Kate had already learned from Lord Glanville that Robert had had to report for training within two days of volunteering. The leisurely process which had carried Brinsley to the front was a thing of the past, and it did not require very much sensitivity to recognise the worry behind Margaret's frown of concentration.

Kate found it curious to walk through the house which she knew so well from holiday visits and to consider its amenities now in such a different light.

"The family will keep the whole of the west wing," Margaret told her. "That's where the nursery suite is, and we don't want to disturb Frisca and little Pirry. Most of the east wing will be made available for the medical staff. That means Alexa loses her drawing room and morning room, I'm afraid. They're going to use the library as a drawing room instead. As for the Tudor part of the house, there are problems in converting it. We've had a surveyor in to look at the long gallery up at the top. It's the perfect shape and size for a ward, but apparently the floor wouldn't take the weight. There would be trouble with stretchers on the stairs as well. The ballroom is more promising, and reasonably straightforward because it's empty. The decisions still to be made are about the opera house."

They walked together through the wood. The path down towards the river was not too steep, but rain the previous night had left it muddy and slippery. Lifting her skirt to keep the hem clean, Kate paused to look back.

"Do you expect to transfer any of the patients from the theatre to the house?" she asked. "It may not be an easy journey. And if doctors are coming and going all day, the mud will get much worse."

Margaret nodded and made a note in the notebook which was tied by string to her belt.

"So we shall need a path with a firm surface and a gentler slope," she agreed. "Gradual enough to push a wheelchair up, in fact. Now then, give me your ideas on this."

They had arrived at a very long brick building, older even than the house. Once upon a time it had been a tithe barn, built right on the bank of the Thames so that tenants of the Glanville estate could bring that part of their harvest which they owed to the church to a convenient place of storage—especially convenient in view of the fact that the Glanvilles had the patronage of the living, and could usually find a member of the family to accept it. During the last century, though, the tithe barn has been allowed to fall into disuse and decay, and only in the past few years, since Lord Glanville's marriage to Alexa, had it been repaired and converted to an opera house.

Even Kate, who was so strongly aware of the need, felt a moment's sadness to see the building which had been Alexa's pride stripped so unceremoniously of its trappings. Already the seats had been taken out, and at this very moment workmen were taking up the raked floor. There would be no need for any of the hospital beds to have a better view of the stage than the rest.

At this moment, however, the stage proved to be in use. A little girl in a white dress was dancing to music which issued from the huge horn of a gramophone. So intently was she concentrating on her energetic but graceful movements that she did not notice the two new arrivals. This was Frisca, Alexa's daughter, made fatherless, even before she was born, by an earthquake in San Francisco and adopted by Lord Glanville when he married her mother.

The record came to an end and Frisca curtsied to the workmen before running to wind the machine up again.

"You ought not to be here, Frisca," said Margaret, stepping on to the stage. "You're distracting the men."

"They like it." Frisca pirouetted as she spoke. Her dimpled smile was infectious. It was impossible to feel gloomy in Frisca's presence—and equally impossible to be strict. Everyone knew that the seven-year-old, angelically blond, was spoiled, but no one could bring himself to be the brute who would dim the radiance in those wide blue eyes. Kate watched with amusement as Margaret did her best to be severe.

"Yes, I'm sure they like it, but they should be getting on with their work instead of watching you. Off you go."

Frisca's pretty face clouded. "Everywhere I go today people tell me to go somewhere else. All the rooms are different and everyone's busy and I can't do anything I want to."

"You should be in the schoolroom, surely," suggested Kate.

"Miss Brampton's saying goodbye to her cousin. He's going to be a soldier like Robert, and she's been crying all morning. She gave me some sweets to keep out of the way for half an hour."

"By the time you get back to the house, the half hour will be up. Run along."

Pouting, the little girl made her way off the stage and out of the theatre, dawdling at first but unable to restrain herself from skipping happily before she was out of sight. Kate continued to smile.

"I've never seen such a child for dancing," she said. "One of these days I'm sure she's going to become as famous as her mother—but as a prima ballerina, not a prima donna. Now then, tell me what you're going to do with all this."

There were so many details to be discussed and so many decisions to be made that Kate was filled with admiration for her aunt's appreciation of each problem and the firmness with which she made up her mind. They discussed catering, and accommodation for nurses. They considered how the actors' dressing rooms could best be used, and whether there was a need for an operating theatre.

On this last point the two women held different views.

"We can hardly hope to equip Blaize as a complete hospital," Margaret pointed out. "I see it only as a place for recuperation and convalescence. Surely it would be a mistake to attempt anything more ambitious. We've set ourselves a limited objective: to free other beds and services for the men in most urgent need by accepting those who need only time and care for their recovery."

"I know that was what Uncle Piers suggested," Kate agreed. "But when I came off duty this morning the corridors of the hospital were lined with beds. These were the men who had been moved out of the acute wards, and these are the cases who will be sent to a place like Blaize if the present rate of casualties continues. They've had their main operations, certainly. But there's gas gangrene in almost every wound. At a guess, I would think that one in ten may need further surgery. I agree that those cases ought not to be sent here. But I suspect very strongly that in fact they will arrive."

Margaret's face paled, and Kate guessed that she was thinking about Robert. She continued to talk quickly, forcing her aunt to concentrate on the matter in hand. More notes were taken, more measurements made. It was a relief, back at the house, to see the calmness with which Lord Glanville accepted the day's new sheets of requirements. He had made himself responsible for obtaining everything Margaret wanted, whether it was equipment such as beds and blankets or labour for the necessary tasks of conversion. His authority and his many friends in the world of affairs cut through the red tape of War Office inefficiency and smoothed away difficulties which would have been daunting to a mere doctor. Kate watched and admired.

For eight weeks she lived a double life. Her work in London would once have been considered full time, but she travelled regularly to the country to undertake what was in effect a second week's work. At first it was only administrative; but even before Blaize could be considered ready to receive its first patients, the ambulances began to arrive, and Kate took turns with Margaret in assisting the hard-pressed admissions doctor. There were times when she could have wept with tiredness, times when she would have paid any price for a full night's sleep. But the survivors of the Battle of Ypres lay in such stoical silence as they waited their turn for attention that Kate found it impossible to turn away as long as there was still work to be done. She had never been a frivolous young woman, but these first months of her working life matured her with remarkable speed. She never ceased to be appalled by the injuries she saw, but with every day that passed she was able to deal with them more competently.

When Christmas came she allowed herself a single day of rest. By now Margaret had closed her London home and it was tacitly accepted that Blaize would be the family centre for as long as the war lasted.

Already, though, the family was scattering. Brinsley was still in France, and Robert too had left for the front. Even to Kate it seemed that his period of training had been very short, and she could see the same anxiety in Margaret's unhappy eyes. But Robert had assured his mother that his role would be to lay the tracks of light railways for the movement of supplies, and this would be done behind the line. Kate could feel no such consolation when she thought about Brinsley.

So it was a small and not very merry group of people who assembled in the library at Blaize to celebrate Christmas—the Christmas which had once been expected to mark a return of peace. Nor were Kate's spirits raised by a piece of news which came from Beatrice. A date had been fixed—two weeks ahead—on which the second women's unit would leave England. But it was not going to France.

Kate knew that there had been great difficulties in getting women doctors admitted to the war zones. The British War Office had remained adamant in its refusal to accept the offer of skilled workers and modern equipment, while the French had proved unable to use the first unit to good advantage. All the same, it was a specific desire to help British soldiers on the Western Front which had prompted Kate to volunteer. It was with dismay that she learned that her unit would be going to Serbia.

Six months earlier she would not even have known where Serbia was. Even now she found it difficult to care greatly about the fervent nationalists whose hatred of Austria had started the war. She sat in silence for a little while, wondering whether to withdraw her application. No one could say that the work she was doing in England was not a valuable contribution to the war effort.

Lord Glanville noticed her silence and guessed at its cause, although Kate was ashamed to admit that her own form of nationalism was making her reluctant to care for anyone but her own fellow-countrymen. It had always been a joke in the family that the Glanville library contained every book, on however unexpected a subject, that anyone could need. Now its owner not only produced a map but proved himself to be the unlikely owner of a Serbo-Croat dictionary, brought back to England by an ancestor whose Grand Tour had once taken in Diocletian's palace. Kate accepted the gift without enthusiasm and continued to consider her future.

But there was no real choice. It would be disgraceful to withdraw from her commitment so late in the day, leaving Beatrice less than a fortnight to find a substitute. And certainly if she did withdraw she would never be offered a place in any other unit and so would lose her only chance of working in a front-line hospital. It was not so long since she had been convinced that it was there, in the places where men were actually being wounded, that she could be most useful, and that conviction had not changed. Perhaps after a little while she would be allowed to transfer to a different theatre of war. But soldiers could not choose where they would serve. Why should she expect different treatment for herself?

Kate allowed herself one long sigh of disappointment and resignation. Then, as the others looked at her in curious sympathy, she forced herself to smile. After only a few seconds the smile ceased to be a pretence as the warmth of her feelings for her family made themselves felt. When she had so little time left in England, she must fill every moment with happiness. Who could tell, after all, when she would be able to spend Christmas at Blaize again?

1915

1

On the Western Front the enemy was the German; in the Dardanelles it was the Turk; in Serbia it was the louse. Its killing power took Kate by surprise, and the battle against this unexpected adversary began almost from the first moment of her arrival in Serbia.

The journey across a continent disrupted by war had been long and uncomfortable. Kate and her fellow-doctor applied themselves to the Serbo-Croat dictionary and by the end of the journey had at least mastered the difficulties of the Cyrillic alphabet. But this achievement proved to be of only limited use. Now they could read and pronounce words in the unfamiliar letters, but they had yet to learn what the words meant.

Communication was the first problem to confront them when at last the party of doctors and nurses stepped off the train at Kragujevatz. They had been invited to come here and they were expected—a reception committee was waiting for them at the station. But their first impression, gained from an interpreter whose English was almost as incomprehensible as the Serbo-Croat of his companions, was that the British team were not wanted in the town. Women in the medical world were so often undervalued that it was easy to see slights even perhaps where none was intended; but to Kate, tired after the journey and still disappointed that she had not been sent to France, the impression that they were being turned away came as a last straw. To keep her temper under control she supervised the unloading of the expedition's

stores while the senior doctor, Dr. Muriel Forbes, established that
she and the Serbs could converse, after a fashion, in German.

"The reason why they're suggesting we should establish ourselves away from the town is that the arsenal is here in Kragujevatz and there are regular bombing raids by Taube aircraft," Dr.
Forbes reported when the situation had been explained to her.
"It doesn't mean that they don't need or want us. Far from it!
Twenty-one of their own doctors have died in the past five
weeks."

"From the bombs?" asked Kate incredulously.

"No. From typhus. There's an epidemic raging. They've had
four thousand civilian deaths in this town alone and nobody
knows how many are dying in the villages. As well as the regular
military hospital here, there's an emergency building filled with
men wounded in the campaign. That's where they'd expected us
to work, but the typhus is spreading through there as well."

"If we split into two teams, could they give us orderlies?" Kate
asked.

Muriel's smile showed that she had been thinking along the
same lines. "Yes. I asked that question, and the answer was that
with the greatest of ease and pleasure we could be provided with
as many Austrian prisoners of war as we needed."

"Is that safe? I mean, would they have to be under military
guard all the time?"

"I gather that they're only Austrians in the sense that they
were conscripted into the Austrian Army because they lived in
land under Austrian occupation. They're Serbs by race—Bosnians
—and delighted to have been captured—in fact, it sounds as
though most of them deserted. They'd work as volunteers."

"Then we ought to establish a separate hospital for the typhus
victims," said Kate. "Under tents, if possible, and a little way out
of the town."

The two women were so closely in agreement that there was
not even any need to discuss where each of them should go.
Muriel, the elder, was a surgeon and volunteered at once to care
for the wounded soldiers who could not be housed in the main
military hospital.

Three days later Kate's tented hospital received its first patients. Those of the British team who stayed with her had been

allocated their own spheres of responsibility—for nursing, the
kitchen, the dispensary, and the stores—and had set to work at
once to train the Serbo-Austrian orderlies allotted to them. Kate
herself had grasped the greatest nettle of all, that of sanitation
and disinfestation. She was only twenty-four years old and all her
training had been done in teaching hospitals run with an almost
military discipline along lines laid down many years earlier—es-
tablishments whose methods of organisation could not even be
queried by a junior doctor, much less completely rethought. But
her recent work at Blaize had provided useful experience of organising a hospital almost from scratch, and from her father she had
inherited the ability to be definite, taking responsibility and giving firm orders even when she lacked the experience to be sure
that the effects would be as she hoped. From her mother, too, she
had from childhood absorbed the principles of community hy-
giene. Lydia's battle in Jamaica had been against the mosquitoes
which carried malaria and yellow fever and against the insanitary
habits which made dysentery endemic. With the same single-
mindedness Kate declared war on the lice which carried typhus
and on the polluted water which spread the equally dangerous typhoid fever.

To save the wounded soldiers in the town from further infection, Muriel would direct typhus patients to the tented hospital
at once. Even though she expected this, Kate was not prepared
for what she saw as she stepped out of the staff tent at six in the
morning. A row of carts stretched from the perimeter of the camp
back along the road until it disappeared behind the brow of a
hill. There were ox wagons and donkey carts and occasionally a
smaller vehicle—hardly more than a platform on two wheels,
pulled between the shafts by the mother of the child who lay on
it. Old men carried babies in their arms; exhausted women slept
on the verge. There was no noise, no jostling for position; the line
of sufferers waited patiently until someone was ready to help
them.

Kate was already dressed in the costume which she had designed for everyone concerned in the reception of new patients. It
was not beautiful, and only time would tell whether it was effective. She had rubbed her body all over with paraffin and was now
wearing a one-piece garment tightly strapped round her neck,

ankles and wrists. One of her first actions when she realised the dangers had been to cut off most of her thick tawny hair so that the short crop which remained could be easily contained inside a rubber cap. Long boots and rubber gloves completed the outfit.

Careless of the impression she must make, she called for stretcher bearers and hurried to the head of the queue. A tall man with only one arm jumped down from the front of the first ox wagon and led her round to the back. He pulled the canvas aside to reveal more than a dozen children. All were between the ages of three and ten and all were either asleep or unconscious. Their hair was dirty and their clothes ragged, but that was of no importance. What made Kate stare in dismay was the state of the little girl nearest to the light. Her leg rested on a pad of folded sacks but there was no flesh on the bone of the foot and the gangrene was spreading above the knee. Several weeks must have passed since she survived the first onslaught of the typhus and it was clear that in all that time she had received no medical attention.

The one-armed man was saying something, presumably in Serbo-Croat. Kate shook her head to indicate that she did not understand, and he made a second attempt in a language equally unfamiliar to her. She put up a finger to silence him as she made a quick count of the children. Three were in need of immediate surgery, five were in the semicomatose stage of typhus which suggested that they were approaching the point of crisis, two others—awake now and moaning for water—showed the brown blotches on their skins which were the earlier signs of infection, and three were already dead. Only one little girl appeared to be free of typhus and her state was the most serious of all, for it was clear that she was suffering from diphtheria and that an immediate tracheotomy was essential.

Kate pointed out this child and two of the gangrene cases to be the first to go to the special admission tents, where they would undergo a routine of cleansing and disinfecting before being admitted to the ward tents. As she turned away, realising that all the reception arrangements must be multiplied, she had to fight down a a sense of panic. In the weeks of waiting to leave she had done her best to fill the gaps in her experience, but even then she had been part of a team and had never been required to attempt

the most dangerous operations. She had had some surgical training as a medical student, but she was not a qualified surgeon. Beatrice, allowing her to join the unit, had expected her to act only
as Muriel's assistant in this field. But to put a child who was already almost dead from diphtheria back onto a jolting wagon in
order that she could be entrusted to Muriel's safer hands would
be a risk too great to take. From now on, Kate realised, everything she did would be a question of life or death for someone.
This was the moment in which the sentimental disappointment
she had felt in being unable to work with British soldiers fell
away from her mind and never returned. The need for a doctor
here was as great as it could be anywhere else in the world.
Within a short time she would have a little girl's life in her
hands, and it was a life just as important as that of a soldier in
Flanders. To a doctor, nationality must never be of any importance.

The one-armed man made a third attempt to communicate
with her, and this time he spoke in French. Kate had learned
French only from books, but she had a natural talent for languages and could both understand what he said and answer him.
Recognising the anxiety in his voice, she paused for a moment, although there was so much to do.

"Can they be saved?" he asked.

"Three are already dead. We will do our best for the others.
But the gangrene is very serious. Why were they neglected for so
long?"

"They are not my children," said the tall man. "They are
orphans. All of them: no mother, no father. I am a Russian. My
name is Sergei Fedorovich Gorbatov. A woman gave me shelter
on her farm. When she died, there was no one left alive on the
farm except her son there." He pointed to a three-year-old whom
Kate had already marked out as the most likely survivor of the
wagonload. "I heard of your hospital and set out to bring him
here. All these others I have found on the road as I came, or they
have been brought out of their houses by neighbours. Their fathers killed in the army, their mothers dead of disease. Who will
look after them?"

Kate was already sufficiently dismayed by the enormity of the
medical task which she faced. This was no time for her to con-

sider how a ruined social order should rebuild itself. She repeated her promise to do her best before turning away more decisively to make the necessary new arrangements.

"May I give you help?" Sergei was at her side as she crossed the field. He made a gesture towards the empty sleeve of his shabby military coat. "I'm no use to any army now, praise be to God. But I can work as a nurse or a messenger. As your orderly, I could help with any problem of language, between French and Serbo-Croat or German. If you will teach me a little English as well, you will find I learn quickly."

Kate had been too greatly concerned with the children to pay much attention to their escort. Now she looked at him more closely. His tangled beard had given the impression of an older man, but he might not be more than thirty. His eyes, unnaturally bright, glittered out of a face which was too pale, almost grey. His clothes were ragged and he himself was dirty. Nevertheless it was immediately clear that he was not a peasant but an intelligent and educated man.

His offer was tempting. Kate had known even before she arrived that she would not be able to communicate in Serbo-Croat, but she had not realised what a disadvantage her lack of German would be. So many of the Serbs had lived under Austrian rule that this was their second or even their first language. Without Muriel, problems of interpretation could arise with an irritating frequency. Kate's knowledge of the political situation in the Balkans was too vague to explain why a Russian should be here. Perhaps he had deserted and now saw the hospital as a kind of shelter. But it was true that his amputated arm must have turned him into a noncombatant, and he had shown compassion by accepting responsibility for so many sick children. It was time to make another quick decision.

"You may stay as long as the children you have brought are patients here," she said. "First you must move your wagon from the road. Then present yourself at the admission tent. Your beard must be shaved. You will have to be stripped and bathed and rubbed with paraffin and given new clothes before you may go near the other tents. And if you leave the compound at any time after that, you may not come back."

Had she spoken in such a way to an Englishman he would not

have been able to believe his ears, but Sergei saluted her now in a
manner which was not a correct military gesture but was clearly
intended to be admiring rather than mocking. The small incident
was reassuring, re-emphasising her discovery that if she was decisive enough about giving orders, even men would obey promptly.

Sergei made himself so useful that there was no further mention of the suggestion that he should leave with the children.
During the next four months at least a hundred thousand Serbs
died in the typhus epidemic, and in the whole of the country
fewer than a hundred doctors remained alive. Some deaths took
place in Kate's hospital, for many patients arrived too ill to be
saved. But her sanitary barriers proved effective and there were no
cases of cross-infection. Even dysentery was kept at bay in spite of
the lack of plumbing. She also found time to organise dispensary
teams to go out to the villages so that when a second epidemic
began—this time of diphtheria—its victims could be treated with
serum in their own homes.

Kate had been taught that typhus was a cold-weather disease,
and as the summer sun grew hotter it did indeed seem that the
plague was coming to an end. Fewer new patients were brought
to the hospital and, now that the side of the tents could be tied
up to let the breeze blow through, those who remained made a
faster recovery. For the first time since her arrival there were
moments—even half hours—when Kate could feel herself off
duty. Sergei, quick to pick up a little English, insisted on teaching
her Russian in return. Kate protested laughingly that of all the
languages in the world, Russian was the one least likely ever to be
of use to her but was disarmed by his sweeping assertion that to
acquire useless knowledge was the mark of the civilised person.
Her good ear for both languages and music enabled her quickly to
acquire a conversational vocabulary. Learning to read and write
was more difficult, but there was an attraction in finding a use for
her previous study of the Cyrillic alphabet, and the unavailability
of any other books gave her an incentive to master those which
formed Sergei's only luggage. Welcoming the necessity to clear
her mind of medical problems for an hour or so, she enjoyed her
lessons and made good progress. Like a dutiful schoolgirl, she
studied grammar and was rewarded by poetry.

Sergei still acted as her orderly but by September had become a friend. So when a message arrived to say that Muriel was ill, Kate took him with her as she hurried to the town. Muriel had already diagnosed her own symptoms.

"It's typhoid, not typhus," she murmured. "I don't understand it. We've been boiling everything. All the milk, all the water, everything. And I was inoculated in England."

"You'll be all right," said Kate, although she was alarmed by her colleague's appearance.

"Yes," said Muriel. "That's only a matter of nursing. I didn't send for you for that. It's the hospital."

"Leave that to me," Kate said. The organisation of the tented camp was running so smoothly that the rest of her team could continue without her for a while. Putting Muriel in the care of a Scottish nurse, she set out to inspect her new territory.

The building horrified her. She could see that efforts had been made to clean it and keep it clean, but the size and rough condition of the converted barracks made sterile conditions impossible. Typhus, which was dying out elsewhere, still lingered here, fastening on soldiers who at the time of their arrival had been wounded but not infected. She set to work with all the energy she had shown on her first arrival in the country, but as the days passed she found herself more and more tired. Then she could hardly drag herself out of bed in the morning, and merely to move about the hospital became an unbearable effort. Yet in spite of the tiredness her head ached so much that she was unable to sleep. Even before the night when she found herself sweating in bed, her body glowing and almost bubbling with heat, she recognised the symptoms. Typhus! She took her own temperature and was just able to read that it was 105° before she collapsed.

Returning to consciousness, she found Sergei's forearm pressing down on her chest. Her lungs were bursting and there was an almost unbearable pain in her heart. She seemed to have forgotten how to breathe, but Sergei's pressure continued until the pain became too great to endure. She screamed, and at once the tensions in her chest snapped and relaxed. Her lungs emptied and filled again, emptied and filled. Sergei slid down to the floor and sat there for a moment, apparently as exhausted as herself.

When he stood up again he was smiling. He began to sponge her—not only her face but her whole body. She ought to have felt shocked, but somewhere in her memory was the realisation that this had happened before when she was almost but not quite unconscious. Like an expert nurse he rolled her first to one side of the bed and then to the other so that he could change the sheets. She was clean, she was cool and—although still too weak to move —she was better.

"In these three weeks you have died twice," Sergei said. "No heartbeat, no breathing. Even Christ was content with one resurrection. You have always been a most demanding mistress. Keep still and I will find you a proper nurse."

Nurse Cameron arrived within a few moments. She took Kate's temperature and gave an unprofessional sigh of relief.

"Crisis over?" asked Kate. Her body was so weak that she could only whisper, but her mind was as clear as though she had never been ill.

"We'll be needing to feed you up, Doctor. But it should be plain sailing from now on."

"And Dr. Forbes?"

"I hoped you wouldn't ask that so soon."

"You mean—she died of the typhoid?"

"I'm afraid so."

Kate was silent for a few moments, but her responsibility for the hospital overcame her sadness.

"Who's in charge now?"

"The Army sent us an officer. Major Dragovitch. He's seen to the general administration while I've done my best to look after the medical side."

"So who's been caring for me?"

"The Russki," said Nurse Cameron. "He's spent three weeks in this room with you. Nursing and talking. Whenever you were at your lowest he'd talk nonstop, almost as though he thought you'd be too polite to die in the middle of a conversation. How he expected you to understand his foreign lingo I can't imagine. I'm not saying a word against him, though. The reason you didn't die is because he wouldn't let you."

He came back an hour later and looked critically at his patient.

"You're not to think that you're better," he said. "There must be at least three weeks of convalescence. As much of it as possible in the sunshine. I shall arrange for you to go back to the tented hospital so that you can lie in a bed outside all day."

"Yes, Doctor," said Kate. "And Sergei—thank you."

They smiled at each other. In this unexpected life, Kate realised that Sergei had become her closest friend. It was an unlikely enough fate which had brought Kate herself to Kragujevatz. She had often wondered what equally surprising story might explain Sergei's exile from his own country, but had never before liked to enquire. But now weakness and gratitude combined to make her feel that there were no questions she could not ask. "Why did you leave Russia, Sergei?" she said.

Sergei sat down on the wooden chair beside her bed. "Do you know what happened in St. Petersburg in 1905?" he asked.

Kate shook her head and he tutted sadly. "The British are interested in nothing but the problems of their own empire," he said.

"If that were true, we should hardly be fighting a war on behalf of Belgium. In any case, in 1905 I was a child living in Jamaica."

"So you've never heard of Bloody Sunday? That's where I lost my arm. You may have thought I was fighting valiantly against the Germans when I was wounded. It's an impression I don't trouble to correct. But I was just a student, marching peacefully with thousands of others to deliver a petition to the Tsar, when the Cossacks charged into us. The Cossacks have a very special kind of whip. Long and strong, and at the end dividing into two thongs with a thin strip of lead between them. It's not intended for use on their horses, you understand. I was one of the lucky ones. At least I was alive when at last the horses galloped away. But while I was lying there in the snow I realised that it would be useless ever again to appeal to the Tsar against the incompetence and cruelty of his own agents. The people must take power into their own hands."

"So you became a revolutionary?"

"All I did was to travel round the docks and factories, suggesting to the workers that they should form committees and con-

sider the possibility of strikes. In October of that year there was a
general strike and it was successful. The Tsar granted us a constitution. But within a week everyone who had been concerned with
the strike was either under arrest or in hiding. Once again I was
fortunate. I was able to escape. But I can never go back to Russia.
There have been sad years." He paused for a little while as
though to remember them. "Now the roads of Europe are filled
with refugees, owning only what they can carry on their backs. I
have become merely one of millions. You remember the children
I brought to the hospital? The orphans?"

"Of course."

"I arranged for those who recovered to go to a monastery in the
north. There's someone there who will never turn away anyone in
need, as I found for myself. This morning I received a letter from
him to say that a new offensive has started. The Germans and
Austrians have launched a combined attack along the whole
length of the northern front. The monastery is under shellfire and
he has had to send the children south for their own safety. So
they're on the road again with nowhere to go—no homes, no
families. What hope have they for the future, these little ones?
Who will feed them? Who will care for them?" He sighed.
"Well, we must give thanks for each extra day of existence that is
granted to us. If we can survive to the end of this trouble, perhaps it will be possible to build up a new life somewhere. As for
you, you must build up your strength as fast as possible, before we
have to go."

"Go where?" asked Kate.

"You've seen the Serbian Army. Brave men, but peasants. They
have good discipline but no equipment, and there are too few of
them. How long do you think they can hold back the armies of
two military nations? For a little while, perhaps, because they
know the terrain and they have the support of the people. But
unless the Allies can spare men from the Western Front to
strengthen them, this hospital will be in the hands of the invaders
before November. The Germans and the Austrians are civilised
enough. At least they obey their officers. But as soon as they win
their first victory, the Bulgars will take the opportunity to invade
from the south, picking the bones of Serbia like vultures. And I

can tell you, the Bulgars are animals. They violate children, they cut off women's breasts. I haven't kept you alive for the enjoyment of devils like these. Before the town is captured, you will have to take your hospital away."

2

In the village where Kate Lorimer had spent her childhood, her father lay ill in bed. The secret of Jamaica's luxuriant vegetation lay in the generous proportion of tropical rain to tropical heat, but the same combination produced a humidity oppressive to a sick man. Soaked in sweat, Ralph Lorimer listened to the pounding of the rain as it hurled itself against the roof. He shivered with cold even while his body burned with fever. A dozen times an hour he flung off his bed coverings but on each occasion was forced to grope for them again almost immediately. This was the most severe attack he could remember since the first bout of malaria had taken him by surprise nearly thirty years before.

Lydia would come as soon as she could. It would be humiliating to send a messenger for her merely in order that he might be made more comfortable. As a general rule Ralph was proud of the dedication with which his wife devoted herself to the medical care of his congregation. He knew how childish it was to wish that for once she would neglect her surgery in the interest of her husband. He knew, too, that his illness was not dangerous. It would burn itself out, as it always had before—and any of the village women would have been proud to come to the pastor's house and nurse the head of their community. It was Ralph's own choice that only Lydia should care for him, and the price he paid for it was her absence whenever anyone else was ill.

As abruptly as it had begun three hours earlier, the drumming of the rain stopped, although for some time longer he could hear the splash of water dripping from the roof on to the edge of the verandah. The wet season was coming to an end. Soon the December days of unbroken sunshine would be here, and Ralph, fit and strong once again, would be able to stride as usual across the land of the Bristow plantation which had been reclaimed from jungle under his inspiration. Violent changes of weather were part of the Jamaican pattern. It was normal that November should bring rain and just as normal that the rain would stop. The only difference between the routines of 1915 and those of previous years was the fear which nagged perpetually at Ralph's mind: the fear that some harm would come to Kate or Brinsley. To Lydia he never spoke of the dangers—there was no need to, for she knew them well enough and shared his anxiety. And sometimes he was able to persuade himself that they were groundless. Kate was not in Flanders; whilst Brinsley, who had spent more than a year at the battlefront, appeared to bear a charmed life. So many of his fellow-volunteers had been killed that he had already been promoted to captain, but so far he had not been even slightly wounded.

In the comparative silence which followed the rainstorm, Ralph could hear Lydia approaching. She came very slowly, her progress tracked by the cheerful shouts of the villagers she passed and her own quieter, breathless responses. The village was built on a double slope: the land fell from the mountains of the interior towards the flat coastal plains and was also cut almost into a gorge by the stream which crashed down in a waterfall before tumbling towards the sea. That might have been enough to explain Lydia's frequent need to pause and rest—but Ralph knew that there was another reason. His resentment of it rose even before she came into the room.

She carried his medicine in one hand and, although everything about her face and body proclaimed her tiredness, she smiled at him with an attempt at her old liveliness. Her other hand supported her ten-year-old son as he straddled her hip. Grant was reluctant to release his clutch of her neck as she set him gently down in a corner of the room and Ralph found himself grinding his teeth in a vain attempt to control his anger.

"Lydia, it will have to stop!" he exclaimed. "You're not strong enough to carry Grant around like this."

"I can manage for a little longer," she said. She gave him the medicine and with cool water and clean sheets applied herself to making him comfortable. But although Ralph was tempted to relax in the ease she provided, he could not control the irritation caused by his son's presence.

"Could you carry me?" he demanded. "If I asked you to lift me out of bed, could you do it? Of course you couldn't. And no more will you be able to carry Grant as he grows. The moment must come when he'll no longer be able to depend on you in such a way, and you're doing him no service to prolong the dependence."

"It's very difficult for him when the paths are so wet and slippery. I don't think you realise. His lameness—"

"I know all about his lameness," Ralph interrupted. "But I also know that he is ten years old. He's not a baby to be pampered and petted, and you're not strong enough to treat him as though he were. He must find some way to move about by himself. I had a crutch made for him, and he ought to use it. Otherwise his other muscles will waste away as well for lack of exercise."

"You ought not to talk like this in front of him," said Lydia uneasily.

"Then he is the one who should go. This is my room and I'll say what I please in it. Go to your own room, Grant." He waited a moment but his son did not move. "I said, get out. Did you hear me? Get out of here."

Naked and very tall, he must have appeared like a giant to the frightened boy as he left his bed and staggered across the room, dizzy with the effects of fever. At the last moment the fair-haired boy twisted away from his father and half rolled, half slithered out of the room.

"You see!" exclaimed Ralph. "He can move well enough when he wants to. It's our duty, yours and mine together, to teach him the best way to use what strength he has. But how can I expect to succeed when you always go behind my back to spoil him?"

Exhausted by the effort, he flung himself back into bed, hoping that Lydia would smooth the sheet and make him comfortable again. But instead she followed Grant out on to the verandah, her lips tight with anger.

Ralph groaned to himself as he lay back on the pillow. Lydia had been the best wife that any man could hope for until the birth of that last, unwanted child; but these days there seemed to be as much quarrelling as love between them. He tossed restlessly from side to side until weakness combined with the humidity to exhaust him. For a little while he slept, and awoke to find Duke sitting beside the bed.

The sight of his assistant never failed to cheer Ralph. Perhaps it was Duke's own smile that worked the miracle. At least three of the young man's ancestors had been white men, so that his skin was lighter than that of most of the islanders, but his flashing white teeth and ready grin were typical of Jamaica. Sometimes when Ralph was angry with Lydia and sickened by the sight of Grant, he longed to proclaim that Brinsley was not the only son of whom he could feel proud, that Duke was a Lorimer as well. But that was a secret which had been kept for twenty-eight years and he recognised how hurtful it would be to reveal the truth now.

"I brought the accounts," Duke said. "But if you too tired, next week good enough."

"No, I'll look at them now." Ralph struggled to sit up, with Duke's help. "Bring me something to drink."

The water from the covered pitcher was too warm to be refreshing. Ralph drank it thirstily but without enjoyment. Half apologetically, Duke took a small bottle from the pouch on his belt.

"Put that away!" Ralph ordered. "If you came more often to chapel, you'd know how strongly I feel about total abstinence."

"A little rum in the water helps fight the fever," said Duke. "Strong medicine, not drink."

He poured it as he spoke, and held it out. Ralph shook his head and then looked in irritation towards the open door as he heard from outside the familiar sound of Grant calling for his mother. He would have gone out to whip the whining child if he had been strong enough, for suddenly he felt that he could bear Grant's petulance no longer. Perhaps that was why he abandoned the principles of a lifetime and in an angry gesture drained the gourd which Duke was holding to his lips.

The rum was not watered at all. Ralph gasped as the spirit burned his throat. For a moment he dared not move or even speak; then his whole body flushed with warmth, balancing the heat of the fever so that for a little while he ceased to shiver and could relax in comfort.

"Mother! Mother!" Outside, Grant was still shouting, more loudly now and with a trace of desperation. "Mother!"

It sounded as though Lydia for once was not near enough to come running to the boy's call. Perhaps, thought Ralph hopefully, she had at last taken some notice of her husband's opinion and had left Grant to look after himself. His anger faded into a feeling of well-being. It might be as well after all to leave the accounts until next week. He was just sliding back into a sleeping position when Grant called again. "Father! Father!"

"Come here if you want me!" Ralph shouted back. The response was automatic and yet even as he expressed his annoyance he was uneasy. It was surprising that Grant should call for someone he knew to be angry with him. And there were other sounds outside by now: a scrambling of bare feet, a murmuring of low voices. Ralph gestured at Duke to go and see what was happening.

"And tell that child to stop shouting," he said. While he tried to keep a normal irritation in his voice, fear was growing in his heart. He stayed in bed as Duke went out, so that for a few moments longer he could pretend that nothing was wrong, but the effects of the rum had worn off already and his body was rigid with cold.

When Duke returned he was carrying Grant. He stood in the doorway for a moment, almost as near to tears as the sobbing ten-year-old. Then he moved out of the way, and four of the villagers carried Lydia inside.

3

The building of Brinsley House at the end of the eighteenth century had been a gesture indicating a change of status. From that time onwards the Lorimers ceased to be merely one out of many shipping families of Bristol and were acknowledged as merchant princes. Magnificently dominating the Avon Gorge, the house was designed to be filled with large numbers of children, servants, and guests. It was in Brinsley House that John Junius

Lorimer had brought up his three legitimate children, William, Margaret, and Ralph; and it was to this same house that Margaret had brought her half sister, Alexa, orphaned at the age of nine. From the ruins of the family fortune after the bank crash of 1878 William had managed to salvage his father's mansion, and had in turn brought up his own three children there. But William was dead; and his elder son, Matthew, had quarrelled with his parents in 1895 and, turning his back on any possible inheritance, had left Bristol for Paris, never since returning. As the end of 1915 approached, Arthur Lorimer lived alone in the mansion, attended only by a few servants who were too young or too old for war work.

It was not a style of existence which suited the old house and, at the moment when one of the Lorimer Line's banana boats was approaching the Portishead docks with letters from Ralph Lorimer on board as well as produce from the Bristow plantation, Arthur had evolved a plan to bring the place briefly back to life.

"I've been thinking about Christmas," he said to his sister Beatrice, who had travelled from London for a weekend free from the fear of Zeppelin raids. "You'll spend it at Brinsley House, I hope. Mrs. Shaw asked yesterday whether she should arrange for the usual decorations to be put in place. At first I thought it unnecessary to go to such trouble when only two of us will be here. But then I had second thoughts. It seems a pity to abandon old customs. So I told her that I should want a tree to be decorated as usual, and holly and candles to be arranged in the galleries. And with that picture in my mind, I've decided to hold a children's party. Or even more than one."

He was amused by the expression of horror on her face. Beatrice had no interest in children and no liking for them. "Whose children?" she demanded.

"First of all the children of my employees. But in addition to them, there are a good many boys and girls in Bristol whose fathers are at the front and whose mothers have trouble enough to provide even the most necessary food. They're not likely to receive many of the presents which you and I could always expect in our childhood. We could give them here, I thought, an afternoon to remember, a little brightness in the gloom. It wouldn't be too difficult to arrange. A few games to play, perhaps a con-

jurer to amuse them, a really good tea and a parcel to take home.
I hope such a prospect wouldn't frighten you away, Beatrice. I
should need your advice. And your help too, on the day."

He knew that he could rely on it. Beatrice's talent for organisation had been increased rather than completely satisfied by her
office work in London. She acted as a kind of remote quarter-
master for all the women's units sent abroad by the suffrage
movement and took pride in obtaining and despatching all the
supplies for which she was asked, although their safe arrival was
not always within her power to secure. As he had expected, she
gave the quick nod which meant that she accepted his proposal in
spite of its unexpectedness.

"I'll buy the gifts for you and wrap them, if you like," she
offered. "Tell me how much you want to spend on each, how
many girls you expect and how many boys. And of what ages."

"Thank you very much. But Beatrice, don't choose presents
that are too sensible."

"What do you mean?"

"I've no doubt the mothers would like to see a warm garment
or a pair of shoes come out of each parcel. But I want to see the
children smile with pleasure rather than gratitude. They should
have toys. Something to play with. Something that their parents
might consider a waste of money."

"You surprise me more and more, Arthur, but very well. I'll
buy skipping ropes and dolls and footballs and tin soldiers."

Arthur was not ashamed that she should think him sentimental. He had never tried to hide the pleasure he took in the
sight of children. The smallness of their neat, slim bodies, the animal energy of their movements, their unrestrained pleasure in
making a noise: all these things won his approval. Perhaps he
envied them a freedom of movement which he had never been
able to indulge—the precision of his mind as he marshalled the
figures which kept his business prosperous was reflected in his
tight, unhurried walk and quiet voice.

"Would Aunt Margaret care to come to your party, do you
think?" asked Beatrice. "I remember how very much she enjoyed
playing with us when we were small."

"I should think she'll have enough to do as commandant of the
hospital at Blaize," Arthur replied. "But I'll invite her, of course.

And Frisca would be the same age as many of the young guests. She might like to come as well."

While he was considering his idea for the party he had needed to remind himself that not all children were like Frisca. It was true that he liked little girls in general, but Frisca was almost an idealisation of childhood made flesh. Blonde, blue-eyed, beautiful, and irrespressibly energetic, she aroused in him a longing to own her so that he could buy pretty clothes for her and show her off and feel proud of her. But the children of his employees were more likely to be shy and badly dressed.

Enough time had been spent on frivolities. Even on a Saturday evening Arthur was not sorry to be interrupted by a messenger from his dockside office. A ship was just in from Jamaica and a lengthy detour made necessary by the danger of submarine attack had put part of her cargo at risk of spoiling.

"I'll come at once," Arthur said. He glanced at the letters which the messenger had brought from the ship. Two of them were from his uncle Ralph—one addressed to himself and one to be put in the post for Margaret. But they, like the rest, could wait until he returned.

"We could ask Matthew," said Beatrice suddenly.

Puzzled, Arthur paused in the doorway. He had already dismissed the subject of the party from his mind and did not take his sister's meaning at once.

"For Christmas," explained Beatrice. "His quarrel was never with us but only with our parents. Now that they are both dead, we could all be friends again."

It was not a suggestion to be adopted too impulsively. Arthur knew how attached Beatrice had always been to the elder of her two brothers, and how much it had upset her when he ran away from home to become an artist. But it was necessary for Arthur to consider his own position.

There was no danger, he decided. Their father's will—in which William recognised that it was his younger son who deserved to inherit the Lorimer business interests and who had the talent to manage them—had been watertight. And if Matthew had wished to challenge it or even to appeal for generosity, he would have done so long ago. As Beatrice said, there was nothing to prevent them from resuming a friendly relationship.

Except, it occurred to him, for one practical difficulty.

"I agree with you in principle," he said. "It would be a good gesture. But how are we to get in touch with him? I've no idea whereabouts in the world he is at this moment."

4

Young men were swept into the Army by dreams of glory, by the shame of being presented with white feathers, or by the prospect of a regular weekly wage. None of these considerations affected Matthew Lorimer, and if anyone had asked him why he had enlisted he would have been hard put to it to find a sensible answer. There was no conscription as yet and his forty-second birthday even excluded him from the voluntary scheme under which men attested their willingness to serve when they were needed. He felt no hatred for the Germans, although it was true that his years in Paris had given him a love for France and a wish to see its soil free once again from the devastation of battle. Nor was he in any sense a combatant. He had joined the Army only because that was a necessary first step towards secondment as an official war artist.

Nobody had compelled or even invited him to spend his time sketching the shell-shocked landscape of craters and barbed wire, with wounded men propped against sandbags and stretcher-bearers ducking low as they dashed from the dubious shelter of one hedge to another—in fact, his realistic pictures of soldiers hardly recognisable as human beings beneath their coverings of mud and blood were not always to War Office taste. He could have continued to prosper as a painter of portraits. There were still plenty of rich women in England. They looked a little more tired than in the previous year and their eyes could not always conceal the sadness of bereavement as their sons or brothers, husbands or fiancés were lost to them in the Flanders trenches or on the Gallipoli beaches. But their commissions for portraits could have kept Matthew alive if he had chosen to make his living in that way; and in addition a new market had opened as the war news grew grimmer and frightened mothers commissioned paintings of sons who might never return from France.

Only restlessness could explain why Matthew should have turned his back on all that. He had been restless all his life, but at first there had been a purpose to his sudden movements. When he left England as a young man it was not solely because he was bored with accounts and shipping statistics: more positively, he had set his heart on a painting career. And when, ten years later, he abandoned his life in Paris, it was not out of dissatisfaction but because of his projected marriage to Alexa. The discovery that Alexa was his aunt—a relationship for many years concealed by her adoption and by the closeness of their ages, had left him in a state of shock. Recognising that he could never marry her, he was unable to prevent himself from continuing to love her. Jealous and unhappy, he had watched from the back of the admiring crowd as she emerged from her wedding at St. Margaret's, Westminster, on the arm of Lord Glanville. Secretly he hoped that she had chosen to acquire a title and a fortune by marriage only as a compensation—because by an absurd accident of birth she was separated from the man she really loved. At some point, he knew, he would have to accept in his heart what his reason had already recognised as an inevitable and permanent separation; but until that point came he drifted without purpose, using the war as an excuse for physical insecurity in order that he need no longer come to terms with the deeper purposelessness of his life.

In the last month of 1915, Matthew was back in England. The Battle of Loos seemed to have existed in a different world from that of his quiet Chelsea studio, but as he worked his sketches up into a large painting of the battlefield at night all its sounds came back to haunt him: the boom of cannons, the spitting of machine guns, the erratic stabs of rifle fire, the deafening explosions of shells and grenades, and, above all, the screams of the wounded. He slept badly, continually waking in a nightmare conviction that he had been blinded and would never paint again. In an effort to tire himself out, he stayed at the easel until the small hours of every morning. So when his doorbell rang late on a December evening, his strained eyes failed to focus immediately on the young woman who stood outside.

She was a working girl whose shabby clothes were too thin to prevent her from shivering in the winter air. After allowing him a few seconds to study her, she gave a resigned laugh.

"You don't recognise me."

Her voice, with its Midland accent, stirred Matthew's memory and he stared harder at the strong-boned face.

"Of course I do." Matthew had abandoned the snobbish class judgements of his parents on the day he left Brinsley House. Even if he had not had a particular reason for kindness in this case, he would never have begrudged politeness to someone whom his mother would have regarded only as a possible applicant for a post as kitchen maid. "It took me a moment to move my mind from the picture I'm working on, that's all. Come upstairs."

She looked curiously at the huge painting as she followed him into the studio and allowed him to take her coat.

"Is that what it's like, then?"

"No. I can't find any way to paint the noise. This is a safe and silent version of hell. The reality is rather different."

"Bit of a change from when you were painting me."

"It's all connected, though. These explosions of light are caused by the shells which you help to make. Well, perhaps these are shells filled by some German Peggy, but yours will be having the same effect on the other side of the line."

She was intelligent enough to be amused at the way in which he let her know that he had remembered her name.

"What happened to the picture you did of me?" she asked.

"The munitions factory one went to be turned into a poster. One of a series to persuade women to take up essential war work. The other one's here somewhere. Sit down, and I'll find it."

Earlier in the year he had been asked to make a portfolio on the Home Front and chose to concentrate on the contribution which women were making to the war. Everywhere he went he found women doing men's jobs, from farm labourers and gamekeepers in the country to bus conductors and policewomen in the towns. Particularly in the factories, as the men moved out the women moved in. Peggy had been making fuses in a munitions factory when he first sketched her three months ago. She worked long hours in conditions which he privately regarded as criminally dangerous and was faced at the end of the day with a long walk to the poor lodgings which were all she could afford. She was not by birth a town girl, and yet not exactly a country girl either. Her father was a coal miner and her home in Leicestershire was a mining village. There had been no openings for girls there, she had told him and, although she could have found employment on a farm nearer to home, she had some talent for sewing and was reluctant to expose her hands to such rough work in all weathers.

Matthew had found the firm boldness of her features intriguing, marking her out from the other girls in the fuse room. He offered her money to spend a few hours sitting for him in his studio, but her exhaustion when she came was such that she fell asleep while he was painting her. The canvas which he now pulled out of the rack depicted her in just that state—a young woman completely worn out by her work.

She stared at it critically for a few moments, then sighed.

"I should've stayed asleep a bit longer," she said. "I've fallen."

The phrase was unfamiliar to Matthew, and she realised that he was puzzled. "A baby," she explained. "I'll be having a baby, come June."

Inwardly Matthew groaned, but he did not allow any dismay to show on his face. "Is it mine?" he asked. There was no denying that he had taken advantage of her in every sense, at a moment when she was only half awake; and there had been other meetings in the month which followed, before he left for France. But she had not been a virgin.

"Oh, yes," she said. "The first time, it were with a lad from our village. More nor a year ago. I were going to marry him. He never come back from Ypres. That were the reason I took this munition work. To get my own back, so to speak. There were no one after him, till you."

"I'll give you some money," said Matthew. "You can go home to your parents, I suppose."

"Not in this state, I can't. I could go home as a wife. Or even as a widow, if it came to that. But I'll not show my face there with a bastard. Me dad would kill me. And me mam's dead."

"I can't marry you, if that's what you're after," said Matthew. He chose the words carefully. They meant only that if he could not marry Alexa he was not prepared to marry anyone at all, but with luck they would suggest that he was married already. If necessary he would tell the full lie, but he still hoped that the matter could be settled without a quarrel.

"But you live alone here."

"That doesn't mean that I'm free."

"It means I could move in," she said. "You'd find it cheaper to support me and the child here than in lodgings. You could do with a bit of housekeeping, by the look of it. And a baby ought to have a father."

"You're asking too much," said Matthew; and some of the spirit which had first attracted his attention flashed angrily into her eyes.

"*You* asked enough, didn't you? You expect me to walk out of here with a pound or two in my pocket and to feed your child on it for fourteen years or so, until he's big enough to earn?"

"Of course not. I'll send you something every week. It won't be a lot, though. I'm not much better off than you are."

Peggy laughed her disbelief. "It won't do," she said. "If you can't marry then I must do without the marriage, but there's no reason why you shouldn't pretend. If I live here with you, me dad'll think all's right and proper. And if it turns out later that you've got a wife tucked away somewhere he'll be sorry for me, perhaps, instead of spitting at me on the doorstep." The anger faded from her face and was replaced by a look of mischievous invitation. "The baby won't be here for getting on six months," she pointed out. "We could have a bit of fun before that. And if I keep on working for a while longer, with no lodgings to pay, I can save enough for clothes to start him off. It wouldn't be so bad, you know."

She stood on tiptoe to kiss him. Even while he returned her embrace, Matthew considered the proposal. He had been lucky so far, he supposed—because she was certainly not the only one of his models over the years who had been persuaded to stay for the night when a sitting was over. It had been a mistake, in retrospect, to expect that Peggy would behave like a professional, accepting any accident as the luck of the game; but since he had made the mistake, he must pay for it. And although he had no very strong family feeling, Matthew recognised his responsibility to the unborn child. It could not be right that his son should be brought up in the kind of poverty to which Peggy would soon descend if she were left unsupported.

There was not even any reason why he should not allow her the marriage certificate which would make her respectable in the eyes of her family. That was not a decision to be taken on impulse now, but it was something to be considered. Peggy was a decent enough girl, clean and hard-working. He might even find himself emerging at last from the squalor in which he had lived for the past twenty years. Certainly, as she reminded him, he could take pleasure in her company. The collapse of his hopes of marriage to Alexa had left him emotionally shattered, and his experience of war in the past year—even as a spectator—made him profoundly pessimistic. His ambition to be a great artist one day had already faded and now he no longer expected to obtain any great satisfaction from life. There were no plans which would be endangered merely because he found himself encumbered with Peggy.

And perhaps, he thought as he kissed her again with more enthusiasm, responding to her invitation, perhaps a permanent relationship of this kind, and the family life which the birth of a child would bring, might have one positive effect. Alexa's marriage to Lord Glanville had not succeeded in stifling his obsession with her. But a new way of life and a woman of his own—surely now at last, if he really made the effort, he could force himself to forget Alexa.

5

The guests who enjoyed the hospitality of Blaize at the end of 1915 wore uniforms of hospital blue instead of the clothes appropriate to weekend house party guests. And they stayed longer. But the mistress of the house continued to regard herself as a hostess. The change from country house to hospital, originally planned to meet a temporary emergency, had by now taken on a permanent air. The old tithe barn which Alexa had earlier converted to a riverside theatre had been stripped of its seats and was used as a single long ward for soldiers who had survived operations in

France or London but were still seriously ill. A scattering of ugly huts around it housed nurses and orderlies and could provide an isolation ward in case of infectious disease. As the men became convalescent they moved up to the house. The orangery was a ward for wheelchair cases. The ballroom was divided into cubicles for men who were learning to walk on crutches. And the east wing was occupied by doctors and a dozen patients, mainly blind, who were able to manage the stairs.

With thoughts similar to Arthur's in Brinsley House, Alexa had been making plans to entertain her many guests for Christmas. In the office which had once been a smoking room she expounded them now to Margaret.

"Each of the men will find two stockings on their beds on Christmas morning," she said. "Khaki ones, of course. All the women in the village have been knitting frantically to get enough finished. And Piers has been collecting little things to put inside. Tin trumpets, false noses, bags of sweets."

"You're treating them like children," said Margaret, laughing.

"They must feel like children, lying there helpless. If they didn't, how would they ever be able to tolerate all the business of bedpans and being washed by nurses? But there'll be adult things as well. Plenty of cigarettes, of course; and we've been offered two hundred copies of St. Matthew's Gospel in a pocket size. Anyway, we shall see to it that the stockings are filled. And I shall provide a Christmas meal. Everything will come from our own resources, the home farm with the help of one or two of the tenants, so you won't need to go through all this ridiculous War Office requisition business. I've already been promised turkeys, sausages, bacon, beer, potatoes, and sprouts; and the plum puddings were made here a month ago. Piers will pull out some port wine to drink the King's health."

"Are you leaving me anything to do at all?" asked Margaret.

"We need some crackers," said Alexa, consulting her list. "The children in the village school are making paper chains and streamers and painting nativity pictures to be hung up. We must make the wards look really cheerful. There's plenty of holly and mistletoe in the grounds."

"Just stop for a moment," Margaret pleaded. "Who's going to put up all these decorations?"

"The VADs could do that in their spare moments, surely," Alexa suggested.

"You'll need to check that with Matron. They aren't allowed to have many spare moments, poor girls. Whatever you ask them to do will be extra to their nursing duties."

"They'll want to do it, all the same," Alexa said confidently. "We'll have carol singing in the ballroom on Christmas Day, and I'll form a little choir to sing in the Theatre Ward."

"The VADs again?"

"Well, we ought to have a few women's voices. I should think there'll be plenty of volunteers. And on Boxing Day you've already agreed that we can put on an entertainment."

Alexa had made it her contribution to the war effort not only to sing to the troops herself but to assemble a concert party which would provide a programme of varied entertainment. Naturally she had reserved the Christmas booking for her home ground.

"Ah now, I have a point to raise on the subject of the entertainment," said Margaret. She searched her overcrowded desk for a letter and read it out with a solemn expression on her face. " 'Dear Commandant Aunt, Mamma is going to give a concert at Christmas and there will be a lot of singing and playing the piano and making jokes but no dancing. I wish to offer my services as a dancer and I shall be very good. Yours faithfully with love and kisses, Frisca.' I take it she's already approached you on the subject?"

"Yes," said Alexa. "I've never included dancing in the programme because so many of these men will never be able to dance again. And because often they can't *see* the concert very well, if they aren't able to sit up, but they can hear it. In any case, Frisca's too young for this sort of thing."

"How old were you when you first sang in public?" asked Margaret.

"My mother was dying. I needed the money." But Alexa had not needed the reminder that she was only nine years old when she made her first public appearance—in a music hall, not an opera house, but to just as much applause as she was to attract later on. She was willing to be persuaded if Margaret felt strongly enough to press the point.

"Some of these men have babies they've never seen," Margaret said. "A good many of them must have wondered whether their children would grow up without knowing what their fathers looked like. They've spent more than a year, most of them, living with death and with other men in a world which hardly seems to include children at all. I think the sight of Frisca might well make some of them cry. But if she's prepared to face this rather special kind of audience, it can do nothing but good to remind them that they can hope to return to the sort of normal domestic life in which little girls smile and show off."

"Whatever you command shall be done," Alexa conceded. "And now I can see that you'd like to be left to your paperwork." She smiled at her sister as she went out, but before the door closed behind her she saw that Margaret was about to be interrupted again and stepped back into the office to give warning. "There's someone else waiting to see you. One of the VADs. And by the look of her, you're going to need a spare handkerchief."

6

The young women who joined the Voluntary Aid Detachment as their contribution to the war effort were conscientious and willingly hard-working. But most of them were girls of good family, brought up in homes run entirely by servants, so that even the simplest chores had to be explained to them. It was easy for Matron and the charge-sisters to become impatient when, out of anxiety to please, the VADs spent longer on some routine duty than a professional nurse would have done. It was tempting, as well, to allocate all the most unpleasant tasks to them on the grounds that they were still only semiskilled.

Margaret sympathised with both sides in the frequent disputes which arose. But she regarded herself mainly as the protector of the girls who were young, inexperienced, and overworked and who in most cases had never lived away from home before. Matron was well able to look after herself.

For this reason she was careful not to show any sign of impatience as Nurse Jennifer Blakeney came in, although the weekly roll of patients required by the War Office still lay uncompleted on the desk.

"Good morning, Nurse," she said. She kept her voice cheerful, although Jennifer's unhappiness was plain enough. "What's the problem?"

"Matron told me to report to you," said Jennifer, and was then apparently unable to go on.

"Yes?"

"She said I ought to consider with you whether I was suited to my work."

"That's a fairly large matter to consider," Margaret said. "Sit down, Nurse. Have I had a chitty from Matron about you?" She began to search through the papers on her desk to see whether there was some complaint that she had overlooked.

"No, Dr. Scott. It's only just happened."

"What has just happened?"

As carefully as though Matron herself were presenting the case for the prosecution, Jennifer recited a list of her offences, culminating in Sister's discovery that she had poured out twenty mugs of tea, left them standing on a tray for half an hour, and had then poured the tea away and washed up the mugs.

"So you're not concentrating properly on your work," said Margaret. "But I've had good reports of you before. I take it that something has happened." She recognised the silence which followed as that of someone who knows that if she tries to speak she will burst into tears. Alexa's quick summing-up of the situation had been correct. "Have you had some bad news?" she enquired.

It was not a guess which required very much intuition on her part. There was hardly a family in England which had not by now been given cause for grief. Margaret herself, with her son and her nephew still unhurt, knew that she was luckier than most people.

Jennifer nodded and the tears began to run down her cheeks. "My brother," she said.

"Killed?"

Jennifer nodded again, doing her best to stem the flow with much rubbing of her handkerchief.

"I'm very sorry, my dear."

"But it's not just that," said Jennifer. Now that the main fact was established, the words came tumbling out. "It was my father who wrote to tell me. He's quite old. My mother died six years ago and now that Geoffrey's dead—well, he's upset, of course, as I am, but more than that." She looked up, red-eyed. "He wants me to go home."

"To give up your work, you mean?"

"Yes. To look after him. Or just to live with him. He's lonely. He didn't mind too much while he could think that Geoffrey and I would both come back in the end, but now he's frightened."

"You're only a volunteer, of course," Margaret said carefully. "Not an enlisted soldier. You have the right to resign if you wish."

"But I don't want—Dr. Scott, I don't know what I ought to do. I've done my training, I think I'm some use here—I know I've been careless this last week, but I could stop that. I'm sure it's my duty to go on nursing, and yet there's my duty to my father as well, and no one else can do that for me." The tears welled into her eyes again and she buried her head in her hands.

Margaret allowed her a moment to bring herself under control. She was a slight girl, probably not more than twenty, with fair hair and a pale, pretty face spoiled only by anxious eyes. It was tempting to be purely sympathetic, and certainly the child needed comfort. But Margaret had spent many years acting as the supervisor and friend-in-need of young women who were training to be doctors and knew that there were times when firmness was more helpful than kindness.

"So you're doing one of your duties badly because you can't choose which of two you ought to accept," she said as Jennifer's sniffs came to an end at last. "I know how tempting it is for parents of my generation to believe that they have a right to their daughters' company and I can see that your love for your father makes this a very difficult choice for you. It's not for me to say what you should decide. There's no right or wrong about it. What is certain is that you must make a decision and when you've made it you must hold to it without regrets. Sometimes, I think, it's better to be definite than to be right." She paused for a moment to consider. "Did you tell Matron about your brother's death?"

"No, Doctor."

"I'll have a word with her. As far as this past week is concerned, I'm sure we can all forget about it and you'll make sure that there's no further cause for complaint. But with regard to the future—I'll give you a week's compassionate leave. A visit to your father will be a comfort to you both, and while you're at home you will make your decision." She opened the leave book which Matron had brought for her approval that morning. All the VADs hoped that they might be allowed home for Christmas, but Jennifer's case seemed stronger than most. "I'll present you with another choice at once. If you think it will mean more to your father, I'll change the rota so that you may have Christmas leave. Or else you may go home at once and come back before Christmas Eve."

It seemed that Jennifer had learned her lesson, for she made her choice without hesitation.

"I wouldn't want to spoil anyone else's hopes for Christmas," she said. "I very much appreciate your offer of leave now, and I'd like to accept it."

Even after Jennifer had left, Margaret was not allowed long without interruption. But the arrival of the post was always welcome and she smiled to see a letter from her brother.

Her smile was quick to fade. Ralph's letter was long and rambling, incoherent almost to the point of incomprehensibility. But although he did not state in so many words that Lydia was dead, there could be no other possible interpretation of the grief and anger and loneliness which he had poured out on paper.

For a long time Margaret stared blankly at the wall in front of her. Lydia had been her friend for fifty years. They were playmates as children in Bristol, and as medical students in London had lived and worked together for the hardest and happiest years of their lives. It was as a direct result of Margaret's matchmaking that her brother had married Lydia and taken her off to Jamaica. And now her dear friend was dead. It was to be expected at her age, she supposed, that she must lose one by one everyone whom she had loved when she was young, until now only Ralph himself remained, but this particular bereavement made her feel that her youth itself had disappeared. There would be no one now with whom she could exchange memories of bicycle rides and theatres and examinations and all the struggles that had been necessary before the two of them were accepted in a profession dominated by men. Lydia—dear, ugly Lydia—had always been so merry, laughing away the tiredness of nights on duty and the drudgery of each new subject which had to be studied.

How merry had Lydia been in the last years of her life, Margaret wondered. She had never complained at the need for her two elder children to spend so much time away from home for the sake of their education, but it must have come as a bitter blow when the war prevented their return just as hopes of a reunion were highest. Brinsley and Kate were such handsome children, sturdy both in body and in the independence of their character. Grant could hardly have provided a satisfactory compensation for their absence. If Ralph's letter were to be believed it was Grant—crippled and clinging—who had been responsible for the final strain on his mother's heart.

Margaret was not a woman who succumbed easily to grief, but the months of war had taken their toll of her nerves. It added an extra dimension to her sadness that a chapter of the past should so finally close at a time when the present was grey and uncertain and when it was not possible to look into the future at all without terror. If a woman surrounded by love on a peaceful tropical island could die, what hope was there for a young man on a battlefield designed for killing? The sense of desolation which overcame her embraced everyone she loved and clouded the future as well as the past. She mourned for Lydia. And at the same time she feared for Robert.

7

The gales of late December had whipped the Channel into a fury almost as spiteful as that of the Western Front, and the troop trains in both France and England were slow as well as over-crowded. By the time Robert arrived at Paddington Station on his first home leave he was exhausted by forty hours of travel. The train which was already pulling away from the barrier was the last of the day, his only hope of sleeping in a comfortable bed at Blaize and waking up to Christmas Day amongst his family. He forced himself to make one last effort and began to sprint as though the widening gap between himself and the end of the train were exposed to machine gun fire. Still running, he fumbled with the handle of the last carriage and fell rather than stepped inside.

As his panting subsided and he looked around, he saw that the only other occupant of the compartment was a fair-haired young woman wearing the uniform of a VAD. She looked startled, even a little apprehensive. Robert glanced at the window and saw the diamond-shaped label which reserved the compartment for LADIES ONLY.

"Sorry," he said. "I'll move at the next stop."

"It doesn't matter." Her voice was shy and attractively soft. She hesitated as though she were either wondering whether it would be proper for her to continue the conversation or else was doubtful about the particular question she wanted to ask. In the end, however, she was unable to restrain it. "Where have you come from?"

Robert was reluctant to answer. He had promised himself that for the next ten days he would forget the canal and the bridge, pretend that Loos had never existed and that he would never return to Hédauville. In any case he had been warned by friends who had been on leave before him that civilians were not genuinely interested in the details of battles. They made polite enquiries but rarely listened to the answers. Perhaps they lacked the imagination necessary to envisage the horror of life in the trenches; or perhaps, imagining it too well, they were embarrassed to discuss it amidst the comforts of England with someone who was enduring it on their behalf.

"What sector of the front, I meant?" She hesitated again. "My brother was killed—"

Now Robert saw what she wanted—the description of some landscape which would furnish her attempts to reconstruct the scene; and, most of all, some kind of reassurance that the death had been necessary, a means of understanding why it had happened.

It was not a reassurance which he could give. There was noth-

ing deliberate about his evasion of her question. It was more than
three weeks since he had last enjoyed an undisturbed night, and
he had not slept at all for the past forty-eight hours. As though
the catching of the train represented the last positive effort of
which he was capable, he gave one deep sigh and felt himself top-
pling sideways. From what seemed to be a deep sleep he was conscious of the girl shaking him by the shoulders. She was worried,
perhaps, about his sudden collapse, because her thumb was pressing his wrist to feel the pulse. He managed to grunt as an indication that he was still alive and the focus of her anxiety changed.

"What station do you want? Where are you going?"

"Blaize," he murmured, and fell weightlessly through the darkness into sleep again.

He awoke in a midmorning light to find Frisca sitting beside
his bed, staring intently at him. He had just time to consider that
this must be the first occasion on which his young cousin had
ever managed to keep still for more than two seconds at a time
when she flung her arms round his neck.

"Steady, steady!" he protested, laughing. "I'm still asleep."

"No, you're not." She hugged him again. "You're scratchy,
though."

"Let that be a lesson to you. You should never come into a
gentleman's bedroom until he's had time to shave."

"Aunt Margaret said I could sit here. She said no one was to
wake you until you were ready, but she wanted to know when you
did wake."

"Off you go and tell her, then."

Frisca must have had difficulty in finding his mother, for he
had time to bathe before he heard her footsteps hurrying along
the corridor. He opened the door so that she could run straight
into his arms and for a moment they stood close together without
speaking. They would both have been embarrassed, though, to say
what they were feeling. Margaret's voice was light and smiling as
she sat down on his bedroom chair.

"You're just in time to help with the carving of all the turkeys."

"What an exhausting business it is, coming on leave," Robert
laughed. "But I can hardly believe that I'm here at all, so a little
strenuous carving may help to persuade me that it isn't a dream."

"If it hadn't been for Nurse Blakeney, you *wouldn't* have been here at all—you'd still have been asleep on the train when it arrived at Bristol."

"Is she one of your nurses? I must thank her."

He found the opportunity to do so later in the day, when he met Alexa leading a group of a dozen VADs and convalescents out of the house towards the Theatre Ward.

"Come carol-singing with us, Robert," she called.

He had been on his way to find Frisca in the stables so that she could show him the puppy she had been given for Christmas, too young yet to leave its mother. But they had fixed no definite time. He joined the group without admitting that the attraction lay in one member of it, the fair-haired girl who turned when Alexa called. She smiled at him, first in a nervous, tentative manner, and then again with pleasure as she saw that he intended to come. It was easy for him to catch up with her as the party walked down the gently winding path which had been built to connect the original tithe barn with the house at a gradient more suitable for wheelchairs than the old woodland walk.

"I'm jolly grateful to you," he said. "Not many people on that train would have known which station I needed for Blaize. I hope you didn't have too much trouble getting me off it."

"The stationmaster helped," she said, smiling again. "And he knew who you were. It was a relief to discover that you lived here and were on leave. I was afraid at first that you'd been told to make your own way to the hospital for convalescence after some kind of injury or illness and that perhaps you were having a relapse which I ought to be able to recognise."

"No. Just uncomplicated tiredness. We'd been having a fairly noisy show. You asked me a question in the train, Nurse Blakeney. I don't remember whether I had time to answer it before I flopped."

She shook her head. "No. But I shouldn't have asked. Of course you don't want to think about that when you're on leave."

"It's all right. I don't expect I'll know much about your brother's sector. But I'd be happy to answer any questions that I can, if it would stop you worrying."

"It's not worry, exactly," she said. "I mean, he's dead now. There's nothing to be done. But we were always very close. It seems terrible that he should go into a world that I don't know anything about and simply disappear forever."

He could see her eyes filling with tears and was tempted to take her hand and comfort her, but the occasion was too public.

"This isn't the moment," he said, referring to her question. "What are your working hours tomorrow?"

"I start at seven in the morning and come off duty at eight in the evening. But we usually have two hours off sometime in the afternoon."

He fixed a rendezvous and then, anxious not to draw attention to himself and the girl, increased his walking pace to catch up with Alexa. Only then did he wonder whether his promise was a wise one. To describe the mud and stench of the trenches, to list all the stupid, useless ways in which her brother might have been killed, could be of no possible benefit to Nurse Blakeney. The truth was that he wanted after all to talk about it for his own sake, to build some kind of bridge, if only of words, between the year he had spent in Flanders and these few days in Blaize. His mother, surrounded by the casualties of the fighting, must have some idea of its fierceness, but in no circumstances could he tell her—when she was already so anxious about his safety—how much worse the conditions were than anything she could imagine.

The patients in the hospital had been given their Christmas meal at noon but it was not until the evening that the family, fully occupied throughout the day with their efforts to make the festival a joyful one, sat down to Christmas dinner. Alexa and Margaret had dressed for the occasion and Piers brought up some of his best wine; while Frisca, overexcited, was allowed to stay up late for once. For a little while they all relaxed as though the evening and the kind of normal domestic life it represented would last forever. But sadness was not far away even from the peaceful candlelit table on which glass and silver gleamed and glittered with a brilliance undimmed by war. When Piers rose to propose the toast of Absent Friends, Robert noticed at once that a name was missing from the list. He made no comment at that moment; but later, as they moved towards the library which was now used as a drawing room, he held his mother back for a moment.

"Aunt Lydia?" he asked.

"I didn't want to spoil your return home with bad news," Margaret said. "She died in November, although the news only reached us here ten days ago."

"I'm very sorry." Robert had had little opportunity to become acquainted with his aunt, but he knew her to have been his mother's best friend. "Do Kate and Brinsley know?"

"Ralph asked me to write to them. He can never feel sure that the addresses he has aren't out of date. Brinsley probably will have heard from me by now. Hardly the most welcome kind of letter to receive at Christmastime. But then, I suppose no one can expect to have a very merry Christmas in the trenches."

"Oh, I don't know." Robert realised that it was his duty to cheer his mother up. He sat down on the floor in front of the log fire and allowed Frisca, sleepy now, to snuggle up to him. "Last Christmas was quite a jolly affair. I remember it very well."

"Tell us," said Frisca.

"Well, I hadn't been at the front long enough to know what was normal and what wasn't, but the first thing that seemed odd on Christmas Day was the birds."

"Birds?" Margaret laughed in surprise. "You never told me in your letters."

"I hadn't seen a bird since I arrived in France. They had more sense than to hang about the front line. But on Christmas Day, there they were, perching on the barbed wire. That was what first made us realise that the firing had stopped. And the rain had stopped as well. A crisp frosty dawn, and sparrows sitting still."

"Did you feed them?" asked Frisca.

"Yes, we did. We scattered crumbs all over the place. And while they were pecking away we saw four Germans walking across No-Man's-Land. They were jolly nervous, I can tell you that. One of our officers went out to talk to them and within an hour there were fifty of us out there, swapping cigarettes and looking at family photographs. Mind you, for every ten men above ground there was probably one tunnelling away below, laying mines to blow up our trenches. But we didn't think of that at the time."

"I remember the newspapers said that soldiers had been singing across to each other from the two sets of trenches," Margaret said.

"That's right. 'Auld Lang Syne' and 'Good King Wenceslas' and 'Stille Nacht.' But that was only part of it. I remember there was a field of cabbages between the two lines. Someone had sown them and was never able to get back for the harvest. By Christmas they were all slimy, even though the ground was frozen. We started half a dozen hares in that field, and coursed them."

"You mean you and the Huns together?" asked Frisca.

"They didn't seem like Huns that day. Just ordinary chaps who didn't want to fight any more than we did." Unusually serious, he looked at his mother. "It was an important day for me," he said. "I'd been frightened when I first arrived at the front. And then to stop myself being frightened I'd had to concentrate on killing and hating. But suddenly, just for one day, I was able to feel like a decent human being again."

"Did you catch any of the hares?" Frisca asked.

"Yes. We got two of them for the pot, and Fritz bagged one as well. The cook didn't quite rise to the Blaize standard of jugged hare, but it was an improvement on bully beef, I can tell you that. I can imagine Brinsley's Christmas well enough. But not Kate's. Where is she now?"

"The last we heard for certain was that she was somewhere in Serbia. I don't expect the name Kragujevatz means any more to you than it did to me at first." Margaret stood up and looked along the lowest of the library shelves until she found a large leather-bound atlas, so heavy that Robert hurried to take the weight. He laid it on the desk and she searched the index for the Balkans. "The national frontier lines in this are probably a century or two out of date; but then, no frontier can be guaranteed for more than a week nowadays." She frowned over the small print before stubbing her finger down. "Here we are, south of Belgrade. But it's three months since I last heard from her, and even that letter was written in July. I've no idea whether any normal postal service gets through. Beatrice was in charge of keeping the hospital supplied, at least until the invasion, so I sent my letter to her and asked her to include it with any stores that she was able to send out. I haven't really much hope of it reaching her, though."

"What invasion?" asked Robert. The war to him was a matter

of a few yards of muddy ground gained or lost. Although he knew about the Dardanelles, nothing but the Western Front was real. Serbia, small and remote, had been responsible for the start of the war, but seemed to have no further importance.

"The Germans and Austrians and Bulgarians launched a joint attack on Serbia two months ago," Margaret told him. "Kraguje-vatz is behind the enemy lines now."

"And Kate?"

Robert had noticed as the evening passed how his mother's face had lost its expression of strained tiredness as she was able to relax in an evening off duty, knowing that her son was safe. Now the lines round her eyes tightened again in anxiety.

"My only news comes from Beatrice and even she isn't sure what's happened. Some of the nurses stayed behind in the hospital to care for the Serbian soldiers who were too badly wounded to move. They're in Austrian hands now, though since they're civilians Beatrice is hoping that they'll be repatriated. The others decided to move as many of the men as they could, hoping to establish another hospital further south. Kate was the only doctor in the unit who was still alive in October, and she took charge of that group. But nobody knows what has happened to the convoy which retreated, or where it is. And the most terrible stories are coming out of Serbia, Robert. It's not just the sick who are trying to get away. The whole Serbian Army is in retreat. And all the civilians are escaping as well, if they can. Those who stay are starving and those who take to the road are dying of exhaustion. I haven't dared to tell Ralph any of this, when he's already distraught over Lydia's death. But I'm very frightened for Kate."

8

Time had changed its nature: there was a difference in kind between living and surviving. No longer did each day present itself to Kate to be lived through, moment following moment—not necessarily to be enjoyed, but at least to be taken for granted. Instead, as the retreat continued, she had to fight for every second of the future, and each pace forward was a triumph of determination.

More than two months had passed since the Germans and Austrians invaded Serbia from the north. Kate had evacuated the patients from the military hospital in Kragujevatz only a few days before the building was destroyed by bombs and the town was occupied. Ever since then they had been retreating southwards as the enemy advanced, and they were not alone. The whole country was on the move, trying desperately to escape before the enemy caught up. With so many of her charges sick, Kate could not hope to cover the ground fast, but as the end of the year approached they had crossed the Serbian frontier into Albania.

There was no comfort to be found there. The sea might promise safety, but between Kate and the sea lay brigands and mountains—high, cruel mountains, covered with snow. It was difficult to believe that the retreat would ever end. As she trudged on towards the top of yet another mountain pass, her mind mechanically repeated the same phrase over and over again: one more step, one more, one more.

Her shoes had long ago worn out, but she had bound her feet and legs with long strips of hide from one of the dead oxen, and had replaced her tattered clothes from the bundles of possessions dropped at the roadside by refugees too weak to carry them any further. There was no element of theft or looting in this. Anything left behind would be snatched by the enemy. Serbia was represented only by whatever could be carried over the Albanian mountains. So by now Kate wore trousers and a military greatcoat as well as a thick layer of dirt. It was three weeks since she had last been able to wash more than her face, hands and feet, and she had been sleeping in her clothes ever since the retreat began. Her head was swathed in scarves, whitened by the snow, leaving only a slit through which her eyes peered down at the path immediately ahead.

In a way the desperate nature of her situation reduced the anxiety she felt. At the beginning of the evacuation she had been almost overwhelmed by her responsibilities. No longer then was it merely her business to keep wounded men alive. She had to provide wagons to transport them, and that meant that every night corn or hay must be found for the oxen or horses. The nurses and

orderlies and patients and men of the military escort must be fed
and there was no system which provided food or even ensured
that it existed. Billets or camp sites had seemed necessary for
night halts, and again it was nobody's business to arrange these
for her. By now, of course, after weeks of enduring freezing tem-
peratures in the open, she had almost forgotten how essential it
had seemed at the beginning that everyone in the column should
have at least a tent over his head for the night.

And then, each morning, there had been the strain of insinuat-
ing her own small unit into the unending stream of people and
wagons which blocked all the roads south. It had been necessary
to shout and bully, allowing artillery units to pass but forcing a
way into the line in front of the pathetic groups of villagers who
hauled their own carts, laden with children and possessions, at a
pace even slower than that of the oxen. And all the time the
sound of the guns had boomed through the air to remind the refugees that the Germans were only eight hours behind them, and
the Bulgars advancing from the side—in each case held up for
what could only be a limited time by the remnants of the Serbian
Army, brave but underequipped. There had been hopes at first
that the British and French might send help, but by now this was
a subject which no one mentioned in Kate's presence.

Ten weeks had passed since the retreat began, and one after another her responsibilities had slipped away. All that was left was a
determination at the beginning of each day to keep the survivors
of her party alive until they reached the sea; but by each evening
it seemed that it would be enough if she could drag her own
exhausted body across the mountains. The Austro-German invasion, which forced the Serbian Army and the royal family to evac-
uate Kragujevatz, had begun while she was still convalescent after
her attack of typhus, and at the beginning of the trek she had
had a horse to carry her south across the Serbian plains. But as
the hospital column reached the foot of the Albanian mountain
ranges and began to climb, there had been no more roads but
only narrow paths marked out by goats and goatherds. There was
no difficulty in finding the way, for every route which led towards
the sea and safety was lined with the bodies of men and horses,
but the tracks had proved too narrow for the ox wagons which
had carried the wounded soldiers from the hospital. In the

foothills it had been possible to transfer the patients to small forage carts for a few days, but by now they were strapped to all the available horses in litters, and anyone with two sound legs was expected to carry his own weight.

As comfort and even hope disappeared, Kate felt increasingly surprised that the men of the military escort did not desert. Almost all of them had wives and children whose homes would by now be occupied by the Germans, and the temptation to protect their families must have been strong. But somewhere in these mountain passes the point of no return had been reached. The soldiers would perhaps starve if they went on, but they would certainly starve if they attempted to return. They might die of exposure in the mountains, but they would be at the mercy of the Bulgars if they turned back to the plains. Probably, too, those of them who had been born in Austrian territory and who had willingly allowed themselves to be taken prisoner by men of their own race would be shot as deserters if they fell into Austrian hands again.

There was one form of desertion, of course, which was amenable neither to discipline nor to the reasonable balancing of alternative dangers, and her party's numbers shrank every day. They could protect each other against the wolves which howled in the darkness and against the Albanian bandits who attacked stragglers for the sake of their clothes; but there was no protection against the increasing weakness of their own bodies. Even able-bodied soldiers were by now collapsing into the snow, unable to go any further, so it was not surprising that the wounded should succumb.

They were nearing the highest point of the pass. In terms of the total journey, that meant nothing. There had been high passes before and no doubt there were more still ahead. But on the southern side of the peak the wind would perhaps bite less fiercely and there would be a better chance of finding a sheltered spot in which to sleep. Kate bent her head lower and forced her feet to keep moving. One more step, one more, one more.

Four hours later she wrapped her blanket tightly around her shoulders and leaned back against the black rock of the mountain, staring up at the sky. The blizzard had ended and the moon was full, reflecting off the snow and frost as clearly as though it were day. Ready to sleep, she felt completely at peace: the peace of someone too exhausted to care whether or not she would wake in the morning.

Sergei came to sit beside her. He pressed close against her side, not in any flirtatious way but in order that whatever body heat they retained might be shared.

"I have brought you your Christmas feast," he said, setting down a plate of beans and stale bread and a tin mug filled with water from snow melted over the camp fires.

"Is it Christmas, truly?"

"Truly."

It seemed incredible that she should not have known, that Christmas Day should not somehow have had a character of its own, impinging itself on her consciousness. Kate dipped the bread into the water without comment. For the first weeks of the retreat there had been few problems with food, for the invasion had begun before all the harvest could be brought in and the peasants who fled from their farms left plums on the trees and grapes on the vines and maize still standing in the fields. But since crossing the frontier it had been necessary to avoid inhabited areas, because the Albanians were unfriendly and fierce. By now their rations were almost exhausted. There were still horses which could be killed for food, but then the wounded men they carried would die, for it would be hard to find stretcher bearers still strong enough to carry any load along the steep and slippery paths.

From further down the mountain came the plaintive sound of a gusla as someone began to draw his bow across the single string. The sound was tuneless and very sad—Kate had never heard a guslar play a gay melody. Even when the instrument was used to accompany the kolo, the dancers required only a firm dignity of rhythm: lightheartedness was not demanded. But no one would have the strength to dance tonight, Christmas or no.

The men were not too tired to sing, though. The sound began as a kind of humming, which swelled as more and more of them joined in until at last it exploded into a cry of anguish. Kate did not need to understand the words to know that the soldiers were singing about their homeland, Serbia, which they had left perhaps forever, and about the wives and children they might never see again. The emotion was infectious, almost unbearable. Kate felt her own heart breaking with sympathy for the singers.

"At home," said Sergei. "What would you be doing now at home?"

Home was Jamaica; and the Jamaicans, like the Serbs, celebrated Christmas with song. Kate remembered the hymns and carols which her father had taught to his congregation and the poignant harmonies with which the people of Hope Valley sang them on Christmas Day. When the Jamaicans sang about death they swung their shoulders and clapped their hands and shouted to the skies in a kind of exultation. But when it was time to celebrate the birth of a baby, their voices dropped to a whisper and the sadness of their singing had often moved Kate, as a little girl, to tears. At the time she had been unable to understand their attitude; but by now it was easier to sympathise with the feeling that a newly born child was condemned to a life of hardship on earth, while a dying man might hope for happiness in heaven.

But Jamaica was too far away. Kate had been cold for so long that she could hardly remember how delightful it had felt to be enveloped in the balmy warmth of a tropical island. Instead, as she gazed at the line of campfires which flickered along the line of the track, she remembered the log fires which burned throughout the winter at Blaize. She had sat in front of one a year ago with Margaret and Alexa and Piers. At the time she had believed that she would never be so tired again as after the weeks of effort needed to equip and staff Blaize as a temporary hospital. Now, of course, she had learned what true tiredness was.

"My uncle will be opening a bottle of champagne now," she said. "If I were with him, I should be drinking a toast to Absent Friends. As it is, he'll be drinking the toast to me. And we can respond."

She lifted the mug of water to her lips, but Sergei put a hand on her wrist to stop her. He pulled a bottle from his pocket.

"I'd been keeping this to celebrate the new year," he said. "But who knows where we shall be on New Year's Eve."

"Still on this mountain, I should think," Kate said. But Sergei shook his head.

"The reconnaissance party has returned. Journey's end is in sight. This is the last high pass. And there are ships waiting at Durazzo to take any members of the Serbian Army to Salonika. Before the old year is over, you and I will have to say goodbye."

"Why, Sergei?" Kate was startled and upset.

"You will return to England, surely. It will be possible, and if I were your doctor I would order you to do so. You need rest, good food."

In a long silence Kate allowed herself to daydream. She imagined herself eating meals—hot, satisfying meals. But even the thought of delicious food was not as tempting as the prospect of sleep. To lie in the comfort of a bed, to be warm, to sink into sleep and to awake in the morning rested and still warm! She sighed at the thought, savouring the prospect but not really expecting to enjoy it again.

It was reasonable that she should return to England. A year away from home, in almost constant danger, must surely qualify her for a short period of leave. And then she would be justified in asking Beatrice to send her to France for her next tour of duty. That was where she had wanted to work, and by now she must have deserved the right to choose.

It should have been simple to decide, and yet it was not. Round the campfires the men were singing again, their inadequate meal quickly eaten. There was no sense in which she could feel them less deserving of care than the British soldiers in France. And there was Sergei. The thought that she would have to sail away from Sergei stabbed at her heart with an unexpected pain.

She glanced at her companion and could not resist a smile. Like herself he was dressed in many layers of ill-fitting garments picked up from the roadside, crowned by a woollen hat which he had pulled down over his ears. He had sewn up the empty sleeve of his greatcoat and used it to carry the paper-bound books which he would not abandon even in this emergency. Shaving had been one of the first luxuries to be abandoned by all the men, and Sergei's beard, like his hair, was long and untrimmed. Its raven blackness made his face appear even paler than normal, and his eyes had sunk more deeply into their dark sockets, although they still flashed with the fire which had impressed Kate at their first meeting. If she had come face to face with such a man a year ago, in the civilised surroundings of Blaize, she would have gasped and hurried away. But now Sergei was her closest friend.

Language, which had once been the barrier between them, had

in the end drawn them together. In the relaxed days of the
almost-forgotten summer, Sergei had begun to teach her Russian
and later, in a curious way, she had absorbed much of what he
was saying to her during the course of her illness, while she was
only half conscious. Since then, she had used the intellectual
effort needed to understand him as a way of taking her mind off
physical problems. She and Sergei conversed sometimes still in
French, but more often in Russian; and it was during these conversations that she felt closest to him. For his part, there was no one
else to whom he could talk in his own language, and he showed
in his smile how much it meant to him. They were speaking in
Russian now, and Kate was not at all sure that she could bear to
part from him.

"Where will the men be going after we reach the coast?" she
asked.

"There's talk of a Serbian division which will be assembled in
Salonika and sent to fight on the Eastern Front."

"And you? Will you go with them?"

Sergei sighed, shaking his head sadly. "No. The Serbs can no
longer fight as an independent army. They will come under Russian command. And I can tell you that the first Russian officer to
set eyes on me would have me shot. Whether you go to England
or not, we shan't see each other again." He filled her mug from
his bottle. "So we'll drink first to the absent friends of this Christmas. And afterwards to those who will be absent friends next
Christmas but for a little while longer are present comrades." He
filled his own mug and they clinked them together.

He had found the slivovitza, no doubt, in the cellar of one of
the abandoned farms they had passed, distilled by the farmer
from his own plums. More cautiously than Sergei, Kate allowed it
to make its fiery way down her throat. The warmth it brought to
her body was comforting, but she could not prevent her eyes from
filling with tears.

"I seem to spend my life saying goodbye to everyone I love."
By now her knowledge of Russian was good enough for her to
choose precisely the word for love which expressed her feeling of
affection and respect and friendship. There was no romantic attachment on either side, but that did not make her any less
unhappy.

"You must tell yourself that if a parting is sad, it's because the comradeship which went before was good. And perhaps after all we shall meet again one day. I shall return to Russia when the revolution comes."

"Are you so sure that it will?"

"You've seen all these people on the road, half alive or half dead, driven from their homes for some reason which they will never understand. What we've endured isn't only the retreat of an army: it's the flight of a nation. And what's happening in Serbia is happening all over Europe. There are French refugees, and Belgians, and Russians. Do you think they will endure such suffering forever? There will come a moment—it *must* come—when they will turn on their rulers and say 'We have had enough.' It may not be in Russia. If the Germans are defeated, it will come in Germany. It could happen in England if the Germans win and your people understand how their generals have sacrificed a generation of young men through their stupidity. If the Tsar's army defeats Germany and Austria, he will survive for a little while, no doubt. But his ministers are incompetent and his wife is German and gives him bad advice under the influence of a drunken hypnotist. No. Russia will be defeated and then the voice of the people will be heard. We shall build a new society."

"There would be no place for me in it," said Kate. "And Russia is so large that I would never find you even if I were there. So it will be a final parting. What will you do, Sergei?"

"I shall go back to look for the orphans. Not just the few I brought to your hospital. A quarter of a million people have died in South Serbia, and who knows how many more must have been caught behind the enemy lines in the north. There must be children wandering all over the country with no one to help them. I shall see how many of them I can keep alive. We will drink another toast. To the children of Europe!"

Brought up in a teetotal household, Kate was unused to drinking spirits and the second mugful of slivovitza had an immediate effect on her tired and undernourished body. She could feel her head swimming, and this was followed by a delightful sensation as though she were floating, warm and peaceful, high above the snowy pass. If this is being drunk, I like it, she thought, and fell asleep.

Sergei had been right when he promised that the end was in sight. Within three days the depleted party which had left the hospital ten weeks earlier made its way wearily down the last steep track and arrived at the coast. After so much hardship it was almost bewildering to be welcomed by an Italian relief unit with hot water and fresh clothes. There was a generous ration of bully beef and flour, as well as a token issue of such almost forgotten luxuries as coffee and sugar. The refugees ate and then, with one accord, lay down to sleep.

Warm and well-fed at last, Kate made a list of her surviving patients. The most seriously wounded had died during the retreat and those who were still alive now could hope to recover. But they still needed medical care. With increasing disquiet Kate tried to discover who would give it to them. Many of the doctors in the Serbian Army had died in the typhus epidemic at the beginning of the year, and others had been killed at the Battle of Kosovo. Of all the soldiers who had embarked on the retreat across the mountains, a hundred thousand had died on the road, and that number included many medical officers. There were no qualified doctors available to sail on the ship which was soon to leave; nor were any known to be waiting in Salonika.

Had Sergei been intending to travel with the Serbs, Kate might have decided what to do on personal grounds. But he had made it clear how impossible that was, so there was no weight of friendship to put in the balance against the prospect of seeing her family again. For the whole of one morning she paced up and down beside the grey winter waters of the Adriatic. She longed to go home, but more and more clearly she realised that her duty lay in a different direction. No real choice existed. She must stay with her patients.

Two days later she watched the last of the sick and wounded men being carried up the gangplank of the ship which would take them from Durazzo to Salonika—if it was able to thread its way successfully through the minefields. Sergei had been standing beside her, checking off the name of each man who went past. As the last of them disappeared down the companionway he handed her the list.

"Goodbye then, my brave, foolish Katya," he said.

A feeling of desolation robbed Kate of speech. She stared at

him in silence for a moment. Then Sergei put his one arm round
her shoulders and kissed her, Russian style, three times. Still without speaking, Kate watched as he strode away.

Darkness fell as the ship moved away from the port. She stood
for a long time on the deck, watching the dark silhouettes of the
mountains gradually merging with the blackness of the sky and
wondering whether she had indeed been foolish. Her spirits were
low. This was New Year's Eve and there was no one with whom
she could drink a toast to a happy new year. Her surviving nurses
had accepted with relief the offer of a passage home, so that of
the original team which had come from Britain, Kate was the
only one who would be staying with her patients. At the time
when she made the decision she had been sure that she was right;
but this was a lonelier moment. She was sailing towards 1916
with no friends or close companions at hand and no hopes that
the year could bring anything more than new tragedies.

Major Dragovitch, her colleague from the hospital, appeared at
the top of the companionway. The ship was blacked out for fear
of submarines, so she did not recognise him until he was close.

"We dance the kolo now for the new year," he said, bowing
and offering his arm. The small gesture cheered Kate at once. It
was an accident of administration which had cast her lot with the
Serbian Army rather than with the British or French. But by refusing the chance to return to England she had demonstrated to
the Serbs that she regarded herself as one of them, and now they
were making a gesture in return, accepting her as a well-tried
companion. She let the major lead the way below into a large
cabin which had been set aside for the use of officers. There she
took her place in the circle of dancers, moving her feet rhythmi-
cally to the sound of a flute and a violin.

After each dance she was offered drinks—for all the officers, it
seemed, had made good use of their two days in the port. It was a
party after all, and as for the second time in her life she became a
little drunk, she pushed the sadness from her mind.

As midnight approached, the music stopped while every glass
was refilled. There was a moment's pause until a blast of the
ship's siren marked the time. The single melancholy note, dispersed by the wind into a mournful diminuendo, was enough to
induce a new mood. A second earlier they had all been deter-

minedly cheerful. Now the same thought entered the mind of
each of them—that they might never see Serbia again. They had
been holding their glasses ready, but the toast which emerged was
not what had been expected. They drank to their homeland and
the day of their return to it.

Kate's homeland was not theirs—indeed, she hardly knew
where it was. Was it Jamaica, in which she had been a child? Or
England, where she had lived as a student? She had left Hope
Valley behind her without putting down roots anywhere else. The
Lorimer mansion perched above the Avon at Bristol: Margaret's
friendly house in Queen Anne's Gate, closed now for the duration of the war: Blaize, rich and peaceful before the war and now
crowded and businesslike—all these had welcomed her, but none
was her home. Not from choice, she had become a wanderer.

It was not important. People mattered more than places. She
was amongst friends, and that must be enough. And suddenly her
companions were cheerful again, with the abrupt change of mood
which she had learned to expect from the Serbs. Their gaiety, un-
founded but determined, was infectious. To the sound of shouted
good wishes for the new year, and the smashing of glasses after the
toast had been drunk, Kate sailed into 1916.

1

On the last day of June, 1916, Robert Scott began to write a letter to Margaret. He was not the only man to be writing to his mother at this moment and to judge by the tense quietness of his companions and the uneasy chewing of fountain pens, he was not alone in finding the letter difficult to phrase. For some days now they had all guessed that a big new offensive was imminent. No one was anxious to put his suspicions into words in case they should be confirmed, but Robert had drawn his own conclusions from the number of Decauville railway tracks which he and his section had laid in the past three weeks and the weight of ammunition which had been hauled along them. The tramp of men moving forward along newly surfaced roads had told its own story. So too had the piles of wooden crosses waiting ready in the villages behind the lines and only partly concealed by coverings of torn tarpaulin.

That afternoon the orders which they had all been expecting had come at last. After almost two years of war, officers and men alike knew the odds against them. Robert calculated that his cousin, Brinsley Lorimer, who was in the front line and would be one of the first to go over the top, had less than one chance in four of surviving the next day and only one chance in three of emerging from it unhurt. Robert's own odds were less daunting, for the sappers would not take part in the first wave of the attack. It would be their task to move rapidly forward after the first line of German trenches had been taken, to repair the damage done to them by the British guns during the attack and to build a road capable of carrying guns and supplies across the shell-pocked surface of what at the moment was No-Man's-Land. But they would be working under fire.

So this letter home could not be composed without thought. If it should turn out to be the last letter his mother ever received from him, she would keep it for the rest of her life. It was an occasion for writing something memorable, some statement of a personal philosophy which would serve as his memorial: or something especially loving, an expression of thanks for all the happy years of his youth.

What was so appalling was that he simply couldn't do it. Strong and healthy and twenty-one years old, Robert was incapable of stretching his imagination to envisage the possibility that within twenty-four hours he might be dead. And if his mother were to receive a solemn letter from him, different from his usual matter-of-fact style, she would be frightened, possibly without reason. With a sigh he bent his head nearer to the lamp and began to write.

"Dearest Mother, Guess who I saw two days ago. Brinsley, no less—for the first time since I waved him goodbye on Waterloo Station. I was sent up to the front line to take a good look at the terrain and check my maps, and I noticed a lot of chaps wearing his regimental flash, so I asked whether Captain Lorimer was around and finished up by having a meal in his dugout. Not much difference in the menu from my own mess. Same old powdered soup, same old tins of meat and peas and potatoes. But someone had brought some quite decent wine back from his last rest period, so we made a party of it. Thanks to a near miss from a howitzer a couple of days ago, Brinsley is down to his last gramophone record so we all had to listen to 'If You Were the Only Girl in the World' about twenty times during the evening. He seems to have had a jolly good time on his last leave, and taken in all the shows.

"I could hardly believe it at first, but Brinsley does actually seem to be enjoying the war. As though it were some kind of game, just a bit more exciting than cricket. A lot of fellows put on that sort of act, of course, but in Brinsley's case it seems to be genuine. I won't pretend that I share the feeling—or even understand it. But his men practically worship him for it. Some of them helped me to find my way back afterwards and we chatted for ten minutes while we waited for a break in the barrage. He's had so many narrow squeaks—and has come through them all without a scratch—that they reckon he has the devil's own luck, and they'll follow him anywhere because they feel safest when they're close to him.

"There's going to be a big push tomorrow. I can say that because by the time this reaches you, you'll know all about it. Brinsley's looking forward to it. And perhaps I am in a way as well, but a different way. We can't go on like this forever, thousands of men sitting in holes and shooting at each other, but obviously things have got to be worse for a while before they can be better. So let's hope that this one is going to be the decider, and that we'll be in Berlin before Christmas.

"I send my love to all the family at Blaize. But most of all, of course, dearest Mother, to you. Your loving son, Robert."

He read the letter through carefully to check that the last sentence was not too sloppy and that the rest contained no information—details of his position or the name of Brinsley's regiment—that would infringe the censorship regulations. Then, although it was still early, he lay down to rest. He did not expect to sleep.

At half-past four the next morning he went to rouse the two men he had chosen to act as his runners. They had not slept either and seemed almost grateful for the opportunity to move. Together they made their way in silence along the communication trench. Then there were thirty yards of open ground to be covered before they could reach the shelter of their observation post.

The front line curved at this point in front of a small hill which had once been heavily wooded. By now only the stumps remained, with a few bare spikes to indicate the original height of the trunks. Once shellfire had destroyed the trees, the debris had quickly been appropriated for firewood, so the observation post was a dugout. Robert had always been good with his hands and eighteen months of war service had provided good practice for his ingenuity. He had made and installed three large periscopes and had also made sure that the post was concealed from air observation by camouflage.

It was not possible to see the German trenches from the British line, nor even from Robert's position on the hill, for the ground of No-Man's-Land rose to a ridge which divided the two armies.

The ground was a mess of craters and hummocks bounded by for-
midable lines of tangled barbed wire and peopled now only by
the decomposing bodies of men who had taken part in earlier attacks. In a few hours Brinsley and his fellow-officers would be
leading their men up the slope towards the German machine
guns. Although he would not be amongst them, Robert found
himself shivering with fear on their behalf. It seemed impossible
that they could break through—and even if the main attack succeeded, how many of those in the first wave could expect to arrive
at the further side?

In the hour of waiting there seemed no alternative to such
thoughts as these. Over and over again Robert looked down at his
map, checking it with the actual contours of the land, making
preliminary choices of the best line for laying a supply route. The
final decision could only be made after the attack had succeeded,
if it did succeed, and when it was possible to assess which section
of the area had been least devastated by shellfire.

Gradually the sky lightened, cloudless and clear, bearing all the
promise of a perfect summer day. Robert found himself suddenly
thinking of his cousin Frisca. Probably it was because he was trying to visualise summer in England, to conjure up a mental picture of girls in white frocks playing croquet on smooth green
lawns or eating strawberries in the shade of cedar trees. Blaize in
peacetime seemed to sum up everything he was fighting for, but
Blaize had changed as unexpectedly as his own life, although less
dangerously. He did not want at this moment to visualise his
mother sitting in her office and signing death certificates or drug
requisitions, nor to think of Alexa endeavouring with all the skill
of a professional actress to conceal the heartache she felt at the
sight of her beloved theatre converted into a hospital ward. Nine-
year-old Frisca, alone amongst his family, had not changed at all.
She was still dancing through life, her golden curls bobbing, her
bright blue eyes flashing with gaiety. He remembered how he had
awoken from an exhausted sleep on the first morning of his last
leave to find his cousin sitting at his bedside, and how the expression on her young face had changed from almost maternal solicitude to delight that he was ready to be talked to at last. With a
rush of emotion that was almost a physical desire he wished that

he could hug little Frisca now and tell her that there was nothing
to worry about.

He thought of Jennifer as well, whom he had wanted to kiss at
the end of that leave. Her shyness had restrained him on the last
occasion when they had been alone together, and their final goodbye had been said with his mother watching. Although there was
nothing to suggest that she disapproved of their deepening friendship, her presence had proved inhibiting to them both. But Jennifer had written to him regularly during the past six months, and
he had replied to each letter. The correspondence was important
to him. To his mother he wrote only in reassurance. He told her
about his rest periods, his billets, the pleasures of buying an occasional meal or cup of good coffee. His letters to Jennifer were
quite different. As though it were necessary to tell the truth to
somebody, he described to her with complete honesty his moments of fear and nausea, disgust and shame. Perhaps he hoped
that the moment would come when she would tell him that she
could not bear to hear any more, so that he would have reason to
hope that she was beginning to care for him; but until that time
he poured out his feelings about the war without reserve.

She, like himself, might be awake at this moment, approaching
the end of night duty in a ward full of men who in their time had
awaited the dawn with as much apprehension as Robert felt now.
He tried to force himself into her mind, so that his own mind
should be distracted. Robert suspected that Jennifer was not a
particularly good nurse. She had none of the controlled compassion which enabled his mother to recognise a need and alleviate it
as far as she could with all the sympathy and skill she possessed
but without allowing any kind of emotional involvement to dis-
tort her judgement. Jennifer was too young and too highly strung
to remain detached. She suffered with her suffering patients, deliberately indulging her own feelings, whether of anger with those
who had inflicted the injuries she tended, of anguish with those
who endured them, or of desolation with the bereaved. She had
confessed to Robert that she chose to work as a nurse deliberately
to ensure that she should not be happy when so many people
were frightened or unhappy. It was an attitude wholly to her
credit; yet in these moments of waiting it proved not to be the
memory of Jennifer which brought most comfort to Robert, but

that of Frisca. He felt almost that Jennifer had a need to suffer and did not want to be spared anything; whereas it seemed important that Frisca should be protected, that nothing should ever happen to sadden those sparkling blue eyes. Dear little Frisca, he thought affectionately. And then suddenly it was not possible to think about England any longer.

The barrage which began at six o'clock was more intense than any he had heard before. As though a conductor had signalled with the sharp double tap of his baton, a symphony of gunfire began with a single, ear-splitting chord. With a rolling reverberation it developed through all its different movements: of surprise, rangefinding, concentration, obliteration, deterrent—all leading up to what must be the finale: the creeping curtain barrage of attack. There could be no crescendo, because the fortissimo was sustained from first to last; and after the first few moments it was impossible even to distinguish the notes of the different instruments: the smacking percussion of field guns, the rasping of the medium artillery, the drumming boom of the biggest guns, and the high-pitched scream of shells. The orchestra became a double one as the reports of guns firing behind him were echoed in sinister fugue by the explosions of the shells out of sight in front. These in turn were joined by another band of instruments altogether when the distinctive notes of the German howitzers began to punctuate the score, their crashing chords coming nearer and nearer as they probed behind the lines for the British guns.

Beneath Robert's feet the ground was shuddering. His ears were battered not only by sound but by the vibrating pressure of the air. His whole body became tense, as though by drawing in on himself, holding every nerve end under tight control, he could give himself immunity from death's flying splinters. An hour passed, and more, but still there was no pause in the relentless battering on his eardrums. The noise hung over him like a cloud, a huge umbrella, filling the atmosphere almost visibly, with no chink or break in its intensity. Nothing but noise existed: nothing but noise was real. Robert felt himself beginning to tremble, his self-control stretching towards snapping point. Only the presence of his two equally dazed companions prevented him from crying.

In the firing trench at the foot of the hill the rising sun glinted

on a row of bayonets. Robert reminded himself that, unlike the
men who held them, he was not just about to walk towards a line
of machine guns. A sudden conviction that he would never see
Brinsley again made him angry with himself. He had said goodbye to his cousin too casually, wishing him good luck with nothing more than a smiling nod of the head. Just as he ought to have
told his mother how much he loved and admired her, so he ought
to have touched Brinsley on the arm, shaken him by the hand,
even embraced him. How ridiculous it was that it should be so
difficult to demonstrate affection even where affection so genuinely existed. Well, it was too late for regrets. He could think
only of himself, and by now the tension had become unbearable.
How much longer would the barrage continue? When would the
attack begin?

In the trenches, no doubt, whistles were blowing. To Robert,
who could not hear them, there was something uncanny about
the manner in which an unbroken line of men, stretching away as
far as he could see, began to move. They scrambled out of the
shelter of the trench, paused, steadied and then advanced, with
rifles held at the port and heads down so that their steel helmets
would provide some kind of shield. The solidity of the line and
the slowness of its pace was almost unbearable to watch. Robert
knew well enough that the speed of the advance was determined
by the movement of the curtain barrage, that if the men moved
too quickly they would run into shellfire from their own supporting guns; but he felt sure nevertheless that if he had been
amongst them he would have found the temptation to run and
zigzag overwhelming.

For the first thirty yards the slope of the ridge gave the at-
tackers some protection. But as they approached the top they
were greeted with a savage burst of machine-gun fire. Within seconds more than half the men within Robert's viewpoint were flat
on the ground. Some of them might have flung themselves down
in self-protection, but as he searched the nearest part of the ridge
through his binoculars he could tell that many would never rise
again.

A second wave followed twenty yards behind and received the
same welcome—although rather more of these, bending low,

broke into a run as they reached the dangerous point of exposure and pressed on towards the German lines. A third wave moved at first much faster than the other two: the artillery barrage was well ahead of them by now. But as they approached the top of the ridge they began to falter. Robert knew from his own experience how great a mental effort was needed to step over or upon a man's body, even when it was quite certain that he was dead.

As they hesitated, they were rallied by an officer who straightened himself ahead of them and turned, gesturing them to follow him at a run. It was not possible for Robert to hear what he shouted, but the effect was immediate. The third wave charged forward, the officer at their head. He was running in front of them, moving diagonally to avoid a large crater, when he was hit. Even without binoculars Robert could see all too clearly what happened. The man's head jerked backwards, either as a direct result of the impact of shrapnel or bullet or because the strap of his steel helmet, dislodged, tightened across his neck. For a moment or two his legs continued their running movement, but his arms were thrown upward and his shoulders forced back. Losing his balance, he fell into the shellhole which he had been trying to avoid. But there was time, as he staggered on the edge, for Robert to see, beneath the displaced helmet, the officer's curly golden hair. So distinctive; so familiar. Surely it couldn't, mustn't be Brinsley.

Yet as he raised his binoculars to his eyes and adjusted the focus with fingers trembling with shock, Robert had no doubt that it was his cousin's face he would see. He had to wait a moment for the smoke of the battlefield to clear briefly. Then his fears were confirmed. Brinsley had not fallen to the bottom of the crater—a huge hole, big enough to stable a team of horses or store an ammunition wagon—but was clinging with one arm to its side. He was writhing with pain, his legs from time to time jerking convulsively. Robert felt every spasm as though his own body were suffering. With a feeling of panic which increased as every moment passed, he waited for someone to carry Brinsley back to the British lines. But Brinsley's own men had by now surged forward, beyond him, and although the stretcher bearers had begun to make their quick dashes out of cover to pick up the wounded, they were bringing the nearest in first. With so many fallen men in need of them, it was hardly surprising that they should leave until last those who lay on the top of the ridge, within the range of the German machine guns.

Robert handed the binoculars to one of his runners. His trembling had stopped and he felt both very calm and very much afraid. "Wait here," he said to the men, though there was little enough danger that they would follow him unbidden into the smoke and chaos below.

He dashed first for the shelter of the communication trench and used that to lead him into the section of the firing trench from which Brinsley had led his men. If one of his own senior officers had seen him, he could well have been court-martialled for leaving his post, but he had only one thought in his head: that Brinsley was still alive and must be brought in. As he climbed out of the trench he automatically crouched low, head down. The ground was littered with men and equipment and made rough by shellholes and mounds of soft earth, but he ran as straight as he could over the first uphill stretch, only beginning to zigzag as he approached the brow of the hill. The noise here was perhaps no louder than it had been in the observation post, but it was more confusing, and punctuated with the shouts of the assault troops as well as the cries of the wounded. All the craters which could be seen through the smoke looked much alike, and others were visible only when he reached the very edge. It was difficult to preserve any sense of direction. Twice he thought he had arrived at the right place and twice was disappointed. He paused briefly and saw across a stretch of exposed ground a shellhole which was large enough to be his goal.

Again he began to run. Then, without warning, there was no more noise. He was floating in the air, turning slowly over and over in a state of bliss. Or at least, part of him was, for it seemed that he had left his body behind on the ground. He could see it, but he was not inside it.

The silence seemed timeless but ended with a crash. Now he was back inside his body, and his body was lying inside the crater he had been hoping to reach. Earth at first trickled and then rushed down its side as though from an erupting volcano. It covered his face as he lay prone. He lifted his head for a second to escape from it, and put up a hand and arm for protection. That was something—that there was nothing wrong with his head or his arms. But he found himself unable to sit or stand or move his legs. He tried to work out where he was injured, but there was no pain to guide him, only numbness as he pressed whatever he could reach and tried in vain to flex the muscles of his lower limbs.

Raising his head again and propping himself up on his elbows, he looked around for Brinsley. But even if this was the right crater, the new shellburst had destroyed its shape, throwing out or burying any previous occupants. Robert lay there alone as the battle raged around him. His mind, still in some curious way detached from his physical state, was unable to make itself care.

In the course of the day he received company. A grey-haired man, too old for war, weeping uncontrollably and unable to advance any further. An injured stretcher-bearer, flinging himself in for shelter as a mortar exploded nearby. Two dead men and a third who died within an hour. And a blood-showering rain of arms and legs which arrived after a shell burst that made the ground tremble as though an earthquake were beginning. Robert observed what happened, but felt no reaction to it. He supposed that he was dying, but the fact did not seem to be of any importance. He tried to remember his mother, and to feel sorry for the grief she would experience, but he was unable to visualise her face. His imagination refused to move outside the confines of the crater. He lay without moving, waiting without knowing what he was waiting for or what he hoped would happen.

The noise around him continued throughout the whole of the long day and so dense was the smoke at the top of the crater that it was impossible to tell for certain when night was falling. But at some point in the early evening the numbness of Robert's wounds began to recede. Uncertainly at first, his mind re-established its link with his body. He became frightened for himself and angry at the chain of events which had brought him where he lay. But these feelings did not survive for long, for they were driven out by a pain so overwhelming that he could not even begin to control his reaction to it. It first attacked his hips and then spread down-

wards through his legs. Finally, as though carried in his blood-
stream, it moved upwards, towards his heart, into his head,
agonising and unendurable. Robert began to scream: uncontrollably, on and on and on.

2

On the morning of July 1, Margaret heard from Kate at last.
The letter—the first to arrive since the brief message which had
announced her niece's escape from Serbia and decision to remain
with the Serbian Army—was a cheerful one. She was on the
Romanian Front, Kate told her aunt, and had established a hospital with a hundred beds at Medjidia. The remnants of the Serbian Army were now under Russian command, so she was finding
it very useful that a Russian friend's tuition had made her fluent
in the language some months ago. She had to spend half her time
arguing with Russian transport officers and quartermasters. The
inefficiency of the Russian Army was almost unbelievable, and
she was glad that her medical supplies came directly from Beatrice's office.

The situation she described sounded appalling to Margaret,
who was accustomed to discipline and efficiency in hospital management, but the letter contained no hint of complaint. During
the long retreat across the mountains Kate had obviously been depressed, facing problems far outside the ability of a single doctor
to solve. At least now she was in a position to be of real help to
those in need of medical care.

Margaret was glad on her behalf and looked forward to passing
on the news. Alexa had been spending the week at Glanville
House in Park Lane, taking her concert party to perform in the
London hospitals. When the time came for her return in the evening, Piers went to the station to meet her train. Glancing from
the window of her office at the sound of the returning motorcar,
Margaret noticed how serious they both looked as they went into
the house. The observation worried her and after a little while
she went to look for them.

She found them in the nursery, beside their sleeping son. The day had been one of the hottest of the year and little Pirry had thrown off all his bed coverings. His soft and seemingly boneless body sprawled in total relaxation on the mattress. One hand stretched above his head; the thumb of the other was in his mouth. The door was open, but Margaret felt it would be an intrusion on the family group to go in. She paused in the doorway and the two adults, speaking quietly to each other while looking at the sleeping child, were not aware of her presence behind them.

"A vigorous offensive!" said Piers. He glanced down at the newspaper he was gripping. "Such an easy phrase to write, but what does it imply? Last week, Alexa, when the House rose, I went out on to the terrace and found myself standing next to Lord Falmouth. His two elder sons were both in the Army and both killed in the first months of the war. He'd heard that morning that he'd lost his youngest son as well. The last. He hadn't been able to face his wife with the news. I think he told me just to see whether he was capable of speaking the words without breaking down. The boy was only nineteen. He'd been in France for five months. That made him fortunate in terms of statistics. Did you know, Alexa, that the average expectation of life of a nineteen-year-old second lieutenant is twelve weeks from the day he arrives at the front? How long can we go on like this? But how can we stop? I never thought I'd live to bless the fact that my son was born when I was already an old man. All my friends of my own age are either in mourning already or expecting the worst. I feel almost guilty that I'm so fortunate."

He turned to embrace Alexa and caught sight of Margaret. There was no reason why Margaret should have felt guilty about her accidental eavesdropping, but equally there was no doubt from her brother-in-law's expression that he had not intended what he had been saying to be heard by her—as though she were not as well aware as he of the risks that faced her son. To reassure him, she smiled as though she had only just arrived.

"Is there anything new in the paper?" she asked.

Piers handed her the copy of *The Star* which Alexa had brought from London. Underneath the black headlines which announced the opening of a British offensive came the brief official communiqué. "At half past seven this morning a vigorous offensive was launched by the British Army. The front extends over 20 miles north of the Somme. The assault was preceded by a bombardment, lasting about an hour and a half."

"I heard the guns," said Alexa. They moved away from the nursery, closing the door behind him. "I woke up at six o'clock this morning. There was no one about in Park Lane: no traffic. The air was very still. And I heard the guns."

"All the way from France? It's not possible, surely."

"I wouldn't have expected so. I can only tell you that it happened. And I wasn't the only one. From time to time throughout the day I've seen people standing motionless in the middle of London, not doing anything, just straining their ears. Everyone's been snappy and uneasy today. Partly because of the heat perhaps. But it's as though we've been having knowledge forced on us when we would have preferred not to know. And if we can hear the sound in England, what must it be like to be only a few yards away from the guns?"

"Brinsley is somewhere near the Somme," said Margaret. Both her son and her nephew were careful not to give anything away in their letters, but Brinsley had recently been on leave and had mentioned the names of villages near to the base town of Albert. Margaret had looked them up later on the *Daily Mail* map which hung in the library, and knew that she had reason to feel anxious. But to talk about her fear would do no good. The day was over now. If Brinsley and Robert were safe, there was nothing to worry about. If they had come to harm, it had happened already. Her own anguish could do nothing to help them, and she had long ago ceased to believe in the power of prayer. She was frightened but determined not to show it. In an attempt to talk of something more cheerful she asked Alexa how London was looking.

"Drab and dowdy," Alexa told her. "There are no flowers in the parks, no water in the lakes, no lights in the buildings at night, no street lamps lit either, for fear of Zeppelin raids. The soldiers on leave are lively enough and there seem to be plenty of overpainted young women ready to go with them to the theatre or music hall. But there's no feeling of style anymore. Hardly anyone wears evening dress to the theatre now, and a gentleman in a tall hat is almost a curiosity. To tell you the truth, there's hardly anyone I know left in London. The museums and galleries are closed, and the shops are so understaffed and understocked that anyone who owns a house in the country has retired to live in it and to buy food from the nearest farm. If I didn't believe that our concert party brought a little glamour to men who deserve to be cheered up, I'd never stir from Blaize. As it is, I think we shall have to close Glanville House. It's becoming impossible to replace the servants as they leave to join up. Even the maids are going to work in factories. It doesn't seem to worry them that their skin will turn yellow from the munitions or that they may even blow themselves up. The last kitchen maid I employed had never been outside her own village before last Christmas and now she's gone off to sell tickets to omnibus passengers."

Once Alexa embarked on the subject of servants, there would be no stopping her for the next ten minutes. Margaret withdrew her attention, trying to calculate when she could expect to hear any personal news, and what value it would have—since a letter received today would only mean that the writer had been safe five days earlier.

In the event, she did not have to wait long. Piers was always the first to read the daily paper. He marked anything in it which he thought might be of special interest to his wife or sister-in-law, but when Margaret arrived for her own later breakfast after an hour spent in her office reading the nurses' overnight reports, she always looked through the casualty lists for herself. They might contain names recognised by her but not known to Piers. On Tuesday, however, there was a name which Piers neither overlooked nor marked. He brought the paper to her office and silently handed her the page which announced that Captain Brinsley Lorimer had been killed in action.

Margaret wept. Her life had not always been a happy one, but for almost the whole of her fifty-nine years she had been able to accept its setbacks without tears. Only within the last few months had each new blow seemed less supportable than the one before. And Brinsley, lighthearted and life-loving, had been a second son to her for ten years—ever since her brother had sent him to her in England at the age of thirteen for his education. She felt Piers's arm round her shoulder, but each of them knew as well as the other that there were no words which could bring comfort.

A long time passed before she was able to control herself. Then she looked again at the page. Her swollen eyes refused to focus on the tiny type, but she could see that the list of names continued for column after column. "Robert?" she asked.

"I've been right through," Piers said. "Not just the Royal Engineers but every single name, to make sure. He's not there."

That was a comfort only in the sense that she could not have endured a double blow. She thanked Piers for staying with her, promised that she would be all right now, and was left with the task of writing to Kate and to Ralph. Brinsley's father would have had the official telegram of notification and so would know already of his son's death.

The morning post brought a letter from Robert. It had been written on Friday, before the battle began, so that the mere fact of its arrival gave no reassurance. And its casual mention of an unusual social occasion brought a new chill to Margaret's heart. If Robert had been near enough to Brinsley to share a meal with him, then Robert was on the same section of the front. Her face was pale as she went out to do her morning round.

Pale enough, presumably, to be noticeable. In the long ward which had been converted from Alexa's little opera house, Margaret was aware of one of the VADs staring at her with an intensity which merited a reprimand. With some difficulty she focussed her eyes and attention on the nervy face and recognised the young woman who had helped to get Robert off the train at the beginning of his last leave. Nurse Blakeney, wasn't it? The girl approached her, visibly summoning all her courage. A VAD was not expected to speak unless she was spoken to.

"Dr. Scott. Please forgive me—I know I shouldn't—but I have to ask. Doctor, have you had bad news?"

"Yes," said Margaret. She was aware that she spoke brusquely —it was because her tears were still not wholly under her control. Only after she had answered did she understand the question. This girl was not a friend of Brinsley's. She might have glimpsed him on his last leave, but she could have no real interest in his safety. It was Robert's welfare which concerned her. "Not about my son, though," she said. "As far as I know, he's all right."

The girl's relief showed on her face. "I had a letter yesterday,"

she said. "But of course it was written last week, before he went
into action. So I was afraid—I'm sorry, Doctor."

Margaret remembered now that Robert had seen something of
Jennifer Blakeney during that leave earlier in the year, but she
had not realised that they were corresponding. Well, that was
none of her business. She felt no need to stand on her dignity
when it was possible to be kind.

"That's all right, Nurse," she said. "When I hear anything
more up to date, I'll let you know."

She moved on, forcing herself to keep her attention on her
work. But it was impossible not to be edgy, not to feel frightened
whenever she caught the sound of bicycle wheels on the gravel
path in case it should prove to be the telegraph boy and not some
unimportant domestic delivery. Each morning the casualty lists
were longer and more delayed, making it clear that the offensive
had developed into a continuing full-scale battle and that the
death roll was running into thousands. She had no interest in the
communiqués which claimed that a few yards of ground had
been won, but spent every free moment obsessively rereading the
lists of names. On Thursday she learned that Robert had been
wounded.

This time Piers did attempt to comfort her. "It's a terrible
thing to say, but a wound may prove to be the best way of saving
his life," he pointed out. "He'll be out of the battle. With any
luck, he'll have been sent home."

"The Blighty one!" said Margaret. Every patient in the hospital
at Blaize had had his own Blighty wound and it was true enough
that some of them were grateful for the small hurt which had removed them from the scene of greater danger. But for many the
price was a larger one than they could ever have wished to pay.
Margaret could not afford to stop feeling frightened until she
learned the details of Robert's injury. "There are too many
wounded," she said. "I've been warned to expect fifty acute surgical cases in the next two days. They know we haven't got the facilities, that we're only equipped for recuperative nursing and convalescence, but apparently there simply aren't enough hospital
beds in England and France to cope with the numbers. Some of
the men have been moved around for up to five days with noth-

ing more than a bit of emergency attention. Five days! And
there's gas gangrene in every wound!"

She realised that she was in danger of becoming hysterical and
was not surprised at the firmness with which Piers addressed her.

"I'm going to London to find him," he said. "You concentrate
on your job here, keeping other people's sons alive. I'll get on to
the War Office and track him down. When I find him, do you
want him here?"

The need to answer had a steadying effect, as no doubt he intended. Neither of them wasted words on the hypocrisy of pretending that they would hesitate to pull any official strings necessary to obtain special treatment for Robert.

"If he's in need of major surgery, he must go somewhere
equipped to do it," Margaret said. "I'll give you the telephone
number of someone who could advise you on the best specialist
units. But as soon as he only needs nursing, yes, I want him
here."

3

Robert had no recollection of being carried from the crater. At
the regimental aid post he had recovered consciousness briefly.
His groan—whether of pain or merely despair that he was still
alive after what had seemed to be the peace of dying—brought a
nurse to his side. He felt the stab and pressure of an injection, the
firm marking of a cross on his forehead. His eyes closed again.

When he was next able to look around him he was in a casualty clearing station, lying on a stretcher at the side of a tent. His
hips were bandaged, but that part of his uniform which had not
been cut away was stiff with dirt and blood. It was night, although presumably not the same night, and he could see a surgeon, his white smock soaked in blood, bending over a trestle
table by the light of an acetylene lamp. It was the beginning of a
new nightmare.

He had become nothing but a helpless body, conscious now,

but to be moved or forgotten in accordance with some plan which he could not understand or control. His stretcher was stacked into a bunk in a railway truck, was swung onto the deck of a ship by a crane, was carried off to another train. From time to time he was offered a drink, a cigarette, or another injection of morphine, but he had no clear idea of how time was passing, except that the smell which he carried round with him grew more nauseous with every hour. No one had time to talk. Doctors and nurses, orderlies and stretcher bearers were all overworked, silent and grey from lack of sleep. It was as though he were on a conveyor belt so badly overloaded that it could only be kept moving if everyone concerned winched it by hand, knowing that if they were to stop for a moment the weight would be too great for any movement to start it again.

The recurrent injections muddled his mind while keeping the pain of his body more or less under control, but it was in a moment of comparative clarity that he found himself lying on the platform of a railway station. There was nothing to tell him where it was. He could only hope that he had reached London at last, that the apparently interminable journey was in fact near its end. Without warning he remembered a day almost two years earlier. He had broken the news of his enlistment to his mother on a station platform just like this one, and almost as crowded with stretchers. It was the day that Brinsley had left for France—and with the memory of that moment Robert recollected for the first time since the explosion of the shell what it was that he had been doing when he was hit. The horror of what he had seen had sealed the picture off from his mind, but now he saw Brinsley running through the smoke, saw his bright yellow curls spring up as they were freed from the flattening weight of the dislodged steel helmet, saw the jerk of his arms and shoulders as the bullet stopped him in his tracks. Remembering, too, the agonised twitching which had continued after his cousin fell to the ground, Robert began to vomit.

The feeling that he had been abandoned was so strong that it seemed a small miracle when he felt his face being sponged. The woman who was bending over him was shabbily dressed and undernourished, but her eyes were full of sympathy. He muttered his thanks as soon as he could speak again and in return she told him that her own son had died of wounds. She met every hospital train now to give to strangers the kind of care which might have eased his pain.

"Where am I? Is this London?" Even talking was an effort, but he did his best to speak clearly.

"That's right, dear. London. Live in London, do you?"

"I want someone to know where I am," he told her. "Will you get in touch with my mother. Or my uncle. Anyone. Tell them where I'm being taken."

She bent again to read the label which had been tied to his tunic, giving his destination as though he were a parcel. "Where shall I find them?" she asked.

"What day of the week is it?"

"Friday, dear. Friday morning."

The battle, he remembered, had begun on a Saturday. But there was no time to wonder what had happened to the missing days. Painfully he groped for the linen bag which had been tied round his shoulder and which contained his papers and valuables. There was some money there. He pressed it all into her hand.

"Take a cab to Glanville House in Park Lane," he said. "Even if there are only servants there, they'll know where to telephone my mother in the country. Speak to her yourself if you can. But tell someone where I am. Robert Scott."

"Robert Scott," she repeated. "All right, dear." She sponged his face once more and left him.

A little at a time, Robert's body, which had for so long been tensed against pain, began to relax. He had been taken from the battlefield where he was in danger of his life; he had survived the nightmare journey; and he had come to the country where strangers were friends. Very soon now he would see his mother again and then everything would be all right. She would tighten her lips when she saw how dirty he was; she would bathe him and be gentle with him and heal his broken body and hold him tightly and warmly close to herself for the rest of his life. "Mother!" he murmured, closing his eyes in an attempt to prevent the tears from forcing their way out. "Mother! Mother!" Half delirious, he was still calling aloud for her when Lord Glanville arrived.

4

Robert's plaster was due to be cut away on the first Monday in December. He longed to escape from the heavy cast which had imprisoned him for so many months, and yet was a little frightened of what his release might reveal. On the Sunday morning he kept his mother back for a moment when she stood up to leave after her usual breakfast-time chat.

"Mother, am I going to be all right?"

"You're almost all right already." But Margaret recognised his anxiety and came back to sit beside the bed for a moment longer.

"Normal, I mean. Back to what I was before. Nobody's ever told me exactly what damage was done, you know."

"The damage was to the bone." With the professional air of a qualified doctor, Margaret touched her own hip and thigh to indicate the areas which had needed repair. "Obviously, the flesh was badly torn as well, and the surgeon had to get out all the shell splinters and broken bits of bone before he could set what was left and allow the healing process to begin. The reason why he's kept you still for so long is to give the breaks the best possible chance to knit. He thinks, and so do I, that, yes, you'll be back to normal. One leg perhaps fractionally shorter than the other, but hardly enough to notice. An extra half inch on the sole of your left shoe and you won't even limp. We caught you in time, thank God, to prevent the gangrene from getting a hold. You're bound to be very stiff and weak at first, though, Robert. You must be prepared for that. You won't simply be able to stand up and walk tomorrow. You'll have to take things slowly. Do exercises. As a matter of fact, I'm going to experiment on you."

Startled, he looked to see whether she was joking, and was not entirely reassured when she laughed.

"*You're* going to be all right, but we've had a lot of men through our hands who aren't. They're alive, but not whole. And very depressed, as you can imagine. I mean, suppose you're used to earning your living as a train driver and suddenly you're blind. What do you do?"

"Alexa has a blind piano tuner," Robert remembered.

"There aren't enough pianos in England to keep the new generation of blind men busy," said Margaret. "I've been trying to think of new possibilities. It started as a search for some sort of therapy—to keep the men occupied while they were still here, to take their minds off the future. And then I thought, it ought to be therapy for the future as well. I've had a friend down here who's helped me work something out. He specialises in muscular diseases. He has evolved a training. Half a dozen of our long-stay patients have gone through it already, and now they're teaching the next batch. To massage muscles which have gone out of use for a while, or have been strained or injured." Robert felt her firm fingers kneading his arm for a moment as she demonstrated what she meant. It invariably surprised him that his mother, who had always been small and by now was not young any longer, should have such strong hands. "As soon as you're out of this suit of armour, I shall send one of them in to pummel you until you're ready to go riding with Frisca again. She can't wait to get you out of bed, you know. You won't have a moment's peace after tomorrow."

"I'm afraid I'm just about to give her a nasty shock," Robert told her. His mother had so often teased him about the devotion which his lively little cousin felt for him that he knew she would understand at once. And she did: he could feel the sudden tension in the atmosphere as she waited for him to speak the words. "I have actually become quite fond of Jennifer," he said.

It could hardly come as a great surprise to her. When he had first been brought to Blaize after a series of operations in London, it was Jennifer who had made it possible for him to find a place in the overcrowded hospital by giving up her leave to nurse him in his own room for the first two critical weeks; and since then she had spent almost all her free time caring for him. Robert knew that his mother would have noticed. He did not expect her to pretend surprise, but had hoped that she might look pleased. Instead, the thoughtful expression with which she received the news came as a disappointment. "You don't mind, do you?" he asked.

"I'm a little anxious, perhaps," Margaret said. "Jennifer only knows you as a soldier and you only know her as a nurse. But those are temporary roles for each of you. When the war is over—"

"Will the war ever be over?" demanded Robert. "And shall I still be alive when it is? I can't stretch my mind to think of the future, Mother, not when it's as far away as that. I can imagine tomorrow. I can just about believe in next month. That's all. I want to be happy now, not one day. I could be happy with Jennifer."

"Yes," agreed his mother. "Yes, of course. I'm sorry if I sounded doubtful, darling. The mothers of only sons are notorious for being possessive. But that was nothing to do with Jennifer. She's a very gentle, conscientious, loving girl. She worries too much, but the best cure for that is happiness, and I'm sure you'll be able to find it together. Have you asked her yet?"

Robert shook his head. "I wanted to tell you first. And to be sure that—that I'd be all right. After tomorrow, you know. But I think she guesses. And I think I know what she'll say."

There were no doubts in his mind at all, in fact. Only a determination not to allow Jennifer to sacrifice her life to someone who might prove to be a cripple, or worse, had restrained him. But he had kissed her, and she had come close enough for him to kiss her again. He knew enough about her shyness and the careful way in which she had been brought up to be sure that she would not have allowed that unless she intended to accept his offer as soon as he made it. He was sorry that his mother had felt unable to show more enthusiasm, but he loved her enough to be charitable. She had given the reason herself. She was a widow, and he was her only son. She would realise soon enough that she would be gaining an affectionate daughter by the marriage. He smiled up at her and was rewarded by her kiss, and the familiar feeling of her fingers riffling through his hair. Then—even on a Sunday— it was time for her to return to her duties.

5

As Margaret left her son's bedroom, she was angry with herself
for having allowed her feelings to show. Robert had been right to
guess that she felt little enthusiasm for the thought of Nurse Jennifer Blakeney as a daughter-in-law. Everything she had said
about the girl's good qualities was true enough, but it was also
true that Jennifer was too tense and anxious, seeming to live on
the edge of her nerves and be easily unbalanced by the need to
make choices. It was not the recipe for the sort of carefree married life which two young people ought to be able to enjoy—but
then, who could be carefree nowadays? To be free of anxiety in
1916 was to be callous or simply unintelligent. Margaret repri-
manded herself for falling into the same trap that she had seen
waiting for Robert. Jennifer had not settled easily to the strain of
a nursing life, but it was a temporary life. In her own home, with
her own loving husband and children, she would be a different
person, calm and contented. And Robert would be happy. They
were all agreed on that, that Robert should be happy.

She was intending to spend an hour in her office before making
her round of the wards, but was caught on the way by one of the
village girls who seemed nowadays to have taken the place of
the under-footmen.

"If you please, Doctor, her ladyship asked me to tell you that
Mr. Lorimer of Bristol is waiting to see you in the library."

Margaret went there at once, wondering what could have
brought her nephew to Blaize without even a warning by telephone. For a moment, as she hurried along the corridors, she was
frightened lest something should have happened to her brother
Ralph. Arthur, whose ships still plied—although less regularly
now—between Jamaica and Bristol, might well have been the first
to hear of any accident.

But the emotion which was causing Arthur to pace up and
down the room was one of irritation, not mourning, whilst Alexa
looked merely perplexed as she waited for information. Ralph

was, however, at the root of the trouble. Arthur was hardly able to go through the politenesses of greeting his aunt before he thrust a letter into her hands.

"This is from Uncle Ralph!" he exclaimed. "Without a word of warning! Without its apparently occurring to him for a moment that we in England have far greater duties than anything he can imagine out there. How can he expect any of us to shoulder his responsibilities for him at a moment's notice? Really, it's too inconsiderate. Read it, Aunt Margaret. See what it says."

Alexa came to stand beside Margaret as she frowned over the almost illegible scrawl. Remembering how neat her brother's tiny handwriting used to be, Margaret could hardly believe that he was responsible for this.

"He was drunk when he wrote it," said a voice from beside the door. Margaret looked up in astonishment. She had not realised that anyone else was in the room. An eleven-year-old boy was sitting on the floor with one leg in front of him, the other at an awkward angle. He had been tugging at the threads of Lord Glanville's Turkish carpet and now, as a spider scurried away towards the corner of the room, he slapped his hand over it and began to pull off each leg in turn with an expressionless face. Instinctively Margaret moved to stop him. But then, disentangling her mind from the puzzle of the unreadable letter and the brusqueness of the boy's comment, she realised who he was.

"You must be Grant, then." She left the letter to Alexa and opened her arms to welcome with a kiss the youngest child of Lydia, her best friend, and Ralph, her favourite brother. "And I'm your Aunt Margaret. We haven't seen each other since you were about six weeks old. I don't expect you remember that."

She smiled at him and was disconcerted by the scowl with which he responded, making no effort to stand or even to lift his arms to return her embrace. He was an unattractive child, pale-faced, podgy, and shabbily dressed. His hair, long and straight and with the appearance of having been roughly chopped with scissors, was so fair as to appear almost white, and his blue eyes were hard. Margaret had spent a great part of her professional life looking after children and took almost for granted her ability to establish an immediate rapport with them. For a moment, faced with this cold sulkiness, she was taken aback. But perhaps the let-

ter would offer some explanation of her youngest nephew's mood
as well as of his presence.

"I'll tell you what it says." Arthur was too impatient to wait for
the two women to puzzle out the words. "Uncle Ralph has sent
us his youngest son. He's not capable of caring for the boy any
longer, now that Aunt Lydia is dead, so he expects us to do it for
him. Without bothering to ask in advance. Obviously it was a
mistake on our part to behave so generously to the others—to
Kate and Brinsley. He takes it for granted that we'll look after as
many children as he cares to ship to England with the rest of his
merchandise."

"You forget yourself," Alexa rebuked him. She turned to the
boy. "I'm your Aunt Alexa, Grant, and this is my house. I have a
little girl almost the same age as you—just a year or so younger.
Come with me and we'll find her. You can play with some of her
toys while we prepare a meal for you."

"I don't play with toys," said Grant.

"All the same, I'd like you to meet Frisca." Alexa opened the
door, expecting Grant to follow her, but the boy did not move.

"He has to be carried everywhere." Arthur was still too out-
raged by the imposition to accept Alexa's hint that it should not
be discussed in the boy's presence. "That's another problem. It
may have been possible in Jamaica, but which of us can carry that
sort of burden?"

"Stand up, Grant," said Margaret gently, while Alexa rang for a
servant. Half helping, half pulling, she steadied the unwilling boy
on his good leg. "Oh, we can soon find a way to deal with this.
We've got a whole storeroom full of crutches. We'll cut one
down to size and you'll soon be running around on your own."

"I don't want to," said Grant, but Margaret took no notice.

"This is a hospital as well as a house," she said. "Anyone who
isn't able to look after himself has to do what the doctor tells
him; and I'm the doctor." She was still smiling, but made no attempt to conceal the firmness in her voice. "Off you go now to
meet Frisca."

The footman who had answered the bell picked Grant up in
answer to her gesture, and Alexa went with them to introduce the
two children to each other. At last Margaret had the chance to
read her brother's letter.

"This is written in grief, not drunkenness," she said. "At the very moment when he'd just learned of Brinsley's death in France. I suppose it was too much for him to bear, that the deformed child should survive when he had lost his golden boy."

"I'm not concerned with Uncle Ralph's reasons. Only with his actions. What he asks is impossible. Quite impossible."

"There's plenty of room in Brinsley House, Arthur."

It seemed to Margaret that Ralph was not the only one behaving selfishly. Her nephew was one of the few people in England who was doing well out of the war. He had no personal attachments and so did not share the strain endured by all those whose loved ones were at risk on the battlefield. The family shipping line and the shipbuilding firm which he had bought more recently were both profiting from large government contracts, and even before the war started he had been a wealthy man. He could keep Grant in a corner of his mansion in Bristol, with a tutor and a nurse if necessary, and hardly even know that he was there. "And I thought you liked children," she chided him.

"Children like Frisca, perhaps. But not a boy like this. Spoilt. Sulky. Ugly. Raging every time he fails to get his own way. He's been at Brinsley House for three days already, because I couldn't get away any sooner, and I can tell you that I've had enough. I'm not surprised that Uncle Ralph wants to be rid of him. I must repeat that I recognise no responsibility in the matter at all. If you can't take him, then I'll send him back to Jamaica on the next available ship."

"I take him?" Strained as she was with lack of sleep, overwork and anxiety about Robert, Margaret hardly knew whether to laugh or cry. How could Arthur imagine for a moment that she could carry this load as well?

"Or Alexa, of course. I realise that she doesn't have your feeling for children. But she has servants. And as she said herself, there can't be more than eighteen months difference in age between Grant and Frisca. They could share the same governess."

Alexa's first words, when she returned to the morning room, were sufficient to throw doubt on that suggestion even before it was put to her.

"I'm afraid there's going to be trouble there," she said. "It's difficult for someone as lively as Frisca to know what to do with a boy who can't or won't move. I suppose I shouldn't say this in front of a doctor, but one wonders sometimes whether it wouldn't be kinder if babies with such disabilities weren't allowed to survive the moment of their birth."

The casual remark had an effect on Margaret which Alexa could not have anticipated, for it was Margaret who had cared for Lydia during her last pregnancy, Margaret herself who had delivered the baby in that steaming West Indian village. She still remembered the moment in which she too had wondered, staring down at the new-born child, whether if he had the choice he would prefer never to draw his first breath. It had been a moment of temptation made stronger by the knowledge that the pregnancy was an accidental one and that the baby was unwanted by either parent. She had resisted the temptation and in so doing had condemned the child to a life in which his father resented him and his mother was weakened by his demands. Unlike Arthur, it was not possible for Margaret to say that she had no responsibility at all.

In any case, the boy was a Lorimer, descended—like each of the three adults in the room—from John Junius Lorimer of Bristol. He was a member of the family, and what was a family for if not to deal with emergencies like this? Inside a family, the question of whether someone had an attractive or unattractive personality was irrelevant. Whether or not Margaret could make herself like Grant, she had a duty to help him.

"When does your next ship sail for Jamaica?" she asked Arthur abruptly.

"Not for some time. The number of German submarines operating in the Atlantic makes the risk not worth taking too often, and that route is one of the government's lower priorities."

"Give me good warning as soon as you know a date, if you please. Alexa, may Grant stay here until then? We will speak of it only as a holiday, so that he won't feel too greatly rejected when we send him back. It's natural that Ralph should have been distraught by the news of Brinsley's death. We must give him time to recover. In the meantime, this is a hospital and poor Grant is in need of treatment. Arthur may be right in saying that he has been spoiled, but it's equally clear that he has been neglected. There are surgeons performing miracles every day in England now. We must see if there's anything to be done for the boy. If there isn't, we must teach him how to live with his own body. I'm too old to bring up another child. But at least for a limited time, I think we should all recognise our family responsibilities even if we take no pleasure in them. If Arthur will contribute towards the cost of any medical treatment and Alexa will allow Grant to live here with Frisca, I will do my best to find some course of treatment which will benefit both his body and his mind."

The decisiveness with which she spoke made it difficult for the others to demur. Alexa no doubt realised that her frequent absences from Blaize and a continuing sufficiency of servants meant that an extra guest would cause her little personal inconvenience. And although Arthur's interest in making money was almost obsessional, he had never been mean about spending it in a cause which touched his pride. Their realisation that Margaret was accepting the responsibility for sending Grant home as well as for keeping him for the time being made it easier for them both to accept her decision. Arthur gave the quick nod with which, like his sister, he was accustomed to approve a new proposal. Alexa, as befitted a chatelaine and prima donna, murmured something which could be taken as a gracious acceptance.

"That's settled, then," said Margaret briskly. "As a temporary arrangement at least. But that still leaves us Ralph to worry about. Do you think Grant was telling the truth when he said that his father drank? Ralph has been a total abstainer all his life. As a boy he never drank spirits because of his enthusiasm for games, and as a Baptist minister he was determined to set a good example. I can hardly believe that he would abandon his principles."

"I'm afraid it may be so," Arthur said. "We must make allowances for the fact that Grant and Ralph are clearly on bad terms, but there's evidence to support what the boy says. Most of the business letters which have reached me recently from Hope Valley have been written by Duke Mattison, Ralph's assistant—because, he explains, the pastor is ill. The nature of the illness is never defined, but it may well be—"

"Then perhaps Kate should come home to look after her father," Margaret said. "She's only a volunteer, after all. Even a

conscripted doctor would have been entitled to leave after two
years. I'll write and suggest that just at this moment Ralph may
be more in need of his daughter's care than the patients in her
hospital are of a doctor. And in the meantime we shall all do our
best to help Grant, shall we not?"

Her smile met with little enthusiasm. Grant had managed to
alienate his relatives in England in record time. But neither Alexa
nor Arthur made any further objection. The war had ushered in a
new world, but some of the old values survived. Even when scattered all over the world, the Lorimers remained a united family.

6

Everything about England came as a bewilderment to Grant.
To begin with, he had not expected it to be so cold. He was accustomed to rainy days, but in Jamaica it was warm even while
the rain was falling and as soon as it stopped the sun came out,
making the air steamy with heat. He had been given no new
clothes since his mother died and now he found that in this chill
December weather everything he was wearing was too thin as well
as too small.

He was astounded, too, by the size of the houses. There was
not a single building in Hope Valley which had more than one
floor—most of the village homes contained only one room.
Brinsley House, his cousin Arthur's house in Bristol, had seemed
like a palace, and yet Brinsley House was quite small compared
with Blaize. Did everyone in England, he wondered, live in such
a grand style?

The immediate problem here was one of stairs. Although
Grant was careful to conceal the fact as much as possible, he had
become quite adept at moving around on level ground, but he
had never before been faced with so many flights of stairs and his
difficulty in coping with them was genuine—even if he could not
make anyone believe this.

It came as no surprise to realise that he was not wanted: he
was used to that. He had not been wanted in Jamaica, either,

since his mother's death. But it had been an unpleasant shock to discover that he was not even expected, that the letter which his father had scrawled had travelled on the same boat and had been delivered, so to speak, by the same post as himself.

It was Miss Mattison, the village schoolmistress, who had really been responsible for his journey. On the day when the telegram arrived from the War Office to announce that Captain Brinsley Lorimer had been killed in action, the whole community had watched in horror as their pastor raged across the length and breadth of the valley, and the Bristow Estate which adjoined it, and even climbed the rocky path to the Baptist Hole, roaring his grief aloud and feeding it with forbidden rum.

Grant had spoken the truth when he claimed that his father had been drunk. His father's flock had accepted their shepherd's lapse more tolerantly than the frightened boy, for they would have behaved in the same way themselves. Most of them had kept out of the way until the fury of his mourning had spent itself. But Duke, on whom he depended, had made it his business to follow the pastor unobtrusively and make sure that he did himself no harm. And Duke's mother, Miss Mattison, had equally unobtrusively arranged for Grant to be carried to the schoolhouse. She kept him out of the way there for several weeks, in case his father's frenzy should vent itself on his unloved youngest child, and it was she who suggested, when she thought the time was ripe, that the boy should go to England. She knew from what Duke had told her, and what rumour in the Valley confirmed, that Arthur Lorimer, master of Brinsley Great House in Bristol, was a very rich man.

But when Miss Mattison's plan had been put into effect and Grant found himself unloaded at Avonmouth with a consignment of bananas, Arthur had made no pretence of a welcome. Grant found that easy enough to understand. What was more bewildering now was the attitude of his two aunts. They had agreed, apparently, that he should stay at Blaize, and yet they seemed to have no interest in him. Aunt Alexa had simply disappeared into another part of the huge house, while Aunt Margaret was always busy, always hurrying on her way to somewhere else, always tired, always worried.

"She's anxious about Robert, don't you see?" Frisca told him when he commented on this. Of all the surprises which England had in store for him, Frisca was the most astounding. In Hope Valley everyone was black—except for his own family, of course, and the Mattisons, who were a light shade of brown. He had known that in England everyone would be white, but Frisca had a brightness about her which was different again. Her golden ringlets were shiny as the sun, her eyes were alight with liveliness, her clothes sparkled with cleanliness, and her whole body somehow had a bouncing brightness of energy. Grant had spent the whole of his life pretending to himself that as long as he had his mother he didn't care whether or not anyone else in the world cared a fig for him. But now his mother was dead. He pined for someone else to like him. Could he persuade Frisca to do so?

"Who's Robert?" he asked, looking up at her.

"Aunt Margaret's son. My cousin. Your cousin, too. He's a hero. He was wounded in the war. Tomorrow he's going to have his plaster cut off and then everyone will find out whether he's going to be able to walk properly again. That's why Aunt Margaret's worried. In case he can't. Would you like to meet him? Come along. I'll take you."

She jumped up and led the way out of the schoolroom, skipping along the corridor. Grant scrambled to keep up. His crawl was ungainly, and he was defeated when she disappeared too fast down a narrow flight of stairs. He managed to bump himself down them in a sitting position, but at the bottom he had no idea where to go. He was stamping and almost crying with vexation when his Aunt Margaret appeared.

"I'm looking for Robert's room," he pouted. "Frisca was taking me, but she's gone too quickly and I don't know the way."

"I'll show you," said his aunt, turning back. She was still looking anxious, but she smiled at him kindly. "Are you warm enough in those clothes, Grant?"

"No." His voice expressed his resentful misery.

"I thought not. We must do something about that." She watched as he pulled himself along. "Your crutch will be ready tomorrow. That will make things much easier for you."

Grant had always refused to use the crutch which his father had made for him in Jamaica. He would have liked to refuse this one too, but already he had realised that although his aunt was small and tired and quite old, she was used to people doing what she said. She made no attempt to help him now, but walked slowly enough for him to keep up.

"Another visitor for you, Robert," she announced as she opened a door for Grant. "Turn them both out as soon as you feel tired."

The young man propped up in bed had bright red hair. He grinned at Grant in a friendly way and persuaded Frisca, who was hanging round his neck, to let go for a moment so that he could greet his new cousin properly.

"Hello, young Grant. Glad to meet you. You're just the chap I've been waiting for."

"Why?" asked Grant, still snivelling.

"Are you good with trains?" Robert asked him.

The expression on Grant's face turned to bewilderment, and Robert laughed.

"Perhaps there are different kinds of toys in Jamaica. What do you play with mainly?"

"I never had any toys," said Grant. "Only books."

"Then I'll have to show you what to do. I ought to have grown out of such things at my age, but I still like playing with trains. I make my own nowadays. And I've had an idea for a new sort of points system—you know, for making the engine go along one track rather than another. I can see you don't know what I'm talking about. I'll ask someone to bring the box in, and then we'll see if you can do a layout for me. I can't get down on the ground, you see, with all this plaster."

"I could do it for you," said Frisca indignantly. "You never asked me."

"It's a man's job," Robert said. "Girls are meant for looking pretty and dancing about and cheering up their sick cousins. Trains are serious business, and something tells me that Grant's going to be very good at them."

Apart from Miss Mattison, who had once remarked that he was clever, no one had ever told Grant before that he might be good at something. It was a new astonishment, that this cousin who hardly knew him was prepared to be friendly. A few minutes earlier Grant had been anxious to attract Frisca's interest, to establish some special claim on her. But although Frisca was polite, even kind, he could tell already that she would never want to slow down to the pace of someone like himself. Robert was different. At least for the time being, Robert was even less able to move around than Grant. He needed help, and the cheerful grin with which he asked for it was so friendly as to be irresistible. Within the space of a few minutes Grant had banished his sulky expression, changed his allegiance, and given his devotion to his cousin Robert.

7

For four days after the removal of his plaster, Robert would not allow his nurse, Jennifer, or any members of his family to visit him when he was out of bed. He was appalled by his own weakness. His left leg seemed as useless as if it had been shot away. Even his arms, after such a long period of inactivity, were hardly strong enough to control the heavy crutches which had been brought him. Every day he practised walking up and down his room, brushing aside the help of the orderly who came to make sure that there was no accident. But after only a short spell he was forced to fall back on the bed, exhausted by even such a small effort.

On the fifth day, however, he waited until he heard Jennifer's knock on the door and then stood up, steadying himself on the crutches before he called her to come in. She clapped her hands with pleasure as she paused in the doorway, her pale face flushed with happiness.

"That's no way to congratulate a fellow on being vertical again," said Robert. "I hoped you'd fling yourself into my arms and smother me with kisses."

"I was afraid of knocking you off balance," Jennifer answered in a whisper. Her shyness revealed itself in her face as well, but she came towards him in spite of it.

"Knocked off balance is what I want to be." He could only spare one arm to hold her as she kissed him, but when his head began to swim again it was with excitement, not weakness.

"Darling Jennifer!" he exclaimed. "But perhaps, having made my little gesture, I'd better sit down again. And you can give me a demonstration of your bedside manner."

"I'm so glad for you, Robert. It's marvellous to see you up after such a long time."

"I'd begun to think it would never happen. But now I really do feel that it's only a matter of time before I'm trotting round normally again."

"Of course it is," she agreed. "And not very much time, either."

"So there's no reason any longer why I shouldn't ask the most beautiful girl in the world whether she'd consider marrying me."

There was a moment's silence, but it was not a pause which caused him any anxiety, for he could feel the pressure of Jennifer's hand on his own. She was savouring a few seconds of joy, that was all.

"There never was any reason, Robert," she said softly.

"Oh yes there was. That standard plot about the beautiful nurse who devotes her life to her crippled patient is fine and romantic in stories, but highly unsatisfactory in real life."

"That would have been for the nurse to decide. But I'm delighted for your sake that it will never be necessary."

"You haven't actually answered me yet."

"You haven't actually asked me yet," she replied. But her head was on his shoulder and her arm round his waist. "Will it be all right with your mother, do you think?"

"Mother will be delighted." Robert spoke with certainty, knowing that whatever his mother's reservations might have been at first, she would welcome Jennifer into the family wholeheartedly once the engagement was a firm one. "I've dropped a hint to her already, as a matter of fact. Made it clear, of course, that it all depended on you and I was only telling her what I wanted. But any mother thinks that her son must be irresistible, doesn't she, so I don't believe the announcement will come as much of a surprise. What about your father?"

"Daddy's sixty-four," said Jennifer. She flushed slightly. "Ever since my brother was killed, he's only got one ambition left in life: to have a grandson. Each time I go home I'm put through a great inquisition to find out whether I'm—what's his phrase?—

'interested in anyone.' He's desperate for me to be married. I can promise that he'll welcome you with open arms."

"Mother would love a grandchild as well," said Robert. "Well, I've no objection to making the old folks happy, have you?" He laughed affectionately to see how Jennifer flushed again. It made her look prettier than ever. "So the sooner we get on with the wedding, the better. All the same, I need to get a few more muscles back into use. January, d'you think? Let's tell everyone the middle of January."

He kissed her again, his happiness so complete that he could think of nothing but the present moment. It was impossible to plan for the future, disagreeable to wonder whether he would have to return to the front, unreal to visualise a peacetime job and a married life in a home of his own. Too many things were beyond his control. The only certainty was that he loved Jennifer and she loved him. His mind clung to those two facts as tightly as his arms gripped her body—a body which looked so slim and fragile but felt surprisingly solid and reassuring.

When the time came for her to go on duty he felt a need to share his happiness with someone to whom he need not explain it.

"Could you find young Grant on your way out and tell him I need company?" he asked. As he expected, it was some time before the boy appeared. He was still dragging himself along the ground, Robert noticed with a frown.

"Where's your crutch?" he demanded.

"I can't manage it. It's too heavy and it won't go where I want it to go."

"I know the feeling," Robert sympathised. "All the same, it's a battle which has to be won. Let's declare war together on old Kaiser Crutch. I'm just getting the hang of mine. It comes suddenly, if you practise. From now on you and I are going to have a session together every day until we've got it licked."

He was as good as his word. At first, because he himself tired so easily, all they could do was to walk in turn up and down his room, but as Robert's strength returned, so did his adventurousness. By the time Christmas came, the two of them were climbing the stairs every day to the Long Gallery in which the Glanville ancestral portraits hung and playing complicated games of football and crutchball with a soft woolly ball stolen from little Pirry's nursery.

"It's not fair really," Grant complained as Robert scored his third goal one morning. "You've got two crutches and I've only got one."

"But you've got one perfectly good leg. You can stand steady even without a crutch. I've only got two weak and feeble legs. If you take *my* crutches away, I shall simply collapse on to the floor."

"You'll be all right soon, though," said Grant. "I'm going to be like this always."

"All the more reason to make the best of it." But Robert looked consideringly at his young cousin even as he spoke, and later that day he brought up the subject with his mother.

"Can anything be done about Grant?" he asked. "This chap who's pummelling me about every morning, for example. Could he do any good?"

Margaret shook her head. "No. He can help to strengthen muscles. But he can't alter the shape of a bone."

"Suppose Grant had been standing next to me when the shell burst," Robert suggested. "Suppose his hip had been smashed up like mine. The doctors could have set it into the position in which it *ought* to be, couldn't they, instead of back where it was before?"

"Sending a boy of eleven out to a battlefield in order that he shall be blown up is rather a drastic solution."

"Of course. But I mean—I can only put it crudely. Wouldn't it be possible for someone to hit Grant with a hammer—scientifically, of course, and under anaesthetic—and break whichever bit of bone is causing the trouble. And then put him in plaster, like me, until it mends, but in a better position. Or wouldn't his leg be long enough to reach the ground even if it were straight?"

"No, it wouldn't," said Margaret. "But that could probably be remedied. He could wear a surgical boot. You're quite right to prod me, Robert. These past few months, with such a never-ending stream of casualties to cope with, it's been difficult to think of anything but the hospital. But it's wrong of me to neglect the family. Before the war there wouldn't have been anything to be done in a case like Grant's, but doctors who've been treating a wide range of casualties are working miracles nowadays. There are all sorts of new operations and techniques. I'll make it my New Year resolution: to find someone who can help Grant."

1

Margaret stared at the sulky face in front of her and sighed. She had gone to a good deal of trouble to have Grant examined by a specialist. The verdict was a hopeful one. The boy's body could never be perfect, but a considerable degree of improvement was possible. An operation which might have been thought chancy in 1913 had become routine by the beginning of 1917. Margaret had felt pleased and enthusiastic as she explained to her nephew what would be involved, but his reaction was all too familiar.

"I don't want to," he said.

"Is it because you're frightened of being hurt?" Margaret asked. "You don't feel anything at all in an operation, you know. The doctor puts a mask over your face, with ether on it. Before you know what's happening you're in a deep sleep, and when you wake up it's all over."

"I don't want to," said Grant again.

"Come with me," said Margaret. She found it continually necessary to fight against irritation in her dealings with her uninvited guest. Grant was no longer quite as unattractive in appearance as on the day of his arrival. Piers had taken him to a tailor to be equipped with clothes which were not only warm enough for an English winter but were also cut to accommodate his distorted limb without looking too ungainly. His hair had been neatly cut and the exercise of moving about on his crutch had helped him to lose a little of the podginess developed in a childhood spent mainly sitting on the ground. But although Robert seemed to have the knack of cheering up his young cousin, Margaret herself was offered nothing but sulkiness in response to her efforts to be helpful.

She led the way now to a large room which had once been the main dining room at Blaize. Half a dozen empty Bath chairs stood against the walls. The men who had arrived there in them were standing in the middle of the room, each helped by an orderly to come to terms with a pair of crutches, just as Robert had been forced to do once. But Robert was now as fit as he had ever been, able to ride or walk as well as any other member of the family. Each of these men, in their suits of bright hospital blue, had one empty trouser leg.

"Take a good look," Margaret said. She did not intend to discuss her plans for Grant in front of the disabled men—but the boy had no such inhibitions.

"Is that what you're going to do to me?" he demanded. "Are you going to cut my leg off?"

"Of course not." More roughly than usual, Margaret pulled him out of the room and into what had once been a serving pantry. It was time, she decided, to stop trying to be kind and to see whether a little bullying would have a better effect. "I brought you here to show you that it's time you stopped being sorry for yourself. You've got a bit of trouble in one leg; just a little bit, and you think that entitles you to spend the rest of your life sulking. All the men you've seen in that room have had to get used to the idea that they've got to live the rest of their lives with only one leg. They'll never be able to run anywhere again, never be able to ride a bicycle; some of them will never be able to work. And it's painful, having only the stump of a leg—did you know that? The part that isn't there seems to go on aching, and there's nothing any doctor can do about it. They've got to get used to that as well. If I offered any one of these men the chance to have a simple operation which would leave him with two good legs, he'd jump at it. He wouldn't be frightened."

"I'm not frightened," said Grant.

"Yes, you are. I don't know whether you're frightened of the operation or whether you're frightened of suddenly finding yourself the same as any other boy, with no more excuses for all these sulks, but you're certainly frightened of something. Well, it's time

you stopped. Do you think your brother Brinsley was frightened
when he led that attack?"

"It's easy being killed," said Grant.

Margaret stared at her nephew, horrified to hear such a remark
on the lips of an eleven-year-old. "Listen to me, Grant," she said.
"When you were born, I was the doctor who looked after you
and your mother. Quite often a new baby needs a little help before it can take its first breath. No one would ever have known if
I'd allowed you to die before you'd even begun to live. But you
wouldn't have wanted me to do that, would you?"

"Yes, of course I would!" exclaimed Grant without a moment's
hesitation. "I'd never have known, anyway. But nobody wanted
me to be born. My parents didn't. It was all a mistake. My father
told me that."

"Oh, Grant!" Overcome by compassion for the unhappy boy,
Margaret opened her arms to him. And suddenly he was crying—
not with the tears of petulance and frustration to which she had
become accustomed, but from a deep misery of spirit. Margaret
found that she was crying as well. Her grip tightened, and she
was conscious of the boy's stiff body relaxing as he came close to
her for comfort instead of holding himself aloof.

After a little while she found her handkerchief and dabbed dry
both her own eyes and Grant's. "I wanted you," she said. "I
wanted you to be alive then, and I want you to be alive—and
happy—now. And your mother loved you: you know that. As for
your father, I realise that you and he have found it hard to be
friends, but you must make allowances for his unhappiness at
your mother's death, and then Brinsley's. I remember him saying,
when you were born, that God must have some special purpose
for you. When you grow up, you must make him as proud of you
as he was of Brinsley. And the first thing is to get you strong and
fit. You came to Blaize at an awkward time, Grant. We were all
unhappy, and too busy to welcome you properly. I'm sorry about
that. Everything's going to be different from now on. You're part
of the Lorimer family and we all love you. Now that Robert's
married, I need to have someone else to care for specially. I want
you to trust me to arrange what is best for you. Will you do
that?"

He nodded. Margaret was relieved—but anxious at the same time. She had already recognised in Grant the all-or-nothing emotions of the fanatic. Until now, it seemed, he had found more people to hate than love. But if he attached himself to her, she would have a responsibility to accept his devotion without disappointing him. To send him back to Jamaica, for example, unless he asked to go, would surely be a rejection too great for him to bear.

It was difficult for Margaret not to feel a little weary at the prospect of adding to her family responsibilities at a time when she was within a few days of her sixtieth birthday. But she had never been able to resist the appeal of a child in need, and Grant's need was greater than most. It was necessary to look on the bright side; 1916 had been a terrible year. There were no indications that 1917 would be any better as far as the war was concerned, but she could make it her business to see that the family at least was kept as happy as possible.

It was a resolution which quickly came under strain. Robert and Jennifer had been married early in January and Margaret had watched her son's firm stride down the aisle with a proud happiness. When she remembered the shattered body which had been returned to England it seemed miraculous that he should have made such a complete recovery. Foolishly, it did not occur to her that his state of health would be of interest to the Army too. She did not expect him actually to be discharged, but had imagined that rather than being returned to active service at the front he would be found some convalescent post such as that of an instructor at a training camp. So it came as a bolt from the blue when one day in February Jennifer burst into her office in a state of hysteria.

"What's happened?" Margaret's first thought, as she jumped to her feet, was that Robert must have had some kind of accident.

"He's got to go back. They say he's fit enough. They're going to send him over to France again. You've got to stop it. Please don't let them."

Margaret sank back into her chair, just as upset as her daughter-in-law, but corseted against shock by her age. Until that moment she had not fully realised how great a relief it had been to have Robert in England. Even at the beginning, when his condition was still a grave one, he had at least been surrounded by people who were trying to save his life, not take it. There was little she could say to comfort Jennifer.

"I hoped, like you—" she began; but to finish the sentence was unnecessary. "There's nothing we can do, I'm afraid. He's a soldier. He has to do what he's told."

"You're a doctor. You could say that he isn't fit. All they did was look at him and make him walk about and take deep breaths. That's not a proper medical examination. You could tell them that he isn't ready yet."

"I can't say that if it isn't true. In any case, they'd hardly believe his mother, doctor or not. And think how humiliating it would be for Robert. What does he say about it?"

"He takes it for granted that there's no choice. But it *would* be true that he isn't ready yet. He has nightmares, terrible nightmares, every night. About walking over dead bodies"—Jennifer was weeping again by now—"and arms and legs falling off when he touches them. And when he wakes up, he's shivering. He trembles for hours sometimes. He'd never admit it, but he's frightened. Deeply, deeply frightened."

"If no one were ever frightened, there'd be no such thing as courage," said Margaret. "He's already proved that he's a hero, trying to save his cousin's life. You should be proud that he's prepared to go back in spite of his experiences."

"I don't want to be proud. I want to be married. He's never told you how terrible it is out there. The mud and the smells and the noise and the danger. He never wanted you to be worried. But he wrote to me. He told me all about it."

"Get a grip on yourself, Jennifer. I've spent two years caring for the victims of the battlefield. Do you think I supposed that people were throwing grenades and gas shells at them during some peaceful country walk? You could give me credit for a little imagination. I didn't need to be *told*. Oh, I'm sorry, dear." She stood up again and put her arm round the girl's shoulders. "It's as much of a shock to me as it is to you. But I'm afraid there's nothing we can do. If there are any choices at all, we must leave them to Robert."

"Then he'll go," said Jennifer flatly.

"Yes." Margaret kissed her daughter-in-law. "Give him as

happy a time as you can until then, my dear. Don't let him see you crying."

In obeying that instruction, Jennifer proved more successful than Margaret might have expected. But when the day of parting came at last and she returned alone from London, it seemed that the effort had exhausted her. Twice during March she fainted in the ward, and Margaret began to receive complaints—cautiously worded, in view of the family relationship—about Nurse Scott's tendency to weep and dream. Before long it became necessary to have an official interview.

"I can think of an explanation for what's been happening," Margaret said. "I'm hoping you're going to tell me that I've guessed right."

She was rewarded for the gentleness of her approach by seeing the shy flush which had won Robert's heart. Jennifer nodded.

"You're expecting a baby?"

"Yes. In November."

All problems of discipline forgotten, the two women hugged each other. Then Margaret, her eyes shining, prepared to exercise her authority as a prospective grandmother as well as the administrator of the hospital.

"This feeling of weakness may not last for more than a month or two," she said. "But all the same, I'm going to suggest that you go home to Norfolk. There's too much heavy lifting in your work here. It's not good for you or for the baby. I know how much your father has longed to have you back with him, and this is the time when you'd be justified in indulging him. Country air and country food and plenty of rest. It's the best recipe. Do you agree?"

"Yes, Mother. Thank you very much."

Margaret was touched by the girl's first use of the word which Robert had from the beginning urged her to adopt. In the first weeks of the marriage the dual relationship had apparently made it impossible for Jennifer to decide whether she was talking to her commandant or her mother-in-law. From now on, Margaret was sure, their relationship would be a much easier one. Her happiness at the news was such that for a little while she was able to stop worrying about Robert. She did not even feel any great uneasiness at first when Piers came into her office a day or two later and enquired whether she had an address for Kate.

"Yes. A new one has just arrived. It's somewhere in the South of Russia." She handed her address book across the desk. "I'm not sure how much one can count on letters reaching her, though. She obviously never received my message about Brinsley's death. You look worried, Piers. Has something happened?"

"Yes," Piers told her. "It may not be important, but she's a long way from Moscow and Petrograd and news may take quite a time to travel. By the time she hears from there, it could be too late for her to get out of the country. And in my opinion she ought to leave. There's some very disquieting news coming through from Russia. Very disquieting indeed."

2

Every day Kate allowed herself two minutes of rage against Russian inefficiency. It acted as a safety valve, making it easier—a little easier—for her to cultivate during the rest of the day a Russian quality of resignation.

There was nothing wrong with the postal arrangements. What was left of the Serbian division was now under Russian command, and if the youngest and most useless of the Russian officers sent a message to his family in Moscow or Petrograd requesting the dispatch of a new pair of gloves or some favourite item of food, the parcel would arrive in the minimum time needed for the courier to make the double journey by train. But none of Kate's letters to the Minister of War or any of the committees which had recently been set up to deal with supplies or transport or hospitals was even acknowledged.

No one, it appeared, was willing to authorise the release and dispatch of the crates of medical stores that were waiting uselessly in some warehouse or other. In vain did Kate argue that the consignment was private property, sent from London specifically to re-equip the volunteer hospital which the Suffragist Movement had re-established after the Serbian retreat, this time on the

Romanian front. Somewhere in the tortuous bureaucratic process through which even the simplest transaction had to travel, some stamp or signature must be lacking. Before she learned better, Kate would have expected that in an autocracy decisions could be made simply and speedily. But in practice she found that no one in any sphere was willing to take responsibility for anything—not even the Autocrat himself.

At first it had been possible to make excuses. Almost before she had recovered from the hardships of the Serbian retreat, Kate— along with the new staff of English and Scottish nurses who had joined her in Medjidia—had found herself retreating again, this time across the Dobrudja plain. It was reasonable that her supplies should be stored securely until the hospital had been re-established in a position which could be considered temporarily safe from capture. But by January 1917 the situation was stable and still the supplies did not come.

It was not only the hospital that was underequipped. The soldiers—Serbs and Russians alike—were short of ammunition. There were not enough rifles for each man to have his own; someone leaving the front line for a day's rest had to hand his weapon over to his relief, together with a ration of cartridges which would be quite inadequate in any full-scale battle. For the time being everything was relatively quiet along the frozen front, but there was talk of a spring offensive. Kate knew little enough about the strategy and mechanics of war, but it was plain to her that if an attack by either side began before the Russians had supplied their men—including the Serbs—with rifles and machine guns, cannons and ammunition, there would be a massacre. And if there were a massacre—or even nothing more than the normal run of casualties after a battle—Kate and her staff, lacking even the most basic drugs and bandages, would be unable to cope with it. Throughout January she waited with mounting frustration.

But the beginning of February brought a possible explanation of the delay. She had asked one of the Russian officers to take the matter up for her while he was on leave. It came as no surprise when he returned empty-handed, for she had already realised that more perseverance would be required than he was likely to display; but it was of some value that he could tell her what the obstacle was. Beatrice—far away in London and aware of the chaos

which had surrounded the hospital unit in the second retreat—
had consigned the stores to Dr. Kate Lorimer by name, presumably as a precaution against misuse. "You will have to go personally to Petrograd to sign the papers and accept delivery," the
officer told her.

"And will that be enough?"

"Who knows? Have you friends? In such matters, it is always
as well to have friends."

Kate knew no one in Petrograd, and for a day or two longer she
hesitated. But her life since leaving England had matured her far
beyond her years. She was only twenty-six years old, but responsibility and the habit of command had given her the authority of
an older woman. The knowledge afforded her little pleasure: she
would have liked to be young for a while longer. But it meant
that she did not lack confidence. And there would be no language
problem. Her lessons in Russian from Sergei had enabled her to
converse with the Russian officers right from the start, and constant practice had by now made her fluent. It did not take her
long to decide that she must make the journey.

She was still in the process of arranging for her duties to be
covered during an absence which might extend itself beyond her
expectation when a bundle of letters arrived from home. She had
written to England with a new address, and here were the answers, more promptly than she could have dared to hope. Had
she judged only by their dates, in fact, the speed would have
seemed nothing less than a miracle. But she knew that Russia—
unlike the rest of Europe—had never adopted the Gregorian cal-
endar and was by now thirteen days behind everywhere else. It
was a small matter, but one which she found typical of the back-
wardness of the country.

Guessing that it would be the dullest, she opened her cousin
Beatrice's letter first. As she had expected, it was devoted to the
business of the hospital unit. With typical efficiency, Beatrice
enclosed a copy of the stores inventory in case the first notification had been lost during the Dobrudja retreat. The supplies had
reached Petrograd in the late autumn, just before the port was
closed by ice. The ship had already returned to England to
confirm the delivery.

Kate sighed as she read the businesslike communication, but it told her nothing that she did not already know. By contrast, Alexa's letter was gossipy and casually organised, hopping from one subject to another. Just as the typed list reflected Beatrice's character, so it was in keeping with Alexa's interests that she should enthuse about the musical life of Russia—the excellence of the bass singers, the grace of the ballet dancers, the taste and discrimination of the aristocratic audiences who were as likely to throw jewels as flowers at the feet of their favourite artists. Kate could not help laughing to herself, so different was the Russia in which she was living now from the Russia which had fêted Alexa during her opera season in St. Petersburg, eight long years ago.

"And if you find yourself in Petrograd, as I believe they call it now," Alexa continued, "you must on no account fail to visit my very dear friend Prince Aminov. Prince *Paul* Aminov, I should perhaps say, because you will have discovered by now that even younger sons in Russia take their father's title, so there are probably half a dozen Prince Aminovs scattered around the family estates. Paul is a great patron of the opera. In one of his palaces, at Tsarskoe Selo, he has a private theatre. It was when I sang there for him that I became determined to have my own little opera house one day. He'll be interested to hear from you that I did at least manage a season or two before this terrible war interrupted all our lives. He had a younger brother—I forget his name, but he played the piano so well that in England he could have been a professional concert soloist. In Russia, of course, it would be unthinkable for a nobleman to stoop to earning his living in such a way. Paul is officially an admiral, and his brother was something in the Army—but I doubt whether he saw much more of his regiment than Paul did of his fleet. I'm writing to Paul by this same post to tell him that my niece is a guest in his country. So I can promise you a welcome if you should ever go north. They have a palace in the city itself, of course."

Of course, agreed Kate, and for a second time she laughed aloud. No doubt it was true enough in peacetime that admirals could amuse themselves with their private theatres and their favourite singers; but in war even the least military-minded officer must recognise where his duty lay. Whether he was competent to discharge it was a quite different matter. However, Alexa's promise of an introduction strengthened her confidence in the success of the journey she planned. The requirement of her personal signature made the visit necessary: the name of a powerful family increased the hope that it might be successful. The warning that she might need friends had not surprised her and, although her claim on the Aminovs was so tenuous, it still might be enough. The Russian officers with whom she messed were all members of the nobility, and she had had time to learn that they were as generous as they were unpredictable when favours were asked.

She was still thinking about her journey when she opened Margaret's letter, but within a few seconds all thought of medical stores had vanished from her mind. She stared at the words with incredulous horror.

Brinsley was dead. Brinsley had been dead for more than six months. Margaret, it seemed, had made two attempts already to break the news, but realised from the cheerful note in Kate's last letter that they must have gone astray. She gave some details of the battle, of the letter which his commanding officer had written praising his gallantry, of his posthumous D.S.O. Kate found it impossible to believe any of this. There had been a moment, as she said goodbye to her brother on the platform of Waterloo Station, when she had been frightened lest she should never see him again, but beneath the fear had lain a belief that someone so young and full of life could not possibly die. Brinsley—his mouth curling with mischief—had claimed to be lucky, and Kate had believed him.

Still shocked, she allowed her eyes to run over the rest of the letter without taking much of it in. Robert had been wounded but was recovering well. Her father, though, was showing signs of breakdown as a result of Brinsley's death. Duke Mattison was writing alarming reports of his increasing irrationality, and there were hints that he was drinking too much. Margaret asked Kate to consider seriously whether her duty now might not lie at home in Jamaica. If she decided to return, Beatrice could find another doctor to replace her.

Kate set the letter aside and began to pace up and down. Almost as though she were sleepwalking she made her way to one of the hospital wards. The night sister looked up in surprise, since it was not the doctor's hour for a round, but Kate did not explain her presence. There was an immediate cry for water from the

men at one end of the ward; whenever anyone new came in, they
renewed their pathetic requests for a drink. Neither doctor nor
nurses could ever persuade soldiers whose stomachs had been shot
away that a sip of water could kill them as certainly as a glass of
poison.

What was it all for, Kate asked herself as she looked at the
faces of the injured men. One of her early grievances had been
that the Russian command had proved readier to risk the lives of
their Serbian allies in battle than those of their own army. As a
result, few of the Serbian division survived: most of the patients
now in the hospital were Russian. Sixteen-year-old boys, grey-
haired fathers of families, uncomprehending peasants who had
probably never travelled more than ten versts from their villages
before the recruiting officer arrived. What were they fighting for?
What were they dying for? For these men, at this moment, it was
possible to say that they were fighting to defend their own country; but that had not been the case at the beginning of the war.
And what had a complicated network of treaties and guarantees
and invasions ever had to do with Brinsley, except to make him
their victim? How much longer could it go on? How long would
women see their sons and husbands taken from them without
protest? How long would the men themselves continue to obey
officers who might have to order them to advance against machine guns whilst armed with nothing more than pitchforks? Kate
knew that such a thing was happening already and would happen
even more frequently in future. Some of the patients in her hospital had arrived with wounds to their feet or fingers which Kate
knew to be self-inflicted. If despair had already reached that
pitch, the time must be near when the men would simply turn
and run away.

The thought increased her sadness. It should have been possible to think of Brinsley's death as glorious. No doubt he had
acted heroically in the moment of battle. But was it worthwhile?
He had not survived to ask the question, so Kate put it to herself
instead. The answer came easily. No, it was not worthwhile.
There was nothing that any politician or general had ever told
her which would justify the death of one young man like
Brinsley, much less millions. Kate suspected that the war continued only because no one knew how to stop it.

The only clear fact was that she was doing some good where she was. Armies would continue to kill each other whether she was in Europe or Jamaica, but every single doctor at the front line saved lives every day simply by being on the spot. It didn't matter whether the lives saved were Serbian or Russian or even Austrian or German. Her responsibility as a doctor was wider than her responsibility as a daughter. She loved her father deeply, but in the middle of a war she could not devote herself to the care of a single man. As a doctor herself, Margaret would surely understand.

All that night Kate wept for her dead brother, but grief served only to stiffen her resolve to stay and do her job properly. That meant that she must have the right equipment. The very next day, grim with determination, she set out on the long journey to the city which had once been Alexa's glittering St. Petersburg— the Russian Paris, the Venice of the North—and was now, simply, Petrograd.

3

The Astoria Hotel was full. Or, at least, not necessarily full, but reserved for accredited members of military missions. Kate was startled and depressed by the rebuff. Tiring and uncomfortable, the journey had been unexpectedly protracted, for the train had twice been halted for several hours by a lack of coal, and on a third occasion had been forced to wait for the removal of an engine which blocked the line after its boiler burst in the extreme cold. She had been looking forward to a comfortable bed and perhaps even a bath.

Disappointed, she paused in the lobby to consider what she would do. All foreigners visiting Petrograd were accustomed to stay at the Astoria as a matter of course. It was the only hotel in the city with international standards of service and language comprehension. Because Kate spoke Russian she could search for the kind of accommodation which ordinary Russians used, but after so many crowded days of travelling she felt desperate for rest and welcome. Even more to the point, she was not adequately dressed to endure the biting wind which came straight off the frozen Gulf of Finland. The south of Russia had been cold enough, but here the temperature was so low that without a scarf across her mouth and nose it was painful even to breathe. She returned to the droshky which had brought her from the station and gave the driver the address of the Aminov town house.

There she used her own language to ask whether Prince Aminov was at home. Even if they did not completely understand, the servants could be expected to get the gist of the request and it seemed a good idea to make it clear from the start that she was a foreign visitor. The prince himself would certainly speak English, although French would be his first tongue. Russian was the language of the peasants.

The numerous servants in the hall were formally dressed in livery, but informal in behaviour. Kate discovered at once that Prince Paul was not in Petrograd; and her attempt to learn the whereabouts of his brother—whose name Alexa had omitted to mention—was greeted with a real or pretended lack of comprehension. They did not realise that she could understand the discussion which they proceeded to hold amongst themselves. From it she learned that Prince Vladimir had arrived home on leave that day but had given orders that he was not to be disturbed. Different opinions were expressed as to whether the arrival of a foreign lady would justify the overriding of these instructions.

Kate's tiredness, subduing her sense of polite behaviour, drove her to interrupt a discussion which seemed set to continue interminably. She demanded to be taken to Prince Vladimir, and by the firmness with which she turned towards the staircase made it clear that she would find her own way if no one was prepared to escort her. Her knowledge of the Russian character was accurate enough. Confronted by determination, the servants shrugged their shoulders and accepted her wishes. Two of the footmen went up the wide marble staircase in front of her to lead the way.

The grandeur of the rooms on the first floor almost took Kate's breath away. She had visited Brinsley House and had lived for several months in Blaize, so she was not unfamiliar with the life of the rich. But this house was built and furnished on an unimaginable scale of opulence. Alexa had not been exaggerating when she talked of palaces—and even then she had been describing one of the family's country homes, giving the impression that what was maintained in the town was merely a pied-à-terre. Kate's eyes widened as she followed the footmen through huge rooms decorated largely, it seemed, with gold leaf. Crystal chandeliers hung from the high ceilings. Carpets of luxurious thickness or of delicate Chinese colours covered the floor. Vases and urns of green malachite stood on Boule commodes. And small ornamental objects, of gold or jade or crystal decorated with jewels, were set out on Louis XV tables as casually as though each of them were not worth a fortune.

Someone was playing a piano, and as they came nearer to the sound, the footmen fell back. The intrusive foreigner, it seemed, should be left alone to face their master's anger at being disturbed. Ready to do so, Kate opened a door and found the pianist. But at first she could not bring herself to look at him, so overwhelmed was she by the room. It was a hall rather than a mere room—perhaps actually intended as a private concert hall, since there was a raised platform at the far end: or perhaps as a ballroom, with provision for an orchestra. Except for the grand piano on the platform and fifty or so gilded chairs arranged against the wall, it was unfurnished: but the proportions were so perfect that it did not appear bare, and the materials of its construction so beautiful that it did not need decoration. The walls were of a pale pink marble into which had been set, as a pattern, panels of other marbles in a range of colours which seemed too fragile to be stone: pale blue and delicate mauve, the sea shades of green, clear yellow, misty grey. It was an aristocratic room in its own right; a fit setting for an aristocrat.

Kate had been an enthusiastic concertgoer in her student days and recognised the work she was hearing as the piano part of an early Beethoven concerto. But the piece was interrupted by the pianist's awareness of her presence. He was a fair-haired man in his early thirties, wearing the style of moustache currently sported by the dashing young officers of the cavalry regiments. But instead of wearing uniform, he was casually dressed, with a scarf loosely knotted inside his open-necked silk shirt. And although a moment earlier he had been hunched over the keyboard, projecting an impression of great physical power and control through the

crashing chords and rapid trills of his performance, in repose he
gave the impression of softness, as though there were no bones in
the wide, long-fingered hands which rested on his knees as he
looked at her. He would have had the right to be impatient or indignant or aggressive, but instead his brown eyes watched her pas-
sively as she walked towards the platform.

"I'm trespassing in your palace and disturbing your practice,"
she said as she approached. "I must apologise. But the servants—"

"Oh, the servants!" He interrupted her with a shrug of his
shoulders. She had spoken in English and, as she expected, he answered her fluently in the same language. "What can I do for
you?"

"I'm Dr. Kate Lorimer, from England," said Kate. "I have an
introduction from my aunt, Lady Glanville, to Prince Aminov—
Prince Paul Aminov."

He stood up and bowed over her hand in languid acknowl-
edgement of the introduction. "I fear your journey is not ended,
Dr. Lorimer," he said. "As an admiral, my brother feels obliged to
be at least within sight of the water while the war continues. He
is at Murmansk. And my sisters and their children have retired to
one of our country estates to avoid the food shortages in the city.
I regret that I am the only member of the family here to welcome
you. But I can see that you are fatigued. I shall not allow you to
continue in search of my brother until you have dined with me
and enjoyed a good night's rest. And if your business is not with
him personally, I hope you will allow me the pleasure of representing him."

"I should certainly be most grateful—"

Again she was interrupted, this time by a clap of the hands.
The two footmen hurried in with a promptness which made it
clear that they had been listening to the exchange. Kate heard
them ordered to take her and her luggage to a room. Then the
prince turned to her again and for a second time formally kissed
her hand.

"When you are rested, we will meet again for dinner," he said.
"It will be an unexpected attraction of my leave to enjoy such
charming company."

To Kate, knowing herself to be tired and dirty and crumpled, the remark sounded like a joke. But during the past winter she had spent enough time with aristocratic officers of the imperial army to know that the compliments which would have signified insincerity in England were only normal politeness with them. In any case, she had come in search of hospitality and did not intend to let pride rob her of it. With so many rooms and servants, her presence was not likely to inconvenience her host—and the speed with which he resumed his piano playing as she withdrew suggested that he would not allow it to do so. She had been received and temporarily dismissed.

How could she discover at what hour she would be expected to appear for dinner? Her enquiry to the maid received the courteous answer, "It is as you wish, madame." So the problem was solved by sleep, which overcame her as soon as she lay down on the huge four-poster bed, intending only to rest for a moment or two. By the time she awoke, the short northern day had long since ended and the maid was standing in the doorway, awaiting instructions.

Over dinner Kate felt it her duty to give more information about herself, especially to a host who clearly thought it rude to ask questions. The first matter to be established was that of Alexa's name. Prince Aminov had never heard of Lady Glanville, but as soon as Kate remembered that Alexa's visit to St. Petersburg had taken place before her marriage, and mentioned Alexa Reni, there was a very different reaction.

"The beautiful Alexa! Oh, but most certainly I remember her visit. I thought her the most ravishing creature I had ever seen. And her voice was as perfect as her face. I dreamt of composing an opera for her. My brother, alas, took care that she should not notice me. I half expected her to become my sister-in-law, but it seemed that Paul was not quite persuasive enough."

"From what my aunt told me, I had the impression that he was offering a little less than marriage." Kate spoke mischievously. At the first moment of meeting she had been tired and uncertain of her welcome and her host had been patiently suffering an interruption: no wonder they had behaved stiffly to each other. Now that they were both relaxed, she found him easy company.

Her professional acquaintance with the Russian officer class had led her to divide it into two categories: one containing drunken boors and the other delightful but often idle dilettantes with the charming manners of international society. Prince Aminov, it seemed to her—although only a dilettante in the sense that his talent for music was not exercised for money—fell into the second group. Already he was flirting with her in the manner of a man who knows he will not be taken seriously, and for this one evening of relaxation Kate was prepared to match his mood.

"You are probably right," he laughed. "When Paul did marry, two years after your aunt left Russia, he chose a grand duchess from the imperial family for his bride—with highly advantageous effects on both his fortune and his career. We are close in age, but he was an admiral before he was thirty, while I, as a bachelor, have to endure the more usual intervals between promotions."

"I hope your brother's marriage has proved as happy as my aunt's."

"Ah, well," he sighed. "Unfortunately my sister-in-law died in childbed last year—and the baby died as well. So you'll find my brother unencumbered. Perhaps you'll have more success than the lovely Alexa in persuading him to take an English wife."

Kate flushed. Too unsophisticated to make a joke of his teasing, she could counter it only with her true reason for coming to Petrograd, although the effect was to make it clear that she was using the Aminov palace as a hotel. Fortunately her host took it for granted that she should have done this, and insisted that she must stay as long as might prove necessary. He listened with a frown to the details of what she needed.

"I can tell you where to go and whom to see," he said. "But the difficulties you face will be no less here than they were at a distance. The inefficiency of the ministries is almost unbelievable. The armies lack ammunition because the trains lack coal, and yet there is plenty of coal in the country. The city bakeries can bake only a tenth of the bread which is required because they are short of flour, and yet the granaries in the east are full. Every department is ruled by incompetence." He sighed. "There must be some efficient officials somewhere, but they are all afraid to act on their own initiative and are strangled by bureaucracy if they attempt to use the system laid down for them. It is my duty as an officer of His Majesty's Regiment of the Imperial Guard to protect the Tsar's life with my own, but I would be doing him a better service if I could persuade him to dismiss his present ministers and committees and give direct power to one or two men who know what the Army needs and would cut through every knot to provide it. We are losing the war. You, on the front, must know that as well as I do. There are too many Russians who are ready to give in, to make a treaty. The rest of us, those who remember Japan and are not prepared to be humiliated again, have only one defence against such defeatism—we must win." He smiled apologetically. "Well, I mustn't start delivering political lectures. What difference does it make to an Englishwoman whether we win or lose?"

"If Russia were to surrender, the German and Austrian armies could turn their whole force against the French and British," said Kate; but even as she spoke she realised that a Russian could not be expected to care greatly about that. Tactfully she tried to rouse the prince from his mood of depression. Would he play to her, she asked him, and the charm of his smile showed at once how much the suggestion pleased him.

It was as well that the evening finished on a restful note, for the next day tried Kate's patience to the limit. To sit in a hospital hundreds of miles away and fume because letters were never answered had been hard enough. Far worse, she discovered, was to wait in a government building and see that her request for an appointment was not even conveyed from the reception area to the office of someone who might conceivably deal with it.

On that first day she tried to cultivate the patience shown by her fellow-petitioners. It did not come naturally to her, and she wondered whether the Russians themselves were not being pressed close to the edge of tolerance. Surely in such conditions even they might abandon the fatalism which had endured for so many centuries. On her way back to the palace on that first evening she noticed the long line of women queueing for bread and realised that they would have to wait all night in the bitter cold for whatever might be available the next morning. Twenty-four hours later, as Prince Aminov's sleigh was carrying her back from a second wasted day, she saw the lines break. The windows of the bakery she was passing were broken by stones and the crowd rushed inside to seize what they could. So great was the crush that the sleigh was brought to a halt. It was able to continue only when the clatters of horses' hoofs on the frozen ground alerted the looters to the fact that the Cossacks were coming.

"One thing surprised me," said Kate when she was describing the incident to her host later that evening. "A friend once described to me the whips which the Cossacks carry."

"Yes?" Prince Aminov showed no interest in whips. "What of it?"

"They were not carrying them today."

It had seemed significant to Kate, but the prince merely shrugged his shoulders. "The crowd was mainly of women, I imagine. It is when students riot or soldiers mutiny that the Cossacks need to establish their authority. Now then, I have an invitation which I hope that you will accept. On Sunday evening Princess Radziwill is giving a gala ball. She has heard that you are my guest here and insists that I bring you as my partner."

Kate considered the offer doubtfully. A society dance would not have attracted her even in England. Here she would find it even more difficult to converse—in French—with the kind of wit and intelligence that would be expected.

"I'm afraid I came to Petrograd prepared only to petition ministers," she said. "My clothes are worse than unsuitable—it would be an insult to a hostess if I appeared in them."

Prince Aminov waved away her objection. "My sister-in-law's wardrobe is still hanging in her dressing room. Paul has not been back here since she died. He will never want to see them again. Please take your choice. No one will be hurt or offended, and each of the balldresses will have been worn only once. You will make me very unhappy if you refuse."

Kate hesitated still. She found it easy to converse with her host, but less easy to know what he was thinking. Except when he was playing the piano, his eyes held a dreamy, faraway look, as though nothing were of any great importance to him. She realised that out of politeness he would have been bound to pass on the invitation to her, but she was unable to guess whether the corresponding politeness on her part would be to accept or to persist in her refusal.

Prince Aminov took her hand and bowed to kiss it as though they had only just been introduced.

"You are too serious," he said. "It is good that you should be so greatly concerned for your patients and I admire your perseverance in battering your poor head against the doors of our bureaucracy, fighting your own private war. But you are too young to be angry all the time. There is nothing you can do for your hospital by staying here in the evening. And a good deal that you might achieve by coming."

"What do you mean, Excellency?"

"I mean that this may prove the way to unlock the warehouse which holds your goods. I shall introduce you to the right people —the highest people, who are never likely to grant an audience to someone who comes without appointment to their waiting room. You will meet them on their own ground, as an equal. Together we shall approach the little difficulty with delicacy. They will realise that you are a friend of mine. Then they will understand that the customary procedures will be observed, and the difficulties you have faced will disappear."

"Are you trying to tell me that they are corrupt—that they need to be bribed?" Kate demanded.

The prince gave an amused smile. "Is it corruption to operate a system which is generally known and accepted? It would certainly be corrupt if they allowed your property to go to someone else for a consideration, but I'm sure they would never dream of doing that. All they expect is a little present—a fee, you could call it. And I only use this argument to show you that you will be serving the interests of your patients in going to the ball, because I could not bear to be disappointed of your company. The evening is a time for pleasure—and how could I enjoy myself if I knew that you were here alone, fuming with rage. You will come, please? For my sake."

His smile was curiously sweet, banishing the dreaminess from his eyes and replacing it with a pleading warmth. Kate was not easily charmed and was well aware that any claim that he would be miserable without her was only a pretence. Nevertheless, she found the mixture of formality and persuasiveness in his manner to be irresistible.

"Thank you, Excellency," she said, half laughing at herself for the weakness of her capitulation. "I shall be most honoured to be your partner."

4

Early on Sunday morning Kate stared out of her bedroom window across the frozen water of the Neva. At this time of day the ice was a pale green, as delicate in shade as the panels of the marble hall. Later, if the sun shone, it would glint with gold for an hour or two before sunset turned it a rosy pink. On the further side of the river the spire of the Peter and Paul fortress, too slim to hold the snow, was golden as well: a beautiful sight but a symbol of ugliness. The contrast was too acute to be believed—on this side of the river, the pampered comfort of the prince in his palace; and on the other, the hardship and oblivion to which political prisoners were condemned.

There was no bureaucracy to be besieged today—its officials would replace obstructiveness by absence. The Aminov palace was equally silent. Kate was growing familiar with the timetable of the Russian nobility, whose day—Sunday and weekday alike—hardly began before nightfall. Still governed by the habit of hospital routine, she herself woke early, but never saw her host at breakfast.

If the prince had known that she intended to go out and explore the city—and unescorted into the bargain—he would certainly have prevented her. There had been a series of strikes on the previous day. No trams or trains had run, and crowds carrying red banners paraded through the streets demanding the resignation of the Cabinet and the expulsion of the German Tsarina. The Army had been called out and some of the demonstrators were killed. But it was rumoured that many of the soldiers had disobeyed the order to fire.

Kate was well aware that the streets of the city were becoming unsafe. Being Kate Lorimer, however, she was not prepared to make any concessions to the fact. After almost a week spent in ministerial anterooms, she felt the need to treat her frustration with a dose of fresh air and exercise.

For more than two hours she tramped over the frozen snow in the boots which the army cobbler had made for her. In spite of the blackness of her mood and the heavy greyness of the sky, from which new snow was falling, the beauty of this most un-Russian city took hold of her. Already she had admired the magnificence of the Winter Palace, and she was able to appreciate the classical elegance of the pale yellow buildings which curved round the facing side of the palace square even though they housed the General Staff offices she hated. The elaborate ceremonial arch in the centre of the curve and the picture-book array of noble palaces, like the Aminovs', which stretched along the river bank, were all part of the same splendid architectural centrepiece with which she had become familiar. But now for the first time she wandered further afield, exploring the network of canals, admiring the decorative bridges which ran so elegantly across them, and the handsomely painted mansions on either side.

It was as easy here as in Prince Aminov's marble hall or golden drawing room to forget the other aspects of the city: the slum tenements with their insanitary courtyards, the poverty of the people on the streets, the deep puddles which formed when the sun shone warmly enough for an hour or two to melt the snow. From the first moment of her arrival in Petrograd she had been appalled by the contrast between the luxuries of her temporary home and the world of pain and misery on the battlefront which she had been attempting to describe to the indifferent bureaucrats of the General Staff. Only that morning she had become aware of another contrast, with the world of the political prisoner. And now she realised that the extremes of luxury and sordid discomfort were to be found inside the central living area of the city. How long could such a state of affairs be tolerated, she asked herself. Her step became firmer and even less ladylike than before as her anger rose.

The sound of singing drew her towards the Cathedral of St. Nicholas. Reminding herself that it was Sunday, she went inside.

It was a long time since she had last been able to attend a Baptist service, and it was likely to be an equally long time in the future before she had any contact with the faith which her father preached so eloquently in Jamaica. But although the form of the Russian Orthodox service was so different from that of a Nonconformist chapel, the same God presumably listened to prayers in all languages, and Kate was in need of comfort.

On the ground floor a funeral service was in progress. A crowd of women, fat and dowdy in their winter coats and headscarves, wandered, weeping, in and out. But the singing came from a higher floor. Kate climbed the stairs and found herself in a treasure house. The light of many hundreds of candles was reflected off jewelled icons and golden mosaics. Even here, it seemed, she could not escape from the contrast between great wealth and great poverty. Gorgeously attired in yet more gold, a black-bearded priest was reading from the Bible to his crowded congregation. Almost imperceptibly his reading voice changed to chanting and the chanting to an operatic style of bass singing. All her life Kate had been susceptible to the influence of music, whether soothing or stimulating. She made no attempt now to listen to the words, but allowed her troubled spirit to be comforted by the beauty of the sound.

The voice of the single singer was joined by a choir in the gallery above. The new sound filled the building, swelling and diminishing, harsh and even discordant at times, its harmonies changing abruptly from major to minor key with that especial Slavonic characteristic that was so difficult to analyse but so easy to recognise. Kate tried to pray but found the atmosphere uncongenial. Her Baptist upbringing had given her a positive attitude to religion and life. She was not prepared—as the Russian Orthodox worshippers were—merely to prostrate herself on the ground and await events. Her father, in his services, was accustomed to converse aloud with God—to put forward problems, and to receive solutions which owed a good deal to the pastor's own conclusions. Kate knew that prayers were not always answered—but that could be the fault of the petitioner: it remained important to continue the dialogue. But above all it was necessary to take whatever action might be necessary to achieve God's revealed wishes, to walk firmly down the path illuminated by His will.

Such an attitude was out of tune with the mood of this congregation. Already in the hospital Kate had learned to recognise what appeared to be a peculiarly Russian aptitude for suffering—an ability to accept separation, hunger, pain, and even death without a murmur of complaint against whatever inexplicable fate had brought all these things to pass. The women in this congregation—for there were few men—seemed to display the same passivity: whatever was God's will was to be accepted.

No doubt the obstructive behaviour of Russian officials was encouraged by this attitude. Their procrastinations or outright refusals to take action would all too often be accepted without complaint: or, if that was too much to hope for, the petitioner would continue to wait patiently for something to happen which might change the situation. More than once in the past few days Kate had longed to leap to her feet in some crowded waiting room, allowing her rage to explode. She had persuaded herself that restraint would be wiser, but now she wondered whether she was right or whether the time had come to protest. In this cathedral too she would have liked to shout out, interrupting the service to tell these submissive women that life ought to be good, that it was not necessary to be always unhappy and—most of all—that to accept the blows of fate or government without complaint was to invite further tribulation. Oh, for the throbbing vitality of Hope Valley!

She held her indignation under control now, just as she had controlled it during the search for the right rubber stamp; but the intensity of her feelings, raised to a higher pitch by the melancholy music of the choir, drew her into a state of exaltation—a trancelike ecstasy, illuminated by a visionary flash. There is no God, she thought, and at once everything was explained.

Her father had preached in the name of God, but it was his own hard work as an administrator that brought happiness to his people, and she suspected that he had always known this himself. For the past two years she had done her best to reconcile the death and suffering she saw with the faith of her childhood, the belief in a loving God who ordered everything for the best. She had failed in the attempt. How could a loving God have wanted Brinsley to die? But if God instead were angry or uncaring, why should He be worshipped? The reconciliation of faith and fact had proved to be impossible. Now she knew that the effort had never been necessary: there was no God.

So there was no excuse for passivity. The world might be destroying itself, but the destruction was not inevitable. There was no God. Men who were the victims of other men must save themselves by their own exertions and build a new society out of love for their fellow men, not from hatred or fear. It was all so obvious that she could not understand why she had taken so long to comprehend it. She even remembered that Sergei had tried to convince her of the need for a change in society. Revolution was the word he had used, and she had been alarmed by it, thinking in terms of the French terror. But a spiritual revolution would be as effective as a political one. All that was needed was a change of attitude, a determination to be positive.

Kate Lorimer's vision was the opposite of Saul's, but Petrograd was on her road to Damascus. "There is no God," she repeated to herself. "No God. Only men, who must love one another."

Around her the service continued, but it had nothing more to offer. Kate pushed her way out of the crowded cathedral and began to walk back towards the Neva. The day was lighter now: the sky seemed to have lifted. Was it only the excitement of her vision which made her want to run and shout? Was it only her imagination which made her see the people in the streets in a light very different from that of the early morning? They were holding their heads higher, surely—were walking with a more purposeful air. Her excitement increased, as though the change in her faith had imperceptibly attuned her to the mood of the city. Her own anger made her sensitive to the anger around her. The Russian people were ready at last to break through the shell of their old passivity and she, Kate Lorimer, felt herself spiritually to be a Russian.

Within sight of the river she paused in surprise. It had not all been her imagination, then. Crowds of people were approaching on foot across the bridge. There was nothing threatening about their pace or attitude: only their number made it clear that this was no ordinary Sunday promenade. And if she had had any doubts, a disturbance behind her would have dispelled them. A line of soldiers, their footsteps quietened by the snow, was marching down the Nevsky Prospekt towards the Admiralty building, leaving a few of their number in a group at each street corner. Hardly more than boys, they looked uneasy in their ill-fitting uniforms. But they were armed.

There was no confrontation. The crowd filled the heart of the city but did not threaten it. The demeanour of the soldiers made it so clear that they did not wish to use their weapons that their officers, equally uneasy, showed no disposition to test their authority by giving the order to clear the area. Nevertheless, the steady increase in the size of the crowd and the silence, which was as sinister as it was surprising, brought Kate down to earth again. In any kind of battle it was important to be recognisably on one side or the other: the man in the middle was too often the target of both. Prudently she made her way by back streets to the Aminov palace.

5

The moment of revelation inside the cathedral had changed Kate's whole attitude to life. She was aware that she would never look at society in the same way again—and yet the knowledge did not affect her actions immediately. She was still the same punctual and efficient woman who kept promises once she had made them. When Prince Aminov had first asked her to go to the Radziwill ball she had felt doubtful. But the possibility that the occasion might prove of practical value had persuaded her to accept, and the mere fact that her doubts about going to a party had deepened did not seem a good enough reason now to disappoint her host. As the maid came into her room that evening with a heavy weight of creamy satin over her arm, Kate's gasp was not one of rejection but merely of incredulity. She had been promised the choice of a gown and had intended to look for the simplest, but it appeared that the maid had taken the decision out of her hands.

"It's unlucky to put on clothes which have been worn by someone who is dead," the girl explained. "But this dress was ordered by the princess to be ready for her after the birth of her baby. She never even saw it."

"It's too rich for me!" Kate exclaimed, for the low-cut, sleeveless bodice and the hem of the skirt were both patterned in hundreds of tiny pearls.

"The others will be too tight," said the maid. Not for the first time, Kate was amused by the frankness of Russian servants. And this one, no doubt, was telling the truth. Kate's experiences during the past two years had hardly allowed her to grow fat through overeating; but she was sturdily built and it was unlikely that even the most vigorous attempt at tight lacing would reduce her waist to a fashionable smallness. If for this one gown the dressmaker had guessed at a slight increase in size on the part of a new mother and had allowed her a little looseness even on top of that, the maid's choice might indeed prove to be the best. Laughing, Kate allowed herself to be taken over. Only when she was ready, with her hair veiled and ornamented, her shoes buckled, her necklace fastened, her long gloves smoothed up to the elbow, was she allowed to look at herself in the glass.

Her first reaction was one of amusement. The maid had turned her into a princess. Kate was tall enough to give the impression of elegance when, as now, the cut of her clothes imposed it. No doubt she would destroy the illusion as soon as she moved, for she had never been able to subdue an unladylike stride. But as long as she stood still, straight-backed, and with her head held high, she recognised that Prince Aminov would not need to be ashamed of his partner at the ball.

For a moment she felt all the ordinary feminine excitement of a young woman who sees herself to be attractive. Her complexion was freckled instead of fashionably white and her auburn eyebrows were too thick. But her wide-set green eyes were clear and bright and her smooth forehead, strong cheekbones, and generous mouth combined to give an impression of freshness and candour. Half ashamed of her moment of conceit, she admitted to herself nevertheless that she was not too bad-looking after all. She lifted her heavy skirt off the ground and walked slowly downstairs.

Two footmen were waiting to throw open the doors of the drawing room. As Kate paused, just inside the doorway, Prince Aminov rose from a Louis XV sofa to greet her, but it seemed

that for a moment he could neither move nor speak. He stared as
though he could hardly believe what he saw, and Kate was conscious that she was staring back in very much the same way. The
uniform which he was wearing for the evening was too elaborate
even to be mess dress. The profusion of gold braid and the jewelled Order on its blue diagonal ribbon must surely have been
designed for attendance on the Tsar. Kate, who despised ostenta-
tion and was accustomed to judge men by their behaviour and
not by their clothes, told herself that she ought to laugh, or at
least not to notice. But instead she was overcome by the dignity
of his presence. Seeing the prince in his informal day clothes she
had already realised that his appearance was attractive, but now
she had to admit that he was outstandingly handsome.

It was an artificial effect, of course. Unmarried though she
might be, Kate had seen so many men naked that she was able
mentally to strip Prince Aminov of all his trappings, and deliberately now she did that. It was the tightness of his high collar, she
reminded herself, which made him hold his head so proudly erect,
when his shoulders more naturally hunched themselves over the
piano keyboard. It was the thickness and embellishment of his
jacket which gave the impression of a strong chest, when really
his figure was slight and unathletic. It was his tailor who had cut
trousers of such elegant slimness, his valet who had polished
hand-made shoes of such smartness. She was looking at a production, not a person, but the very fact of recognising this made her
see the man more clearly, and what she saw had an effect which
she could not have anticipated. Both as a medical student and as a
doctor working amongst soldiers, Kate had counted a good many
men as her friends, but she had never fallen in love with any of
them. To be attacked by first love at the age of twenty-six was so
overwhelming an experience that she was silenced by the pain of
it.

She tried to fight against the realisation of what had happened, but Prince Aminov did nothing to help her. She could feel
his hand trembling as he raised her own to his lips; and although
only his eyes told her how much he admired her appearance, they
spoke so eloquently that she knew she was not mistaken. Neither
of them spoke as, in answer to his pull at the bell, a footman ap-

peared with a full-length sable cape to protect Kate from the bitter cold of the evening.

Even during the journey to the Radziwill palace—short in distance but lengthened by the need to take their place in the long
line of equipages which were bringing the guests to this gala occasion—they made no attempt to converse. Kate could think of
nothing but the strong, smooth hand which was holding her own
beneath the fur of the cape. Only when at last they stepped inside the reception area, dazzlingly lit by scores of chandeliers, did
Prince Aminov laugh in what seemed a deliberate attempt to
break the spell and to bring to a glittering social evening only the
gaiety it deserved. They were surrounded by warmth and light
and music and champagne. As soon as Kate had been presented
to Princess Radziwill, and curiously but graciously received, the
prince led her into the first of a series of reception rooms. A gypsy
orchestra was playing, almost drowned by the noise of conversation. Kate accepted a glass of champagne and switched her
thoughts into French and her expression into the vivacity required to accept meaningless compliments from the strangers to
whom she was bewilderingly introduced.

The ostentatious display of wealth took her breath away. Kate
had often heard Alexa describe how the women of the Russian
nobility wore their dresses cut almost indecently low in order to
adorn the décolletage with the maximum number of diamonds;
but she had been talking about the early years of the century. It
had not occurred to Kate that the same fashion would still pre-
vail at a time when Russia had endured two and a half years of
war and was on the verge of defeat. She thought of the bewildered Russian peasants who lay wounded in her hospital and
found that she could not pretend to smile any longer. Even
the champagne seemed less sparkling, although all around her
the effervescent chatter continued unabated.

Prince Aminov was sensitive to her change of mood, although
not prepared to indulge it.

"I've just seen the Grand Duke Boris disappear into the card
room," he said. "To continue, no doubt, his conspiracy against his
cousin Nicholas. My own belief is that it's safer to do one's plot-
ting in public. So I am going to present you now to someone
whom you must charm. You may think him stupid, as indeed he

is, but you must use his stupidity to make him believe that he would have a conquest if only I were not here to guard you."

Flirtation was not Kate's style, and to pretend to flirt was even more degrading. She was about to demand an explanation and was ready to behave coldly if she did not receive one. But Prince Aminov gave her no time to ask questions before introducing a white-haired gentleman of distinguished appearance, conspicuous even in this company by the number of medals he wore. His name caught her attention at once, for this was the titular head of the Committee of War Materials which was so stubbornly refusing to hear her case. Kate knew as well as his staff that he rarely went near his office. But she also knew that without his authority no one would ever take action.

That she should attempt to flatter a man whose criminal inefficiency was responsible for so much suffering made Kate feel sick with disgust. But as long as she had the power to relieve that suffering by any action of her own, it would be equally criminal to let pride hold her back. Like any simpering ninny, she forced herself to smile at his jokes and blush at his compliments. Whether she could have brought herself to ask him a favour she did not need to discover, for Prince Aminov was doing it for her.

"Bandages? Medicines? Of course she must have them. Who is the idiot who has been holding them up? Well, it will be Lev Ilyich Kharsov. He must be shown where his duty lies. Tomorrow, my dear young lady, you must take tea in my office. At four o'clock. Or five. I shall expect you. Everything will be arranged. And in the evening you must join me in my box at the ballet. The whole of St. Petersburg is in a state of civil war, disputing who is the greatest dancer. Is it Pavlova, or Kschessinska? Or even Karsavina? You must form your own opinion, so that you can argue with the same heat as the rest. Till tomorrow, then."

Kate's face was pale with anger as someone else claimed his attention. Prince Aminov misunderstood her expression.

"Don't worry. He won't try to seduce you. There will be secretaries in and out of his office all the time. He'll want them to see that he's still irresistible to beautiful young women, but that's all. You must go, in order that Kharsov, whoever he may be, understands that you are a friend of his master. By tomorrow evening, all your difficulties will have disappeared. And now that our business is over, we may give ourselves up to pleasure. Will you dance?"

Still too disturbed to object, Kate allowed him to lead her through a series of imposing rooms, each crowded with guests. In the first two chambers the white walls and ceilings had been covered with a filigree of gold so delicate that it might have been spun by a spider. But the walls of the ballroom, and the surfaces of the pillars which supported its high roof, were covered with sheets of mirror, each set at a very slight angle so that the light of the chandeliers was dazzlingly reflected and magnified. Another orchestra was playing here. As Prince Aminov turned to face Kate with a formal bow, she slipped her finger through the loop on her skirt to lift the hem from the floor, and was ready to dance.

Her French conversation had not disgraced him, and neither did her waltzing. The disquiet she felt stiffened her back and increased the dignity of her bearing, but did not distract her feet from their rhythmic movement. As though she were watching from outside, she was conscious of herself moving round the ballroom with as much grace as any other of this aristocratic company. From time to time she glimpsed her own reflection in the mirrored wall but hardly recognised it. She, just as much as Prince Aminov, had become a clotheshorse and not a person. What she saw had no connection with the way she felt.

The prince, delighting in the dance, was holding her more tightly than he ought. Only an hour or two ago his closeness would have given her pleasure, but now she resisted it, refusing to remember the flash of desire she had felt as her host rose to greet her. Her mind had established control over her body again, and all the pride she had felt in Prince Aminov's admiration, all the pain and excitement of her own reaction, had been devoured by an anger which left her at once hot and cold. When the dance came to an end she stood for a moment without moving before raising her head to look steadily at her partner.

"I'm very sorry, Excellency," she said. "I can't stay here. I must ask you to be good enough—"

He interrupted her anxiously. "Are you not well?"

"I will say that I'm not well, because I don't wish to disgrace you by letting anyone guess any other reason. But really I am perfectly well. I ought not to have come here tonight, that's all."

"You must explain more than that." The orchestra began to play again and he led her out of the ballroom, opening a door at random so that they could talk in private. Surrounded by their host's collection of musical clocks, Prince Aminov waited to hear what she had to say.

"I can't give you a good explanation. It's just that I feel this occasion isn't a suitable one for the times. When there's so much poverty in the city and so much pain and death all over Europe."

"If princesses never gave balls, the poverty in the city would be far greater," Prince Aminov pointed out. "Because Princess Radziwill entertains her friends today, there will be money tomorrow in the pockets of servants, grooms, florists, jewellers, dressmakers, caterers, musicians."

Kate was tempted to voice her suspicion that princesses took a good deal longer than a single day to pay their bills, but she had no wish to quarrel. Instead, she tried as sincerely as possible to make him understand a little of what she had felt earlier that day.

"I was walking in the city this morning, Excellency," she said. "You must know far more than I do about what is happening here. But it seems to me that there is an inexorable division—a chasm—opening between the sort of people who are here in this palace tonight, and all the others."

"The division has always been there," he pointed out.

"Then I suppose it must always have been accepted. Until now. I don't believe it's going to be accepted any longer. And I have to make it clear which side I'm on."

"I would like you to be on my side," he said.

"You don't need me. And there are so many others who do. I can't in honesty say that I'm on your side, because that would mean supporting everything which has helped to create that hell out there on the battlefield. I thought perhaps I could forget that just for one evening, when it seemed that to come here might be of practical use, but—"

"But we have talked of bandages and drugs, and you have remembered." His voice was still soft, but it had lost the languid drawl which sometimes gave the impression of insincerity. It seemed to Kate that he was sympathetic, but she did not dare to accept sympathy. Just because she had found him so attractive earlier in the evening she needed now to distance herself from him.

"I'm ashamed," she said. "Ashamed that I came here in the first place, and ashamed of asking you to take me away. I know I'm behaving unpardonably. Enjoying your hospitality, wearing your sister-in-law's dress, your family jewels. A complete stranger, and you've been so generous to me! I'm more grateful than I can say, but all the same—" She sighed, angry with herself and with the whole situation.

"But all the same you have a headache and I have insisted that you should let me take you home. Come, then."

They made their way back through the golden rooms, thronged with people who were now not entirely sober. Nor, Kate suspected, was the Aminov coachman, who had not been expecting a call so soon; but fortunately the horses knew their way home. Back in the Aminov palace the prince himself took the sable cape from Kate's bare shoulders and smiled at her.

"May I ask you an impertinent question? How old are you, Dr. Lorimer?"

"Twenty-six." Kate had promised herself she would never be the sort of woman who was ashamed to admit her age.

"When I first saw you, you looked older; did you know that? But tonight, for three hours, you have looked twenty-six—or even younger. If I tell you that you ought to wear satins and jewels always, I suppose I shall make you angry. But beauty deserves to be adorned. I hope you will stay young for a little while yet, Dr. Lorimer."

Kate wasted no time in protesting that she was not beautiful, although she did repeat once more her apologies for her behaviour. But when she returned to her room she could not resist the temptation to stand in front of the glass for a second time that evening—for if anything in her life was certain, it was that she would never look like this again. She made an attempt to rebuke herself for vanity, but instead she found herself flushing with pleasure because Prince Aminov had called her beautiful.

What of it, she demanded, working her self-criticism into indignation. Not to flirt with a young woman was by the standards of his class to be uncivil. It didn't mean anything. She didn't want it to mean anything. Even in England Kate had held strong views about the social obligations of the aristocracy—but most British landowners, when compared with the Russian nobility, might be considered impoverished and full of social concern. Although more fortunate than others, they were members of a community, not merely of a social caste, isolated by its wealth from the rest of society, as was the case in Russia.

In other circumstances, perhaps, she could have enjoyed a friendship with Prince Aminov, for she found his company congenial and his conversation excitingly different from anything she had enjoyed since she said goodbye to Sergei. In other circumstances, indeed, she could have fallen in love with him. Even as she formulated the thought, she knew that she was being dishonest with herself. She had already fallen in love—but if she could continue to pretend indifference on her own part and attribute insincerity to him, perhaps she could cure herself of the affliction. Circumstances were what they were. The prince was a representative of a privileged class of which Kate could not bring herself to approve. It was unfortunate, but it was final. Slowly she unfastened the tiny buttons at her waist and slipped the low-cut bodice off her shoulders, stepping out of the gown as it fell heavily to the floor.

That night there was shooting on the Nevsky Prospekt. But the soldiers who fired on the workers during the hours of darkness streamed out of their barracks the next morning, killing the officers who tried to stop them. They joined the demonstration and by their own desertion turned it into a revolution. When the hour arrived at which Kate might have seen her papers stamped at last beside a samovar of tea, her prospective host was already a prisoner of the Duma. In the Tauride Palace, Kerensky took into his hands the power which the Imperial Cabinet had abandoned, and did his best to prevent a massacre. But in the city outside ministries were burned, police stations besieged, and the streets were crowded with students, workers, and soldiers destroying every trace of the old regime.

Only thirty hours after Kate had stared across the frozen Neva at the beautiful golden spire of the Peter and Paul fortress, she watched again as it fell to the forces of the revolution, and saw the political prisoners and their military guards streaming together across the bridges. Her instinct had been a true one. She herself would never look like a princess again, and nor would anyone else in the country for very much longer. The face of Russia, too, had changed forever.

6

The Tsar had abdicated, but the liberal Provisional Government, sharing power and premises uneasily with the Petrograd Soviet of Workers' and Soldiers' Deputies, was no more willing to interest itself in Kate's medical supplies than the old regime had been. While the struggle for authority continued, no one would spare the time to take a decision about such a trifle, although it would have taken only a moment for someone to stamp a paper of release—freeing himself with a single thump of the nuisance of Kate's daily attendance at the supplies office.

Prince Aminov had returned hastily to duty as soon as the troubles began, telling her before he left that she must stay as long as she needed. It was with increasing anxiety on his behalf that Kate read the various proclamations which issued from the Soviet, for their intention and effect was to destroy discipline in the Army, robbing officers of any power to enforce their orders and encouraging mutiny and desertion by the abolition of the death penalty. One of these orders provided that local soviets of soldiers or sailors should in future control all arms and equipment. Kate saw how she could use this to suit her own purposes. It would need a good deal of courage, but in the interests of her patients she steeled herself to be brave.

She went as usual the next day to the offices of the General Staff, and as usual found them swarming with petitioners like herself. Also as usual nowadays was the presence of the troops who lounged in the huge entrance hall with red ribbons tied round their arms, content to show themselves without posing any great threat to anyone. There was a junior officer ostensibly in charge of them. Kate had had plenty of time during the past few days to study his increasing nervousness and the care he took to give no direct orders which might lead to trouble.

She began by making a fuss at the desk of the man who had so often before told her to wait. He did so again, but this time she did not move far. Instead she climbed on to the desk and made a speech.

Even in Russian the words came fluently, fuelled by all the frustrating weeks in which she had had time to rehearse them. Her appeal was made directly to the soldiers. She was speaking on behalf of their comrades at the front, she told them, men who were dying for lack of the drugs withheld by these other men who had been careful to keep themselves at the greatest possible distance from danger. The property *belonged* to the soldiers in the hospital. It had been refused them by ministers and generals, but now it was true, was it not, that generals no longer had any right to obstruct the needs of the people? She herself knew where the goods were held. If they could not be extracted by the production of the right piece of paper, they could be taken without permission, by force. Kate promised that they would be handed over to those who needed them and were entitled to have them. She appealed for help. Looking straight at the young officer, she asked him to lend her a section of his men.

As she had calculated, he hesitated and her point was won. Ten men were instantly ready to follow her. Anxious not to delay, lest the impetus of her vehemence should be lost, Kate nevertheless needed to press further demands on the officer. When she returned, an official permit for the transport of the goods must be ready, she told him, and an escort to help load and guard them. She expected the necessary papers to be prepared within the hour.

They would be ready; she felt no doubt of that. The men were anxious to exercise their new powers over officers, and the officers would wait for more important issues than this one on which to make a stand. Striding out victoriously, Kate led the way to the warehouse.

Three hours later she returned to the Aminov palace to collect her bags. Was it only the triumph of her achievement which made her feel that spring was on the way at last? After weeks of bitter cold the sky was filled with pale sunshine; the snow was melting and it was possible to fill her lungs with air which seemed almost warm. She was singing aloud with happiness as she approached the palace door.

It was open. That was unusual enough, but the scene inside was more unusual still. The floor of the entrance hall was awash with wine and half a dozen of the servants were sprawled around in a manner which made it clear that what had not been spilt had been drunk. From their quarters behind closed doors came the sound of singing and shouting. Kate found herself tiptoeing through the confusion and up the stairs, uneasy lest some obstacle might arise at the very moment when success was in sight.

Still quietly, she opened the door of her bedroom and then was alarmed into silence. Prince Aminov, standing in the middle of the room, was pointing his revolver at her.

He put the weapon away as soon as he saw who it was, and apologised for frightening her.

"I needed to speak to you, and there was no other room in the palace where I could feel safe from discovery while I waited. Even this room will not be safe for long. You must leave Russia at once, Dr. Lorimer. I have come to warn you, in case you are not aware how dangerous the situation has become. You should go immediately to the British Embassy and arrange for your government to get you away. It may be that these people have no good reason to attack foreigners, but they have ceased to be ruled by reason."

"What has happened, Excellency?" Kate asked. She could see that he was shocked and upset, and at first she assumed that it had been caused by some event on the battlefield.

"Mutiny has happened," he said. "Murder has happened. My brother has been killed—on his own ship, by his own men! And the Imperial Guard itself has proved disloyal. Who could have believed it? I was ordered back from the front to command the garrison at Tsarskoe Selo, but when I arrived I was greeted by a disorderly mob who first of all demanded that I should join them and wear the red cockade. And then they recognised me as a member of the nobility. I was lucky to escape with my life. And when I return here, thinking that at least I can rely on the loyalty of my own people to protect me, I find—I find—"

"They're drunk, Excellency. This isn't their normal behaviour. It's not the expression of their true feelings."

He shook his head in disagreement. "There are different kinds of drunkenness. If all they wanted was their own pleasure, they would have drunk only vodka. They don't like wine. They are consuming it only to show that I am no longer master in my own house. The same thing has happened in our theatre palace at Tsarskoe Selo—it has been completely sacked. Not looted. Spoiled. The chandeliers cut to the ground, the pictures slashed, the panelling defaced. Now I shall never be able to show you the theatre where Alexa sang. But what does all that matter beside my brother's murder? You must understand that he was not like me. I am a reluctant officer, serving because it is my duty. But he —his ship was his whole life. What has happened to loyalty?" He buried his head in his hands for a moment. "But for you now the important thing is that you should go. Go back to England. That was why I waited, in case you did not understand how grave the position is."

"No!" Kate cried. "It's impossible. I have my supplies at last. After waiting so long, I can't leave now. I must take them to the hospital. It is you who should leave the country."

"There is no way of doing so. The British and French will send ships to take away their own people as soon as the ice breaks, but they will not use precious space to save Russians from each other."

"Then where will you go?"

He threw out his hands in a gesture of helplessness. "There is nowhere. Yesterday I owned three estates. Today, after my brother's death"—his voice faltered again—"I own seven. But it seems that the places where I am known are the most dangerous. Ever since our father died we have cared for our people, Paul and I. I truly believed that they loved us. But now—"

He sat down on the edge of the four-poster bed and for a second time buried his head in his hands. It was not fear which made him tremble, Kate realised—although he had good cause to be afraid—but the shock of his brother's death and the servants' disloyalty. Like the ice on the Neva, the established order had cracked and there was nowhere he could feel safe.

Kate took a little time to consider the question seriously before she spoke. This was not an occasion for impulsive gestures. She must be sincere, and practical in regard to details. It proved not to be too difficult. Only a little time had passed since she had regretted the way in which circumstances made it impossible for herself and the prince to develop a true friendship. But circumstances had changed with a vengeance. No longer overprivileged, he lacked at this moment even the precarious security of every other class of society. Yet there were no crimes for which he could be held personally responsible.

"You could come with me," she offered. "For a while, at least, until this first violence subsides. For all we know, the revolution may not yet have spread outside Petrograd. In any case, as you've already recognised, you'll be safer where you aren't known. Come south with me. I can arrange it. The train leaves in two hours."

"You don't know what you're proposing. For a woman—and especially a foreign woman—to travel across a country in a state of anarchy is foolish enough. As your companion, I should double the danger. It's out of the question."

"Listen to me, Excellency," Kate pleaded. "I arrived here unknown, uninvited, tired, and not even very clean. You've made me welcome. You've treated me like a princess. It's not just that you provided me with the first taste of comfort that I've had for two years. I've been spoiled by your kindness, your conversation, your music. Was it presumptuous of me to hope that we might become friends?"

"Of course we are friends," he said. "And for that very reason—"

Kate would not allow him to finish. "As your guest, I have an obligation to give you a present as an expression of thanks for your hospitality. It's an English custom. And as my friend, you have an obligation to accept whatever I choose to give you." She forced herself to laugh, trying to deflate the solemnity with which she had spoken. "Although it may prove in the end that I have nothing to offer except words. But I can try, and you must let me try."

They were discussing what might well be a matter of life and death—and yet it seemed to Kate, as she gazed steadily into

Prince Aminov's eyes, that he was not really listening. She waited for his answer, and it did not come directly.

"I remember—it can be only a short time ago, but it seems to have been in a different lifetime—how I danced with you at Princess Radziwill's ball," he said. "You were wearing my sister-in-law's balldress, and you were magnificent. Magnificent! I had never seen a woman looking beautiful in quite that way before. Not a Russian way, not a fashionable way. It was your eyes, I think, so green, so full of fire. Of course, I could not understand at once what it was that made you hold your head so high. I would have liked to kiss you, but before I could do it you were telling me that society was divided and that you and I were on different sides. And now again I would like to kiss you: but today the division is a real one, not a theory, and I must keep in my own place if I am not to drag you down."

"This is not the time to speak of kissing," said Kate severely. "And as for the rest, you're talking nonsense. If we were both on the same side there would be no need of help and no opportunity to offer it. But if we waste any more time in argument, the opportunity will be talked away. Is it that you don't trust me?"

His eyes showed that she had hurt him, and he gripped her hands fiercely with his own, as though that were an answer.

"Well then," she pointed out, "the division isn't as great as it seems. I'm on the side of the revolution because even in such a short time I've seen a whole nation being pushed to its doom by stupidity and greed and inefficiency. I don't pretend to understand the causes: I only know that the system has to be changed. But I've also seen that you share most of my feelings—of compassion and a wish to help poorer people, to protect your dependents. It's only your birth which puts you on the other side. You can't change that, but I'm not going to let you suffer for it if I can help it. I shan't speak to you in English again. From now on we must talk in Russian. Nor shall I address you again as Excellency. You are my comrade—Comrade Vladimir—and you are going to work in my hospital."

Her forcefulness was enough to bring the sentimental moment to an end. He even forgot his family grief for long enough to laugh wryly at her, and himself. "That a woman should speak to

me so!" he exclaimed, shaking his head unbelievingly. Yet there
was no sign of resentment. If anything, Kate suspected that he
admired her most when she was at her most determined. From
his nursery days he would have been accustomed to give orders
and expect them to be obeyed. The necessity for command and
discipline must be so much a part of his character that rather
than flounder in a chaos of equality he was prepared to obey
someone else's equally arbitrary instructions.

"Well then, Comrade Katya," he said—speaking, as she had ordered, in the language which was almost as foreign to him as to
her. "I am your friend, so I accept whatever you have to offer. I
am your slave, so I obey. What would you have me do?"

"Get out of that uniform," she said. "Take some clothes from
the servants. They're too drunk to notice. Shabby clothes, but
warm. Then make your way to the station. I'll meet you there in
about an hour. Will you bring my bag for me?"

Unexpectedly she remembered Sergei, whom she had ordered
about in exactly the same way at their first meeting. That meeting had been the start of an affectionate friendship—no, more
than that: they had loved each other, in a way. Was she becoming one of those bossy women who only liked men they could
bully? Later on she would need to consider that and be careful.
But for the moment she must not allow the impetus of her determination to slacken.

"You speak Russian very well," the prince said. "Not just
fluently, but with the right amount of passion. No Russian who
didn't know you would recognise you for a foreigner. He might
think you came from a different province from his own, with a di-
alect which he couldn't quite place, but that would be the only
question in his mind."

"I feel almost as though I *am* Russian," Kate said, turning
briefly back from the doorway. "I'm sorry, truly sorry, about your
brother's death, Vladimir. It wasn't right and I don't believe it
was necessary. I don't like to think of anyone being in fear of his
life. But I can't help being excited. To be in this country, at this
moment! For more than two years Europe has been destroying itself, and now at last a new society is being built, and I'm here. I
intend to be part of it, to help."

"The fire has returned to your eyes," said Prince Aminov softly.

"And the beauty to your face. And all because you feel so passionately about people who are strangers to you."

He was about to kiss her. Kate wanted him to do so. She had
wanted it once before, and had been able to control her emotions
only because she had recognised the barriers of class and idealism
which separated her from Prince Aminov. Now that those barriers
were broken down, there was nothing to hold her back—and indeed, she found his new vulnerability even more attractive than
his earlier kindness and glamorous appearance. What made her at
this moment long to step forward into his arms, to press her body
close to his and to comfort him in his distress was the lost look in
his eyes. His whole way of life, from the moment of his birth, had
been supported by the service of other people, and all those sup-
ports—except hers—had been abruptly withdrawn. He had
believed himself to be loved and respected, and found himself
hated instead. He must have expected that his wealth would
cushion him for the whole of his life and even now it would be
possible for him to fill his pockets with jewellery or Fabergé trifles
which alone would represent more wealth than a Russian worker
would see in the whole of his lifetime: but such riches, if they
were discovered, would betray rather than sustain him. He had
never needed to earn a living, but now he must step out into the
ordinary world. It was a tribute to his courage that he showed no
sign of fear, for the prospect must certainly be alarming. Even if
he escaped physical harm, he was so badly equipped to adapt his
life to the demands of a new society that he was bound to suffer.
Kate saw all this, and felt her heart swelling with the wish to protect him.

But this was not the time to confess her feelings. Far more important was the need to maintain her earlier mood of excitement
and determination. The same forcefulness which she had used to
appeal for help and to demand authorisation must be maintained
at its highest pitch if she was to be of any help to Vladimir.
Keeping her voice brisk, she repeated the arrangements for their
meeting and hurried from the room.

The papers which awaited her appeared to cover all the checks
and emergencies which might arise on the journey, authorising
the movement of the supplies as well as of herself and a soldier
who had been left on guard at the station. It was this young Es-

tonian, Vassily Petrovich Belinsky, who was an important part of Kate's plan to smuggle Prince Aminov out of the capital. He had enjoyed helping to break open the warehouse door and carry out the crates; but his pleasure had turned to sulkiness when he found himself appointed as the escort. Clearly he had no wish to exchange his lazy life in Petrograd for the long and uncomfortable journey south.

Kate set to work on him as soon as she had congratulated him on defending the reserved wagon containing the crates of supplies. The train was so overcrowded that this was a considerable achievement, even allowing for the fact that civilian passengers were accustomed to observe military priorities.

"You are in luck, Vassily Petrovich. There is no need for you to make the journey. I have a volunteer to accompany me."

"Why should anyone wish to do that?"

"He has a son, five months old, whom he has never seen: and two weeks' leave but no money or permit to travel. He will gladly take your place for the sake of a day or two with his wife. All he asks is that you should keep away from your officers and comrades for two weeks, so that they believe you to be obeying instructions. And he has sent this basket in order that the two weeks need not be too dull."

As she left the palace she had picked up some of the bottles of wine which littered the floor. Prince Aminov had been right to suggest that vodka would always be more welcome, but in these days of shortages no sort of drink was likely to be rejected. It required little persuasion to show the young soldier that he could enjoy a fortnight's leave. If he remembered that he had left his identity papers at the office, in order that his details might be entered on the travel permit, he presumably thought that they were still there, instead of folded inside Kate's money belt. It would be two weeks before he discovered the truth—and then he would find it safer to claim that he had lost them in the confusion of the journey than to confess what had really happened. Kate allowed him no time to think about them, but hurried him on his way as soon as she saw approaching a shabby, rather furtive peasant figure whom she recognised as the prince.

"Your name is Vassily Petrovich Belinksy," she told her former host as he climbed into the wagon. "It's hard that I have to learn to call you Vassily when I've only just become used to calling you Vladimir."

It was partly relief which made her chatter on, but in addition she was excited by the adventure. By her own efforts she had achieved what she came to Petrograd to do and had a good chance of taking her friend to safety at the same time. But the prince looked dazed, and as the train pulled out of the station on its long journey she noticed how sadly he looked back at the city which had been his home. Whilst she looked forward, seeing little good in the old regime and eager to take part in the building of a new way of life, he was conscious only of what he was losing. For him, the future promised only danger and hardship.

Her sympathy silenced her. She gazed at her companion as he leaned a little way out of the wagon, still watching the receding city. There had been a moment once before when she had been forced to admit to herself how attractive she found him. On that occasion she had controlled her admiration first of all by mentally stripping away the uniform which made him look so handsome. Then, as she realised that it was the man himself, unadorned, who excited her, she had in a manner of speaking dressed him again in order that the gold braid and jewelled Order should act as a barrier between them, reminding her that the two of them lived in different worlds.

Now the splendid trappings of nobility had disappeared. Beneath the shabby overcoat was not a prince but a man. But Kate, assuming authority, had changed in the opposite direction, so that in a sense she was not a woman but a doctor. Would that, she wondered, be any protection during the long journey? Did she want to be protected?

The train picked up speed. Vladimir pulled the heavy wagon door across until it clanged into place. He gave a single deep sigh, a groan of loneliness and misery and insecurity. Then he turned towards Kate and, still without speaking, took her into his arms. She did her best to comfort him, and found that it was no longer possible to control the love she had felt and concealed since the night of the Radziwill ball.

In the days and nights that followed, Kate should have been worrying about her patients and nurses, for the journey across Russia would have been complicated enough even for a passenger who had only himself to move from one train to another. When it was a complete wagon which had to be uncoupled and then attached to another engine, the difficulties at times seemed insuperable. As one obstacle succeeded another, Kate would in normal circumstances have become indignant. But the new experience of love made her for a little while unusually passive. It was easy to live from moment to moment, accepting each delay as it came, because she was so completely overwhelmed by the happiness of her honeymoon.

This was not the sort of honeymoon that might have been envisaged either by the daughter of a missionary or by a Russian prince. But Kate felt no qualms about the fact that she lacked a marriage certificate; nor did Vladimir complain about a honeymoon suite which consisted of a nest of blankets, extracted from one of the hospital crates, in a corner of the goods wagon. To the nurses who greeted her when at last they reached the Romanian Front, Kate announced that she was married, because that was how she felt.

7

Born in a spring of despair and hope, the revolution stumbled through a summer of chaos towards a winter of defeat. From her field hospital on the Romanian Front, Kate watched with dismay the disintegration of the Russian Army. The orders and decrees which flowed from the capital effectively sapped all discipline, and the Germans and Austrians were quick to take advantage of the fact that their opponents no longer had any firm chain of command. Their summer offensive found Kate's medical unit well enough equipped to deal with the casualties, but lacking any military protection. Those of the Tsarist officers who had been born into the nobility had been killed when the first news of the revolution arrived. Most of the others had fled; and the few who remained were well aware that if they ordered a counterattack or tried to impose any punishment, the rifles of their men were as likely to be turned on themselves as on the enemy. What followed was not a mutiny in any active sense, for most of the Russian soldiers simply slipped away to their villages, knowing that they could no longer be shot for desertion. The Serbs remained in the line, because they had nowhere to go—but of the men who had sailed with Kate for Salonica in 1916 only a handful were still alive.

Without Vladimir at her side Kate might well have despaired, overwhelmed by the responsibility for the safety of her nursing team and her patients as the enemy advanced. At first his support was only that of a lover, for he had few practical skills. But in order to establish him as one of the medical team she taught him how to administer anaesthetics: he had the strong hands necessary to hold the mask down over the face of a struggling patient and, although he never overcame his distaste for watching an operation in progress, he did not allow his squeamishness to distract him from watching the patient's breathing. In addition, he was recognised as Kate's personal assistant, and if at times he seemed quiet and withdrawn and uncertain of himself, this was assumed to result from the natural reluctance of a man to obey the orders of a woman, of a husband to run errands for his wife. Kate, not daring by any word or gesture to hint at the difficulties which he faced as a result of his birth and upbringing, watched with loving anxiety as he gradually learned to get the necessary tasks accomplished not by giving orders but by taking part in the work.

Even though she no longer felt alone, she was still left to take many decisions with which no one else could help. In the disorganised conditions which now prevailed, she realised that there could be no possibility of further support from Beatrice and the suffragists' movement. She alone had to decide, as the Germans advanced, when it was necessary to pack up the unit and retreat; and with increasing clarity she saw that she would have to recognise the moment when the nurses on her staff had done as much as could reasonably be expected of them.

The moment came on a night in the autumn of 1917. For the third time since the beginning of summer they were retreating. So many Russian soldiers were taking the same direction, whether as deserters or as the ragged remnants of an army, that it was difficult to find billets for the night. The peasants in the villages were suspicious, and unwilling to part with any of the food they had hidden, for they saw that the coming winter would be a hard one. For this night, Vladimir had found a river-side site and had supervised the erection of tents, and Kate had already made her evening round of the wounded. She knew that after a day of jolting over rough roads in carts with wooden wheels, their best treatment was to sleep in peace. So she had no duties to disturb her enjoyment of the night, and for a little while it was enough to be alone with Vladimir in the small tent which they shared.

Later, though, she lay awake in the darkness, listening to the noises of the night—the croaking of frogs, the rustling of the wind in the reeds, the gentle tapping of the willow trees against the canvas, the rippling of the river over the stones near the bank. How much longer, she asked herself, would her nurses be safe? Behind them was an advancing enemy army and in front of them was a country in anarchy. The hand-to-mouth existence they had been leading during the past three months had been only just tolerable in summer: how could they hope to survive a Russian winter in such conditions? There was talk of famine, and Kate believed this to be well-founded.

All the nurses had been serving abroad for more than a year. They deserved to have leave, but they would know as well as she did that if they went back to England it would not be merely for a holiday: they would never return. In those circumstances many of them no doubt would be willing to stay on a little longer, but as Kate considered the situation it seemed to her that a choice which might exist now would very soon disappear. At the moment the sea route from the Crimea was still open, and foreign nationals were being taken out of the country, although no Russians were allowed to leave. But the unit was being pressed steadily further north. Very soon it might become impossible to reach Odessa or Sevastopol; very soon there might be no more ships.

What disturbed Kate most was the unexpected change in the attitude of the Russians towards the nurses. Always before, their profession by itself had been enough to earn them respect, quite apart from the fact that they were women. But in the last few weeks she had been aware of a change. Deserters would rob anyone they met unprotected on the road, and serving soldiers showed no chivalry in grabbing for food or shelter. If their uni-

forms no longer protected the women, it was difficult to see how
else they could be made safe.

The nurses were not, of course, Kate's only responsibility. She
must think of her patients as well. But during this evening's
round she had counted that out of forty-three Russian patients,
thirty-seven had self-inflicted wounds. They had chosen with
some care where to shoot themselves, so none of the wounds was
likely to prove dangerous. Kate had given them the treatment
they needed and in the circumstances it seemed reasonable that
they should be handed back to the care of the Russian Army. Her
own unit, after all, had been directed specifically to the care of
the Serbs. There were so few of these left that she could take care
of their wounded alone, and could count on the protection of the
fit survivors.

All this time, she realised, she was taking it for granted that she
herself would stay. The assumption was an important one, and
she forced herself to examine it. Why should she not take the
chance to escape from a country which held as much danger for
herself as for the nurses? The answer was confused, even paradox-
ical. She was able to accept the chaos around her as an inevitable
—and temporary—result of changing a complete social order: she
still had the same ideals, the same vision of a new society, which
had so much excited her in Petrograd, and would be grateful for
any opportunity to contribute to the task of reform. Stronger
even than idealism, though, was her love for the man whom those
ideals had turned into a fugitive. If she could have seen any way
of taking Vladimir to safety, she would not have hesitated to do
so. But this same society in which she had so much faith kept
him a prisoner inside his own country; and as long as he had to
stay, she would stay with him.

Perhaps it was not a paradox after all, merely a double reason
for a decision which had really been made by her emotions and
not by her reason at all. As the long hours of the night passed
and the current of the river flowed and splashed only a few feet
away, she forced herself to think the decision through, to be sure
that she understood all its implications.

The task was impossible. There could be no assurances in a period when history itself did not know which direction it was tak-

ing. Only uncertainty was certain. As far as consequences were
concerned, she must assume the worst and decide whether she
could accept them.

The sky was lightening now as her sleepless night came to an
end. Without disturbing Vladimir, she slipped out of the tent
and sat down on the river bank a little way away. There was a
chill in the air, and frost had touched the spiders' webs: winter
would soon be here. Remembering the last two winters, she could
not help shivering, and for a moment or two it was difficult not
to feel melancholy as in her mind she said goodbye to the past.
Never again would she feel herself wrapped in the balmy air of
her tropical birthplace. Her father would die, and she would
have no chance to say goodbye. Would she ever visit Blaize again,
to see Margaret growing old and the younger members of the
family growing up? Perhaps it would be possible one day, when
this time of upheaval was over; but if her choice now was to be
sincere she must tell herself that, no, she would never return.
She gave a sharp nod of her head, a gesture to mark the promise
to herself that there would be no regrets.

"Is it decided, then?"

Startled, she turned and saw Vladimir leaning against a tree.
How long, she wondered, had he been watching her.

"Is what decided?"

He shrugged his shoulders. "How should I know? But there is
something, I know that. For two days I have watched you balancing arguments in your mind." He came to sit beside her on the
bank, pulling a reed and dangling it to trouble the surface of the
river. Without interrupting, he listened while Kate detailed her
plans.

"So your nurses will return to England. But you have not
spoken of yourself."

"I shall stay, of course."

"All the dangers you have recognised, the dangers which you
wish the others to escape, will still face you. And the ships which
will take them away would have room for you."

"But not for you. Vladimir, do you believe that there's any
frontier you can safely cross? Can you think of any way in which
you can leave the country?"

Vladimir shook his head.

"Well then, there's no choice. I won't go without you."

"It may be forever," said Vladimir. "If you stay now, you may never see your own country again. Or your family, all the people you love in England."

"I've been thinking about that," said Kate. "I've had to put my family into the balance. But I love you. However I hold the scales, the fact that I love you weighs down all the rest."

He took hold of her shoulders and pressed her back on the ground, kissing her passionately. Then he raised himself a little, so that Kate could look up at his face, framed by the golden lattice of the willows above.

"And I love you," he said. "Katya, will you be my wife?"

"I'm your wife already."

"I mean, in the old way. With a certificate."

"Is it possible?" asked Kate.

"It's possible to try. The people in these little towns we pass are frightened, ready to run if the Germans come any nearer. Everything is unsettled, so we should be believed if we claim that we ourselves have had to abandon our home and friends. You will have to be the wife of Belinsky, I'm afraid."

"Shall I have to show my British passport?"

"I think that would be unwise. Too unusual. You must tell them that you were in Petrograd at the time of the revolution. Your papers were already lodged at the marriage court when it was burnt down. Before we go, we will decide on a name, a Russian name, and a place of birth."

"They may be suspicious."

"Within an hour we shall have passed on, and they will be on the road themselves soon. If they're suspicious, they may refuse us, but they can't hurt us. I want you to marry me, Katya. I've nothing to offer you. Nothing but danger. But I want to be your husband forever. Will you take the risk?"

"Of course." She stretched up her hands to grasp his head. But for a moment he resisted her efforts to pull him down so that she could kiss him again.

"There will be no going back," he reminded her. "You will have become a Russian. That's not a destiny to be embraced lightly."

Kate was not interested in destiny. It was Vladimir she needed to embrace. "I'm a Russian already," she said.

8

The people of Hope Valley, in Jamaica, knew almost nothing of what was happening in Russia during the spring and summer and autumn of 1917. What could a revolution in a cold and far-away country have to do with their own warm and contented lives in a remote tropical village? But their pastor, Ralph Lorimer, learned of every new development with the deepest distress. As accurately as anyone in Europe, he could foresee what effect it was likely to have on the course of the war. From the very outbreak of the February revolution the Germans were able to profit from the crumbling of opposition to their armies on the eastern front; and by facilitating Lenin's return to Petrograd from his exile in Switzerland they were actively promoting an early ending of hostilities with Russia, which would leave them free to concentrate all their forces in the West.

The gloom engendered by conclusions such as these was not peculiar to Ralph. What struck home to him personally was the conviction that his only daughter had become a victim of the terror. She would surely have escaped if she could—or at least have let it be known that she was safe—but the enquiries which Lord Glanville made through the British ambassador in Petrograd proved fruitless. In the months between the February and the October revolutions almost all the British subjects who had applied for repatriation had been brought safely back to England. But Kate was not amongst them and those who returned had no knowledge of her whereabouts.

Lord Glanville and Margaret both attempted to persuade Ralph in correspondence that at a time of such upheaval the absence of any message did not necessarily mean that the worst had happened: few letters of any kind were coming out of the country. But Ralph was not to be convinced. Already robbed of two of his babies, the wife he loved, the elder son he adored, he knew that God was punishing him for the wrongdoing of his youth by the destruction of everything he held dear. Kate had become a victim of revolution as yet another scapegoat for her father's sins.

The biggest sin lay like a millstone on his conscience. Ralph had never confessed to anyone—not even to his wife—the subterfuge which had resulted in the Bristow plantation becoming his personal property instead of being owned by the Hope Valley community of which he was the pastor. His claim that he was the rightful heir to what had long before been a Lorimer estate had been a lie. Almost as soon as he had spoken the words he had realised that the lie was unnecessary—but it was no more excusable for that. Later he had persuaded himself that all was for the best and that he had won God's forgiveness because of his good intentions and practical achievements. Under his control the estate had developed a prosperity which it could not possibly have attained as a collection of smallholdings.

For many years Ralph had suppressed his qualms and at times he almost forgot that there had been any deception about the ownership of the rich coastal land. Now the news from Russia fanned his feelings of guilt into fear. The Russian peasants, he learned, were dividing amongst themselves the huge estates which they had worked for their landlords. Hungry for land, they killed any landowner who resisted them. The authority of the Church was under attack too. It was not Ralph's church, but what was happening meant that temporal and spiritual authority were equally at risk: and in his own community Ralph represented them both.

Commonsense told him that the members of his congregation concerned themselves little with the world outside their island and did not know a great deal even of what went on in Jamaica, outside their own village. Nor could any agitator invade the valley without Ralph knowing of his presence at once. But he was unable to believe his own attempts at reassurance.

The thought obsessed him that God was intent on punishing the wicked in France and Russia—and soon in Jamaica. In the beginning, when the first news of the February revolution arrived from Russia, it had been possible to believe that Kerensky might be capable of controlling the forces of anarchy which had been unleashed. But the October revolution was a different matter.

Lenin and Trotsky made it plain that the message they preached was for the whole world to hear, not for the people of Russia alone. Bolshevism was contagious, Ralph recognised. Once the foundations of society began to rot, wherever in the world it might be, the rottenness would spread until no form of law or decency was left uncorrupted. When he had drunk too much rum he saw himself pressed backwards by an army of black workers, falling beneath the blows of their machetes, hearing in his dying moments their triumphant cries as they staked out their own plots of land. And the times when he drank too much rum became more and more frequent.

He took the rum to control his fever. So at least he told himself and Duke, his young assistant. Both of them pretended not to notice that it was after the bottle was empty, not before, that his hands began to shake and his head to spin with dizziness. There were some moments of calmness when he realised what was happening and vowed to control both his fears and the remedy; and there were other moments, equally calm, when there seemed no point in pretending that he had anything to live for any longer. God would soon summon him to account. Although he still led the services on Sundays and paced the fields during the weekdays, exhorting his people to prayer and work, little of his time was spent in the estate office. But in his lucid moments Ralph looked clearly enough to the future of Hope Valley and considered how best to provide for what remained of his family.

As the end of 1917 approached he studied the accounts which Duke prepared and made a series of careful notes. As soon as his mind was made up, he sent for his assistant.

"We must consider what will happen when God has taken me to Himself," he said without preamble. "This letter is to Mr. Arthur Lorimer. I'm going to tell you what is in it. You had better sit down."

The permission caused a moment's delay, since Ralph's office contained only one chair. Duke fetched his own from the adjoining cubicle. For a while Ralph stared at the young man's intelligent brown face and was satisfied that he had made the right decision.

"If Brinsley had lived, he would have taken over the management of the plantation," he began. "But Brinsley is dead. Whom the gods love, die young." He fell silent again, not concealing his bitterness at the loss of his son.

"You have another son, sir," Duke reminded him.

"Grant is only a child. And in any case—well, there's no need for me to pretend any longer." He laughed at the admission. "Never did pretend very much, did I? I can't bear the thought of him taking over the work that I've built up over so many years. He's not fit to manage. He's not able even to walk over the ground. If I try to picture it, I'm revolted. That is un-Christian of me, but we must be honest now. And practical. You understand?"

"Yes, sir."

"I recognise my duty to Grant," Ralph continued. "I've made due provision for him. It's all in this letter to my nephew, Mr. Lorimer. I have funds in England, and they are to be managed in Grant's interest until he is twenty-one and then used to buy him a business or a partnership or an estate somewhere else—whatever his talents at the time suggest. But not in Jamaica."

His silence this time lasted so long that Duke must have wondered whether the conversation was at an end. Then Ralph broke it abruptly.

"I have one more son," he said. "Has your mother never told you who your father is, Duke? Never discussed him with you at all?"

"No, sir."

"But you must have wondered. And guessed the truth, perhaps, although we have never spoken of it."

This time it was Duke's turn to be silent. "I'm guessing now, sir," he confessed at last. His eyes, unshocked, stared steadily at Ralph. Duke was accustomed to wait for instructions. It was an indication, perhaps, of the strength of the Lorimer strain, for any full-blooded Jamaican would have wept and flung himself into his father's arms.

Perhaps the restraint was imposed by Ralph's personality. He had long prepared for this interview, promising himself that it must be conducted on strictly business lines.

"You had little help from me in your childhood," he said. "But I shall make up for that now. You've proved that you're honest and competent. You know the work, what needs to be done. And

I can trust you, can't I, to remember that the land must be used for the benefit of all the people here? They will be your people."

"Yes, sir. But not for a long time, God willing."

"Perhaps not for ten years. Perhaps tomorrow. God alone knows. I shall leave you the whole plantation when I die. But there's one condition. Kate."

"Kate is my sister, then," said Duke softly.

Ralph glanced across at the young man. Surely he could never have hoped . . . no, of course not. Duke was married to an island girl, and his son, Harley, was already four years old. He had been such a close friend of Kate's when they were both children that he was bound to be pleased by his discovery of the relationship. That was all.

Ignoring the interruption, Ralph continued his exposition. In his heart he feared that Kate was dead. But it was necessary to act on the presumption that she would one day return; he must give formal recognition to hope. He had given thought to the necessary details and, although his concentration was flagging and he wanted to be alone so that he could have a drink, he forced himself to explain to Duke how a second trust fund must be created, with Arthur Lorimer as trustee, into which the profits of the plantation would be put for the next ten years. "One third for you, as well as the salary you pay yourself. One third for the people. One third for Kate, if she is alive, or for her children, if she has any. After ten years, if she cannot be traced, my nephew will divide her portion between yourself and Grant. You understand why you have to wait?"

"Yes, sir. But I don't ever want to take what's hers. If she comes back, it must all be for her. All the land."

"No." Ralph saw no need to mention his fear that if Kate did survive the revolution she might prove to have been infected by its philosophy. From childhood she had been a passionate defender of the underdog and it was too easy to imagine her refusing an inheritance or accepting it only to give it away. "No," he insisted. "You are the heir. The land is not to be divided, and it's for you. Kate's a doctor. To have an income would be useful to her, but she doesn't need land and she wouldn't know how to run it. I want you to have it. You have always been obedient, and you must obey me in this. Is that clear?"

"Yes, sir." Duke rose to his feet. As always, his head was held high and his back straight. He had inherited his bearing and fine features from his mother, Chelsea Mattison, whose beauty as a young woman had proved irresistible. From his father he had inherited a powerful physique and a shrewd head for business. His body was as strong and athletic as Brinsley's had been—and he shared the same love of cricket—but his nature was more industrious and his character more serious. He was serious now as he looked at Ralph. "Maybe you don't want I tell anyone outside about this," he said. "But just once I have to say it out loud. Thank you, Father."

The emotion of the moment, unexpected because he had thought to have it under control, caused Ralph to choke and cry out. He opened his arms to embrace his son, allowing his senses to register the feel of the strong muscles and the smooth skin. It was right for him to be ashamed of his responsibility for Duke's birth, but he was proud to have such a son. He had lost his merry, hard-working wife, his golden boy, his lion-hearted daughter, but after all there was still someone to love. There had been occasions before this one when he had wept in Duke's arms, but his tears then were caused by rum and depression. Now he cried for joy.

Afterwards he made a copy of his message to Arthur, in case a U-boat should sink the ship which carried the original. The next day he travelled to Kingston and arranged for the separate despatch of the two identical letters. Then, in his lawyer's office, he signed the will which had already been drawn up in accordance with his instructions.

The reminder that he still had family ties apart from Grant should have renewed his interest in life and restored him to cheerfulness. Instead, the assurance that he had settled his affairs on earth led his thoughts more towards the next world, as though he had not only chosen an heir but already handed over the inheritance. Knowing that it was in good hands, he no longer even pretended to interest himself in the management of the plantation. But he was still the pastor, and still every Sunday, shaved and sober, he preached to the congregation with some of the old fire and taught the Sunday school with some of the old patience. For the rest, he grew listless and slovenly.

His congregation were tolerant people. Conscious of their own transgressions and mindful, too, of the prosperity he had brought them during the thirty-five years of his pastorate, they took little notice of his bouts of drunkenness. Under the influence of rum he now became silent, not rowdy. He was waiting, they realised, for God to call him Home. In a curious way their respect for his holiness grew with this realisation. Patiently and lovingly they waited with him.

9

The music room at Blaize had been preserved from the hospital's increasing demands for space. In it, Alexa spent an hour every morning practising her vocal exercises. If Piers, her husband —or anyone else—had asked her directly, she would have had to admit that she did not ever expect to return to the stage as a prima donna. The nights of triumph, the applause, the curtain calls, the bouquets—all these were gone forever.

Were she to be honest with herself, she would admit also that this was not entirely the fault of the war. Her international career had effectively come to an end when she consented to become Lady Glanville. The interruption was intended to be no more than temporary, but the task of producing an heir had proved less simple than she anticipated. It was part of the bargain she had made with Piers that he should have a son, and a good many months had been wasted on the baby daughter who died within a week and the renewed hopes which ended in miscarriage.

After the eventual achievement of Pirry's birth there had been just one season in which, with health and voice restored, she had sung the leading parts in her own opera house; but she was as well able as anyone else to recognise that this was only a hobby, a tiny tributary of the main stream of opera. The war had robbed her of even this, but it would scarcely have been possible in any event for Lady Glanville to have stepped back into the place which Alexa Reni had vacated.

For one thing, she had already—earlier in 1917—passed her fortieth birthday. As a young woman she had scornfully dismissed singers who spoiled the great reputations of their youth by continuing to perform after their voices passed their peak, vowing never to make the same mistake herself. If her career had not been interrupted, she confessed to herself, that vow would have been broken. But she was realistic enough to recognise that if she were now to attempt a full return to the stage she would be using her reputation only to ruin it.

To her surprise, the discovery did not depress her. With a husband who adored her, she no longer felt the need to make conquests and collect tokens of admiration: her private life was contented to the point of placidity. As for her professional life, it was enough that she had once been at the very top of the tree. She had been ambitious as a young girl and her ambitions had been fulfilled. No one could deprive her of the memory of success and so she was able to let the experience of it slip away.

Not that any of that made any difference to the perfection of her approach. The soldiers to whom she sang nowadays, whether in camps or hospitals, had little interest in opera, preferring to hear "Keep the Home Fires Burning" or the hit songs from *Chu Chin Chow*. Either alone or in the concert party she had organised she gave them what they wanted, but with a quality of voice which would have satisfied the most meticulous critic of a performance at the Royal Opera House.

On a frosty day in November 1917 her first engagement was at a rehabilitation centre. Margaret had asked her to inspect the various training schemes in operation there, in case any of the ideas and techniques could be put to use in the convalescent wards at Blaize; and the commandant of the centre had expressed himself delighted to give her lunch and act as her personal guide before the afternoon recital began.

"Our chief problem here is one of morale," he explained as they moved quietly from one room to another. "All our patients have been too severely wounded ever to return to the Army. In a medical sense, they've come to the end of their convalescence by the time they're sent here. They're as fit as they ever will be again, but all of them are disabled for life. We try to train them for some new career, but naturally they arrive in a state of great depression, and they're very reluctant to leave here and face the world again. We have to be rather brutal with the men who have finished their course—push them out, in point of fact. On the other hand, we sympathise with those who are just arriving and haven't yet come to terms with their disabilities. The first classes they attend are what you might call therapy rather than formal training. In the old barn, for example"—like the hospital at Blaize, the centre was a temporary conversion from a country house—"we're running an art class for men who've lost the use of one or both legs but still have their hands and eyes undamaged. One of our patients—the only civilian here—turned out to be a professional artist. A very talented chap. He acts as instructor— that's *his* therapy. The idea is that if one of them turns out to have any talent, he could be more intensively trained either to teach art or to take up commercial drawing; but in any case it does them all good to feel that they're capable of producing *something*. They'll be packing up in the next few minutes, ready for your concert, so they won't mind being interrupted."

He pushed open the door. Outside, it was a bitterly cold day. But inside the barn the air was made hot and stuffy by three paraffin stoves grouped round a makeshift platform on which a model was posing. A dozen men in hospital blue sat round the platform, their chairs and easels widely spaced so that the instructor could move between them in his wheelchair. The opening of the door allowed the cold air to stab into the barn. The model was too well trained to move, but the instructor looked round in slight irritation. Alexa gasped in a sudden shock as she recognised the man who had been her first love. She felt her arm being seized by her companion. Before she had time to understand what was happening she was outside again, with the door slamming behind her.

Dizzily she leaned for a moment against the wall of the barn while the commandant exploded into an apology which she did not understand.

"I'm so sorry, Lady Glanville. My fault entirely—I should have warned them—you must forgive me—I do apologise."

"What are you talking about?" Alexa asked faintly. It was clear to her that she was expected to reassure him, but since she saw nothing for which he could be blamed she found it difficult to choose the right words.

"The model," he said. "Mr. Lorimer wasn't expecting a lady visitor, of course. I allowed him a free hand in the choice of subjects. But of course if I had told him you were coming, he would have found something more suitable today."

"Was the model naked, then?" Alexa had a vague impression of the profile of a young man, almost certainly blind; but she had been distracted before her eyes could take in the rest of his body.

"You didn't see? I was afraid—you looked so startled—and quite justifiably so."

"Not by the model," said Alexa. "No, I didn't see. It was Mr. Lorimer himself who startled me. He's a relation of mine, as it happens. But we'd lost touch. I didn't even know he'd been wounded. It was a shock. Is it serious?

"I'm afraid so." The commandant shook his head sadly. In relief that he had not after all caused offence to an influential visitor, he was willing to talk freely. "Very considerable injuries to the spine and abdomen. Wheelchair for the rest of his life, I'm afraid, and basic nursing care. No reason, of course, why he shouldn't continue to paint. You might say he's lucky, for an artist. Blindness would have been far worse in his case. But there was no injury to his eyesight at all. Nor to his manual dexterity. Count your blessings, I tell him. But he's as downcast as any of the others. Nothing worth living for, never going to be a great artist now, all that sort of thing. It's only to be expected. He's a good teacher, though, and it's getting through to him that he's helping some of the others. With any luck, that will be a help to him in turn, given time."

"After the concert, perhaps I could talk to him privately." Alexa could barely bring the words to her lips. "Is there anywhere we could meet?"

"Of course, Lady Glanville. I'll see to it."

She felt a moment of panic at the ease with which the arrangement was made. On the day of their engagement she had promised Piers that she would never see Matthew again. But neither of them then could have envisaged the circumstances of this new encounter. A happily married woman, mother of a four-year-old son; and a severely disabled man. What harm could a conversation between them do? And it would be unthinkable to turn her back on a member of the family. She had spoken the truth when she claimed a relationship with the instructor. Matthew, after all—in spite of being three years older than herself—was her nephew.

It was not an easy meeting. The commandant put his own office at their disposal and Alexa waited until Matthew had arrived there before she joined him. She had sung all her songs that afternoon for him—and he, meeting her gaze steadily, had known it. So there was no longer any element of shock in the encounter, but the constraints imposed by their past relationship remained. It was impossible, naturally, for Alexa to kiss him; but equally impossible, for quite different reasons, to shake hands as though they were mere acquaintances.

Twelve years had passed since they last saw each other. At the ball which Lord Glanville had given in 1905 for Alexa Reni, the star of the new season at the Royal Opera House, she and Matthew had danced together, their eyes bright with love and excitement. And then Alexa had been forced to tell him what she had only recently learned herself—that her father, the mysterious man who had had a liaison with her mother in the last years of his life, was Matthew's grandfather, John Junius Lorimer.

She had done her best to persuade Matthew then that the discovery was of little importance. It was true that they could no longer contract a valid marriage, as they had hoped, but what did that matter to an artist and a singer? Alexa had been sincere when she said that she cared nothing for convention. That had made all the greater the shock of hearing Matthew declare that she must be free to marry one day, to be respected and to lead a conventionally happy life in the class of society which her beauty and talent entitled her to enter. He had kissed her with a fervour which left no doubt of the passion he was renouncing. Then he had run from the ballroom, never to see her again. Until now.

"I don't know what to say." Alexa felt her voice shaking. She leaned back against the door, trying to laugh at her own inadequacy.

"Well, I do," said Matthew. "I have to say that you're more beautiful than ever. I wouldn't have thought it possible, but you've grown even lovelier than when you were eighteen. Lucky Lord Glanville. I was glad when you chose him to marry. He seemed a kind man. Why don't you sit down? You've been told, I suppose, what's wrong with me."

He was talking too much for the same reason that Alexa was talking too little. Neither of them was quite certain what their relationship was or could be. She sat down and did her best to conduct an ordinary conversation.

"Not in any detail," she said. "How did it happen, Matthew? You weren't in the Army, were you?"

"At my age? Don't be ridiculous! Well, I shouldn't say that. I gather that even old men like me are being swept into the general carnage these days. No. The really ridiculous part of the whole business is that I could have stayed safely at home if I'd wanted to. I actually chose to go up in an aeroplane. I had to beg people to let me. I must have been mad."

"An aeroplane!"

"That's right. I was an official war artist, doing a series of battle paintings. I got it into my head that I'd like to see what the whole thing looked like from above. On the ground, it's all a mess. Dead bodies, live bodies, none of it makes any sense. There must be a pattern somewhere, I thought, and it might be possible to see it from the air. They let me go up on an observation flight, to take photographs of the enemy lines. I knew how to work a camera."

"And was there a pattern?"

"If it counts as a pattern to see rows of ants bustling around. All keeping to their own tracks, trying to achieve some invisible goal, occasionally diverting round some invisible obstacle." He hesitated and for the first time the note of bitterness left his voice. "Well, as a matter of fact, it was beautiful. There was snow on the ground—you remember how late spring was. Impossible to believe that armies were killing each other down there. Little dots of people. Little puffs of smoke. Peaceful. The aeroplane was noisy, but everything else seemed to be silent. Until at last one of the puffs of smoke pointed in our direction and we fell out of the sky."

"You were shot down? Oh, Matthew!" It was impossible to restrain her affection for him any longer. She seized his hand and pressed it against her cheek. Gently, but definitely, he took it away.

"Don't, Alexa," he told her. "I didn't want this meeting. I

knew you were coming to sing, of course, but I hadn't meant to be at the concert."

"But we could be friends again," Alexa said. "Twelve years of separation is long enough, surely. And when we're members of the same family, it's absurd. We've got nothing to be ashamed of. Nothing that happened was our fault."

"What happened?" asked Matthew wryly. "Nothing, alas!"

"And how much I regretted that, when you left me," said Alexa. "That night in Paris, after *Salome*—I would have stayed with you, you know, if you'd asked me."

"And instead I asked you to marry me and we found ourselves trapped by all the Lorimer conventions of correct behaviour between a gentleman and his fiancée. But now you're married to Lord Glanville, and another set of conventions comes into play."

"Piers couldn't possibly object—" began Alexa. But Matthew interrupted before she could move too far away from the truth.

"In view of my condition?" he suggested, still with the same forced smile on his lips. "It's certainly true that he'd have nothing to fear from me. Well, to be honest, I'm not much bothered about what he thinks. I'm speaking out of selfishness. I couldn't stand it. I'm having trouble enough in coming to terms with everything I've lost as a result of the crash. To be reminded of what I lost even before that would be too much of a burden. I'm sorry, Alexa."

Alexa was silent, recognising her own selfishness in her reluctance to let him go. She did her best to accept his decision without letting him see what an effort it cost her.

"But where will you go when you leave here?" she asked.

Again the wry smile twisted Matthew's lips.

"I have a house—a very small house—in Leicestershire," he said. "Whether any of the doors will be wide enough to admit a wheelchair, I don't know. And inside the house I have a wife. Whether she'll have any use for a cripple is another thing I don't know. I even have a baby son, John. With any luck he'll get on with me for a year or two, until he feels the need of a father who can kick a football around with him."

"A wife!" Alexa was dumbfounded. It had never occurred to her that Matthew would marry anyone else.

"A wife to whom I can never be a husband again."

"But you can still paint." She did not know what else to say. Her beloved Matthew reduced to this! And married.

"Oh yes," he agreed. "I'm a very lucky chap. I can still paint."

Alexa realised that whatever comfort she tried to give would increase his bitterness rather than assuage it. She longed to put her arms around him, to feel his arms around her, to give him one last kiss. Instead, she said goodbye quietly and went out of the room before he should see her cry.

10

As the time of her grandchild's birth approached, late in 1917, Margaret went to Jennifer's family home in Norfolk. She felt entitled to some leave, for this was her first absence from Blaize since she had taken charge of the hospital there. By now her work was almost entirely administrative: there were plenty of doctors on the staff to deal with medical emergencies.

She found her daughter-in-law in good health, but strained and apprehensive. Margaret herself had been forced to approach the birth of her only child without a husband at her side for support, and sympathised with the young woman's fears about the coming ordeal. She did her best to be reassuring and was rewarded by Jennifer's increasing serenity of mood.

The sea was not far away from the Blakeneys' home, Castle Hall, but the flat land between was low and marshy, making it difficult to walk there easily. Its presence made itself felt mainly by the sea mists which spread inland every evening and often, at this time of the year, did not disperse until noon. They made outdoor exercise undesirable for Jennifer, who by now was in any case too big to move easily. The baby's head had dropped, making walking difficult. Mr. Blakeney, Margaret's host, was elderly and frail even for his years. He too kept to the house in these cold days. Margaret, more active than either and for too long confined to her office, felt the need to spend some time each day in the open air.

She went out in the afternoons during Jennifer's rest period, using the first day to explore the Blakeneys' own grounds. The grey stone house, shabby but comfortable, had a modest garden of lawns and flower beds at the back, with a spinney at what appeared to be the boundary. But on the far side of the trees, still within the estate, were the ruins of the old castle which gave the house its name.

Except for a single tower at one corner, little of the structure had survived, but enough of the outer wall remained to show what an extensive area it had once protected—and because the stone foundations were set in a high bank of earth, there was still a feeling of shelter inside. Outside, on the other hand, the wall was steep, an effective defence. At its highest point it was set on an outcrop of rock immediately above the marsh which twice a day filled with tidal water and twice a day drained itself back into the narrower channel of a river running out to the sea.

In the days before the war, when gardeners were easy to come by, the grass inside the walls had probably been kept neat, but now a thick growth of nettles and brambles made it impossible to cross. Round the circumference ran a well-trodden stony path, however, and as Margaret walked along it both on that first day and on later occasions she revelled in the peace of the deserted site. If she paused to look out, either inland or across the marsh to the sea, she could see birds by the hundred, but no people at all. The change from the bustling grounds of Blaize and the constant demands made on her there was so restful that for the first time she was able to appreciate how tired she had been when she arrived.

On other days she explored some of the nearby villages, marvelling at the richness of the huge churches which had been built in the centuries when the wool trade made Norfolk wealthy but which today dominated only shrunken and impoverished communities. She was returning from one of these walks when she saw approaching from the other direction the elderly village postman. He had returned to his old employment when his younger successor went off to the war. He got off his bicycle to open the gate, and recognised Margaret as the guest at the Hall.

"How's Miss Jennifer, then?" he asked.

"Very well. It won't be much longer. Can I save you the journey up to the house?"

"If you'll sign for this. Telegram. Name of Scott."

"That must be for me." Margaret frowned as she signed. Only that morning she had read in the paper that more than two hundred thousand British soldiers had been killed or wounded in the Third Battle of Ypres. Blaize, no doubt, like every other hospital, would be under pressure to increase its number of patients. She hoped that her deputy was not calling her back just at the moment when she could be of use to Jennifer. She opened the telegram.

"Is there any answer?" asked the postman.

Margaret shook her head, unable to speak. She stood still, leaning against the gatepost, as the old man mounted his bicycle, wobbled, and pedalled slowly away. Then, equally slowly, she walked up the long drive.

She could not face Jennifer yet. Instead of going into the house she continued to walk across the garden and into the ruins of the castle. Only when she was sure that no one could see her did she sit down on the stone wall and take the telegram out again.

It was intended for Jennifer. Margaret had forgotten that Robert's wife had the same surname as Robert's mother. It was Jennifer who had become Robert's next of kin, Jennifer to whom the War Office expressed its regrets.

She read the words again. They were not an announcement of death: not quite. Robert was missing, believed dead. Earlier in the war she would have seized on the uncertainty. It was unbelievable that Robert should have been killed, and in 1915 or 1916 she would have refused to believe it. But now any attempt at optimism was crushed by the weight of probability. Too many women had been widowed, too many widows had lost their only sons. It was no longer possible to pretend that such things could not happen: they happened every day. She tried to cling to the element of hope—that if he were known to be dead, certainly dead, someone would have said so. In this moment of shock, though, she could not make herself believe anything but the worst. "Missing, believed dead" meant only that no one had found the body.

The thought of Robert being only a body was too much for her to bear. He was all she had. His cheerful grin and mischievous eyes, his lively kindness and affection, had been everything in the world to her for twenty-three years. Without him she had nothing left. Clutching the telegram to her chest she rocked backward and forward, trying to control her emotions. Whatever she might think of the Kaiser and his advisers, she had never before hated the Germans as a race. The men in the enemy army were doubtless as puzzled and frightened as most British soldiers by what was happening to them. But at this moment she hated the man who had fired the bullet or the mortar or the shell which had killed her son. Had Robert been frightened, she wondered; had he been for long in pain? When he was a little boy she had shared his pains with him and she felt this one as well. Not exactly sobbing, not exactly screaming, she began to wail as she rocked, throwing the despairing sound out across the marsh to join the desolate cries of the water fowl.

It drew to an end at last. She had come to Castle Hall to support her daughter-in-law and it was time to consider how best to do this. The first decision was an immediate one. The news must be kept from Jennifer until after the birth of the baby and if possible until she had completely recovered her strength. Margaret knew enough about the depression which often followed childbirth to realise the danger of providing a real rather than an imaginary cause for it. That meant that newspapers must be destroyed, the telephone guarded and visitors interrogated and if necessary warned. But most of all it meant that Margaret herself must be as cheerful and businesslike as usual, allowing nothing in her manner to suggest that anything was wrong.

Never in her life had she found it easy to lie, even when it was kind or sensible to do so. And Jennifer naturally liked to talk about Robert. Sometimes she asked her mother-in-law to describe his boyhood, but more often she was concerned with her life with him after the war. If Margaret was to join convincingly in such conversations from now on she must first convince herself that nothing too terrible had happened. She set herself to do so.

Robert was missing. That was bad, but it was only temporary. There would be more news soon. Until it came there was nothing to mourn. And when it did come, the news would surely be good. Almost certainly he had been wounded, but the lack of definite information must suggest that he had been taken prisoner. She would not believe that he was dead until someone proved it to her. There was bound to be a period of suspense and she had the power to spare her daughter-in-law that anxiety. If the news could be kept from Jennifer for a little while, she might never need to hear it at all.

Margaret brushed the stone dust off her coat as she stood up. She straightened her shoulders and walked back round the castle wall towards the house with the firm step and all the determination which had enabled her to survive earlier tragedies in her life.

She had hoped to reach her bedroom and to wash some of the strain away from her swollen face before anyone saw her; but Jennifer, restless, was waiting in the front hall. Margaret took one look at the young woman's wide, frightened eyes and gripped her hands.

"Has it started, dear?"

Jennifer nodded. "Should I lie down?"

"Only while I examine you," Margaret said. "There may still be quite a long time to wait and you'll be more comfortable moving around at first. Give me a moment to wash and change my clothes. I'll come to your room."

The monthly nurse was already in the house, so would not have heard any news from outside. Between them they could guard Jennifer from any careless word. Mr. Blakeney would have to be told, but that could wait until the printed casualty lists in the newspapers began to include the victims of November 30. For the moment, Margaret applied herself to the task of welcoming a new life into the world, and found some comfort in the familiar routines.

As she had warned Jennifer, it would be some hours before the birth could be considered imminent. Margaret prescribed a hot bath and took the opportunity to shut herself in the library and telephone Lord Glanville. Piers received the news with a groan of sympathy which revealed his personal distress. He had known Robert since babyhood and loved him almost as his own son. Anxious to complete the conversation before she was interrupted, Margaret pressed the only important question.

"What are the implications, Piers? What are the chances that he's only missing? He doesn't necessarily have to be dead, does he?"

She was asking for reassurance and Piers did his best to provide it, although the uncertainty in his voice gave the clue to his real opinion.

"No, of course not. Not necessarily. I'll find out everything I can, Margaret. The Germans are supposed to send lists of their prisoners, as we do of ours. It's bound to take a little time before details come through. I'll make enquiries—and make sure that any information which arrives reaches us at once. But Margaret—"

"Yes?"

She heard him sigh. "I'll do what I can," he repeated. Margaret knew what the hesitation meant. He was warning her not to hope too much, because he was already almost sure that she would be disappointed. It was a question of statistics, of probabilities. In any kind of normal society a young man of twenty-three would have an expectation of life of forty years. But a young man in France was lucky to survive twelve weeks. Robert had been lucky, in that sense. The telegram which Margaret had hidden in her drawer could have been expected at any time in the last two and a half years.

She ended the conversation with a reminder that any news should be communicated only to herself. Then for the second time that day it was necessary for her to conceal her heartache under a cloak of cheerful efficiency.

The baby was a girl, small but healthy, her downy hair suggesting that the blondness of her mother's Danish ancestors had only slightly subdued the bright red of her father and grandmother and great-grandfather. Margaret tried to feel joyful but found it impossible. She could control her grief only by suppressing all emotion. Fortunately Jennifer was too tired and too happy on her own account to notice. Margaret waited while Mr. Blakeney was shown his granddaughter, checked that mother and child were comfortable in the care of the nurse, and went back to pace up and down her own room.

The charade continued for eight days. When at last Margaret was called to the telephone to speak to Lord Glanville her immediate reaction was one of hope. But the sympathetic gravity of his voice allowed the hope no encouragement. He had managed to get in touch with Robert's commanding officer and had learned the details of the German counterattack at Cambrai—which had recaptured almost all the ground gained by the British in the

Third Battle of Ypres. The number of confirmed British casualties was already over forty thousand and it was thought that almost ten thousand had been taken prisoner.

"Then if Robert's missing, surely it's most likely that he's a prisoner-of-war!" Margaret exclaimed.

"His name hasn't yet appeared on any of the lists, I'm afraid."

"But if he had been killed, someone would have seen."

"The German attack took place during a snow blizzard. It sounds as though there was little visibility. And a great deal of confusion as our men were pressed back. But in fact he was seen to fall. His sergeant and a linesman both reported it, and they were each of the opinion that he had been hit in the head."

"But afterwards." Margaret had to force herself to say the words. "Afterwards, if he were dead, his body would have been found."

"He was hit right at the beginning of the enemy attack, and the area where he fell was overrun by the Germans. Later in the day our troops made a sortie and recovered the ground temporarily, although it was lost again the next day. They brought in any wounded they could. But Robert wasn't amongst them."

"Then surely that's good news!" exclaimed Margaret. "The Germans must have found him first and taken him prisoner. Taken him to hospital if he was wounded. They wouldn't trouble to move the dead body of an enemy in the middle of the battle. Surely it must mean that he's still alive, Piers. What other possibility can there be?"

The silence which followed was almost as terrible as the explanation which gradually she forced out of him. Margaret had known Piers long before he married Alexa. They had been friends for twenty years and their honesty with each other was a fundamental ingredient of the friendship. Piers might try—as he was trying now—not to tell her the whole truth, but he could not bring himself to lie. Little by little, as he gave reluctant answers to her direct questions, Margaret built up a picture of a desolate countryside in which snow turned to slush and slush seeped into the pulverised soil and turned it into liquid mud. In mud like that even living men drowned. The body of a dead man would simply sink beneath the surface and never be seen again.

In more than thirty years as a doctor Margaret had seen a good many deaths, but she could not think of Robert's death as being like any other. When she replaced the receiver at the end of the call, her mind was numb but her body was retching. She needed to be alone, and it was the worst possible timing which allowed Jennifer at that moment to come slowly downstairs for the first moment since her baby was born.

Jennifer was radiant with happiness. Her fears of childbirth had been forgotten, her body had recovered from its tiredness and she was delighted by her beautiful daughter. Contentment enveloped her as she came into the library.

"The vicar has just left," she said. "He came to arrange for my churching."

At any other time Margaret would have registered a protest. She disapproved strongly of the service prescribed for the churching of women. On her wedding day a bride was exhorted by the church to have children and it seemed illogical that when she had obeyed that instruction she should immediately be regarded as unclean. It was a pagan ceremony which ought to be resisted. But today she was in no mood for argument, and Jennifer's happy mood allowed no opportunity for it.

"He asked at the same time about a date for the christening," she said. "I imagine there's no hope of Robert having leave in the near future, so I shall have to choose a time to suit the godparents. And before that I must make a final decision on a name for Baby. It's a great difficulty."

"Did you and Robert not discuss it and have your choices ready?" To her own ears Margaret's voice sounded unfamiliar, a low expressionless mumble; but Jennifer appeared not to notice anything unusual about it.

"Oh, Robert refused to be serious. I suggested that a daughter might be called Roberta, and he wrote back to say that that would be perfectly all right as long as he was allowed to call her Bobbie or Bertie. I wasn't having that, of course, so then I asked whether he would consider Florence, because I so much admired Florence Nightingale. He didn't like the name, but suggested that if I really wanted to call a daughter after a city there was plenty of other choice: Paris, for example, or Troy or Petra. Berlin, he thought, might be a little unwise in the circumstances." Jennifer giggled at the memory of what had clearly been a long-running discussion by correspondence. "He makes a joke of every-thing, doesn't he? I don't think he could really make himself be-lieve that there was going to be a baby. He had to wait until it arrived. Well, of course, I wrote to tell him straightaway, and pointed out that we really must settle the matter and suggested three more names. So the question is, how long will it be before I get an answer? Our letters have been taking about five days each way, so I should hear by Christmas. Mother, what's the matter?"

Margaret did not answer, *could* not answer. Her voice was no longer under her control. It would be unforgivable to disturb the young mother's joyful lightheartedness, but it was impossible to pretend any longer. She could not even think of any excuse to take herself out of the room, but remained frozen in silence and misery and on the verge of fainting.

"Mother! Mother, what's happened? Is it Robert? What's hap-pened to Robert? Is he dead? Oh God, don't let him be dead."

"Prisoner." Margaret forced out the small lie in order to save herself fron attempting the larger one.

"How do you know?"

"Telegram."

"Where is it? I want to see it."

"I threw it away. No, wait a moment, Jennifer. Don't go away. We must talk about it."

"I'll come down again after Baby's next feed. I'd like to be alone till then with her. We'll talk afterwards." Jennifer's face, al-ways pale, was drained of all colour as she stood up; but her eyes were calm, almost blank. Still moving slowly, she went out of the library, leaving Margaret to indulge the same need for solitude.

She was joined some time later by the monthly nurse.

"I'm sorry to bother you, Doctor, but I'm a little disturbed. Mrs. Scott's lost her milk."

"She's had a shock," said Margaret. "Some bad news. The trou-ble may only be temporary. Have you tried making up a bottle?"

"Yes, Doctor, but Baby won't take it."

"I'll see what I can do. Will you go into the village and ask Dr. Nelson whether there's anyone who could act as wet nurse if it becomes necessary."

In the nursery the baby was crying. Jennifer had returned to bed. On the sheet in front of her was the War Office telegram.

"I may have had to steal it from your drawer," she said. "But it was addressed to me. And it came more than a week ago."

"I felt—" Margaret's explanation was interrupted by the shrugging of Jennifer's shoulders.

"Yes, I can understand what you felt. I'm grateful. Thank you very much for those few days. But now it's time to stop pretending, isn't it? This says nothing about Robert being a prisoner."

"I've been talking to Lord Glanville. He's made enquiries. The Germans took thousands of prisoners. It may be a long time before all the names come through."

"That's not what it says. It says that he's been killed."

"No!" protested Margaret. "Nothing as definite as that. That telegram was sent when nobody knew. And since then—if he were dead, he would have been found."

"Death isn't the existence of a dead body," said Jennifer. "It's the absence of a live one. Absence without end. That's what's happening now. It's only just beginning. But it will go on forever."

For the second time since the arrival of the telegram Margaret forced herself to close a part of her mind and to control the trembling of her body in order to provide comfort. In a curious way she found it easier this time. The first shock had been a general one. With no details of what had happened she had been unable to imagine Robert's death and so what little hope she had been able to pretend was based on the belief that a son could not be snatched from the world without his mother experiencing some instinctive sense of disaster. Her recent conversation with Piers had given her a second shock which provided all too many details. It was easy for her imagination, feeding on them, to build up a picture of what might have happened, but the picture was so horrifying that neither her mind nor her body could admit it. As she sat down on the edge of the bed and held Jennifer tightly in her arms, she was not pretending any longer. Her demand for optimism was sincere. Robert must, *must* have been taken prisoner when the Germans captured the territory on which he lay wounded. She had asked Piers what alternative there could possibly be, and nothing that he had suggested was acceptable.

"We must both hope for the best," she said. "And we mustn't believe the worst when it isn't certain. We're lucky to have been

given that much uncertainty, that much hope. I think he's a prisoner, Jennifer. I *feel* it. You must feel it too. The war can't last
forever. When Robert comes back, he'll want to find you and
Baby both strong and beautiful. Have a rest now, until the next
feed."

As obediently as a child Jennifer slid down beneath the sheets
and closed her eyes. Neither on that day nor on those which followed was she seen to cry.

11

Once it was recognised that Jennifer's letter would never have
reached Robert, there was no reason to delay the christening in
the hope of an answer. Castle Hall bustled with activity as servants and family alike did their best to return, for one day at
least, to peacetime standards of hospitality. A long white christening robe, finely pleated and delicately embroidered, had been
taken out of its cocoon of tissue paper and ironed with the rever-
ent care imposed by a garment already two hundred years old.
Bedrooms had been prepared for the godparents, who would be
staying overnight, and there would be a christening tea for friends
of the family who lived locally. Precious sugar and jam had already been set aside over a period of several months to be squan-
dered now in a single baking session. So much was going on that
when, on the morning of the service, the wet nurse came to say
that the baby was missing from her cradle, it took Margaret some
time to discover that Jennifer likewise was nowhere to be found
in the house.

There had been a frost in the night and, although a pale sun
was shining now, the December day was still very cold. Hurrying
outside without a coat, Margaret shivered as she looked quickly
round the garden. The hoarfrost that whitened the lawn had
been flattened by footsteps leading through the spinney. Margaret
followed the track and came to the castle ruins.

Jennifer was standing on the broken wall at its highest point,
where it thrust out into the marsh and gave a view towards the

sea. She had her back to Margaret, but the trailing end of a white shawl suggested that she was holding the baby in her arms.

The situation made Margaret uneasy. For a moment she was tempted to dash through the tangle of nettles and brambles, taking the shortest line towards Jennifer. Or, moving faster round the circumference, to creep up from behind without a sound, giving no warning of her approach. Both these ideas she rejected, tutting to herself at the wildness of her imagination. Instead, she called across to tell Jennifer she was here and began to approach round the wall as though it were the most natural thing in the world to take a walk in her house shoes and best Sunday dress.

It had come as a welcome surprise that Jennifer had succeeded in being brave and sensible. Margaret herself had emerged from the grief of her first shock persuaded that she was right to hope and that grounds for such hope existed. Piers had agreed that there would necessarily be delays before the full list of those who had been taken prisoner was known, and this had proved to be the case. Although Robert had not been mentioned in the first batch of five thousand names released by the Germans, more were being added to the list in a steady trickle every day. Every day Margaret encouraged Jennifer to expect good news and every day Jennifer, calm and dry-eyed, nodded her head and agreed that the nightmare must soon be over. It was not a pretence on Margaret's part. She had genuinely made herself believe what she said and so she was sure that Jennifer must believe it as well. Or at least, believe that it was worthwhile to wait. And Jennifer would never hurt her own baby. The flash of fear at the sight of the motionless woman on the rampart had been irrational and unjustified.

Nevertheless, it would be as well if Jennifer did not stay there too long. Margaret greeted her in a normal manner but suggested almost at once that the air was too cold for the baby.

"In so many layers of wool she can hardly be conscious of temperature," said the young mother, and it was true that the little girl, although restless for her feed, showed no sign of discomfort. "I needed a little peace and quiet, and there isn't much to be found in the house. With the christening this afternoon, I can't put off the choice of a name any longer."

"I thought you must have decided already and that you were

going to surprise us," Margaret said. "Have you made your choice, then? Will you tell me?"

"Her second name will be Margaret, for you. I'm sure Robert would have wanted that. As for her first name, I shall call her Barbary."

"Barbara, you mean."

"No. Barbary."

"But dearest, that's not a name."

"It's an old form of Barbara," said Jennifer. "If you look in the graveyard when we go to the church this afternoon you'll see the tombstone of Barbary Anguish. She was twelve months old when she died in 1704. When I was a little girl I used to run out of the church sometimes because the sermon seemed too long. I'd sit on that grave and think about Barbary Anguish. The whole name seemed so sad, as though her parents had known even before she was born that she would bring them nothing but tears."

"But this baby is going to bring you great happiness, Jennifer."

"Look down there," said Jennifer, and Margaret followed her gaze down the steep cliff of the rocky outcrop and over the marsh, half flooded now by the tidal water that forced its way through the tall reeds. Not far away, in the deeper channel of the river, the surface of the water became more turbulent as the incoming tide fought against the current surging down towards the sea. On the further side of the water stood a row of windmills. The wind had dropped, leaving them for the time being motionless, which made all the greater the contrast with the life of the river and the marsh. Tern and crested grebe cruised over the water, curlews called from the meadow beyond, swans in formation flew overhead with the air screaming through their wings. A heron stood amongst the reeds as though made of stone and one by one the wooden posts which marked the river channel were occupied by sleek black cormorants which stretched their wings to dry and then crouched without moving, waiting until a fish should pass below.

"It's very beautiful," said Margaret; but she shivered a little as she spoke, and this time with more than the crispness of the air. It was not a welcoming beauty but an alien one. Even as she watched, a low sea-mist spread across the further bank of the river, swallowing the windmills one by one. If she had not seen them a moment earlier, she could not now have guessed that there was anything there. It seemed that her companion shared something of the same feeling.

"The Romans built this castle," Jennifer said. "Everything inside it was safe. Part of the civilised world. Everything outside was hostile. Barbary. The barbarians came from the sea and destroyed the land. My own ancestors were amongst them. The castle walls survived for a little while and kept the people inside safe, but when they decayed the barbarians were waiting. They're always waiting. In the mud of Flanders, in the mists of Norfolk. As we stand here, the guns are booming and men's bodies are shattering into pieces. And there are more ways of ending a life than with a gun. The world is full of people who can only kill and destroy. There's no refuge any longer. The whole world is barbary."

"For you, perhaps. But not for your baby. She has her own safe place, in your heart. And certainly she's not one of the barbarians herself, to be given such a name."

"Perhaps not," agreed Jennifer. "But she's the daughter of anguish. I've made up my mind. I shall call her Barbary."

Her voice, although definite, was calm enough, but suddenly Margaret was frightened again. The wall was high and the white bundle in Jennifer's arms was tiny and helpless.

"We ought to get Baby back into a warm room," she said. "Let me hold her while you climb down. It's a steep path—and it's too soon, really, for you to be scrambling about like this."

Jennifer gave no sign, as she obeyed, that she had been looking for anything more than fresh air and a quiet place in which to reflect. But that did not prevent Margaret from drawing the nurse to one side as soon as the baby had been fed and tucked up again in her cradle.

"Mrs. Scott is very depressed," she said. "It's natural in the circumstances. You should encourage her to rest as much as possible and to eat a little more. And for the next few days, until I speak to you again, you shouldn't allow the baby to be left alone with her mother. Tell the wet nurse as much as you need to."

She saw the woman's eyes open wide and was satisfied that her anxiety was understood. Later Margaret was to ask herself how she could have been foolish enough to channel her anxiety so narrowly. What she suspected might indeed have been in Jennifer's distracted mind as she climbed the steep slope of the earthworks, but it was only half the danger.

That afternoon the baby was christened in the little flint church to which so many members of the Blakeney family had brought their newborn and their dead. Still unhappy about the choice of name, Margaret hoped that the vicar might protest that it was not a Christian name in the literal sense: but he—presumably sharing Jennifer's familiarity with the child's name which had been carved on a tombstone two hundred years earlier—did not demur. Jennifer came calmly to the tea party which followed the service. Afterwards she claimed to be tired by all the excitement and went early to bed. The next morning her bedroom was empty.

It was three days before her body was found entangled in the reeds on the river bank. Margaret, who did not sleep at all during that time, received the news with a numbness she could not explain. It was as though she had expended all her grief on Robert and had no tears left to shed. This did not prevent her, though, from feeling guilty at what she saw as a failure of sensitivity on her part. She had not wanted to act as a prison warder but realised now that she should have done so. Sitting with Mr. Blakeney in a room which felt cold in spite of the log fire burning in the grate, she tried to express her regrets.

"Jennifer was always highly strung," he said. "She never found it easy to cope with difficulties. Perhaps she led too sheltered a life here. I know that she found her hospital work very distressing when she first went to Blaize, even though she had no personal involvement."

What he said was true. Margaret remembered her own earlier observation of the nervous strain induced in Jennifer by the need to take a difficult decision. But that was no excuse for her own shortcomings.

"There's the question of the baby," Mr. Blakeney said. "When I die, she'll inherit everything I have. And I shall make a settlement of part of it to take effect at once. It would be a comfort to me, once she's a little older, to have her company sometimes. But I can't look after a baby. I'm an old man. And not well. If she stays here, she'll be brought up by servants. And even though she might learn to love me, she'd lose me before very long."

Margaret made no attempt to argue, and not only because she was too tired. At their very first meeting her trained eye had identified Parkinson's disease in the trembling of Mr. Blakeney's fingers, and under the strain of tiredness and bereavement his hands were now shaking uncontrollably. In years he was not yet seventy, but the greyness of his complexion suggested that his estimate of his own future might not be far from the truth.

"I'll take her back to Blaize," she promised. "You must come to visit her there as often as you wish. And she can come here for holidays as well."

It could not be a permanent solution. Margaret was certainly in better health than her host, but she was not so very much younger. The war had made thoughts of retirement impossible, but she had already passed her sixtieth birthday. Like an old woman, she allowed herself a moment to remember all the other members of the family for whom she had at one time or another assumed responsibility. Robert, of course, had never been anything but a joy to her, while Kate and Brinsley had come under her roof when they were old enough to be independent to some extent. But Margaret could still recall the doubts she had felt on three other occasions when she had found herself in much the same situation as today. She had adopted Alexa without having any assurance that she could afford to support even herself, much less a child. When Alexa herself had become pregnant with no husband to support her, Margaret again had come to the rescue, relinquishing the care of little Frisca only when Alexa's marriage provided a new home for her. And then the last year had seen Grant's arrival, with Ralph's increasingly confused letters making it clear that the boy would never be welcomed back in Jamaica.

This case was different. Margaret felt sure that she would have no difficulty in loving her granddaughter, but she could not count on living to see Barbary grow up into adulthood.

It didn't matter. No better arrangement suggested itself. And one of the curious effects of the war that had been going on for so long was that it distorted the idea of the future. Like everyone else Margaret habitually used the phrase "after the war," but this was an unreal concept as long as no date could be attached to it. It meant "sometime" but carried the connotation of "never." Nothing could be less satisfactory than to live from one day to the next when every single day brought news of fresh unpleasantness; but it had become the only way to survive. All that mattered was that Barbary needed a home and a substitute mother today, and that for today and probably tomorrow Margaret could provide her with it.

"I shan't call her Barbary, though," she said. "I don't like the name and I don't like the spirit in which Jennifer chose it. I can't unchristen the baby, but I suppose I can call her what I like. Would you mind if she were to become Barbara?"

"I shall leave every decision to you," said Mr. Blakeney. "And I think that to be a good one. I'm very grateful to you. It's a comfort. Thank you very much."

Neither of them could truly be comforted, but the decision at least served the purpose of reminding Margaret that other responsibilities were waiting for her and that it was time to pick up the threads of her own life again. Two days after Jennifer had been buried in the same graveyard where once she had sat out boring sermons on the tomb of Barbary Anguish, Margaret took her baby granddaughter back to Blaize.

1918

1

Every night Margaret dreamt that she was drowning. Sometimes it was the reeds of the Norfolk marshes that entwined themselves round her ankles and tugged her under the water as she kicked and struggled. At other times it was the liquid mud of a battlefield crater that sucked her down, and then her body seemed not to resist but merely to stiffen as inch by inch it was drawn below the surface.

Whichever nightmare it was that attacked her, the effect was the same. She awoke each morning at four or five o'clock, drenched in sweat and unwilling to return to the terrors of sleep. She had been tired enough before, but now she was exhausted. Piers, concerned for her health and knowing that she had passed her sixtieth birthday, more than once suggested that she should retire. But the German offensive in the spring of 1918, sweeping again over the Somme battlefield on which Brinsley had died, seemed about to press the British Army back into the water. Once more the demand for hospital beds rose as casualties flooded back from a battleground that was no longer a place of retrenchment but of retreat. Like everyone else in England, Margaret read with a feeling near to despair Field Marshal Haig's grim admonition: "With our backs to the wall and believing in the justice of our cause, each one of us must fight to the end." Defeat was very close. This was no time to consider retirement. If her nightmare had any basis in reality, it meant that she was in danger of drowning in a bottomless sea of work.

Yet the impression left on her waking mind by the recurrent

dream was so strong that when Arthur arrived from Bristol one day in May to break the news that Ralph was dead, it hardly seemed to come as a shock. Her emotions had been numbed by too much bad news. That a man who had spent his whole working life in an unhealthy tropical climate should die at the age of fifty-eight could not be thought of as surprising. Margaret was sad, because she had loved her younger brother dearly, but she was too tired to weep.

"How did it happen?" she asked.

"There's some kind of deep pool on the Hope Valley estate, apparently," Arthur said. "A waterfall feeds it from above and a stream trickles out from the edge to pass through the village."

"I've been there," said Margaret. "Ralph called it the Baptist Hole. He used it for baptismal services." She remembered, though, how she had once crept towards the pool by night and had seen a very different kind of ceremony in progress, an orgy of music and movement which seemed to have come straight from the jungle, surviving the years of slavery without change. For a moment she wondered wildly whether her brother had fallen victim to some pagan rite, but it appeared that the truth was less dramatic.

"There's no doubt, I'm afraid, that he was drinking more and more heavily in this past year. My information comes from Duke Mattison. Brinsley's death must have been a terrible shock, of course, and on top of that Uncle Ralph had convinced himself that Kate must also be dead, since there's been no news of her from Russia."

"You mean, he fell into the Baptist Hole when he was drunk, and drowned there?"

"It seems so." Arthur hesitated. "There are some business aspects of his death to discuss. But no doubt you'd prefer to wait until you've recovered from the main shock before I inflict any others on you."

Margaret shook her head wearily. "Tell it to me all at once," she said.

What Arthur had to say came as less of a surprise than he apparently expected. Margaret had never known for a fact that Ralph had had an illegitimate son in Jamaica shortly before his marriage to Lydia, but from his unhappiness at the time and the

hints that he had dropped she ought to have guessed—and indeed she had wondered but had not liked to ask. She remembered
how Duke's intelligent face had impressed her on the only occasion when she had met him—and remembered, too, how Kate
had praised his head for figures and willingness to work hard.

"I'm glad," she said. "It must have been some comfort to
Ralph to have the company of one of his sons in those last days.
But has he been fair to Grant, Arthur? Duke may deserve to in-
herit the plantation on the grounds of the work he's put into it,
or even because he's the most capable person to manage it. But
Grant is a legitimate son and more in need of support."

"Grant is well enough provided for," Arthur assured her.
"Uncle Ralph never intended to allow him a share of the plantation—the original intention was that Brinsley should inherit it
all. Do you remember that in the first months of the war I
invested in a ship-building company? Uncle Ralph had funds to
spare at that time, the profits of his trading, and asked to be associated with me in the investment, on Grant's behalf. The German submarines have been making his fortune for him—every
ship sunk in the Atlantic has needed immediate replacement."

Margaret found it distasteful that anyone should have made
money out of a war which had wrecked so many lives. But Grant
himself had no responsibility for what had happened.

"This means that Grant will never go back to Jamaica," said
Arthur. He was warning her, presumably, that she now had no es-
cape from her unofficial adoption, but that was something which
Margaret had accepted long ago.

"Perhaps when he's older he could share in the management of
this company in which you've invested," she suggested. "I remember you intended to make an offer of that kind to Brinsley."

Arthur shook his head. "Can't stand the boy. I'm sorry, Aunt
Margaret. I don't know what it is about him. Uncle Ralph
couldn't bear to have him around, and nor can I. I'll see that his
money is well managed until he needs it, and then it can be used
to buy him whatever kind of business or estate appeals to him.
But not mine."

"You saw him at his worst," said Margaret. "He arrived in England neglected and unhealthy—and made unhappy, naturally, by

his mother's death and his father's rejection of him. But come and meet him now. He's a different boy."

She took her nephew out into the spring sunshine. The early months of the year had been wetter than usual, but May had brought dry weather at last, and all the soldiers who were well enough to leave their beds were taking advantage of the spacious grounds. They greeted Margaret as she passed them, and she did not like to move on without a friendly word, so it was a little while before she was able to discover Grant's whereabouts.

He was pushing Barbara's baby carriage up the slope from the river. Her nursemaid walked beside them but did not need to help. Grant's arms—which he had used for many years as a means of pulling himself about—were exceptionally strong. The operation on his hip had been as successful as could have been hoped: he still walked stiffly, but the surgical boot which added a necessary two inches to his stunted leg was placed as firmly on the ground with each step as the normal boot of the other foot. Not only was he walking with ease and confidence, but he had become much thinner. In the last few months, like any thirteen-year-old boy, he had begun to shoot up in height almost visibly; he had shed the fat which gave him such an unattractive appearance when he first arrived in England.

In addition to the improvement in his physique, the boy's temperament had changed in a way which must surely impress Arthur. Grant was talking to Barbara as he pushed her, pulling funny faces and jigging the baby carriage up and down in an attempt to make her smile. Whether or not the five-month-old baby was responding, Margaret could not see; but certainly Grant was laughing at his own jokes.

Barbara's arrival at Blaize at the turn of the year had gone almost unnoticed by the adults who lived there. Margaret had written in advance to Alexa to discover whether there would be any objection to the presence of another baby in the house, and had received the answer she expected. But Alexa and Piers had been as stunned as Margaret herself by Jennifer's death and the uncertainty about Robert's fate. Their embraces had been reserved for Margaret as she came wearily into the house after her stay in Norfolk; it was the wet nurse who was left to carry Barbara up to the nursery quarters.

So many young lives had been snatched away from Margaret's love and care that she had felt a need to pause before she could commit her emotions yet again. She knew that the baby would be well cared for by little Pirry's nurse. Once a day she paid a routine visit to the nursery and stared for a moment into the cradle. But she had not felt able to lift the baby and cuddle her. For the first time in her life, it seemed, she had lost the ability to show love.

Alexa had never pretended to be interested in any children except her own, and Piers spent most of each week in London. So Barbara was left to servants—and to the other children of the family. Four-year-old Pirry saw her only as a rival who had caused his expulsion from the nursery to the more disciplined world of the schoolroom, ruled by a governess, while Frisca was too active to be interested in a baby who could not move from her cot. Barbara's first friend in the Lorimer family had been Grant.

"He was very fond of Robert, you know," Margaret told Arthur as the nursery group moved away up the slope. "Robert had the knack of teasing him into cheerfulness. So of course the news upset him badly. He doesn't believe that Robert is a prisoner any more than Jennifer did. When Barbara first came here, he'd sit by her cot for hours, just staring. I suppose he doesn't understand about babies. He must have been trying to see the connection between Robert and Robert's daughter." It occurred to Margaret even as she spoke that it was time for Grant to be given a little information on such subjects. It was unlikely that Ralph had ever had a fatherly chat with his unloved son. She made a mental note to ask Piers if he would take on that duty, and then continued with her explanation. "So Grant was one of the familiar faces in the baby's life. When she gave her first smile it was to him, just because he was there. It was his finger she gripped when she began to play. He has a talent, I think, for all-or-nothing devotion. That may be why it took us all so long to make a good relationship with him when he first arrived. He'd been wholly devoted to his mother all his life and he wasn't going to let anyone take her place."

"And you think he's devoted to Barbara?" Arthur's voice revealed his incredulity.

"I'm sure of it. Oh, he's very fond of me as well. But he's grabbing at Barbara just as he grabbed at Robert. Well, it will be good for both of them. When he first asked me whether he could push her out in the afternoons, I said he'd have to prove to me that he was safe with her, absolutely steady on his feet. Until then he'd been reluctant to admit that his operation had been a success. He still limped around in a very exaggerated way, and wouldn't wear his boot. But when I insisted that the baby carriage must be pushed smoothly, he taught himself to walk normally almost overnight."

"*Almost* normally."

"Well, when you consider his state when he arrived here!" It seemed to Margaret—who regarded the improvement in Grant as a small miracle—that Arthur was being overcritical. "And it's not just walking. He's become fanatical about getting himself fit. He goes to the exercise classes that we run for the men. And he's asked Piers to let him ride. He's still on a leading rein at the moment, but if he can really learn to grip with his knees he'll bring back into use all the muscles which must almost have wasted away while he was a child."

For a moment she was cheerful. Then she remembered that she now had to break the news to Grant that his father was dead. Probably he would not care greatly, but Margaret cared on her own account. Arthur seemed to understand her sudden silence. He refused her invitation to stay the night and left her to her memories.

The wooded slope between Blaize and the river was too steep for most of the convalescent soldiers to tackle. Margaret made her way there, hoping to be undisturbed. May was the month in which the azaleas were at their best. One of the patients, shell-shocked and silent, had devoted himself all winter to the task of clearing the winding stream and the azalea walk from the mud and weeds which had threatened to choke them after the last of Lord Glanville's gardeners had been conscripted. Margaret sat down beside the water which was once again flowing cleanly along its path of flat grey stones and tried to think about Ralph.

The picture was too confused. There seemed no way of reconciling the golden young man, confident and handsome in the white braided blazer of a schoolboy captain of cricket, with Ralph as she had last seen him, thin and stooping in a shabby black suit, his eyes wrinkled against the sun. And since that time his burdens had grown even heavier. He should have died sooner, Margaret thought to herself; before Lydia's death—and certainly before Brinsley's.

Yet when Brinsley had died, it had seemed too soon. Had they been wrong, Margaret asked herself suddenly, to feel so much sadness and regret for a life cut short. Brinsley, like his father, had been a golden boy—but Brinsley would never be tired and old and disillusioned, wondering whether his life's work had been worthwhile. He had always thought of himself as lucky. When Margaret considered her brother's life, and when she looked at some of her patients—alive, but facing years of pain and dependence—it was difficult not to wonder whether perhaps Brinsley's luck had held after all. Death was a disaster only for those who were left behind.

She could persuade herself, no doubt, not to mourn too much for Ralph, who in his last months had been lonely and without hope. But it was impossible to carry the thought to its logical conclusion and hope that Robert was no longer suffering, that he was dead, not sharing the pain she felt on his behalf. She had begun by feeling sad about her brother's death; but by the time she arose to walk back to the house her thoughts had returned, as they always returned, to her missing son.

Someone was calling her name. She heard it faintly while she was still in the woods, and then more loudly as she stepped out into the open. It was possible to recognise Lord Glanville's voice, although she could not see him; and the sound startled her. Piers was not a man who shouted. Nor did he ever use her Christian name in public. In private they had been close friends for many years, but in the world of the hospital she was always Dr. Scott. Margaret began to hurry, fearful that some accident had occurred to Alexa or one of the children.

She saw him hurrying up the paved path from the theatre ward; he must have been to look for her there. In his hand was a card which he waved in the air as soon as he caught sight of her. That was another departure from the norm. Even in these days when formality had almost disappeared, letters were carried by servants. Margaret froze into stillness. She refused to allow her mind to think or guess; and as though in sympathy, her body ceased for a moment to breathe.

He came towards her and it seemed that he was no more able to speak than she was. Without allowing her a chance to look at the message he held, he took her into his arms, almost crushing her in the tightness of his embrace.

How could she share his emotion when she still did not know whether the tears in his eyes were of sorrow or joy? She struggled to pull his arm away, to take the card from his hand. Then it was her turn to feel the tears flooding into her eyes. The postcard—printed and formal, except for a blank space in which a name had been written in ink—was little more informative than the telegram which had arrived five months earlier. But it provided the only piece of information that mattered.

Captain Robert Charles Scott was not dead but a prisoner of war.

2

Almost every month some new messenger arrived from Moscow; to announce a new decree, to investigate the working of an old one, to explain some aspect of Bolshevik policy, to make it clear that the blame for the poor harvest of 1918, and the consequent food shortage, must be squarely placed on the shoulders of the peasants, who had generously been given land and had responded with indolence and selfishness instead of free-handed gratitude. The orator on this occasion had been sent by the Commissar for War.

That was all Kate knew as she hurried to the September meeting, a little late because of an emergency in the operating theatre and so tired that she wanted only to sleep. But she knew that her absence would be noted by the soviet of the military hospital to which she had been attached since disbanding her own medical unit a year earlier. In any case, there had been rumours that Commissar Trotsky himself was in the area. He was known to be touring the country in his armoured train, recruiting for the Red Army. Since the assassination of Uritsky and the shots which wounded Lenin, all Trotsky's appearances were made without advance warning. But stories of the Red Terror had reached even this remote part of Russia, and Kate was curious to see the man who was presumed to be responsible for the shooting of so many prisoners and hostages.

As soon as she opened the door, however, she knew that the speaker was not Comrade Trotsky. Even if the empty sleeve of his greatcoat had not given her the clue, she could not have failed to recognise the voice which had taught her to speak Russian. Sergei's pale yellow-grey complexion was even less healthy than before and his fanatically glittering eyes had sunk even more deeply into their black sockets, but his intensity of manner and shabbiness of appearance had not changed at all.

He recognised her with equal speed. His eyes, drawn by the movement of her late entry, fixed her for a moment with their hypnotic gleam. But he did not allow himself to be distracted from his theme; and that was directed to the men, not to her. He was describing the atrocities perpetrated by the White Army, the intention of its generals to restore land to the old nobility if they won, the need for all who were faithful to the spirit of the revolution to join the Red Army and fight both the enemy within the country and the invaders from outside.

When the meeting was at an end, Sergei asked a quiet question of the chairman of the soviet, who looked around and pointed out Kate. There was another brief discussion, and then an announcement that Comrade Gorbatov wished to speak to the Comrade Doctor. Kate deduced from this that Sergei had not admitted that he even knew who the doctor was, much less that they were old friends. In the current atmosphere of suspicion and betrayal, she found this disquieting; and she could see the same uneasiness in Vladimir's eyes as he watched her follow the speaker out.

At their parting, Sergei had kissed her. For two years Kate had remembered him with affection, but now she did not know how to approach him. She had seen too many personal relationships snap under the strain of divided political loyalties. She waited; and so, for a moment, did he. Then he laughed.

"So you have remained faithful to your Serbs, foolish one."

"There are not many of them left," Kate said. "Those who survived the second retreat were badly treated. When the officers of
the Russian divisions found that they could no longer rely on
their men to obey orders without mutinying, they used the Serbs
instead to take the force of the German attack—but without
doing them the favour of giving them any weapons. Yet later,
when the death penalty was abolished and the Russians began to
desert to their home villages, the Serbs were forced to stay in the
line because they had nowhere to go."

"I'm delighted to hear you speak so fluently. I was a good
teacher, was I not? But the words you use are bitter."

"I'm speaking of the past," said Kate. "Like everyone else, I
hope for better things in the future. Are you having success in
building your new army?

"It goes well, yes. The difficulty is in finding officers. We're
having to recruit from amongst the officers of the old Imperial
Army."

"I thought most of them were in hiding."

"This is their opportunity to emerge. Those who don't take advantage of it will proclaim themselves as enemies of the people.
There will be no second chance."

Kate was careful to keep her voice under control so that Sergei
should not guess her personal interest in the subject. "And do you
find them reliable?" she asked.

"Every unit of the army is to have its own political commissar,
who will soon report any disloyalty. And of course, not all officers
are equally welcome. If any of the old nobility expect to obtain
an amnesty in this way, they very soon discover that they are
mistaken."

"How do you mean?" asked Kate.

"We shoot them. Except in a few cases—of men who handed
over all their land and property to the people voluntarily, right at
the beginning, before it became impossible for them to do anything else."

Kate felt that her sudden pallor must be too visible for Sergei
to ignore; and now that she had heard what she feared she was
anxious to change the subject as quickly as possible. But it
seemed that her old friend had his own anxieties.

"You shouldn't be here, you know. You should have gone long ago, while it was still possible. You could be in great danger."

"Why?" asked Kate. "I mean, I've been in danger almost without pause for three years now. Why should this be any worse?"

"The news isn't generally known outside Moscow and Petrograd," Sergei said, "but the Intervention is becoming more serious. The British have landed troops at Vladivostok and Murmansk. That's too far away for them to give any protection to you. But their presence on Russian soil is bound to stir up great anti-British feeling. In fact, hatred of foreigners has become Party policy. We have no choice."

"I speak Russian all the time," said Kate. "I have a Russian name. Nobody knows that I'm British."

"Your Serbs know."

"They would never betray me."

"You can never be quite sure. It only needs one. By mistake, even—mentioning the English doctor when he thinks no one is listening. Would you leave if I could find a way? It may be too late already. The French and British have both sent warships to take off some of their own people: I doubt if there will be a second chance. But if I could find a route, would you go?"

"If what you say is true, you would surely be putting yourself in danger by helping a foreigner."

Sergei smiled. "Do you remember that I once saved your life?" he asked.

"Oh, Sergei, how could I ever forget!"

"Well then, when a man saves someone's life he's responsible for that person forever."

"Sergei!" They were both laughing with happiness as they embraced. "I couldn't be sure—I didn't want to get you into trouble."

"I'm the one who gets people into trouble," he said. "You may trust me not to be sentimental. But of course what makes the decision easier in this case is that I know you have never been an enemy of the people. Will you go?"

Kate needed a moment longer to think, and it was a reminder of the new barriers which had sprung up between friends that she could not afford to let Sergei know what she was thinking. She would not go without her husband, and in the eyes of a Bolshe-

vik, Vladimir would undoubtedly be an enemy of the people.
They could try to deceive Sergei—but the documents which were
adequate to support Vladimir's identity in a place where he was
established with no reason to arouse suspicion might not stand up
to the more detailed investigation which the issuing of a passport
would involve.

"No," she said. "You are kind, as you have always been kind to
me. But I believe in the new society as passionately as you do.
I'm a Russian now. And soon I shall be the mother of a Russian
as well."

"Ah!" he said. He drew away and looked at her more closely.
"And I thought you were wearing three overcoats to keep out the
cold. The father is Russian, then, not Serbian?"

"Yes."

He thought again. "It's still my opinion that you aren't safe
here. You should go to some place where you aren't known. As a
doctor you can make yourself useful anywhere. If I may speak
without immodesty, your speech is a credit to my teaching. You
can pass for Russian as long as no one has any cause to suspect
that you are not. I'll give you a travel permit. No journey is safe
now, I'm afraid. If the train is stopped by bandits, you'll have to
hope for your pregnancy to protect you. If the line's cut by the
Whites, I suppose it might be worthwhile to reveal your nationality. The British are supposed to be supporting them, after all.
This authorisation will only serve if it's the Cheka who stop
you."

"I should want my husband to travel with me," said Kate
firmly.

"Greedy, greedy." But Sergei was smiling. He sat down and
opened the briefcase he carried, taking out a selection of papers
and rubber stamps. "You'd better have an official posting to another military hospital, in order to keep your ration entitlement.
What's your husband's name?"

"Vassily Petrovich Belinsky."

"And occupation?"

"Anaesthetist."

Sergei laughed in incredulity. "You have been able to get anaesthetics for your hospital?"

"No," said Kate, joining in his laughter, although with a trace of bitterness. "Not any longer. His function now is to hold the patient down while I operate."

"There'll be fewer problems in keeping you together if we choose something less specialised," said Sergei. "Medical assistant should do." He scribbled and stamped for a few minutes before considering again. "I'll send you to Petrograd," he said. "I don't recommend that you stay there too long. The food shortages are worst in the big cities. But it's the best place to establish a new identity, and it's a place where doctors are badly needed. After a year or so you could move on to somewhere smaller if you wanted to—Novgorod, perhaps—and settle down. There you are, then. I'll tell the chairman of your soviet that I've transferred you, but I won't say where you're going. You need to muddy your tracks if you're to be safe."

"Thank you. Thank you very much. And Sergei—I am so very glad for you, that you've been able to return to your own country. I know how much it always meant to you."

"You were kind to me when I was an exile," he reminded her. "I don't forget that. I only hope that you won't regret cutting yourself off from your own country and your family."

"From each according to his ability; to each according to his need," quoted Kate. "I believed that, you know, long before I ever came to Russia. I can see the need here, and I have the ability to help. Shall we meet again, Sergei?"

He shrugged his shoulders. "It's a big country—even after the Brest-Litovsk Treaty. But I shall know where you are, at least to start with. And if you are in any trouble, you can write to me in Moscow. Cautiously, of course—other people will read the letter. In the meantime, I wish you all happiness."

"And you, Sergei." They embraced for a second time before Kate went off to find Vladimir.

"I wish it were anywhere but Petrograd," she said, when she had told him of Sergei's fears for her safety. "There must still be people there who know you. But I dared not risk raising difficulties, in case he should ask too many questions."

"I doubt if I could be recognised with my beard and shabby uniform," he said. "And we shall hardly be moving in the same social circles as before. What worries me more is the danger to the baby of the train journey. It's difficult to believe now that there was once a time when a journey on a Russian train was the most luxurious form of travel in the world. I'm afraid we're going to find it very different now."

3

There were people on the roof of the train and people travelling on its outside steps. Kate looked at the jostling crowd on the station platform and at the packed wagons which were drawing to a halt beside it and saw no possibility of finding a place. She felt Vladimir's strong fingers gripping her arm.

"Hold onto my shoulders and follow me," he said. "Don't let anyone push in between us. Now!"

He thrust forward towards the nearest wagon door. Those who were already on the train did their best to push the new passengers away, whilst those at the back of the platform pressed forward. More frightened than she had ever been in the middle of a battle—since now it was her baby that was at risk—Kate longed to use her arms to protect herself. The pressure was so great that she could hardly breathe and it was difficult not to panic. All her self-control was needed to obey Vladimir's instructions in the five-minute struggle which seemed to last forever.

The wagon was divided into compartments and the sides of each compartment were fitted from floor to ceiling with sleeping shelves. The compartment into which Vladimir eventually forced an entrance already held at least a hundred people, instead of its official maximum of thirty. There were three or four people on each shelf and the floor between was stacked with bundles and baggage. Vladimir looked quickly round and discovered a top shelf which was occupied by only three people. Ignoring their loud protests that there was no room for more, he hauled Kate up to join them, himself standing on the edge of one of the lower shelves to make sure that she did not fall from her precarious perch. Kate, breathless and bruised, listened to the thumping of

her heart and was frightened again, but her anxiety for the baby
came to her rescue. She forced herself to relax, to breathe deeply
and lie as still as though she were sleeping. Still grumbling, but
accepting the presence of the intruder, the old woman beside her
allowed her a few more inches of the shelf.

The first struggle might be over, but the discomforts of the
journey had only just begun. It was impossible to move. Even
after twelve hours had passed it seemed risky to produce what
food they had managed to carry with them, in case it should be
snatched away by their hungry fellow-passengers. The few windows of the wagon were tightly sealed against the cold outside
and the atmosphere became steadily more stifling. The smell was
appalling. All the travellers were dirty and a good many of them
were visibly verminous. They spat, they smoked and they uri-
nated. How long, Kate wondered, would it take to reach Petrograd?

Her defence was to retreat into what was almost a trance,
removing her mind from her body so that she could feel peace instead of disgust. Occasionally she was aware of Vladimir's hand
stroking her cheek or his lips softly kissing hers, but she did not
speak. The train crawled on across the huge subcontinent.

From time to time it came to a halt. This might mean that it
had arrived at a station, but the density of bodies within each
wagon was such that it was impossible for anyone else to enter.
Once—or so the rumour came down the length of the train—it
was because there was no more fuel to fire the engine; all the passengers at the front had been ordered out to chop wood from the
forest. If Kate strained her head downward she could see out of
one of the windows, but there was little variety in the view—
sometimes an unbroken sheet of snow, stretching to the horizon;
sometimes a dark forest, equally silent and uninhabited. Sometimes the moon was shining and sometimes there was daylight,
but she made no attempt to keep track of the passage of time.

She was asleep in the middle of an afternoon when the train
stopped yet again, but this time with a shuddering jolt which
aroused and alarmed all the passengers. All of them were well
aware of the various dangers of which Sergei had warned Kate. So
many different armed bands were at large that no one could feel
safe.

The door was opened from outside. Kate's first feeling was one of relief as the foetid atmosphere was disturbed at last by a shaft of air which was icy cold but so clear that its invasion of the wagon was visible. She breathed deeply through the scarf which she had pulled across her mouth, but at the same time listened with anxiety to the shouted commands coming from near the front of the train. More sinister still, there was the sound of gun-fire; somebody screamed.

"Who is it? Who is it?" Everyone was calling to those nearest the door. The answer was brief and sinister.

"Cheka!"

A wave of fear swept through the passengers. The Cheka was supposed to be on the side of the peasants and proletarians and only against the bourgeoisie and what was left of the nobility, but there was no one who had not heard stories of the Red Terror, of hostages taken and executed, of innocent men shot merely as an example to others. And there were few people—even amongst the poor—who could feel sure that they were not offending against one of the new regulations which flooded out of the Bolshevik headquarters. It was generally known that anyone who denied carrying firearms and was then found in possession of a revolver would be shot immediately; but Kate detected a feeling of terror in the old lady lying beside her as someone else on the same shelf shouted a reminder that it was against the law now to possess more than two of any article of clothing.

Kate had more reason than her neighbour to be nervous. She spoke Russian fluently enough to persuade anyone who had no grounds to suspect otherwise that she was indeed Russian, al-though he might presume that they must come from a different district from his own—the huge Russian state contained so many nationalities that there was necessarily a wide variation of dialects and accents, especially amongst those for whom Russian was a second language. But it would be impossible for her to sustain a plausible identity under interrogation by somebody who was look-ing for irregularities, and Sergei's warning about the danger of being British had been a valid one. Nor was she anxious only on her own behalf. Vladimir, like any other aristocrat, had been brought up to speak French, with English as his second language, so he, like Kate, had learned Russian only as a foreign tongue. And he too would have difficulty in producing acceptable answers if his life before the revolution was investigated too closely. His identity papers were those of an Estonian, and any interrogator from that area would realise immediately that he had no right to them. He and Kate were equally at risk. Their only hope was to remain inconspicuous, two anonymous and insignificant figures in a crowd.

Vladimir had scrambled towards the door when it opened, in order to look outside. Now he climbed back again and spoke quietly into her ear so that no one else could hear.

"Groan," he said, and repeated the command urgently as Kate looked puzzled. "Groan. As though the baby were coming. As though your labour had started."

Kate did as she was told, moaning faintly to begin with and then panting more loudly. She was not clear what the purpose of the charade was. The baby was not due for several months and she could not produce it now merely to create a diversion. She continued to groan, though, as Vladimir muttered to the old lady beside her that his wife's time was approaching, that he must go and see whether there was a doctor anywhere on the train, just in case one should be needed. Kate grabbed at his hand.

"You're not really going to leave me."

"Listen," he said. Once again his lips were close to her ear. "When the Red Guards come, you groan again. You don't speak. Whatever happens, you don't say anything. The old lady will tell them what the trouble is. They won't do anything to help, but your travel papers are in order, so with any luck they'll leave you alone."

"But why won't you be here?"

"They're calling all the men of military age off the train to have their papers checked," said Vladimir. "You're not to worry. It will be all right, of course. But just in case anything goes wrong, you mustn't be associated with me. I'll step out from a different compartment."

"No!" exclaimed Kate. Too frightened to be cautious, she tried to sit up, but Vladimir held her down.

"As a couple, we could make them suspicious. Separately, we can get away with it. I'll be further down the train, and I'll be watching. I shan't let them take you off. That's a promise. If there's really trouble, I'll come back to you. But there won't be trouble."

"But suppose—oh, dearest, suppose they take *you* off, to join the Red Army. It might happen. Sergei said there was compulsory recruitment."

"It wouldn't be the end of the world. It would give me a better set of papers when I was discharged. I'd come back to you."

"Where? How should we ever meet again?"

"Ssh!" The warning was necessary, for Kate's voice was rising as her fear increased. She could tell, though, that Vladimir recognised the difficulty as a serious one.

"Listen, then," he said. "If we're both on the train when it moves off, then I shall see you at the station at Petrograd. If I'm taken off, you must go first to the hospital and take up your post there. I'll know where to find you. But when the time comes for the baby to be born, go to Tsarskoe Selo. I expect it's called something else now that the Tsar is dead, but you'll find it. It's not too far from Petrograd. We had a theatre palace there. We'll use that as a rendezvous. Not the palace itself, of course; it was looted in the February revolution. But there's a lodge by the south gate. The lodgekeeper's wife was my wet nurse. Two years ago I would have trusted her with my life. Now, one can't be quite sure. Take it carefully. You should be able to find out whether she's loyal to the family, whether she'd help you to care for my baby. If you're doubtful, protect yourself by saying that you were seduced and deserted. Beside the gate of that lodge there's a hollow tree. I used to put messages there when I was a boy. That's where I'll look for a letter from you, to tell me where you are and who can be trusted. If I get there first, I'll leave the same information for you."

"Vladimir, I want to stay with you. Please don't leave me."

"I'm a danger to you," he said. "And to our child." He put his hand gently on her abdomen to feel the movement of the baby. "I love you, Katya. I'll love you till the day I die. Be brave just for a little while. We'll be together very soon, I promise. But if the baby is born before I can come, sing him the lullaby I composed for him. I shall be able to hum it in my own head and think of the two of you together. Now, remember to groan."

Not gently, but passionately this time, he kissed her again. She clung to him, still unwilling to let him go. As he released himself from her grip he muttered something about the doctor to anyone who might be listening, and then climbed down to the floor and swung himself outside.

Kate had hardly needed the reminder to groan, although it was fear rather than pain which caused her fists to clench and her eyes to flood with tears. But she was sufficiently in control of herself to know that at all costs she must refrain from making a fuss. It might be true that Vladimir saw himself as a danger to her, but certainly she was a danger to him. He had told her not to speak, and she must obey his instructions for his sake as well as her own.

The search of the train took several hours. When it came to the turn of Kate's wagon, all the men in it were ordered out. Kate counted that almost forty jumped down from the door. By the time the engine had begun to hiss again, and the shouting outside to take on a different note, only seven of the forty had returned. It was possible to move now, for in addition to the absence of so many travellers, much of the baggage had been hauled off the train. Stiff after the long period of immobility, Kate climbed down from her shelf and leaned out of the doorway.

The Cheka had made a good haul. A long line of men was tramping away from the train under armed guard. But a few remained behind, sprawled in the snow, the victims of execution without trial. Fighting hysteria, Kate strained her eyes in an attempt to recognise Vladimir amongst the group of living men. But the distance was too great and the unwilling conscripts were all dressed much alike.

Two of the Red Guards came running down the length of the train. Kate was pushed roughly inside in order that the door might be slammed and locked. The engine gave a piercing signal and began to move, carrying its cargo of silent or wailing passengers on towards Petrograd. Kate was one of the silent ones, dry-eyed again after the panic which had almost overwhelmed her. Even more than before she could sympathise with the helplessness which Vladimir had felt in the first weeks of the revolution, when he found himself condemned by his birth to be an outsider in the new society. In her case it was nationality which was likely to prove more important in the eyes of strangers than all the sympathy she felt for the downtrodden people of Russia, and she was angry as well as upset at the way in which the landing of British troops at a port hundreds of miles away had forced her to keep quiet when she ought to have been able to protest, to cry, to cling to her husband.

As the train thrust steadily on, she stared out of the window at the empty countryside. The first snow had fallen in the previous week, covering the vast plains which stretched to the horizon. Its smooth surface was unbroken here, so different from the area around the train's stopping place which had been churned up and spattered with blood. She felt utterly alone in this enormous, uncaring country. How would she ever find Vladimir again? She tried to persuade herself that he was on the train, not daring to return to her under the eyes of the Cheka; but in her heart she did not believe it. What she could manage to hope was that his papers had been good enough to protect him from the fate of those who had been shot out of hand.

When the train at last reached Petrograd she was faint with hunger and anxiety and lack of fresh air. Hauling out her baggage, she sat down on it without regard to the chaotic movement and shouting all round. For an hour she waited to hear her name called or feel Vladimir's hand on her shoulder, but he did not come. It was scarcely a disappointment; only a confirmation of the fears which she had already been forced to accept.

She allowed no sign of emotion to show on her face. If anyone noticed her, it must only be as a pregnant woman, tired after a long journey, resting or waiting to be collected. But inside her head, silently, she was screaming.

At last, bringing her panic under control for the third time, she rose to her feet and picked up her bags, consoling herself with the reminder that they had had time to arrange a rendezvous. Russia had become a country of forced partings, but this parting need not be forever. She knew what to do, and she must do it. Exhausted and unhappy though she was, Kate picked up her baggage and began to make her way towards the hospital.

4

The speed with which the war changed direction in the autumn of 1918 took almost everyone by surprise. At one moment the Allies were on the verge of defeat; almost at the next, their ar-

mies were once again pressing forward. There were rumours of a
new weapon, the tank, which would transform battle tactics once
its mechanical unreliability had been overcome. More certainly,
there was a promise that five million American soldiers would be
sent to Europe in 1919, and the advance force which arrived in
time to take part in the new offensive had a value out of all proportion to its numbers, bringing healthy and bright-eyed young
men to a continent whose own youth were dazed or dead.

By October the Turks had been defeated and the Bulgarians
had surrendered. Even without victory on the Western Front, a
way into Austria and Germany had been opened through the
back door. Little by little Margaret allowed herself to hope. A
hospital in a prisoner of war camp must be as safe a place as anywhere on the Continent. One day, and perhaps quite soon, Robert would come home.

In the meantime there was no relaxation in the pressure of
work at Blaize, for a new problem had arisen. England had been
invaded not by the German Army but by an enemy more difficult
to fight. No cannons or machine guns could hold back the advance of the influenza epidemic. It had taken the lives of sixteen
million Indians, it had swept across the Near East and had
reached France earlier in the summer. Now it crossed the Channel and, on a scale comparable with that of a battle, began to
claim the lives of civilians whose resistance had been lowered by
the shortages of food.

The patients at Blaize, weakened by their wounds and the am-
putations which many of them had suffered, were especially at
risk. Margaret saw the danger and did her best to divide the long
ward in the converted theatre and introduce barrier nursing procedures in the hope that any infection could be contained. It was
a further burden of work on someone who had been under strain
for so long. Although only too well aware that the disease was a
killing one, she felt almost relief when after two days of indisposi-
tion she awoke one morning to find her body heated to fever
pitch and her head swimming with dizziness. Now at last she
could shed all her responsibilities and lie back to sleep.

In her illness she was more fortunate than most victims of the
epidemic, for there were trained nurses on hand to care for her.
The time came when she was able to stare up at the ceiling, too

weak to move but cool and comfortable for the first time since the attack began, and confident that the worst was over. She accepted a drink of hot milk. Within a few hours she even began to feel hungry.

"What day is it?" she asked as a tray was brought and she was propped up on pillows to receive it.

"Sunday, Doctor." The nurse sat down to help her eat, for she hardly had the strength to lift a spoon.

"Then Lord Glanville will be at Blaize, I imagine. Will you tell him how much better I am." No doubt he had come to sit beside her during her illness, but she had been conscious only of a confusion of comings and goings and could not recall who her visitors were. It was too soon for any of the children to be admitted to her sickroom, but she looked forward to showing her brother-in-law that she was on the way to recovery, and to hearing all the news of the family and the hospital.

"Lord Glanville isn't here, I'm afraid, Doctor. He's in London."

That was a surprise. It was true that within the last month or two, as peace came into prospect at last, Piers had spent more time at the House of Lords. Political life was beginning to revive. Lloyd George had united the country behind the single aim of winning the war, but once it was won the parties could be expected to separate again, each with its own policies. Lord Glanville had never been a member of the government, but he was politically active. The campaign to allow women the vote, which was one of his chief interests, had achieved its first great success earlier in the year, but there were other battles to be fought. Younger women were still excluded from the suffrage, and a whole range of social problems would need to be solved if peace were not to bring as much hardship as war.

So although most of the house in Park Lane had been closed for the past four years, with its staff dispersed and its furniture under dust covers, one chilly bedroom in Glanville House had been kept open for his use, with a cook to prepare any meals which he did not wish to take at his club. For some months now he had been spending only one day a week at Blaize—but that day was Sunday, so that Margaret's hope of seeing him had been a reasonable one.

"And Lady Glanville?" she asked instead.

"She's in London as well."

That was even more of a surprise. None of the concerts which Alexa organised for soldiers in their camps or hospitals ever took place on a Sunday. The nurse, seeing her puzzlement, began to talk in an ill-concealed attempt to change the subject. The war was almost over, she said. The Germans had appealed for an armistice and the terms were being negotiated at that moment.

Perhaps it was not such a change of subject after all. If events were really moving with such rapidity, Alexa might be preparing to reopen Glanville House. Margaret lay back again in the bed and tried to imagine a world at peace again.

She had fallen ill in October; it was November by the time she recovered. The fog which shrouded the river valley imprisoned her in her room even when she was ready for the stimulus of fresh air and exercise. She was still confined to the house when the chief physician of the hospital brought in a letter.

"Lady Glanville asked me to give you this, but not until I considered that you were strong enough."

Alexa's message was a brief one, written from Glanville House.

"Piers is very ill. Come if you can."

Margaret looked at her colleague, who answered the question before it was asked.

"It's the influenza again, the same that attacked you. But unlike you—"

"Are you trying to tell me that he's dying?"

"Lady Glanville wrote to me by the same post. She's very much alarmed by his condition."

"How long have you had the letter?"

"Two days. If you'd left the house in that fog, it would have killed you. Even as it is—"

Margaret wasted no time in arguing. Dressed in her warmest clothes, she set out at once for London.

Even before the cab which carried her from the station had come to a standstill she knew that she was too late. The curtains of Glanville House were drawn, and outside in the road a boy was sweeping up the straw which had been laid in front of the house to muffle the sound of traffic. She sat without moving until the cab driver realised that his passenger was too weak to walk and rang the front door bell for a servant to help her.

Alexa came into the drawing room as she sat there, still shocked, shivering in spite of her heavy coat. For a little while neither of them could speak or move. When at last Alexa broke the spell and began to pace the room, her voice was bitter rather than broken-hearted.

"When I think of the years I wasted!" she exclaimed. "We had such a short time together, and it could have been so much longer. I was a fool to send him away when he first asked me to marry him. And even before that, when I was singing in Italy—he may not have said in so many words what he felt for me, but I knew. I knew all the time, right from the moment his wife died. And I kept him away all that time. Eight years, Margaret, that's all we had together; only eight years, when it might have been twenty."

Margaret's own marriage had lasted for only a few months, and the years of separation from Charles which preceded it had been made necessary by the complications of her family history rather than her own waywardness. There had been a time, too, when she had loved Piers herself and found it difficult not to resent his infatuation with the beautiful young singer who seemed not to care for him at all. But this was not the time to admit any feeling of jealousy to her heart. The man who had died had been loved by both of them; but although Margaret had lost her closest friend, only Alexa was widowed by the death. Margaret did her best to provide some kind of consolation, reminding Alexa that at least during those eight years of marriage she had brought her husband great happiness. Yet there was nothing she could say which would provide real comfort. The evening was filled with silences, until in the end they took their separate sorrows early to bed.

The next morning there were decisions to be made. Alexa was as a rule more practical and businesslike than might have been expected of a prima donna, but now she was numbed not only by the shock of bereavement but also by the sudden realisation of the huge responsibilities she would have to shoulder until her son was old enough to take over the Glanville estates. It was Margaret who decided that the funeral should be held at Blaize and who made all the necessary arrangements—and for the printing of cards, the wording of newspaper announcements, the listing of friends and political allies who must be informed, the planning of a memorial service in London later. In a way it was a relief to concentrate on the mechanical decisions which were so unimportant compared with the loss of her dear friend. She was not aware of the passing of time, and it was only when she paused to shake her chilled fingers back into life that she realised how dark the afternoon had grown without the appearance of luncheon.

Alexa had been too upset to give domestic orders, no doubt, and Margaret herself had not yet recovered her appetite since her illness, so the omission was of no importance. But later she rang for a servant to post her cards, and no one came. Yet Alexa, she knew, had summoned staff from Blaize as soon as she realised that her husband was too ill to be moved to the country. Margaret rang the bell again.

It was answered at last by a young girl. She had been left behind to do anything that was needed, she explained with a trace of sulkiness, while the others were out celebrating.

"Celebrating!" For one horrified moment Margaret, unable to think of anyone but Piers, assumed that for some ghoulish reason the servants were rejoicing in the death of their master. The girl noticed her incredulity and was surprised by it in turn. Then an explanation occurred to her.

"You've heard the news, I suppose, ma'am," she said. "At eleven o'clock this morning it happened. The war's over."

"No," said Margaret, "I hadn't heard. I see. Thank you. Post these letters straightaway, please."

After the girl had gone she walked across to the window. Drawing the curtain slightly to one side, she looked over Park Lane to Hyde Park. It was dark by now. A bonfire was burning in the park. Round it danced a circle of people, hands linked, while others searched the ground for wood to throw on the flames. The street, too, was full of people, all pressing towards Buckingham Palace. There seemed to be a great deal of hugging and kissing going on. Not everyone in the crowd was completely sober.

Margaret allowed the curtain to drop again and tried to open her heart to happiness. This was the moment they had awaited so long. For more than four years the phrase "after the war" had summed up every future pleasure, every future hope. And now, it seemed, the moment had come. "After the war" had arrived. Why was it, then, that she found it impossible to feel any pleasure, any hope—impossible, in fact, to feel anything at all?

She had waited too long and lost too much. "After the war" had been a time to enjoy with those she most loved, and where were they now? Lydia was dead, Ralph was dead, Brinsley was dead, Kate had disappeared, and now Piers was dead as well.

A series of bangs came from the direction of the park, startling Margaret by its resemblance to gunfire. She looked out again and guessed that children were throwing firecrackers onto the bonfire. It was going to be a noisy night.

Disturbed by the sound, Alexa came down from her bedroom. She had been crying. Margaret moved to one side so that she could see out of the window.

"The war's over," she said.

"When?"

"Seven hours ago. Odd, isn't it, that it should just slip away. One had imagined something dramatic happening. But in France, I suppose—"

In France there would be silence. At eleven o'clock that morning the guns would have ceased to spit out death; by now the ground would have stopped trembling. Tired men would fall asleep that night and expect to wake in the morning. The change was dramatic enough for them. Margaret's present sadness was in one sense a selfish one. War or no war, men in their sixties were liable to fall ill and die. That was no consolation, but she could not expect the whole world to mourn with her. The people in the streets outside were quite right to sing and dance. The years of partings had come to an end at last. Grant and Frisca and Pirry and Barbara would grow up without needing to know the anguish of saying goodbye to someone who might never return.

And Robert would come home. There was no need to be frightened for him anymore. The war was over.

PART II

THE AFTERMATH

(1919–1920)

1919

1

The rumour that the war was over in Europe reached Kate early in 1919, three weeks before her baby was due. There had been similar rumours before, but this one was slower than the others to fade. At one time she would have greeted the news with thankful relief, but now it seemed more likely to increase the danger which would face her if her nationality was discovered. Both in Petrograd itself and in the Butyrky prison in Moscow a number of Englishwomen were under arrest for no crime other than that of being English. It was just conceivable that the allied powers which had provided troops for the Intervention might use the armistice as an excuse to withdraw. But far more likely was the probability that with the Germans defeated they would throw an even stronger force into the battle against Bolshevism—and at the same time the German surrender would increase the bitterness of those within Russia who believed that Lenin and the other Bolsheviks had conceded an unacceptable amount of Russian territory in the Brest-Litovsk Treaty. So the civil war was likely not only to continue but to increase in bitterness.

That meant that there could be no hope yet of Vladimir's return. Because the alternative was unthinkable, Kate had succeeded in persuading herself that he, like most of the other male passengers on the train, had become a conscript in the Red Army. He would have been careful not to do anything which would single him out from the others or suggest that he had once been a Tsarist officer. There was no reason why he should be in any greater danger than any other soldier; but she could not expect the western armistice to secure his release.

Once that fact was clear in her mind, Kate realised that it was time for her to leave Petrograd and establish herself at the second rendezvous which Vladimir had suggested, near the home of his old nurse. There was in any case another good reason for leaving —that if she did not make the journey soon, she might be too weak ever to embark on it. She had not yet reached the point of starvation, but like everyone else in Petrograd she was fast approaching it. The granaries of the steppes and the orchards of the Crimea had been cut off from the city by an exceptionally hard winter. Shortage of fuel meant that few trains even began the long journeys needed to bring in supplies, and bandits and Cossacks alike ambushed and plundered whatever stocks did move. The smaller estates nearer to Petrograd had suffered from the disruption caused when the peasants divided into smallhold- ings the land confiscated from the nobles, but proved incapable of raising more than subsistence crops.

For six weeks now Kate had lived almost exclusively on a diet of boiled rye gruel and a thin fish soup made from herring heads —no one was able to discover where the more edible parts of the herrings went. It was not a diet which she would have recom- mended to an expectant mother. For the sake of the baby, if for no other reason, Kate saw that it would be wise to leave. In the country at least there would be firewood to provide a little warmth, and it was bitterly assumed in the city that in defiance of orders the peasants had hoarded cabbages and potatoes and were secretly cooking and eating them.

With the decision made, Kate applied for leave, slightly exag- gerating the imminence of the expected birth. It took little time to pack up her few possessions. For weeks looters had been roam- ing the city, ensuring that no one any longer owned more than he could keep in his own hands. Kate possessed only two treasures. Into the waistband of her skirt she had sewn the ring which Vladimir had given her after their marriage; it was the only jewel he had dared to take with him when he fled from his palace. With less concealment she carried her bag of surgical instru- ments. For the rest, when the time of her departure arrived she wore every article of clothing she owned and strapped a bedding roll on to her back. Ponderously huge, she left without regret her quarter share of the icy room which had been allocated to her by the hospital soviet and climbed onto one of the trams which was still running between high walls of snow.

It was a journey into an uncertain future. As Vladimir had expected, the village of Tsarskoe Selo had changed its name after the murder of the Tsar and his family, but she had discovered where it was and ascertained that trains were still running to it. She had no idea, however, whether the Aminov palace was still standing. And an even greater doubt was whether she would be helped or denounced if she revealed any part of the truth to her husband's old nurse.

The wind when she arrived was bitterly cold, and she could hardly drag herself from the station to the ridge on which the village was built. Had she not had a strong constitution she would have been dead long ago, and even as it was the weight of the baby and her undernourished state had brought her very near to collapse. Only anxiety forced her on. She dared not enquire for the Aminov palace by name, but instead asked anyone she met on the street what building she was passing at that moment. The colonnaded square and magnificent domed church still indicated what an elegant centre the village had once provided for the noble families who used it as a healthy escape from the Petrograd swampland; but their palaces, each in its own estate, were scattered through the surrounding countryside.

At last a landmark enabled her to follow the directions which Vladimir had given her. As she trudged along the narrow track which had been beaten down through the snow, the light began to fade and she grew anxious at the possibility that she might have to retrace her steps in the dark. But the lodge, when it came into sight, was at least inhabited, even though it might prove to hold no welcome for her. The windows were obscured by frozen snow, but it was possible to see a gleam of light in the upper room.

First of all she must look to see whether there was any message. The dead tree by the gate was easily identified, but Kate stared with dismay at the blackened slit in its trunk which Vladimir must once have used as his postbox. It was far too high for her to reach. He, as a boy, would have been agile, climbing the tree next in the row and dropping down to the leafless branch which stretched jaggedly out like a pointing finger. But for her, now, such a climb was impossible. Could even Vladimir have managed it in such icy conditions? Kate set down her bedding roll and moved round the tree, looking for some lower hiding place which he might have used instead.

There was nothing. Frantic with frustration, she fixed her eyes on the aperture, so near and yet so tantalisingly far. She found soft snow and carried it to pack round the trunk of the tree. She leaned her bedding against it and began to inch her way upwards. Her fingers touched the branch, searching for a hold. There was a crack in the surface and the wood was rotten; she pressed inwards, tightening her grasp, willing her arms to take the weight and allow her to pull herself upwards. But the bedding roll began to slip. She felt herself being stretched, uncertain whether to hang or to fall. Suddenly she was conscious of a violent pain, as though a horse had kicked her in the stomach; and at the same time she knew that the waters had burst and that the baby, too soon, was about to be born. She gave a single cry, of distress as much as of pain, and fell back to the ground.

It was not a long drop, but she fell awkwardly and was unable to move. Her muscles, tense with the first contraction of labour, refused to relax themselves. She remembered how Vladimir had commanded her to groan when the Cheka had stopped the train. It had been only a pretence then, but now—when the sound of pain would have been justified and might have brought help—her body seemed too tightly clenched to allow even the smallest whimper to make itself heard. Perhaps she was unconsciously defending the unborn child, endeavouring for a little longer to protect it in the safe warmth of the womb.

The black canopy of night unrolled itself above Kate's head and the snow began to fall again. As the chill of the ground penetrated her clothing she shivered for a while. Then, little by little, she relaxed in the soft warmth of the snow. From time to time her muscles tensed again, forcing her breath out in a grunt of pain: but between contractions she felt herself sinking into unconsciousness.

It was still dark when she awoke, but instead of bright stars in a wide velvet sky the blackness was broken by a spark which she recognised as the smouldering tip of a pine-bark taper. She was wrapped so tightly in blankets that she could hardly breathe, but although her skin was sweating with heat, her bones felt cold. Her head, too, seemed to be frozen, so that she needed to lie for a little while without moving while she tried to remember what had happened.

As she struggled with her memory, so she absorbed the atmosphere. She was indoors, certainly, and to judge by the warmth which comforted her back she had been given the place in which any children of the house would normally sleep, on top of the big stove which served a country family for cooking and heat. There was a smell of smoke and uncured wolfskin, and the steady sound of a spinning wheel.

Cautiously, in case her head should hit the roof, Kate tried to sit up, but was at once conscious of pain. Her hand, swaddled inside the blankets, moved to feel her swollen abdomen and found instead a tender flatness. Even then, alarmed and uncomfortable, she did not call out at once because she could not remember what language she ought to speak.

The sound of spinning stopped and a candle came near. Standing on the ledge at the side of their stove, a peasant couple looked down at her.

"I told you she was alive," the woman said; and then, to Kate, "He was sure you were dead, comrade. But I said no, you were an icicle but icicles can be melted."

"The baby," said Kate. Her mouth was swollen, so that the words emerged indistinctly, but the woman understood.

"Yes, you have a baby. A baby girl."

"Alive?"

"Alive, yes." But the woman crossed herself as she spoke and Kate was afraid.

"May I see her?"

"She's not here," said the man. He spoke more roughly than his wife. "Do you think we could feed two extra mouths?"

"Be silent," said his wife. "How much food has the comrade taken from us? A spoonful of gruel, nothing more."

"Where's my baby?" said Kate. As well as being frightened, she was unhappy. She had so much wanted to experience the birth of her child but it had happened in the end without her knowledge, as though her body were only a machine.

It was the man who answered again, in the same gruff voice. "At the orphanage. What better place? It seemed that she was an orphan in the moment she was born."

"Where is the orphanage? I must get her back." For a second time Kate tried and failed to sit up.

"The orphans live in the old palace of the Aminovs," said the woman. "You can walk to it in ten minutes once you are strong enough. The child isn't lost."

"But who will feed her? Who will look after her?"

"The holy saints will provide. Go back to your chair, Ivan Ivanovich, and leave me to women's work." She fetched a bowl of water and set it down near Kate's head. But instead of washing her she leaned close and spoke in a whisper. "You've come from *him*, haven't you? It's twenty years since he last slipped his messages into that tree, the young rascal. But no one has ever used it since. I watched you searching before you fell. You were looking for a letter. Tell me I'm right. It's *his* baby, is that right too?"

Kate did not answer immediately. Vladimir had been right to warn her that even the most devoted old servant could no longer be trusted to remain faithful. It could be a trap on the part of a clever old woman to send her surly husband away before making a show of friendship.

But she was probably not clever. And she had not yet abandoned her old faith. Now that Kate's eyes were accustomed to the lack of light, she could see the icon in the corner. Besides, if the baby was alive, her life must have been saved by the old woman's care, and who in such circumstances would harm a newborn child? If the baby was dead, Kate did not at this moment very much care what happened. "Yes," she whispered.

"Don't tell *him*," said the old woman, making it clear that on this occasion the emphatic pronoun referred to her husband. "He's afraid of the Red Guards. But he's not unkind. Truly, when he took the child away, he thought you were dead. Have you papers?"

"Yes." Kate tried to fumble for her pocket but realised that her clothes had been taken off her. In any case, the woman gestured for her to be still.

"Not for me. How should I be able to read them? But I can tell *him* that there's no need of concealment. That will make his mind easier." Her hand moved bonily over Kate's body, feeling her breasts. "And you have milk. Good. Then the little one will not be a burden. Sleep now. Tomorrow, in the daylight, we will bring your baby back to you."

2

Eight days later, with baby Ilsa in her arms, Kate stepped over the threshold of the Aminov theatre palace. Once upon a time—and not so very long ago—it had been a miniature Versailles, surrounded by terraces and fountains and by a park planted with trees in the English fashion. Inside the dignified building with its classical design and pale yellow walls, Vladimir and his brother and sister, with their Russian nurse and French and English governesses, had spent much of their childhood, surrounded by every comfort and luxury. Alexa had sung here—less than ten years ago—to an audience of grand dukes and duchesses, princes and princesses. Kate—even in those far-off days disapproving of privilege—had stared in amazement at the diamond bracelet which represented the fee for a single evening's entertainment.

Alexa would not have recognised the palace now. The theatre itself was made of wood, although the fluted pillars which pretended to support the high painted ceilings gave the impression of being marble. They alone—perhaps for that reason—had survived undamaged. Everything else had been pillaged. The chandeliers had probably been smashed only out of spite, but the draperies must have been useful for clothing. The wooden balustrade of the tiered gallery in which the audience sat had already been chopped down for firewood, and now the elaborately patterned parquet floor was being prised up, block by block, for the same purpose.

The thickness of the atmosphere made it difficult at first to see the whole of the former auditorium. Smoke from a fire which smouldered in the middle of the hall mingled with the smells of

cabbage and urine and body sweat. Stepping carefully over the
bodies of children who lay alive but unmoving on the floor Kate
began to explore the building, her eyes widening in horror as her
rough count of the inmates increased. The old woman, whom she
had already learned to call *babushka,* had told her that the old
name of Tsar's Village had been changed to that of Children's
Village because as many of the parentless children of Petrograd as
could be found were sent up to this higher area for their health.
Kate held her baby even more tightly in her arms than before,
realising that if she had died, this would have been Ilsa's home.

Her explorations brought her in the end to what had once been
a kitchen. On the only bed she had so far seen—its iron frame
having presumably survived because it could not be burned—a
middle-aged woman lay dead. A girl of about twelve or thirteen
sprang to her feet at Kate's approach, almost attacking her in despair and anger.

"You're too late!" she cried. "It's three days since I sent the
message. How could she keep alive so long? Three days!"

"The message didn't come to me," said Kate. "Who is in
charge here?"

"Who is there, now that *she* has gone?" The girl began to wail,
as though for the first time admitting the death which must have
taken place twenty-four hours earlier.

"But so many children! They can't just be abandoned. Hush
now, don't cry. If I'm to help you, you must help me first. Tell
me how you came to be here. And when you last had food. And
how many of the children are sick. But first of all, tell me your
name."

The girl's name was Vera; between sobs she told her story. Her
father had been killed at the front; her mother had died of typhus. She had been one of the first to be sent to the Aminov palace, and was amongst the oldest. There had been about eight
hundred orphans in the building two months earlier, but almost
all of them had had influenza. At first they had nursed each
other, but by now they were all too weak. Vera did not know how
many had died. Comrade Nina, the woman who lay dead on the
bed, had done her best to provide rations for the children, but
since she had become ill three weeks earlier they had had only
what they could steal.

"Did she ever tell you who it was who allowed her the rations? Did the food come through the Red Guard or from the District Revolutionary Committee?" It was impossible for a stranger in any area to know whether the civil or military authority was locally in control, and important not to guess wrong.

Vera shook her head. But it was to the Red Guards that she had gone for help three days later. They had seemed kind enough, promising to pass on her message for a doctor to visit Comrade Nina and to arrange for a supply of food. But no doctor had arrived. They had given her a sack of frozen potatoes on the spot, but the man who offered to drag the sack back for her had stopped on the way and demanded to be paid for his trouble. When Vera had explained that she had no money, she had learned that a different kind of payment was envisaged.

At the memory she began to wail again. Kate comforted her briefly, but too much needed to be done for time to be wasted on what was past. Responsibility would provide the best distraction for Vera.

"I want you to look after my baby," she said, putting Ilsa in the girl's arms as she spoke. "She's very tiny and very precious to me, but I'm sure I can trust you to take good care of her while I go into the village and talk to the Revolutionary Committee. I've just fed her, so she'll be happy with you for the next three hours. And you can feel sure that I shall come back. I'm going to look after all of you here—and you will be my chief helper."

She spoke more confidently than she felt. But the need was so great that action of any kind was bound to lead to some improvement. An hour later she was locked in argument with the chairman of the committee, a young railway engineer, as he pointed out the impossibility of finding food where no food existed and Kate reminded him of the community's responsibility to the children of their dead comrades. They both spoke with passion, and the argument would have become heated had Kate not remembered how dangerous it was in these times to make enemies. Even under a self-imposed restraint, however, she could see that her arguments were having some effect. By midafternoon she was back at the palace, congratulating Vera on her success as a nursemaid and collecting a group of the oldest children to act as her aides.

None of them was over twelve and all of them were shabby

and emaciated. Starvation had made some bright-eyed and others
dull and apathetic, but they all lacked energy and Kate saw few
signs of intelligence. Patiently she explained to them several times
how she proposed to put them into pairs and give each pair the
responsibility for one room of the palace. They must bring her a
report on the number of children in their room and say how
many were dead, how many were ill, how many were hungry, how
many were healthy.

While they were gone Kate—with Vera's help—drew a rough
plan of the palace on the whitewashed wall of the kitchen, for
she had no paper. She wrote in the numbers they brought her,
she supervised the removal of those who were dead, she made
quick plans for future organisation. In the evening she went back
to the committee, this time in full session.

"The children will become robbers," she said. "For three weeks
already they've eaten only what they could steal. They've taken
the food which the peasants provide for their horses and they've
burrowed into farm storerooms. Until now they've gone out in
twos and threes, but they're becoming desperate, comrades. If
nothing is done you'll have an army of young bandits on your
hands, organised and violent. If the peasants have food, it's better
that they should surrender it to a legal authority."

Kate knew well enough that this was already happening. Every
town dweller in Russia believed that the countryside was full of
hoarded food. Seizure was taken as a matter of course; only distribution was under debate.

The committee proved sympathetic enough in principle. Its
chairman explained that one official orphanage had been established a year earlier in the palace formerly belonging to the
Tsar. No one has realised how many children, drawn by the
promise of shelter but failing to secure admission to the main orphanage, had established themselves in the neighbouring palaces
of the old nobility. It seemed incredible to Kate—whose months
in Petrograd had been regularly disturbed by official searches and
checks and head counts, with a continuing survey of papers and
permits—that the men responsible for local administration should
not have known the extent of the problem, but she accepted that
this was the case as she saw them in turn accepting her right to
speak for the inhabitants of the old palace.

In theory, at least, the battle was won. For one more night the children would have to exist on promises, but a supply of cabbage would be sent up the next morning and as soon as Comrade Katya supplied a written list naming all the living children a regular ration would be allotted.

With success in sight Kate tried to relax and found herself unable to move. She had started the day still weak from childbirth and from the hypothermia which had followed her collapse in the snow, and had committed herself to a timetable which was emotionally and physically exhausting. She was conscious of the blood draining from her face and the strength leaving her muscles as she tried, but failed, to stand.

The chairman of the committee looked at her curiously.

"You're not well, comrade. When did you yourself last eat?"

Kate was reluctant to mention her stay with the old lodge-keeper's wife. So many actions these days which were innocent and even kind could cause trouble. Instead she muttered something about the recent birth of her baby.

"Then you will eat at my house before you return," he said. "My wife too has had a child and she assures me that every meal she takes herself keeps two people alive."

For a moment Kate hesitated. Ilsa would be sleeping now, but would she be safe with Vera as the thirteen-year-old grew sleepy herself? And was it right to eat when the orphans were starving? The answers came quickly. Whatever food she was offered could not rob them in any way, and it was certainly true that an undernourished mother would not be able to breast-feed her baby for long. She accepted the invitation with gratitude.

The soup contained scraps of bacon fat, and there was bread on the table; it was a feast. But Kate dared not relax, for she found herself being interrogated as she ate—about the future as well as the past. It was necessary to come to a quick decision, and what she decided was that she would stay with the orphans. Their need for someone like herself was desperate. Kate knew herself to be capable of organisation; and once she had obtained the basic essentials of food and warmth, her medical skill would also be needed. It would be worthwhile work—and it would have the inestimable advantage of keeping her in the place which Vladimir had chosen for their reunion, without any of the suspicions which would have been aroused had she continued to visit the lodge without excuse.

But it was one thing to come to a decision and another thing to obtain permission. Since the first heady days of the revolution, Kate had had plenty of time to realise that a desire to do a particular job was often regarded as the most absolute disqualification. So when she was asked about her plans, she took care to mention her medical qualifications but replied in the properly orthodox manner.

"I shall be expected to return to Petrograd. My leave from the hospital was only granted so that I could travel to relations for my confinement. The baby came early, before I had reached them —and as a result I shall not be expected back for another three weeks. So I can afford to spend a little time here. I see the need to stay longer. But naturally my official duties as a citizen of Petrograd must come first."

"I shall apply for your transfer," he said abruptly. "You are more use to us than to them. Your papers, please."

Kate knew better than to go anywhere without them and had no doubts about handing them over to be inspected. Every move increased her security by distancing her from the time when she had been identifiable as an English doctor. Her marriage certificate had given her an official Russian name and Sergei's documentation had ensured that her qualifications and transfer to the appointment in Petrograd were thoroughly authenticated. This man, although brusque, would not be looking for discrepancies but seeking to use her medical skills for the benefit of his community. Even before he nodded and moved the dishes off his end of the table so that he could laboriously copy down details and prepare a letter, Kate recognised that—for the moment—she was safe. And Vladimir's child would be safe with her.

1920

1

Peace had come to England in drab dress. Even now, in 1920, with the second anniversary of the Armistice approaching, people in the London streets seemed shabby to Frisca's critical young eye, and the November sky was heavy with damp, grey clouds. She stared down from the window of Robert's study, waiting for him to come home, depressed by what seemed a conspiracy of gloom against her.

Yet even when her spirits were low, Frisca herself illuminated the unlit room. There was a brightness about her which no temporary depression could subdue. Her golden hair and pale, clear complexion caught the eye, and an exuberance of personality, penetrating even her present sulkiness, uplifted the spirits of anyone who met her.

Frisca herself was well aware of the impression which she made even on strangers, and as a rule she traded on it shamelessly. But for the moment she was concerned to preserve the resentment she felt against her mother. She turned towards the door as she heard her cousin coming up the stairs, but did not move towards him.

A year earlier she would have rushed into his arms, demanding to be hugged and kissed. What held her back today was more than the sense of grievance which she was about to pour out. Ever since she was a baby, Frisca had made it clear that Robert was her hero. Over and over again she had told him that she loved him. It had only been after her thirteenth birthday that she had begun to suspect that she *did* love him, in a manner quite different from anything which her earlier extravagance of compliment might suggest. And so—although her mother would have found the fact difficult to believe—Frisca had grown shy in Robert's presence.

Robert, it seemed, had not noticed any change. But then Robert himself had changed in the year which he spent as a prisoner of war. Frisca had been at Blaize on the day he returned there. She had found herself staring at someone who was almost a stranger, looking far older than his twenty-four years, with the skin stretched tightly over the bones of his face and his sunken eyes withdrawn and blackened with tiredness. His hair had only just begun to grow again after the shaving made necessary by a series of operations. Its bright red waves, which she had once loved to ruffle, had been replaced by a prickly stubble, with a small circle of baldness remaining to indicate the entry point of the bullet which had so nearly cost him his life.

On that day of his return, Frisca had run away to weep. And she had wept again often in the five weeks which followed when, sitting beside the bed in which he drowsed the days away, she realised that he was not exactly sure who she was.

It was her aunt who comforted her then, in a way which perhaps Margaret herself did not realise.

"He's had a bad time, Frisca, and he's very tired. You must be patient. It will take a little while before he sorts out what really happened and what he only dreamt. It's one of the effects of a wound in the head. Nightmares become more real than reality. He doesn't even remember very much about Jennifer, you know. I had to tell him she was dead. He told me how much he'd clung on to the thought of the happiness he'd had with her, and yet he wasn't absolutely sure whether it was something he'd truly enjoyed or whether he'd only dreamt it because he wanted it so much."

It was in that moment that Frisca had realised how completely her rival for Robert's affections had disappeared. Jennifer was more than dead: she had never quite existed.

By now, of course, Robert had recovered and remembered. He would always be deaf in one ear and Frisca had noticed that he was apt to become dizzy and lose his balance if he lowered his head too far—for example, to tie his bootlaces. He was more serious, as well, than before he went to fight. But he still seemed to regard Frisca only as a little cousin, to be romped with and teased. He greeted her now with a pretence of shock.

"And who is this long-legged creature? My, Frisca, how tall you're growing! Have you come up to London for Armistice Day?"

"Mamma wants to spend the night at Glanville House. It's more because it's the anniversary of Poppa's death, I think." Frisca's real father had died before she was born. "Poppa" was Lord Glanville, whom she had loved even before he married Alexa and became her stepfather. "I came round to find out how your examinations are going."

"Over," said Robert. "Last one today."

"How did it go? Did you know all the answers?"

"Hope so. I'll be pretty fed up if I have to take any of them again. I can manage any practical job they set me, but all this book work gives me a headache."

"What's the point of it, then?"

"Assuming I've passed, I'm now a qualified civil engineer. Rather different from being a military engineer. Instead of blowing bridges up or laying temporary railway tracks, I now know how to build them so that they'll last forever; and the certificate which proves that I know should get me a job anywhere in the world."

"But you won't go anywhere in the world, will you?" Frisca expected his reassurance and did not receive it. "Robert! You're not going away?"

Robert's expression was a curious one, mingling excitement and uneasiness. "I can't tell you anything yet, Frisca," he said. "I must talk to Mother first."

"Oh, do tell, Robert. I can keep a secret. I promise I won't say a word. Honour bright."

She could see how much he wanted to share his news, and all her shyness disappeared as she took his hand and set herself to charm the secret from him.

"Well, not only must you keep quiet now, but when you hear the news from Mother you mustn't let on that you already know."

"Promise!"

"All right, then. I was offered a job this morning—a job I applied for a few weeks ago. It depends on passing the exams, of course. But if that's all right, I shall go off to India in January."

"India!" Frisca made no attempt to conceal her dismay but Robert was too excited to notice.

"That's right. Down in the south. There's a big project on foot to build a series of dams. The people who live there have a terrible time. Either it rains too much and all the land floods and they get drowned. Or else it doesn't rain at all and all the crops die and they starve. The dams will help them both ways. They'll hold back the floods and then release the water down irrigation canals when it's needed."

"But it's so far away," Frisca wailed, making no attempt to conceal her distress.

"I want to do something worthwhile, Frisca. If that bullet had killed me, I should have died without ever having been of any use to anyone. It wouldn't have been my fault then: I was too young. But if I die in ten years' time I want to leave something behind me which will make somebody grateful that Robert Scott was once alive. I spent too long killing people. Now I have the chance to help people live a little longer. Do you understand?"

"Aunt Margaret won't let you go."

"I think she will," said Robert. "She won't like it. She'll be unhappy at first. That's why it's very important that you mustn't say anything to her at all. You must leave it to me. But Mother has spent the whole of her life helping other people. She'll be pleased, in her heart, that I want to do the same, even if it's in a different way and in a different place."

Frisca was not convinced. Although in some respects she was selfish, demanding to get her own way and taking for granted the admiration she excited, she was sensitive to other people's feelings. She knew, for example, that Alexa, her own mother, had no very deep feeling for her, and she had learned this by recognising the overwhelming love which her aunt Margaret felt for Robert. Frisca herself had been in a position to see how her aunt had changed in the two months after Robert's return. Once she had survived the shock of first seeing his appearance, all the strain and tiredness of her work at the hospital had fallen away. She looked ten years younger, and the bustle and energy with which she had organised the return to her London home while still occupied in winding down her responsibilities at Blaize had been those of a woman made happy by the presence of the one person to whom she was devoted. Frisca understood the feeling, because she shared it. Aunt Margaret would be very miserable indeed if Robert were to leave.

With such an ally, Frisca decided that she need not upset herself too much just yet. And even as she assured herself that Robert would not be allowed to go, she began to wonder whether it would after all be such a disaster if he did. In India, presumably, he would meet only Indian girls, and he would surely not want to marry one of them. He would work hard while he was out there and then at some time—when he was about thirty, perhaps—he would decide that it was time he looked for another wife. He would come home on holiday to find one—and in the meantime Frisca would have had time to grow up. It had been the only tragedy of her life that she was too young for Robert, and when he married Jennifer she had thought that she must have lost him. But now she had another chance, and she was growing older all the time. Four years would be enough, or even three. If Robert went to India in January for three years she would be just seventeen when he came back. She was so intent on her calculations that she did not notice the firmness with which her cousin changed the subject.

"And now suppose you tell me why you were wearing such a face of thunder when I came into the room."

"Was I?" Frisca had genuinely forgotten; but not for long. "Oh yes. Robert, do you know what Mamma is going to do with me?"

"Tell me. One secret in exchange for another."

"This isn't a secret, worse luck. It all started with my ballet teacher. Beastly old Benina. She measured my feet and my fingers and pretended she could tell from that how much I was going to grow. And she says I'm going to be too tall to be a ballet dancer. So I'm to be sent to prison instead."

"Sounds a rather drastic solution," agreed Robert, but he was laughing. "I take it you mean you've got to go to school at last."

"Yes. But why does it have to be beastly old boarding school? I agree with Mamma that Mademoiselle is useless and that we've both only put up with her because a ballet dancer doesn't need to be brainy. But there are other kinds of dancing besides ballet, and other kinds of school."

"Not near Blaize. The village school would hardly be suitable."

"Well, I could live in London and go somewhere every day instead of being bullied and starved and made to wear a beastly uniform."

"I expect your mother wants to stay at Blaize, though."

"Well, that's exactly it." Frisca put on her most conspiratorial voice. "She has her reasons for that, and for wanting me out of the way. She can't confess them, so she has to make up this ridiculous story about me being a giant."

"I'm sure you're going to be an absolutely perfect height for being a beautiful woman, Frisca," said Robert firmly. "All that Benina means, I take it, is that it's no good if one cygnet or sugarplum fairy is waving her wrist about several inches above all the others. And you'll like boarding school. I did, tremendously. Even Grant's enjoying himself now, although at a boys' school it's difficult if you don't play games. You'll make hundreds of friends and have lots of fun. Why should Aunt Alexa want you out of the way, anyway?"

"So that I don't find out about the new man in her life. He's coming to live at Blaize. She's trying to pretend that he's family. In fact, she says he's a cousin of mine, but that's ridiculous. I've seen him. He's older than she is."

"Who is he?"

"Matthew Lorimer, his name is."

"Well then, he *is* your cousin," said Robert. "He's Arthur's elder brother. What's more, he was very badly hurt in the war. If you've seen him, you must know that he's in a wheelchair."

"What's that got to do with anything?" Frisca demanded.

"Well, it means that he can't exactly be the new man in your mother's life in the way you seem to think."

"Why not?" Frisca waited for an answer but was not given one. "I've seen the way they look at each other, Robert. *I* know when people are in love. She pretends it's all work, that he's just going to design a bit of scenery for her opera house. But that would only take a few weeks, and she's fitted up a whole new studio for him, big enough for him to move around in his wheelchair and paint people's portraits. He's moving in for good."

"It's not easy for a man who's been badly wounded to build up his career again, Frisca," said Robert firmly. "You should be more tolerant. Your mother is Matthew's aunt, and if she's decided to help him, that's just generosity on her part. I'm sure she's very fond of him, but there couldn't be any question—"

Even if there had not been an interruption he would not have succeeded in convincing Frisca, but at this moment the maid knocked on Robert's door.

"If you please, sir," she began; but she in turn was interrupted by his mother's voice calling from below.

"Robert! Robert, come quickly. There's a message from Russia. It's about Kate. She's alive!"

2

It was a new miracle, a second rising from the dead. Margaret read the message over and over again. First Robert had returned to life, and now Kate, although she had not come in person. Margaret looked at the one-armed stranger who had brought the letter. He had introduced himself in careful English as Sergei Fedorovich Gorbatov, but without explaining how he came to be acting as Kate's messenger.

"It gives no address," she said.

"She lives as a Russian. No one at the orphanage where she works knows she is English. If the letter had been read and had contained anything to identify her as an Englishwoman, it would have had bad consequences for her. You must understand that the Civil War has caused harsh feelings in the country, and the support which the Whites have received from England is well known. It was the British blockade, too, which caused many deaths from starvation last winter. Katya has asked me to tell you that she dare not receive letters directly from you. If you care to give me any news of your family, I will write to her in Russian and pass it on in a way that does not reveal where you live."

"If it's so dangerous for an Englishwoman to live there, she

ought to come home," said Robert. "If you were allowed to leave
the country, sir, presumably she would be as well."

"It's not easy to get permission," Sergei said. "I'm allowed to
travel because I'm on a government mission. I don't think Katya's
papers would stand up to the inspection needed for a passport.
But the truth is that she has chosen to stay."

"Read the letter, Robert." Margaret passed it across. In the excitement and shock of its arrival she had kept it to herself, only
exclaiming aloud over the facts it revealed. "She's married a Russian, but apparently he's disappeared. She has to stay where he
can find her if he ever turns up. She has a little girl, as well, who
must be about the same age as Barbara."

"This is not only a matter of family," said Sergei. "The work
she is doing is of great value. If I were to tell you how many children were orphaned in our country by the years of war you would
hardly be able to believe me. Katya is the doctor for two thousand of them. They are all undernourished and some of them are
maimed and in winter most of them are cold. There is plenty for
a doctor to do, I can tell you. I have the greatest admiration for
your niece, madame. I met her first in Serbia—it was she who
taught me my first words of English. From the very first day
of our friendship one thing has been clear to me; that she has no
barriers of nationality in her mind. When she sees a need, she
hurries to fill it. She has seen such a need in the orphanage. She
told me that you yourself had undertaken the same kind of work
once and that you would understand." Sergei paused for a moment. "My affection for your niece is very deep. You must believe
that. If she had asked me to help her leave the country, I would
have done everything in my power. But she made no such
request. She has made the decision to stay, and I respect her for
it."

"What happened to her husband?" asked Robert.

"She married a prince. A dangerous choice in these times. At
the moment when his identity was discovered he was travelling
on permits signed by myself, so for a little while it seemed that
the danger might be contagious. But I was able to prove that he
must have stolen them. His rank, of course, makes it impossible
for Katya to enquire openly about his fate, and in her own interest I have made sure that no one could connect the doctor at

the orphanage with a man—one of many men—arrested by the Cheka."

"Was he killed? Does she know what has happened to him?"

"She will not believe that he is dead. She hopes."

"And you. Do *you* know the truth? Have you told her?"

Sergei gestured with his hand in a manner which could have meant any of several contradictory things, and Margaret felt a moment's uneasiness. They had greeted the stranger as a friend because he brought good news, but everything they knew about Russia since the revolution, and everything he was telling them now, built up a picture of a society ruled by suspicion, in which any kind of knowledge might spell danger. Could he be a government spy and not a friend at all, looking for information which might incriminate Kate in a way her English relations could not even imagine? Or could he, on the other hand, be more than a friend—in love with her, perhaps, and anxious to keep her in Russia so that he could marry her himself one day? So many horrifying stories of betrayal and death had come out of Russia in the past three years that Margaret did not know what to believe. If Kate's husband were really dead, she ought to come back to the safety of her own country. There was plenty for a doctor to do in England as well. As definitely as she could, Margaret made her opinion clear to the Russian, but once again he merely shrugged.

"Any message that you give to me, I will pass on," he said. "If you tell me that you have a home and a welcome waiting for her here, I promise that I will explain that to her. But I think you should not hope too much. Katya is a woman of great determination and strong loyalties. You know that for yourselves, I'm sure. She could have returned to England when she was forced to leave Serbia. When she made the decision to stay with a defeated army, she was well aware that nothing but danger and discomfort lay ahead."

Margaret was silent, knowing that this was the truth. She excused herself for a moment while she sent a message to Alexa at her house in Park Lane. By the time she returned to the drawing room she was already half reconciled to accepting what Sergei had said. She invited him to stay for the night but was not surprised when he refused, agreeing only to dine with them. Doubtless he was no more anxious than Kate to be suspected of having friends in England. So all that remained when the meal was over was to dictate to Sergei the news of everything which had happened to the family in the past four years.

"She knows of her brother's death," Sergei said. "The news upset her very greatly and it was because he died, I think, that she was committed to the ideals of the revolution even before it began. And it's because of his death that she cares so deeply for the orphans who are still alive."

There were other deaths to report: Kate's father, Alexa's husband, Robert's wife—although Kate would not even know that Robert had ever married, or that he was the father of a daughter who was almost three years old by now.

"But there is good news as well," Margaret said. "Her younger brother, Grant: tell her that he lives in England now and that an operation has made it possible for him to walk much more easily. And as a result he has become a happier boy."

"And a fitter one," said Robert. "I've never known such a chap for doing exercises. When I think how fat and lazy he was when he first arrived! Now he seems determined to set himself endurance tests. Where an ordinary boy would do an exercise ten times, nothing less than a hundred is good enough for Grant. He's becoming very tough indeed."

"He will take over her father's property in Jamaica when he is old enough, I suppose," suggested Sergei.

"No." Margaret hesitated, wondering how far it was safe to entrust a stranger with news which would come as a shock to Kate. "No, the land was left to one of Kate's childhood friends, Duke Mattison."

"She has spoken of him to me. The clever black boy, with a talent both for figures and for—" The word for "bowling" had obviously escaped Sergei; instead he swung his one arm vigorously to indicate what he meant.

"Yes, he's a good cricketer. Kate ought to be told, perhaps, that he inherited both his talents from his father. Her father."

By his smile Sergei showed how confident he was that Kate would not mind. He waited with patient interest for the next piece of information.

"What other good news is there?" asked Alexa, who had joined them for dinner to celebrate Kate's being alive. She had been pale when she first arrived, interrupted in a vigil of remembrance for her husband, but now her normal vivacity had returned, as though she had consciously made a decision to change her mood. "You could tell her that her cousin Arthur has been given a baronetcy to go with his fortune—which may now be a little less than before the honour was bestowed. So when he chooses a wife, she will be Lady Lorimer. He must be the most eligible bachelor in Bristol, for he's still unmarried. Be sure to tell Kate that."

It was unkind of them all to laugh, Margaret thought, as she saw that the family reference could only puzzle Sergei. But he added the name to the notes he was making without showing any reaction and then looked across at Frisca, who had been specially allowed to join the adults at dinner.

"And from the evidence of my own eyes I can tell her how beautiful is her young cousin," he said, bowing slightly as he paid the compliment. Margaret, who agreed with it, noticed that Frisca glanced at Robert and flushed very slightly before laughing it off in her usual self-assured manner.

"Since it may be years before we see Kate again," Frisca said, "she'd better have our future news as well as what's happened in the past. You can tell her that I'm going to be a great dancer, even if I *am* a foot taller than anyone else on the stage."

"Well, if we're to talk about the future, she may like to know what's happening at Blaize," Alexa added. "That's the name of my house in the country," she explained for Sergei's benefit. "Before Kate left for Serbia, she helped to turn it into a hospital for wounded soldiers. Now the house has been restored as a home, and the theatre will open again for opera next summer."

She went on to give details of the productions she planned in a way which Margaret felt would be of limited interest to Kate, so far away and in such a different society. Margaret allowed her attention to wander, realising that the significance of the conversation only indirectly related to what was being said. Alexa's emergence from her bereavement was almost complete. She was no more than forty-three years old and it was right that she should have picked up the threads of her life again and made plans for the years to come. When the enthusiastic flow of words came to an end, Margaret looked at her son.

"And what about you, Robert? What message will you send to Kate about the future?"

In the silence which followed, Margaret knew at once that something was wrong. The Russian was merely waiting politely to hear what else he should note; and Alexa's expression, too, revealed nothing more than a normal interest. But Frisca was almost literally holding her breath, while Robert's face reminded his mother of that earlier occasion when—knowing that she was bound to disapprove—he had broken the news to her that he had volunteered for the Army.

"Well?" she asked.

"I have some plans, certainly," said Robert. He made the admission with reluctance. "But I'd like to discuss them first of all with you, Mother."

"That means that Kate will never know. And after such an ominous hint, I shan't be able to sleep until I know what you're proposing. So you might as well confess at once."

She tried to keep her voice light as she spoke, and with a similar effort sought to maintain an untroubled expression on her face as Robert, still reluctantly, told her of his intention to go to India. The blow fell on her like a landslide. He must have realised it, because he came across and sat on the arm of her chair, putting his hand on her shoulder.

"You have responsibilities here," was all she allowed herself to say. "Barbara."

"Yes, I know." His grip tightened for a moment. "I can't go without your cooperation. That's why I wanted to talk about it privately with you."

"We'll think about it tomorrow, then," she said. Her attempt to pretend that nothing disturbing had taken place evidently did not deceive her visitor, who put away his notebook and stood up to take his leave.

"But you have to let us know where Kate is!" exclaimed Margaret. Her voice quavered under the two shocks of the evening. Just as Robert, who had earlier returned from the disappearance which might too easily have signified his death, was about to leave again, so too it seemed that Kate had only briefly come back to life and would now slip into invisibility in the blackness of a closed society. "I understand everything you've said about the danger to her of having connections in England. But in case something really important should happen—here or there—we must have some idea of where to look for her. You've told us that because of your own affection for Kate you would never do anything to harm her. Well, you must believe that our love is at least no less than yours. We won't write to her, but we need to know where she is."

Sergei had already taken Margaret's hand as he prepared to say goodbye to her. For a moment he stared steadily into her eyes. "Knowledge that cannot be used is like a long fuse leading to a hidden bomb," he said. "The day comes when it is tempting to light the fuse, just to see where it leads." He lifted her hand to his lips but, although his manners might be prerevolutionary, Margaret recognised the ruthlessness with which he was rejecting her plea.

After he had gone and Frisca had been taken home to bed by Alexa, Robert lingered for a moment in the drawing room; but Margaret knew that she was too upset to be either kind or rational.

"After the service tomorrow," she said. "We'll think about it then."

But the next day, Armistice Day, imposed thoughts of its own. Margaret's house in Queen Anne's Gate was so near to Westminster Abbey that the family party did not emerge until an hour before the procession bringing the body of the Unknown Warrior for burial was due to arrive at the abbey. They found the streets already packed with men and women dressed in black. Margaret had not expected that the crowd would be so great, and—because she was not tall—realised that she would see nothing of the ceremony.

She would hear it, however. Six years earlier Brinsley had left for France to the sound of a military band. Now the sound of another military band brought back memories of his departure, but it was a different sound—not the cheerful strains of Tipperary, with fifes and piccolos disporting themselves in high-pitched mischief, but the slow, muffled drumbeat of a funeral march. And it was greeted not with the cheers of a crowd which could have no conception of what lay ahead, but with the tears of a nation which had had time to count the cost. Three quarters of a million men had gone out to fight and had not returned. Now one of them was being brought home.

The sound came nearer, masking the slow footsteps of the escort. Military orders were given: the music stopped. There was a curious stiffening as the men in the crowd straightened their shoulders and held up their heads until, without any ostentatious movement, they were standing at attention. The women, by contrast, bowed their heads as though they were in church. During the hours of waiting there had been conversation and movement, but when the slow drumbeat came to an end, the crowd became quiet and still. Thousands of living people, sharing a single emotion, were together—and spontaneously—paying tribute to the silence of death.

Intense and oppressive, the absolute silence extended for what seemed a very long time. It was broken in the end not by any sound but by an almost imperceptible change in the atmosphere as the men and women in the crowd began to listen for the muffled sounds of the burial rites. Margaret's concentration, too, was broken, and she could not prevent her thoughts from returning to the bombshell that Robert had dropped on the previous evening.

In her mind the two subjects merged. There was a connection between what was happening in the abbey and Robert's plans for the future—although an hour earlier she would not have been able to recognise it. She had not been conscious of any change of heart during the long and emotional silence, but at the end of it she had accepted a new idea. The partings and losses of the war must be seen for what they were—memories, not a continuing part of everyday life. Those who had died were dead: those who were still alive must make plans for their future lives—otherwise, what point would there be in their survival?

It was right that everyone should look ahead: that Frisca should dream of dancing, that Alexa should shake off the grief of her bereavement and plan for the reopening of her theatre, that Matthew should come to terms with his injuries and refuse to let them bring his career as an artist to an end. It would not be reasonable to expect that Robert alone should stand still, frozen in the role of the only son of a widow, returning from the dead and bound to stay within her sight in order to reassure her that he was still alive. Margaret was glad that she had managed to control her first reaction of distress at Robert's news.

He would come back, after all. This would be a different kind of parting from those of the war years. Robert would build his dams and then come home again. And in the meantime he would leave Barbara behind to give her grandmother, like everyone else in the family, a window to the future.

From the door of Westminster Abbey came the clear, poignant sound of a bugle playing the Last Post. Margaret could see tears on many of the faces around her, but she lifted her own head high in a determination to be happy. Frisca still needed her love and support, and for Grant and little Barbara she would for many years be the only family they could call their own.

I am a lucky woman, Margaret told herself—for what pleasure would retirement have had to offer with nothing to do? When the crowd began to disperse she put her arm round Robert's waist, hugging him gently; and as he looked down at her she accepted all his plans by her smile. The war had cast a long shadow, and perhaps she had been slow to recover from its pains and partings. But it had ended two years ago, and it was time to free herself of its fears, to step out of the gloom and into the sunshine. It was right that her son should look into the future and see only peace and happiness ahead.

BOOK TWO

The Lorimers at Peace

PART I

NEW LIVES

(1923–1926)

1923

1

The deluge came to an end as abruptly as it had begun four hours earlier, startling Robert by the silence which replaced the persistent drumming of water on the roof of the rest bungalow. The monsoon season was drawing to a close at last—but still, at this moment, there was water everywhere. It puddled the red earth of the paths, trickled from the roofs of the village houses, and rose from the ground in a carpet of steam as the sun beat down from a suddenly cloudless sky. Robert had left England at the end of 1920, so this was his third year in the south of India, but he still found it an extraordinary thought that a village which seemed in danger of flooding each October would undoubtedly be parched in May. The wells would be dry, the animals gaunt, and disaster only a week or two away from the whole community —until the rains came again.

Well, it was his business to break that pattern, if they would let him. That was why he was here. He dressed after his siesta and, anxious for exercise, strolled to the edge of the ridge on which most of the village huts were clustered.

At this time of the late afternoon the centre of activity was the swollen river below. In the separate areas ordained by custom, small boys were scrubbing the grey skins of water bullocks, women were washing clothes, and men were performing their own ablutions. The fronds of coconut palms and banana plants, made heavy by the weight of rain, were almost visibly stretching themselves, rising again towards the sun.

Robert sat down on the trunk of a tree which had fallen during

the previous year's cyclone and enjoyed the coolness which came
with the setting sun. As the light faded, the villagers made their
graceful way home, climbing the slope in single file, straight-
backed beneath the loads which they carried on their heads. Further up the river from the washing area, oil lamps began to
flicker. They were in the temple area, the cause of his visit to
Chotapur. He heard the raucous blast of a wind instrument—it
was something between a trumpet and a clarinet, but he did not
know what it was called—and the beating of drums, slowly at
first, but gradually increasing in tempo. On the previous evening,
careful to remain out of sight in the shadows outside the temple,
he had watched the evening ceremony, so he knew what would be
happening now. Siva the god was being brought out for food and
recreation.

Robert had not been able to see the god, who was enclosed in a
silver litter, and he had found the procession a rather scruffy
affair. It was conducted at a run by the priest and the boys who
carried the litter, pausing in only the most perfunctory way beside
the plates of food left by worshippers and tossing flower petals
ahead as carelessly as Robert back in England might have tipped
a shovelful of coal on the fire. At the end of it all, Siva was not
returned to his own shrine but left with the goddess Meenakshi
for the night. It was, Robert supposed, a reasonable routine for a
god whose chief attribute was fertility.

Under the next stage of a project to dam three rivers as part of
an irrigation scheme, the temple area—a considerable distance
from the village, and at a lower level—was due to be flooded.
Robert himself, busy with the practical construction of the first
dam, had not previously been involved in the actual siting of the
next stage. But the workmen who had been sent four months
earlier to peg out the ground had been chased from the village
with stones when it was realised that their strings and poles were
condemning Siva to death by drowning. It had been thought ad-
visable for a sahib to explain the necessity for the exercise with all
the authority of his white skin. By arriving at the end of the monsoon, Robert had hoped that he would find the temple flooded by
the swollen river, as yet undammed. But the stone wall which
enclosed the area had been soundly built. The water, although

lapping against one side, did not penetrate the huge blocks of granite.

A meeting on the site had been arranged for the next morning. He made his way there at the appointed time, breathing the air deeply as he went. There was no sign of rain. Later in the day, no doubt, the humidity would rise again, but the dawn coolness was delightful. The air seemed to sparkle with freshness, and his step was almost equally light as he found himself almost running down the slope.

The old men were waiting for him—not just the priests, but all the elders of the village, most of them so thin and shrivelled that their bony knees and shoulders almost concealed the rest of their bodies as they squatted silently on the ground.

The schoolteacher, however, had not yet arrived. He was a young man attached to the big mission school in Trichinopoli, whose task was to travel amongst a group of villages, holding classes which were a mixture of ordinary school and Sunday school. Robert could have brought one of his own staff to act as interpreter, but had decided that a man from another village might be regarded as even more dangerously foreign than an Englishman; so he had made an arrangement with the teacher, who had been born here. It was almost certain that the head priest and most of his supporters could speak English, but Robert accepted their right to pretend otherwise.

For a little while after the first motions of greeting had been performed he waited, as silent as those who faced him. Robert was by nature punctual—no one brought up by Margaret could be anything else—but he was also patient. Unlike many of his countrymen, he felt no urge to convert India to a European pace of life. When at last he summoned one of the small boys who were always within earshot, the message he sent was a reminder of the disrespect being shown to the guardians of the temple. The sun rose higher in the sky, and Robert had time to study more closely the temple which he was proposing to destroy.

It was not a beautiful building. The tower above the sanctuary was crudely carved with figures which had been equally crudely painted, giving them the bright pink-and-blue look of a fairground. The pillars of the temple were black and heavy, and round the outside of its walls was another set of carvings, less garish but more disturbing. They showed Siva in all his aspects: Robert knew the stories well enough to recognise them. The most striking was in the porch: a relief of Siva dancing. His legs and four arms formed a decorative pattern but the expression on his face was sly and tempting—the face of a human seducer allowed to have divine powers.

The teacher, Padan, arrived at last, taking care over his distribution of apologies and excuses. To Robert he explained that one of the English teachers from the mission had arrived without warning to inspect his class. That would be Eleanor Dunlop, Robert thought, controlling his amusement. Eleanor was new to the country and had not yet accepted its ways. In a little while she would learn the importance of preserving the dignity of subordinate teachers in front of their classes, even at the expense of efficiency. He felt sorry for Padan, torn between two duties, but was not prepared to release him from his promise of help.

Speaking slowly, so that the old men could understand even before the translation began, Robert explained the benefits of the dam which was to be built. He reminded them of the flood which had so often washed away animals as well as crops. He pointed the way into their own memories. Everyone in the village knew how often a harvest failed for lack of water, but the listeners here were old enough to recall the great drought, when the monsoon had failed for three years in succession and there had been starvation throughout the country. "How many men and women live in Chotapur today who were born in those years?" he demanded rhetorically. "I can tell you the answer. There are none: because the women had no milk and their babies died. When the dam is built, such a terrible time will never come again."

The answer was simple and dignified. The gods had been consulted on the matter and had agreed that it would be good for the land and the people that water should run in canals throughout the year. There was no objection to the construction of a dam. But it could not be built where the poles of the workmen had been placed.

Robert tried again. The line of the poles had not been chosen without good reason. A dam must have a particular shape. It must be placed in exactly the right position to take the weight of the water which would press against it. It must have regard to the strength of the land on which it was built, making use of natural rock, curving in conformance with the contour of hills and valleys.

Suddenly the old men, until then so quiet, burst into a babble of sound from which Padan extracted a single objection.

"They say that a little distance could make no difference—just so that the high wall would pass behind the temple instead of through the enclosure."

"But it would make much difference." Robert turned to point towards the ridge on which Chotapur itself stood. "If the village itself is not to be in danger, there must be no gap between what we build and the line of the hill. The curve of our wall will hold the water back, but only as long as there is no escape. That some of the land nearest to the river will be under water all the year cannot be helped. And although the dam cannot be moved, the temple could. I would send my men. They have machines to lift heavy stones and they are very skilful. We could rebuild your temple for you—either only a little way away, or in a new place which would be more convenient for the villagers. Where we are now is a long way for a sick man or an old man to walk in the heat of the day."

"To be moving the sacred stone is not possible." This time Padan spoke for himself, without needing to be prompted by the priest.

"Which one is that?"

Padan spoke to the priest, asking permission. Then he led Robert up the steps in the porch to the edge of the sanctuary, although preventing him from going further inside. Robert needed a moment for his eyes to adjust themselves to the darkness. But gradually he was able to make out the phallic shape of the Siva lingam, its tip daubed with vermilion paint.

"We could move that," he said. "It could be done with great respect, under the supervision of the priest."

The priest himself came up to join them. As Robert had suspected, he spoke English well.

"You are not understanding," he said. "It is not the stone which makes the ground sacred. It is the ground which makes the

stone sacred. The temple was built here because this is holy
place."

"Why?" asked Robert. Doubtless some story would be produced, that Siva himself had stopped here on one of his amorous
adventures. It should, he thought, be possible to twist such a
story to suit his own wishes. But the priest, having made his
point, had retreated again into noncomprehension, and Padan
could only shrug his shoulders. "It has always been so," he said.

It was difficult for Robert not to feel irritated. That work of
such importance should be delayed by an objection which could
hardly be regarded as rational was difficult to accept. The porch
was cool, and he used it as a forum for his argument while the
villagers clustered round the foot of the steps. He offered prosperity and health and he offered them reasonably, but was met only
with stubbornness.

"Let me show you," he said at last. He walked briskly down the
steps and out of the enclosure and began to draw on a patch of
still-muddy earth with a stick. After even a brief period in the
shade the sun struck at his eyes. And the stick was too short. He
was forced to bend down, to press hard into the mud, and
realised too late that he was using the stick to support himself as
his head swam with the dizziness which had often attacked him.
He anticipated the snapping of the stick even before it happened,
and was still conscious as his forehead hit the ground.

When he opened his eyes again he was in bed in his own darkened room, cooled by the steady swish of a punkah. He called for
the bearer, but it was Eleanor who came.

"On the first day after the monsoon ended, it was foolish to
stand for so long in the sun," she said severely.

"It wasn't sunstroke," he said. There was something in
Eleanor's assertive voice which brought out the argumentative
side of everyone who met her, and Robert was no exception. "I
was wounded in the head during the war. This happens from
time to time. As long as I don't happen to be standing on the
edge of a cliff, it's not important."

He could have stood up, brisk and well-balanced, to prove his
point, but was trapped beneath the sheet by the realisation that
he was naked. Eleanor possibly surmised this and prepared to
withdraw.

"I've brought my cook over to your bungalow," she said. "We can have dinner together."

It was one of the first things he had noticed about Eleanor when she arrived in Trichinopoli. As an unmarried woman confronted with an unmarried man in any merely social situation she became shy, even frightened, although she was no longer a young girl. But if in any way she could control the relationship, twisting it into some aspect of her own life in which she felt confidence, she became opinionated and bossy. This was clearly going to be one of those occasions. She was a teacher, not a nurse, but at least for this evening Robert had been fitted into the stereotype of a patient being bullied for his own good.

He didn't mind too much. Most of his working days were spent in country areas where he was the only European, but there was a club at Trichinopoli at which he spent his rest periods. The head of the mission and the unmarried ladies on his staff tended to restrict their social contact with the English community to those members of it who attended church on Sundays, and Robert was not amongst them. But one day the mission's sewage system, never efficient, had developed a fault beyond the power of any local plumber to diagnose. It had been cured at once after Robert had explained the simpler principles of water levels, and Eleanor and her colleagues had since that time been prepared to recognise him as a respectable acquaintance. Robert, for his part, was not a recluse by inclination and accepted any social contacts with pleasure. He had no feeling of warmth towards Eleanor but was always prepared to argue with her.

Over an almost tasteless English dinner—Eleanor obviously had no intention of going native by allowing curries to be served —it became clear that argument was on the menu.

"You're not going to let them get away with it, I hope." Eleanor was on the attack even before they had settled themselves at the table.

"With what?"

"Making you change your plans just for the sake of a heathen temple."

"It wouldn't be impossible," Robert said. "I wasn't going to admit that in the first round, so to speak, because it will mean extra work for me, and a very slight extra risk for them while the construction is in progress; but it could be done."

"Why should it, though? We're here to destroy Hinduism. What better way to start than by sweeping away one of their gods for such an excellent reason?"

"*You* may be here to destroy Hinduism. I'm most certainly not. Indeed, if that's really your aim, I think it utterly misguided."

He was amused to see how deeply he had shocked her, so that for a moment she was forced to struggle for words.

"But you agree—you must agree—that Christianity offers the only hope for these poor people."

"I lost four years of my life while the Christian nations were killing each other," Robert told her. "And now I come here and I find no wars, no murders—"

"That's due to British rule," Eleanor interrupted.

"Partly, I agree. But it has something to do with the fact that the Hindus are gentle people, passive, accepting life as they find it. I have a great deal of sympathy with that attitude."

"You're trying to change their lives as much as I am."

"I'm trying to remove some geographical disadvantages so that they can continue to live their lives in the way they wish but for rather longer than before. When this scheme is complete, it will be possible for a farmer to grow three paddy crops a year where now he can only manage one, and that only if the monsoon comes at the right time. You're telling them about miracles which happened two thousand years ago. I'm performing a miracle here, on their own doorstep, in their own time."

He wished that he had the gift of words, so that he could convey to Eleanor the love and respect for the people of the villages and the satisfaction which his work gave him. India had won his heart almost as soon as he arrived—but what he loved was India as it was, not as Eleanor would like it to be. His argument, unfortunately, had played into her hands.

"Well then," she said triumphantly. "That all goes to show that you shouldn't let superstition get in the way of your miracle. You could get the temple moved, you know, by doing a little damage."

"How do you mean?"

"It's important, they say, that everything should be perfect.

There's something inside a Siva temple. I don't know what it is, but I've been told it's obscene."

Robert remembered the lingam and once again suppressed a smile. He strongly suspected Eleanor of being so unsophisticated that if she were to see it for herself the shape would have no significance for her: it would have to be explained before she could be shocked. For the time being it seemed simpler to agree.

"Well, if it were cracked," she said, "it wouldn't be sacred any more. Just another stone. They'd move the temple then, without thinking twice about it."

"What a ruthless young woman you are," he said, smiling openly now. He saw her take a breath to argue again, but the conversation was too predictable. She would talk about the importance of spreading the Truth, and it was a truth which Robert felt to be irrelevant; but he did not want to quarrel. Deliberately he changed the subject, enquiring about the education of the children in Chotapur.

Eleanor, like Robert himself, went to bed early in order to take advantage of the cool working hours of early morning. He moved towards the door as she stood up to leave, ready to escort her back to the village house which the mission owned, but she paused as her attention was caught by his photographs.

"You carry your family round with you."

"Yes." There were three photographs in the folding leather frame which could be opened out like a triptych. "That's my mother. And that's my daughter."

"Your daughter! I didn't know—" Eleanor checked herself. "So that's your wife, I suppose. She's very beautiful."

"No," said Robert. "My wife died soon after Barbara was born." He looked at the third photograph. Frisca sent him a new picture of herself every year, and the change from child to young woman was proving to be a startling one. For one thing, she had had her hair cut short. And this year she had patronised a professional photographer, whose lighting had emphasised her blondness even in black and white. He had taken her with her head thrown back, laughing, and had faded the background into mistiness. The effect was to make her appear a beautiful woman of twenty-six rather than a schoolgirl of sixteen—and either she

was wearing lipstick or else the appearance of it had been added
in a touching-up process. "No, Frisca's only a cousin of mine."

"A rather special sort of cousin, judging by her looks."
Eleanor's voice held a touch of tightly controlled criticism.
Eleanor herself strained her dark hair back into a tight bun, and
her well-scrubbed skin, innocent of makeup, was rapidly losing its
English bloom under the attack of the Indian sun. She was thin
and flat-chested rather than slim, and her clothes were chosen to
cover, not adorn her. She was not ugly—in fact, her strong features might have been described as handsome—but everything
about her appearance proclaimed the fact that to take any interest in it would be sinful vanity. If she were condemning Frisca as
frivolous on the strength of a photograph which so clearly
projected a wish to impress, it would hardly be surprising.

"Oh yes," Robert agreed lightly. He opened the door of the
bungalow for Eleanor to precede him. "A very special sort of
cousin, certainly. But only a schoolgirl still."

2

Running away, running away, running away, finished with
school now, finished with school now, finished with school now.
The train screamed with excitement as it rushed towards a tun-
nel, plunged into darkness, emerged to a landscape of peaceful
stone villages and grazing sheep. Out of the lavatory window flew
grey felt hat, grey flannel skirt, grey flannel blazer, grey woollen
stockings. A demure schoolgirl had left her seat ten minutes
earlier. The young woman with bright bobbed hair who made her
way now to a different part of the train was wearing makeup
which did not conceal the flush of excitement on her normally
pale cheeks. Her short skirt revealed a slim length of silk stocking
and her eyes sparkled with hope. Clutching the bag which held
her dancing shoes and clothes, Frisca sat on the edge of her seat
and waited for London to arrive.

It was not part of her plan to cause anxiety or distress to anyone. Her mother thought she was still at school. And Miss

Brownlow, noting the royal connections of the lady whose signature Frisca had so carefully forged, had easily been persuaded to issue an *exeat* for her pupil to attend a christening service as godmother. There had been a few well-chosen words on the Christian responsibilities of such a role and some routine questions about the arrangements for meeting Frisca off the train. Miss Brownlow was a snob whose attitude to her pupils was largely determined by the titles of their parents. Frisca was not an Honourable, but she was the daughter of a Lady, which was the next best thing.

Miss Brownlow also lacked the suspicious instinct essential to the task of running a school. It had never occurred to her that one of her pupils might subscribe to a periodical which advertised opportunities to appear on the stage, and allowed ladies and gentlemen who were temporarily available for such opportunities to mention the fact in print. Frisca was on her way to an audition.

She felt no guilt about deserting her studies. The school had been given a fair chance to prove itself useful, but after three years her French and German were worse than when she had arrived, her maths were as bad as they always had been, she had been introduced to Latin and biology and found them both boring, and even English had been reduced to incomprehensible rules about parsing and participles. The optional extras should have proved more fun, but although she was the best actress in the school she was always made to take a male part because she was not only tall but slim-hipped and small-breasted. She was by far the best dancer in the school as well, but in the annual concert was allowed only a single solo because her grace in an ensemble showed up the awkwardness of the other girls. It was true that she had discovered the pleasures of gymnastics, but that seemed a small return for the enormous fees which her mother was paying for her education. Smugly, Frisca assured herself that in a week or two she would not only be saving on the fees but even earning her own living. The train gave one last whistle to announce its arrival in London and began to slow down.

"I hope you're not expecting me to solve the unemployment problem single-handed," said the dance director, Mr. Watts, two hours later to the crowd of girls assembled on the small stage. If he felt any enthusiasm for the task of picking twelve dancers out of the dozens who had arrived for the audition, he was careful not to show it, and Frisca tried equally hard to conceal her dismay. She had not expected so much competition—and to judge by the conversations in the changing room, most of her rivals, even if they were not established performers, were at least thoroughly accustomed to auditioning for chorus work. She had assumed that talent and determination must ensure her success; but probably most of these girls had talent and were as determined to escape from poverty as she was from education. She pinned the number she had been given on to the left shoulder of her leotard and hung back so that she need not be in the first line of dancers to high-kick their way from the back of the stage to the front.

The audition continued for longer than she had expected. A third of the girls were dismissed after the first attempt at precision dancing, and a dozen more failed the tap-dancing test. Divided into groups, the remainder were made to perform a more complicated routine after a demonstration from the dance director, and this also led to eliminations. But when the rest were told to line up across the stage in order of height, there were still twice as many dancers as were needed.

Frisca was at the end of the line. Not for the first time she cursed her height. As unobtrusively as possible she bent her legs and pushed her hips back, trying to level with her neighbour. There was a shout from the darkness of the stalls, where the producer and dance director were conferring: "You at the end, stand up straight."

Frisca did as she was told, and at the same time stretched out one leg in a ballet dancer's position. At least one advantage of being tall was that she had good legs, long and slim. She flashed her eyes in what she hoped was a seductive fashion, practised in the mirror on returning from holiday visits to the movies. "And cut out the glad-eye," said the voice. "All right, girls. Relax, but stay in line."

Frisca was too tense to join in the chattering which broke out. She watched anxiously as Mr. Watts made his way on to the stage, followed by another man who was presumably Mr. Goldie, the producer—a dark-haired man in his late thirties who seemed, from the difficulty with which he climbed the steps, to have an artificial leg.

Mr. Watts came first to Frisca. "Sorry, darling," he said, crossing through her number on a list. "Thank you for coming."

Frisca could feel her face sagging with disappointment. She had been nervous as the time of the audition approached and in the days before that she had told herself over and over again that no one could expect to succeed at the first attempt. Nevertheless, that was exactly what she had expected to do. It had never really occurred to her that she could fail.

Her misery must have been clear to the dance director, for he lingered a moment longer than was necessary. "Too tall, I'm afraid, darling," he said. "You dance very nicely. If I had another beanpole as good as you, I'd see what I could do about it. But I can't do much with just one. Sorry."

"Just a minute," said the producer. He had caught up by now and was staring hard at Frisca. "Where have I seen you before?"

"I don't think you have, Mr. Goldie." His name had been printed in the advertisement which brought her here.

"No previous experience?"

Frisca shook her head. She was so near to tears that it would be too dangerous to lie. But another emotion fought with her disappointment. The producer was looking at her so closely that she began to be frightened. She knew from films and magazines what was sometimes expected of young girls with stage ambitions. She was not, of course, afraid of being coerced. Surely no one would dream of making an improper suggestion in such a public place— and if he did, she could always say No and walk away. What frightened her was the intensity of her own ambition. Would she have the courage to resist an advance if the films and magazines turned out to have been painting a true picture of the price to be paid for a girl's first stage job?

"What's your name?"

"Frisca Glanville." She had been legally adopted by her stepfather and given his name at the time of his marriage to her mother.

For a moment longer he stared at her, frowning, and then suddenly laughed in recognition.

"Glanville. Got it! You're Lady Glanville's daughter."

There was a groan from the man at his side. "Not another deb!"

"Lady Glanville is Alexa Reni." Mr. Goldie turned back to Frisca. "Christmas 1916. The theatre ward at Blaize. You did a song and dance act, the whole length of the ward, down one side and up the other. And when we'd finished cheering, you did the whole round again, kissing every man who'd got his eyes open."

Frisca felt herself blushing. "I was very young," she said.

"Yes, you were. You were indeed. So how old are you now?"

"Nearly seventeen," she told him, reluctantly truthful.

"And does your mother know you're here?"

"Well, not precisely here at this moment, but she knows I want to follow her on to the stage. And dancing is what I can do."

Mr. Watts interrupted impatiently. "Hugo, however sweetly she may have kissed you when you were at death's door, and whoever her mother may be, she's still too tall for the chorus."

"Clear the stage!" called the producer. He turned back to Frisca. "Have you got a party piece?" he asked. "If so, give your music to the pianist. Or tell him what you want and he'll play it anyway. I won't ask you to astonish my friend here, but see whether you can impress him. You have two minutes."

Frisca wasted no time. She was ready for exactly this opportunity to show off—lacking experience in chorus auditions and not expecting such a crush of applicants, she had assumed that each girl would be expected to dance individually. Although realising that they could never provide her with a career, she was still having ballet lessons, but a classical solo had not seemed an appropriate offering for a musical comedy. Instead, she had prepared an acrobatic dance which showed off her athletic grace as well as the nimble neatness of her footwork. To end it, she leapt into the air and landed by doing the splits. The girls in her dormitory, enjoying a preview the previous evening, had applauded with a vigour which had brought the house monitor indignantly along the corridor to send them back to bed with conduct marks all round, but today Frisca was received in silence. The dance director refused to look interested and the remaining girls clearly resented the special treatment. Even Mr. Goldie was not prepared to praise her.

"Wait in the wings and see me afterwards," he said. "Right, Bert, what are we left with?"

Frisca, shivering with cold after the exercise but not daring to move away for her coat, watched as more names were crossed off the list. She counted the girls who remained. There were twelve of them, and twelve was the number needed. As they were put through one last routine to check that their appearance as well as their dancing abilities combined well, she set herself to control her disappointment.

Half an hour later, the stage was empty except for the pianist.

"Frisca Glanville, back on stage!" called the producer. The lights had been dimmed by now, so she could see him as he sat halfway back in the stalls, huddled in a black overcoat. "Can you sing?" he asked.

"Of course." By her mother's standards, Frisca had no voice at all, but her mother's standards were impossibly demanding. Frisca had none of the power required of an opera singer: her voice was high, but too light. But she had inherited Alexa's perfect ear. She sang in tune and made a pleasant enough sound. Correctly interpreting Mr. Goldie's gesture, she crossed to the piano and from the music on offer chose a song from *Lilac Time*.

"Now something a little less ladylike," said Mr. Goldie when she had finished. "Give me 'Yes, We Have No Bananas,' and belt it out."

This too was received in silence.

"All right, Jack, we shan't need the piano anymore, thank you very much," called the producer. "Miss Glanville, get something warm on and come back here."

Some of Frisca's anxiety returned as five minutes later she sat down a few seats away from him. She wished that he would smile, instead of staring at her with such concentration.

"I need to have a word with your mother," he said. "Will you fix up a meeting for me?"

"No," said Frisca. "If I go to her and tell her that I've got a job, that's one thing. She'll be surprised, but she'll be pleased as well. But if she finds out that I'm only *trying* to get a job, she'll tell me not to be stupid."

"I remember the first time I ever saw your mother," he told

her. "Alexa Reni she was then, not Lady Glanville. I was just a boy, and she was marching in some sort of procession. Votes for Women, I think it was. Singing at the top of her voice as she marched. Her voice was still one of the best in the world, and she was the most beautiful creature I'd ever seen. More than just beautiful. Determined, as well. A strong personality, I would say. Someone who would respect ambition in her daughter, and encourage it."

"What my mother respects is success," said Frisca. "She expects everyone to be at the top of the tree. She hasn't got much use for anyone who fails."

"You're not going to fail," said Mr. Goldie. "All we have to decide is how you start. Before the war, I was a dancer. And then my leg was shot away. There's not much scope for one-legged dancers on the London stage. That day in Blaize, I was lying in bed feeling pretty sorry for myself. No career, no money, no house, no girl, no future. It's not quite like Bert said. I wasn't at death's door. But you—how old were you then? Eight or nine?— you brightened up the ward. Brightened the day. Nothing changed, but nothing seemed quite so black again." He gave her a sudden severe glance. "I don't propose to be sentimental about this. Bert's quite right that you're useless as a chorus girl. Not only because you're too tall and he hasn't got anyone to balance you. It's because you catch the eye too much. You're a soloist. I can see you as a star, but I can't see you as an unobtrusive hoofer in the back row. The problem is that stars don't spring from nowhere. They have to have experience, they have to be professional, and on top of their talent they have to provoke the sort of bally-hoo that builds up a queue at the box office."

"Then how does one begin?" asked Frisca bitterly. "If you can't start at the top and people won't let you start at the bottom, what are you supposed to do?"

"I might be able to offer you a slot as understudy. That's in my sphere, not Bert's. You'd go into the chorus whenever anyone fell out: he wouldn't object to you for an occasional evening. But on top of that, you could understudy for the soubrette. It's not much of a life, being an understudy. Rehearsing, hanging around. All the tedium and none of the glamour. But then, when you'd worked your way into the company, if you showed you could do the job, it wouldn't be impossible to arrange for the understudy to get her chance one evening. And if the buzz went round in advance that she was Alexa Reni's daughter, we'd have a good chance of getting the critics back again. There are a lot of people who remember your mother. Not just the opera buffs from before the war, but all the chaps in the Army who went to her concerts. I'd need to be sure that she'd cooperate, though, if we ever got that far; that she'd let her name be mentioned."

"I don't want to owe a career to the fact that I'm Alexa Reni's daughter," Frisca protested. "I want to earn it for myself."

"Now you're talking like someone out of a Victorian Sunday school prize book. You can do the earning part when somebody's watching you. What you have to do before that is to get yourself into a position where you can be watched. That's a matter of luck, not talent—always. And to have a useful mother is a more respectable sort of luck than most sixteen-year-old girls can count on. Of course, it may be that you're only trying to get away from your mother, and don't really care about a stage career at all. If that's the case, I can understand your objection."

"No," said Frisca. "We get on well. But I want to show her that I can stand on my own feet."

"That comes later. I'd bet my bottom dollar that if you asked your mother how she got started in opera, you'd find that there'd been someone to give her a helping hand. It's one thing to climb to the top of a tree once you're on the bottom branch. But for the first bit, the smooth trunk near the ground, you need a ladder. Of course, it may be that you're too young for this sort of offer. Or maybe you're simply not ambitious enough. You just thought it would be fun to have a go. Is that it?"

"No." Frisca frowned as she shook her head. She realised that he was deliberately provoking her and saw no need to conceal the fact that he had succeeded. While she pouted, he smiled at her for the first time.

"You really are an extremely pretty girl," he said. "I don't suppose you go around kissing crippled men quite so freely these days though, do you?"

Frisca's eyes widened in anxiety. This was just the kind of invitation she had feared. But at least his laughter was reassuring.

"Oh, you needn't worry," he said. "I distinguish between busi-

ness and pleasure. I'm putting my own money into this production, and if I offer you a job, it's because I think you're capable of
doing it, as well as bringing in some extra publicity. Well, speak
up. Do you want the chance of making your mark in this show?
And if you do, are you prepared to start off as understudy? And if
you are, will you arrange for me to meet your mother and persuade her to cooperate?"

At the beginning of the day Frisca had been a schoolgirl, and
perhaps Mr. Goldie had been right in thinking that the whole adventure had started as rather a lark. But behind the gesture lay a
confidence in her own ability that persuaded her that it was time
to be sensible. The future might well be alarming as well as exciting, but there was no question of turning back. She was not a
schoolgirl any longer. Education had flown out of the train window with the grey felt hat and the grey woollen stockings.

Frisca looked Mr. Goldie straight in the eye. "Yes," she said.
"And yes. And yes."

1926

1

England had become a daydream rather than a memory.
Throughout his long voyage home on leave in the spring of 1926
Robert had looked forward to the cool peacefulness of the English countryside. He did not expect to spend much time in London, for his mother had given up her house there, accepting
Alexa's invitation to take Barbara and Grant to Blaize as company for Pirry. This was good news, for Robert had spent many
boyhood holidays at Blaize, as well as the months of his convalescence during the war, and had no trouble in thinking of it as
home.

While he was in the trenches, the ancient house had provided
him with a picture of what he was fighting for—a picture of
maids in black dresses and white aprons and footmen in pale grey
livery carrying silver tea trays out to the table beside the cedar
tree. The sun was always shining—but was never too hot—and at
the far end of the terrace, safely out of range of the rose-pat-
terned tea service, children would be playing with balls or hoops.
That scene—already long out of date before his departure for the
East in 1920—had sustained him through many exhausting days
of frustration at the inefficiency which seemed endemic in India.

Such a recollection of gracious living had not survived his first
step ashore. India might be disorganised, but the working people
of England, he discovered, were devoting their considerable
powers of organisation to the task of bringing the country to a
standstill. Only half an hour before the liner docked, an announcement was made to the effect that a General Strike had

begun and that there would therefore be no boat trains to take
passengers from Southampton to London.

From the height of the promenade deck Robert looked along
the quay, hoping that Alexa might have sent her Rolls-Royce to
the port instead of to meet him at London. But the strike must
have taken her by surprise, or perhaps she had not realised what
its effects would be, for there was no sign of the car with its distinctive coat of arms. Undoubtedly she would be willing to send
it for him if he joined the crowd of passengers who were struggling to discover whether the telephone service was operating.
But that would mean a wait of several hours, and he had seen
something else on the quay which gave him a better idea. The
railwaymen might have gone on strike, but they had left their
train behind—complete with an engine and a full tender of coal.

Robert's work as an engineer had made him resourceful and
practical, and during the war he had learned how to keep machines running even with half their innards blasted away. He
joined the group of undergraduates who were willing and ready to
drive the train to London if only they could persuade it to move.
It took him only an hour to discover what parts the railwaymen
had removed before they went on strike, to cannibalise another
engine and to announce that the boat train was now ready to
depart. In return for his contribution, he appointed himself the
driver.

There was no Rolls-Royce at the terminus either, but by now
Robert was enjoying himself. He transferred his luggage to a west-
bound train, and on this occasion, since he would not be travelling the full distance, volunteered to put in a stint as stoker.

The taxi driver who agreed to take him from the local station
up to Blaize looked at him doubtfully, forcing Robert to realise
how dirty his clothes were. But he was too excited by his nearness
to home to worry. He looked impatiently out of the window as
the taxi drove up the long, winding approach. Now it seemed
that his daydreams were coming true. The sun was shining and
the family was indeed taking tea in the garden—although not on
the terrace at the back; they had chosen a sheltered place on one
of the side lawns so that they could watch for his arrival.

As soon as they heard the sound of the taxi, his mother and
daughter stood up and came running to the front of the house,

with the little girl tugging impatiently at her grandmother's hand
to hurry her. Barbara's pale chestnut hair was swept neatly back
into two plaits and she wore a white dress, immaculately clean,
just as Robert had imagined she would. Yet as he stepped out of
the car, his heart surging with happiness, he saw the excitement
in Barbara's eyes change to fear. She stopped dead in her rush towards him and began to back uncertainly away.

Behind her, Margaret was laughing.

"Robert, darling, how could you! Your poor daughter must
think that living in India has changed you into an Indian. A very
black Indian, at that. Have you seen your own face? What *has*
been going on?"

Robert silently cursed his own thoughtlessness as he explained
how it was that he had succeeded in making the journey from
Southampton.

"You always did love playing with trains." In a gesture which
came straight from his childhood Margaret took a handkerchief
and wiped his lips clean, as though they were jammy rather than
sooty. Then she kissed him—but now it was Robert, realising at
last that he was covered with greasy black smuts, who drew back
from hugging her as he wished. His mother was too level-headed
to be upset as, still laughing, she packed him off to the bathroom
with instructions to start his visit again from scratch in an hour's
time; but Robert was angry with himself for making such a bad
start to establishing a relationship with his daughter.

It was hopeless, he thought as he soaked and scrubbed the
smuts away. Barbara hardly knew him. She had been only three
years old when he first left for India. At that time Margaret had
provided all the love she needed, and probably the child had not
noticed how difficult her father found it to be natural with her, to
show—or even to feel—any special affection. She was part neither
of his old life, before the war, nor of the new one which began
after he had qualified. Her place was in a kind of limbo of past
years and events which were good for nothing but to be forgotten.

Two and a half years later he had come home on his first furlough, and she had been more aware that he was her father, flirting with him a little, and showing off. But even then he was only
a visitor, a temporary disturbance of her real life at Blaize.

Now she was eight, and he was so completely a stranger that she could not be expected to know what about him was normal and what was merely accidental. As for himself, he still seemed to lack any kind of paternal feeling. He couldn't think of himself as being anyone's father. And Barbara was too quiet, too shy. Robert had never spelled it out to himself before, but it occurred to him that he had always been surrounded by women with strong personalities. His mother had been unusual amongst women of her generation in working and accepting heavy professional responsibilities, and his cousin Kate had shown an equal determination to put her medical training to good use. Alexa, talented and beautiful, was exceptional by any definition, and as for Frisca—why couldn't Barbara be more like Frisca, Robert wondered; energetically pulsating with life and so positive and graceful in all her movements that she gave pleasure to everyone who saw her. Motherless and almost fatherless as she was, it was not Barbara's fault that she was so withdrawn. But it did not help Robert to feel like a father.

When, clean and smiling, he went downstairs, he obeyed Margaret's instructions to start the visit again from the beginning. But as far as Barbara was concerned, he never properly overcame the bad impression of his first arrival. She continued to be shy of him. And even with his mother he could not feel entirely relaxed. Although only on one occasion during the weeks which followed did she express the thought in words, he recognised her need to remind him that she could not continue to be responsible for Barbara forever. The moment would come when he would have to look after his daughter himself.

He knew, of course, that his mother was sixty-nine, and noticed that she was walking more slowly than before, stopping more frequently to rest, forgetting what she had said and either repeating it or becoming anxious about her forgetfulness. But the practical difficulties of taking over his daughter defeated him. His work in India was valuable and still unfinished. He was not prepared to abandon it, but he knew that the climate would be unsuitable for an English child. Barbara was much better off where she was—and because he found it impossible to envisage a future in which his mother was no longer alive, he put off from day to day considering alternatives to the present arrangement. Silence on this one matter led to a slight constraint between him and his mother. She was waiting for him to raise a subject which he could not bring himself to discuss, and the small barrier of reticence made them both uncomfortable.

Relations with Alexa were less complicated. The part of hostess had always been her favourite role. But even she on this occasion seemed unusually tense, snapping at servants in an unaccustomed manner or leaving the room abruptly to nurse a headache. Robert commented cautiously on the change.

"She's a little under the weather," Margaret agreed. "It's a difficult time for her. She's nearly fifty and she's had to accept the fact that she can't sing professionally anymore. After so many years, it leaves a big gap in her life, as you can imagine. She's thrown herself into the management of her theatre, and it's a great success, but she misses actually being on the stage herself."

"Hasn't she ever considered marrying again?" asked Robert. His aunt was still a very good-looking woman; and although Blaize and Glanville House would presumably belong to thirteen-year-old Pirry once he came of age in 1934, Alexa had a considerable fortune at her own disposal—enough to attract a husband if she wanted one.

"She won't do that," said his mother. "I told you—did I tell you?"

"What did you tell me?"

"There's someone she sees when she's in London. A producer. Younger than herself. But she won't marry him. There's Matthew, you see."

Robert did not entirely see. It came as a surprise to him on the first evening of his return to be introduced to a first cousin who was a stranger—he had heard about Matthew Lorimer, but had never met him.

Matthew was in every way the opposite of his sharp-witted and sharp-featured brother, Arthur. He was a heavy man, perhaps as a result of the years confined to a wheelchair. His thick hair still from a distance seemed fair, but was rapidly turning white. Alexa had converted the coach house for him, giving him a suite of rooms on the ground floor with accommodation above for the two menservants who looked after him. She had built him a studio as well—and to judge by the number of titles he mentioned as he showed Robert the portraits on which he was working, she had also introduced him into her own circle of society friends.

Although he could not put his finger on the cause, Robert found Matthew's presence unsettling. Perhaps jealousy was at the root of it. His daughter treated the man in the wheelchair as something between a father and a large teddy bear. Lifted onto his lap, she snuggled up to him or hugged him or beat her fists against his chest in mock anger. It was natural, Robert told himself; but that did not make him like it.

And Matthew himself, although friendly enough, emitted an uncomfortable impression of concealed power. He could not walk, but the arms with which he propelled his wheelchair were very strong. His portraits were superficially pretty but at the same time extraordinarily revealing of character, sometimes disquietingly so. He spoke very little in company, but the mental alertness with which he observed everything that went on could not be hidden. More successfully he concealed his feelings about Alexa. Occasionally one of them would touch the other in passing, but they rarely seemed to look at each other. Robert found this unnatural, making it difficult to understand whether their relationship was that of patroness and artist, aunt and nephew, or two friends with independent careers.

All these strains in the atmosphere made it hard for Robert to settle down to the lazy holiday he had expected, and he used the general strike as his excuse to escape. He had no very clear idea what the strike was about—and no ordinary newspapers, which might have enlightened him, were being published. Alexa's opinion was made plain enough: the strikers were holding the country to ransom and should be made to return to work—by force if necessary. Margaret, always more sympathetic towards people less fortunate than herself, suggested that it was asking a good deal of the miners, already doing a dangerous job for low pay, that they should work longer hours for even less money, as had apparently been proposed. But even she did not understand why the discontent of this one group of workers should have persuaded railwaymen and printers, bus drivers and builders, steel workers and factory hands to withdraw their labour in support. Unexpectedly, it was Matthew's opinion which proved to be the most abrasive.

"In India, I suppose you're a sahib and the rest are just natives," he said, with an edge to his voice which Robert would not have accepted from anyone but a cripple. "And during the war you were an officer and the rest were just other ranks. The other ranks have become workers, but you're still an officer. As Pirry would say—and as Lenin said before him—the world is divided into those who rule and those who are ruled, and those who rule haven't the faintest idea how some people in this country live. There are men who joined the Army in 1914 because they couldn't believe that anything could be worse than the hell of poverty they were living in. They were wrong, of course, but only because the new hell destroyed their bodies while the old one had merely attacked their souls. And now they're either unemployed or underpaid, back in that same hell of idleness and near-starvation, watching their children grow up to the same prospects. Can you blame them if they feel the need to make a desperate gesture?"

"You're becoming as much of a Bolshevik as Kate," said Alexa lightly. "What do you know about the starving masses, Matthew?"

"I've lived amongst them," he replied. "Not for long, but for long enough." But he accepted her warning that he should not press the argument to a quarrel, and shrugged his shoulders. "Well, I suppose that if the trains are going to be run at all, it's better that an engineer should do it than an undergraduate."

"Now you've got to the heart of it, Matthew," Margaret told him, laughing. "Robert doesn't care who's right and who's wrong. He just wants to go on playing trains."

Robert recognised that his mother was not far from the truth. The certainty that he could be of practical use enabled him to forget his inadequacy as a father. He arranged to sleep for the duration of the crisis at the London club of which he was an overseas member. Then he enrolled himself as the driver of an Underground train. His fellow-volunteers were all ten years younger than himself, but they accepted him instantly as a companion, taking it for granted that they would spend their free time together in a pleasure-seeking group. Robert's own twenties were a casualty of the war—there was a sense in which he had never been a young man at all. Although by now he was thirty-two, he

found himself almost for the first time in his life enjoying the
kind of light-hearted gaiety which he should have had at twenty.

With five of his new Cambridge friends, he held a lavish dinner to celebrate the fact that they—and their passengers—had
survived their first day's work without accident. They were stroll-
ing away from the restaurant when his eye was caught by a name
on one of the posters outside a theatre. He had known, of course,
that Frisca was in London, and had fully intended to get in touch
with her as soon as he had established when his free time would
be. He knew also that she had begun a stage career—and from
one or two hints which his mother had dropped, had gathered
that the energetic way in which she was flinging herself into the
life of a Bright Young Thing contributed to Alexa's bouts of bad
temper. But he had not expected that at the age of nineteen
Frisca would have her name in such large type. She was not the
star of the revue, but it seemed that she did not come far behind.

"Cousin of mine," he told his friends, to explain why he was
lingering.

"What, the blonde with the legs?"

"I don't know about that. She's blonde, certainly. And tall."

"If you don't know, then I can tell you. Frisca Glanville's got
the best legs in London, and she doesn't mind who sees them.
Your cousin, indeed! Pull the other one. Or prove it. Come on,
chaps. Let's all go and meet Scott's cousin."

They hustled him towards the stage door. The audience was
just leaving the theatre, suggesting that the time was a reasonable
one for a call. Robert recognised that his friends were drunk. But
he was not drunk himself, was he? He allowed himself to be propelled through the cluster of admirers waiting to see their favourites leave.

The stage door proved to be an expensive tollgate. Even after a
generous tip had changed hands, Robert was required to send in a
scribbled note and wait for an invitation in return. Frisca's dresser
opened her door to his knock and Frisca herself turned on her
dressing table stool to face him. Robert stood still in the doorway,
so unexpectedly that the others behind him stumbled, pushing
each other forward in their eagerness not to be shut out.

For a moment the shock was so great that he could neither
move nor speak. At the end of his last leave he had said goodbye

to a schoolgirl in a sober grey uniform, pouting with sulkiness as the car carried her away to school. There seemed no connection between that child and this slim young woman whose dress was cut so low both front and back that she could hardly be wearing anything beneath it. Even her hair, although it had retained the golden sheen he remembered, had been shingled and in some way varnished into waves, more formal than the fluffy curls through which he had once run his fingers. But her eyes were as bright and lively as before. Her smile was welcoming. She laughed—a light, mischievous laugh—as she took in his astonishment.

"Yes, it's still me," she said. "I've grown up, that's all."

2

As her seventieth birthday approached, Margaret found it more and more difficult to keep a grip on the passing of time. Instead of progressing smoothly and steadily, it seemed to move in waves which she rode as though she were on a switchback—at one time climbing up an inch or a second at a time, so slowly that she seemed on the verge of falling backwards, and at other moments careering along at such a pace that her mind could not keep up with events. She had always prided herself on being a good organiser, but nowadays she often found herself late and flustered. And it was almost as bad when she was early—so obviously prepared for some meal or outing that other people were forced into unnecessary apology.

Recently the rest of the family had begun to ignore these lapses, and that in a way was more distressing than if she had been kindly but firmly put right. They pretended not to notice when she repeated something she had said only half an hour earlier, without realising that Margaret herself was conscious of the repetition almost as she embarked on it. And they made a point of reminding her frequently of anything which had been arranged. When she had remembered the plan, she was irritated: when she had forgotten it, she was frightened.

In an attempt to keep her responsibilities under control, she sat at the little bureau in her bedroom and made lists of what had to be remembered and done. At the top of the list, ever since Robert's arrival home, had been the question of Barbara. It was necessary that decisions should be made, especially about her education. Pirry would be starting at Eton in September and Alexa might not want to maintain a tutor and schoolroom for Barbara alone. In any case, she ought to go to school like other girls. But what kind of school? She was such a solitary, highly strung child —as her mother had been—that it was difficult to tell whether boarding school would bring her out of her shell and give her friends, or would make her miserable. Robert must be made to express views and to make plans which reached even further into the future. The general strike had ended—sooner, she suspected, than he liked—so he could no longer claim to lack time to consider the subject.

Of more immediate importance on the current list, however, was the reminder that today was Grant's twenty-first birthday. Alexa was giving a family luncheon party for him. The choice of luncheon rather than dinner was in order that Frisca could be present and still reach the theatre for the evening performance, but Margaret could not help contrasting the modest scale of the celebration with the last twenty-first birthday party which had been held at Blaize. It was perhaps because Alexa did not wish to remind everyone of the handsome young man who had danced the night away twelve years earlier—and who had died within two years—that she was not prepared to repeat her lavish hospitality this time. But more probably it was because she had no great affection for Grant.

Arthur came to the luncheon—as Grant's trustee as well as his cousin. He had changed very little as the years passed. Margaret sometimes thought that like William, his father, he had been born middle-aged. It was rumoured that the shipping industry was running into difficulties, but undoubtedly Arthur had tucked away enough money during the boom to keep him comfortably in his Bristol mansion for the rest of his life. Whenever Margaret read in the newspapers about the hard-faced businessmen who had done well out of the war, she could not help thinking of Arthur, who had emerged from those terrible years with a baronetcy and a fortune. And yet—at least within the family circle—he was not an unsympathetic man. He had confided in Margaret some years earlier his distress at learning that he would never be able to have children, and this knowledge condemned him to a double loneliness. It had always been clear that he would only be prepared to go to the trouble of courting a wife in order that she should produce a family for him. With that possibility removed, he had accepted the inevitablity of spending the rest of his life as a bachelor.

At the end of the birthday meal, while they drank their coffee on the terrace in the sunshine, he explained to the rest of the family what he had already discussed with Grant.

"Grant's father set up two trusts before he died," he said. "One was straightforward. He'd set aside a considerable amount of money out of his trading profits over thirty years or so, and this capital sum was to be invested and kept till Grant was twenty-one. It was to compensate him for the fact that the plantation in Jamaica was left to Duke. The investments have done well enough to buy a small business or an agricultural estate somewhere, as Uncle Ralph had in mind. I told Grant two months ago how much he could expect to have, and we've been making enquiries together."

"I've decided to go abroad," Grant said. "There's an opening in Malaya. A rubber estate on the west coast. I haven't enough to pay the full price, but apparently there's a well-established system there—an exporting company which will give a mortgage on the balance of what I need, in return for an option on a certain amount of the crop at a fixed price."

"Why does everyone want to go so far away?" asked Margaret sadly. "What is so special about Malaya?"

Grant, his fair hair looking almost white in the bright sunshine, set down his coffee cup and came across to put his arm round her shoulders. She felt the firmness of his muscles and marvelled, as often before, that a podgy, whining child should have grown into this thin, tough, and wholly controlled young man. Sometimes she felt frightened by the intensity with which he pursued any enthusiasm, whether for a person, an idea, or a method of keeping fit, but it had been a long time since she had felt sorry for him.

"It's not just to get away from you, Aunt Margaret!" he told her. "This is a bargain offer. Most people won't consider it, because the climate is bad and there won't be another white man within miles. But I was brought up in heat and humidity. I like it. And I can do without company, as Robert can."

"Oh, I'm not completely isolated," said Robert lazily. He was sitting on the grass, leaning against the side of Frisca's chair. "There's a gaggle of spinster missionaries ready to fight for my soul whenever I give them the opportunity."

"I'm jealous," laughed Frisca.

"If you saw them, it might put your mind at rest. Did your botany degree teach you much about rubber, Grant?"

"Not much. But it's made me interested in the possibility of developing new plants. Not rubber trees, probably. But just as a hobby, I'd like to experiment with orchids. To breed a new one."

"Call it after me," murmured Frisca.

"I might, if it were beautiful enough to be worthy of you. If it turns out to be ugly and horrid, I'll call it after Barbara instead."

"*You're* ugly and horrid," protested Barbara, but she was laughing then and spoke the truth only when she said, "I wish you wouldn't go."

"I'll come back," he promised.

Arthur interrupted them with a dry cough. "To get back to business. As I said, the first trust was straightforward, and it will be wound up now. But there was another one. A third of the profits from the Hope Valley plantation has been accumulating for the benefit of Kate, or any child of hers. If I knew that she was dead, without issue, some of that money would also revert to Grant."

"She's not dead," said Margaret. The thought that Arthur was sweeping his cousin Kate aside in such a way made her heart beat too fast. "And she has a child."

"Quite so. Quite so. We know that they were both alive in 1920, but that was six years ago. Anything might have happened since then. And that's my first question. Has anyone had any more recent news?"

There was no answer, and Arthur pressed on, pursuing his narrow line of thought. "I haven't liked to make enquiries in Russia, or try to send any information to her, because you told me, Aunt Margaret, that it might be dangerous for her to be known to be English. Do you think that's still the case?"

"How can we tell?" Margaret's anxiety rose again, almost as though merely to discuss Kate was to put her at risk.

"Precisely. We can't. I'm going to make a suggestion, and I shall be glad of your comments, although of course the final responsibility will have to rest with me. I don't consider that there's any possibility of Kate receiving the money to which she's entitled while she remains inside Soviet Russia. Even to offer it to her would put her at risk as a foreigner and a capitalist. We can only wait until she communicates with us. And until then I propose that the money which has accumulated for her should be invested in her brother's new estate. It can be secured on the land in a perfectly proper manner, and it will reduce Grant's need for a mortgage."

Margaret's anxiety persisted. Arthur was talking as though none of them would ever see Kate again. And yet wasn't it Arthur who once upon a time had wanted to marry her? Perhaps that was the trouble. She had rejected him, and now he was not prepared to be kind to her. Margaret herself knew little about investments. She was not even clear about the sources of her own income. She had lived on her salary until she retired, and although Alexa had tried at that time to explain the provision which Piers had made for her, Margaret had never completely understood it. It came as a relief when Alexa, who had a good head for business, voiced her own feeling.

"As a source of income, a plantation in Malaya isn't as safe as stocks and shares in England, is it?"

"Not in the sense of paying so many pounds every quarter day. But we have no reason to believe that's what she wants. It has as good a chance of capital appreciation as anything else. She may not wish even for that. We have to assume, don't we, that she's in sympathy with Communist ideas? Otherwise she would surely have left that country by now."

"I think it should be put on a completely businesslike basis," Alexa said firmly. Then she smiled, so that Arthur should not be offended. "As I'm sure you've already decided, in order to safeguard yourself as trustee. The capital amount which has accumulated for her out of the profits should be secured on the land, as you say. And either Grant should pay interest on it into a bank account here, or else an amount representing the interest should be compounded with the capital each year, on the same security."

"I think you can trust me to look after Kate's interests so far as I can understand them," Arthur said. "What I needed to discover was whether any of you had news which might indicate her plans or inclinations. You'll get in touch with me if you hear anything, won't you? And now I have to make my way to a meeting. Would you like a lift to London, Frisca?"

"When a ride in your magnificent Morgan is on offer, I hardly even care about the destination," Frisca said, laughing. "You've no idea how my stock goes up with the rest of the cast on the evenings you call for me after the show, Arthur."

Margaret noticed the startled reaction on Robert's face to this casual remark. But it did not linger there for long. Robert could hardly expect that he was the only man who had ever taken Frisca out to supper; and a forty-seven-year-old cousin who visited London only infrequently could surely not be regarded as a serious rival.

There was a brief period of bustle as Frisca and Arthur said their goodbyes and left. The coffee cups also disappeared, but after that no one seemed inclined to move. The sun was hot on the stone terrace and the lawn beyond was peaceful. The whole garden held its breath in the warm stillness, and even the bees and butterflies seemed to be taking a siesta. Margaret felt her head nodding on to her chest, and after a little while she ceased to jerk it upright again and allowed herself to sleep.

She awoke cautiously an hour later, not making any movement which would indicate to the others that she was emerging from a nap. Equally cautiously—as though to reassure herself that Blaize was still there, that it had not somehow been spirited away during her sleep—she began to look around her, checking all the familiar features of the garden. That was when she noticed the boy.

He was a small, undernourished boy, about ten years old, with a head which seemed too large for his body. The bicycle he was standing beside also looked too large for him and so, most definitely were the clothes he was wearing. They were shabby in a manner which was familiar to Margaret. She had spent long enough working in the slums of London to recognise the custom whereby clothes, whether bought or handed down, were always acquired a size too big so that the child could grow into them—and were always worn out before that moment arrived. This boy's appearance was dominated by a pair of grey shorts which fell shapelessly to a point an inch or two below the knees.

But Margaret paid less attention to the boy's clothing than to his face. It was, at this moment, a frightened face with a trace of hurt and bewilderment in its expression, but it reminded Margaret of another boy she had known almost fifty years earlier. That little boy had had thick fair hair, neatly cut into a fringe, whereas the stranger's hair was brown, and tousled. The resemblance, nevertheless, was very strong. Afraid of feeling dizzy if she stood up too suddenly after her sleep, Margaret waited quietly for someone else to notice that a visitor had arrived.

Robert was at the far end of the lawn, throwing a cricket ball for Pirry to catch. Pirry hated all team games. The world, he had announced plaintively, was divided into those who took a sadistic pleasure in bashing inoffensive balls about and those who could let them live in peace. There was no doubt which group he belonged to himself—but he had realised that boarding-school life would be intolerable if he flaunted his lack of interest in games too blatantly.

Nearer to Margaret, Matthew was sitting under the cedar tree in his wheelchair, with Barbara on his lap as he read her a story. She was really too old to be snuggled in such a way, but they both enjoyed it. Grant was sitting on the grass beside them, staring at Barbara as she listened to the story. It was never possible to tell from his face what he was thinking, but it could always be assumed that his concentration would be undivided.

Alexa had been in the house and it was she, coming out to join the others, who noticed the intruder and frowned.

"One of the village boys?" asked Margaret.

"No." Alexa took her duties as mistress of the house seriously enough to be sure of recognising all the children on the estate. She called Pirry and told him to send the stranger packing unless he could produce some message which justified his presence. Pirry's usual languid air was disturbed by surprise as he returned.

"He says he's John Lorimer and he's come to see his father."

"And who is his father?" demanded Alexa, but Margaret had guessed the answer before she heard it.

"Mr. Matthew Lorimer, he says."

Alexa's face, like Pirry's, showed surprise but nothing more. It was clear to Margaret that she must have known that Matthew had a son, even if his sudden appearance was unexpected. With the efficiency which she directed towards the running of her theatre, Alexa at once set herself to stage-manage this encounter. Barbara was sent into the house with a message that there would be one more for tea, so that Matthew was unencumbered when he was given the news that a visitor had arrived claiming to be his son. Then Alexa went over to the boy.

"That's a very smart bicycle," she said.

"I won it in a painting competition." He spoke in a heavy Midlands accent.

"Let me hold it for you while you go and say hello to your father."

"That 'im in the chair?"

"Yes." Curiously, she asked, "Didn't you know?"

The boy shook his head.

"Well, we'll leave you to have a chat," Alexa said. "We'll all come back and have tea out here in about half an hour."

She leaned the bicycle against the cedar tree and came across to help Margaret up from her chair. Margaret found herself confused and dizzy, in need of the support of Alexa's arm round her waist as they walked slowly towards the house.

"Had Matthew told you?" she asked.

"That he had a son? Yes."

"How could he let it happen? The child's half starved. And those clothes!"

"You mustn't blame Matthew."

"I'll have tea in my room," said Margaret. Whether or not anyone was to blame, she was upset and unhappy. The boy was a Lorimer. He should never have been abandoned in such a way. Matthew himself had been brought up in comfort. Margaret remembered the nursery teas she had shared with him, the velvet suits he had worn for special occasions, the huge rocking horse on which he had galloped to imaginary countries. He had quarrelled with his parents later, but as a child he could never have accused them of neglect. Margaret walked restlessly round her room, muttering to herself.

Later that evening a message came, asking her to visit Matthew; it was not possible for him to come upstairs to see her. She answered the call and found him alone.

"Where is the child?"

"Gone to bed. Tired out. He's cycled more than eighty miles today. Not bad for a ten-year-old, is it? And he started at four o'clock in the morning."

"Why didn't you tell us, Matthew? We could have helped. We could have done something."

"Alexa told me you were upset. That's why I wanted to talk to you. John hasn't been neglected. He's been brought up in poverty, certainly, but that's a different thing. That was his mother's choice."

"I didn't even know—"

"Alexa knew. That I was married, for a start. And that my wife had washed her hands of me. I don't blame Peggy for that. She married someone rather different from a cripple in a wheelchair. She may have thought that she'd have to support me. But even if it wasn't that, she needed male company, and I wasn't a man any longer. All that was settled long before I came here. Alexa didn't entice me from a wife; she rescued me from a hospital. You must be quite clear about that, Aunt Margaret."

"But the boy!"

"I couldn't steal Peggy's son from her."

"You could have sent money."

"For four years I didn't have any money. A disability pension, that was all. Hardly enough to keep myself in cigarettes. It was Alexa who put me back on my feet again." He paused, and laughed with a trace of bitterness. "Well, you're right, in a way. But when Peggy needed help, I gave it her. When I needed it, she turned me away. If she'd asked for money when I had it, I would have sent it. For John, not for her. But she never asked. I sent him presents, for Christmas and his birthday every year. He told me today that she always opened them first and took my letter out. She pretended that they'd come from an uncle. Until his birthday this summer, John believed that his father was dead."

"What happened this summer?"

"He got to the parcel first. Normal curiosity. And curiosity again has brought him south. But only to look. Not to stay."

"We should feed him properly. He should have clothes—"

Matthew put a hand on her arm. "Aunt Margaret, you mustn't distress yourself about this. Of course we're feeding him. And Robert has promised to take him to London tomorrow to buy him something better to wear. But we have to be sensible about it. We can't send him back to a mining village in Leicestershire in the sort of clothes a young baron like Pirry will be wearing at Eton. Robert will get him something warm for the winter, a pair of stout boots, that sort of thing. It would be no kindness to cut him off from his friends or his mother. He knows where to find me now. My name and my address. If he needs me, he can get in touch. But he can't live in two places at once, and his home isn't Blaize."

Well, it ought to be, thought Margaret, but she understood what Matthew was telling her. It was none of her business. As she kissed him good night and went back to her own room, she was still unhappy, but now it was for a different reason.

It was not something she had ever put to herself in so many words before, but as she looked back on the past she recognised that for almost fifty years she had been the emotional centre of the Lorimer family. On the day of her father's death, her brother William had shouldered all John Junius' business responsibilities, and his son Arthur had inherited them in turn. But it had always been to Margaret that any kind of domestic trouble had been brought. Matthew himself was only the first of many Lorimer children who had been able to rely on her love, with a home whenever it was needed. And now she was not needed anymore. It was only a short time since she had worried because Robert did not appear to realise that she would not be there forever to look after Barbara. Matthew, on the other hand, took it so much for granted that she was an old woman that it would not even occur to him to ask for help. Well, he was quite right and she must not allow herself to be distressed by it. He was right, too, to remind her that to take a child out of his familiar surroundings was not always a kindness.

Her memory tugged her back into the past, recalling the day on which she had first learned that lesson, and the remembrance turned her restless disquiet into decision. She opened her bureau and began to write.

"In 1878 a nursery governess, Claudine, who had been employed for a time by my brother William, gave birth to a son in France. He was christened Jean-Claude and brought up on a farm called La Chalonnière, halfway between Sarlat and Les Eyzies in the Dordogne. Claudine's husband agreed to bring him up as his own son, so he goes under the name of Grasset. But his father was my younger brother, Ralph. Jean-Claude is a Lorimer. Someone ought to know."

With the brief statement pinned to her will and both of them put away, she felt at peace again. The matter was not likely to be of any importance. Brinsley was dead and Kate might never return from Russia; Grant was not the kind of young man likely to feel sentimental about the existence of an illegitimate half brother, and the link with Duke was too tenuous to be of importance. Still, one day somebody else would become the person who kept track of the Lorimers and the threads which linked them. It would be Alexa, probably—perhaps she had already taken over the role. She would not be interested in Jean-Claude any more than the others were; and the boy himself—the man, rather—would not even be aware that he had any connections in England. There had seemed at the time to be good reasons for secrecy and it was unlikely that anyone would wish to break the silence after so long. Margaret, though, was a believer in the truth. The facts of a family history were what had actually happened. The secret would not die with her now. Somebody would know.

3

For a good many centuries the floorboards at Blaize had been squeaking their betrayal of anyone who crept from his own bedroom to another. Robert, knowing how lightly his mother slept, did his best to be discreet but guessed that he had probably failed. She would be shocked, no doubt. Although Robert himself felt little guilt, Frisca's youth must weigh heavily with someone of his mother's generation. Yet Frisca Glanville at nineteen was far more sophisticated than Margaret Lorimer would have been at thirty.

Had Margaret ever challenged him, he would have tried to justify himself by saying that this was not just a love affair. He wanted to marry Frisca. He wanted it more than anything else in the world. The incredible fact that she allowed him to love her almost overwhelmed him with joy, but it was not enough. He needed to own her. Only marriage could give him the security of possessing her forever. His mother might have been reassured by the intensity of his wish to behave honourably—and although he knew that she disliked the idea of first cousins marrying, he and Frisca were not full cousins. Because Alexa's birth had been illegitimate, her daughter and Robert shared only one grandparent out of four. That could hardly matter very much.

More of a problem than their family relationship was the extreme unlikelihood of Frisca's ever agreeing to marry him. Her pattern of life was so different from his own that it was hard to see how they could ever live together even in the most literal sense. In India Robert was accustomed to a working day which began early in the morning, before the sun rose. He was usually in bed by ten o'clock in the evening, and always before midnight. Frisca, on the other hand, emerged from the theatre at half-past eleven every night hungry and wide awake. After supper she expected to be taken on to a nightclub to drink and dance until five or six in the morning. She went to bed at almost exactly the time Robert habitually rose; and slept, except on matinee days, until two or three in the afternoon.

There were no nightclubs in South India; no smart restaurants, no vivacious company. For the past two years Robert had been living in the village of Chotapur in order to be near the last of the three dams which was under construction. But even if he moved back to Trichinopoli in order to provide a wife with a club for recreation, some female company, a small circle of white faces, how exciting would Frisca find such a setting? It was all too easy to imagine, for example, what Frisca would think of Eleanor, and Eleanor of Frisca. Marriage was impossible. In his heart he knew it was impossible and yet he was desperate to achieve it.

His leave was drawing to a close and still he had not spoken his mind. In the end it was Frisca who introduced the subject, although indirectly. She had her own almost self-contained flat within Glanville House in London, and lived there during the week. To the wall of her practice room she had fitted a barre; for although she recognised that she would never be a ballet dancer, the exercises which she had practised from childhood provided a disciplined routine. Frisca very often gave the impression of being careless and frivolous, but in one sphere she was a perfectionist. The revues and musical comedies in which she appeared required her to sing, and she did so adequately enough; but dancing was her vocation. She was a professional, and Robert's teasing always produced the same answer: "Nothing but the best will do."

After the collapse of the general strike, he ought to have returned to Blaize for the rest of his furlough. At first he had invented excuses for lingering in London, but his mother had guessed the truth the first time she saw him in Frisca's company. So now it was understood by both Margaret and Alexa that just as Frisca came to Blaize every Sunday and Monday for his sake, so he spent the rest of the week in London to be with her. He liked to watch her practise—the contrast between the sweating, dishevelled girl of the afternoon and the slim, soignée young woman of the evening gave him repeated pleasure. Today, however, it seemed to him that she was not putting her usual effort into the exercises.

"You're slacking!" he accused as she flopped down on the floor beside him. Over her leotard and practice tights she had pulled a thick sweater and a pair of equally thick stockings which came to just above the knee. The effect was both ludicrous and exciting.

"Yes. I'm not sure how energetic I ought to be. I forgot to ask the doctor." She gave the back of her neck a vigorous rub with a towel and then smiled at him with something less than her usual assurance. "Which is my subtle way of telling you that I'm pregnant."

Robert's reaction was spontaneous—enthusiastic and sincere. It was not because he had any great wish for another child that he gasped with delight at the news.

"How absolutely ripping!" he exclaimed. "Frisca, dearest darling Frisca, will you marry me?"

"Why else do you think I told you, if not so that you could make an honest woman of me?" She was laughing, but she was nervous as well. "Is it all right, Robert? I mean, you're not to feel trapped."

"I've spent the past three weeks wondering how I could manage to get myself trapped. No, longer than that. From the moment I walked into your dressing room." He lifted the heavy sweater and rubbed his hand over her taut, flat stomach, amazed that there should be no visible sign of the miracle. "Can you feel anything?"

"No. It's terribly early days yet. With anyone else I'd have waited another month, to be absolutely sure. But you'd have slipped through my fingers by then."

"Will your mother be upset?" he asked.

"I sometimes suspect that Mamma in her youth may have had one or two moral lapses," Frisca said carefully. " 'Liaisons' was the word they used in those days, I believe. She may not approve of my behaviour, but I doubt whether she'll be surprised, and she would need to phrase her disapproval very carefully. There will be words about social stigmas, no doubt."

"I'll get a Special Licence," Robert promised. "It will seem reasonable enough, with the end of my leave so near. And then the baby will appear only a week or two on the wrong side of respectability. Come on, you'll catch cold if you sit around like this."

The next hour was the happiest of Robert's life. He looked down at Frisca and marvelled that he should be allowed to possess something so beautiful. It was too good to be true, he told himself—and he was right.

The difficulties began to present themselves almost before the first excitement was over, and it was little consolation to Robert that he had been aware of them all in advance: from this point of view Frisca's pregnancy was a complication as well as a delight. Her first assumption was that he would be able to arrange a transfer to work in England, and he had to explain that he was employed by a contracting company which operated only in Africa and India.

"Then you could change your job," she suggested, as though this were the simplest of matters. "You're a qualified engineer."

Robert wondered whether to remind Frisca how many ex-servicemen, many of them as well trained as himself, were currently unemployed in England. But it would be equally truthful to give a more personal answer.

"By the time I get back to Chotapur the monsoon will be over and it will be time for the main working season to begin. There has to be someone who knows what he's doing to supervise the work. A dam, after all, can be a killer if any kind of weakness is hidden away in it. I can't just walk out on the job. It could take the company a good many weeks to find a replacement and get him out there. And even then—I've been concerned with the project right from the planning stage. I know all the complications and snags. Some of them it's impossible to put into writing. And there's only about six months to go. I can't abandon it now."

Frisca considered the problem for a few moments before asking whether India was a good place to have a baby. "And don't tell me that Indian women do it all the time," she said, keeping her voice light. "Would it be healthy for me?"

"It would be hot," Robert admitted. "And a lot of people get stomach upsets when they first go out. But it's not a White Man's Grave, or anything like that. I find the climate perfectly supportable. You'd be all right, I'm sure. But the baby—" His voice faded in unhappy doubt. "I'd have to ask about babies."

"Well, listen," said Frisca. "Suppose I travel out with you now. And then leave again in about five months' time. Come home here to have the baby. With a bit of luck, your dam might be finished by then. If it isn't quite, you'd return a few weeks later, as soon as you've wrapped the job up, and look around for work in London."

"London isn't the right place for me," he said.

"Why not? I can tell you, we need a new bridge over the Thames."

How could Robert explain to someone whose life had always been comfortable and happy the need that he felt to use his skills amongst people who lived in poverty and insecurity? He had committed himself to India six years before, and his work there was a vocation, not just a job. Frisca seemed to understand his silence, and was worried by it.

"Darling, you understand that I have to come back to London, don't you? I mean, I'll take a year off for you and the baby, of course I will. But it would be silly to give up the stage completely when I'm getting on so well. You do see that, don't you?"

"I can afford to support a wife," said Robert. "I *want* to support a wife."

"Oh heavens, it's not the money. It's not even the being famous thing, although one oughtn't to pretend that that isn't fun as well. But I'm good at it, you see, Robert. At dancing, I mean. It's not just that I enjoy it, but that I do it well. I'm going to be the best dancer of my kind in England one day. I'm almost there already. I don't know what I'd do without it. I need something to be proud of."

"You'll be proud of your baby," said Robert.

"Yes." Frisca's voice was extremely doubtful. "I mean, yes, of course I shall, but there's not much credit to producing a baby, is there? Any woman can do it. I suppose I'm being silly and selfish, but I don't see why I shouldn't have a husband and a child and my name in lights all at once."

"But not a husband who works in India," said Robert.

The silence which fell between them offered no meeting place.

"We'll have to think about it, shan't we?" said Frisca. Her voice was unhappy. "It might be best not to mention it to anyone else just yet."

Robert looked at her in alarm. "You won't do anything silly, Frisca, like trying to get rid of the baby?"

"Of course not." Her shock at the suggestion was reassuring. For a day or two, separated from her by a visit previously arranged to the home of a school friend, he struggled with the problem and was able to persuade himself that they were bound to find an acceptable solution. It was not he who was trapped, but Frisca—and so in the end it would be Frisca, not himself, who would have to surrender. Because he loved her, he did his best to plan for a future which would offer her satisfaction. But because he thought she had no real choice, he was not prepared to abandon his own career. So it came as a shock when she greeted him on his return with an air of forced brightness.

"The pressure's off," she said. "The panic's over. No baby. Sorry I frightened you." She laughed affectionately at his dumbfounded expression. "I was a bit too quick off the mark, I'm afraid. I've had these false alarms before. The thing is, I've been dotty about you ever since I was knee-high. My hero, you were, even in your spotty schoolboy years. It seemed too good a chance to miss, to tie you up in the chains of your own standards of proper behaviour. It *was* a trap. Sorry, sweetheart."

"I wanted to be trapped," he said. "You know that. I wanted to marry you. I still do, baby or no baby. Frisca darling, you know how much I love you. I adore you. You didn't need to tell me it was a mistake." But he understood why she had confessed. She was setting him free only because she wanted to be free herself.

"It wouldn't work, would it, Robert," she went on, confirming his suspicions. "I love you too, and it's breaking my heart to say this, but I've got just enough sense to see it straight. If I kept you in London you'd never forgive me. And if I went out to India—well, as I say, it simply wouldn't work. I'd be snapping your head off within a month. I haven't got the memsahib mentality. I can't imagine living without something to *do*. And I don't mean patting children on the head or—well, what *do* British women do in Indian villages? Lovely nights, I can imagine that, but all day while you're out at your dam? You knew all the time that it wouldn't be possible, didn't you, Robert? I mean, you wouldn't even have suggested it if it hadn't been for the baby. Remove the baby from the situation, and we're back where we started."

Robert's disappointment was so great that he was unable to speak. Recognising this, Frisca drew him into her arms.

"Nine more days before you have to go back," she said. "Nine more nights. And then a happy parting, Robert. A love affair that can never spoil or go stale. I've loved you all my life, and I shall love you all the rest of my life. But we weren't made to be married to each other. It was love that was the trap, not just the baby. Say you understand that, Robert, and we can be friends forever."

Robert gave a groan of deprivation. But as his arms tightened about Frisca, he had to admit that everything she said was true. India was calling him, and he would have to return. Alone.

4

Siva was dancing on the verandah of the bungalow. As his luggage was carried inside, the carving caught Robert's eye and he stared at it in bewilderment. He had seen it before, in the porch of the temple which he had tried to move. But now, he noticed, the relief was cracked. The expression on the face of the dancing god had always been sly, but the crack distorted his mouth, making him appear to laugh. It was a mocking laugh, arousing uneasiness. Robert called for his bearer to give an explanation.

To discover the full truth took time and involved an inspection of the site. Robert had warned the villagers at Chotapur that the slight change made in the line of the dam to protect their river temple might cause problems, especially before the whole project was completed. He had been right. A heavier monsoon than usual, coupled with the partial blockage of the river, had flooded the temple enclosure and its surroundings, eroding the soil. There had been a cyclone, too, while he was in England. Its worst effects had been felt on the coast, but the last flick of its tongue had been enough to uproot a fig tree in the sacred precinct. Falling, this had broken through the roof of the temple. The Siva lingam had been chipped and the reliefs in the porch cracked. The elders of the village had carried the carving up to the bungalow on the day after the cyclone. Nothing imperfect could be allowed to stay in a temple.

The enigmatic expression on Siva's face was disturbing enough even in its proper place. Its presence on his verandah seemed distinctly sinister to Robert, as though it had been brought as a warning of reprisals to come. He made cautious enquiries and was reassured. Now that the temple—and in particular the lingam—was no longer perfect, the site had ceased to be holy. With none of the fuss which might have been expected after the indignation aroused by the first plans for the dam, another position had been chosen, more convenient to the village, and a new temple was already under construction. Nobody seemed to feel strongly about it. The villagers had resisted change while they still had a choice but accepted it when it was forced on them by their own beliefs. It was all so simple that Robert wondered why he had not done a little secret sabotage long ago. In fact, he remembered now that Eleanor had suggested it. He had been shocked at the time, but perhaps she was right after all. Being right was one of Eleanor's most irritating characteristics.

The first weeks after his return passed in a flurry of work. It was necessary for him to make the rounds of his area, inspecting what had been done in his absence, checking the effects of the previous year's achievement, giving instructions for the new season. Continually on the move, talking to different groups of people almost every day, it was easy to put England out of his mind. But the moment came, as it was bound to, when he returned to his own bungalow and saw the prospect of two and a half lonely years stretching ahead.

The days were not too bad, and he had always slept soundly at night. But the evenings were unendurable. He had brought back with him a good stock of books and a further supply of records for his gramophone; and before too long bundles of newspapers would begin to arrive from home, dispatched after his departure, for him to read one each day in proper order. But the books could not hold his interest, and the only record he played was a selection from a musical comedy. Over and over again he wound up the machine and listened to the tinny notes to which Frisca had danced. As he listened, he stared at the dancing Siva until the two images blurred in his mind: the golden-haired girl with her pale skin and long, straight legs, and the dark stone god with his many arms and legs bent into a decorative pattern. The god of fertility aroused his lust, and Frisca was not there to satisfy it.

There were beautiful girls in the village. Early each morning Robert watched them walking in single file through the fields, brass pots steady on their heads, graceful in brightly coloured saris. But they, like the stone Siva, were dark. Everything in this country of sunshine was dark. Robert longed for Frisca's blondness until his longing could be borne no longer.

The letter he wrote was a complete surrender. He loved her, he confessed, too deeply to endure life without her. If she would come out to India to marry him, he would take her back to England as soon as the contractors could find an engineer to replace him. And then he would find some kind of work to do in London. He didn't care what it was as long as it would keep him close to her.

The relief of writing the letter was so intense that he was overcome by a great peacefulness. There would be many weeks to wait before he could expect an answer, but life seemed to wear a rosy dress as he prepared to endure them. So marked was the contrast with the fidgeting unhappiness which had overwhelmed him earlier that even Eleanor, entertaining him to dinner at the mission, commented on it. But Robert was not prepared to share his secret. He smiled at her more affectionately than usual because he was happy, but treated her to no explanation.

His happiness was not to last long. Only ten days later a letter arrived from Frisca; it must have come into Bombay on the same mail ship which was now bearing his own back to England.

"I love you, Robert," Frisca wrote. "I'm saying that now because I shan't ever be able to say it again. It wouldn't be fair. But I always shall love you. I sent you away with a lie, though, and I ought to put the record straight.

"I am—truly—going to have a baby. When I told you I was pregnant it wasn't a mistake and it wasn't a lie. It wasn't an accident, either. Whether you can understand how much I've always loved you and always wanted to marry you, I don't know, but it's the only explanation I can offer for what I suppose is unforgivable behaviour. All the same, we were both right, weren't we, when we realised that a marriage between us wouldn't work? We'd have ended up hating each other. I couldn't bear that, because I want to love you forever. That's why I had to send you away, and I could only send you away by being dishonest. The lie came when I said that the pregnancy business had all been a mistake, a false alarm. Now I'm frightened that you're going to hate me for that instead. Please forgive me, Robert, for giving your child to someone else.

"It hasn't taken me long to find a willing father for the baby. I married Arthur—our cousin Arthur—last week. It makes it easier, somehow, that I've known him all my life and he's not young anymore and he isn't passionately in love with me. I didn't want to marry anyone who would expect me to love him in the way I loved you. You might say that Arthur is going to take pleasure in 'owning' me, and I don't really mind that. We've always got on well together in a father-and-daughterly sort of way. He likes buying me presents, especially clothes. He wants me to go on with my career, so that he can feel proud of me. The other side of it is that I could tell him the truth about the pregnancy, and I have. It means that I have something to offer him, you see. Ever since he got his baronetcy he's wished he could have an heir for the title and Brinsley House and all his money, but he was told by his doctor ten years ago that he'd never be able to have a child of his own. Now he's going to get his heir—we're both praying it will be a boy. Everyone will think that the baby is Arthur's own. You and he will be the only people to know the truth. I told him that the baby is yours, and even that seems to suit him. Keeping things in the family, I suppose.

"So everything's settled and I feel aboveboard again. It was horrid, being deceitful. Don't be angry with me, Robert. Dearest Robert."

Of course he was angry. He screwed the letter into a crumpled ball and then was forced to smooth it out again so that he could reread it. How dare she give his child away? What right had she? Why couldn't she have waited, told him the truth, given him the chance to find a solution? There was no consolation to be gained from the knowledge that they had agreed about the impossibility of a continuing relationship. He paced up and down his verandah, kicking at Siva as he passed.

After anger came calculation. Arthur was an old man, surely. How old? The effort to work it out produced an unsatisfactory result. Nearly fifty, perhaps, but not more. A rich man, taking care of himself, could live for twenty or thirty years after fifty. Except that men of that age, marrying young wives, sometimes overexerted themselves, died of heart attacks. It took a little while for Robert to admit to himself where his thoughts were leading him, and then he was appalled by them. It was not even that he disliked Arthur, who was a decent enough chap and had probably thought he was doing a favour to everyone concerned.

Given a choice, he would hardly have chosen Eleanor as a confidante, but there was no one else to whom he could speak. In any case, she led the way into the subject herself. He was returning her invitation to dinner when, always abrupt in her speech, she asked him outright.

"What's happened, Robert? One day you were on top of the world, and now suddenly you seem to be in the depths of despair. No trouble at home, I hope."

Perhaps she had noticed that the photograph of Frisca was no longer on show. Perhaps she had even guessed part of what had happened. Robert was not prepared to tell her the true cause of his unhappiness, but he made an admission of a sort.

"How can one control one's thoughts, Eleanor? I find myself wishing for someone to die. I know that it's shameful, wicked even, but I can't stop myself."

"This is where I feel the Roman Catholics have the advantage over us," Eleanor said. "Their people can confess, which is a help in itself. And then they're told not to do it again and that gives them the requirement of obedience to balance against their own desires."

"But since I'm not a Roman Catholic?"

"Are you seriously asking for advice? It's not easy, without knowing the circumstances. I should say that you ought to spell out to yourself all the benefits you might gain if this man *were* to die. And then take whatever steps are necessary to make sure that you wouldn't be able to take advantage of them if that did happen. If you're expecting to inherit money, for example, you could write to the man and ask him to change his will so that you wouldn't get anything."

"No, it isn't that particular benefit. But what a very drastic solution if it were—when after all, one might have a perfect right to inherit when the time came." Robert was talking too fast to cover the shock he felt. Eleanor was not particularly intelligent, yet she had produced exactly the right solution. If Robert himself were to marry, it would no longer matter to him whether Frisca was a wife or a widow.

Knowing how easy it was to be pushed in the wrong direction by loneliness and unhappiness, he did not take any decision at once. Instead, over a period of several months, he set himself to observe Eleanor in her daily life, noticing the firm fairness with which she managed the children in her classes, the firm unreasonableness with which she expected perfection from servants who did not know the meaning of the word. In every sphere of her life except one she gave orders with confidence. Only where personal relationships were concerned was she insecure—and Robert suspected that once she was married even this area of uncertainty would disappear and her husband, like everyone else, would be told what was best for him.

Did he mind? In an odd way the years in the trenches and, even more, the months of headache and dizziness which had followed his second wound, had changed his character. The robust energy of his youth had faded away, leaving him passive, prepared to drift with the tide. He was still able to take responsibility, for his work or for anything else. But he felt no great need to be the ruling partner in any relationship. His one attempt to stand up to Frisca with the refusal to abandon his work had been inspired by the belief that her pregnancy would give her no choice but to accept what was more or less an ultimatum. Such a disastrous miscalculation did not inspire him to repeat that kind of gesture.

There was a difference of religious belief, certainly, between himself and Eleanor, but his view was to have no view at all, so why should they quarrel? They had in common the wish to help the people in whose country they were living. It was his love of India which had wrecked his prospects with Frisca. With the greater passion thwarted, he must at all costs preserve the lesser. He had already been approached to see whether he would sign a new contract for a railway-line extension after his dams were finished, and since there was no longer any reason for him to return to England, he would accept. Eleanor would want to continue her teaching, so there would be no difficulty on that score.

Eleanor would surely be grateful to have a husband. Missionary teachers even at the best of times must expect to remain celibate, and this was not the best of times. So many of Robert's contemporaries had been killed that the number of women in England who had no hope of marriage was recognised as a social phenomenon. Eleanor, thin and desiccated, was scarcely beautiful, and her tubular cotton frocks looked dowdy and faded even before the dhobi had begun to beat the colour and shape out of them. But Frisca's looks were so much out of the ordinary that no one in the world could compete with them. It was as well, really, that there should be no comparison.

The moment of decision came when he read a second letter from Frisca. He had not been able to bring himself to answer the first one, not even to congratulate her on becoming Lady Lorimer. Receiving the letter that had crossed with hers, she would have known how he felt. Now, more briefly, she wrote to tell him of the birth of a son, Bernard Lorimer, who should have been Bernard Scott.

Robert's first reaction was to have the stone relief of Siva dancing crated up. Eleanor disliked it and had already expressed her surprise that he could bear to live with such a nasty heathen thing on show. It was to be regarded as a combined wedding and christening present, Robert wrote to Frisca. "It seems a suitable gift for a dancer. It's very old, of course. I'm sorry about the crack but that's part of its history. I can remember what you used to say when you were a child and I used to tease you for practising those interminable dancing exercises, on and on for hours. 'Nothing but the best will do.' But by now I expect you've grown up enough to realise that sometimes one has to settle for the second best."

He checked his own bitterness and tore the letter up, rewriting it more formally, more kindly, more affectionately. They were, after all, cousins. Arthur would not expect them to have become strangers overnight.

After he had posted the letter and arranged for the despatch of the stone, Robert asked Eleanor if she would marry him. It was ironic that after forcing himself to consider the possibility for almost six months, in order to be sure that he was not simply over-reacting to a disappointment, it needed only the single moment of watching acceptance and happiness brighten her eyes to tell him that he was making a mistake.

"Nothing but the best will do," he reminded himself for a second time and, again for a second time, he pushed the bitterness to the back of his mind as he waited for Eleanor to say yes.

PART II

FAMILY TIES

(1930–1937)

John.

Margaret had written the word in her diary on the page headed December 15, 1930. Now she copied it onto the notepad which she used to jog her increasingly erratic memory. She felt sure that there was something which ought to be done, but now she could not even remember who this John might be. She stared at the name and spoke it out loud, putting to it any surname which seemed to fit. There were several boys and men called John in the village. Margaret tried to make herself useful by visiting any of Alexa's tenants who were sick or old, so she might have come across some case of need attached to the name. Suppose the need was urgent. Margaret worried about her forgetfulness but was reluctant to confess it. She gave herself a few days in which to solve the problem but without success. She would have to ask Alexa.

Only over the luncheon table could Margaret hope to see her half sister. Alexa's years as an opera singer had accustomed her to late hours. It was her habit to have breakfast brought to her in bed, never earlier than nine o'clock and more often at ten. The post would be brought up at the same time, and half an hour later her secretary would come into the bedroom to fill in the diary and take instructions on the social letters.

By eleven Alexa would be dressed and in her office. Lord Glanville, while he lived, had been enthusiastic about the conversion of the old tithe barn into a river-side opera house, encouraging his wife's natural aptitude for business. She had a head for figures that he might have described as masculine, had his fervent support for the Women's Rights Movement not guarded him against that kind of inadvertent insult. His accountant had shown her how to keep accounts and how to draw up the financial forecasts essential for opera, and he himself had always been willing to give advice; but only when she asked for it. His reward had been the knowledge that if—coming to fatherhood so late in life—he did not live to see his heir come of age, Alexa could be trusted to see that her son's inheritance would be preserved.

The confidence which Lord Glanville felt in his wife's judgement had been enshrined in the will drawn up after the birth of his son. Pirry would automatically inherit all the property and estates which were entailed in the male line, as well as the title; and sufficient money was put into trust to ensure that they could be adequately maintained. But a large part of Lord Glanville's disposable fortune had been left directly to his widow. Some of it she had used to buy the best singers in the world for the productions of her little opera house when it reopened after the war. But by 1930 she no longer needed to entice them with money; the reputation of Blaize was sufficient attraction.

Summer was the hectic time of the year; but the present period, before Christmas, was also a busy one. Production details for the coming season had to be decided and bookings made for the season after that. Alexa took all the important decisions herself, and Margaret knew how hard she worked in the middle of the day. But she would break off at two o'clock for luncheon and a chat. Then she might leave for London, to visit a dressmaker or go to a theatre or a dinner party.

Margaret was aware that her sister had a regular escort for these evening occasions, but thought it none of her business to ask questions. Alexa had spent her life being flattered and loved and showered with presents. She could not be expected to change her nature merely because she had passed the age of fifty; and Matthew could not fill the need. But when she was not in London she was regular in her visits to Matthew. Margaret herself went to bed early, at ten o'clock, and at about the same time Alexa would walk across to the coach house and sit with Matthew in his studio until the small hours. They had never attempted to conceal the fact that their affection for each other was far stronger than a family tie; but the tension which had once left them looking tired and unhappy seemed now to have charged them both with creative energy. Alexa's working hours were shorter than Matthew's, but they were equal in concentration.

Margaret's day, by contrast, began early. As a medical student in the 1880s she had discovered that the hours between six and eight in the morning were the best time for studying, and she had been an early riser ever since. Ten years had passed since her retirement in 1920, but she still felt guilty if she did not leave her bed as soon as she awoke. Alexa's attempts to provide her with breakfast in bed were always resisted.

These days, though, it took her a long time to bathe and dress. The task of brushing her long hair—completely white now—and twisting it into a bun was a tiring one. She needed to rest her arm from time to time before she could raise it again to her head. If Alexa had known, she would have insisted on sending a maid, but Margaret was not yet prepared to admit to any of the weaknesses of age, nor to accept any lessening of her independence.

Often she breakfasted alone, but not when Pirry and Barbara were home from boarding school. The meal that morning was made cheerful with their chatter but was over too soon, leaving another day to be filled. The need to be useful and busy was so much part of Margaret's nature that she hated to find herself without occupation and rationed her few duties carefully through the week. There could be no question of her making any contribution to the running of the big house. It was lucky that Alexa allowed her to help with the visiting of tenants, but she had long ago discovered that they preferred her to call in the afternoon, when they or their neighbours had made their cottages spick and span. In the morning she could only read the newspaper and write letters.

She had regular days for Robert and Grant, writing to each of them at length once a week. Some of the men who had been patients at Blaize when it was a military hospital still kept in touch with her, and she spent an hour writing cards to thank them for their news. But the name at the top of her memory pad still worried at her mind. Who was John?

She intended to approach the subject cautiously over luncheon, in the hope that no one would become aware of her lapse of memory. But it was some time before she could get a word in. Alexa, it soon appeared, had something special to say.

"Your school report arrived this morning, Pirry," she announced. A general gloom descended. This was a conversation which took place three times a year and was never a happy one. "I'm inured by now to the insults which every subject master is accustomed to hurl at your academic performance. But your housemaster has found a new stick to beat you with. Exactly what does he mean by unsuitable friendships?"

Pirry flushed. He had inherited his mother's red-gold hair and pale complexion, and although he was seventeen he had not yet any need to shave. The effect was curiously feminine. At thirteen he had been an outstandingly pretty boy and since then had somehow managed to avoid the normal adolescent coarsening of feature and roughening of manners.

"They're all sports-mad at that hell-hole," he said. "Maniacs, the lot of them. Why you condemned me to five years at such a place, I can't imagine. The world is divided into mothers who love their sons and those who send them to Eton." He gave Alexa his most winning smile. "Well, I realise that since my father and grandfather and great-grandfather went there, you had no choice. But if you picked up one of the poorest boys from the village and set him down in the middle of one of our playing fields in winter, he'd sue you for common assault. And if Aunt Margaret then saw the conditions in which he had to clean off a thick layer of mud, she'd close the whole institution down on grounds of indecency and insanitariness, if such a word exists. One of these days I shall be brought home on a stretcher with all my ribs broken where some fourteen-stone thug sat on me and then you'll be sorry and it will be too late."

Barbara giggled and Margaret could not resist a smile, but Alexa merely sighed.

"And the unsuitable friendships?" she asked again.

"Well, there are one or two methods of escaping compulsory games. One can't do it too often, of course. And if one does, it's naturally important to keep out of the way, not to be seen. I managed to find a little cubby hole. Private and reasonably sound-proof. I keep a gramophone there. One or two other chaps know about it. Two of us were caught red-handed listening to

Mahler. It might not have been as bad if it had been Sousa or Johann Strauss, but it appears that Mahler is decadent. The other young gentleman concerned is the only son of a duke. Unsuitable friendship, indeed! If you were looking for a friend for your eldest unmarried daughter, assuming you had one, you'd think that no one could be more suitable. All Pruneface means is that I should have been playing games and if I wasn't playing games I should have been doing extra prep and if I wasn't doing extra prep I should have been doing anything at all except listening to music and if I happened to be listening to music it shouldn't have been Mahler and if I had to listen to Mahler I should have done so alone. It's nothing to do with the particular chap who was listening as well. No doubt the Duke of Caversham is at this very moment having precisely the same conversation with his son about the unsuitability of knowing Lord Glanville."

"Caversham?" Alexa's attention was diverted by the name. There had been a long period, as Margaret well knew, when its owner had followed Alexa all over Europe, showering her with presents of jewellery. "I know the Duke of Caversham. His son's only thirteen."

"All the more credit to the little lad for appreciating good music so early in life. His dad's an opera buff. They've got the same records as mine at home. It's ridiculous to expect a chap who's been brought up in a civilised manner to become a philistine the moment he's hurled into compulsory education."

"Right," said Alexa. "You've said your bit. Now you can listen to mine." Her voice was unsympathetic. The note of harshness disturbed Margaret. If there was going to be a quarrel it would be humiliating for Pirry to know that other people were listening. She began a counterconversation with Barbara, asking her about her plans for the day. The answer was unexpected. Alexa's chauffeur was going to give her a driving lesson.

"But dearest, you've only just had your thirteenth birthday. You're too young. It's against the law."

"Not as long as I stay on a private estate. Merriman's fitted a dual-control brake on the van so that he can stop me if I'm going wrong. He says I'm making myself so useful, helping him with the retuning and all that sort of thing, that it's only fair for me to find out what everything's used for. I like engines. I'd like to be an engineer when I grow up, like Daddy. But not dams and roads and railways. Cars and aeroplanes, that sort of thing."

"My poor Barbara, I don't think anyone's ever going to let women build aeroplane engines."

"Why not?" asked Barbara. "When you were my age, no one was going to let women be doctors, but it happened. The nice thing about engines is that either they work or they don't, and you can tell. I mean, if someone comes to *you* with a pain, you can give them some medicine but you can't feel the pain yourself and so you can't exactly know whether the medicine's doing any good. But if I clean a sparking plug, something will start which wouldn't start before. It's very satisfactory. Pirry says that the world is divided between people people and things people and that I'm a things person."

"Oh, I hope not, dearest."

"Why?" asked Barbara, but Margaret was given no time to reply. Pirry, more flushed than before, was pushing back his chair and tugging at his cousin's arm.

"Yes, all right," said Alexa, giving the two young people permission to leave the table before they had time to ask for it. She sighed as the door closed behind them. "It's not right for a boy to be brought up in a house full of women. I asked Matthew once if he couldn't take more interest, but he said that Pirry would resent any attempt on his part to be a kind of substitute father, and that may have been true. The housemaster's doing his best. But Pirry's not his kind of boy. They just don't get on. Well, only another year. Perhaps university life will be more congenial."

"You'll send him to Oxford, I suppose." Pirry's father, Piers, had been an Oxford man.

"I'm not sure, Margaret. I don't want to cut him off from the rest of his generation, but Oxford seems to have become terribly effete these days. Lots of precious young men writing poems and drinking too much."

"They're not all like that, surely."

"No. As Pirry himself might say. Oxford is divided into aesthetes and hearties. He's clearly never going to be a hearty, and I'm not sure that I want him to be that sort of aesthete. I wondered about a university in Germany. It would be useful from the language point of view, and the musical life is very good.

Pirry isn't a singer, but he genuinely does love opera. I'd like to feel that he'd take over my opera house with the rest of the estate one day, and keep it going. But the important thing at the moment is that he mustn't get himself kicked out of Eton, or no decent university will take him. Well now." She made it clear that she was changing the subject. "Christmas. I had a letter from Frisca this morning. Bernard's chicken pox turned out to be a very slight attack. He's been pronounced germ-free, so they'll be able to come."

"And what about John?" Margaret realised that the question might not make sense; but to her relief, Alexa seemed to understand.

"John? I'm leaving Matthew to deal with John."

Then Margaret remembered. John was Matthew's son, the undernourished boy who had appeared unexpectedly at Blaize one day on his bicycle and two days later had departed with an equal lack of warning. Twice a year since then, after Christmas and his birthday, thank-you letters had arrived for the presents which his mother now admitted were from his father. So far as words were concerned, the letters were brief and formal, written in a neat copperplate hand; the reason why Matthew showed them round the family was that John decorated them with ink caricatures of himself, using whatever the present happened to be. It was odd, thought Margaret, going off at a tangent yet again, it was very odd indeed to see how tastes and talents were inherited. That Pirry should love music was not too surprising, since he had been brought up surrounded by it. But Barbara hardly knew her father and could not have developed a taste for tinkering with engines from watching him. And for ten years John had believed his father to have been a miner, killed in a pit crash. His neat draughtsmanship—and, more important, the pleasure he took in practising it—could only have been instinctive.

But something had happened recently to worry her about John. Yes, she remembered that too. His mother had died; he had written to tell Matthew.

"Did Matthew go to the funeral?" she asked.

Alexa shook her head. "No. Peggy had told so many lies. All her neighbours thought she'd been a widow for years. It wouldn't have been kind to her memory for a deserted husband to bob up."

"So what's happening to John now? He's only fourteen."

"He's living with the family of one of his school friends in the village. As a matter of fact, he wrote to Matthew again yesterday, asking if he could come here for Christmas."

"Asking! Oh, Alexa, he shouldn't have had to do that. We should have invited him. Straightaway, before he had time to feel lonely." That was why she had written the name down. She remembered it all now. "Poor little boy. Fourteen. That's only a year older than Barbara. Just think, if Barbara were to find herself all alone in the world! Alexa, we must look after him."

"It's not quite as simple as that. Peggy told lies to the boy as well. When she was caught out in the first story she made up another one. John doesn't *like* his father. He blames him for everything that's happened. On that visit four years ago, they didn't get on at all, you remember. Naturally Matthew didn't want to say anything that would set the boy against his mother. Now Peggy's dead, perhaps he'll feel able to explain what really happened: I don't know. Of course John can come here for Christmas. I've told Matthew that. But I don't think any of us ought to expect too much from it. You're right that the boy must be feeling lonely and miserable. But I'm not sure that the sight of the rest of us, all happy together, is going to do much to help."

"It mustn't be only Christmas. Matthew must take the responsibility for him. I'll go and talk to him. It's very important."

"He knows that," said Alexa soothingly. "But you mustn't lose sight of the fact that they rub each other up the wrong way. It's not only that John resents Matthew. Matthew can't help remembering that if it hadn't been for John, he wouldn't have had to marry Peggy. Hardly the basis for a warm relationship. But Matthew *is* thinking about it. He's going to have a word with Arthur over Christmas. John's left school already, it seems. He got a job on his fourteenth birthday, to look after his mother when she was ill. A dead-end boy's job that won't lead anywhere. With all this unemployment he could be on the dole by the time he's sixteen if he stays in Leicestershire. He seems to be neat-fingered: you've seen his letters. If Arthur likes the look of him, he might give him an apprenticeship in the drawing office of his shipbuilding firm. And John might find it easier to take a favour from his uncle than from his father. Anyway, he'll be here for Christmas and you can mother him as much as you like."

"You're humouring me, Alexa," said Margaret sharply. "I won't be humoured. You don't seem to understand, any of you, how important it is for a family to hold together. We're all lonely sometimes. Some of us are bad at making friends, and some of us lose our friends when they die. But anyone who's part of a family ought to be able to feel that there are people who'll accept him for what he is and love him and care for him whether they like him or not. If we don't have that sort of comfort, what is there?"

Alexa came round to Margaret's end of the table and put her arm round her sister's shoulders.

"Do you think you need to teach me that lesson now?" she said softly. "Do you think I shall ever forget how you took a dirty, shabby little girl into your home when you hardly had two pennies to rub together, just because she was the daughter of your father? Illegitimate. Hardly a member of the family at all. Haven't you realised how important it is to me that I've been able to make this house into a family home. I can't pretend that I'm as warm-hearted as you, but anyone with Lorimer blood who wants to be loved and looked after can come to Blaize: you will love him and I shall look after him. We're not really saying different things. A family can't force itself on one of its members. All it can do is exist, and be there when it's wanted. John very understandably feels the need of a family at Christmas, and he's going to get it. He's going to have lots of presents, and we shan't let him leave until between us we've worked out what kind of work he'd like to do and what training he'll need to qualify for it. It's for him, not us, to say what he wants of us after that."

It wasn't good enough, Margaret thought. Everything Alexa said was true, but it wasn't good enough. Nevertheless, she held her tongue. At the time of adopting her orphaned half sister, Margaret had been twenty-nine, young and determined, professionally qualified and hard-working. The responsibility she undertook at that time was one which she could reasonably hope to carry through to its natural end. But now she was almost seventy-four, too old to make promises and be sure of keeping them. If, as she believed, a family ought to offer security to all its members, that kind of security could only come from someone younger. She would have to trust Alexa.

In Russia in the mid-thirties any visit from an official was a cause of anxiety. The higher the rank of the visitor, the greater the reason for alarm. Kate Lorimer had as many guilty secrets as anyone else, not the least of them being the fact that she had been born Kate Lorimer. Nevertheless, when no less a person than People's Commissar Gorbatov arrived—unaccompanied and unannounced—at her room in the Children's Home in 1935 and called her name, Kate turned towards the door with an instant smile.

"Sergei! How very good to see you! What are you doing so far from Moscow?" They embraced affectionately and he stood with his one arm around her shoulders, looking down at the bench where she had been working.

"What are *you* doing?" he asked, and Kate was quick to understand that he did not intend to answer her own question.

"We're short of medicines," she replied. "The children are bound to fall ill sometimes, and I've no drugs with which to treat them. The Home has a partorg now, whose job it is to supervise their political education and social well-being, so if I can't give them medical care, I'm useless. I've been experimenting with herbal remedies—with a good deal of success as far as poultices and infusions are concerned."

"And how many of your charges have you poisoned in the course of your experiments?"

"I've taken advice from every babushka in the village," Kate told him. "Many of these remedies have been used for generations. And when I was a child I studied the same kind of medicine in my own home village. My mother was a doctor there, and often found herself in competition with folk magic."

"But you can't expect to grow the same herbs and roots here that you found in Jamaica," he said. The reference to her past was so unexpected and so unwise that Kate could not prevent herself glancing at him in alarm and found his sunken black eyes staring deeply into hers.

"Even you, even here!" he sighed. "Is there no one in Russia who is not afraid? You asked me why I'm here, Katya. Did you know that in Leningrad alone five hundred people have been shot since Kirov was assassinated? I have been sent by Stalin to discover whether that is enough or whether those who ordered the executions also have something to hide. Yet Nicolayev, the assassin, who still claims that he acted alone and only out of jealousy on account of his wife's affair with Kirov, may well be telling the truth. Now I am making you uneasy again, am I not? Well, you will show me round the Home and we will talk of the children and say nothing of which your commandant can disapprove. But I hope I may eat alone with you tonight?"

"I'll arrange it," Kate promised, trying not to reveal how much the strangeness of his mood disturbed her. She had no kitchen of her own, but Sergei was such an important figure in the Party that his name was enough to authorise the service of food in her own room. Sergei himself contributed two bottles of vodka, refilling his own glass so frequently that the first bottle was soon empty.

"Does Ilsa sleep with you here?" he asked, looking around the room. The bed was concealed by a curtain.

"No. Until a few months ago she slept with the orphans. But now—" Kate's face brightened as she accepted a refill of her glass. "She's a marvellous pianist, Sergei. If you were to hear her, you'd hardly believe that she's so young. And she's in good standing with the Party. She's been a Pioneer since she was eight, and recently she's become a member of the Komsomol. So she's been officially recognised as especially talented and goes to the School for the Musically Gifted in Leningrad. She comes home for holidays, but lives in the city during the term."

"She inherited her talent, I suppose, from her father. Prince Aminov was a brilliant musician, was he not?"

The silence in the room was so tense that Kate was unable to break it even by breathing. She stared wordlessly at Sergei. He was a little drunk—the narrowing of his eyes showed it—but there had been nothing careless about his choice of words. She felt him take her hand and lift it to his cheek. "He's dead, you know," he said softly. "He's been dead for sixteen years."

For a moment Kate's body seemed to freeze into a hard, heavy lump. Unable to think or to feel anything, she began to shiver uncontrollably. Sergei's hand tightened on hers. "Were you still in love with him?" he asked.

"I was in love with the memory of him." Her voice seemed to come from a long way away and she was surprised at her own honesty. "There's never been anyone else. But we only had a short time together, and I've grown older, while he stayed the same in my memory. If I'd met him again, we would have been strangers. I needed the memory. But—" She struggled to collect her thoughts. "Those first years after we were separated, I loved him so much. I cried. I prayed that one day he'd come. Just walk into the room, as you did today, and call my name and be happy with me. But then—oh, it took a long time, but I began to ask myself what sort of life he was enduring if he was alive and yet not able to look for me. About three years ago there was a man who arrived and said he was the father of one of the orphans. The poor girl believed he was dead; hadn't seen him since she was two years old; thought of him as a hero, a gallant young man killed in the struggle against the enemy. Then suddenly she found herself staring at a stranger. An old man—in his thirties, but old. Alive and yet somehow dead. Dead eyes, dead skin, dead spirit. He'd been in Siberia. I watched them together and I thought of Vladimir and I hoped he was dead. I *hoped* it. After that, I made myself believe that it was so, because every alternative was too terrible to bear. I suppose I couldn't make myself believe it quite certainly enough to leave the Children's Home. There was always that little doubt, the thought that if an old, broken man arrived for me, I must be here. But now you tell me that Vladimir is dead and I can answer, Yes, I know. And I'm glad. Glad for him." She was crying, though: the tears trickled through her fingers as she buried her head in her hands.

Sergei sat without speaking until her emotions had exhausted themselves. Only then did he say quietly, "There are questions you should ask me."

Not much imagination was needed to guess what he meant. How long have you known? Did you know before his death, or after? Then those questions would lead to another. Could you have saved him? Kate stared into Sergei's eyes and did not speak at once.

Vladimir had been travelling on a permit signed by Sergei on that fateful journey in 1918. Even so early in the revolution, Sergei had been a man of importance. His signature was not to be taken lightly. Vladimir had known that his stolen papers were not perfect. He was older than the man whose identity he had assumed, and he would be caught out at once by anyone who came from the town in which he was said to have been born and brought up. But the Cheka would not have dared to shoot him until they had cleared the execution with the man who had authorised his journey.

What real choice would Sergei have had then? Kate had put him in danger by asking him to help a man she knew was not entitled to such help. He had known the risk and had accepted it because of their old friendship. But Vladimir must have been doomed from the moment his interrogation began and if Sergei had tried to protect him further the only consequence could have been that both of them would have died instead of only one. So Sergei, almost certainly, had claimed to have been deceived.

Why, she wondered, was he giving her the opportunity to accuse him of betrayal? Whatever the reason, she did not propose to take it. She had lost her husband, but in her heart she had known for many years that she would never see him again. The time of mourning had ended long before her tears began to flow; and if she had no husband, would never have a husband again, she could not afford to lose the friend of her youth, the man she had loved less passionately and less protectively than she had loved Vladimir, but for longer.

She stood up and moved across to the stove in the corner of the room, warming one hand against its tiles. It was the stove which had heated Vladimir's nursery suite. Kate had chosen the room specially so that she might indulge herself with thoughts of his childhood. Now she used the same movement to steady herself before she looked back at Sergei. "No, my friend," she said. "I have no questions to ask."

He moved more quickly than she could have expected, pressing her body close to his with his single arm, so that she could feel her heart beating against his chest. Without making any attempt to kiss her, he allowed his feeling for her to communicate itself through their closeness. How well we know each other, Kate thought. Just as she had not needed to ask Sergei for his confession, so he had realised that she understood the truth and accepted it.

"Do you want to go back to England?" he asked at last, moving a little away from her.

"I suppose I ought to consider it. But I have no life there. No friends. It would be more comfortable, I suppose, and perhaps less frustrating." She spent a moment thinking of the discussions and arguments which were necessary here in Russia before any sensible decision could be made, the inefficiency which it seemed hopeless to fight, the constant suspicion and threat of denunciation. "But then I remember the ideals of my youth. They're not quite dead yet. 'From each according to his ability.'" She laughed at herself a little as she quoted. "What ability I have is put to good use here—and I don't only look after the children; I love them as well."

"Then let us drink to the children, who keep you in Russia." Suddenly Sergei was gay, his excitement brightening his eyes as he filled their glasses. The earlier conversation was over and done with. Neither of them would ever refer to it again. Kate had drunk far less than her companion, but even she felt her head beginning to swim. For safety's sake she sat down on the ledge of the stove, enjoying its warmth and remembering another, even colder, evening.

"We drank almost the same toast together once before," she said. "To the children of Europe—do you remember?"

"I remember everything." Sergei stared down at her, and there was a look in his eyes that she had never seen before. They gave no warning of his sudden change of subject, but only of the depth of his feelings. "Katya, something terrible is happening in Moscow. Trust is no longer possible. There's no one in whom I can confide. Not even the boys who lay beside me in the snow in

1905, bleeding from the same whips that cut away my arm. Not even the comrades who made the revolution with me in 1917, who created a new society. I couldn't have believed, if anyone had tried to warn me, that it would come to this. That we, the old Bolsheviks, should no longer dare to speak freely to each other. Stalin is a monster, Katya. I have to say it to you."

For a second time that evening Kate's body seemed to freeze, and not even the stove could warm her blood. "Those are dangerous words for you to speak, Sergei, and for me to hear."

"Yes," he agreed. "But they must be spoken. There must be someone, one person in the whole world, to whom I can say without fear whatever is in my heart. Otherwise we have killed friendship, destroyed love. I must have one person to trust."

"Your wife?" suggested Kate.

"Three months ago my wife denounced her own brother. She reported something he said while he was drunk and now he's dead. Shot. How can I ever talk freely to her again?"

"And you trust me more than her?"

Unexpectedly the sadness in his eyes was banished by a glint of mischief. "I know so much about you that you wouldn't dare denounce me because we should fall into disgrace together. A foreigner, living under a false name, with false papers, and once married to a prince of the old nobility! You're as good as dead already, Comrade Katya! But I shall never need to blackmail you with that. The poison of Moscow hasn't yet infected you. Instead, I must make you believe me when I tell you that I love you. I love you so much that if you were to betray me I would be glad to die rather than live in a world in which you were no longer my friend."

The best of their conversation that evening seemed to be taking place in the silences between the words. Kate stared at Sergei, and he answered the question she did not ask.

"Yes," he went on. "This is why I had to tell you about Vladimir. I needed to ask for your forgiveness before I could ask you to accept my trust. And only after that could I ask you to take me to your bed."

Kate was not a romantic young girl waiting to be swept off her feet by a passionate lover. She was forty-three years old. An unbalanced diet caused by the food shortages had thickened her tall and always sturdy body. Her complexion had been weathered first by the strong sunlight of a tropical island and later by the extreme cold of Russian winters. Ever since she cropped her hair to discourage the Serbian lice she had worn it short, trimmed severely with the same scissors which kept the orphans neat. From the moment when she had ceased to excite herself with fantasies of Vladimir's return, it was as though she had taken a deliberate decision: to make herself, if not unattractive to men, at least neutral, so that she would never invite their lust. The smile of her generous mouth was still as warm as ever, and nothing had dimmed the brightness of her green eyes or the forceful excitement with which she pursued her enthusiasms; but she had taught herself not to expect that any man would ever again desire her body.

Had she dreamt of a love affair, it would not have been with a one-armed man in his fifties. If rumour was to be believed, the People's Commissars in their comfortable Moscow flats suffered few of the deprivations of the rest of the population. But Sergei remained thin and hollow-chested, his complexion still the same unhealthy yellowish-white colour which had shocked her at their first meeting. If anything, he looked worse now: his hair had always been dark but now was dyed; the unnatural raven-black sheen made him appear even older.

For a moment she was tempted to laugh at the ridiculousness of it all. But at the same time she understood what Sergei was asking and offering. He would be giving her—if his loyalty was indeed beginning to crack—the power of life and death over him, but at the same time he would be exposing her to the same risks which he faced himself. It was the duty of every citizen to denounce anyone who was guilty of disloyalty. Failure to do so was a criminal offence. Denunciation was the only defence against a charge of conspiracy, of guilt by association. When men of importance fell from power, their friends and supporters and all who had been shown their favour shared their disgrace. Disgrace, these days, meant death. A children's doctor in a country village, obeying the instructions of the district committee and attending the necessary meetings and political education classes, was remote from danger. The mistress of a commissar was not.

She felt ashamed of herself for even considering the risk. Had it not been for Sergei, she would have been lying in a Serbian grave for the past nineteen years. He had a right to claim some of the years for which he had saved her. They had loved each other, in a way, for a very long time, and Kate had thought that way sufficient. But Sergei was asking her to make their friendship complete, to create a relationship of mind and body in which nothing at all should be held back. He was right to do so. There must be one person in the world for him to trust. And one for her.

1

It was in 1937 that Sergei began to prepare for his own death.
During a visit to Kate in the middle of June he tried to persuade
her to let him send her away from the Children's Home.

"But why?" she asked, bewildered.

"You're too near Leningrad. You'd be safer in some more
remote area. Down in the south, perhaps. With a warmer climate. It could be arranged."

"I'm safe enough here," she said.

"It's known that you receive visits from me. If anything should
happen—"

"What is likely to happen?" she demanded, alarmed for Sergei
rather than herself. "Do you need a warmer place yourself? Are
you ill?" He had looked unhealthy ever since she first met him, so
his appearance gave no clue to any change. "If it's necessary for
your sake, of course I'll think again. But Ilsa is doing so well with
her musical studies. I want to stay here if I can."

"I see." He considered for a moment. "All right. I'll arrange for
the partorg to go instead."

Nothing could have told her so clearly how seriously he was
worried. Like every large institution, the Children's Home had a
commandant whose duty it was to make sure that all the staff
were politically reliable, as well as maintaining the proper discipline in the Home. Sergei had always done his best to pretend
that his visits to Kate were imposed by his official duties, but it
was unlikely that the partorg had been deceived. As long as Sergei
remained a commissar, the association could do Kate nothing but

good. But if he should be disgraced, his visits would be remembered and held against her.

"Tell me what's wrong," she asked quietly.

"Do you know what is happening in Germany?" Sergei began to pace up and down, his restlessness showing the strain he was under. "Have you heard what Adolf Hitler is doing to the Jews?"

"I've heard rumours."

"The rumours are true. The Jews are being sent to labour camps—just because they are Jews. Whether they're dying because of overwork or poor treatment or whether they're being deliberately killed is less easy to determine, but our information is that none of them ever return to their homes. So would you expect a Jew to be a supporter of Hitler?"

Kate shook her head.

"Last year, and the year before, at the public trials of the Trotskyite conspirators, I tried to make myself believe that they were guilty, that their confessions were true. Well, perhaps I couldn't believe quite that, but I told myself that there must have been some guilt to inspire such feelings of shame. But now there's been a new trial. Not in public this time. I suppose the men accused weren't trusted to confess so readily. It's over already. The verdict will be announced in a few days. After they've all been shot."

"Who was on trial?" asked Kate.

"Marshal Tukhachevsky and seven of his generals. Accused of spying for the Germans. Giving information to Hitler's Army. And Katya, three of those men are Jews. It isn't possible. It simply is not believable." He thumped the wall with his fist as he spoke. "I have been given a new appointment. As Political Commissar to the Red Army. It's a sign of Stalin's high regard for me. I have to find out how far these treacherous generals have infected their subordinates with their disloyalty and stamp it all out. Remove every officer who can't be trusted, even if it means that in the end there is no army left at all. And I take on this task without believing for a moment that the generals were guilty."

"Why should people confess to crimes they haven't committed, knowing that the penalty is death?"

Sergei gave a sigh of hopelessness. "Sometimes they're deluded, made to believe that they're being asked to confess only in order to trap and incriminate others, and that they'll be pardoned after the trial. Sometimes there are—what shall we say—hostages; a son or a wife who can be saved only by a public admission of guilt, so that the choice is between the death of one man only and the death of that man and everyone he loves. I suspect that sometimes drugs are used. But do you see what is happening, Katya? Our army is being destroyed. If I do my task as efficiently as I'm expected to, I shall merely advance its demoralisation. And one day—I don't know when, but the day must come—we shall need our army to fight against Germany. Those Jewish generals knew that. They *wanted* that. And so I have to ask myself, who is responsible for this great act of destruction? And why? There are only two possible explanations. Either Stalin is mad, or else the German intelligence service has somehow infiltrated his advisers to make sure that our military power is weakened before the fighting begins."

"Or both," suggested Kate in a whisper.

"Or both," he agreed. "So what do I do? Do I remain loyal to my leader? Or do I do my best for my unfortunate country? And if I choose the second, have I any hope of success?"

"You must get out." Kate now was thoroughly alarmed. On many occasions during the past two and a half years she had heard Sergei express his doubts about Stalin's methods of government, but never before had he admitted his own involvement so openly. "There must be some excuse you could find to leave the country. To study new weapons, perhaps, new tanks or aeroplanes. You could go to England. My family would welcome you. And after a little while I would join you."

"A stupid general might be allowed abroad to look at tank trials, with an interpreter and a bodyguard to make sure that he returns when he's told. But not a political commissar who speaks five languages and knows too much. Even to ask for permission would be dangerous. The train is travelling too fast for me to jump off it now. No, I think time is running out, Katya. You must be prepared. And you must be separated from me. There's a woman in Leningrad. To my friends in Moscow I've been pretending for a long time that she's the one I come to visit. Now she's dying, and when she's dead, my visits must stop. We must have a story to explain my interest in the Children's Home. Once the partorg has been transferred to Komsomolsk, there'll be no one to contradict it. If I can ride the storm, we will come together afterwards."

Kate looked at him in silence, understanding that he had no true hope to offer. She did not weep, because the only farewell gift she could give him was their last night together.

Nor did she cry four months later when the committee of interrogation arrived from Moscow. After they had left she walked away from the Children's Home to the top of the ridge, turning her back on the city in which she had first embraced the ideals of the revolution. It had been called Petrograd then, and now was Leningrad—the difference in name was only one of many changes in the past twenty years. This was one of the golden days of autumn, a day when the sunlight danced on the leaves of the trees and dappled the ground beneath them. When the nobles built their palaces here they had set their serfs to cut back the dark severity of the evergreen forest and in its place had planted spacious parks in the English manner. Oak and maple mingles their shades of yellow and orange and brown and flaming red, a bright frame for the forest which stretched to the horizon behind them. Kate felt as though her heart was being torn in two. How could it happen in the same world that Russia should be so beautiful and that Sergei should be dead?

They had tried to trap her. Suspicious, but unable to prove their suspicions, they had hurled the shock of his execution at her. And Kate, expecting the worst from the moment she was summoned in front of them, had acted the part which Sergei had already forced her to practise. The pretence of indifference was her only defence, but it seemed to her now, as she struggled with her tears, like a betrayal.

After the first horror, the details—carefully rehearsed—had come easily. Commissar Gorbatov had made regular visits to the Children's Home during the past few years to visit one of the orphans. Kate had understood that the child's late father was an old comrade of the commissar's. Unable to take full responsibility for his friend's son, he had wished to assure himself regularly that the boy was being well looked after. Such solicitude was unusual, and Kate had once or twice wondered whether Commissar Gorbatov might be the boy's real father. But to voice such a suspicion of an important man without proof would have been dangerous. In any case, Kate was not responsible for the admissions to the home but only for the health of the community. The boy had died four months ago, and the commissar's visits had come to an end.

Because she gave no sign of knowing herself to be on trial, her defence had been good enough. No doubt the committee had made enquiries before they sent for her and had discovered that her reputation stood high in the community of Pushkin. Kate was a good doctor and a politically reliable citizen. She spent two days a week at the local hospital and over eighteen years had given many people cause for gratitude. Unless someone reopened the case by denouncing her, she could consider herself safe; but the feeling that she had betrayed a friend lingered, causing her to shiver in the autumn sunlight.

To calm herself she turned back to the building and went in search of Ilsa, who had come home for a two-day visit. The sound of a piano guided her. It was Vladimir's piano, although of course Ilsa did not know that. In the first two cruel winters of her life in the palace, Kate had managed to save it from being chopped for firewood only by a strong warning of the dangers of taking an axe to something strung at such high tension. Later, she had had it moved to safety in a small room which could be locked and forgotten. Not until the struggle for survival had given place to a more secure way of life did she suggest that music should be part of all the children's experience and unlocked the door for anyone willing to treat the instrument with care.

Ilsa was playing the lullaby which Vladimir had written for her —her only legacy from the father she never knew. Vladimir had begun to work on the song as soon as he knew that his wife was pregnant. It had never been written down, but Kate's ear and memory for music was good and she had sung it over and over again to her baby. There was a period, as Ilsa grew older, when she discarded the lullaby with the rest of her babyhood loves, but recently she had begun to improvise from it on the piano, using it as a theme on which to base variations in the styles of all the composers she studied. To judge from the harmonies emerging

through the open window, Brahms was the current favourite—
but the tune was still Vladimir's.

Kate stood without moving, remembering the last journey
which she and Ilsa's father had taken together. If Sergei had tried
to defend Vladimir after his arrest he would have been dragged
down by the association. Kate had understood that well enough—
she had hardly needed even to forgive Sergei. In exactly the same
way Sergei had made it clear how unnecessary and wasteful it
would be for her to link herself with him in disgrace. Like Kate
earlier, he would not see anything to be forgiven. There was no
need to add guilt to her desolate feeling of loneliness.

The rhythm of the piano playing changed, distracting Kate
from her unhappiness. Still in the style of Brahms, Ilsa was playing something almost as familiar to Kate as the lullaby, yet she
could not quite put a name to it. She went into the music room
and watched her daughter giving a vigorous imitation of a complete orchestra. One day, she thought, Ilsa would be a beauty. For
the moment the eighteen-year-old was in love only with music,
and relaxed from its disciplines in a tomboy untidiness. She had
been slim as a child, and would be again later, but at the moment
she had the sturdy appearance of a healthy country girl, like her
mother at the same age. Her dark chestnut hair was plaited, but
not very neatly, and her ruddy cheeks gave her a fresh, outdoor
look. Her eyes were as green as Kate's, and just as likely to glint
with stubbornness: when Ilsa had decided what she wanted, no
one had much chance of budging her. She had high cheekbones
and a very slight slant to her eyes which made Kate wonder
whether any of Vladimir's ancestors had come from Mongolia. At
the moment those distinctive cheeks and eyes gave her the look
of a kitten, to be petted and teased. But she was still growing and
the length of her fingers—she had beautiful hands—suggested
that she would be a tall woman. When that happened, her face
would lengthen as well and the kitten would become a beautiful
cat, elegant and proud.

Kate controlled her thoughts. No one in Russia was elegant, or
dared wish to be. She smiled at her daughter as the music ended
and asked what she had been playing.

"You should know. You taught it to me. You used to sing it

when we went for walks. And the words were always nonsense, because you couldn't remember the real ones."

"I can't recognise it in that disguise. Play just the tune."

Ilsa obliged, tossing her head to the syncopated rhythm.

"It sounds African," she said. "Where did you get it from?"

Kate did not answer at once, for she had identified the tune now, and it was Jamaican. Not one of the hymns which the Hope Valley congregation sang in her father's church, but a wilder one to which they clapped and rocked around the Baptist Hole. "It comes from the jungle," her father had said, but he had never been able to suppress it.

"I don't think you ought to play that," Kate said. "I shouldn't have sung it to you. Will you try to forget it?"

"Why?"

Even to her daughter Kate could not admit the truth, that she had spent her childhood as an English girl in Jamaica. She replaced one confession with another.

"It was a hymn," she said—honestly enough. "I used to sing it as a little girl. Before the revolution, of course, there was no harm in it. But now . . ."

Ilsa looked puzzled, as well she might. There were still churches in which services could legally be held, and she had probably heard enough Russian Orthodox music to know that it bore no resemblance to what she had just played. But she shrugged her shoulders, not troubling to argue.

"Just as you like. It doesn't fit with Brahms, anyway. I must get back now. What did all those men want this afternoon?"

"They were asking about one of the children," said Kate. "A boy who died a few months ago. It was nothing important."

It was difficult, after what had happened, not to cling on to her daughter as they said goodbye, as though any parting might prove to be a final one. But she controlled the impulse, smiling as she waved Ilsa on her way.

The heartbreak of her bereavement returned as soon as she was alone. She sat down at the piano and picked out the dangerous tune, remembering her home in Jamaica. She had been happy there as a child—and yet excited when the moment came for her to leave. As though it were yesterday, she recalled the moment when she said goodbye to her parents before sailing to England to train as a doctor. As young and healthy then as Ilsa now, she had looked at the strained faces of her father and mother and wondered whether they had ever regretted the vocation which had led them to spend their working lives so far from their friends and family. It had never occurred to her that she too might one day regret the path she had chosen.

But if she were to be honest now, she must admit that her excitement and confidence were dead. The world was closing in on her, stifling the spirit which once had been eager and optimistic. As a child she had been brought up to love God and to believe in His all-embracing love; but it was a belief which had not survived the horrors of war. The faith which replaced it—a faith in the power of men to build a new society out of their love for each other—had been almost equally intense, but this in turn could not endure under the disappointments and betrayals of life in a Communist society. Almost without recognising the change, Kate had looked for happiness instead in a personal relationship between two people who loved each other with no reservations. It had been perfect while it lasted, but a single bullet had been enough to end it. What was left, Kate asked herself.

Ilsa was left. Not just because of the talent in her fingertips. Not even because she was all that remained of Vladimir. She was Kate's own future. Nothing else in the world made life worth living except the knowledge that Ilsa would still be alive after Kate herself was dead. Kate shivered again at the danger of pinning all her hope and love to the mast of a single life—especially in Russia, where the life of an individual was regarded as so unimportant. Russia had killed Vladimir, killed Sergei, killed her own idealism. Somehow she must escape from the country with Ilsa and return to England.

There she could become a Lorimer again. The family would be waiting, welcoming and forgiving. Was Aunt Margaret still alive, she wondered. During Kate's years as a medical student in England her aunt had acted as a mother to her, not merely providing a home, but making up for all the love that Kate's own mother, kept in Jamaica by her work, had been unable to show. Margaret must have been hurt when a silence that could have been explained at first by the disruptions of war and revolution had extended itself indefinitely. But the ties of family were strong enough to survive silence and neglect. Kate knew that if she were to walk into her aunt's room now she would be welcomed as though she had never been away. The thought provided a warming contrast with this fear-ridden regime which stifled criticism and did not require disloyalty to be proved before it was punished.

How could she get away, though, when even to express a wish to travel was an antisocial act? Perhaps Ilsa herself might provide the solution. Already she was recognised by her teachers as their most brilliant pupil; already she was giving recitals in Leningrad. Within two years, if her progress continued, she would be ready to embark on an international concert career. It was state policy to allow the best of their young soloists to perform abroad as an example of the excellence of Soviet cultural education. But even in two years' time Ilsa would still be under twenty-one. It would not be unreasonable that her mother should ask to accompany her as a chaperone. Kate had never allowed her daughter to know anything at all about her family background. Ilsa had never heard the name of Lorimer. She knew nothing of her mother's childhood in the West Indies. It was dangerous to inflict secrets on a child.

So if Ilsa was able to leave the country, it would be with no expectation of remaining abroad and so with no feeling of guilt or anxiety which could transmit itself to any Soviet official. There would be no reasonable grounds for forcing her mother to stay behind as a hostage for Ilsa's safe return. Kate knew well enough that reasonableness was not something on which she could rely where officialdom was concerned; and she was taking a good deal for granted even in thinking in terms of a European tour. But in this moment of sadness, with her lover dead, she needed something to which she could look forward with hope. She would endure two more years here. And then, in 1939, she and Ilsa might go home together. To England. To Margaret. To the family.

2

Night was the richest part of India, when the sky widened and lifted, a canopy of black velvet pricked with stars. There was a weightlessness about the atmosphere, a spaciousness of silence, as though the whole vast subcontinent was drifting timelessly, effort-lessly through space. Robert sat in the darkness and stared at the thin, pale moon.

Ten years had passed since his marriage to Eleanor. There was little warmth in their relationship. His love affair was with India, and it was one which Eleanor could not share. At one time he had liked to sleep outside on his verandah during the dry season. There he could savour the coolness and enjoy, too, the knowledge that in the morning he would be awakened gently by the sun's first probing fingers of light. But that was before his marriage. Eleanor from the first had refused to join him, had forced him in-side. Initially she had made the mosquitoes responsible for her de-cision and later, with more embarrassment, had claimed that even beneath a net she would feel too exposed, too public. But Robert came to understand the true reason. India was too large for Eleanor.

It was not just the size of the land. Its history, its population, its problems were all too big to be grasped, let alone controlled. Eleanor could survive only by fencing off a tiny area with a lim-ited number of inhabitants—most of them children—and holding them tightly in her grip. Any reminder of the alien world outside the safe walls of the mission compound was unwelcome, because she was powerless to change it but unable to accept it.

This difference between her and Robert proved ineradicable. Eleanor remained determined to change everything; there was nothing, nothing in the world which was not capable of improve-ment. Robert wanted to change nothing. "As long as they're happy . . ." he would say, shrugging off Eleanor's frustrations in a gesture of tolerance which embraced superstition and ineffi-ciency with an equal lack of indignation. If a man was unhappy enough to ask for help, certainly it should be offered him; but if he was at peace with his old customs and beliefs, then it was a cruelty to force on him the expectation of greater happiness.

Just once during their married life Robert had expressed the opinion that a faith which brought contentment was more impor-tant than truth. This had upset Eleanor so deeply that he would never say it again. Instead, he held his tongue and got on with his work. He provided water against the days of drought, but forced no one to use it. He built roads along which lorries could trans-port food and fertilisers but was careful to leave beside them a dusty track along which plodding bullocks could draw their carts while the drivers slept.

In a word, he had acquired by tolerance the same habit of acceptance which ruled the lives of the Indian villagers. They were amongst the poorest people in the world. Robert could not be unaware of their never-ending struggle to feed themselves—bending to plant or weed the paddy fields, reaping the rice harvest a handful at a time, spreading the grains out to dry in the sun, or threshing and winnowing in the wind. He knew that biologists were working to develop new and sturdier strains of rice, to strengthen resistance to drought or flood, and certainly he approved of such efforts. But he found himself ranged on the other side when he heard other agriculturalists arguing for the introduction of tractors or threshing machines. These undoubtedly would release the pressure which kept the villagers working for the whole of one day merely to be sure that they would be able to survive the next; but who had considered what new social pattern would arise to replace the old?

He knew well enough that in resisting change he was on the losing side. Already discontent in the cities was beginning to spread. The disciples of Gandhi, the little man with the spinning wheel, were travelling through the country like a new kind of missionary, spreading by secret murmurings their criticisms of British rule. Moslem and Hindu communities that had lived side by side for a good many centuries with barely a quarrel were being encouraged to consider themselves separate and irreconcilable. Eleanor and her fellow-teachers were making their own attack on the social pattern, not only by their Christian teaching but also by their determination to offer education to girls as well as boys. Everybody, without doubt, was acting for the best as he saw it. But Robert viewed all their good intentions with silent scepticism. He had lived through one example of what happened when people cared passionately enough for some belief to fight for it, and it was not something he ever intended to do again. His motto now was live and let live.

The ten years of his marriage to Eleanor had been more than long enough for him to accept that he had made a mistake but long enough also for him to have come to terms with it. Their incompatibility could be concealed by avoiding argument and working hard in their separate spheres. Nothing had happened in all that time to pose a serious threat to their relationship.

Nothing, that is to say, until that morning. In the cool of the evening Robert sat on the verandah, pulling at his pipe and waiting for the peacefulness of the atmosphere, lit by the pale moon, to exert its calming effect. His tenseness showed in the unusual speed with which he rocked himself. Eleanor had disapproved of the rocking chair when he first acquired it; it was an article of furniture which she associated with grandmothers in kitchens. By now he had managed to convince her that the movement brought him relief whenever he was afflicted with headaches. But usually the rocking was slight and soothing. Tonight was different. Calmness was taking a long time to come.

Robert had arrived back at the mission bungalow at ten o'clock in the morning after a five-hour journey from the road construction site where he had spent the week. There had been letters from home waiting for him. Like a good mother, Margaret wrote regularly once a week, but shipping schedules frequently caused two or three to arrive together. As soon as he had bathed and changed and eaten he sat down to read them in order and learned from the first that his cousin Arthur was dead. Sir Arthur Lorimer, Bart, had been buried eight weeks ago. Frisca had lost her husband. Nine-year-old Bernard had been deprived of the man he thought was his father.

Eleanor had glanced at her husband anxiously as she saw him lower his head in the way which experience had taught him could best control his dizziness, the legacy of war, which still attacked him from time to time. She said nothing, and after a moment he had recovered himself, staring unseeingly at the page, turning it over as though he were reading on, then opening the second letter and rereading both—this time with more concentration—before handing them over to Eleanor, as his custom was, as though they contained no news of any significance.

"How old was your cousin Arthur?" Eleanor asked when she reached that paragraph in her mother-in-law's letter. She was instantly full of condolences and consolation. "I don't think I met him, did I?" They had spent two leaves together in England since their marriage.

"No." Neither Robert nor Frisca had been able to face a meet-

ing, and Frisca had taken steps to make one impossible. "He lives
—lived—in Bristol, but he and Frisca were away in the West
Indies each time while we were at Blaize. He was a lot older than
me. Getting on for sixty. Too old to be scrambling around cargo
ships, anyway." Arthur, usually so careful, had fallen down the
companionway of one of his own fleet of ships, hitting his head
on an iron rung. He had been unconscious for five days before he
died.

There was no reason why the subject should be mentioned further, and, to make sure that it was not, Robert managed to
remember one of the other topics mentioned in the letter.

"Arthur was the younger brother of Matthew, whom you *did*
meet at Blaize. You remember, in the wheelchair."

"He was the one who was knighted in the New Year's Honours
List, wasn't he?"

"That's right. The Victorian Order. For painting princesses
prettily. I hope you realised what a distinguished family you were
marrying into. A baron, a dowager baroness, a baronet, and now a
knight. Sliding down the social scale, I suppose, but that can't be
helped." He was talking too fast and in a way which was out of
character.

Eleanor seemed not to notice. "Which is the baron?" she
asked.

"Young Pirry. Piers Alaric Charles, Baron Glanville."

"Oh, of course. The one who lives in Germany. You certainly
scatter yourselves round the world, don't you?"

The exchange of trivialities had carried him over the first dangerous moment that morning, but now, rocking his chair on the
verandah in the evening silence, he remembered how, on another
verandah, he had once wished for Arthur to die.

Ten years. He should have waited for Frisca. He knew now
that he could have waited for more than ten years. If only he had
kept himself free! But there was nothing to be done about it.
Robert was not a practising Christian, yet he accepted unques-
tioningly the traditional morality of his family. Ten years earlier
there had never been the slightest possibility that Frisca, after
marrying Arthur with no concealment of the truth, could have
been persuaded to divorce him. It was equally impossible now for
Robert to consider leaving Eleanor. Her religious convictions

made divorce an impossibility for her, and even to suggest it would have been cruel. No, there was nothing to be done. He had made a mess of his life, and nobody but himself must suffer for it. What was, was to be accepted.

Rocking and smoking under the stars, he prayed for the night to heal his disturbed spirit. When Eleanor came out to join him, he pretended to be engrossed in a book, hoping that she would take the hint and be silent. Untouched by nature's magic and incapable of sitting for a moment without occupation, she had brought a pile of exercise books with her, but Robert noticed that she did not open them.

"What are we going to do about Barbara?" she demanded.

Since his mother naturally devoted a great part of every letter to news of his daughter, this was a question which Eleanor was frequently prompted to ask on mail days. Pretending not to have heard, Robert continued to read his book. He had been deaf on one side ever since being wounded in 1917. He could still hear perfectly well on the other side, but when Eleanor was in one of her tiresome organising moods, it suited him to be deaf in both ears.

Efficient as always, Eleanor well knew how to deal with this. She touched his knee to attract his attention, forcing him to turn his head.

"What are we going to do about Barbara?" she repeated.

"Do we need to do anything?"

"Really, Robert! You can't put this off forever. She's your daughter and you're hardly acquainted with her. I've always been willing to give her a home here; you know that. With so many servants available in India, it would be no trouble. You may have been right until now to say that she should finish her schooling in England and not have to travel back and forth for holidays. But she's had her eighteenth birthday. She'll be leaving school soon, and your mother's getting on. It's not too early to make arrangements."

Robert cast a despairing look at the stars and closed his book with a sigh which he almost, but not completely, suppressed. When Eleanor was in this sort of mood there could be no retreating from the argument. He might manage to persuade her or he might, to her distress, lay down the law on a matter which was, after all, his business rather than hers. But he could not hope to escape.

"You know that Mother and Alexa have been discussing this," he reproached her. "Alexa wanted to give her a season as a debutante. She thought that to present her at Court might cure Barbara of her shyness. But Mother managed to persuade her that it would be a form of torture for the poor child. So the latest idea is that she should go off to France to be finished instead. I must have shown you the letter at the time."

"But *whose* latest idea?" demanded Eleanor. "Wasn't it Alexa's again? What do *you* think ought to happen? You're her father."

"But as you've pointed out so often, I hardly know her. I trust Mother and Alexa to do what's best for her. And Barbara's got a tongue in her head. If she doesn't like a plan, she'll say so. If there's something she actively wants to do, she'll say that as well. If her great-aunt and grandmother don't agree with it, no doubt she'll appeal to me for support. Until that happens, I don't see any need to interfere."

"But it's so useless, being 'finished.' What will she be good for then? Arranging flowers and spending money on clothes?"

Robert's lips tightened as he tried to control his irritation. "Not everyone can be as useful as you, Eleanor."

"Of course they can. She could take some kind of training. Whatever happened to suit her taste. But how can she ever develop a taste when she's being overpowered by those two old women."

"You're talking about my mother, Eleanor."

"I'm sorry, dear. Yes, I'm really sorry. I didn't mean that. Your mother, of course, has led such a useful life herself as a doctor, and Alexa had a career which—whatever one may think of it—must have given pleasure to a lot of people."

She makes Alexa sound like a retired prostitute, Robert thought, but he said nothing.

"What I mean about Barbara," Eleanor went on remorselessly, "is that I feel strongly that she needs the chance to breathe. To get to know herself, and to get to know you. I don't necessarily mean that she should come and live here for good, though you know how delighted I'd be if she did. But for a few months, perhaps, after leaving school. It would help her to grow up. And it would give her confidence in your affection. I know there's always been some good reason why you couldn't look after her yourself, and I'm sure she's accepted that. But if you don't make some kind of move now, she'll begin to wonder, Robert. She's never had a mother, and that's sad to start with. If she has to ask herself whether even her father loves her, that could make her very unhappy."

The trouble about Eleanor was that her intentions were always good and, surprisingly enough, her conclusions were very often correct. And then, being in the right, she nagged. Her rightness was a black-and-white kind of rightness which made no allowance for other people's greyness. It was true that Barbara might wonder whether her father cared for her, but would a few months of living together do anything to change her mind? In his letters Robert had been able to make a good show of affection. But face to face, how could they pretend that they were anything but strangers? To send an invitation would certainly be the right thing to do. But would Barbara understand that it might be dangerous for her to accept? "I'll think about it," he said.

It was a phrase which never failed to annoy Eleanor. She did not press the argument further at that moment, but her suppressed irritation would have been enough in itself to spoil the calm of the evening. Robert, however, put Barbara out of his mind almost immediately. It was the thought of Frisca which tormented him. For the whole of that night he lay awake, remembering how he had loved her, torturing himself with the memory of her body, so slim and yet so softly rounded, so pale and yet so generous.

There had been no single moment in his life with Eleanor when he had come anywhere near the joy he had shared with Frisca. Had Robert been more passionately in love with his wife in the first place, he might have been better able to persuade her to enjoy herself. As it was, he had made little impression on her curiously Victorian attitude to marriage. On one occasion Robert had actually heard her express the opinion that the institution was necessary in order that a man might have the opportunity of indulging his animal nature and that it was a wife's duty and function to make herself available for this purpose. She was talking about the Indians at the time, but it was difficult not to suspect that it represented her attitude to her own marriage as well; and by so thinking she had made it come true.

Exhausted, but recognising at last that he had no hope of sleeping that night, he rose at five o'clock and wrote a note for Eleanor to find at breakfast. Sunday was always a difficult day. It was the only full day which Robert could be sure of spending at home, since his work so often took him out to wherever the section of road under construction was being surveyed or blasted. By contrast, it was one of Eleanor's busiest days. In addition to attending Early Service, Morning Service, and Evensong, she took a Sunday school class in the late afternoon. Since Robert had long ago given up going to church even once a week, Eleanor hardly saw him all day, and found it hard to conceal the fact that she thought God and herself both entitled to his company on the Sabbath.

Today his mood would stand no further arguments. First he spent an hour or two in the workshop he had built for himself. Mechanical invention had become his hobby, and he was working on a new kind of axle for railway carriages. This was not part of his salaried work, but rather an extension of his boyhood love of playing with trains. One of India's many problems was that separate railway systems had been developed at the same time, using two different gauges of track. Although—as in Trichinopoli itself —the two sets of lines often came very close together, it was impossible for the engines or coaches or goods wagons to be changed from one to the other. It should not be impossible, Robert felt, to design an adjustable axle that would enable the width between the wheels to be varied, making the same stock usable on either gauge of track. The problems posed by the heavy engines might prove insoluble, but he had considerable hopes of inventing a compatible wagon chassis that could be moved from one system to the other by a light shunting engine.

After working on the prototype he drove out with it to a deserted spot where a few hundred yards of track branched off to form a passing place on a single-track line. The side line was seldom in use, and the points were operated by hand. With some difficulty Robert manhandled the heavy pair of wheels and their connecting axle from the trailer which had drawn them behind

the car on to the track. Then he began to carry out tests with the
points in different positions, to make sure that the wheels would
not use their adjustability to splay out at the wrong moment. The
work was tiring and, as the run rose higher in the sky, he could
feel the sweat pouring down his face, but he forced himself not to
stop for a rest or even to drink. He had taken a decision not to
think of Frisca again for twenty-four hours, and was determined
to concentrate on his self-imposed task.

By noon, though, he knew that he had had enough. His head
was throbbing with the heat of the sun; and the dizziness which
still affected him from time to time, even so long after the
wounding which had caused it, was reminding him that he ought
not to continue to bend down and straighten himself. He heaved
at the points lever for one last test and, clattering the metal
wheels over the junction once again, did not hear the whistle of a
railway engine which was hurrying back to Trichinopoli after an
overnight repair.

It was approaching from his deaf side, but there should have
been no danger, for he was clearly visible to the driver, and so was
the obstruction he had placed on the line. What was not apparent was the fact that he had changed the points. The engine
driver, pulling the whistle more as a salute than a warning, did
not slacken speed as he approached, expecting as usual to take the
main track. By the time he realised that he was being turned on
to the side line, it was too late to stop.

Robert, alerted at last by the vibration of the track, looked up
too suddenly. The sun was in his eyes, the engine towered above
him, with sparks flashing from the screaming metal wheels as the
brakes bit. He tried to fling himself to one side, but his head was
spinning and his balance and judgement were equally affected.
The engine came to a halt, shuddering and hissing, but it was too
late. Distraught, the driver jumped from his cab and found that
there was nothing to be done. Out of an empty sky a dozen vultures appeared and hovered for a little while on huge ragged
wings; but the steam engine which held the dead man in its
talons was too powerful a rival, and after a while they returned to
the city.

The sun beat down on Robert's crushed body, seeming to gloat over the violence of his end. It had finished what a German bullet began twenty years earlier. He had played with trains once too often, and now his love affair with India was over.

3

Grant Lorimer was a man who held strictly to routine. Neither as a boy nor as a young man had he ever been frivolous, frittering his time away, and in 1937 he was thirty-two years old, his own master, serious and methodically hard-working. Drawn to the East like his cousin Robert, he too was an early riser. By five o'clock every morning he was moving through his Malayan plantation, supervising the tappers as they made their swift but delicate cuts in the rubber trees. Only when the sun became too hot for tapping did he return to the bungalow for breakfast.

Later in the morning there were decisions to be made about the next stages of draining, felling, and replanting. He had taken possession of the estate ten years earlier—in the same month that Robert had married Eleanor. He had found then that many of the trees were old, producing little, while others had been badly cut. Much as he would have liked it, they could not all be replaced at once, for new trees would not come into production for six years. But by now his programme of clearance and replacement was in full operation.

In the first of the new sections to mature he was experimenting with two different styles of cut. The old criss-cross method was inefficient, he felt sure. So he had trained three of his best tappers in a new style, cutting only one side of each tree, but with each narrow incision close to the one above it. A year of instructing and bullying had not, however, succeeded in persuading the coolies who collected the latex to remember that the yield of the experimental area should be kept separate, so that it could be weighed and compared with the results of the older method.

For this reason Grant was forced to take charge himself of an operation which normally could have been left to the overseer, but the speed with which he moved, defying the heat and humidity, enabled him to fit in the extra task without trouble. Although he would always limp from the deformity with which he had been born, he had made himself so fit with exercise and hard work that he could cover the rough ground as fast as any Tamil or native Malay.

By noon he would be back in his bungalow. He ate very little lunch, but took a bath and changed his clothes. The midday heat seemed not to affect him at all, and he rarely took the siesta which his fellow-planters regarded as essential in such a humid climate. Instead, after doing his office work, he devoted an hour or two to his hobby of orchid breeding.

An orchid garden had been constructed to his specifications at the side of the bungalow; a series of wooden trellises over which palm leaves could be laid in a way which broke the directness of the sunlight without providing complete shade. The orchid house nearby he had built with his own hands, acquiring over the years such necessary equipment as a culture chamber, an autoclave, an agitator, and enough racks to hold a hundred germinating or rooting flasks. He kept meticulous records of his crosses, and had managed to find a secondhand machine which stamped out the necessary details on to metal labels.

The late afternoon was the time when most of the other planters in the area assembled at the club; but a planters' club—a twenty-mile drive away—had little to offer Grant. He neither drank nor smoked nor played cards. On the tennis court he was ungainly, needing his specially built-up shoe to enable him to play at all. Although his game was in fact of a reasonable club standard, it had not taken him long to realise that other people found it difficult to play naturally against him: a shot of which they would have been proud in other circumstances made them feel guilty when he was the one who failed to reach it.

For an opposite reason he was reluctant to swim in the club pool, tempting though this was on a hot and sticky afternoon. Grant was an excellent swimmer. A large part of the therapy which Margaret had designed to help him during his boyhood had taken place in the water; he could swim fast and almost forever. But he was ashamed of his misshapen leg and would not display it in public. Instead, he drove down to the coast every Sunday and swam alone in the sea. No one could accuse him of being unfriendly to his neighbours, but his reputation for unsociability was well deserved.

Grant didn't care. Just as he disciplined his body, keeping each muscle in good condition and being careful never to succumb to the lethargy which the humidity imposed on anyone who did not guard against it, so he had adjusted his mind to solitude. He was almost, although not quite, self-sufficient. His need for friendly intercourse showed itself only in the long letters which he wrote regularly to a few scattered correspondents. Several were fellow orchid breeders. Two others he had met on the voyage out to the Federated Malay States ten years earlier; the friendships struck up on board would not have survived had they all been living near to each other, but the exchange of experiences by post allowed the casual relationship to remain alive without needing to develop. Another correspondent was Grant's old university tutor, to whom he reported his experiments with orchids and with rubber. Another, the most regular, was his aunt Margaret. And yet another was Barbara.

Evening was the time when Grant read his letters. There was no regular hour of the week or day when a postal delivery could be expected, and it was a useful curb on impatience to make the rule that he would open his mail only at the time which other men used as the signal to start serious drinking: after sundown. At half-past six his Malay houseboy would bring a lamp out to the verandah, and Grant would open his correspondence.

On this day in 1937 there were two letters, both from Blaize. They had come by air mail, which was unusual. Family chat was not normally reckoned to be urgent. It was confusing sometimes to receive an answer to a letter written some months earlier when three or four other letters might have been despatched in the meantime, but everyone had adapted himself to the time lag; and in lives which were much the same from day to day, a leisurely pace seemed no handicap.

Equally unusual was the fact that one of the letters came from Alexa. Her monogram identified the envelope and there was no mistaking her Continental style of handwriting. The second was addressed in Barbara's round, still immature hand. Grant put it aside for the moment. He could make a fair guess at its contents. She would have read some of the books which in every letter he recommended to her and would comment on them carefully. If Alexa had subjected her to one of her holiday bursts of cultural education, there would be descriptions of operas or art galleries; but if, as was more likely, Barbara's presence at Blaize had hardly been noticed, she would be more concerned with the details of her great-aunt's latest car. Grant looked forward to reading his cousin's letter, but curiosity led him to open the other first.

Once a year it was Alexa's habit to send Grant a present which was intended to arrive at Christmas, although it rarely succeeded in doing so. Apart from that, she never wrote to him. Even before he slit open the envelope he felt anxious.

His fears proved justified. "I have bad news for you, I'm afraid," Alexa wrote. "A letter has come from India to say that Robert is dead. It was Eleanor who wrote—to Margaret, of course." Alexa described the details of the accident.

"As you can imagine, the news has caused great distress to everyone here. Poor Barbara is very confused. She hardly knew her father, but she'd hoped that now she's left school she might be able to spend some time with him. So I think she feels more that she's lost a possible future relationship than a past one, and she doesn't know quite how to cope or what to do. Frisca is also terribly upset. She recovered from Arthur's death earlier in the year as well as could be expected—there was so much business to be settled, with solicitors and all that sort of thing, that she hardly had time to think. But naturally it was a depressing time, and this second shock has hit her when she's down. She spent her early childhood in Margaret's home, while I was still travelling from one opera house to another, and Robert was almost an elder brother to her. She'd always been greatly attached to him, and the news has made her very unhappy.

"But of course the one who's really suffering is Margaret. It's almost breaking my heart to watch her. So many of her friends and relations have died already. That she's been able to accept as something which is bound to happen as one grows older. But for children to die before their parents seems to offend against some kind of natural law. She's had to go through it all once before, when she thought Robert had been killed in the war; and from the moment when he returned she must have taken it for granted that he'd be there for the rest of her life. His going off to India was hard enough for her, but at least he was alive to be loved.

"So suddenly she's lost her main reason for living. My dear Grant, I can't really describe how devastating the change in her has been—and just in a matter of days. Barbara and Frisca are young, and they'll recover, but I don't think Margaret will. She doesn't cry and she doesn't talk, but her eyes are dead and she really isn't interested in anything anymore.

"I do hope I'm not exaggerating and alarming you too much. I'm not trying to organise a great deathbed scene. There's nothing actually *wrong* with Margaret at all. I mean, she's almost eighty and for the past few years she's been getting more forgetful and more arthritic: growing old, in fact. But she's certainly not suffering from any recognisable terminal illness. All I'm trying to say is this. I know that you and she have always had a very special relationship. If you want to see her again, I don't think you ought to delay your next home leave too long."

Grant stared at the letter for a little while and then read it again, doubly upset by its contents. Alexa was right in recognising his special relationship with Margaret, who had adopted him—in fact if not in law—after his own mother had died and his father had rejected him. But he had had a special relationship with Robert as well. Alexa had acknowledged the shock which Robert's death had inflicted on his mother, his daughter, and his one-time mistress—she had not admitted the last relationship in so many words, but Grant had been twenty-one and living at Blaize during the summer of Robert's love affair with Frisca, and well aware of what was going on. But long before that, Robert had been a very special friend to the podgy, whining, crippled boy who had arrived without warning from Jamaica.

Grant remembered how his cousin, himself recovering from the first of his war wounds but still lively and laughing, had shown him how to use crutches with agility and not rely on other people to help him move around. They had played together with Robert's trains—except that it was not really play but earnest concentration, setting themselves problems and solving them. From Alexa's letter, it sounded as though the same kind of problem and the same degree of enthusiasm had been responsible for the fatal accident on the railway line.

The moon rose and the heavy scents of night swelled in the air as Grant, unmoving, mourned Robert's death. Not a man who found it easy to make friends, he had found the link of cousin-ship a peculiarly congenial one. It existed from the moment of birth and could be as important or as insignificant as the two peo-ple concerned wished. He and Robert had thought of each other as cousins, but within that relationship they had been friends, making no demands on each other—not even keeping directly in touch—but linked, all the same, by everything which their family background had given them in common.

Well, Robert was dead. There was nothing to be done there. But Margaret was still alive, and Grant appreciated Alexa's warn-ing. Knowing that Alexa had never liked him, that probably she was writing for Margaret's sake rather than his own, did not dimin-ish his gratitude. He could take no action at this hour of the night. But tomorrow morning he would drive to the club and telephone to Singapore as soon as the shipping offices opened. His rubber trees and orchids would have to do without him for a few months. He must book himself the earliest possible passage home. To say goodbye to Margaret. To mourn with her for the loss of one of his cousins, Robert. And to comfort, if he could, another cousin: Barbara.

4

"What a very beautiful young woman you've become," said Grant.

He was not accustomed to paying compliments to girls—any more than Barbara, to judge by her flush, was accustomed to re-ceiving them. But he had remembered his cousin as a shy and un-gainly schoolgirl and was startled by the ladylike smartness of the girl who had driven Alexa's Riley down to meet him. Her light chestnut hair, fine and straight, fell to shoulder length, swaying whenever she turned her head. Her complexion was pale, and her high cheekbones and the delicate line of her straight nose gave her long face an aristocratic appearance, as though she were descended from the Glanville companion of William the Conqueror rather than from a slave-trading Bristol sea captain.

Even more surprising to Grant than Barbara's appearance was the discovery of a strong desire to kiss her. As he could easily do if he chose. They were cousins, after all, and she would accept—she might even be expecting—a family embrace, a routine brushing of lips against cheeks. But that was not the sort of kiss he had in mind. Unsure of himself and confused by his own emotions, he decided to wait.

Barbara drove fast, but capably. Grant repeated the regrets at her father's death which he had already written in an air letter, and she nodded her appreciation without taking her eyes off the road.

"How's your grandmother?" he asked.

"Still terribly cut up. I don't think she's ever going to get over it."

"That's really why I've come home," Grant said. "Not that there's anything I can do. But just to be here for a bit."

Barbara nodded again to show that she understood. She had always been sparing with words. Only as the car wound up the long drive which led towards Blaize and came to a standstill outside the ancient house did she return to the subject.

"Grandmother's mind wanders rather nowadays," she said. "Perhaps it's the same with all old people. She remembers everything which happened years ago, when she was a child. But she gets mixed up sometimes with her nephews and great-nephews. You mustn't be hurt if she doesn't recognise you at first."

"Thanks for the warning." Without it, Grant would have hurried straight from the car to his aunt's room. Now he forced himself to move slowly, taking time to greet Alexa and chat with her, then to go up to his room and wash while Barbara told Margaret who was coming. It was a necessary reminder that he had made the journey for his own sake as much as his aunt's. He had come to say goodbye—not in so many words, of course, but with an expression of his love for her, in order that he should not later regret an untidy ending of his relationship with the woman who had been a second mother to him.

Barbara appeared in the doorway and nodded to indicate that he was expected. Nervous of what he might find, Grant went to his aunt's bedroom.

How tiny she was! To be sure, when first Grant had arrived in England as a boy he had seen that Margaret was small. But as the woman in charge of a wartime hospital, her every word and movement had been charged with authority. Grant she had made a particular point of bullying—for his own sake. Physically—and morally too—she had seemed to tower over him as he sat, lame and sulking, on the floor. Now he was the one who towered over her, a fragile little woman. White-haired and white-faced, she seemed to have shrunk, so much diminished from his earlier memories that he felt he could pick her up with one hand. She was sitting in a chair by the side of her bed, tucked in tightly with shawls and blankets as though to stop her blowing away.

He fell to his knees in front of her chair, bringing himself nearer to her level and grasping her hands with his own.

"Hello, Aunt Margaret," he said. "Do you remember me? I'm Grant."

Whether or not she needed the reminder, she was hurt by it.

"How could I forget you, Grant dear?" she said reproachfully. "You're Ralph's son; and Lydia's. Lydia was my best friend. We were medical students together—did you know that? While he was alive, my father wouldn't let me be a doctor. Women couldn't in those days. But then he died."

She stared for a long time at the black-framed portrait of her father on the wall facing her. Once upon a time, Grant remembered, its place had been in the minstrels' gallery. She must have asked for it to be moved to her bedroom.

"Robert is dead as well." Margaret was pursuing her own train of thought. "Did I tell you that? Robert died in India."

"Aunt Alexa told me," said Grant. "I'm so sorry, Aunt Margaret. So terribly sorry." He kissed her again, his arms embracing her tightly.

"He was a very rich man," Margaret said when the moment was over.

"Robert?" Grant was surprised.

"No, my father. My father was a very rich man. He kept two carriages. When I was a girl, I never needed to carry money. I could go into any shop in Bristol and it would be "Good afternoon, Miss Lorimer. What can we do for you, Miss Lorimer? We'll send it up right away, Miss Lorimer." I never knew what anything cost at all. It made things difficult later on. My father killed himself in the end, you know. Did you know?"

"No," said Grant. "I knew that he owned a bank and that the bank failed. And that he died soon afterwards."

"We all pretended it was an accident," Margaret told him. For the past few minutes her voice had been vague and inconsequential, but now Grant was aware of a change to a firmer tone. "It wasn't because he was afraid of being poor. At least, I don't think so. It wasn't even because he'd made mistakes, although he had, and they were what brought him to it in the end. It's like that boy of Alexa's says—" She paused, searching for the name.

"Pirry."

"Pirry, yes, that's right. Pirry likes to divide the world up. Often what he says is silly, but I remember once when he was right. There are those who do things, he said, and those to whom things are done. My father, all his life, was a man who did things. He wasn't prepared to let people do anything to him, tell him how to live the rest of his life. He made the choices himself, always. He chose to die. I didn't blame him; I was glad, in fact. But it was hard for your father. William had the shipping company and Alexa had the jewels and it was enough for me that I had the freedom to do what I wanted. But Ralph was only a schoolboy when the bank failed. He had nothing. I never understood how he came to own that land in Jamaica. He did very well for himself, but I don't know how. It didn't do him any good. His eldest boy was killed. You remember that? Brinsley. It's a terrible thing, for parents to see their sons die before them. My Robert has died in India. Did you know?"

"Yes, I did." Suddenly Grant could not bear any more. Alexa, seeing Margaret every day and watching her grow older, had told him how shocked she had been by the abrupt deterioration after Robert's death. It was far worse for Grant himself, who still remembered his aunt as the efficient substitute for his mother who had guided him firmly through the years of his adolescence.

"I'll come back to see you again later," he promised, kissing her tenderly before he left.

For a little while he walked round the gardens and woodlands of Blaize, forcing his eyes to look at the plants and trees, but unable to keep his thoughts away from the tiny old woman tucked into her chair. He was not alone in seeking silence. As he made his way up the steep hill from the riverside theatre, he came across Frisca sitting motionless on the bank of the stream which ran beside the azalea walk.

Earlier that day Barbara's appearance had taken him by surprise. His first view of Frisca created a different impression. She had always been exciting to look at. Her blond hair, pretty face, pale, clear complexion, and slim, athletic body combined with her bright-eyed smile to create an exuberance of personality which overwhelmed everyone who met her and had carried her to stardom on the stage. But there was nothing exuberant about her now. It was the first time that Grant could remember seeing her sitting still.

As he approached, she looked up and smiled. She was still as beautiful as ever, but it was a more mature beauty than he recalled. Ten years ago she had been a Bright Young Thing, restless and adventurous. Now her eyes suggested that she was more peaceful but less happy.

"I was sorry to hear about Arthur's death," he said, sitting on the bank beside her after they had greeted each other. "It must have been a great shock. He wasn't so very old."

"No," said Frisca. It was clear she did not want to talk about it.

"It must be very complicated for you, with Bernard still too young to take over the business. Are you going to stay on in Bristol?"

Frisca shook her head. "I was never there much anyway, and now I'm going to Hollywood. I've been making pictures in England for the past few years. I don't expect they've come your way."

"I'm afraid not."

"They've been successful enough, but Hollywood is the real place to be. When I was offered a contract before, Arthur told me that making pictures in England was just about all right, but to do the same thing in America would be unutterably vulgar. Not at all suitable for a Lady Lorimer, he thought. So I stayed here. But now there's nothing to hold me back. It's exciting for a dancer to be filmed, you know. One can't go on doing high kicks forever. But if it's trapped on celluloid one can hope that any skill one has won't be entirely forgotten. Has it upset you, seeing Aunt Margaret?"

"Yes." Grant assumed that Frisca was changing the subject, but it seemed that she was still following the same line of thought.

"Me too. When I remember how marvellous she was and how hard she worked! I don't suppose she's conscious of the change herself, but it certainly frightens me. If I had to choose—and then forget what I'd chosen—I'd want to have someone creep up behind me on my fortieth birthday and hit me very hard on the back of the head. While I'm still me, and before any talent I have starts slipping away."

"I don't expect you'll still think that on your fortieth birthday."

"I don't suppose I shall. That won't mean I shall be wiser then than now. But like everyone else I shall grow old and wrinkled and arthritic and then I shall sit and play my old movies back to myself and think, well at least there were good years once. Rejoice, O young man, in the days of thy youth."

"That was one of the gifts Aunt Margaret gave me," Grant said. "Without her, I'd have sulked my way through the rest of my life."

"So I suppose she has her old movies too." Frisca smiled to dispel the gloom from their talk. "Not just you, but me and Barbara —and even Mamma. All happy, well-balanced adults because one woman was prepared to love us when we were children." An owl hooted from the depths of the wood. "That's Bernard's signal. He's been building a tree house. Will you come and inspect it with me?"

She led the way into the wood. There was a slithering sound above their heads and a ten-year-old boy appeared at high speed down a rope.

"This is my son, Bernard," Frisca said. "Bernard, your cousin Grant."

Bernard stretched out a hand, but then studied its dirty palm critically and withdrew it, grinning cheerfully instead. For the third time that day Grant was completely taken aback at the sight of one of his relations. Barbara and Margaret had both changed from the way he remembered them. This boy, by contrast, bore a resemblance so close as to be uncanny to a man who was dead. Not Frisca's husband, Arthur, but Robert.

Silenced by surprise, Grant stared at the boy's bright red hair and his mischievous freckled face. But it was the grin which made it incontrovertibly clear who his father must have been. That was the grin which had helped to tease Grant himself out of his dumps when he first arrived from Jamaica. Even while he was saying hello, Grant was mentally counting the years since the General Strike in order to confirm his guess.

"Coming up?" Bernard held the rope out hospitably.

"For the sake of my stockings, I'm prepared to regard your new home as private to you," laughed his mother. "But congratulations on your housebuilding abilities. It looks very safe and smart. Are you coming in for tea?"

"No, thanks, I've got my own rations." Hand over hand, he pulled himself up the rope again. Frisca took Grant's arm as they moved away. She could not have had very much difficulty in interpreting his expression and realising what he had guessed.

"Yet another kind of old movie," she said, and for a moment her hand tightened its grip. "It's a very curious relationship, isn't it, one cousin with another? You know each other well enough to be comfortable together, to feel affection long before there's any question of love. It doesn't prepare one for surprises. When two unrelated people fall in love and marry, they take it for granted that they're going to make discoveries, perhaps unwelcome ones, and adapt to them. But cousins have this feeling that all they have to do is to go on as they started. I'm not sure that it's a good basis for a marriage. With Arthur and me, it didn't matter, because neither of us expected too much. But with Robert . . . He'd known me all my life. When he came back from India and found that I wasn't a child anymore, it knocked him off balance. And me too, because that was what I'd always wanted, in a way. But only in a way. I hadn't sat down and waited for it to happen. I'd set to work making a life of my own, and it was a good life.

With a stranger, I'd have thought of all the snags before I ever got involved. But Robert and I were never strangers. That was why it went wrong. Because we were cousins."

"But which was the mistake?" Grant asked. No doubt the question was impertinent, but their own talk reinforced what she was saying. It was because he and Frisca were themselves cousins that they could fall so quickly into discussion of the most private aspects of another cousinship. "Were you wrong to fall in love with Robert? Or wrong to leave him?"

"I was right to leave him," Frisca said, not answering the first question. "Right for me, that is. For him, who can say?"

"But you're unhappy now."

"Because he's dead!" she cried, making no attempt to disguise her anguish. "While he was alive I could go on loving him. Somehow it didn't matter not seeing him. It didn't even matter that he was married to Eleanor. We had a love affair and we could preserve it against anything that happened in life. But now he's dead and, yes, of course I'm unhappy."

It was a disquieting conversation, for reasons which probably Frisca would not have guessed. In bed that night Grant thought about Barbara. There was a parallel of a sort in that he, like Robert, had found himself confronted by a beautiful young woman whom he had remembered only as a schoolgirl. But the two cases, surely, had nothing else in common. Robert had come home on leave wanting to be married. It was true that for a man with limited time away from a place where few possible brides were to be found, a family relationship was dangerous, offering opportunities at the expense of real choice. But Grant in Malaya had never felt any longing for a wife. He could manage very well by himself for as long as he chose. It was only the sight of this one girl which had made him consider changing his choice.

The women, too, were quite different. Frisca's talents had been on public display, attracting admirers, but Barbara's was a more private kind of beauty, guarded by her shyness. Frisca had admitted that it was her own career which proved the stumbling block in her relationship with Robert, but Barbara had no career, no real life of her own. She was devoting herself to her grandmother, and when her grandmother died she would be very nearly alone in the world. She would feel the need then for another life, someone to look after her. The two situations, his and Robert's, had nothing in common at all, he told himself. Not yet asleep, Grant began to dream of Barbara in Malaya.

The next day he sat for longer with Margaret, telling her about his life on the rubber plantation. Barbara was waiting when eventually he came downstairs. "Would you like to swim?" she asked.

"In the river?" Grant did not try to hide his surprise. It had been part of his fanatical pursuit of fitness as an adolescent that he should not be daunted by the temperature of the water, but his young cousin had never pretended to such spartan tastes.

"We've got a pool now, a covered one. Aunt Alexa had it specially designed for Matthew, with a kind of hoist to get him in and out. It has to be kept very warm for him, so it suits me as well. It's next to the tennis lawn. I'll meet you there in ten minutes."

Did she realise what she was asking, Grant wondered. Did she remember about his leg? In Malaya, he never appeared in company in shorts. He swam alone. For his infrequent games of tennis he wore long trousers. Even when he was relaxing on his verandah, the cloth that he twisted, Malay fashion, around his waist, was long enough to reach the ground. He was thirty-two years old and until the previous day had taken it for granted that no woman would ever be able to love the body which had so much angered him as a child and which he had disciplined so severely ever since. Perhaps it would be wise to take it for granted still, but for the first time his determination to be self-sufficient was faltering.

Barbara had grown up with him. More even than Margaret, who had studied his deformity with a medical eye and had done her best to improve it, Barbara might take his crippled leg for granted. It was simply a part of him, and even after this interval she would not be shocked by it. There was no one else in the world of whom that could be said.

To check that he was right, he watched her eyes as he took off his towelling robe on the edge of the pool a few minutes later. He could see them studying his body with interest, not flickering away in embarrassment. "You're not very brown," she said.

"When you live in a hot country, the idea is to keep out of the sun as much as possible."

"What a waste!" She sat on the edge of the pool, splashing her toes through the water. "How does this temperature suit you?"

"Too hot for serious swimming. But much the same as my local patch of ocean."

"Lucky you. When are you going to invite me over for a swim?"

"Now," said Grant. "Will you marry me, Barbara?"

So great was her astonishment that she lost her balance and fell into the pool. Her pale auburn hair darkened and flattened itself against her head, emphasising the length of her face as she straightened herself in the water and stared at him.

"*What* did you say?"

"I want you to marry me. You're the most beautiful girl I've ever seen." He lowered himself into the pool beside her and touched her freckled shoulders with his finger. She did not move; but her surprise remained.

"But you hardly know me. I mean, not *really* know me."

"I've known you ever since you were in nappies."

"I call that negative knowledge. The kind of knowing that has to be forgotten."

"And in these last few years through your letters."

"That's different, as well."

"Then would you accept love at first sight—the sight of you standing beside the car yesterday?"

Uncertain what to say, she was silent for a very long time.

"I can't leave Grandmother," she told him at last. "You won't be able to stay here for long, I don't expect. You'll have to say goodbye to her and go back to Malaya. And Frisca is going as well, with Bernard. So I must stay. For however long it may be."

"One of my virtues is patience," Grant told her. "And one of my vices is tenacity. Of course you must stay with Aunt Margaret as long as she needs you. All I ask is a promise that you'll come when you can; and I shall love you and wait for you as long as need be. I've startled you now; I can see that. There's no need for you to answer yet. But soon, I imagine, you'll have to consider what you want to do after—after Aunt Margaret dies. I don't imagine you have much in common with your stepmother. Eleanor has never really joined the family. Now that your father's gone, presumably you won't ever be going out to India. So you'll start making other plans. I want to be part of them, that's all."

He kissed her then as he had wanted to kiss her at their earlier meeting—not as a cousin but as a lover—and was rewarded by her quick gasp of pleasure. She was still a little puzzled and shy of him, so he kept his own emotions within bounds, both then and during the weeks which followed. He had come home to see Margaret, and he spent much of each day with her. But his dismay at his aunt's frailty no longer obsessed him. Instead, he looked ahead to his own future and saw Barbara and happiness there together.

5

Margaret so rarely left her room that she was surprised to be told that her presence was needed downstairs. It was Barbara who brought the message, with Grant waiting behind her in the doorway, ready to help.

"What for, darling? Who wants me?"

"Matthew does." Barbara was wrapping a shawl around Margaret's shoulders, looking for a rug. "He wants to take a family photograph before Grant leaves."

"Grant, you're not going already? You've only just arrived."

"I've been here seven weeks, Aunt Margaret. I can't neglect my plantation any longer, I'm afraid."

"He's convinced that all his rubber trees will die of broken hearts if he isn't there to stroke them every night," Barbara laughed. Margaret noticed that her granddaughter's voice was affectionate in its teasing, but she was struggling with too many thoughts to accept another one for the moment. Grant stepped forward as she looked round for her stick.

"May I carry you down?"

"No, thank you. I can walk perfectly well." She smiled to herself at one of those memories which nowadays always seemed clearer than what was happening at the moment. "I remember the first time you asked whether you could carry Barbara. When she was just a tiny baby. You'd had your operations by then, but you were still walking around in a lopsided way, as though you wanted everyone to know that you were different. I said you could hold her as soon as you stopped limping. It took you exactly three days to walk properly!"

She had begun to walk herself by now, moving stiffly and slowly, but although it was necessary to watch for any unevenness in the floor, she did not miss Barbara's delighted smile at the reminiscence, or the way in which her hand was squeezed by Grant's.

For the photograph Matthew had chosen the great stone staircase which led up to the front entrance of Blaize. He was waiting there in his wheelchair, checking his exposure as the family assembled.

What a small group it was! Margaret felt overwhelmed by a sudden dismay at so many missing faces. Her two brothers, William and Ralph, had died so long ago that it was pointless to regret their absence, but where were all their children and grandchildren? Brinsley had been dead for twenty years and for almost the same length of time Kate and her daughter in Russia had been cut off from the rest of the family. Arthur had died, and now Robert too. With an effort of will, Margaret pulled her mind away from the thought of Robert dead. Every night she remembered him and wept for him, but after the first numbed days of shock she had made it a rule not to indulge her grief when anyone else was present.

There were other cousins missing, but still alive, of course. Beatrice ran an East End Mission with the same efficiency that her brother Arthur had applied to his shipping company. She and Alexa had never been friends, and she was never invited to Blaize. Matthew's son had distanced himself from the family more deliberately, making it clear that he was not prepared to maintain any kind of relationship with his father.

A more unexpected absentee was the actual owner of Blaize. Under the terms of the entail, Alexa's son, Pirry, had come into his life interest in the house on his twenty-first birthday in 1934. But he seemed content to leave the estate in his mother's care, and showed no sign of wishing to return to England. University courses were longer in Germany, he explained on each of his Christmas or summer visits, and all his friends were on the Continent. He was ready to admit that the political climate in Heidelberg was unpleasant. From childhood he had amused himself by dividing the people of the world into opposing groups. But to assert—for example—the contrast between cat-loving people and dog-loving people was quite different from listening to Adolf Hitler proclaim that the world was divided into those of pure Aryan race, who should rule it, and others, who seemed by implication to be allowed no right even to live in it.

His letters did little to reduce Margaret's bewilderment about what was happening in Europe. To someone like herself, who had lived through what must surely be the most terrible war in history, it was unimaginable that anyone could embark on a course which might lead to another conflict. But Pirry gave her no reassurance. The world, he incorrigibly declared, is divided into those who tolerate people different from themselves, and those who exterminate them. For this reason he was planning to leave Germany—but not to return to England. He hoped to find in Vienna a cultural atmosphere more congenial than that of philistine England.

Matthew was ready for them at last. Margaret allowed herself to be settled into a chair while the rest of the little group arranged themselves around her. Alexa, the mistress of the house, stood behind with her hands on Margaret's shoulders. Frisca and Grant were placed on either side of her, while the two representatives of the younger generation, Barbara and Bernard, sat at her feet.

Margaret looked down at the two young heads. She remembered her father only as white-haired, but knew that as a young man his hair had been as bright red as her own had once been. The colour of Barbara's had been subdued by her blond mother to a pale auburn, but Bernard's tousled curls were as bright and unmanageable as Robert's at the same age. Bernard, of course, had a double share of the Lorimer genes. She ran her fingers over his head, half in affection and half scolding.

"Didn't anyone tell you to comb your hair, young man?"

He grinned as he looked up at her. "I thought you'd all want to be able to recognise me," he said, and Margaret gave him a loving

slap. She never called Bernard by his name because at every meeting his appearance disturbed her. There was always a moment in
which she was not quite sure whether or not he was Robert, mi-
raculously returned to her. Alexa and Frisca had noticed her hesi-
tations and come to the wrong conclusion. They thought she was
losing her memory, becoming senile. It seemed they had even
warned Grant that she might not recognise him when he came
home. That had been apparent from the way in which he had introduced himself seven weeks ago and his affectionate relief when
he realised that she remembered everything about him. There was
nothing at all wrong with her memory for family relationships. It
was only this one likeness, between Bernard and Robert, which
confused her.

"Do you all have to look so unhappy?" Matthew demanded.
"I've got four of the most beautiful women in England in my
sights, and not a smile between them."

Margaret heard Bernard snigger and slapped him gently again.
It was true that she herself had never been beautiful, not even in
the days when her hair had flamed and her eyes flashed with a determination to get her own way. But Frisca was truly an out-
standing beauty. Her face appeared not only on theatre and cinema posters but on postcards and even cigarette cards. Alexa,
whose own loveliness had taken Europe by storm at the turn of
the century was still, at sixty, a remarkably handsome woman. As
for Barbara, her sensitive face needed only happiness to make it
radiant, and in the past few weeks it seemed that this was happening.

They were all smiling now. With one strong hand Matthew
moved his wheelchair round, changing the angle of his shots,
while he held the camera in the other. A scene for somebody's
photograph album, thought Margaret. Perhaps in fifty years' time
Barbara would show it to her grandchildren, pointing out her
own grandmother, the old lady who had been born in 1857,
unimaginably long ago. What would they make of her, she wondered. But there was no time for speculation, for already
Matthew was indicating that he had finished, and the family
group was scattering.

Later that day Grant came up to her room to say goodbye.
Margaret knew how unlikely it was that she would ever see him

again, and succumbed to the temptation to repeat some reminis-
cences of his own childhood and his father's. In the middle of
them she interrupted herself abruptly.

"Poor little Barbara. Both her parents dead. She's never really
had anyone but me. What's going to happen to her, Grant?"

She felt his arm tighten round her shoulders.

"I'll look after her," he promised. "You can rely on that. Goodbye, Aunt Margaret. Dearest Aunt. Thank you for everything."

It must have been arranged that someone would keep her company to prevent her from feeling upset, because Alexa came into
the room even before the car doors slammed and the gravel
crackled below.

"Barbara's driving him direct to the ship." Alexa stood by the
window, watching them disappear.

"I hope she doesn't go too fast. Are they going to marry?"

"That's what Grant would like, certainly."

"Then why didn't they tell me? Why isn't she going back with
him?" Margaret was frightened of the answers to her own questions. She did not want to be told in so many words that Barbara
felt it her duty to stay with her grandmother. She might find herself refusing to accept the sacrifice.

"I think she's right to give herself a little time, to consider it
away from him," Alexa reassured her. "Grant's a very possessive
young man, you know. If she's not careful, Barbara could find
herself gobbled up. I've never thought it was a very good idea to
move straight from one's family home to a husband. You and I
didn't make that mistake—nor did Frisca. It would do Barbara
good to live more independently for a while before she makes up
her mind. Not that it's any of my business."

"I've never believed that it's wise for cousins to marry," Margaret said. "Not good for their babies, I mean."

"You didn't try to dissuade Frisca when she announced her engagement to Arthur."

"Ah well, I already knew, from Arthur himself, that he couldn't
have children." She enjoyed her sister's startled gasp.

"Margaret! Have you known about Bernard all the time?"

"Not all the time, no; but most of it. He's so much like his father."

"Were you angry when you realised?"

"What happened between Frisca and Robert I've got no right to know. If he was unhappy—well, that's all in the past now. But that Frisca's son should prove to be my grandson as well as yours, that's something very important. I would have liked to have a lot of children, you know, but there wasn't time. Those few months were all I had with Charles. Only one child and only one grandchild, it seemed. That was too fragile a line. You must feel it too, Alexa—how important it is that the family should go on, even after we're not there to see it anymore. Bernard and Barbara and the others—the young ones—they're our future. Ancestors aren't important in a family. Descendants are what matter."

Suddenly she was too tired to talk anymore. It had been a long day. Her eyes closed and she allowed herself to sink towards sleep. For the first time since the news of Robert's death she felt at peace. The young ones would look after the family. Barbara would go out to Malaya one day: she would marry Grant and have children, Margaret's great-grandchildren. Frisca's boy, too, who was Robert's son, would marry one day. Yes, for as far ahead as it was reasonable to look, the Lorimer line was secure.

BOOK THREE
The Survivors

(1938–1947)

1938

1

The rough December wind plucked at the surface of the River Thames and tousled the bare branches of the trees as it whirled up the hill towards Blaize. It eddied and howled between the dark Tudor chimneys, which clustered in decorative groups on the roof of the old house. The flagpole above the great hall staggered beneath its attack and the black and white standard of the Glanvilles soared and stretched in a flurry of energy and excitement. Then the gale abated and the flag drooped to reveal that it was flying at half mast.

Barbara Scott, returning from an early-morning walk in the woods, ignored the wind which tangled her hair and dried the tears on her cheeks. Today was her twenty-first birthday, but in the sadness of watching her grandmother gradually slip away from life the date had been forgotten. She paused to stare at the lowered flag. Margaret Scott, whose death the previous evening it signified, had not been a member of the Glanville family, but Blaize had been her home for more than twenty years. It was Barbara's home, too, but as she stepped across the threshold now she felt as though she were a stranger, not belonging in the house. With her grandmother dead, there was no longer anyone who would truly care whether she stayed or left.

Inside the house, she tugged the knots out of her wind-swept hair, staring in the glass at her long, pale face, its eyes black circles of tiredness after so many sleepless nights. Then, tidy again, she made her way to her great-aunt's bedroom.

Lady Glanville took breakfast in bed as a lifelong habit, not for any reason of health or age. As Alexa Reni, thirty years ago, her triumphs both on and off the operatic stage had accustomed her to a day which began long after the sun rose. Her late and leisurely breakfasts were social and sometimes even business occasions, so Barbara knew that she would not be intruding.

"You look worn out, child. You should have stayed in bed."

"I couldn't sleep." Barbara bent to kiss her great-aunt's cheek and picked up one of the newspapers which covered the bed.

"You can have them all." Alexa pushed the others towards her. "Either they're full of gloom or else you can't believe a word they say."

Barbara knew what she meant. Ever since Mr. Chamberlain's dramatic flight from Munich in September with his talk of "peace for our time" there had been an unspoken conspiracy to pretend that the danger of war had receded. But her cousin Pirry's letters from Vienna made clear his opinion that the goose-stepping Nazis who had invaded Austria in March would not be content until they controlled the whole of Europe.

Today, though, Barbara's interest was not in the headlines. She turned to the back page of *The Times* and read the notice which Alexa had telephoned through for its Deaths column. "It's sad," she said.

"That Margaret's dead? Of course it is."

"Not just that." Barbara began to read the notice aloud. "'On December 5, 1938, peacefully at Blaize, the home of her sister Lady Glanville, Dr. Margaret Scott, M.D., in her 82nd year, daughter of the late John Junius Lorimer of Bristol, wife of the late Charles Scott, mother of the late Robert Scott—'it makes everyone connected with her sound so very dead."

"Well, that's how it was." Alexa sighed. "Certainly it's sad. But if you think that death notice is all depressing, just consider the letters after her name. They stand for a triumph of hard work and determination. She was born in 1857, remember. There was no way then in which a woman could become a doctor in England. She was one of the first to fight her way through to qualification." It was not in Alexa's nature to be demonstrative, but briefly she patted Barbara's hand. "It's one thing to feel unhappy because she's dead. Of course you do, and so do I. But you mustn't feel unhappy about her life. She was the most marvellous woman I've ever known, and her reward was the love that everyone felt for her."

Barbara recognised that this was true. Quite apart from the family, the letters she had read aloud to her grandmother during the past few months testified to the affection with which she was still remembered by dozens of men who had been her patients during the war.

Alexa did not allow the sentimental moment to last long but reached for a notebook. "Now then, who else is there to notify? I sent off cables last night to Pirry in Vienna and Frisca in Hollywood. Pirry must certainly come to the funeral. Frisca will find it more difficult to get away; and I doubt whether she could arrive in time in any case."

"Matthew knows, I suppose."

"Yes. I'd better telephone his sister, Beatrice. I don't know whether she'll make the funeral, though. She's getting very old."

Barbara tried not to smile. She rarely met Beatrice Lorimer, who ran a charitable centre for women in the East End of London, but guessed her to be the same age as Alexa. The difference was that Alexa, who had been beautiful, took pains to guard her looks even at the age of sixty-one: while Beatrice, sharp-featured and plain, was equally at pains to demonstrate how much she despised the cosseted rich.

"There's my stepmother." It was a natural association of ideas to move from the charitable Beatrice to Eleanor, the missionary teacher who had been Robert Scott's second wife. She was still working in India where Robert had met her, and the rest of the family had known her only for the duration of a few brief furloughs. They were antagonised by her sharp bossiness and intolerant belief in the rightness of her own opinions and, with Robert no longer alive to act as a link, it was to be expected that the relationship would fade away. But she had been Margaret's daughter-in-law, and Barbara recognised the need to be polite. "Shall I write to her?"

"If you would, dear, yes. We can't do anything about Kate, because we haven't got an address."

"Is she still alive?" The question was a foolish one. There had been no news of Kate, either good or bad, since the visit of her Russian friend three years after the 1917 revolution. Kate's surviv-

ing brother, however, was more accessible. "Did you send a cable
to Grant?" Barbara asked.

"No. An air letter will be quick enough. Cables are so bleak,
and he made it clear on his last visit that that was his goodbye to
Margaret and he wouldn't be returning."

"He might have changed his mind."

"Grant never changes his mind." Alexa made the statement
firmly. "In any case, Malaya is even further away than Hollywood. He couldn't possibly get here in time for the funeral."

"I'll write to him as well then, shall I?"

"Thank you, dear." Alexa looked up from her notebook with a
sudden sharpness. "Are you going to marry Grant?"

The question was disconcerting, not merely because it touched
on such a private matter but because Barbara had made a determined and successful effort not to consider the possibility at all
while she devoted herself to her grandmother. She flushed now as
she answered.

"I shall have to decide. He asked me, certainly. You wouldn't
have any objection, I take it?" But as she asked the question, Barbara reminded herself that she was twenty-one today. She could
do what she liked. Instead of being pleased she felt only a new
sadness that there was no one who would care enough about her
plans to stop them.

"Your grandmother wasn't enthusiastic. She saw how things
were going while he was here. It was nothing to do with Grant
himself. Just that, as a doctor, she always thought it a mistake for
cousins to marry. If they want to have children, that is."

"And do you think it would be a mistake as well, Aunt Alexa?"
Barbara knew she would be given an honest answer. Her great-
aunt had always regarded tact and hypocrisy as the same thing.

"What worries me is nothing to do with cousins and babies. It's
—well, both Margaret and I were in our thirties before we married. I'd made a career for myself as an opera singer. She'd made
a career as a doctor. I think that's a good way to do it. To be independent, to have your own life before you start living someone
else's."

"You make it sound as though Grant would bully me into
doing whatever he wanted."

"Oh, not *bully*, dear. That's far too strong a word. But you have to admit that Grant is—what shall we say?—single-minded. He's older than you and he's made a life for himself in the East. He'll expect his wife to fit in with it. That's natural. And if you go out straight from here, with no experience of fending for yourself, you'll find it difficult to do anything *but* fit in. That'll be natural too, at first. But after a little while you'll begin to develop your own ideas about how you want to live, and you might find it too late. Grant isn't a man who will bend very easily."

Barbara flushed again, this time with resentment that she should be considered so weak. "I can remember both you and Grandmother regretting what a short time your marriages lasted. You wished you'd married when you were younger, didn't you, Aunt Alexa?"

It was not a kind question to put to a woman who had been married for only nine years and widowed for twenty. But Barbara, still lost and lonely after the death of the woman who had brought her up, could not help feeling that Alexa too was being unkind. Most girls, surely, were married straight from their family homes. It was all very well to say that she should live independently, but what could she do? Her great-aunt and grandmother, at her age, had both been talented and ambitious; but she was neither. She didn't want to be independent. She wanted to be wanted. Now that Margaret Scott was dead, the only person who truly loved her was Grant Lorimer, in his lonely bungalow in a Malayan rubber plantation.

Her resentment must have made itself obvious. For the second time Alexa gave her a sympathetic pat, this time dismissing as well as consoling her.

"It's the wrong time to talk about it. And none of my business in any case. It's your life, Barbara dear. You must make your own choices. Off you go, then, and write those letters."

2

The wind which chased its tail round the chimneys of Blaize as Barbara tried to walk her unhappiness away had earlier whipped the English Channel into a storm. The overnight crossing took longer than usual and there was a general feeling of relief at the sight of land. The engines slowed and the cross-Channel steamer ceased to pitch and shudder as it drifted through the smooth water of the harbour.

Tall and elegant, the young Lord Glanville smoothed down his already sleek fair hair before putting on his hat and gloves. Yachting was his hobby and he had endured worse gales than this in far smaller vessels. He strolled to the covered deck and studied the crumpled figure of the young man who was sitting on one of his trunks.

"Collins!"

The man did not move—gave no sign, in fact, of having heard.

"Collins!" The sharpness in Pirry's voice as he repeated the name had the desired effect of command and reprimand. The young man leapt to his feet.

He had been sick during the crossing—the odour of his unhappiness clung to his ill-fitting overcoat, and his face was yellow. Pirry nodded as though the effect pleased him. He took hold of the man's scarf, which was hanging loosely round his neck, and tied it in a way which would cover and warm his chin. Without speaking, he pointed out a violin case and a shabby leather grip to be carried: then moved to the rail to attract the attention of the porters who were waiting on the quay. He wanted to be one of the first to pass through Customs.

As always, the tying up of the steamer and lowering of the gangplanks took an interminable time. When Pirry at last approached the immigration desks he snapped his fingers to hurry the three porters who staggered beneath the weight of his luggage. He called to his companion in the clear high drawl of the English aristocrat.

"Collins! For heavens' sake, keep up with me, Collins. You can carry this bag now. And the coat. But don't get lost. And watch those porters." He thrust a briefcase under the valet's arm and tossed a heavy fur-lined overcoat over his shoulder. The young man, with no hand free to control it, was forced to press his chin down to one side in order to prevent it from sliding to the ground.

"Some people think they own the world!" The immigration officer's muttered comment was just loud enough to be heard, just soft enough to be ignored. Pirry's expression was bland and bored as he set the two British passports on the desk.

The immigration officer checked the expiry dates and stared at each photograph in turn. He could hardly fail to reconcile that of Lord Glanville with the long face, straight nose and superciliously raised eyebrows of the traveller in front of him. A rich young man, Pirry had been well-groomed when the photograph was taken and was well-groomed still.

The valet, on the other hand, had suffered a sea change. Pirry had sent Collins off to be photographed for a passport on the day he engaged him. It was a self-satisfied, rather plump face which stared up from the page, above the severe collar and tie and dark jacket which were correct dress for a gentleman's gentleman. Little of that formal correctness or smug expression could be recognised in the miserable and crumpled figure who was still struggling with the fur-lined overcoat on one side while with the other encumbered arm he tried to dab eyes which were streaming from the effects of the cold wind. The immigration officer gave a sympathetic shrug as he closed the passports and nodded the two men through.

The next stop was at the Customs table. Pirry did not anticipate any trouble for an Englishman returning to his own country.

"How much of this is yours, sir?"

"The two portmanteaux, the trunk, those three suitcases, the violin and the briefcase. That other bag belongs to my man."

"That's quite a lot of baggage, sir."

"Yes—the reason why I had to endure this filthy journey instead of flying. I've been living abroad. One accumulates objects."

"So these are your household effects; is that it, sir?"

Pirry nodded. The arrogant expression with which he had approached the immigration barrier had disappeared. His voice was pleasant and less high-pitched than before. "You probably know what's been going on in Vienna since the Nazis marched in. It's no longer a civilised place to live. They haven't disturbed the foreign residents so far; but whatever Mr. Chamberlain may say, it's clear to me that there's going to be a war. I didn't want to get caught, having to run for home at the last minute, with no time to pack properly."

The Customs officer hesitated, no doubt conscious of the press

of passengers behind. The blue chalk was already between his
fingers when he changed his mind. "If you'd just unlock that suitcase, sir."

Pirry produced the key without fuss. "Reading isn't one of my
vices, if you're looking for dirty books," he said, smiling.

It was not a book, obscene or otherwise, which emerged. The
skilled rummager knew his business. He untied the leather jewellery roll and stared at the diamonds which flashed from each
velvet-lined pocket. "Would you describe these as your personal
effects, sir?"

"No, those are my mother's. She travelled with me as far as the
French coast, took one look at the state of the Channel and decided to stay on dry land until things settled down. She doesn't
trust foreign hotels, though, so she gave me these for safe keeping. As a matter of fact," Pirry added thoughtfully, "although it's
my mother who wears them, they do really belong to me. Family
heirlooms, and I'm the head of the family. No wife, so I've never
suggested to Mother that she should hand them down. But
strictly speaking: yes, they *are* my personal effects. You must be
very experienced in the Channel weather. How long do you
reckon this storm will last?"

"Should blow itself out by noon. May I see your passport, sir?"
He studied it, no doubt noting its owner's title, before coming to
a decision. The jewels were rolled up again, the suitcase locked,
and the blue chalk at last scribbled on each item. Pirry wondered
whether he would make any kind of check afterwards. Well, it
wouldn't matter. The Glanvilles did indeed have family jewels in
plenty, and his mother would back up his story as long as she had
not been doing anything too conspicuous in England on the same
day. He signalled to the porters and led the way to the boat train.

Neither Pirry nor his companion spoke during the unnerving
wait while the train filled up. At last the whistle blew. Doors
slammed and the guard moved along the platform, waving his
flag. The train moved very slowly out of the station and then,
gathering speed, began to hurtle towards London. As though he
had been holding his breath all night, Pirry let out a sigh which
was almost a groan of relief. He stood up to release the blinds
which earlier he had pulled down for the sake of privacy. For a
few moments, steadying himself against the swaying of the train,

he stared out at the peaceful English countryside, almost empty at this early hour of a winter morning. Then he turned to smile down at his travelling companion.

Had the immigration officer been present, he would have found it hard to believe that this compassionate traveller was the same person as the arrogant aristocrat whose passport he had stamped half an hour earlier. On the other hand, his sympathy for the hard-pressed valet would have been confirmed. Clutching the violin case in his arms as though it were a baby, the crumpled young man was weeping. Soundlessly at first the tears streamed down his cheeks, but soon he began to sob aloud.

Still without speaking Pirry untied the scarf which had partly covered his companion's chin. From his breast pocket he took the handkerchief which the real Herbert Collins had folded crisply for him in Vienna and held it out.

"*Jetzt bist du in Sicherheit, Leo,*" he said softly. "You are safe."

3

When Alexa had dressed and finished her letters, she walked over to the old coach house to sit for a little while with Matthew. He was not painting today. Heavily immobile, he sat in his wheelchair, staring at the canvas which one of his menservants had brought down from the racks in the loft to set up on an easel. Alexa looked at it in surprise. It was almost a puzzle painting, a medley of shapes superimposed on each other in varying shades of green—very different from the portraits of children and beautiful women from which he made his living.

"If it were brown, I'd guess it was Braque in his Picasso period. And if it were blue, it might be Picasso in his Braque period. But it's Lorimer in his Lorimer period, is it?"

Matthew nodded, pushing the wheels of the chair to move himself nearer to the fire and the sofa on which Alexa could sit.

"Last night I was thinking about Margaret," he said. "Wondering if there was anything she would have done differently if she had her life over again. And then, egoist that I am, I put the same question to myself. When I was in my twenties, I was sure that I was going to expand the frontiers of art. This sort of thing" —he gestured towards the easel—"was in the air, but only a few of us were trying to translate a particular vision into paint. Why did I give up? Braque was wounded almost as badly as I was. But he went on and I turned soft."

"You didn't give up. You're an extremely good portrait painter. You might have turned out to be only a second-rate Cubist."

"But suppose portrait painting as a genre is second-rate. I should have painted what I saw inside my head instead of the heads which presented themselves to my eyes. 'Nothing but the best,' you used to say to Frisca when she was a little girl, remember? Perhaps you should have said it to me as well."

"You *are* the best. The best portrait painter in England. It's pointless to compare different strands of art. It's as though I started worrying about whether I'd done well to be a good opera singer when I might have been a lieder singer instead." She would have continued to argue, anxious to raise both their spirits from the gloom engendered by Margaret's death, but was interrupted by the ring of the telephone.

It was the internal line from the main house. Matthew answered, needing to listen only for a second. "Pirry's here," he said.

"I'll come back later." Surprised and delighted, Alexa hurried across to the morning room of the big house.

"Pirry!" She looked lovingly up at her son as they embraced. Alexa was tall, but Pirry was taller. "Did you fly? I didn't think you could possibly be here so soon. I only sent the cable last night."

"Cable? I've been travelling for two days. I haven't had a cable."

"Margaret died yesterday."

"Oh. Oh, I'm so very sorry to hear it, Mother." He kissed her again, and Alexa knew that his sympathy for herself and grief on his own account were both sincere. But it seemed he had too much on his mind to indulge in the kind of reminiscence which Barbara had invited, and Alexa was eager to express her own anxieties.

"I'm so glad you're safely out of Vienna, Pirry. I was worried. You must settle down here now. This is your home, your land.

There's a lot of work in managing the estate. I was glad to look after it while you were a child, but it's time you took over. You're not going back to Austria, are you?"

"Yes, I must. There's a lot to be done, and not much time. I've brought someone with me, Mother. I want you to look after him for a little while. Leo!"

A young man appeared in the doorway. Too small for the clothes he wore, he appeared ill-at-ease, almost furtive, as he waited for Alexa to acknowledge his presence.

"Leo was born in Russia," Pirry said. "His father was a Georgian. His mother was a Jew. They died in one of Stalin's purges. Leo escaped to Vienna. Now he's not safe there either. He's had a rough time, Mother. Please be nice to him."

Alexa shook her head in bewilderment. What claim on her could this stranger have? Although she tried to close her eyes to her son's way of life, from time to time attempting to interest him in a girl who would make a suitable wife, in her heart she suspected the truth about his relationships with the young men who in turned shared his flat in Vienna. But surely this shabby and unattractive youth could hold no appeal for someone as cultivated in his tastes as Pirry.

"Why should I?" she asked, angry that she should be expected to involve herself in his affairs. "I've made it clear—"

"It isn't because he's a special friend that I've brought him here," Pirry said. "I hardly know him personally. He doesn't understand English, incidentally, so you can speak your mind. There are two reasons why I had to get him out of Vienna. One was that if he'd stayed, he'd have been dead within a year."

"You're exaggerating, Pirry. Civilised people—"

"Herr Hitler is not a civilised person, Mother. The Germans you remember—the opera-lovers of forty years ago—don't exist anymore. Or if they do, they're too frightened to show themselves. I've been reading *The Times*. I can see how you're trying to deceive yourselves. The Anschluss was just a family visit, not an invasion! Well, maybe some Austrians did welcome it. But for the Jews there, it's a death sentence. Herr Hitler has divided the human race into Aryans and others, and made it clear that Europe will be a purer place without the others."

"You used to play that game yourself once," Alexa reminded

him, and quoted: "'The world is divided into those who do and those to whom things are done.'" Some of those boyish divisions had been witty, and many of them had been true.

"It was only a game for me, though," Pirry pointed out. "A form of words—with no penalty for being in the wrong half. I've got to tell you what's happening to the Jews, Mother. Every male Jew between eighteen and sixty is being sent off to a labour camp. While he's there, his wife is forbidden to work, to eat in a restaurant, to go to the synagogue or the park or any public place. His parents may not rest on any public seat or benefit from insurance. If they sell any possession to avoid starvation, they're allowed only a tenth of its value. And meanwhile the man who ought to be the breadwinner is being worked literally to death. In three weeks' time Leo will have his eighteenth birthday. I had to get him away."

"*Vielleicht hat die gnädige Frau Juden nicht gern.*" The young man spoke softly, but Alexa caught the words. She had lived for long enough in Germany as a young woman to be fluent in the language, but chose not to reply in it.

"It's ridiculous for him to pretend that I'm prejudiced, Pirry. The musical world is full of Jews and many of them are my friends. Explain to him that he must wait a moment, until I understand."

The German explanation, she noticed, included a suggestion that she was upset by her sister's recent death; but she did not protest.

"You said there were two reasons," she reminded Pirry.

"Leo is a violinist. In the first rank. That's the only way I know him, from his concerts. He was a boy prodigy in Russia, giving recitals before he was twelve. When he was fourteen he broke his wrist. If it hadn't been for that, he might have survived his parents' disgrace. But the Russians thought he was finished as a player. It's been a long haul back for him, but now—I brought his violin in my luggage. Will you let him play for you, Mother? If you could just listen, hear what he has to offer the world, I'm sure—"

"No!" Alexa interrupted more sharply than was necessary and saw the sudden despair in the eyes of the young man who had not understood the conversation but recognised the single negative. "If I'm to believe what you say, that must be enough. I can't expect the boy to audition for his life. Presumably a bad violinist would be in as much danger as a good one. How did you get him out?"

"He travelled as my valet. I left Collins in Vienna and used his passport. That's one reason why I have to go back, to get Collins out. I don't expect to have any trouble in Austria myself until we're actually at war."

"You think—?" But Alexa did not finish the question. She believed, as clearly Pirry did, that only war could halt the German occupation of Europe. "Has your friend any right to stay here?"

"No. There *is* a scheme for getting Jews out of Austria. If they can find a country which will give them an entry visa, they can leave. But they can't take any money with them. The British are only granting visas when there's someone in England prepared to guarantee the support of the refugees. If they already have a quota number for the United States, it may be only for a year or two. But for the others—it could mean keeping them for life: that's a lot to ask. It's hard, when you realise that a good many of the Jews are well off, able to support themselves if only they were allowed to bring their money out."

Pirry pulled from his pocket a leather jewellery roll. Alexa, who owned a great many jewels and had a good eye for value, was impressed by the diamonds and emeralds and opals he displayed.

"I carried these through for five people I know," Pirry explained. "If I can get a good price for them it means that five families can ask for guarantees and then visas by giving a private promise that the guarantors will never be called on to pay anything."

"Then why did you have to smuggle this man out? Couldn't you simply have provided a guarantee yourself?"

"I tried, but his papers weren't good enough. Coming from Russia, he was a refugee already. I had to do it this way. If we wait a little and then produce him as someone who is here and has adequate support, I can't believe that anyone would send him back."

Alexa, though she did not remind her son of it, was a friend of the Home Secretary. She could help Pirry there, just as she could introduce him to a jeweller who would give a fair price for the smuggled stones. And there was plenty of room at Blaize for Leo to stay and practise until he was ready to take up his own life again.

"I'm sorry to have seemed ungracious, Pirry," she said. "You've been living with this sort of knowledge, I suppose, but I hadn't realised. I'll do whatever I can. Introduce your young protégé to me, will you?"

"Mother!" Pirry hugged her again. "I knew I could rely on you."

But he had not been quite sure, Alexa realised. There was relief as well as love in his embrace. And the stranger's expression was still apprehensive as Pirry beckoned him to come close.

"Mother, may I present Herr Leo Mikhailovich Tavadze. Leo, *meine Mutter, die Baronin Glanville.*"

Alexa smiled at the young man as he approached, and in German welcomed him to Blaize as her guest. Almost gasping with gratitude, he lifted her hand to his lips.

"May I leave him here, then?" asked Pirry when the two had chatted for a few minutes. "As soon as I've arranged the guarantees, I must get back to Vienna. Collins—"

"Collins can look after himself for a few more days." Alexa had never liked her son's valet. "Naturally, Pirry, you must stay for Margaret's funeral."

4

The tiny church on the Blaize estate was crowded with Glanvilles. Long-nosed and long-faced, their likenesses—carved in alabaster, engraved on brass or painted in wooden memorials—dominated the east end of the old stone building. Their elaborately ornamented tombs filled the side chapels and pressed close to the altar, leaving little space for their descendants to continue the ceremonies of worship.

On the day of Margaret Scott's funeral, however, the living for once outnumbered the dead. Members of the family, in the re-

served Glanville pew, sat at right angles to the rest of the congregation. As the organist gently filled the time of waiting with
music, it was easy for Barbara to study her fellow-mourners.

Many of them she recognised. There were few of Alexa's tenants who had not benefited from Margaret's quickness to notice a
need and to supply whatever comfort was required. Wrongly, but
without hesitation, they thought of her as one of the Glanville
family and had come with affection and gratitude to pay their last
respects. Other faces were unfamiliar, but could be identified by
their sticks and their soldierly bearing as onetime patients of Margaret's, still remembering her care for them after twenty years.

A young man who belonged to neither of these categories appeared at the west end of the church. Barbara heard Alexa
whispering instructions to one of the ushers that he should be
brought to the family pew—for by now the church was full.
Looking in their direction, the young man began to approach
down the aisle in acceptance of the invitation. Then he stopped
as he caught sight of Matthew.

The Glanville family pew was square and enclosed. In earlier
centuries it would have contained a brazier to warm the aristocratic feet of the lords of the manor. More recently it had allowed
the younger worshippers—including Barbara herself for some
years—to fidget or play on the floor without distracting others.
Cushioned and draught-free, it provided comfort and privacy. But
its wooden door was too narrow to admit a wheelchair. Matthew
sat apart from the others, in the transept.

At this moment he was studying his prayer book and did not
notice—as Barbara did—how the young stranger paused and
turned away to the back of the church. Barbara would have asked
Alexa to explain, but now the sound of the organ was swelling to
fill the whole church and the congregation was rising to its feet.

Margaret herself had chosen the hymns to be sung at her funeral, and her favourites were Barbara's as well. The vicar was an
old friend of Margaret's, able from his own knowledge to speak of
her life since she had first come to Blaize in 1914 to organise it as
a military hospital. Everything about the service—the building,
the words, and the people—was familiar to Barbara, and until the
last words were spoken she was comforted by the feeling that she
belonged in this setting. Only outside in the churchyard, as they

reassembled for the interment while an icy wind chilled their bones and tugged at the women's hats, was she again overcome by desolation at her grandmother's death. Barbara herself had no claim on Blaize. This part of her life must soon come to an end.

Margaret herself, at exactly Barbara's own present age, had left the house in which she had been brought up and set out to make a new life for herself. Her situation had been far less enviable than her granddaughter's, for her departure was forced on her and the man she loved had disappeared. She could not possibly have foreseen, sixty years ago, that she would end her life in comfort and security, surrounded by love and respect. So why should Barbara feel afraid? No one would make her leave Blaize until she chose, and a new home with a man who loved her was waiting. Why was it that when she tried to visualise herself sixty years on, or even ten, she felt herself shivering?

It was the winter wind, of course. Back in Blaize the cheerful warmth of log fires in the huge stone fireplaces raised her spirits as well as warming her body. "Who is John Lorimer?" she asked Alexa.

"Why do you ask?" Alexa glanced across the hall at Matthew.

"There was a wreath. 'With love and thanks from John Lorimer.' And there was someone at the church I'd never seen before. He hurried away afterwards."

"He's a talented young man. Margaret and Arthur arranged for him to have an apprenticeship in the drawing office of the Lorimer Line. He did so well that the company's board sent him to the university, at Bristol, to do a degree course in engineering. They gave him a kind of scholarship. He's a rather touchy young man. Always found it difficult to say thank you. But he knew how much he owed to Margaret. She was the only one of us who could get near him."

"But who *is* he? With that name—"

"He's Matthew's son," Alexa explained. "He won't speak to his father because he believes that his mother was badly treated. No one can persuade him that it was the other way round. There's no scandal involved, if that's what you're wondering. Matthew was married to John's mother. No skeletons in that particular cupboard."

"You're surely not accusing Margaret of having guilty secrets?"

Matthew, moving silently in his wheelchair, had come up beside them in time to hear Alexa's last sentence but not to know the context.

"Traditionally this is the time when we find out. The lawyer is here, all ready to read Margaret's will in the time-honoured way."

"I remember at the last family funeral—Arthur's—we all learned about that family living in Jamaica," said Barbara. This had not been Arthur's own secret: it was only because he had acted as trustee for his uncle's estate that the younger Lorimers had learned for the first time what Margaret and Alexa had known for some years already—that Harley Mattison, who had the reputation in cricketing circles of being the best spin bowler ever produced by the West Indies, was the grandson of Ralph Lorimer.

Margaret's will was not expected to provide any dramatic surprises. Her small pension had died with her, and she had never had more than a life interest in the settlement made by Piers Glanville. Yet there was a secret to be revealed after all. Pirry laughed aloud as the lawyer read out a note which had been attached to the will, telling the family about the existence of yet another unacknowledged branch of the Lorimer line, this time in France.

"Well, I must say, for a Victorian missionary, Uncle Ralph led an interesting life!" he exclaimed. "Babs, you'll have to break it to Grant that he's got a French half brother as well as a Jamaican nephew."

Barbara joined in the laughter; but her temporary cheerfulness had faded by the time Pirry, anxious to return to Vienna as soon as possible, came to say goodbye to her.

"You'll have left for Malaya before I'm here again," he said. "All the best, Babs. Tell Grant from me that he's a lucky chap. Always remember that the world is divided into the British and the barbarians. And keep in touch, won't you?"

The cliché was a reminder of what Barbara had already realised. In a curiously decisive manner Margaret's death had robbed the family of its heart. While she lived, she had linked all the cousins in her web of love, but now the invisible strands had snapped. Blaize remained as a physical centre, but in a sense the family had died with Margaret. What survived would be only a scattered group of relatives, individuals leading their separate lives, unless they themselves took pains to ensure that their links should not be broken.

More than most of the others, Barbara needed the support of her relations. "Yes," she agreed. "We must keep in touch."

By the first week of September 1939, Barbara Lorimer had been married for five months and was five months pregnant. Frisca and Alexa had seemed shocked to learn that she was expecting a honeymoon baby. Polite congratulations failed to conceal their opinion that she would have done better to settle down in the role of wife before taking on that of mother as well. In Barbara's view this was an unfair reaction. After all, Alexa had wasted no time after her marriage to Lord Glanville before trying to produce an heir—while as for Frisca, her healthy, full-weight son had been born less than seven months after her wedding.

In her letter of reply Barbara had tried to explain how useless she felt when she first arrived at the rubber plantation in Malaya. So well had Grant organised himself as a bachelor that there were no household duties for his wife to undertake. Because she was anxious to share his interests, she insisted on helping him with the records of his orchid crosses, but even here suspected that she was robbing him of a pleasure rather than saving him a chore. When the pregnancy was confirmed, Grant had been delighted because he wanted a child, but Barbara herself had been pleased mainly because preparing for the baby would be something to do.

There had been other reasons for relief, but these were secret. Almost from the first moment of her marriage, Barbara had suspected that she had made a mistake. Margaret and Alexa, at different times, had both expressed doubts in advance, but these were easy to dismiss because they were the wrong doubts. The problem had nothing to do with the fact that she and Grant were cousins; nor with the other fact that Barbara had never earned her own living. Its causes were less easy to comprehend. Barbara had known Grant all her life, and they had always been friends. She could not understand why she should feel frightened now by the intensity of his love, the fierceness of his need for her; but only by a desperate effort of will could she prevent her body from shrinking away from his. The fear was not only physical. She had always been shy and, whether he was being kind or stern, Grant's attempts to regulate her life made him an intruder on her privacy.

If the marriage was a mistake, Grant must never be allowed to guess. Mistakes should be paid for only by those who made them. And perhaps after all she was making too much of the natural complexity of adjusting to someone else's life. It was her duty to try harder, to transform her genuine affection into something more than a pretended love. But it came as a relief when Grant, observing the lethargy induced by her first attacks of morning sickness, decided to treat her as an invalid, leaving her body undisturbed to nurture the developing child. Everything female was a mystery to Grant. He marvelled at the whole business of producing a baby. It was an odd reaction, Barbara thought, in a man who spent two hours each day in his orchid house as a practical geneticist, protecting the virginity of his beautiful plants against the moment when he should fertilise them with a delicate brush and stamp out the details on a label. He seemed to regard pregnancy as a full-time occupation: and for her own reasons Barbara had accepted his view.

Was that why she was still being sick, five months into the pregnancy? No, it was ridiculous to imagine that she could wish such discomfort upon herself. Not only did her persistent nausea leave her weak herself: she was naturally worried about its effect on her child. How could she be nourishing the baby if her own body could accept no nourishment?

Dr. Parry did his best to be reassuring. When the morning sickness first began he had told her that many women—most women—suffered in the same way. It would clear up of its own accord after the third month. Now that she was five months pregnant and still could not look at food without distaste, he had produced a new explanation. The climate was a difficult one and she, as a newcomer, had had no time to accustom herself to the heat and humidity. But she must force herself to eat. The cook had been instructed in the diet she needed and, except at breakfast, Grant watched to see that she consumed it.

On this morning in September, the breakfast tray was a work of art. To tempt his mistress to eat, the Chinese cook had arranged slices of pineapple, mango and paw-paw in a decorative pattern. He had covered the eggs so that the sight of them should not upset her eyes before her appetite was ready to accept them, and had wrapped trimmed slices of toast in a warm napkin. A delicate vase contained a single orchid. Almost equally beautiful was the antique tea-bowl in which thin slices of lime floated on weak China tea.

It was all to no avail. As the Malay houseboy prepared to set it in front of her, Barbara uttered a sound which was unintelligible but immediately understood. He was just able to save the tray as his mistress flung herself out of bed and staggered to the bathroom. After she had been sick—or rather, had retched for a little while—she took a shower, but found no refreshment in it. At no time of the day was the water ever cold.

Grant's working day began at five o'clock every morning, but he did not disturb her when he rose. She noticed now, though, as she returned, that he had left a message on her bedside table. It was brief. "England and Germany are at war."

A wave of misery swept over her as she climbed back into bed. It was only partly caused by Grant's news. Even before leaving England she had known that war against Nazi Germany was inevitable if its policy of aggression continued, and news of the invasion of Poland had arrived the previous day. She was sorry for Pirry, who would have to fight and would certainly not enjoy it; and she felt a sense of loneliness, almost desolation, in being so far from home when so much was happening. But there was no complete explanation for her unhappiness. She seemed these days to be continually on the verge of tears without any good reason.

After a little while she managed to face at least the bowl of tea before she dressed. She spent the morning sewing clothes for the baby, using the smocking and embroidery stitches which Margaret had taught her. As midday approached, she strolled through the plantation, asking the tappers where Grant was so that they could walk back together for lunch. She moved slowly, for the rubber trees which provided shade could offer no protection against the steamy heat which rose from the ground. Even the slightest exertion in this humidity made breathing difficult: but Dr. Parry had told her to take a little exercise every day.

The afternoon passed in the same relaxed fashion. There was nothing she could afterwards regret or blame. At about ten o'clock that night she was lying in bed, half asleep, when she began to miscarry.

It was as though someone had kicked her violently in the stomach. The unexpectedness of the attack made her grunt with pain and, as she tried to sit up, she was gripped by a new spasm. She tried to call out but could not open her mouth even to breathe. All her muscles were taut, imprisoning her in a rigid trap.

As suddenly as it had gripped her, the pain ebbed away. She felt herself pushing it out, ridding herself of it. There was a moment of evacuation when her whole body seemed to be voiding itself, out of her control. And then—as Grant, alarmed into wakefulness, lit the lamp—there was blood everywhere: more blood, surely, then a body could afford to lose. Barbara was not squeamish, but she could not help but be frightened by the sheer volume of the flood which was soaking the mattress.

She heard Grant shout for the servants, who lived in separate quarters. She felt him pull the pillows from beneath her head to raise the lower part of her body. He called for clean linen and tried, but failed, to check the haemorrhage. The pains continued to grip and release her, grip and release.

"Let yourself relax," said Grant. "Keep absolutely still. I'm going for Dr. Parry."

It was a sensible decision but increased Barbara's feeling of panic. Even driving at top speed along the unlit tracks, Grant could not do the return journey in less than two hours. How long could she continue to lose blood at this rate?

Time passed. The servants murmured outside the window. A stranger came in—a Chinese woman, very old and so stooped as to appear tiny. She carried a tumbler filled with a dark brown liquid. The cook was behind her. "Good medicine, mem," he said.

The glass was put to Barbara's lips. It could do no harm, she supposed. But the first sip was so bitter that she pushed it away.

The Chinese woman, stronger than she looked, pressed it back. Barbara felt the cook holding her head, forcing the liquid between her lips as she tried, spluttering, to twist away. She was drowning, freezing, burning; she was being poisoned. Her head fell back on to the bed while at the same moment the old woman pressed down on her abdomen with a force which for a few seconds was agonizing but suddenly became reassuring. Barbara breathed more deeply, panting the pain away. Then she fell asleep.

When she awoke it was morning. She was clean, and the room was full of orchids. Dr. Parry's finger was on her pulse.

"What went wrong?" she asked him.

"Impossible to say. Your surrogate doctor whipped the evidence away before I had a chance to see. It was very bad luck. Unusual, at this time. Lots of women miscarry in the first three months, and there's a dicey patch around the seventh month, but there's not often any trouble in the middle."

"Well, why, then?"

"Only one suggestion I can make. Nature keeps an eye on the process of making a baby. Very often a baby that aborts like this has something wrong with it. Your body somehow discovers that it isn't going to be perfect, and rejects it. In a way it's comforting to know that that can happen. That's why I'd have liked to see the evidence. You'll think this is just professional jealousy, no doubt, but tangling with native medicine is a dangerous game."

"It won't do any harm, will it—for the future, I mean?"

"It tends to kill or cure," said Dr. Parry. "And I'd better be fair and admit that this time it cured. No, don't worry about the future. This won't happen again. Give yourself a month or two to get over it. I'll drop a hint to your husband that he needs to be patient. But in three months, say, there's no reason at all why you shouldn't try again. In fact, it's the best thing to do. I'll send you something to make up for the blood you've lost. Take it easy for a while."

After expressing his sympathy once more he went outside. Barbara could hear voices without being able to distinguish the words. When the car had left Grant came in, kissing her gently as though he were not sure which parts of her body might still be tender.

"I'm terribly sorry, Grant." It was ridiculous to feel guilty when she had done nothing wrong: but the blame must lie somewhere in her body.

"Don't be silly. I know how disappointed you must feel."

"We'll have another shot."

"Yes. When you're strong enough. Dr. Parry suggested that we ought to wait three months."

Whatever Dr. Parry might have meant by waiting, Barbara realised at once how Grant intended to interpret it. The relief which she needed to conceal increased her feeling of guilt. For three months she could be alone again, belonging to herself and not to a husband or a baby. She promised herself that she would deserve the respite by teaching herself to regret it. Then in three months' time they would try again.

1940

1

The first of June, 1940, was a perfect English summer day. Out of a serene blue sky, the sun flooded Blaize with light and warmth. The gardens were at their best, for the azaleas were still in flower and now the roses in the formal rose garden were coming into bloom, while the scents of lavender and honeysuckle mingled in the still air. But there was no one to enjoy them except the bees which droned like distant Messerschmitts as they went about their wartime duty of providing honey to the Glanville household. Alexa sat indoors, listening to the wireless and waiting for the telephone to ring.

For more than two weeks the war news had been bad. The Belgians had asked for help but then collapsed into retreat, leaving a gap in the front line which the crumbling French Army was unable to fill. By now the King of the Belgians had formally surrendered: and the Dutch, too, reeling under the bombing of Rotterdam, had laid down their arms. The British Expeditionary Force was in retreat. Soon there would be nothing between the Germans and England except a narrow channel of water.

Only one ray of hope illuminated the news bulletins. The Army, it appeared, was making its escape. Every day for a week the number of men reported as rescued had grown. Alexa knew that she could not hope to hear on the wireless the only news which personally concerned her. But the need to hear that the evacuation was still in progress held her as tightly as a drug addiction. Nor was she the only one to spend that beautiful day indoors. The whole of England, on that windless afternoon, was holding its breath.

By midafternoon she could no longer bear to be alone. Pausing only to say where she could be reached, she walked to the old coach house and found Matthew sitting outside it in the courtyard.

"I need to talk," Alexa said. She brought out a chair to set next to his wheelchair.

"Not too hot for you?"

It was very hot indeed. The flagged floor of the courtyard and the stone walls which surrounded it had trapped and absorbed the sun's rays so that the heat radiated from every side. But Alexa was not concerned with her own comfort.

"Earlier this morning I was remembering another very hot day," she said. "The first day of July, 1916. This same unrelenting, angry heat. I was in London, and I heard the Battle of the Somme begin. No one believes that now, but it's true. The air was so still. All over London people were standing, listening. That was the day Brinsley died."

"There's no comparison," Matthew told her. "This isn't an angry heat. It's a miraculous heat. How could so many of our men be getting away if the sea wasn't a millpond? And this isn't a battle like the Somme, with men hurling themselves against guns. It's a retreat. Either Pirry will be evacuated or else he'll be captured. Being a prisoner of war may not be a pleasant prospect, but it's better than being killed."

"He could be killed. It's still a battle."

"You're not to think like that," said Matthew. "Pirry may pretend that he's a bit of an ass, but he's really a very resourceful young man. Have faith for a few more hours. And pray that the sea stays calm."

He reached out towards her and Alexa felt her hand clasped in his strong fingers. As the sun beat down on their heads they sat close together, trying to imagine what was happening to Pirry.

Over Dunkirk, the sky was distinctly less serene than at Blaize. The oil tanks which had been bombed earlier in the week were still sending up clouds of black smoke, with no breeze to disperse it; and from time to time a flight of Stukas would appear, dive-bombing or machine-gunning the men who were queuing' to leave and the boats on which they were embarking.

As he helped to marshal the long lines of weary men who waded out from the shore to wait shoulder-high in the water for another shallow-draught ship to arrive, Pirry indulged in harsh thoughts about the selection board which had refused to believe that a peer of the realm could be both unwilling and incompetent to be an officer. Pirry had been right and the board had been wrong, but he was the one who was paying for it. In an attempt to raise his spirits he began to play the game which had enlivened his boyhood. "The world is divided into those who queue and those who catch the boat for which the others are queuing." But there was no choice. It was the duty of an officer to see his men safe.

A Thames pleasure steamer, dangerously low in the water, pulled away from the mole which stretched into water deep enough for some of the rescue vessels. If it could dodge the minefields and the Luftwaffe, its passengers would be back in England within four or five hours. Lucky devils. Pirry strained his eyes to see which of the ships still approaching the shore was likely to come in his direction.

The answer would have been comic had it not been a matter of life or death. A flotilla of large yachts, as neatly spaced as though starting a race at Cowes Regatta, headed straight towards Pirry's line. It was crazy, he thought, anxiously searching the sky with his eyes for Stukas. If they were to ferry a respectable number of men to the naval corvette which for the past hour had been waiting unreachably in deep water, they would need to make repeated journeys in and out of danger. The helmsmen were risking their lives for a mere handful of passengers at a time. Thank God for crazy men. And thank God too that, from the sound of it, the yachts had diesel engines.

A naval officer stood at the front of the line of men, responsible for seeing that the rescue vessels were not dangerously overcrowded. Pirry waded out to join him, helping to drag nonswimmers into deep water and to push exhausted men up ropes and ladders into the yachts which shuttled between the beach and the waiting corvette. At the end of five hours of extreme exertion, the line of waiting men seemed as long as before, but several hundred were safely aboard the naval vessel and the yachts were heading out to sea again with the last of the troops who could be accommodated on this particular ship. Pirry made his weary way back towards the beach.

"Well done!" said the colonel, for once arriving at a moment which did not catch Pirry at a disadvantage. But even under engine power the yachts moved slowly and both officers knew the danger of the next few minutes. Even as they watched, three Stukas dived from the sky. There was an explosion in one of the smaller boats.

The others were making progress after all. Now that one yacht was stationary Pirry could see the widening distance between them. A shout went up from the stricken craft. "Engine's dead, sir. And the skipper."

The colonel turned to Pirry. "Could you handle her? Under canvas?"

"Yes, sir." Pirry's uniform was tattered and soaked and he himself was unshaven, but he produced a smart salute. No doubt he could thank his blue blood for this opportunity as well, but this time the assumption was justified. Pirry had sailed since the age of eight: first on the Thames and later on the Austrian lakes. With a sincerity that came straight from every Hollywood war film he had ever seen he wished his colonel good luck and made for the yacht.

The pennant which the dead skipper had hoisted drooped listlessly against the mast, with no breath of wind to stir it. And the corvette, not prepared to risk the lives of the men already aboard by waiting for a straggler, had begun to move away towards England. Pirry did not share his anxiety with the tired men who hauled him out of the water, but forced optimism on them instead.

"Two men into the dinghy to row it as a tug. Two men on the tiller to swing the rudder. Let me show you." He began an energetic sculling movement and was conscious of a gasp of hope as, gradually but unmistakably, the yacht began to move. "Once we get away from land we'll pick up a breeze. And as soon as we're in deep water, someone will give us a tow." He handed over the tiller and hurried forward, showing one man how to keep the dinghy line taut and another how to hold the spinnaker. For his own part, he took the mainsail sheet and began the delicate task of feeling for a wind.

Two hours later it seemed that his optimism was justified. The yacht had made enough way to carry it out of range of the guns along the shore. And it had been rescued by a Thames lighter, whose skipper first shouted a warning that they were heading into a minefield and then threw out a towline. There was a scramble to catch and fasten the line and then a cheer as it tautened and they began to move again—slowly, but with a steadiness which the wind had not provided. To avoid the mines, the lighter's course took it westward at first, almost parallel to the French coast, so that for the first half hour England was no nearer than before. But there was a profound security in the steady throbbing of the engine. And the sun was setting. Soon they would be invisible.

Then out of the sunset came the Stukas again, diving steeply in an arrowhead formation. The lighter exploded like a Roman candle, throwing burning fragments high into the air. "Slip the towline!" shouted Pirry desperately; but the men in the prow were staggering from the blast and perhaps could not hear the order amidst the chaos of secondary explosions and the screaming of the men on the lighter. The nose of the yacht was tugged down, still under tow but now heading for the bottom of the sea. As the stern reared into the air, Pirry left the tiller and jumped.

Others must have jumped too, but in the deepening darkness he could not see them. Nor could he hear the expected sounds of shouting or splashing. It was as though men who had twice been offered the chance of safety and had twice seen it snatched away no longer had any energy left with which to struggle. Pirry understood how they felt. Instinct kept him afloat. He trod water with the minimum effort necessary—but he could feel weariness dragging him down, making his limbs as heavy as his sodden uniform, and his mind sluggish. For almost six days he had gone without sleep. For three he had been fighting and for the last two had endured the equal strain of waiting as an exposed and defenceless target. He had had enough. All he wanted to do now was to let go, to sink into the water, to get it over quickly.

But not all his unwanted training had been wasted. An officer should allow himself time to appreciate a situation before taking a decision. Pirry forced himself to appreciate. The situation was that it was already too dark for anyone to see him in the water, even had there been any boats near. To tread water for the eight hours until daylight would require almost as much stamina as to swim, and would impose a greater mental strain. So what about swimming? England, at the most optimistic estimate, was twenty miles away. France, on the other hand—thanks to the route imposed by the minefields—was only three or four miles distant. Only! Pirry was young and in normal circumstances considered himself fit, capable of a long swim in calm water if he took it slowly. But these were not normal circumstances. Could he force his exhausted body to cover such a distance? Was it worthwhile even to try?

He changed the course of his thoughts to consider his mother —but the picture which presented itself was not that of someone distraught and bereaved, but of an indignant dowager. "Do you realise what you're doing, Pirry?" she was demanding. "If you die now, without any children, that odious Duncan will inherit Blaize as well as the title. He'll throw me out the day he reads your name in the casualty lists. You have to stay alive, Pirry. Do you hear me? You have to stay alive."

The words came not from imagination but from memory. Alexa had spelled out the details of the entailed estates often enough in her efforts to persuade him to marry. Pirry knew how much she hated his father's brother, whom she claimed had once tried to rape her. There was no doubt that to drown now, just for the sake of a quiet death, would be a dirty trick to play on his mother. And yet he was so tired.

Pirry turned himself round in the water. The real sunset in the west had already been overwhelmed by the black clouds of night. But to the east, the sky glowed crimson as the fires burned in Dunkirk. They acted as a compass point from which he could calculate the nearest point of the coast, at Calais. And exhaustion, it could be argued, was all in the mind. He had kept going for six days. What difference was there between six and seven? Taking a deep breath, he spoke aloud to the smooth, dark sea. "The world is divided into those who sink and those who swim." Very slowly but very doggedly, Pirry began to swim.

In Southern California the heat was scorching. Bernard was still splashing about in the pool, but Frisca had retreated to the shaded cloister of her home in Beverly Hills. She had some thinking to do. From time to time she reached for the telephone to consult other members of the British community in Hollywood, but she listened only to the opinions closest to her own. By the time Joe arrived she had made up her mind.

Joe Stern was one of the best agents in Hollywood. If he looked pleased with himself now it meant that he had won her a good deal. Frisca gestured towards the drinks trolley as she smiled in greeting. He would need a glass in his hand when he heard what she had to say.

"Well, Frisca honey, here we are. All ready for you to sign. This contract's going to make you the highest-paid hoofer in the studio."

"Got a shock for you, I'm afraid, Joe. I'm not ready to sign."

"What d'you mean, not ready? You've got leading-man approval, dance-director approval, more money than you've seen in your life. What else is there, for Christ's sake?"

"I want to take a break. My current contract runs out on Monday. Once I sign the new one, I'm a prisoner here again until it ends. A well-paid prisoner, I grant you. But I shan't be able to get away."

"Why d'you want to? Where could you go that would give you more than Hollywood?"

"I'm going back to England."

"England? Frisca honey, don't you read the news? England's through."

"I don't think so."

"Well, a week or two, that's all I'd give it. Look, if you want to take a vacation, visit your family, that's O.K. I can get the dates altered, give you a month's break. How about that?"

Frisca shook her head. "I don't want to commit myself here."

"You pass up a chance like this, it doesn't come again. You leave Hollywood, Frisca baby, and you're dead."

"I was first signed up here because I was already a star in the theatre. To go back to the theatre for a year can't be bad."

"Three years ago you were a hot new property. You've had three years' promotion. If you walk out now, you're an unreliable property. And what makes you think the Germans will keep the theatres open?"

"The Germans aren't in London yet."

"And Bernard, what about him? You plan to take him back?"

"No," admitted Frisca. She had had to arrange for her son to stay with friends in California. The British Government had already evacuated all children from London to the country, encouraging parents who could afford it to arrange private evacuation across the Atlantic. To take a thirteen-year-old in the opposite direction, into possible danger, could not be justified. "No, he'll stay. So I'm bound to come back."

"People in Hollywood have short memories."

"I'm sorry, Joe. I know it's tough on you. But I feel a need to be there, to cheer people up a little. There's a flying boat service operating by way of Lisbon. I've booked a seat for next week."

A few hundred miles north of Beverly Hills, Bradwell Davidson, Executive President of Davidson Security Systems, Inc., stood looking out of his office window as he considered the extraordinary suggestion which had been put to him. On the other side of the desk, a mousy Englishman waited patiently for an answer.

"Why the hell should you think I'm prepared to go to a country that's just about to be invaded?" Brad demanded.

"Your father was English." The man who called himself Mr. Talbot made the reminder with diffidence.

"My father was Scottish. And England kicked him out without a penny to his name. He built this up from rock bottom." Brad's father had established a safe-deposit business in San Francisco at a time when gold and silver mines were making poor men rich overnight. Greg Davidson had filled their need for an honest banker to hold their gains and for an investor to finance the purchase of mining machinery when the days of river panning were over; and Brad, his only surviving son, inherited a fortune when his father died. The colourless Englishman in his crumpled suit had already conceded that he could offer nothing meaningful in financial terms to tempt Brad from his comfortable Californian life.

Brad had inherited more than money. Greg Davidson had had an uncanny ability to invent and operate delicate mechanisms, and his son possessed the same talent, harnessing the infant science of electronics to the business of making locks and safes, developing sophisticated time switches, remote-control systems, and surveillance operations. His inherited money gave him financial control over his company, but what made the business successful was his own ability as an inventor.

Mr. Talbot had been aware of that as well—had known enough, in fact, to make Brad uneasy. For masquerading as a potential customer he had enquired about the feasibility of a device that would open combination locks by moving through every combination of numbers at very high speed. It was a disquieting question to put to a man who had just invented such a device but believed that no one yet knew about it.

"I'm not an industrial spy," said Mr. Talbot, showing an equally disconcerting ability to read Brad's thoughts. "I've come from the embassy in Washington and I have the authority of the British Government to issue this invitation. I can't buy you with money or tempt you with patriotism. You may not care very much that this could be literally a matter of survival for England. All I can offer, I suppose, is the challenge of an almost impossible problem to be cracked."

"Which you're not prepared to describe."

"When you arrive in England and realise what's at stake, you'll appreciate the need for secrecy. You'll want to think about this, Mr. Davidson. There's a flight to London through Lisbon next week. But if that's too soon, we can put you on a diplomatic flight whenever you're ready. I'll call tomorrow, if I may, to hear your decision."

After his visitor had left, Brad continued to stare across the grey-green water of San Francisco Bay. How could anyone imagine that he would leave his comfortable home and his profitable work to travel to a country which was wet and foggy and almost certainly dangerous, a country where he didn't know a soul?

To be fair, San Francisco was often wet and foggy as well. And only three weeks earlier the marriage which had been teetering on the edge of collapse for years had finally ended in divorce. Brad was anxious to avoid new emotional entanglements until he had sorted himself out. There was something to be said for escaping the attentions of the smart young women who knew the value of Davidson's to the nearest cent.

Most persuasive of all was the mysterious problem. Many of Brad's inventions evolved as solutions to particular puzzles. It could be worth the trip just to find out what was wanted. If it wasn't worth his while, he needn't stay. The Lisbon flight would be too soon for him to leave the business. But given time to organise his affairs, a trip to England would not be impossible. Not impossible at all.

2

England had been at war for more than a year, but Blaize was at peace. Halfway up its long carriage drive, Brad Davidson of San Francisco switched off the engine of his car and sat without moving, marvelling at the serenity of the ancient house. Not so many miles away to the south the young heroes of the Royal Air Force were still twisting and diving in their dance of death: the Battle of Britain had been won but was not yet over. But here, on the wooded slopes of the Thames valley, nothing moved except the bronze and golden leaves which fell from the trees in a golden shower at each stirring of the autumn breeze.

Brad had arrived at Blaize earlier than he intended. Every signpost in the country had been removed some weeks earlier to confuse the expected invader, so it had seemed prudent for a foreigner to allow plenty of time for a journey across unfamiliar territory. But his maps had served him well and he made good speed on roads emptied by petrol rationing. He had been long enough in wartime England, though, to know that the arrival of an unexpected visitor at a mealtime could be embarrassing when no one was allowed to buy more than a few cents' worth of meat a week.

Two o'clock was the earliest respectable time for an afternoon call.

While he waited, he studied the imposing building. In the four hundred years since the Glanville who was one of Henry VIII's courtiers began to build, Blaize must have endured its fair share of alarms. Within the past few weeks the present Lady Glanville would have been listening to wireless reports of the threatened German invasion. But Brad had read enough history to know that behind the mullioned windows of Blaize, other Glanvilles must have waited with equal anxiety to learn the fate of the Spanish Armada or the movements of Napoleon's armies. Both then and during the English Civil War, no doubt, men had stood on the roof amidst the clustered chimneys, watching for distant signs of fire—whether beacons of triumph or portents of approaching destruction.

Now the descendants of those men would be patrolling the roof each night, ready to extinguish incendiary bombs: but the atmosphere of the house remained one of undisturbed peace. Blaize had survived four centuries and its calm proportions proclaimed that it intended to survive many more.

Its confidence was built on the flimsiest of foundations. Everyone in the world knew that the British had lost the war—except the British themselves. The expulsion of their Army from the continent of Europe had only by a small miracle escaped from being a massacre, yet they had celebrated Dunkirk as though it were a glorious victory instead of an ignominious retreat. And now that the air raids expected for the past year had begun in earnest they were preparing, it seemed, to sit the winter out as though merely to endure would be a victory of another kind. Without allies, without weapons—and, after what might prove to be the Pyrrhic victory of the Battle of Britain, almost without an air force—they had set themselves the impossible task of defeating Nazi Germany, already the master of the rest of Europe.

Well, that was their choice and their war. In the first gloomy days after his arrival in England, Brad had been tempted to remember that it was not his war, and to wash his hands of it. But although at his first breakfast at Bletchley he had stared incredulously at the minute cube of butter which looked inadequate for a single meal but was apparently his personal ration for a whole week, and although one shoulder still ached from encountering an inanimate object in the blackout, he had been swept off his feet by the charm and intelligence of his colleagues.

Brad realised that the company in which he found himself was unusual. One of the promises made by the mousy Mr. Talbot had been that if he accepted the invitation to England he would find himself working with some of the cleverest men in the world. He had not believed this at the time, but it proved to be true. His colleagues were all geniuses. There was no other word for it. Yet the fact that in civilian life they were professors of Classics or Egyptology or Higher Mathematics did not make them despise Brad's skills. On the contrary—already they were goading him to build a chess-playing machine in his spare time.

Brad had also been told the truth when he was promised that the problem to be solved was of vital importance. The Germans, he had learned by now, used a machine looking like an electric typewriter to encode their messages. The principle on which this worked was known, but it incorporated so many variables, and these were so frequently changed, that an intercepted message could not be manually decoded fast enough to be of use. Only an electronic system could provide the vital speed. Brad's talents precisely fitted the task.

But the intense intellectual concentration demanded of him induced a wish to escape occasionally. One of the few conditions he had put to Mr. Talbot was that he should be provided with a car and a generous petrol ration. He had no friends in England, though, and the thought of having an evening out alone was uninviting to a sociable man. It was when the Station X music club advertised a performance of *Carmen* on gramophone records that Brad had remembered his meeting with Alexa Reni.

Brad had been thirteen years old when the famous singer came to San Francisco in 1906 to be the star of the opera season. She was chaperoned by her guardian, Dr. Margaret Scott, and Dr. Scott brought her son Robert, almost exactly Brad's age. Robert and Brad became friends, while Brad's elder brother, Frank, was soon engaged to marry Alexa. When Frank was killed in the earthquake, Alexa, weeping, returned home. But before she went she had invited Brad to look her up if he ever came to England. Now, thirty-four years later, he proposed to take her at her word.

Naturally there were problems. No Alexa Reni was listed in any telephone directory. Brad was not surprised. He remembered her as the most beautiful woman he had ever seen. When she recovered from Frank's death, she would soon have found another husband.

Help was at hand. An interesting fact about the Bletchley Park geniuses was that almost all of them were musical. It was odd that an aptitude for cryptography and chess and music and either dead languages or mathematics should so often be found in the same mind—but useful. Over dinner one night Brad tossed the name of Alexa Reni into the conversation and was not disappointed. Within two minutes she had been identified as the Singing Suffragette and as a turn-of-the-century prima donna, had been married off to Lord Glanville and later widowed, and had been brought almost up to date as the owner of the Riverside Opera House at Blaize. Many large country houses had been commandeered, so no one was sure whether she was still living there; but someone remembered that there was a Glanville House in Park Lane.

The housekeeper at Glanville House informed him over the telephone that Lady Glanville was in the country, and in a sudden fit of impatience Brad had used his free afternoon to drive over without warning. Would Alexa remember him? He left the car where it was and took a short cut towards the house up a woodland path lined with rhododendrons. On reaching the terrace, he paused, looking across the gardens and the sunken ha-ha towards the smoothly undulating acres of park and farmland. English scenery was small in scale, but its serenity delighted his eyes.

The silence was broken by the strident ringing of a bell. Within seconds the peace of Blaize was shattered even more effectively by the eruption of dozens of schoolgirls wearing white blouses and navy blue gym slips. Waving hockey sticks like offensive weapons and shouting as shrilly as though each of them inhabited a separate mountain top, they poured out of the house and disappeared at a run towards the lower lawns.

It was a disconcerting welcome. Brad pulled the bell at the top

of the stone steps and explained his business. The secretary of the
school led him round the outside of the building to another entrance in one of the William and Mary wings. He would find
Lady Glanville's private apartments here, he was told.

An elderly butler showed him into a large, galleried room
which had clearly been designed as a library. Shelves of leather-
bound books, their spines stamped with gold, served as wallpaper
for what had been converted into a comfortable living room.
Three sofas formed a square with the massive stone fireplace in
which a log fire glowed. The rest of the room was crowded with
desks and tables, with a grand piano at the far end. Every surface
was covered with photographs. Many of these showed Alexa in
her various operatic roles. Others were presumably of her family.
Brad paused in front of one as he moved round the room on his
tour of inspection. It must have been heavily touched up, for
surely no woman was naturally as pretty as this—no eyes could be
quite so blue, no hair quite so golden. And yet the face was familiar. He puzzled over it for a moment before recognising it as the
face of a film star. He was still wondering what her connection
with his hostess might be, when Alexa herself came into the
room.

He had sent in his card and a note, so she had had time to
remember who he was. Nevertheless, there was a moment in
which they stared at each other, trying to reconcile what they saw
with what they recollected. Thirty-four years, Brad reminded himself, was a long time. In 1906 Alexa had been unforgettably beautiful. He remembered in particular her reddish-blond hair, coiled
on her head like a crown. Tall and slender, straight-backed and
long-necked, she had moved and danced like a princess. But by
now, of course, she must be in her sixties.

The change was less than he might have expected. Alexa Reni
had been elegant in 1906 and Lady Glanville was elegant in 1940.
Slim and straight-backed still, she wore a well-cut tweed suit and
neat, expensive shoes, showing off fine ankles which had not been
on display in 1906. But her hair was white—or rather, a bluish
purple to match the heather fleck of the tweeds. Her face, naturally, had lost the pale transparency of youth. But she had taken
care of her complexion, and her delicate nose and high cheekbones gave her an imperiously distinguished appearance. She was

a woman of whom strangers would say admiringly, "She must have been very beautiful when she was young," and the beauty had not completely disappeared. Only her eyes betrayed her, bird-bright and mischievous where once they had been liquid and loving. At this moment they were startled as well.

Brad was not surprised. Alexa was still recognisably Alexa, but she had last seen Brad when he was a thirteen-year-old boy in a knickerbocker suit. Now she was confronted by a man of forty-seven, tall and heavily built, with dark hair which still curled luxuriantly at the back of his head but which had begun to recede from his forehead.

Surprise did not inhibit the warmth of her welcome. Within a few seconds he was sitting beside her on one of the sofas, laughing and reminiscing. It came as little surprise to discover that Margaret Scott was dead. Brad knew that she had been considerably older than Alexa. "But Robert is still around, presumably," he said. "I'm hoping to meet up with him while I'm over."

Alexa gave him a curious look. "You didn't keep in touch?"

"My father wouldn't let me. You left in such a hurry that I didn't have time to get an address, and when I asked my father later, he just said, 'That episode is closed.' He was knocked out by Frank's death, I guess. He couldn't bear to think about it."

Alexa sighed. "No, there was more behind it than that. A lot of old family history." She gestured towards an oil painting which hung between two of the windows. Brad turned his head to see the portrait of an old man with imperious eyes, wearing the black clothes of Victorian England. A man to be reckoned with, he was prepared to concede, but he did not see what the connection would be with Greg Davidson.

"That's John Junius Lorimer of Bristol," Alexa explained. "My father, and Margaret's. He was your father's employer—the owner of a bank which your father managed for a short time before he left England for America. There was a great scandal when the bank collapsed. Your father was blamed. It's old history now, but he never forgot it, or forgave. Robert was John Junius' grandson. Not likely to be approved as the friend of a young Davidson."

"Was?" Brad stared at her with concern.

"Robert went right through the Great War," Alexa said, and then corrected herself. "The First War, we have to call it now.

He was wounded twice, badly. The second wound, in the head, left him a little deaf and liable to attacks of giddiness. After the war he went to work in India. He died there—from his war wounds, in a way."

"I sure am sorry to hear that." Brad was sincerely shocked.

"Yes. Poor Robert." Alexa sighed for a second time. "He left a daughter. Have you any children, Brad?"

"Like any normal American citizen I have an ex-wife and an alimony problem. But no children. Is that his daughter?"

Alexa was pointing out one of the photographs, hand-coloured to show the light auburn hair and pale complexion of a girl in her late teens. It was a studio portrait and the sitter, unsmiling, looked tense, with the wary eyes of a young animal. "Yes, that's Barbara, taken a few years ago. She married one of her cousins, Grant Lorimer. They live in the Federated Malay States."

"An interesting face," commented Brad. "And I noticed another pinup girl." He indicated the blue-eyed blonde. "I've seen her at the movies, I guess. Is she kin of yours?"

"My daughter, Frisca. Another girl who married her cousin. It seems to be a bad habit in this family. She's really Lady Lorimer, but if you've seen her in films you'll know her as Frisca Glanville. You ought to meet her. I'll be delighted to see you here any time you call, but I'm no use to you socially, stuck away alone in the country."

"Alone?" queried Brad, laughing. "I was charged by four hockey teams as I arrived."

"Ah yes, my war effort. In 1939 six evacuees were deposited here straight from the London slums—and each with a full head of lice. They cried for their mothers, they wet their beds, and they regarded a bath as a form of Chinese torture. One of them"—it was clear that this had made a deep impression—"had been sewn up in brown paper for the winter and had no intention of exposing his skin even to air, much less to water. My domestic staff gave notice en masse at the end of the first week."

"So what did you do?"

"I put the billeting allowances into a staff benefit fund and gave the children time to discover that there was no fish-and-chip shop, cinema or Woolworth's within walking distance. When the full horrors of country life had registered, I was generous with stamps for their letters home. The bombing hadn't started as soon as people thought it would, so the last child was hauled back to London by its mother within seven weeks. But I couldn't hope to go on rattling around by myself in a house this size. I heard of a school on the South Coast which had been disconcerted when a shell scored a goal on the netball field one day. I rented it part of the house for the duration. All the Glanville ancestors must be turning in their graves. The house really belongs to my son Pirry, but he's a prisoner of war in Germany so—. Well, as I say, Blaize doesn't have much to offer you. Whereas Frisca can introduce you to her young friends. Her house in Bristol has been taken over by the BBC, and anyway, she's starring in a London show, so she lives at Glanville House. Give me your address and I'll tell her who you are. I'm sure she'll get in touch with you directly."

"I'd appreciate that." Brad picked up the photograph and studied it again. "Is Lord Lorimer at Glanville House as well?"

"He was never a lord," Alexa told him. "Just Sir Arthur Lorimer. He died a few years back." But it seemed that the casual note in his voice had not deceived her, for she gave him a sharp look from her bright eyes. "I'm about to be an impertinent old woman. But it's easier to say this before you meet Frisca, and it might be too late afterwards. She's very attractive. Well, you can see that for yourself. When I was a girl, Brad, I got myself into a great tangle with my first love affair. It wasn't my fault. It happened because nobody told me the truth about who I was and what relation other people were to me. I wouldn't like you to get into the same spot. What you do with the information is your own affair, but I want you to know. Frisca is your brother's daughter."

Brad stared into Alexa's eyes as he digested this information. It was not the kind of talk he had expected from the English aristocracy. "Does she know that herself?" he asked when he recovered his voice.

"She knows that her father's name was Frank Davidson. She's been told that he died a few hours after we were married. She's a big girl now and no doubt she could take the truth if you felt it necessary to point out that there wasn't actually much time for a wedding ceremony between the announcement of my engagement to Frank and the earthquake which killed him. But that's not the point I'm trying to make. A great many men fall in love with Frisca. Before you meet her, I want you to be quite clear about your relationship. Frisca is your niece."

Brad laughed with rueful amusement. "Tough having to turn my back on what could be the greatest love affair of the twentieth century before it even begins," he said. "But O.K. Thanks for the warning. I'll be sure to remember."

3

Brad surveyed his surroundings with distaste. The mean window in front of his desk was crisscrossed with sticky tape to prevent it from splintering in an air raid, but this was not enough, unfortunately, to obscure the view. An avenue of elms led his eyes inexorably towards the monstrous house at the centre of the country estate: a nineteenth-century mishmash of mock Tudor and Victorian Gothic. In its park sprawled a fungoid growth of wooden huts. It was one of these jumped-up chicken coops which had been allotted to Brad for his office and workroom. The ground surrounding them was muddy underfoot and damp overhead. Although it was not actually raining at this moment, water continued to drip from the trees on to the puddled paths which linked the huts. The sky was grey, its heavy clouds pressing down his spirits. Brad was not a sentimental man and had no children to have built up a tradition of family fun. Nevertheless, this seemed no way to spend Christmas Day.

He was glad to be interrupted, if only by Sergeant Jenkins.

"You're wanted on the telephone, Mr. Davidson. A personal call." The sharpness in her voice reflected disapproval of people who received personal calls in working hours and resentment at her own lack of Christmas leave. It contrasted with the warmth of Frisca Glanville's voice when he picked up the extension.

"Brad. Why aren't you at Blaize? Mamma promised she was going to invite you."

"I'm doing my martyr act," he explained. "So many guys were longing to get off to their wives and kids that I promised to keep

a few of the roster duties going. Since there's no one to put anything in my own stocking."

"I would have filled your stocking," Frisca protested. "I specially brought back an orange for you and a banana for Mamma.
Well, you may laugh"—and Brad was indeed laughing—"but
have you set eyes on an orange since you left California? Anyway,
when shall I see you? You'll get some free time to make up, I
hope."

"Yes. Next weekend."

"The twenty-eighth? Stretch it to include New Year's Eve,
then. I've got two performances on Saturday and I'm giving a
shelter concert on Sunday, so you'll have to come to Glanville
House. Mamma says you'd be crazy to go to London with the
blitz still on. Will you be crazy?"

He agreed to be crazy, and the warmth of the invitation carried
him through the rest of the cold and rainy week. After his first
visit to Blaize, Alexa had kept her promise to tell Frisca that her
uncle was in England, and Frisca had written promptly to arrange
a meeting. He had already spent three weekends with her—the
Saturdays in London and the Sundays in the country. It seemed
odd to him that people should still be going to the theatre in
what had become a front line of war. But since Frisca took it for
granted that she should continue to appear in *Touch and Go*, her
current revue, it did not befit a foreigner to reveal how disturbing
he found the noisy, dangerous nights.

With his glamorous niece he had established an immediate rapport. No doubt their family relationship was mainly responsible
for the ease they felt in each other's company. Frisca needed to
spend so much of her life keeping admirers at arm's length that
she seemed delighted to relax with someone who could provide
the interest of a new relationship but would not presume on it—
while Brad, disillusioned after the collapse of his marriage, was in
no mood to embark again on the ritual of hunting and being
hunted. Knowing that Frisca did not expect him to flirt with her
and would have been shocked if he demonstrated any serious sex-
ual interest, he too could relax, enjoying an unusual kind of inti-
macy with a beautiful woman.

Frisca was an ideal companion—so pretty, and so well known,
that when Brad took her dancing he could feel every man in the

night club envying him. She was in her thirties, so that although he was fourteen years older she did not make him feel old, as a young girl might have done. She took pains over her appearance. Brad's first sight of her had been on stage, wearing a black sequinned dress which glittered in the footlights and was slit to the waist to reveal her perfect legs and permit the acrobatic dancing that was her speciality. But even off stage she was always well turned out. Brad could not feel surprised that with each passing week of sleepless nights and food shortages, most of the Englishwomen he met became progressively more shabby. But in California he had been accustomed to the company of women who were tall and slim and well-groomed—and in this sense Frisca was a Californian.

The years she had spent on the West Coast pressed another seal on their friendship, giving them in common a place and a way of life. Unlike many actresses, Frisca had been brought up in an aristocratic household and her sophistication and sense of style were wholly British; but they had not subdued an impulsive friendliness which Brad liked to think of as American. As though they were alone on an island built up of the best of British and American life, and surrounded by an ocean of the people who were familiar only with one society, they had become instant friends.

In order to stretch his leave to include New Year's Eve, Brad went this time to London on Sunday rather than Saturday. Thanks to the parcels which his sister Cassie sent him, he was able to delight his hostess with presents of ham and whisky and silk stockings. He had intended, too, to take her out to dinner, but earlier than usual the air-raid sirens began to wail, each eerie undulation picked up by others until the air itself vibrated. Within seconds their eardrums were battered by the noise of the anti-aircraft guns in Hyde Park. On previous occasions Frisca had claimed to find this barrage reassuring. It was near enough, though, for falling shrapnel from the spent shells to prove as dangerous as any German bombs, so Brad and Frisca agreed without fuss to postpone their visit to the restaurant until the night was quieter.

While the guns continued to thunder, they took the whisky down to the old kitchen of Glanville House. For Frisca to heat the whole of the Park Lane mansion would have been impossible as well as unpatriotic and the task of blacking out the windows of the magnificent entertaining rooms had proved too daunting to attempt. So part of the floor above the ballroom had been converted into a flat for her. This had its own kitchen. The below-stairs rooms in which once upon a time cooks and maids and footmen had slaved under the orders of a butler and housekeeper now provided sleeping quarters for the married couple and personal maid who were the only living-in staff left—and also acted as Frisca's air raid shelter.

There were cellars even deeper below ground, Brad had been told, but the bottles of port and fine claret laid down in their dozens by generations of Glanvilles could be converted by blast into lethal weapons. At the time he had marvelled at the matter-of-factness with which Frisca made that comment. He still on such occasions felt like a man who had gone out for a peaceful country walk and suddenly found himself on a battlefield; but with each visit he became more successful at adopting the custom of the country and pretending that nothing untoward was happening.

By the standards of some of his previous visits, the night was not particularly noisy. Either the Germans were dropping incendiary rather than high-explosive bombs, or else the main raid was concentrated on a different part of the city. Brad and Frisca enjoyed the whisky—a rare treat these days—without anxiety.

Their tranquillity made the bomb, when it came, all the more alarming. It was one of a stick of five screamers, which shrieked their way down from the sky in a straight line, each falling nearer than the one before. Brad gave little attention to the first explosion. The second caused them both to prick up their ears, and by the time the third fell they knew that the line was coming their way. There was no glass to shatter, and the underground room was probably safe against anything but a direct hit. Nevertheless it seemed impossible just to sit and wait. Brad was relieved to see Frisca fling herself to the ground and within a split second he was lying on top of her, shielding her body with his own.

The last of the five fell in Hyde Park, only just the other side of Park Lane. With no buildings to take the force of its explosion it buried itself in the ground and detonated a small earthquake.

By the light of the single bulb which swung on its flex like a pen-
dulum, Brad was able to watch the walls of the room curving out-
wards like a fully-drawn bow, until it seemed that another inch of
movement must snap them, allowing the ceiling and the whole
building above to collapse on their heads. As his muscles uselessly
tensed, he felt the house hovering between its own life and death,
and probably theirs as well. Then, very slowly, the walls
straightened themselves, the light steadied, and he allowed his
held breath to expel itself at last.

"You O.K.?" he asked, disconcerted to realise how reluctant he
felt to move away from Frisca. He tried to rationalise his feeling
by looking down at her warm, strong body and realising that it
might easily by now have been lying shattered and still.

"Fine, thanks." As soon as he allowed her to move, Frisca sat
up and dusted herself down. "But I'm going back upstairs. I think
Mamma must have taken me to a performance of *Aïda* when I
was too young. I'm terrified of being buried alive. This is such a
heavy house. The thought of it all coming down on top of me
. . . The air raid warden said that this room would be safe, but
I'm not sure that I like this kind of safety."

"It will be far more dangerous upstairs." Brad helped her to
stand. "Why do you stay in London when all this is going on,
Frisca? You've got somewhere to go in the country. Why hang on
here?"

"My job of course. But other reasons as well: two, at least."
She sat down at the table and nodded towards the whisky bottle.
Brad refilled their glasses. "I'm frightfully fond of London. It's
not the most beautiful city in the world, but—oh, I don't know
how to put it. There's a kind of continuity of life. It's stuffed
with history—every building, every street, even the names of the
streets—and the history is still being made. We're part of it."

"A vulnerable part."

"That makes it more valuable. I don't think anyone believed
that a city could take as much bombing as we've had in the past
four months and not develop a collective hysteria. The Germans
expected us to panic. Our own government expected it. I don't
see why I shouldn't boast. I feel *proud* to be a Londoner. I
wouldn't expect Mamma to move in here. Her mission in life is
to keep Blaize safe for her son. But sometimes I wonder about *my*

son. Bernard's only thirteen. He couldn't be any use in England. He could only reduce my usefulness by making me anxious. I deliberately left him in California to be safe. He *is* safe, and I'm glad. But I wonder whether he'll forgive me, when he grows up, for cutting him off from something which is going to be part of the collective memory of his generation."

She paused, as though putting the question to herself again.

Brad prompted her gently. "You said there were two reasons why you live in London when you could be safe."

"If safety was all that mattered, I could have stayed in Hollywood," Frisca pointed out. "It wasn't easy, turning down a good contract. And it wasn't easy leaving Bernard behind. I came back because I hoped I could be useful, cheering people up."

"Your films do that."

"I suppose so." She hesitated, and then laughed. "I don't want to grow old. It's as simple as that. The most important thing in my life is the way I can move my body, and when I lose that I shan't have any reason to go on living. I went into films to get my dancing put on record while it was still good. Well, that's done. For the rest—it's a kind of gamble. I wouldn't ever kill myself. I'm as frightened as anyone else when a bomb falls—you saw that. I don't exactly look forward to dying. But I'm quite clear that I'd rather be dead than old. So when I make plans, safety doesn't have to loom large in them. The thought that a bomb may hit me on the head doesn't worry me in advance—only for the split second when it's on its way."

"You need to fall in love. That always provides a great incentive to go on living."

"I did once," Frisca said. "But he died. Perhaps that's provided part of the incentive *not* to go on living."

"Your husband?"

"No. Not my husband."

No great sensitivity was required to see that she did not wish to pursue the subject, but the moment in which they had waited together for the bomb to explode had made Brad feel very close to her. "You surely wouldn't argue that anyone can only fall in love once."

"There are ordinary love affairs which can happen any time, and once-in-a-lifetime loves which define themselves. I was thinking of that kind. The others aren't important enough to act as an incentive for anything. Listen!"

The sirens which had announced the approach of the bombers began to wail again, but this time they swooped up to their highest note and held it in the All Clear signal. The air raid was over.

4

Frisca was glad to escape both from the underground kitchen and from her conversation with Brad. She had said more than she intended. It was enough, she thought, that she should always appear carefree, bringing delight to everyone who saw her. This was a talent she had possessed from childhood. Whether or not she herself felt the gaiety which she was able to induce in others was nobody else's business. She paused briefly to make sure that her housekeeper had not been hurt or unduly alarmed by the explosion, and then switched on her torch and led the way upstairs.

On the ballroom floor she looked out of the window to see what damage the bomb had done. There were people standing in the park, pointing upward, as though at the roof of Glanville House. It was odd how clearly she could see them on what ought to have been a dark and unlit December night. And as she wondered what they were indicating, she was aware of an unusual sound: a crackling, almost a roar—quite different from the earlier drone of the bombers.

"Something's burning," she told Brad. Like most Londoners, she had attended fire-fighting sessions and recognised the sound of fire. "It doesn't sound too close—but all the same, I'd like to check the roof. Do you mind?"

Without waiting for an answer she led the way up three more flights of stairs. The main doorbell of the mansion rang as she was passing her own flat, but the sound prompted her to hurry rather than hesitate. The housekeeper would answer; and if it was an onlooker reporting a blaze, the sooner she reached the roof the better. A ladder on the narrow top corridor of Glanville House led up to a trapdoor. Still in the darkness, she opened the trap and climbed out to the walkway which surrounded the pitched roof.

"Careful!" she warned Brad, who had followed close behind her. The narrow walkway was obstructed at intervals with buckets of sand, and the balustrade on the outer edge was only eighteen inches high, intended for decoration rather than safety. But for a few moments neither of them moved at all. Instead they stared unbelievingly towards the east.

The sky was on fire. Like a stage sunset, the crimson glow in the distance transformed all the nearer buildings into black silhouettes, cardboard-thin. There was little smoke to be seen. The only clue to the intensity of the blaze lay in the haziness of the air, which blurred their vision as though they were staring through a fine mesh. Frisca gazed speechlessly at the angry sky, trying to imagine what must be happening on the ground to produce such an effect.

The roaring which she had heard faintly inside was louder now, as though the air from miles around was being sucked towards the inferno and expelled through a high, invisible chimney. She watched the taller buildings blaze and topple and, as her eyes began to focus better, she could see the flames themselves bending in the wind and then leaping upwards again in a high wall.

There was no danger to Glanville House. She tried to work out the location of the fire. "It's nearer than the docks," she guessed. "I was up here the night Poplar and West Ham burned. This is closer. The City of London, I should think. I wonder if they've got St. Paul's, the bastards. The whole of the City must be burning down."

"Will anyone take notice?" asked Brad. "Poplar yesterday, the City tonight—tomorrow the whole of London may go up in flames. When is somebody going to start wondering whether it's all worthwhile?"

"Don't let any Englishman hear you say that."

"But do you really reckon you can win?"

It was not an easy question to answer. Probably that was the reason why the English themselves rarely asked it. Frisca did her best. "If someone claims to be victorious in a war, it may not necessarily be true," she suggested. "But if someone claims to be undefeated, it's true just because he says it. I don't know how we're going to win. But we shan't lose."

"And is it worth it? Look at the price you're all paying, and think how much more there may be to come. Is it worth it?"

"I suppose we may all be fighting for different things." Frisca switched off the torch and leaned against a chimney stack. "You don't know my young half brother, Pirry Glanville. He's not really a hero type. But in the year before the war he helped twenty-three Jews to get out of Vienna. I read some of the letters from people who wrote to him for help. They knew what would happen to them if they couldn't get away from Austria. Twenty-three, Pirry helped, out of millions. Millions! I don't suppose, if I think about it, that I cared all that much about the Germans taking over bits of Czechoslovakia or Poland. But what they're doing to some of the people who live there—it's a sort of devilry, Brad. It's too late for us to be of any use. We've lost that chance. But we can't let them get away with it." She tried, without much success, to laugh at herself. "I suppose you think I'm falling for a lot of propaganda. And I suppose every country, in every war, believes that God is on its side. From everything I've read about the Great War, it seems to have been the most ghastly muddle, with not much to be said for anyone. But I truly believe that this war is different. There's a right side and a wrong side—an evil side. Sorry to make a speech. But you asked me." She paused for a moment. "And you were wondering earlier why I stayed in London. I've never asked you why you came to England. You could truthfully claim that all this has nothing to do with you. What made you choose to help us?"

"A lack of any good reason to stay home, I guess. There are times when nothing seems worth doing, and then you pick up the first offer that comes along—strictly because you don't care."

Frisca didn't believe the answer, and realised that she ought not to have asked the question. She knew that Brad was divorced, and sensed that he had not yet recovered from the experience. But she had no wish to discuss it with him. He was good company, but she wanted to keep her friendship with him on its present social level. Deliberately she turned away, to face back to the blaze.

"There's one thing to be said. Not a lot of people actually live in the City—sleep there at nights, I mean. Somewhere inside that fire thousands of share certificates and insurance policies and bank statements must be burning, as well as scores of Wren churches and perhaps a cathedral, but with luck, not many people. Will you go down first?"

She closed the trap and followed him down the ladder. He was standing so close to its feet that when she reached the ground she could turn only into his arms. Once already that evening, as the bomb fell, she had known that he wanted to kiss her. Deliberately now she moved his hands away and slipped out of reach in the darkness.

"I'm sure Mamma made your status as my uncle very clear to you before she let you meet me, Brad," she said. "Certainly she rubbed it in to me. Did she tell you why she was worried?"

"There was something about an old love affair."

"She had a very raw deal," Frisca explained. "You've met Sir Matthew Lorimer, haven't you—the artist who lives in the coach house at Blaize. He's three years older than Mamma, and she fell in love with him when she was eighteen. Nobody had ever told her who her father was."

"John Junius Lorimer of Bristol, she said."

"She knows that now, but she didn't then. She was illegitimate —born when the old man was almost eighty, which was how the generations got mixed up so much. Matthew was John Junius Lorimer's grandson, so she was Matthew's aunt. But nobody spelled that out to her. People made up stories to keep her and Matthew apart. Years later the two of them managed to fix a wedding date, and that was the first time they were told the truth. They couldn't marry, of course. I suppose Mamma loved my father—and she certainly loved my stepfather, Lord Glanville. But Matthew was her once-in-a-lifetime love and she never quite got over having to leave him. They didn't meet again until she was a widow, and by then he was a paraplegic—a casualty of the first war, in a wheelchair for life."

"You're talking about forty years ago," Brad pointed out. "People were prudish then."

"It was a matter of law, not prudery. And anyway"—Frisca laughed, relaxing the intensity of their conversation—"I'm not sure that Mamma was notably strait-laced in her youth. I often used to wonder, for example, whether she was really married to my father—and even, in my naughtier moments, whether she knew who my father *was*. You've no idea how reassuring your arrival has been. If Bradwell Davidson is my uncle, then Frank Davidson must have existed. I intend to hang onto you as an uncle. I'm short on uncles. Mamma's two half brothers died years ago. I've got a step-uncle, an ancient Glanville who's longing for Pirry to die so that he can scoop up Blaize and the title and most of the money; but he's horrid and I don't count him."

"You're talking too much." Brad's voice came out of the darkness.

"Yes. I'm on Mamma's side, you see. Wanting to keep relationships in their place. She couldn't help getting hurt, because people lied. But she's told us the truth, and I think we ought to play fair."

"And anyway you don't care."

That was unkind, Frisca thought, when she had been doing her best to make him understand that feelings could not alter facts, that it could make no difference to their relationship whether she cared or not. But as well as being unkind, the accusation was true. If her brief and passionate affair with Robert had taught her anything, it was the importance of stopping to think before allowing oneself to be overwhelmed by that kind of once-in-a-lifetime love which was the only kind that mattered. Brad was not stopping to think—probably because until a few minutes ago he had been protected by the anger and scorn he had felt for his ex-wife and by his determination not to take the same risk again. If that determination was slipping now, Frisca thought to herself, he was in a dangerous state—liable, like the prince in the fairy story, to fall in love with the first person he met. All Frisca could do was to make sure that she was not that person.

Interpreting her lack of argument correctly, Brad abandoned the subject.

"If any more bombers are on the way, they've got one hell of a marker," he said. "Eating out may not be such a good idea after all."

Cooking was not one of Frisca's talents, and she had told the housekeeper that she would be out for dinner. Brad's own present, however, would solve the problem.

"We'll have your sister's lovely ham." She switched on her torch again and together they went down to her flat. Frisca herself went straight into the kitchen, leaving Brad to check the blackout in the sitting room before he switched on the light.

"Who is Barbary Scott?" he called through.

"A cousin of mine. Daughter of your friend Robert Scott. Nobody ever calls her Barbary, though. It's generally assumed in the family that her mother was out of her mind when she chose the name."

"I like it. Barbary." Brad repeated the word two or three times. "How did you find out about it?"

"I'm just reading her passport."

"What!" Frisca hurried into the sitting room. Now that the light was on she could see that it was cluttered with luggage. "Babs!" she called. "Babs, where are you?"

The door of the bathroom opened, and her cousin appeared, weary to the point of exhaustion. The complexion that went with her light chestnut hair had always been pale, but now her long face appeared almost white and her brown eyes were ringed with black circles. They held a suggestion of unhappiness. Barbara had always been shy and unsure of herself but now appeared even more fragile than when they had last met.

Frisca allowed herself little time to consider the change, however, before embracing her cousin in a flurry of kisses and questions. "Babs, how marvellous to see you! But what on earth are you doing here? To leave a safe place like Malaya and come to London! What possessed you? Oh, but I must introduce you. This is my uncle, Brad Davidson. Brad, Barbara Lorimer."

Barbara smiled shyly as she held out her hand. She was good-looking, Frisca realised with surprise. In spite of her tiredness and strain she had acquired a taut and nervous beauty in the two years since their last meeting. Brad had noticed it as well. He was staring at her, not moving yet to take her hand. Barbara herself, confused at meeting a stranger, could not have noticed anything unusual in Brad's behaviour; but the earlier events of the evening had made Frisca sensitive to his feelings, and she was aware at once of the almost electric effect of the introduction on him.

It was only a short time since Frisca had recognised how susceptible her uncle might be to the first beautiful woman he met.

Barbara was disqualified by her marriage from filling his needs, just as Frisca herself was by the family relationship; but in the space of only a second, it seemed to have become already too late to say so.

5

"I've decided that I'd like to be called Barbary from now on."

"Because my Uncle Bradwell thinks it suits you?"

"*I* think it suits me as well. Barbary. Barbary." She enjoyed the lilt of the syllables on her tongue as she continued to unpack while her cousin Frisca watched.

"You've taken long enough to decide."

"I didn't even know that I'd been christened anything but Barbara until I applied for a passport. Grandmother and Aunt Alexa never called me anything else. And you and Pirry have always called me Babs."

"And are unlikely to break the habit of a lifetime. What about Grant?"

"Since we married he's called me Ba. I don't like it much, but he wanted a private name. You've always been Frisca. You wouldn't know how it feels to have everyone addressing you differently. It's as though you're three or four different people."

"To add yet another name would seem to increase the problem."

"No," said Barbary. "It will solve it. I shall think of myself as Barbary no matter who's talking to me. I shall be the same person to myself all the time."

"Have you left Grant?" asked Frisca.

Startled by the abrupt question, Barbary looked up from the drawer she was filling. "Of course not. It was Grant's idea that I should come."

"It's a very peculiar idea."

"So I discovered when that bomb fell last night. Our news must have been out of date even before I left. Everyone we asked said that nothing was happening in England."

"All the same, you must have known the risk from torpedoes. What made it worthwhile?"

Barbary sat down on the edge of the bed. "Baby trouble," she said. "I've had three miscarriages in one and a half years. They've got us both worried. And they've left me anaemic."

"So you've come to a country where food is rationed!"

"Don't bully me, Frisca." It was one of the effects of pregnancy that Barbary seemed to cry very easily. "Perhaps we have made a mistake. But Grant felt there must be something wrong—something a good doctor could discover and cure. So when I started another pregnancy we waited just long enough to get past the first danger period and then he sent me off. I'm to have hospital tests. And I've promised to stay in bed for the next five months if I'm told to. Not here, of course," she added hastily. "I hope Aunt Alexa will let me go back to Blaize."

"I'm sure she will. You must want a baby very badly."

"Grant does. Well, I do as well. For one thing, I haven't got much to do in Malaya. Grant's out on the rubber estate most of the time, or in his orchid house, and there are servants to cook and clean, and the club is twenty miles away, and our nearest neighbour is almost as far. There doesn't seem to be anything that a white woman is *allowed* to do, except swim and play tennis or bridge or something like that. It sounds fun, but it gets a bit boring. A baby would pass the time. All the same, if it had been only my own affair, I would have given up by now. Nature does rather seem to be saying that I'm not cut out to be a mother. But it means a tremendous amount to Grant."

And that was understandable, Barbary had always thought. A boy who had been born with a deformed body must often have been mocked. Although the series of operations which he had undergone in his teens went far to correct his disability, so that in a built-up boot he could walk almost without a limp, he would always have felt himself different from other men. In one respect he had bent the difference in his own favour, punishing and exercising his body until he was stronger and tougher than anyone else Barbary knew, but it was natural that he should wish to prove his normality as a husband as well.

"How are things going between you and Grant?" asked Frisca.

"I mean, stop me if I'm being impertinent, but you know me, always avid for gossip. Does married life suit you?"

"Oh yes, everything's fine." Barbary hesitated for a moment. "Though of course I seem to have been pregnant most of the time."

"And Grant leaves you alone when you're pregnant, does he?"

"Yes. That probably made it easier for him to send me here."

"Funny," said Frisca. "I would have expected Grant to be a passionate sort of man. After all, as you say, what else is there to do?"

"Oh, he is!" exclaimed Barbary. "But he's got this ability to cut off. His body will always do what his mind tells it to. I remember, before I went out to Malaya, Aunt Alexa summoned me one day to find out whether Grandmother had told me the Facts of Life."

"And had she?"

"In some detail, actually, as you might expect from a doctor. But Aunt Alexa had something different in mind. She wanted me to realise that a man of thirty-three, which was what Grant was then, couldn't have been expected to keep himself virgin for his innocent young bride, me. That almost certainly he'd got some Chinese or Malay woman whom he was now hastily packing off to her village, and that I wasn't to be upset if I found out about her."

"And was she wrong?"

"Absolutely." The extent of Alexa's wrongness had provided a traumatic start to the honeymoon. There were some details which must remain private even in the exchange of confidences inspired by this reunion after more than two years. But the answer to Frisca's specific question was straightforward enough. "Even before he asked me to marry him, he'd decided that his eventual wife must be the only woman in his life, just as he must be the only man in hers."

"And you don't think the same way?"

"Well, yes, I do, from the moment of the marriage," said Barbary earnestly. "I mean to say, one makes promises. One ought to keep them. In my case, it comes to much the same thing. I was young when we got engaged, and living at home with Grandmother had hardly exposed me to irresistible temptations. But I hadn't expected the same of Grant. Aunt Alexa might well have been right. I wouldn't have minded."

"Is he jealous, then?"

"I think he could be, but he's never had anything to be jealous about. He takes it for granted that I see things the same way as he does. And I do, so that's all right."

"So he's not nervous about exposing you unchaperoned to the licentious advances of a ravaging British Army?"

"He probably thinks everyone shares his own attitude to pregnant women."

"Chivalry, you mean?"

"No. Nervousness. It's odd. He wants the baby, desperately, but he finds the process of producing it rather nasty. As though the womb contains a kind of abscess, and if anyone should press on it—"

"Oh, shut up!" Frisca wrinkled her nose with distaste. "Well, you won't get much social life at Blaize, so you must have a bit of fun in London between your tests. I'm having a New Year's party here after the show tomorrow. I'll lend you my Uncle Brad. He's lonely."

"I shouldn't have thought he needed to be lonely. He's a very good-looking man." To her dismay, Barbary felt herself blushing, as though Brad himself were listening.

"You noticed? Well, of course, you would. In any room full of pasty-faced Britons, a hefty, sun-tanned Californian makes an impression. He noticed you, as well. You'll need to make it clear to him that you're wholeheartedly married, if you are, because he's unattached."

"Well, in that case—"

"There won't be any problem as long as you know your own mind. And when you write home to Grant you won't need to tell any lies. Brad is a member of the family: my bit of the family, anyway. What's more, he's old enough to be your father."

"Is he?" Over their snack supper on the previous evening Barbary had been too tired and too shy to ask questions or stare. She had listened to Frisca joking with her American guest, but had given no thought to his age.

"Precisely old enough. He went to school with your father for a few months in San Francisco. They were friends. Grant couldn't possibly be jealous. As far as the party's concerned, I shall be busy hostessing and you won't know anyone but Brad and Brad won't know anyone but you, so you'll do me a favour if you look after each other. Is it a deal?"

"He won't want—" But Barbary checked her own bashfulness in midsentence. It would be up to Brad himself to say what he wouldn't want. It was true that this interlude between the restricted life on the rubber plantation and the limitations soon to be imposed by her pregnancy would necessarily be short. And if she were to enjoy any male company at all, it was equally true that Brad would be the safest person to provide it. She smiled at her cousin. "It's a deal," she said.

1941

1

Healthily huge, Barbary walked back from the hospital towards
Park Lane, revelling in the crisp March sunshine. Before going to
live in Malaya she had thought of herself as a sun-lover and expected to enjoy the tropical climate—but in practice had found
the heat and humidity enervating. In London, by contrast, the
freshness of the air filled her body with energy. She felt well. She
was well. Everything, this time, was going to be all right.

Even London's special problems could not dampen her sense of
well-being. Her weekly hospital checks involved a good deal of tedious travelling. All trains these days were overcrowded, sometimes so packed that it was physically impossible to force one's
way inside. What had once been a quiet country line serving
Blaize was now part of the rush hour service for city workers who
had moved their families out of London when the blitz began. In
the darkness of a blacked-out train it was difficult for Barbary to
demonstrate to anyone who tried—whether intentionally or not—
to sit on her lap that she had no lap left.

Transport inside the city was equally under strain. Buses arrived irregularly, able to accept only part of the long queues
which formed at every stop: often they were diverted far off their
usual routes by bomb craters in the roads. Tube trains, too, were
liable to stop short of their normal destinations; and although the
stations were cleared each day of the shelterers who slept on the
platforms by night, a claustrophobic stuffiness remained. Whenever the distance was not too great, Barbary covered it on foot.

These city walks proved more than merely healthy. London was battered, dirty, and dangerous, but there was a kind of electricity in the air which revived the spirits even of those whose weary eyes proclaimed their regular lack of sleep. Its effect upon Barbary— who by comparison with the Londoners was well fed and normally rested—was exhilarating. It brightened her eyes and put a spring in her step even while pregnancy was changing her normal long stride to what Frisca unkindly described as a waddle. She whistled now in a cheerful and unladylike fashion as she took a short cut across the park.

Approaching Park Lane, she slowed in surprise as she caught sight of Brad. He was sitting on his mackintosh on the grass, leaning back against a tree. Barbary's whistling stopped in midphrase and she stood still for a moment, looking at him. She was struck, as often before, by his ability to relax. It was an ability which her husband completely lacked. Even when Grant was at leisure, there was always some indication of tension to reveal that his mind was concentrated on something even though his body might be at rest.

There were other differences between the two men. Brad was not fat, but he was a big man, and Barbary had noticed, when they danced together on New Year's Eve, how soft his arms were compared to Grant's, and how comfortably his body filled his clothes. He had a sense of humour, as well, an attribute which Grant had never attempted to develop. Barbary felt that she had never laughed as much as during the past few weeks—and because Brad teased her, she was no longer shy of him. But what she liked most about him was his lazy, catlike ability to stretch out and be still.

Like a cat, too, he could sense the approach of his prey without turning his head. As Barbary, treading quietly, came nearer, he raised a hand in her direction.

"Hi! Come and park yourself beside me."

"Daren't," said Barbary. "Once I got down to ground level it would take a crane to get me up again."

"I shall be your crane." As bonelessly as a snake raising its head to strike he rose to his feet. "I shall lift you gently up into the air like a barrage balloon."

"An extremely apt simile." They both laughed as they looked up at the huge silver sausage, with wires dangling from its inflated

belly, which hovered above them. Barbary lowered herself ungrace-
fully to the grass. "What are you doing in London in the middle
of the week?"

"Not playing hookey, if that's what you think." He sat down
again close beside her, so that they could share the mackintosh.
"I've finished the job I came over to do, but I've had another idea
which might be useful. London University has agreed to let me
use one of its engineering labs. With its students scattered all
over the country, there's space for anyone who's fool enough to
ask for it."

"What exactly do you *do*, Brad?" asked Barbary. "Why do you
need a lab?"

"If you ask me that question again, I shall deliver a short
prepared speech vaguely related to time-control devices on bombs.
But I hope you won't ask, because I'd like to be able to think
that I'd never told you a lie."

"Sorry. I should have realised. Where will you live if you come
to London?"

"Frisca seemed to think there might be room in Glanville
House. I'm prepared to act as janitor while she's away on tour.
And I can pay for my board in silk stockings and food parcels as
long as my sister keeps the lifeline open. How about you? You
look disgustingly healthy for a woman in your condition."

"That's the result of living at Blaize. I don't believe Aunt
Alexa has the faintest idea that food is rationed. The whole of
the walled garden has been turned over to fruit and vegetables
and there are hens and rabbits all over the place. As for the number of piglets which get accidentally run over by tractors on the
tenants' farms, that's nobody's business. There's a new form of
droit de seigneur these days—and it's measured in hams, not vir-
gins."

"So everything's going O.K.?"

"Yes. I'm to go into hospital tomorrow for five days, to be im-
mobilised through the danger period at the seventh month. But
that doesn't mean that anything's wrong."

"Have the doctors discovered why you had such trouble before?"

"You'll never believe it!" exclaimed Barbary. "They say it was
all psychological! When I think of the tortures my body has had

to endure"—for, although she did not intend to go into details to a male, there had been weeks of blood tests and urine tests, internal examinations and temperature charts, corsets outside and a hideously uncomfortable steel contraption inside—"and now they tell me that the problem was in my mind all the time. The first three babies aborted themselves, it seems, because they realised that I didn't sincerely want them to live."

"But you did, surely."

"I *pretended* I did. I deceived myself. But not those superintelligent babies to be. *They* knew that really I was frightened."

"Of what?"

"Well, my mother died just after I was born, so I could have been frightened that I'd go the same way. And my husband was born with a badly deformed body. He's more or less all right now, but he certainly wasn't a perfect baby. And he and I are cousins, so if his trouble had any genetic cause there could be a little risk. Even one subconscious dread, I'm told, could be enough to put me off. To have a choice of two means it will be a miracle if mother and baby survive unscathed."

"You have the look of someone about to perform that miracle."

"I think so. Brad, why are we sitting here when we could be comfortable inside?"

"Because the sun is shining. We may be developing frostbite, but the sun is shining. I swear that at Bletchley Park it has rained every day since September. If you're due back at the hospital tomorrow, you'll be staying over at Glanville House. How about the two of us stepping out tonight?"

Barbary hesitated. Even across thousands of miles Grant's influence was strong. He disliked frivolous social occasions and was never pleased to see his wife laughing in the company of another man, however innocent the friendship. Brad misinterpreted her reluctance.

"There hasn't been a night raid for almost six weeks," he pointed out. "And even if they start again tonight, the bomb that has your name on it is as likely to find you at Glanville House as anywhere else."

"It's not that." Barbary was hurt by the suggestion that she was afraid. But if she confessed the truth, Brad would laugh incredu-

lously. "I'm not much of a companion for a night out in my present state," she said instead. "I couldn't get near you to dance, for
example."

"You shall choose what we do. If you want to stay home and
play gin rummy, that's O.K. by me. But it's my birthday. I need
to celebrate, and one can't celebrate anything alone. You
wouldn't leave me lonesome in the big city, would you?"

"Many Happy Returns! Won't the people you work with celebrate with you?"

"Their idea of a merry evening is to debate whether the theory
of relativity is more or less important to mankind than the dating
of the Minoan Invasion. I don't even know what the Minoan Invasion is. What I need for this evening is someone lighthearted."

"I'm not lighthearted."

"You are with me." He turned his head and smiled at her.
"Hadn't you noticed? Frisca has. She told me that before you
went out to Malaya you used to be a rather sad girl, very quiet
and shy. Now you've changed. At first she thought it must be
Grant and marriage that had done it. But now she reckons that
it's because you're away from the marriage. There's no one
watching to accuse you of being happy."

"That's a terrible thing to say!" But Barbary wondered whether
it was true. With Frisca's description of her as a sad girl it was
hard to quarrel. As a child she was lonely, as an adolescent she
was hurt by her father's lack of interest, and the months before
her marriage had been shadowed by her beloved grandmother's
slow decline into death.

She recognised, too, that she was cheerful now—as though she
could only worry about one thing at a time. Any anxiety she felt
was concentrated on the need to produce a healthy baby. While
that seemed to be going well, she had no worrying power to spare
for Grant's loneliness in Malaya or her own risk from German
bombers. But Brad—or Frisca, prompting the words—had used
an odd phrase. "Because no one's watching to accuse you of being
happy." Surely no one would make happiness an accusation. Yet
the thought rang true even as she tried to dismiss it. Grant was
passionately in love with her. There was no doubt about that. But
he scorned the pleasures of normal social life. He did not encourage his wife to drive to the club without him, although he was

away from the bungalow for so much of the day; and when he accompanied her, his impatience with gossip and badinage made him an uncomfortable companion. No one in Malaya would have dared to flirt with Barbary.

Well, her cousin's uncle was not flirting with her either. A little entertainment could do no possible harm. "I'd love to celebrate your birthday," she said. "But I don't know how to play gin rummy."

"Your choice, then. What would you care to do?"

"Could we see *Gone With the Wind?* Everyone's talking about it."

"And everyone who isn't talking about it is standing in line for it." Brad gave a mock sigh. "I guess you know how many hours it runs. I need your promise that you won't give birth in the middle. Why don't we go early, at four o'clock. Then we could eat afterwards at the Café de Paris, practically next door and safely underground. Right?"

"Right." Too cold for comfort, she tried and failed to stand. Brad helped her to her feet and they walked together to Glanville House.

Later that day she wondered whether she had been wise to accept Brad's invitation, for they emerged from the cinema to find that the six-week respite from raids had ended. The moon was shining with a dangerous brightness, but brighter still were the long fingers of searchlights which probed the sky, crisscrossing in a moving pattern of triangles. Instinctively Barbary strained her ears to catch the droning of enemy bombers, but it was impossible to hear anything above the noise of a nonstop ack-ack barrage. Like her companion she observed the convention of pretending that nothing out-of-the-way was happening.

"After seeing that film, you'll know what to do if my baby decides to arrive tonight," she remarked conversationally as they stood for a moment in the doorway of the Empire, waiting until their eyes could adjust to the blackout in the streets.

"Don't count on it, ma'am." As though infected by the sound track Brad's voice slipped into a southern drawl. "I'm no Scarlett O'Hara. I faint at the sight of blood. Are you ready to run." He grasped her elbow. "It's only a few yards."

The Café de Paris had become popular during the past few

months because it lay beneath ground level, with a cinema above
it. As they made their way down the staircase to the balcony bar,
Barbary saw that the restaurant was packed. The excitement she
had felt earlier in the day swept over her again. Safely sheltered
from the outside world, the lights here were bright, their reflec-
tions sparkling from the mirrors which lined the walls. The contrast between this and the unrelieved darkness of the streets during blackout hours was enough in itself to induce gaiety.·
Vivaciously chatting couples were quickstepping on the dance
floor below to the sound of a West Indian band, and champagne
corks popped at the tables around the floor. Most of the men
were in uniform and all the girls were pretty and smiling. It was a
happy place. The only cloud in the sky was the possibility that
there might not, in spite of Brad's earlier telephone booking, be a
table for them.

But this was an evening when everything was going well. The
headwaiter pointed out a balcony table which was being relaid at
that moment. Next to it, glasses were raised in celebration of a
girl's twenty-first birthday. Flushed with pleasure, she listened as
her friends began to sing and blushed even more deeply when the
band, catching the sound, joined in—converting Happy Birthday
to a quickstep.

"They're playing my tune!" exclaimed Brad. "I'll get you a
drink while we're waiting. What's your poison?"

"A soft drink, please." Barbary was observing all her doctor's
rules. She recognised that it would take Brad some time to get
through the crush to the bar, and turned to watch the dancers
below. The band changed its tune again. "Oh Johnny," they
played, their hips swinging; "Oh Johnny, how you can love." Barbary, happy, began to sing with them quietly—although no one
could have heard her in the general hubbub. "Oh Johnny, oh
Johnny, heavens above, you make my sad heart jump with joy."
She turned away from the balcony railing—still singing, still
smiling—and caught sight of herself in one of the wall mirrors.

The smile faded from her face. She was not vain, and was not
in the habit of studying her appearance even when it was normal,
so perhaps it was not surprising that she had failed to realise how
enormous she was. She had joked about it often enough, but
without *realising*.

How could she have allowed Brad to bring her to a place where everyone else was so glamorous? He deserved better than this—a girl he could dance with, a girl of whom he could be proud. Barbary found herself wondering why a wealthy, attractive, and sociable man should choose to spend almost all his off-duty time with an elderly ex-prima donna, a girl so heavily pregnant that she hardly counted as a female at all, and another woman who—though certainly glamorous—was his niece. It was as though he was making an unspoken declaration that he was not interested in women. Barbary knew that he was divorced but had never talked to him about his marriage. Now, for the first time, she wondered about the damage which his wife must have done.

The thought was not enough to distract her from the shock of her own appearance as she continued to stare at her reflection. She was wearing a maternity smock of Siamese silk over a black skirt. The fabric was beautiful, but by catching the eye only emphasised the swollen inelegance of the body beneath.

All at once the band ceased to play. Barbary saw herself, in the mirror, disintegrate into a thousand splinters. Something very heavy and very hard was pressing down on the top of her head and against her ears, yet at the same time her body was being lifted above the balcony. For a moment she seemed to hover in the air and then, in slow motion, began to fall. Putting out her arms to protect herself, she hit the ground with a crash.

Completely numb, she lay face downwards for a length of time she could not measure. Was she dead? Nothing else, surely, could explain such a complete and dense silence.

Testing her muscles, she managed at last to turn her head, and with the movement the comfort of her temporary deafness disappeared. All around her people were groaning or shouting and from somewhere close came the sound of a woman's screams. Barbary held her breath to check that she was not the one screaming. But in fact she felt no pain. Her inability to move was caused by her brain's inability to give its usual instructions to her body. A great tiredness swept over her and she sank into darkness and silence again.

2

Brad was still in the bar when the bomb exploded. The press of bodies shielded him to some extent from the blast and, though he was thrown to the ground, he was almost immediately able to struggle unhurt to his feet. His first movements were not entirely rational. He helped the men nearest him to stand, but then began to set upright a confusion of fallen glasses, lest they should roll to the ground and break. It was as though he had no recollection of the fact that he had not been alone in the restaurant. Only when he saw that the barman was dead, stabbed in the back by a dagger of glass from the mirror behind him, did this second shock release his memory. He was overwhelmed by something near to panic. Where was Barbary?

He had left her further round the balcony, but when he tried to make his way back he found that a large section had broken away, with the edges sagging dangerously. Approaching as near as he dared, he stared down at what had been the dance floor. Surprisingly, a few of the lights were still burning and as the dust settled it was possible to see the confused mass of bodies below. There must have been more than a hundred people there and, although some were stirring and others were screaming, it was clear that many were dead. Brad felt a sharp sickness in his throat as his eyes searched amongst the bloodstained and sometimes severed limbs for a glimpse of turquoise silk or pale chestnut hair. "Oh my God!" he muttered to himself. "Barbary, darling. Oh, my God!"

By now there was a good deal of shouting. Some of the uninjured were making their way out to call for ambulances: others were lowering themselves on to the dance floor to rescue those who were trapped. Three girls in torn evening dresses were tearing tablecloths and bandaging wounds with the firm professionalism of trained nurses. Brad began to work his way round the undamaged section of the balcony.

He was still looking for Barbary's bright smock and so almost failed to recognise the half-naked woman who lay face downward on the floor. And even when he took a second look his relief at identifying her was subdued by fear at her stillness. He dropped on his knees beside her.

"Barbary! Barbary, dear girl. Are you all right?"

Slowly, as though the effort were too great, Barbary moved her head. He saw her lips move, and strained to hear.

"Turn me over," she whispered.

It was not an easy instruction to obey. Her bare shoulders were slippery with blood and he could feel that he was pressing fragments of glass into her skin. She seemed unable to help and he wondered anxiously whether her back might be broken and whether it was wise to change her position. But he could see that she was distressed by the feeling of pressing down on her baby, and did what she asked.

His success made an immediate difference. For a few seconds, holding his hand for reassurance, Barbary enjoyed being able to breathe deeply again. She even managed to smile. "Like a stranded whale," she said. "But I don't think anything's broken."

He watched as she tested her muscles, moving each foot, knee, arm: only one hand refused to lift. On nearby tables he found—surprisingly unsmashed—brandy for her to drink and champagne in which he could wash the blood and dirt from her face. Raising her to a sitting position he took off his jacket and helped her to put it on. The extreme slowness of her movements contrasted with the scene of urgent endeavour below, where the wounded tried to free themselves from the weight of other bodies and the first rescuers flashed torches and shouted orders.

"If it's bad, sweetheart, you must stay till an ambulance comes. But with so many casualties it's going to take a while to clear the place. If you could make it up the stairs, I could get you into a cab and direct to a hospital."

"I don't need a hospital." She turned on all fours as a preliminary to standing.

"Yes, you do, honey." Brad slipped his arms beneath her shoulders and raised her to her feet. "For a start, you have to have a bath in disinfectant." In all his forty-eight years he had never received any serious physical injury, but he had read that pain was not always felt immediately. Barbary did not, apparently, realise how badly she was cut.

The main staircase was wrecked, but behind the kitchens they found a narrow flight of service stairs. Other diners were staggering in the same direction. Brad persuaded one of them to take Barbary's other arm and between them they almost carried her up to ground level.

"Just a minute, please." Barbary leaned against a wall, breathing the fresh air and gathering her strength. Brad found it unbelievable that Coventry Street should look normal, with no indication of the chaos underground. A crowd had gathered to watch the wounded emerging. "Could somebody find us a cab?" he called, and saw one of the spectators nod and move away.

The taxi driver, when he came, made clear his distaste at being expected to carry not the smart WRNS officer who had summoned him but two filthy scarecrows, one of them covered in blood as well as dust. But judging that the crowd would be hostile if he tried to move on, he grudgingly opened the door.

Brad turned back to Barbary and was alarmed by a change in her appearance. A moment earlier she had looked exhausted but on the way to recovery. Now her body was tense. For a second time that evening she was unable to move, but on this occasion it was because she had locked herself into an iron cage of her own muscles. She was holding her breath.

The moment passed. Her fists unclenched and her hunched shoulders straightened. Two heavy tears rolled down her cheeks, followed by others which she made no attempt to dry. He supposed that until now she had been in a state of shock. The horror in her eyes would be a natural reaction to her first understanding of what had happened. He took her hand.

"Everything's O.K. now, sweetheart," he said. "Get into the cab."

Barbary shook her head, and as she did so her body tensed for a second time. "I'm going to lose the baby," she cried.

Twenty hours after delivering Barbary to her obstetrician Brad returned, unrecognisably clean, to the maternity ward. He had telephoned earlier for news, and was alarmed by the sympathy in the voice which announced the premature arrival of a little girl. Not wishing to ask questions of Barbary herself, he stopped the first nurse he saw.

"Where would I find the babies, Sister?"

"Are you a father? Only fathers are allowed in the nursery."

Brad knew the importance of producing a lie quickly if it was to be believed. "Sure," he agreed amiably. "Who'd want to look at any other guy's baby? It's little girl Lorimer I'm after."

Sister remained suspicious. "Mrs. Lorimer's aunt, Lady Glanville, visited her this afternoon and mentioned that Mr. Lorimer was abroad."

"Was, not is. I came straight over when I heard. I haven't called Aunt Alexa yet to say I'm back. And now"—he broadened his accent to make it more likely that he was the out-of-England Mr. Lorimer—"I'm mighty impatient to see that baby."

She led him through a swing door into a room in which more than a dozen babies lay in cradles. Most of them were crying. Most of them were warmly wrapped so that only their faces, all mouth and indignation, could be seen. Most of them had red lips and rosy cheeks. Only one was different.

Sister stood near as he stared down through the glass of the incubator. The other babies were small, but Baby Lorimer was tiny: it seemed impossible that her thin body could contain all the essential mechanisms of life. Unlike the others she was naked, lying on a bed of cotton wool which emphasised her fragility. Her wrinkled skin was an unhealthy white and her lips had a bluish tinge. Surprisingly, she had a good deal of hair, but this too was almost white. Brad felt as though he were looking at a ghost, attached to life only by tubes. He made no attempt to conceal his dismay.

"What chance has she, Sister?"

"She's very small. And her heart's weak. Two months' premature, it's always touch and go. We're doing everything we can, of course." The nurse paused. "But perhaps you should have her christened."

Brad understood the implication at once. "I can't tell her mother that. She's had a rough enough time already."

"Yes, I've seen her notes. If it's any comfort, Mr. Lorimer, there was nothing wrong with this pregnancy—none of the same troubles that she had before. If it hadn't been for her bad luck, being caught in that raid, she should have had a healthy child at full term. If the worst comes to the worst she must think of this as a kind of war wound. She shouldn't let it put her off having another child. There's no need for her to know about the christening if you don't want to upset her. The hospital chaplain is used to this situation. You'd only need to tell me what name you want to give the baby."

Brad nodded. He was upset in a way he had not expected by the sight of this miniature person, hovering on the frontier of death—and by the thought of Barbary's desolation if the baby did not survive. "Is there anyone with my wife now?" he asked.

"Evening visiting is for fathers only. I'll show you the way."

Barbary was lying back in bed, almost as pale as her daughter. One side of her face was bandaged and one wrist was in plaster. Brad leaned over to kiss her on the lips.

"I'm your husband," he murmured, to prevent her expressing surprise at his affectionate greeting. "The dragons in charge wouldn't let me in on any other terms." He was being unfair to Sister, who had rules to be kept and had made her sympathy clear, but the first necessity was to cheer Barbary up. He sat down and held her hand in an uxorious manner.

"Have you seen the baby?"

"Yes. I've just come from the nursery."

"What's wrong, Brad? They won't let me see her. Only for a second when she was born, and I was too muzzy to look properly. Is there something wrong with her? Like Grant?"

"She's perfect," said Brad. "Tiny, of course, but perfect. She doesn't weigh much. They've put her in an incubator to keep her warm. That's the only reason you haven't seen her. They can't bring her to you, but you can trot along and see her as soon as you're strong enough."

"What does she look like, Brad?"

"Blond. Ash blond. I've never seen such pale hair."

"Grant has it. Almost white." It was clear that the mention of her husband upset her. "Aunt Alexa came this afternoon. She said you told her about the bomb when you phoned. Brad, I don't want Grant to know where it happened. I've asked Aunt Alexa to forget what you told her."

"Anything you say. But why?"

"Grant would never forgive me for putting his baby at risk by going to a place like that. If she dies and he finds out why, he'll say I killed her."

"What do you mean, 'A place like that'? A respectable restaurant."

"Oh yes. I didn't mean—but I shouldn't have been enjoying myself in that sort of way. Going to the pictures. Eating out with you. I should have been concentrating on the baby all the time."

"That's crazy. In any war, safety is a matter of luck. If you'd spent the evening at Glanville House, that might have been bombed. If you'd come into the hospital here, that might have been bombed."

"But they weren't," said Barbary flatly.

Brad was not the kind of bumptious man who would never admit to making a mistake. But he had always been wealthy and self-confident, sure of his own talents. He was sure, too, that Barbary was wrong to feel any kind of guilt. So the feeling of regret and responsibility which now overwhelmed him took him as much by surprise as his earlier distress on seeing the baby. He wanted to kiss Barbary's anxieties away, playing the part of a husband with even more conviction than before. But a married woman who within the past twenty-four hours had suffered bombing and childbirth would be alarmed rather than delighted if he were suddenly to announce that he loved her.

"Barbary darling, I'm sorry. It's all my fault. If I hadn't asked you—"

"You had every right to ask me." Barbary managed a weak smile. "I oughtn't to have accepted, that's all. If the baby dies, I shall feel bad enough on my own account. I'm not tough enough to take a lecture from Grant on top of that. He'd have the right to give it. I couldn't make him understand. He's not sociable, not frivolous like me."

"You're the least frivolous girl I know." Brad made an effort to bring his emotions under control. "And you're not to worry about your baby, because she's going to do fine. What will you call her?"

"I don't know. I wanted to wait and see. Even babies have personalities, don't you think?"

"I've never been a baby-worshipper," said Brad truthfully. "Any newborn baby always looks to me like itself at the age of seventy.

I think of the years it will have to live through before it returns
to that same wrinkled, angry look, and I wonder whether it's
worth it."

"Is that why you never had a child yourself?"

"No. That was more complicated. Joanne didn't want a baby
to start with—afraid it would spoil her figure. She changed her
mind later, but by that time things were rocky between us. She
thought a child might hold us together. I thought—" What had
he thought? His safe, comfortable life in California seemed now
to be part of someone else's history. "I thought that a child deserved to be brought into a stable family situation, and we didn't
have that. And I thought then that I would want to be sure that
any baby which was called mine really was mine, and I didn't
have that certainty either."

"You say you thought that then. Have you changed your
mind?"

"Could be. Looking at your little girl, I felt protective even
without any relationship. I had to pretend to the nurse that I was
her father, and for a moment I even kidded myself. She looked
so"—he wanted to say fragile, but that was too alarming a word—
"so helpless, so dependent on the rest of the world to keep her
alive. Barbary, reverting to the name, you'll find that the hospital
will want to know quite soon what you're going to call her. Until
you have a name you can't be registered, and until you're registered you can't be put on the ration strength."

"You've seen her. If she were yours, what would you call her?
Or did you see only a wizened seventy-year-old when you looked
at her?"

"No," said Brad. "I saw a beautiful blonde. Tall. Slim. Wil-
lowy. Gorgeous. If she were mine, I should call her Asha." He
checked himself, wondering why a name which he had never
heard, which perhaps did not exist, should have floated into his
mind—and uncomfortably realised the explanation at once. It
was because he had seen the baby as a ghost, an insubstantial
wraith, an illusion of light rather than a body of flesh and blood.
"Because she's an ash-blonde," he added hastily. "Or you could
call her Diana. The pale moon goddess."

"Diana Lorimer is difficult to say." Barbary tried it once or twice. "I like Asha, though. I've never known an Asha. It would be nice for her to have a name all of her own."

"Like you. Barbary love, you're tired. I'm going now." He was feeling the strain of too many concealments. "Just remember that I'm your husband. Otherwise I shan't be allowed back. And please don't blame me too much for what happened."

"I don't blame you at all."

"Then you have no right to blame yourself. Some things truly are acts of God. I've never understood why we should be expected to thank God for all the good things in life without cocking a few snooks in the same direction for the bad things." Full of compassion for her anxiety, and very much in love with her, he kissed her again. "I'll be back tomorrow. Get well."

Sister looked up as he passed her cubicle. "Did you choose a name for Baby, Mr. Lorimer?"

Brad hesitated for a second. Barbary had not knowingly made a decision. But if the baby died, the name would be of no importance. And if she lived, presumably it could be changed. Christening and registration were not precisely the same thing. He nodded as though there were no doubt, and the small decision made him feel even more like the father he had claimed to be.

"We're going to call her Asha."

3

Grant Lorimer sat on the verandah of his bungalow, enjoying his regular evening entertainment. The hillside on which most of his rubber trees were planted fell away steeply, so that he was able to look over the plantation to the sea. This was where the Straits of Malacca opened into the Andaman Sea. The sheltered water provided a wide canvas on which the setting sun could paint a changing picture.

Throughout the day the intense heat had been aimed at the earth from a tiny, concentrated circle of light overhead, but by six o'clock the sun became huge. It was a wide crimson disc which rushed towards the horizon and slipped silently out of sight—

leaving behind it a sky which reminded Grant of autumn leaves in the woods of Blaize. At this very moment in October the trees there might be afire with just these shades of gold and red.

Gradually the colour faded, changing to a cool turquoise across which stretched the first fingers of darkness. The clouds of night extended themselves as the light faded. No longer was it possible to distinguish between land and sea, and a stranger might have expected that nothing would disturb the darkness until the sun rose next morning over the eastern hills of Malaya. But Grant sat on and was rewarded by a second vivid display of colour—as though, on the island of Sumatra across the Straits, an erupting volcano was filling the sky with fire.

A passion for sunsets might have seemed an unlikely taste for a man whose way of life was so austere. But Grant had always appreciated natural beauty. The hours he spent in his orchid house owed something to his botanical training but much more to a desire to create a new and beautiful flower. He continued to sit without moving even after the houseboy brought a lamp out to the verandah. This cool hour of the evening was the best part of the day.

The darkness below was disturbed by the headlights of a car moving along the coast road. The driver would be Ted Croggan, who played bridge at the club from four to six every day and dined at home at eight. All the planters were creatures of habit. When Grant first arrived in Malaya he had vowed never to let himself fall into the social rut of gin and bridge, and it had taken a long time for him to realise that his choice of a solitary life had made him just as set in his ways as his neighbours. Marriage had changed that for a little while, but it was almost a year now since he had sent his wife to England.

The car reached the group of Chinese shops in the nearest village to Grant's plantation but, instead of continuing along the coast road, turned up towards the hills. For a little while Grant could see the headlights winding towards him. Then they were hidden by the trees—but the track led to nothing but his bungalow, so it seemed he was to have a visitor. This was unusual. Although the planters occasionally invited each other to dinner, distances between the estates were considerable: it was more generally assumed that anyone in need of society would look for it at the club.

He had been right to guess that the car was Croggan's. For a while the two men discussed the price of rubber—almost the obligatory opening to any conversation. But Grant saw that his neighbour was worried and allowed the conversation to lapse so that the true object of the visit should emerge.

"How's Barbara? Getting on all right?"

"Fine, thank you. She got over the bombing very quickly. The reason she's stayed so long in England is that the hospital wouldn't discharge the baby. Asha was premature, you know— tiny when she was born—and they found something wrong with her heart. They had to operate, and they couldn't do that until she was strong enough. It's been a worrying time for Ba. But I had a letter only yesterday to say that Asha had had the operation and was recovering well. A great relief."

"Pretty name, Asha."

"Yes," said Grant shortly. He disapproved of fancy names and thought it had been agreed that the baby, if a girl, should be named Margaret after his aunt. The need for an emergency christening was to his mind an insufficient explanation for the curious choice of name. His wife had offered reasons—she wanted to associate the name Margaret only with the one person they had both loved dearly, she wrote; and the baby was so pale and blond that once the name Asha had been suggested, it was impossible to think of her as anything else. To Grant they had the sound of excuses, but it was too late to argue. He talked more freely than usual to hide his disapproval.

"The baby should be leaving hospital just about now. Ba said she'd like a week at home with her, while they get used to each other—she hasn't had to look after her at all up till now. But they should be back here for Christmas."

"That's really what I called about." Ted Croggan's face looked more worried than ever. "I'm thinking of sending Ellen and the children home. If they do go, I wondered whether there was anything you'd like them to take back. We thought Barbara might be staying in England."

"That's never been the intention. We didn't know how things

were going to turn out, of course. We'd expected that the baby would be born in May and that they'd be ready to leave in June."

"Do you get the impression that England is a safe place to be?"

"The countryside is safe enough. London certainly wasn't when Ba first arrived, but the raids seem to have eased off now. She's driving an ambulance—she wanted to stay in London so that she could see Asha every day. Women with young children aren't called up, so she'll be able to stop work as soon as she takes the baby home."

"I can't decide what's best for Ellen and the youngsters. The journey's dangerous, for a start. But—you don't come down to the club much, Lorimer. You don't hear the gossip. I've tried to kid myself that it's only rumour, but I don't believe that any more. The Japs are moving their troops through Siam to the frontier. Half a dozen of us went to see the Resident the other day, to find out what's going to happen if they decide it's time to stop looking enviously at our rubber and to appropriate it instead. The answer wasn't reassuring."

"The Australians have brought in a lot of men."

"In the south, yes. Maybe they could hold an invasion there. But it would sweep past us first. When that time comes, I want to be travelling light. What can you do when you've got two children under five?"

"They'd be safe in Singapore."

"I agree, the Japs aren't likely to get in there. But they might get to the causeway and put the island under siege. And then who's going to feed them all, and what happens if some general decides that he can't cope with civilians and sends them all off in boats? The sea will be even more dangerous by then. I don't know what the answer is. I could be blowing it up a bit—but last week I signed up with the Straits Settlement Volunteers and the chap filling in the form said, 'Any hostages to fortune?' I asked him what he meant and he said, 'Children.' Well, I realised he'd got it right first time. How could I agree to go off wherever I was wanted if it meant leaving a woman and two small children unprotected? Sooner or later they'll have to go, and in that case it might as well be sooner, because I shan't sleep easily for wondering whether we might all be taken by surprise. Well, that's my problem, not yours. I just came to say, if there's anything you'd like to send back, Ellen would be glad to take it. And she'd like Barbara's address anyway, to look her up."

"She's living with a cousin of hers, Lady Lorimer, at Glanville House in Park Lane." Grant watched his visitor make a note of it. "Will you stay for something to eat?"

"No, thanks. Ellen's expecting me. Well, keep in touch."

Grant was thoughtful as he ate his solitary meal. Barbary's stay in England had been extended for reasons which he accepted as valid—indeed, essential—and so he had not fretted about the length of their separation. But his desire for her return was so strong that until this moment he had not paused to consider whether it would be wise. Ted Croggan was a bumbler—but had managed to identify a problem, even though he lacked decisiveness in dealing with it. Grant, by contrast, prided himself on his ability to take decisions. What he had failed to do until now was to realise that a decision was necessary. He allotted himself a day to think about it, and went to bed.

Next morning, as usual, he rose before dawn and walked down the hill to the lines in which the coolies lived. He looked on as his Tamil overseer called the names and divided the workers into gangs; then Grant himself assigned the work. He watched the men moving off: some to weed, some to clear ditches, and some —the most skilled, to tap the rubber trees.

What would they do, he asked himself, if the Japanese were to appear one day between the neat rows? The Chinese traders in the villages—knowing what had already happened in China— might try to resist if they had failed to run in time: but they were unarmed shopkeepers, not soldiers. The Indians, who were the hardest workers on the estate, lacked military spirit and would have no reason, unless it were loyalty to their employer, for abandoning their essentially passive philosophy of life. Some of them, indeed, might have been infected by the disaffection which had already attacked the Indian subcontinent. The Malays, too, might see little difference between Japanese rule and British. In case of trouble they would disappear into the jungle, waiting to see which of two alien rulers was likely to win before taking sides.

The whole British Empire, Grant sometimes thought, was like a banking system—sustained only by confidence. A single failure to meet a demand could result in a panic rush of withdrawals. The assumption that the Malay States would survive as a stable colony was based on the further assumption that its subjects would never consider the possibility of any other form of rule. But incorruptible administration and even-handed justice were often not appreciated until they had disappeared. Until now, Malaya had been kept safe for the planters by an absurdly small defence force which could hardly deal even with a small local rising. It would certainly not halt a full invasion. Ted Croggan had been right to worry; and now Grant was worried as well.

There could be no question of leaving Malaya himself. Unlike many of the other planters, who acted as managers of estates owned by one of the huge rubber companies, Grant's plantation was his own property. It represented his only capital and provided his only income. He could not hope to protect it personally if the Japanese invaded; but if he could lie low for a little while, he would be at hand to take control again when the necessary battle had been fought and won. In any such plan, there was no place for a baby.

By midday Grant had made up his mind. At three o'clock he drove to the club and telephoned a cable to be sent to Barbary, telling her to remain in England at least until Christmas. By then she would have received the letter which he wrote the same day to explain the situation. By then, too, it should be possible to see more clearly which way the Japanese were likely to move, and how effective the defence of Malaya might be.

That evening Grant was lonely as he sat on the verandah and waited once again for the sunset. He was impatient to see his baby daughter and, with a passion which made his whole body ache, he longed to have his wife beside him again. But he was confident that no separation, whether of time or distance, could change the love they felt for each other. And Grant had never been a man to regret or reconsider a decision once it was made. It was right that his wife and daughter should remain in England. There was nothing more to be said.

Two months later, when the bombs fell on Pearl Harbor, he knew that he had made the right decision—though he had not expected the Japanese to provoke the United States before mop-

ping up the British and appropriating the Malayan rubber.
Grant's age and lameness made him ineligible for any formal military service, but with a group of other planters who were familiar
with local tracks and waterways he planned a form of guerrilla resistance. They could never expect to achieve more than harass-
ment and were prepared to be pressed southwards to the impreg-
nable fortress of Singapore. But the Japanese, instead of
advancing by land in orthodox fashion, sent their troops by plane
and in small coastal craft to appear behind the British and
Australian and Indian troops who were waiting for them. Grant's
plantation was not occupied at once, but it was cut off almost
from the moment the attack began.

Unlike the bewildered troops, Grant knew the country. He had
lived in Malaya for fourteen years, and frequent holiday expedi-
tions in search of new orchids had taught him how to survive in
the jungle and, indeed, to live off it. As the Japanese planes
roared low overhead and his wireless set crackled out the news of
fresh disasters—the sinking of the *Prince of Wales* and the
Repulse, the abandonment of Kuala Lumpur, the retreat towards
the doomed island of Singapore—he buried his personal treasures
in a waterproof and antproof metal chest, took a last sad look
around his orchid house, hoisted his pack on to his back, and
disappeared into the jungle.

4

On the day when Grant left his plantation forever, his niece
Ilsa—the daughter of his sister Kate—sat in the darkness of a cellar near Leningrad, like him, in hiding from an invading enemy.
Ilsa had never known of her uncle's existence. She would have
been incredulous if anyone had told her that her mother was by
birth an Englishwoman and that she herself had cousins living in
England. Because she had been brought up surrounded by children who had lost their parents, she felt herself fortunate to have
a mother. It had never seemed odd that she should know of no
other relations.

For more than three months she had been living in the cellar beneath the orphanage. The speed of the German invasion of Russia had been as amazing as that of the Japanese invasion of Malaya. One day the Nazi-Soviet Pact tied the two countries in a treaty of friendship; while almost at the next moment, it seemed, the Russian Army was retreating before a major offensive. But official communiqués during the late summer of 1941 were uninformative. There were rumours, fanned by the flood of refugees who fled east before the German advance, but when, at the end of August, 1941, Ilsa made the short journey from Leningrad to her home, it had never occurred to her that the orphanage could be in imminent danger of capture.

Not even a bombing raid provided an alert, for the enemy army was making good use of undamaged roads. A breathless message from a village less than ten versts away was the only warning. There was no way in which two thousand children could be moved in time—and nowhere for them to go, for it quickly transpired that the enemy had already pressed east to the bank of the Volkov, cutting off the neck of land on which Leningrad stood. The city itself was the only remaining bolthole, but must be doomed either to bombardment or to starvation. The best hope, Ilsa thought as she watched her mother and the political superintendent anxiously conferring, was that the Germans would pass through Pushkin without stopping. If the children stayed where they were, they would be in occupied territory but not in the middle of a battlefield. And although she had heard many horror stories about the behaviour of German troops, they would surely not harm innocent children.

One category of innocent child, however, was not safe anywhere in German-occupied Europe. No one knew precisely what was happening to the Jews who were sent west by the trainload from the conquered territories, but Nazi theories of racial purity made it unlikely that their special treatment would be pleasant. There were not many Jewish children in the orphanage, but enough to make precautions necessary. While the political administrator hurried off to destroy their records, Ilsa and her mother assembled all the children at risk. The other orphans were told that their playmates were being sent into Leningrad, so that no indiscretion by a child too young to understand the consequences would betray his comrades. In fact they had another destination.

It was Ilsa who suggested the cellars. As an adventurous young girl she had explored them until her mother, unable to control the rats with which they were infested, put the whole range of underground rooms out of bounds and sealed off the two staircases which led there. The two entrances were still firmly blocked with cement which had not been disturbed for ten years, and it would be safest to leave them untouched. But there was another way down.

The princely Aminov family, who owned the building before the revolution, had their private theatre in the centre of the palace. Nowadays it was the room in which the children ate, but in the middle of the small stage still remained the trap which had been used for dramatic disappearances. The mechanism to operate it was controlled by one of a row of handles. The others had opened and closed the curtains, raised and lowered the scenery flats, dimmed or brightened the lights. Now that there were no longer curtains, flats, or lights, every control in the row would look to a stranger equally unused.

Ilsa herself descended first on the trap platform. She jumped down to the ground, ready to help the eighteen children who were lowered three at a time to join her. After the last batch she went up again to talk to her mother.

"The rats are still there," she said, grimacing. "And it's very dark. Would you like me to stay down with the children?"

Before her mother could answer, they heard shouting outside. A group of women tugged their daughters along the street, wailing in panic. Kate leaned out of a window, calling them; but only one would stop.

"The Germans are here, and what will become of our daughters?"

"What should you fear?" demanded Kate.

"Haven't you heard? They rape anything in a skirt. There's no respect even for a grandmother. What hope can there be for my beautiful child? Fourteen years old and a virgin. I must hide her." Still wailing, she hurried to catch up the others.

Ilsa saw the fear in her mother's eyes and tried to dispel it. "It can't be true. They're not animals."

"Anything can be true. They're a long way from home. Oh, Ilsa, I never thought that all this could happen again. We suffered so much, twenty-five years ago, and it seems that we've learned nothing. Nothing."

Ilsa's heart ached for her mother. In the past three years she had watched her ageing, suffering in ways which she found difficult to understand. Although she never spoke of it, Ilsa had recognised the distress which Kate managed to conceal from everyone else when the visits of Commissar Gorbatov came to an abrupt end. But she had been mystified by Kate's apparent despair when news came of the alliance with Germany, and there had been no good explanation for the depth of her mother's disappointment when Ilsa's first foreign concert tour, originally planned for Paris, had been changed to Berlin.

Ilsa herself did not share the disappointment. She was twenty-two years old, a healthy, cheerful young woman, confident in her talent as a pianist. The war was an annoying interruption to her career, but would not last forever. It worried her that her mother, whose courage she had always admired, should seem so defeated.

But Kate's sigh of despair did not interrupt her activity.

"These peasants exaggerate everything," she said. "But they could be right this time. It's not a good idea for a pretty young woman to show her face. Yes, go down with the children. We ought to have made plans. I'm to blame for not realising the danger. I'll get as much as possible down to you—food, candles, mattresses, water—before the Germans arrive. After that, it will be a case of adding to it when I can. At night, probably. Keep someone near the trap—but out of sight—all the time. Find a place for the others as far away as possible. There's no reason why the Germans should stay here long. Leningrad must be the prize they're after. They'll search every building once, I suppose, and leave a garrison somewhere in the village; but after a day or two I should be able to come down and talk to you."

Almost four months had passed since that conversation, but the Germans were still in the palace, trapping Ilsa and the Jewish children as effectively as though they had been tried and sentenced to imprisonment. The ridge on which the village of Pushkin stood had been chosen by the Tsars for its healthy air, but its height was of military significance too. Some of the German troops pressed further east to isolate Leningrad from the rest of the country: but a strong garrison had remained at Pushkin to play its part in starving out the inhabitants of a city which stubbornly refused to surrender.

All this Ilsa learned from her nightly vigils beneath the stage of the old theatre. The orphanage was now a barracks. The remaining children had been crowded upstairs, and the theatre used as a military canteen. Ilsa had learned German at school and practised it during her visit to Berlin. She understood the conversations which took place above her head and was chilled to realise how effectively the area was controlled. Those who resisted were shot and those who were strong enough to work were sent to labour camps in Germany or occupied Poland. The Jewish families had been the first to go—a fact which at least gave Ilsa the comfort of knowing there was some point to her hardship—but many of the Germans seemed to despise Slavs almost as much as Jews.

In order to discover when the canteen was empty, Kate needed to visit it frequently at night. When, as often happened, she found a group of soldiers still quietly talking, she had to pretend that she was checking that they were comfortable. Necessarily she spoke in a friendly voice and Ilsa, listening below, could tell that the Germans liked her and admired her work. They were not likely to saddle themselves with the responsibility for so many children by deporting their middle-aged medical superintendent.

When Kate did find the canteen empty, she lowered bread and hot soup on the trap. For the rest of the time the little group was forced to survive on raw cabbage and water. The children grew pale in the candlelit darkness and weak from hunger: they huddled together against the cold. Ilsa had feared that it might be difficult to keep them quiet, but found that they rarely even whispered.

Her own mind needed occupation if frustration was to be avoided. Conscientiously Ilsa exercised her fingers, practising brilliant cadenzas on an unresponsive slab of stone, but mock practice was not enough. Although she had never thought of herself as a composer, the special school for musical children had given her a thorough training. Using paper and pencils lowered by her mother, she set herself a series of exercises in composition.

For this activity at least conditions were favourable, for there was no noise and no danger of interruption. Ilsa became more ambitious. Instead of imitating other composers she tried to develop her own style, to listen to the sounds in her head, the sounds in the silent air. The music was there, she found, hovering invisibly, intangibly, inaudibly, waiting to be caught and organised into a formal framework. Her talent as a pianist prompted her to attempt a piano sonata first: but almost at once she was aware of a force outside herself that swelled through her imagination, forcing her towards the richer texture of a concerto. She could hear violins, cellos, percussion, an oboe. In the shadowy half life of the cellar there was all the time in the world, but she found herself writing the notes as frantically as though she could never hope to reach the end.

Her fears were justified. One day in December the silence was broken by something more positive than unheard notes of music. Crowbars crashed against bricks and mortar. The Germans were breaking their way into the cellars through one of the sealed doorways.

Had they been betrayed? Ilsa moved fast, hurrying the children to the point furthest from the breach. But she knew that darkness was their only concealment: they could not escape a search by flashlight.

Her mother, breathless with alarm, arrived at the top of the stairs to remonstrate. Kate's German was less fluent than Ilsa's, but she managed to convey that the cellars were unsafe—that was why they had been unvisited for the past ten years. The German response was precise. Every building in the village was to be mined. There would be no danger as long as the occupation lasted. But if the Russian Army counterattacked and returned to the area, it would be given a noisy welcome.

The officer spoke reasonably, revealing that he had a good relationship with Kate and was warning her of the need to take the children to safety if the Germans left. Briefly Ilsa was relieved. Why should the soldiers laying the explosives need to penetrate to the furthest of the cellars? It would make more sense to blow up the centre of the building.

But she had reckoned without the smell. Ilsa had made rules for sanitary arrangements and was reasonably successful in keeping the children clean. But there had been few opportunities for waste disposal. After living for so long in the undisturbed air Ilsa herself no longer noticed how foul it was, but the first German to come down the stairs made his disgust clear.

After that it was only a matter of time, for there was nowhere to run. Within half an hour the eighteen children, blinking their eyes against the light, were standing with Ilsa in the canteen. The senior officer strode down the line, whipping with his cane at each of the children in turn. "Jew. Jew. Jew." He snapped his fingers. "Take them away."

Only Ilsa was left, to be scrutinised more closely than the others. "Are you also a Jew?" She could tell that he would believe a denial. Ilsa had inherited not only her father's musical talent but also his high cheekbones and straight nose. Through her mother came her chestnut hair and the wide mouth that until recently had found it so easy to laugh. She was tall and straight-backed, and, although she was frightened, she would not allow herself to cringe like the terrified children. She thought of herself as a Slav: but in appearance she had more in common with the German who was interrogating her even than with the Russians amongst whom she had been brought up. "No," she said.

"But you must love the Jews very much to expose yourself to such danger. You know, of course, that the penalty for harbouring a Jew is death. Who else was concerned with this? Whose idea was it?"

In the doorway at the far end of the room Ilsa could see her mother, pale with fear, pressing against the armed soldiers who guarded the entrance. At all costs she must be made to realise that there was nothing to be gained, and everything to be lost, by sharing the responsibility. Ilsa answered the question very loudly and in Russian.

"No one. No one helped me. No one knew. Everyone—even the other children—thought we had gone to the city."

"If you understand German, you will speak it."

Ilsa repeated the claim. She saw the officer turn towards the door, staring speculatively at Kate. "Please, God," she thought, "keep her silent. And if he suspects, make him kind." It was impossible to interpret his expression as he turned back.

"I could shoot you now, here. I have the right. There is no defence for your crime. But you are strong, and the Fatherland needs workers. I will be generous. Since you are a Jew-lover, you may go with your Jews." He snapped his fingers again. "Take her with the others."

"No!" Even as Ilsa felt both her arms roughly seized from behind, Kate broke past the guards, shouting hysterically at the officer. The words, neither Russian nor German, made no sense to Ilsa and the German did not attempt to listen. He thrust Kate aside so that she fell sobbing to the ground, and nodded for the prisoner to be taken away. Ilsa felt her knees buckling in fear and despair. She struggled to go to her mother, but was dragged backwards out of the room.

Part of the nightmare that was just beginning was that Ilsa was never afterwards able to recapture the memory of the loving woman who had sung lullabies to her as a little girl, the calm and silent woman who had walked with her through the forests, the competent and compassionate woman who had cared for so many motherless children. Whenever she tried to visualise her mother from this moment on, she could see only someone who was almost a stranger, shabby and distraught, screaming in a language which Ilsa could not understand.

Barbary watched proudly as her daughter took her first steps along the terrace at Blaize. As a tiny baby, Asha's hold on life had been so frail that her very survival was a miracle. It was thrilling that she could walk at all. The fact that she was later than most children in achieving this was of no importance.

Nor did it matter that those first staggering steps were bearing her not towards her mother but to Brad. While Asha remained in hospital, Brad had frequently accompanied Barbary on her visits and so had needed to maintain the fiction of being Mr. Lorimer, the baby's father. It had become a joke between them and, long before Asha was well enough to be taken to Blaize, had progressed to something deeper than a joke. At this very moment, as Asha's legs moved forward—at first hesitantly, then in a sudden rush of confidence and pride, and at last in a desperate effort to reach safety before she overbalanced—Brad, his arms open to catch her, was calling, "Come on then, Asha. Come to Poppa."

He picked the little girl up with cries of congratulation and swung her in the air before setting her down by her mother's feet.

"You shouldn't let her call you Poppa, you know," Barbary warned him.

"She doesn't call me anything. She surely is the most backward child. And the most beautiful. She makes me see what I missed before. All those years. A marriage isn't a marriage without a child."

"But you mustn't let yourself get too fond of her. One day—"

"One day a stranger will arrive and announce that he's her father by blood and that a substitute father who merely loves her has no rights at all. Is that it? You could be right. But I reckon she deserves to be loved now, by a father as well as a mother. And I also reckon that when a man loves a woman—even a very tiny woman—he ought to show it and give her as well as himself the chance to enjoy it. Wouldn't you agree with that?"

Barbary made no reply. She knew what Brad was trying to say because he had said it, equally obliquely, before. She had no answer to his question. Her only defence was to prevent him from asking it.

She was no longer to be allowed that escape. As Asha began to crawl away—for on all fours she moved at a great pace—Brad checked Barbary's attempt to hold her back.

"Leave her. She can't get anywhere dangerous. I have to talk to you, Barbary. I want to be Asha's father. I want to be your husband. Will you marry me?"

"It's impossible. You know it's impossible."

"Because you're married already, you mean? But you don't know that Grant's still alive."

"I don't know that he's dead. You must see that I couldn't—"

"You know that his plantation is under Japanese occupation. And you know that he hasn't escaped from Malaya. In nine months he'd have had plenty of time to contact you if he'd got away."

"That doesn't prove anything. There are thousands of British prisoners in Singapore."

"If we believe the Swiss lists, he's not one of them." But Brad knew as well as Barbary that this was not decisive. "O.K., so we have two possibilities to consider. Suppose Grant is dead already. I've been making some enquiries in London about whether it's possible to presume death without proof. The answers don't favour me. There's no way you and I could contract a legal marriage now. All we could do is anticipate it and wait. But on the other hand, suppose Grant is still alive. If that's so, you have to make a decision. Do you see yourself going back to live with him again? Or would you want a divorce anyway if he were to appear? It's two years since you last saw him. I could be wrong, but my guess is that you never loved him. Maybe you thought you did, but now you've learned better. Is that right?"

Barbary did not answer. Although she had found Brad attractive from the moment of their first meeting, she had fallen in love with him so gradually, so imperceptibly, that there had never been a point at which she had known that she ought to draw back. At first he had been safe—a relation, Frisca's uncle. They had become friends on that basis, teasing each other, laughing together. It was the bomb which changed their carefree relationship to something deeper. They shared both a feeling of guilt and a fear that the baby might not survive. It was perhaps because their emotions were concentrated on a third person that Barbary had failed to notice immediately how close together they had been drawn.

She knew now. She had guessed during the months in which they had both been living at Glanville House, and had known for sure ever since Asha left hospital—for Brad came to stay at Blaize on every free weekend and no longer made any secret of his feelings. This was the first time he had mentioned marriage in so many words, but she could hardly pretend to be surprised.

Nor could she contradict him. Even while she was living with her husband, Barbary had known that what she felt for Grant was not the passionate love he needed. She had married her cousin because she liked him, because she was sorry for him, but more than anything else because she was a coward, too shy to leave the shelter of home to face a life peopled entirely with strangers. She had never known with Grant the breathless tension which overcame her in Brad's presence—the longing to touch him, the hope that some accident of movement would bring them close together, the overwhelming joy when he, scorning to leave such contacts to chance, took her hand or held her in his arms. She had never before experienced the pain of loving, the yearning to be with her love—so intense that small disappointments became tragedies and sudden surprises transformed the world with delight. She had known for a long time that Brad loved her—and he knew that she loved him, although he had not yet been able to make her admit it.

She did not admit it now. Brad waited, not looking at her.

"The time has come for action," he said. "Starting tomorrow I have an empty week. One project has finished; another hasn't begun. I want to spend the week with you. Anywhere you like—

at Blaize, in London, anywhere. I want to have a honeymoon with you. On account, you might say. I want you to promise yourself to me."

They both had their eyes on Asha, but Asha was no problem. She could be cared for at Blaize. Alexa almost certainly believed that Brad and Barbary were sleeping together already but showed no sign of disapproval. Asha, though, was the least of Barbary's difficulties.

"I couldn't ever divorce Grant, Brad," she said. What she meant by that was that divorce was unthinkable, something which simply didn't happen in her family, however lightly it might be taken in America. But Brad interpreted the remark as referring to legal grounds.

"Then he divorces you. Either way we end up together."

"It wouldn't be fair." The words she had to speak ran so directly against the emotions she wanted to express that she could hardly bring herself to articulate them. "How could I do something like that to him? He may be suffering now. Hanging onto his memories and his hopes. I have to be here, waiting, if he wants me."

For a second time Brad was silent. "All right," he said at last. "Forget the marriage bit. We'll take that as it comes. If you ever find you're free, we'll talk again. Meantime I still have that week. No promises, no strings, but we could make the world stand still for a moment. I love you, Barbary. I want you so much. Will you come?"

She wanted to say yes more than she had ever wanted anything in the world before. With one word she could be in his arms, kissing him, loving him. The word emerged almost as a sob. "No."

"Why not? What possible reason—?"

"The same reason. Because I'm married."

"For heavens' sakes! Be realistic, girl. What harm can it do to a man who'll never know? What's being married got to do with this?"

"Everything. That's what being married is. Making promises. Specific promises. And keeping them even when you don't want to."

Brad stood up, his fists clenched. It was the first time Barbary had ever seen him angry. She searched for some way to keep him near, so that she could continue to enjoy at least the same painful pleasures of the past few months.

"I love you, Brad. You must believe that. I do love you. But—"

"You choose a fine time to tell me at last." He sighed, bringing his anger under control. "It looks as though this is where we say goodbye, then. I'm going back to the States in ten days. Or sooner, in the circumstances, if I can fix it." Her dismay must have shown on her face, for he did not walk away immediately. "Hell, Barbary, you can't have reckoned that I'd stay in England forever. I finished the job I came over to do way back. You could say that I've been making work since then to stay near you. But my own country has first claim on my time now—and I need to keep an eye on my factory. If you'd picked up the plan for next week, I was going to ask you to come home to San Francisco with me. Or if that wasn't possible, I could have fixed it to get back here after a bit. But I guess you don't care which side of the Atlantic I'm on."

"You know I care. It's unkind of you to punish me for doing what I think is right, when doing it is enough punishment already."

"I'm not going just to get at you. There are limits to the punishment I can take, that's all. Well, I've put it on the line. You know what I'm offering. I'll ask you again. Are you prepared to accept anything at all from me?"

Frozen into unhappy silence, Barbary watched the last hope fade from his eyes. He turned and strode away towards Asha, who gurgled with pleasure, holding up her arms. Bending down, Brad put out two fingers for her hands to clutch, and supported her as she walked jerkily back to her mother. At the last moment he picked Asha up and cuddled her.

"Look after my girl for me." He handed her back to Barbary. "And forget what I said. My own fault for getting serious. I should have known . . . Bye, honey."

He had not called her honey since the day of Asha's birth. It was a step backwards towards the first easygoing stage of their relationship. Barbary was trapped by the child in her arms. She wanted to embrace Brad, to kiss him, to plead for a moment of warmth with which to remember him, but he had deliberately made that impossible.

Watching him walk away, she knew that she could still catch him. His manners were good and he would not leave without thanking Alexa for her hospitality. In London, too, he would pay a last visit to Frisca. But what was there to say? She had tried to be honest. Not kind, perhaps, but honest. And surely she must be right to put loyalty to Grant above her own happiness. Her grip on Asha tightened as she realised miserably what a lonely emotion loyalty might prove to be.

1943

1943

In the spring of 1943 Barbary received an unexpected visit from two strangers. One of them—a slight man in his early thirties—was blind, moving with the tentative air of someone still overwhelmed by his disability. The other was a Scotsman well over six feet tall, walking with a limp but sturdily protective of his companion. His accent was so thick that Barbary could not understand the words with which he introduced himself and his companion. Her bewilderment must have been clear, for he nudged his companion as they sat down. "Tell her, Nobby," he said.

"We've got a message for you, Mrs. Lorimer. We promised your husband we'd come to see you if we ever got back to England."

"My husband!" The simplicity of the statement took Barbary's breath away. "You've seen my husband? Where?"

"In Malaya. He got us away."

"Bloody hero!" said the Scotsman, and followed the exclamation with what Barbary took to be an apology for bad language.

"Tell me. Tell me all about it."

"We were cut off at Slim River," said Nobby. "The Nips moved south so fast that we found ourselves behind their lines. I'm talking about a year or so ago. There were about three hundred of us. But scattered. No officers left alive in our lot, so we had to make our own guess at the best thing to do. Some went south towards Singapore. Didn't know it had already surrendered. But I stayed, and so did Jock here. Thirty of us all told. Hoped we could sit it out in the jungle till there was a counterattack. *We* didn't know about Singapore either."

"Go on." Barbary could hardly endure the details. She was interested only in Grant. But she realised that her visitor must be allowed to tell his story in his own way.

"It was O.K. for a few weeks. We found a friendly village. Not something you could count on. The Nips were paying for information. We didn't live *in* the village. Built ourselves a shelter a couple of miles away. But they helped us with food. And they played straight."

"Bloody good lot," agreed Jock, nodding his head vigorously.

"After six weeks the breeze got round that we were there. The Nips didn't know for sure, and they didn't know where, so to help them find out they started shooting the villagers. Ten a day till someone spoke up. So we couldn't stay. We made the village a present of two bodies—men who'd died of malaria. Told them they could stick knives in and pretend to have killed them if they thought it would help. They promised to bury them in the end. The rest of us made for the coast. You've lived in Malaya, Mrs. Lorimer? You know what the jungle's like?"

Barbary nodded and then, remembering that he could not see her, said, "Yes." The rubber plantation had always been kept obsessively neat. But she knew that wherever the land escaped the discipline of cultivation it produced an almost impenetrable tangle of vines and bamboos, and that most of the unclaimed area consisted of swamps, waist deep in water and swarming with leeches and other parasites.

"We'd never have made it if it hadn't been for the planters. Three of them. They passed us along. One led us through the jungle to a river. One took us downriver in a couple of sampans. Your husband took us along the coast—north, not south. Singapore was no good, he said. He'd got a boat hidden. We were the fifth lot he'd sent off. Didn't know whether the others had got anywhere. Wasn't promising us a pleasure trip. All he could do was stock us up, point us in the direction of India, and hand us a compass and a chart to show the islands on the way. That was when he gave us the message. 'If you make England, tell my wife I love her,' he said. He told us where to come. And then—"

He stopped, unable to go on. The Scotsman took up the story, but Barbary still found it difficult to understand what he said.

"The Japanese arrived?" she checked.

"Ay. Just after we were away. We lay off in the dark when we heard the shooting, thinking he might swim out. But they had him."

"Half an hour later they brought him back to the beach." Nobby took up the story again. "They knew we were somewhere around in the dark and they wanted us to see."

"See what?" Barbary felt as though her voice was coming from a body which had nothing to do with her own empty shell. "You mean, see that he'd been taken prisoner?"

Nobby shook his head. Both men had suddenly become reluctant to go on. "I don't like having to say this, Mrs. Lorimer, but after the main surrender, the Nips didn't go in much for taking prisoners."

"You mean they shot him?"

"Not that either."

"Bloody bastards," growled the Scot. "Thought shooting was too easy. They liked to see the blood. Feel the thud. They beat him down, four of him. Then they carried him away."

"Are you sure it was him? You must have been some way away. And you said it was night."

"I've never seen a man before or since with hair as fair as his," said Nobby. "They'd pulled off the hat he wore to keep himself dark. And he was set up by torchlight. As an exhibition."

Barbary felt her body beginning to shudder. She stood up, fighting to control her trembling lips, trying not to cry out, not to be sick. "Excuse me," she said. "I'll get someone to bring some tea."

She only managed to reach the hall before she collapsed, sobbing aloud. Alexa came hurrying to see what the trouble was, and listened as the almost incoherent story poured out.

"Go and lie down, dear," she said. "I'll look after them."

"Ask them the dates. When did it happen? Why have they taken so long to come? Call me when they're going. I ought to thank them."

This last request Alexa ignored, coming into Barbary's darkened room only after her visitors had left.

"They quite understood you were upset," she said. "I gave them a drink and a few things from the farm, and thanked them for you."

"Did you find out anything more?"

"They were hazy over time. March last year, probably. They took four months to reach India and arrived in bad shape—one went blind on the way. They've only been back in England three weeks. The blind man—he wasn't blind at the time, of course— said to tell you that they don't *know* that Grant was killed. Not for certain. He was knocked unconscious, but that doesn't have to be the same thing. In fact, if he were dead, it's more likely that he'd have been left on the beach."

"They said the Japanese weren't taking prisoners."

"There's a doubt," said Alexa. "As long as there's a doubt, you must hang onto it. We'll get in touch with the Red Cross tomorrow. Now that we know when Grant was captured, there's a better chance of checking the lists of prisoners. Don't give up hope yet."

But Barbary had begun to cry again. No one now but Grant himself would be able to persuade her that her husband was not dead. When Alexa had gone, she abandoned herself to a frenzy of tears. She wept for Grant and the pain he must have felt. For Asha, who would never see her father. For herself, because her married life had been so short. But even as she told herself that this was no time for self-pity, another thought intruded. If Grant had died in March, had already been dead when Brad left England, there had been no need to send him away.

Barbary's first bout of self-pity had been hypocritical. This second one was genuine but monstrous. Hardly able to believe that she could harbour such a thought at such a time, she gave herself up to shame and guilt and sobbed herself to sleep.

1944

1

Brad Davidson returned to England in the summer of 1944. For fifteen months he had devoted his efforts as an inventor to his own country's war needs. Now the British had requested his help again, to advise on a weapon recently launched by the Germans. Britain's war was America's war now, so that arranging to return was easy.

The new weapon was a pilotless plane, programmed to fall and explode in a predetermined spot. Defence experts first took Brad to inspect the wreckage of one in Kent. Then he studied their detailed drawings of the missile's components.

"What's the objective?" Brad asked. "To build these things ourselves, or to divert the German ones to harmless places?"

"Diversion. Or premature explosion in the air. At present we're shooting a few down and releasing incorrect information about where the others land, hoping that the German programmers will think they've got the range wrong and adjust the target data on the next wave. We're taking a certain amount of flak on that ourselves. People in Kent don't see why they should be blown up by a bomb meant for London."

"Do they do a lot of damage?"

"It's not like the concentrated bombing of the blitz, but people are getting killed. And these have their own kind of nastiness. Some people call them buzz-bombs. They make a loud noise, something between a hornet and a spluttering motor bike. As long as you can hear one coming you're all right, because it's going somewhere else. But when the engine coughs and cuts out, it begins to fall. There's about a five-second glide. If you're out-side when you hear one stop, you'll see everyone listening, work-ing out angles and distances. The bombing in the blitz built up a community feeling. But when one of these appears, you find your-self willing it to go on further, to hit the next street, not yours."

"Natural enough," suggested Brad.

"Yes. Once they get through to London, there's not much to be done. There's no pattern of arrival, and it's difficult to give a meaningful warning. Sixty or seventy are coming down in London every day, and the blast does enormous damage to buildings. Short of keeping the whole population in shelters for twenty-four hours a day, there's no way of reducing the casualty rate. So any bright ideas will be welcome."

Brad had arranged to use the same facilities that the University of London had put at his disposal in 1941. He found himself a room in a nearby Kensington hotel. No doubt Frisca would be prepared to put him up at Glanville House again; but before he angled for such an invitation he must decide what he felt about Barbary.

Very often in the past year the memory of Barbary had invaded his thoughts. It was difficult to understand why he should be obsessed with someone who had turned him down, when there were so many girls in the world who would not play hard-to-get with him. One reason was her strangeness—her unusual, with-drawn beauty and curious adherence to an old-fashioned code of morality. But in the end Brad decided that what most attracted him to Barbary was her vulnerability. Not because he liked it, but because he was sure that he could change it, making her feel wanted and secure. He knew enough about her to realise that in a sense she had spent the whole of her life camping out under someone else's roof, never truly at home. What she needed was a place of her own, a way of life which she ordered for herself, and freedom from the feelings of guilt and obligation which played so large a part in her life.

He reminded himself now that he had seen her at the most dis-turbed time of her life, worried first about her baby and then about her husband. By now she would be more settled. Would that mean that she needed Brad less or that she would be more ready to accept what he had to offer? Was he prepared to risk a second rejection?

He postponed that decision until he had more information. Frisca would tell him what to expect and perhaps—though not certainly—keep his presence in England secret if he asked her to. Her voice over the telephone at eleven o'clock on a Sunday morning was sleepy. He had forgotten her taste for late nights and late breakfasts. But she woke up into excitement when she heard who was calling.

"Where are you? Come straight over. No, look, why don't you walk across the park?"

"You're asking an American to *walk?*"

"Definitely. It's a lovely day. A gentle stroll will take you just long enough for me to have a bath and put my face on. Right?"

"Don't hang up," said Brad. "Tell me, is there anyone else at Glanville House?"

"If you mean, is Babs living here, yes she is. And Asha."

"Is London safe for a child?" asked Brad in surprise.

"Until a few weeks ago it wasn't too bad. Currently we're suffering from a plague of doodlebugs—vicious little insects which I hope you won't encounter. But with luck they'll go away soon. And Babs has a job in London and wants Asha with her."

"Don't tell her I'm here. Not yet, anyway."

"She'll want to see you," Frisca assured him. "There's been a certain amount of weeping on my shoulder in the past year."

"Has she had any news of her husband since I left?"

"Yes. Not good news, but not definite enough to be final news either. She thinks he's dead."

"And do you?"

"Probably," said Frisca. "Almost certainly. Not *quite* certainly. Mamma and I can live with the doubt. But Babs couldn't take it. She had nightmares for weeks about Grant being tortured by the Japanese. In the end we told her that if a tenth of what she imagined was true, he must have been dead for a year already. She went very quiet and then said that yes, that was what had happened, and she'd known it ever since she heard he'd been captured. It's easier for her to believe that he's dead than to imagine the alternatives. I sympathise—but that doesn't necessarily make it true. Why are we chatting at long distance when we could be face to face? Get walking, Brad. See you in half an hour."

As always, Brad's spirits were raised by the sound of Frisca's voice. She was so warm, so overflowing with vitality. Cheerfully he set out from the hotel, striding into Kensington Gardens and past the Round Pond towards Hyde Park. From here to Park Lane there was grass all the way. Children played energetically with balls, but their pale parents, stripped to the waist to enjoy the sun, looked tired, strained by the hardships of a war which had been battering their bodies and minds for almost five years. Brad felt almost ashamed of his good health but could not prevent himself from humming as he walked.

Frisca's information had not been helpful, because he did not completely trust Barbary's strength of mind. She might be using Grant's death to ease her own anguish but was quite capable of resurrecting him to hold Brad at arm's length.

He paused by the Serpentine, leaning over the bridge. Even in a time of food rationing, children still found crumbs of bread to throw to the ducks who converged on the largesse from every part of the lake, squabbling amongst themselves and dodging the raiding pigeons.

He couldn't keep away. To be in the same country as Barbary and not to see her was impossible. All he could do was keep his distance and make Barbary herself take the first step if she regretted having dismissed him.

The ducks were still squawking so loudly that Brad did not at first pick up the sound which the families near him heard at once. It was their silence which alerted him to the approach of one of the weapons he was studying. Even the children were quiet, the little ones running to grip their parents' hands. No one looked up. Listening to the approach of the spluttering engine was, it seemed, the only concession to be made to anxiety. But Brad was not bound by the same constraint. He looked towards the south, where barrage balloons were tethered in a line like a herd of pachyderms hovering in the sky.

It came as a surprise to discover that the missile was as visible as it was audible. Propelled by a tail of flame, its silver body approached the park. Once it was overhead they would be out of danger: the silent glide would carry it further on before the explosion. In such a peaceful setting—the trees, the lake, the ducks, the family outings—it was hard to imagine that in a few seconds someone might be dead who was now alive; and even harder to feel any personal risk. Yet, like everyone else, he found himself waiting for the bomb to pass.

It had almost reached them when the engine cut out and the flame was extinguished. Brad watched it falling until it disappeared behind the trees at the eastern end of the park. The explosion which followed brought leaves off the trees to swirl round their heads in a premature autumnal fall. The family parties next to Brad relaxed.

"Grosvenor Square, I'd say," suggested one woman, shaking the last crumbs from a paper bag. Her husband shook his head.

"Park Lane, more like. One of those big houses."

Startled, Brad stared at the man as though his expression would reveal that he had been joking. Then he looked at the pillar of dust and smoke already settling back towards the ground. The houses along Park Lane were palatial and few in number. Brad began to run.

He was still running, although panting with the realisation that he was growing too heavy, when he saw Asha, picking up leaves and counting them aloud. She was three years old now—a little girl and no longer a baby—but the startling fairness of her hair identified her. He paused, and Barbary, sitting on the grass nearby, rose to her feet.

His resolution to keep cool vanished as he took her into his arms. With all her doubts and scruples, this was the woman he wanted. Barbary's amazement at seeing him lasted only a second. Then she was responding to his kisses as wholeheartedly as he could have hoped. His relief at finding her unhurt swelled into ecstasy as he realised that she still loved him and sensed that this time she would be prepared to surrender to her love.

It was a good deal to discover in the course of only a few moments—in which neither of them spoke—but he knew he was right. His arm hugged her tightly as they sat down together on the grass.

"I was afraid Glanville House had been hit," he said.

"No. It went further. Grosvenor Square, I think. Brad, you must explain. What are you doing here?"

"First you must introduce Asha to me. She doesn't remember me." The little girl was staring at the two adults with her thumb doubtfully in her mouth. But before Barbary could call her, Asha came running to her mother, anxiety on her face. Another doodlebug was on the way.

It must have been programmed to the same target: the engine cut out at the same spot as the earlier one. But even allowing for the distance Brad had run, he was startled by the nearness of the explosion. Barbary, too, jumped to her feet in alarm.

"That was closer," she said. "And Frisca's at home."

She picked up Asha and hurried towards Park Lane. Catching up, Brad tried to carry the child, but Barbary shook her head. Running, they emerged from the last band of trees to find the ground beyond covered with debris which had not yet settled. Brad stared in horror across the wide avenue.

The top three floors of Glanville House had ceased to exist.

2

For an hour already Barbary had been waiting on a bench in the corridor of the hospital. Only one visitor was allowed at a time. She felt Brad take her hand as he sat down beside her. He had been looking into the possibility of bringing Frisca's son home from California, and had promised to discuss this with the doctors—for the family had agreed that Bernard should not be hurried into a long emergency journey unless there was some hope that his mother would still be alive when he arrived. When the bomb fell on the Café de Paris, Brad had taken over the role of Barbary's husband. Now again he was acting without fuss as the man of the family.

A door opened and Alexa came out. Barbary and Brad both stood up, but she walked on down the corridor as though she had not seen them, her eyes fixed on something a long way away. Her back was as straight as ever, and she was neatly dressed, but for the first time in her life she looked old. Usually she wore makeup so discreetly that it was hard to tell whether her complexion was natural; but this morning there was nothing to conceal the ravages of sleeplessness and distress.

A nurse approached from the same doorway. "Are you Babs?"

"Yes."

"Would you like to go in? But not for too long, please. We'd like to get her back to sleep again soon."

At the time of Barbary's last visit Frisca had still been drowsy from the anaesthetic of her emergency operation. Today her eyes were wide open. One arm lay stiffly beside her, splinted to accept the tubes which fed blood and nourishment into her veins. She raised the other to touch Barbary's cheek as the two cousins kissed.

"I made them stop giving me drugs for a little while," she said. "I wanted to be able to think straight. Yesterday was so muzzy. You came, didn't you? I remember talking, but I don't think I made sense."

"What sort of drugs?"

"Painkillers, I suppose. I must say, without them my left foot hurts like the very devil."

Startled, Barbary bit back the comment she had been about to make and glanced at the frame which held the weight of blankets off Frisca's legs. It was possible, she supposed, that her cousin did not yet realise. Both legs had been badly crushed when Glanville House collapsed and it had been necessary to amputate one foot before she could even be extricated from the wreckage.

"Don't worry." Frisca gave a wry smile. "I know it isn't there. You're not old enough to remember Blaize when it was a military hospital during the First World War, are you? A lot of the patients had lost a leg. I remember Aunt Margaret saying that a limb which didn't exist could be as painful as one which did. I didn't believe her then. I do now."

"It won't last," said Barbary. "As soon as it heals—"

"What may not last is your visit. There are two things I want to say. Do you know that Brad's in England? He phoned me. Just before."

"He's here now. Hoping to see you, if you're up to it."

"Well, listen Babs, you mustn't send him away again. Tell yourself you may be dead tomorrow, so sleep with him tonight. Tonight. Promise?"

"If he asks—"

"Why should he have to ask?" demanded Frisca. "If he didn't want you, he wouldn't have got in touch again. Why shouldn't you offer? Be brave. You know you love him. He could make you happy. Have you ever been happy, Babs? Love him tonight. Promise?"

"Well, I'll try." Barbary flushed with embarrassment. This was not the kind of conversation she had anticipated.

"That's a promise then. And deathbed promises are like deathbed confessions: binding."

"Now, Frisca—"

"The other thing." Frisca was growing tired. Barbary could see her grasping for control of her thoughts, saving her breath for the words. "Bernard. Poor Bernard. I've been a rotten mother."

"Nonsense. He adores you."

"That's because he doesn't know. I've been selfish, always. He oughtn't to have been born, for a start. That was selfish. One day, someone will have to decide whether to tell him the truth."

"What truth?"

"That Robert was his father, not Arthur. Does it matter? I don't know. Mamma's always known. But Mamma's too old, really, to look after Bernard for me. And you're his sister, you see. Half sister, anyway."

"Frisca, there's no question of anyone but you looking after him."

"He's not grown up yet," said Frisca. "Nearly, but not quite. He still needs help. A family. He's clever. Clever in Brad's sort of way. He'll be a scientist. Mamma doesn't know about universities. Will you and Brad keep an eye on him, Babs? He's a nice boy and he's had a bad deal. I shouldn't have left him in Hollywood. That wasn't selfish. It seemed right. But it was a mistake. Except that if he had come, if he'd been in Glanville House—" Her voice trailed away.

"I don't know what they're dripping into you down that tube." Barbary tried to smile. "But it's having a distinctly depressing effect. What you need now, Frisca, is lots of sleep."

As though in response Frisca's eyes began to close, but she continued to talk. "I've had a good life," she said. "Always been lucky. Except with Robert, I suppose. But even there, perhaps it was better to have something short and perfect than ordinary and spoiled. I'm still lucky now. I've always known that I'd be no good at growing old gracefully. A quick curtain call, that was what I wanted. This one could have been quicker, but it will do. For a dancer, dancing and living are the same thing. Hobbling through life isn't surviving; it's going under. Pirry would have a phrase for it. 'The world is divided into those who are alive and those who don't know that they're dead.'"

"Frisca, please." Barbary found it difficult to control her tears.

"I've always known what I wanted." Frisca was no longer listening. "And I've always gone out to get it. I don't believe in waiting to be given things. I make the choices myself. Just like you're going to choose Brad. Remember, you promised." Her eyes now were closed, but she made an effort to open them again. "Did you say he was here? Can I see him? Just for a minute."

Barbary nodded and kissed Frisca goodbye. Brad frowned at the signs of her distress as she emerged, but she gestured him to go in. As unseeingly as Alexa earlier, she made her way to the shabby canteen in which her great-aunt was sipping tea and sat down at the same table.

"She was such a pretty little girl," said Alexa. "Such a lovely woman."

"Isn't there anything we can do?" asked Barbary. "Aren't there any drugs which would cheer her up?"

"Nothing but the best," Alexa remembered. "That's what I used to tell her when she was practising, and she made it her own motto. Everything had to be perfect." Her eyes focused on Barbary for the first time. "I talked to her doctor. It's touch and go, he says. A lot depends on the strength of her constitution and on her will to live. There's nothing wrong with her constitution, but . . . They're doing everything they can, of course. But she's decided to die."

"People can't simply decide to die."

"When they're as ill as that, they can refuse to fight. It's the same thing. Almost to the last minute we have some kind of choice. Frisca has made her choice and I can't find the right words to change it. What can we offer? Only Bernard, and she doesn't care quite enough for him. This tea is disgusting. They must have made it out of the floor sweepings." She stood up as Brad came in. "I'm staying here. I hope she'll sleep now, but I'm staying anyway." She patted Brad's shoulder as she left them.

"What did the doctors say about Bernard?" Barbary asked.

"That she wouldn't live till he arrived."

"But if we told her he was coming, wouldn't she hang on?"

Brad shook his head. "She's given in. She has the right, you know, to look at her own future and reject it. It will be sad for us. But Frisca isn't unhappy. And the doctors may still save her in spite of herself." He took her arm and they made their way out of the hospital. "Are you going back to Blaize now?"

"Yes, to reassure Asha. It must have frightened her, being dumped like that. I'll come back to London tonight, to let Aunt Alexa sleep."

"And I must do some work." They stepped into the sunshine.

"Did Frisca talk to you about me?" asked Barbary abruptly.

"Yes."

"Did she tell you that I loved you?"

"Yes. It's even better to hear it from you."

"And did she tell you that I wanted to do something about it?"

"Yes, that too." His arm tightened round her waist.

"She made me promise to go to bed with you tonight." Barbary did not find the words easy to say. "If you wanted me, that is. I did promise, but that part of the promise I can't keep. I do love you. I do want you, so very much. But if Frisca were to die to-night, while I—while we—"

"Sure. I understand." His voice was deep and loving and comforting. "When you're ready, I'll be waiting. And then we'll be together for the rest of our lives."

3

Frisca Lorimer died, and on the same day in July 1944 another member of the family was sinking towards death in Birkenau, part of the Auschwitz complex.

For three weeks Ilsa had been suffering from typhus, and for the past four days had been afflicted with dysentery as well. Too feeble to reach one of the few toilet buckets in the infirmary hut, she lay naked on a straw mattress soaked in her own excrement. Her wasted body, by now weighing as little as that of a child, seemed to consist only of a swollen tongue, an aching head and an excruciatingly painful gut. She could do nothing to help herself and knew how unlikely it was that the women who had been her companions during the past nightmare months could find any way to save her. The hut was called the infirmary, but contained no medicines or nurses. Ilsa lay on the lowest tier of bunks, staring upwards with unblinking eyes and waiting for the agony to end.

That morning a new form of torture added to her physical discomfort. Somewhere in the block an orchestra was playing. Was that possible? She knew that an orchestra did exist in the camp, but it performed only for the entertainment of the SS officers, or for the trainloads of newly arriving Jews who must not be thrown into panic by realising too soon that they had arrived in an extermination camp. An orchestra would never be allowed to play for the labouring prisoners in the camp—especially for those too ill to work.

Again and again Ilsa told herself that she must be imagining the sound. And yet, if it were only imagination, surely she could have imagined players who kept in tune, instead of producing such an unmusical cacophony. Half delirious, she began to mutter to herself, criticising the performance in a mixture of Russian and German.

"What do you know about music?" The demand came from the blockowa, who strode up and down while the concert was in progress.

Too tired to answer, Ilsa continued to mumble, but was conscious of another voice replying on her behalf. "She was a concert pianist in Russia. Didn't you know?" That must be Sigi, on the tier above. Sigi had had typhus as well and, until the dysentery struck, Ilsa had helped to hold her head for the foul-smelling soup which arrived twice a day.

The blockowa's feet marched away towards the rasping sound. By the time she returned, Ilsa had forgotten the brief exchange.

"You. The orchestra needs you. Report to the musicians' block." Something cotton was flung across Ilsa's face. Raising her arm wearily to pull it away, she discovered it to be a dress. She lay without moving.

"Go on." Sigi's voice was urgent. "Aren't you strong enough? Come on, we'll help." Her feet appeared over the edge of the bunk. She slithered uncertainly to the ground, calling as she did so to some of the less seriously ill women who were still able to walk.

Ilsa turned her head away. Hands pulled at her thin legs, trying to turn her. "No," she said. "I won't play for them. I've picked food for them, I've carried cement for them, I've built a railway for them. But I won't play the piano for them."

"Listen to me." Sigi knelt on the ground so that her head, shaven and lumpy with bites, was close to Ilsa's. "There hasn't been a selection for three weeks. There's bound to be one in the next seven days. When the doctor tells you to run from your bunk to the door, how far do you think you're going to get?"

Ilsa knew that Sigi's warning was true. In the infirmary block, non-Jewish blood ceased to provide protection. Any patient who could not prove herself strong enough to resume work on the day a selection was made would be taken to the gas chamber the same afternoon. What Sigi didn't know was that her friend no longer cared.

Perhaps she came near to guessing, though, for her whispering hissed with intensity. "Listen to me. Are you listening? You know as well as I do that there's only one way to get out of this place. You've got to stay alive. It's the only thing that matters. Nothing that you do here is important as long as it keeps you alive. Are you listening?"

Other voices joined in. "They have bread every day in the musicians' hut." "And shoes." "And showers, sometimes soap, to make sure they don't contaminate the Krauts. You're being offered a chance that any of us would give our eyes for."

Ilsa didn't care. What did life mean but a few more days or months of hopelessness? The women of the Birkenau orchestra might be privileged but were still prisoners, still liable to be sent to death at the whim of the camp commander. What use was it to go on living for a week or two if she would never see her mother or her own country again? Death on this foul bed was the quickest way to find peace.

"Don't give them the pleasure of killing you." Sigi's voice was more urgent than before. "If you've given in, you might as well go on the fence, choose your own death. But if there's someone you love, something worthwhile you've dreamed of doing with your life, you've got to stay alive. For as long as it takes. Are you listening, Ilsa? Think. You haven't got much time."

Ilsa still did not turn her head, but some flicker of energy stirred within her and her mind began to respond to her friend's plea. Remembering her mother and her home, she remembered also the months she had spent in the cellars below the old Aminov palace. The children she had hoped to save were all dead now, despatched to the gas chambers as soon as they arrived at Auschwitz. But during that period of enforced silence she had composed a piano concerto. By now the score would be lost or destroyed, but the notes were still inside her head. She could write it again one day. And there was other music as well. It hovered in the air, waiting to be caught and written down one day when this terrible tiredness had lifted from her body. Sigi was right. There were still things to be done.

Sigi had made one mistake, though. It was true that Ilsa had been a concert pianist once, but she would never play again. Slowly she turned her head. Half a dozen women were clustered round her bunk. Ilsa raised her hands to show them the swollen joints, the chapped knuckles, and the two fingers whose tips had fallen victim to frostbite.

"It doesn't matter," one of the women urged. "I heard the blockowa talking to the kapo of the orchestra. It's not a pianist they want. Just someone who's musician enough to orchestrate for them."

"They certainly need that." It was the first time for three weeks that Ilsa had attempted to smile. As though a signal had passed she felt bony hands tugging at her legs, setting her feet on the floor, raising her emaciated body. Two of them steadied her while another dropped the cotton dress over her head and helped her arms into the sleeves. They supported her as far as the door. Then she was on her own.

At no time of the year did the swampy ground on which

Auschwitz had been built dry up completely. Summer was worse than winter—when at least the mud froze hard. Had Ilsa been wearing shoes, she would have lost them in her first steps. As it was, she hardly had the strength to extricate each bare foot in turn from the slime.

Pausing to rest, she stared at the high electrified fence which surrounded the camp, a permanent invitation to suicide. Sigi had been right to remind her of the choice. As long as it was possible to run to the wire and embrace death, the action of not running meant that she had chosen to live. Slipping and slithering, Ilsa resumed her slow progress towards the musicians' hut. Somehow or other she would keep herself alive: for however long it might need.

1

The Allies were advancing. As the Russians swept towards Auschwitz from the east, its surviving prisoners were hurried west, into the heart of Germany. For three days Ilsa travelled without food or water in a wagon packed so tightly that it was possible only to stand upright. For four more days she was marched through mud and snow. There were two thousand women when the march began, but only a few hundred reached their destination. Ilsa was one of them. The members of the Birkenau orchestra had received the same meagre rations as the other inmates, but because they were not forced to exhaust themselves on manual work, it was just sufficient for survival. Sitting all day at a table as she wrote out parts for the orchestra's eccentric combination of instruments, Ilsa had been able to build up her strength before the evacuation of the camp. And it had been one of the musicians' privileges that they were issued with shoes.

The new prison for the survivors was Bergen-Belsen, but the established camp was already full. In spite of the wet and freezing conditions, new arrivals were forced to sleep on the ground under canvas. In return for heavy work in factories or forests, they received little food. Watery soup was the standard issue and bread a luxury. Those who were sent out to work in the fields stole whatever they could see that was edible. Here there was no orchestra and Ilsa, assigned to clear blocked drainage ditches, was soon exhausted as with every day that passed she slid nearer to the border of starvation. In a matter of only a few weeks they all shrank into skeletons, moving their cadaverous bodies slowly to conserve their energy, and almost too apathetic to use their minds at all. Fighting off the lethargy which was only a short step from death, Ilsa wondered every night whether she would wake the next morning.

Some time in the middle of April, 1945, the atmosphere changed. Sunshine and the melting of the snow raised the prisoners' spirits. Their guards, by contrast, were becoming nervous and indecisive. One day they no longer barked out orders: no working parties were despatched and no rations were issued. Speculating on what could be happening in the world outside, some of the women gathered in groups round the standpipes and waited for the water to be turned on. Others, too tired to care, collapsed onto their mattresses.

Ever since they left Auschwitz there had been daily rumours and wild guesses about the future. Now the rumours merged and confirmed each other until everyone agreed on two facts. The liberating armies were only a few miles away, and the Germans had decided to destroy the camp and shoot all its inhabitants before the Allies could reach them. No one could know the truth, but the rumours provoked their own reaction. Ilsa was conscious of a wave of panic sweeping over the women in her tent.

Before it had time to take hold, the sound of machine gun fire froze them all into silence. Had the killing already begun? Or was it, could it be . . . ? Moving at the slow pace which all of them had adopted as their energy drained away, Ilsa drifted towards the fence.

Other women came too, congregating in the striped shifts which were their prison uniform. Their faces were little more than skulls over which the skin had been tightly stretched, but in their eyes fear and hope and curiosity were struggling. All morning they had been chattering hysterically, but now, as the gunfire stopped again, they waited in a tense silence.

Half an hour passed. There was a new sound, of marching feet. A column of soldiers appeared—their uniforms not grey but khaki.

The tension snapped and now everyone was shouting. The soldiers were identified as British. They formed a line outside the camp. Inside, a cry went up: "Mind the fence!"—for the electricity had not been cut off. There was a period of inaction at

Ilsa's section of the perimeter: more troops must be making their way in by the main entrances. Some of the women were rushing about, anxious to be the first to touch their liberators. But most, like Ilsa, stood where they were, weakened as much by relief and incredulity as by lack of food. Could it be true? Was their captivity ending at last?

Outside there was a second flurry of movement: a line of military ambulances bumped across the ground, led by an officer and his driver in a small open vehicle. The officer jumped to the ground and strode towards the fence. He was a tall man, broad-shouldered and strong, well-fed and healthy. Ilsa stared at him and, as he stared back at her, his eyes widened in horror. "Oh, my God!" he exclaimed. "Oh, my God!"

He was in charge of the ambulances, Ilsa supposed, and she sympathised wryly with his problem. What use would a few dozen stretchers be when there were thousands starving and hundreds already too sick to be saved? He turned away, and Ilsa's attention was distracted by a new surge of movement. The first British soldiers had entered the camp.

An hour later she saw the medical officer again, his height making the shrunken survivors around him seem like dwarfs. He was shouting at the soldiers who had been handing out food and sweets from their own pockets to the starving women. Ilsa did not understand the words of the officer's orders, but she could tell that he was trying to stop them. She tugged at his sleeve, trying first in Russian and then in German to make him understand.

"We are hungry. We must eat. The soldiers are kind."

"When did you last have food?" He spoke in careful German.

"Soup, two days ago. Water, last night."

"But solid food? Bread, vegetables, meat."

It was tempting to laugh. The last taste of meat was not days but years away. "Bread five days ago, or six," she said.

"Then listen." He took hold of her wrist, its thinness jerking his eyes down in surprise. "If you—any of you—have rich food, or too much food quickly, it will poison you. You must teach your body to accept nourishment again. Slowly." He felt in his pouch. "Here."

Compared with the largesse which the ordinary soldiers were

distributing he offered a meagre present, but Ilsa greedily accepted two treasures: a glucose tablet and a plain, hard biscuit.

"Sit here," he ordered her. He watched as she lowered herself to the ground and leaned back against a sentry box. "Eat the biscuit as slowly as you can. A small piece every minute, or every five minutes. Make it soft in your mouth before you swallow. I will come back in one hour, to this place, and you give me more. I promise that. Do you believe me?"

It was not difficult to obey orders. Ilsa had been doing nothing else since she left Russia. She did not believe that the officer would remember her, but in less than an hour he was back, leading a group of about fifty women. He gave a little bread to each of them, and to Ilsa, and repeated both the warning and the promise.

Twice more during the day the officer came himself, and twice he sent an orderly carrying a canteen of hot soup. Not all the women were prepared to wait when they saw others gloating over the chocolate which the soldiers had handed out from their own rations, but Ilsa sat on where she had been left. Food and hope together nourished her body and little by little she felt her strength seeping back.

Late in the evening the officer returned again. "What's your name?" he asked.

Automatically Ilsa displayed the Auschwitz tattoo on her arm. Then she realised that she was no longer a number. "Ilsa," she said.

"You seem to be one of the strongest. Could you help me? We've cleared some of the barracks to act as infirmaries. We need nurses."

"I'll try to help," said Ilsa. "My mother is a doctor. But I've never—"

"For the next few days nursing only means feeding. Helping the weak ones to take soup. My name is Major Laing. I'm a doctor too. Will you come with me then, please?"

Please! He repeated the request to others who had been prepared to accept his warning and make a gradual return to normal eating. They were unable to keep up with his brisk pace, but shambled after him as best they could. On the way they passed a squad of British troops, with handkerchiefs over their faces, digging pits and shovelling in bodies which were already skeletons. Major Laing tried to distract the attention of his little group.

"We've seen it all before," Ilsa told him. She saw no point in pretending to a horror which they had all long ceased to feel; but she saw that the major found her indifference almost as shocking as the appalling conditions of the camp. During the next few days, as he struggled to keep alive women who had endured so much only to slip towards death at this very last minute, he often came to sit beside Ilsa, pressing her to describe her life before and after the German invasion.

"We didn't know," he said more than once. "None of us knew we were going to find anything like this."

"It's not your fault." It was odd that she should try to reassure him. She could not imagine his life any more than he could believe hers. Ilsa watched him trying to bridge the gulf of incomprehension which separated them. From a village now under British occupation he brought her a dress. He gave her a lipstick, and cigarettes, and held her to a restorative diet with an attention which he could not possibly devote to the hundreds of other starving women. She did not understand why he should single her out but was more grateful for the special treatment than she could express. She was an individual again, and someone minded about her.

She found it easy to accept all his gifts except one. After she had been working in the makeshift infirmary for almost four weeks he took her one evening to a building once occupied by the SS.

"There's something to celebrate," he said, unlocking the door.

"What?"

"The Germans have surrendered. Tomorrow will mark the official end of the war. This half of the war, anyway. Victory in Europe. You'll hear the church bells ringing. It will be a big day for you."

"Our big day was when you opened the gates." But he was right, all the same—it was something to celebrate. She followed him inside, but then stared without speaking at the piano to which he led her. She had described her training to him but had not made it clear enough, she supposed, that that part of her life was over.

"Would you like to play?" he asked.

She shook her head. "You."

Surprised, he sat down and played a Chopin étude which she had learned as a young girl. He was only an amateur, and out of practice, but it was not a bad attempt—enough at least to show that he cared for music. Just once since she was snatched by the Germans—in the train which carried her away from her mother and home—Ilsa had cried with self-pity. In the years which followed she had often felt afraid or defeated or in pain, but never again allowed herself to weep. Now, as she listened, the tears, hot and salty, splashed down on her useless hands.

"Your turn." He twisted round on the stool. This had been planned as a treat, of course, and he could not conceal his dismay when he saw how upset she was. Ilsa had formed the habit of keeping her left hand in a tight fist when she was not using it, so perhaps he had never noticed her fingers. She forced the muscles to unclench, straightening her hand so that he could see that two fingertips were missing. "Frostbite," she said. "Compared with most people's, a very small war wound."

"I'm so sorry." His sympathy was awkward. He did not know what to say next—because of course it was true that the injury was trivial compared with the suffering around them, and yet of great importance to Ilsa. She was ashamed of herself for spoiling his gesture. Too many years had passed since she last needed to consider other people's feelings. She would have to learn social behaviour again from the beginning. Smiling apologetically, she made a gesture of her own.

"I know that étude you just played," she said. "We could try it together, with you playing the left hand and me the right."

She enjoyed his pleasure as he made room for her on the piano stool. He was a big man, so it was lucky that there was still so little flesh on Ilsa's bones. She felt his right arm encircle her waist to hold her steady. "Just a moment," she said. It would have been brave to strike straight into the Chopin, but risky. She flexed and relaxed her fingers before touching the keys tentatively, and played first a scale and a series of chords, trying to force the stiffness out and to stretch her hand. Then she nodded and they began to play together.

The result was terrible. There was nothing wrong with Ilsa's memory, but her fingers were slow and clumsy. Only by a hectic scramble could she keep in time, and the effect was scarcely musical. Yet her benefactor grinned with a boyish excitement.

"There! You see! It's going to be all right." The major's arm remained round her waist as he asked where she would go when the repatriation committee arrived to make arrangements.

"Home to my mother. To Russia."

"You must be prepared for shocks," he warned her. "Millions of people have died in the countries occupied by the Nazis. Some places have ceased to exist. I don't know anything about your home, of course, but—" He pulled a card from his wallet and wrote an address and an army postal code on the back. "If ever you need help, Ilsa—if your mother isn't there, if your home isn't there—let me know. I shan't be able to keep track of you. But I hope you'll keep in touch with me."

"I don't understand," she said. "Why have you given so much time to me when there are so many hundreds, thousands, here who've needed your help?" He had saved her life with his warnings on the first day, for many of those who thought themselves luckiest in receiving food from the well-meaning soldiers had died during the night after their liberation.

"But that's the answer," he explained. "There are too many people here. And for most of them we've come too late. No doctor enjoys seeing his patients dying on him by the hundred. We're keeping some alive—but again, there are too many to make it possible to think of them as individuals. When I arrived here you were the first woman I saw as an individual, not one of a mass. I suppose I think of you as a kind of symbol. I can watch you growing a little stronger every day and hope that you represent a thousand others. So don't just disappear, will you, Ilsa?"

He helped her to stand, recognising that she would not want to play again. As she looked up at him, Ilsa was conscious of an odd expression in his eyes. It revealed compassion and friendliness, but something else as well.

An hour earlier she would not have been able to interpret it. Everything in her background and history separated her from this man, who had spent all his early life in comfort and even during the war had the satisfaction of continuing his vocation. They had nothing in common with each other at all. But for the first time now she could see into his mind. He had answered her question honestly, and she understood the answer. It was as though, like Pygmalion, he had been trying during these past days to create a woman from the most basic material of skin and bones and frozen emotions. And now his pride in his achievement was changing to possessiveness and even a kind of affection, just as Pygmalion's had done. She wondered how long it would last.

As she pushed his card into her pocket to join her only other personal treasure—the lipstick he had given her earlier—gratitude overwhelmed her. Major Laing had not only kept her body alive. He had dragged her mind out of the rut of day-to-day survival which for three years had been the only defence against despair. He was reminding her that she had a future—and she knew how she was going to use it.

"May I stay here, with the piano?" she asked.

"Of course. You're a free woman now."

"And could I beg some paper from you? Large sheets. And a pencil?"

Even in the musicians' hut at Birkenau there had been no time for her own music. Now she could write down the piano concerto first composed in the cellars of the orphanage. She felt her eyes brightening with excitement. Even her blood seemed to be moving less sluggishly through her veins. She could hardly wait to begin.

"I'll see what I can do." He was staring at her as though unable to believe what he saw. "What's happened? Suddenly you're looking better."

"I've had time to learn that there are only two states of health. Either you're alive or you're dead."

"And you've decided that you're alive?" He bent down to kiss her lightly on the forehead. "Welcome back to the world, Ilsa." He went off to look for the materials she had asked for.

Alone at the piano, Ilsa stroked a key with one finger and drew a deep breath of happiness. The nightmare was over. She had survived.

2

London was packed with shouting, cheering people. Alexa
recognised that even if she could find a taxi it would not be able
to move along the thronged streets. As she made her way cautiously through the jostling crowds, she found it difficult to banish
from her mind memories of other crowds celebrating the end of
another war. November 11, 1918, had been the first day of her
widowhood. But May 8, 1945—V-E Day—would bring happier
remembrance. Barbary's second daughter had been born that
morning.

Brad and Barbary had set up house together in the month following Frisca's death. Brad, already over fifty, made no secret of
his wish to have a child of his own and, although it was still impossible for him to marry Barbary, they were not prepared to be
either patient or ashamed. Alexa might think their decision to
have a baby unwise, but her own experience made it impossible
for her to disapprove, and Barbary's radiant happiness disarmed
criticism. They had found it easy and cheap to buy a house in
London, for the flying bomb attacks had prompted a second
exodus from the city. Barbary had flung herself into the task of
turning it into a home, working almost single-handed at everything from the first sweeping up of broken window glass to the
final hanging of home-made curtains against the home-painted
walls.

Because of her problems with earlier pregnancies she had chosen to have her second baby in hospital, but this time there was
nothing to cause anxiety. Brad's telephone call to Alexa earlier
that day had announced the uncomplicated arrival of a seven-
pound girl.

She found Brad already sitting at Barbary's bedside. He kissed
Alexa warmly and hardly gave her time to congratulate the
mother before showing off the baby. Pink and healthy, the little
girl lay contentedly asleep in a cot at the end of the bed.

"Lovely!" Alexa exclaimed with the effusiveness of a good actress. Babies were not one of her enthusiasms, but her pleasure in Barbary's happiness was genuine. "What's her name?"

"Have we a choice, on a day like this?" asked Brad. "Victoria Europa, naturally."

"Don't be an idiot, Brad." Barbary giggled happily.

"Well, what then?" asked Alexa.

"One thing's for sure: this baby is as rosy as Asha was pale. I reckon we should start from there. Rosie, Ros, Rosebud."

"Rosemary, Rosalind, Rosamund," said Barbary. It was clear that the light-hearted argument had been in progress for some time already.

"Christen her Rosamund and call her Ros," Alexa suggested.

"Three cheers for the British art of compromise!" Brad hugged Alexa again. "Agreed, Mother?"

"Agreed, Father." The two parents kissed to seal the decision. It was delightful to see them so much in love with each other. Alexa produced the presents she had brought and was content to listen to their badinage until the staff nurse, breathless at the discovery that her timetable had slipped out of gear in the euphoria of victory, hurried in to say that Barbary must be allowed to rest.

Alexa had been invited to spend the night at Brad's house, so they left together. "Will you rebuild Glanville House now?" he asked as they made their way slowly through the celebrating crowds.

"With so many thousands of homes destroyed, I doubt if there'll be either the materials or the labour to rebuild such a huge property just for a single family," Alexa said. "Not that I'm one of these socialists. But I can see that other people's needs will be greater, for a little while at least. It won't be my decision, of course."

"How's that?"

He had forgotten, Alexa thought. No, it was more than that. Brad had never met Pirry. He must know that she had a son, but he could not be expected to feel much interest in the prospect which had brought happiness to Alexa even before she heard about the baby.

"My son is head of the family," she reminded him. "The house belongs to Pirry. And now that the war is over, he'll be coming home."

Pirry arrived at Blaize without warning, wearing a demob suit which looked shabby in spite of being brand new. His appearance was so unexpected that Alexa could only cling to him wordlessly.

"Five years is a long time," Pirry said as they drew apart at last. He was recognising, no doubt, that they had both aged since their last meeting. "Let's go out and talk in the rose garden. I've dreamed of roses. Five minutes while I take off this terrible suit. It seemed undemocratic to turn it down, but I'm hoping a deserving member of the staff will accept it."

"You have to think before you're generous these days. Clothes are rationed. Make sure your old suits fit you before you throw anything away." She laughed. "What a ridiculous way of welcoming you home!"

"Recognising that I'm a foreigner in my own country is very wise. I shall need to be educated. You go and choose the sweetest-smelling bush and I'll come and join you there."

In an open-necked shirt and a pair of grey flannels—their cut curiously wide to an eye accustomed to utility styles—Pirry looked younger and more relaxed. Alexa sighed with happiness. "We must have a welcome party," she said as they strolled through the garden. "No, two. One for our friends and one for the tenants."

Pirry shook his head. "No thank you, Mother. I think the tenant and young master thing is finished. As for your friends, most of them have sons who are heroes, fighting men. With the best will in the world they wouldn't be able to conceal their suspicions that I've enjoyed a cushy billet and a fast demob."

"But it wasn't your fault."

"Of course not. One doesn't feel guilt, exactly, or shame. But one can't be proud of having a much safer war than a good many civilians. Like Frisca."

Alexa's chin jerked up and her hand tightened its grip on his arm. She recognised Pirry's need to speak his sister's name, to refer to her death, but she did not want to talk about it now. Pirry, always sensitive, understood at once and allowed her to change the subject.

"What was it like, being a prisoner for so long?"

"Boring," he said. "Of course, for the regular officers it was far worse. The only war to take place during their fighting careers, and they were missing it! No hope of promotion. They were intensely frustrated and they took it out on the rest of us with ridiculous regulations. But for chaps like me, civilians at heart, it was simply a waste of time. Five boring years. The Red Cross arranged some correspondence courses, though. Chaps qualified as lawyers, accountants, doctors of philosophy."

"What did you study?"

"Norwegian. There was a Norwegian in the camp. I chose it for its lack of practical use—but in fact I got quite interested and started making translations of Ibsen. I picked up some Swedish as well. And I taught German—anyone who knew anything was expected to take classes. We must be the best-educated bunch of soldiers in the world. Graduate of the Universities of Heidelberg and Oflag VIIID, that's me." Without warning, he put both arms round Alexa, holding her so tightly that she could hardly breathe. "Dearest Mother. It's so very good to be home."

At that moment, and in the summer weeks which followed, Alexa was happier than she had been for years. She was surprised to find Pirry content to drowse the days away, for she had expected that after such a long confinement he would be extra-energetic, and anxious to look up his old friends. But he claimed that his greatest deprivation had been the lack of freedom ever to be alone, and she was content to indulge him.

There was, however, business to be settled. The family lawyers wrote for instructions on the subject of claiming war damage compensation for Glanville House.

"What's your feeling about houses, Mother?" Pirry asked as he studied the conditions. "Are you happy to have a home only at Blaize? Or do you want to keep something on in London—and if so, would it have to be a proper establishment or just a pied à terre? I don't see much chance of rebuilding Glanville House as it was or as it ought to be. Everything which was part of the family history has gone. And the site will be immensely valuable. If we were to take the compensation and sell the land, you could afford to choose anything else in London."

"I quite agree, darling. I shall spend most of my time here. It would be nice to have a flat in London. But two or three rooms in your home would be ideal. If you could bear that in mind when you do your house-hunting."

"We'll find you a self-contained flat. I don't propose to have a London home."

"You mean you're going to live at Blaize?" Alexa would have felt excited had instinct not told her that Pirry meant something different.

"I'm going to live abroad, Mother. As I did before the war."

"You were only a student before the war. It's time you settled down now, Pirry."

"I am going to settle down. But not here, I'm afraid."

"You know what I mean. You should get married. Have a family."

"Do I have to spell it out to you, Mother?"

A feeling of panic almost choked Alexa. She did not want to hear the truth, although she already knew it. "You're very rich, Pirry. There are girls who'd like the sort of life you could offer—who'd agree not to bother you too much if you made it clear—"

"Mother! You've never been a hypocrite. It's one of the marvellous things about you. A girl who'd accept an arrangement like that isn't a girl you'd want for your daughter-in-law."

"But you don't need to go abroad." In Alexa's mind was the hope that the atmosphere of Blaize would exert its own magic and persuade him to make the family's hold on it secure.

"I met someone in the camp, Mother," Pirry confessed reluctantly. "Five years is a long time. We think of ourselves in a way as married."

"Well, you can't be. To another man! That's ridiculous."

"I know we can't. But—" His voice strengthened and he looked his mother more steadily in the eyes. "We're going to live together. Openly. If we try to do that in England we shall be sent to prison—and the Sunday papers will have a field day. So we've got to go abroad. Now listen, Mother. There's no problem about Blaize until I die. I'm thirty-two years old and in perfect health and I promise, I absolutely promise, to outlive you. So you can stay at Blaize for the rest of your life. What happens after I die won't matter to either of us. In the meantime, I shall come back every summer. And you can visit me in winter. I shall choose a sunny place. The West Indies, perhaps. Being rich can't help me to get round the law, but it can prevent us both from being miserable about it."

"You don't understand, Pirry. About looking after Blaize, I mean. It's been so difficult during the war. Shortages of materials, no labour. An old house needs such a lot of attention. It's a big responsibility—and it's *your* responsibility. I'm sixty-eight, Pirry. The only incentive I've had to keep Blaize in good order is because I've been waiting to hand it over to you. A heritage is a burden unless one loves the heir. Why should I bother to get the roof repaired just to keep that odious Duncan or his odious son dry one day? And how can you possibly guarantee to outlive me? You might have died at Dunkirk after your boat sank."

"The point is that I didn't. I kept that promise to you even though you didn't know I'd made it. I knew what would happen to you if I drowned, and so I didn't drown."

"You're talking nonsense, Pirry. Selfish nonsense. You're upsetting me."

"I'm sorry. I'm truly sorry. But I'm not a child anymore. I can't change my nature."

"How do you know? You've never tried." Appalled that they should be quarrelling so soon after their long separation, Alexa hurried away before either of them should say anything too hurtful to be forgotten. As always when she needed comfort, she sought out Matthew and sat beside him as he painted. He had a sitter, so she could not confide in him, but in the silence which his concentration imposed she was able to calm herself with arguments which convinced her even while she was half-aware of their speciousness.

She must make allowances for the unnatural conditions of a prisoner-of-war camp. As Pirry had reminded her, it had been a long time. He would probably not have set eyes on a woman for five years. Who could blame him for looking elsewhere for companionship and affection? Alexa told herself that she must not nag or argue. Sooner or later Pirry's love for his mother and the peaceful atmosphere of Blaize would have their effect. If she could only be patient, everything would be all right.

3

Not long after Alexa had welcomed Pirry home, she said good-bye to the wartime occupants of Blaize. It was during the last week of July, 1945, as she switched off the wireless which had just announced the incredible news of Winston Churchill's election defeat, that she heard the strains of the end-of-term hymn. "Lord, dismiss us with Thy blessing." Three times a year for the past five years the words had roared out of the ballroom which acted as the school's assembly hall, but she would not hear them again. With Pirry at her side she stood on the terrace to watch the girls leave. They came up in little groups to assure her that they would never forget Blaize.

"Nor will Blaize ever recover from them." Alexa tried to conceal from Pirry that she had been touched by their words. "The grounds, for example." Many of the girls had just presented her with little bunches of flowers—all of them cut without permission from Alexa's own gardens. "Quite apart from playing hockey, they had a Dig for Victory campaign in 1941 and planted potatoes everywhere. Like gold prospectors, they'd stake out a claim in the middle of the croquet lawn because that looked easier to dig up than the field I offered them."

"If they've all gone, let's look round," suggested Pirry.

It was a depressing tour. Alexa had naturally moved out her own good furniture. In its place were iron bedsteads, shabby desks and chairs, ugly trestle tables. No redecoration had taken place during the war, so that all the walls were grubby and many had been defaced by scribbled names and messages.

"The furniture's due to go out tomorrow," Alexa said. "Then it's in the contract that they have to make good any damage and redecorate."

"The building seems to have adapted remarkably well," Pirry commented. They were standing in Alexa's old drawing room, a large and once very beautiful apartment. At present its eight full-

length windows were half concealed by shabby blackout curtains
and a miscellaneous collection of chairs revealed that the room
had been used as a staff common room. "Do you see yourself
coming back to this, Mother? I was just thinking how incon-
venient the old arrangements were. I didn't notice at the time,
but I'm struck by how much cosier you are in the west wing. The
library makes a marvellous drawing room, and it's so handy being
able to walk straight into the dining room instead of trekking
across the banqueting hall. And when I think that until you had
that new kitchen built every bit of food had to be carried along
corridors and up stairs, I can't think how we ever managed to
enjoy a hot meal at all."

"But we did," said Alexa. "The servants knew how to cope."

"And do you think you'll still be able to get servants? Enough,
I mean, to carry coals and trays and jugs of hot water and to keep
all this clean and polished?"

"What are you saying, Pirry?"

"Just thinking aloud, that's all. I certainly don't want you to
feel restricted in any way. If you're looking forward to having the
spaciousness of the whole house at your disposal again, then
that's how it's going to be. But the west wing is large on its own.
You might find it less of a burden if you only needed to look
after that."

"Someone still has to be responsible for the rest. To start with,
we have to keep it warm. It's been allowed to get damp. That
couldn't be helped: but it mustn't go on."

"You're right; someone has to be responsible. And you're right
to think that I mustn't leave it all to you. But suppose we could
make another arrangement like the one that's just ended."

"You mean another school?"

"Why not? This time there'd be no need to rush. You could
lay down conditions, make sure that your private grounds really
are private, insist that the school should install central heating,
that sort of thing. Or, of course, to give you full control, it could
be your own school."

"Pirry! I thought I was to have less responsibility, not more!"

"Sorry. But I remember once talking to Leo Tavadze in
Vienna. He told me about the Russian tradition of helping chil-

dren with special talents. Under the Tsars there were conserva-
toires. You might have thought that the Communists wouldn't
approve of special treatment, but they did. Leo went to the
School for Musically Gifted Children in Leningrad. Its job was to
turn out virtuosi. We ought to have something like that in England. Not as large as the school that's just left. Twenty or thirty
children, perhaps, getting a decent general education but an out-
standing musical one."

"It wouldn't be economic," Alexa objected. Years of managing
her own theatre had made her a shrewd businesswoman. "They'd
need so many teachers compared with the number of pupils that
there'd be no money for installing central heating. Unless the fees
were astronomical."

"We could set up a trust," Pirry suggested. "A charity. Ask
music lovers to contribute. Then there needn't be any fees at all.
Scholarships to make sure that no gifted child was refused a place
for lack of money. Leo would help. He'd give a recital in London
and donate the proceeds. He's longing to show how grateful he
is."

The young Jewish violinist whom Pirry had brought out of
Vienna had been interned in the Isle of Man as an enemy alien
until Alexa succeeded in persuading the authorities that a man
with his history could not possibly be a Nazi supporter. She had
secured not only his release but an American visa, and the press
cuttings which he enclosed with his frequent letters revealed the
success of his renewed career.

"Don't count on me to help," Alexa warned her son. "I shall
have quite enough to do, getting the opera house going again. I
couldn't take on a school as well."

"But would you object if someone else did? It would only be
worth considering if you were content to go on living just in the
west wing. And if you wouldn't mind having children around—
dedicated, hard-working children who'd be too busy practising to
dig up your croquet lawn."

"Would you organise it, Pirry? Be responsible?" Alexa foresaw
problems; but if the proposed venture held Pirry in England for
some time longer, the price might be worth paying. Their discus-

sion continued over a period of several days; but in the end—
more cheerful than at any time since their quarrel—she agreed
that if he would do all the work, she would accept all the consequences.

4

That first summer of peace saw many arrivals and departures—
not all of them as easily arranged as that of the schoolgirls. Alexa
was not surprised to learn that Brad intended to take his new
family back to the United States—but either Grant's permission
in writing or else a certificate of his death had been required by
the British authorities before Asha could have a passport and by
the United States before Barbary could be issued with a visa.
Only after a good deal of time and argument was persistence rewarded. Using the implausible excuse that a young relation
needed to be collected and escorted home—implausible because
Bernard was by now eighteen years old—Barbary obtained permission to enter the United States with Asha for a limited time.

It was a delight to Alexa to observe her great-niece's happiness.
The little house in London was filled with laughter as preparations for the move were made. Brad and Barbary were deeply in
love but had never stopped teasing each other. As for Asha, who
might have been expected to feel jealous of a new baby, she sat
for long periods beside the cot, singing tunelessly or dangling toys
for Ros to clutch.

Not long before Barbary was at last due to leave, her stepmother returned from India. It was difficult for Alexa to think of
Eleanor Scott as a true member of the family. She did her best to
appear cordial by inviting Eleanor to stay at Blaize—since Barbary was in the throes of packing up and selling her home—but it
was a relief to learn that the missionary society maintained a retreat house for the benefit of its overseas workers on home leave.

"How much have you told her?" Alexa needed to check with

Barbary before following her in paying a visit to Eleanor. Eleanor
would certainly disapprove if she learned the true state of affairs.

"I hadn't intended to say anything," Barbary confessed.
"When I went to see her, I left Ros at home. But how do you
persuade a four-year-old to be discreet? As soon as we'd finished
tea, Asha stood up and announced that it was time to go home
and bathe baby. Collapse of respectable façade. Eleanor's always
been nosy. As soon as she realised that there were questions to be
asked, she asked them."

"What did you say about Grant?"

Barbary's answer contained no hint of doubt or deception. "I
told her that he was dead."

At the end of October, some weeks after Barbary had said her
goodbyes and sailed away, a message was brought to Alexa: a Red
Cross lady, Mrs. Mostyn, had called in the hope of seeing Mrs.
Lorimer. The caller was invited in but told that Mrs. Lorimer was
not available.

"Do you know where I can get in touch with her?"

"Can you tell me what it's about?"

Mrs. Mostyn hesitated. "Are you Mrs. Lorimer's mother, Lady
Glanville?"

"Her great-aunt. Her mother died when she was a baby. As it
happens, I'm also her husband's aunt. We're a close-knit family.
So if your visit concerns him . . . ?"

"Yes," said Mrs. Mostyn. "I have some good news for Mrs.
Lorimer. But there's bad news as well."

Alexa waited.

"Mr. Lorimer is alive." Mrs. Mostyn paused, expecting some reaction to her dramatic announcement. She was not offered it.

"And the bad news?"

"The bad news is that he's ill. Very ill indeed. I don't know
how much you've read about the survivors of the Japanese camps,
Lady Glanville?"

"Very little." The first of the released prisoners of war had arrived in England only three weeks earlier. These had been the
fittest of the liberated men, yet their condition had prompted
comparisons with the condition of the Belsen survivors.

"Your nephew was one of the prisoners sent to build the

Burma-Siam railway," Mrs. Mostyn said. "The conditions—" She broke off, upset. "I was a nurse in the first war, Lady Glanville. I thought I'd seen every horror that one man could inflict on another. But these men were used as slaves. Worse than slaves, really, because a slave owner has an interest in keeping his workers healthy. The Japanese regarded these as expendable. If they died, there were more where they came from. They didn't feed them properly. They refused to give them medicines. It's incredible that any survived at all."

"But my nephew—?"

"He must have had an immensely strong constitution. He was older than the soldiers—but of course he was used to the country and the climate. Apparently he knew a great deal about local trees and plants. He helped to find food and to invent medicines."

"But he's still very ill, you say."

Mrs. Mostyn accepted the need to be businesslike. "It's not just a question of starvation—though he only weighed eighty pounds when he was put on the boat at Singapore. During the past three years he's also suffered from cholera, malignant malaria, severe ulceration, almost continuous dysentery, and extreme malnutrition. He's enduring the effects of vitamin deficiency over a long period. He's still got beri-beri. His eyesight has been affected and his bones are very brittle."

"Is he expected to live?"

"There's a good chance, given careful nursing over a long period. He was taken straight to the Hospital for Tropical Diseases and he'll have to stay there for quite a while. His wife needs to be warned that she may not recognise him. I've had to watch some of these meetings. It's very upsetting—two people who've been looking forward to a reunion for so long, and then the woman finds that her husband is somehow not the man she married. Not physically, and often not psychologically either. This is why we're taking the news round in person—so that we can give a warning."

"Mrs. Lorimer has had no expectation of his return. She's never known for sure that he was a prisoner. We tried to find out what had happened. We were told that the Japanese were supposed to provide information about everyone they captured, and to give each prisoner a postcard to address. But my nephew's name has never been on any list."

"As far as I am aware, the Japanese ignored every single part of the Geneva Convention. Lack of information was the least of it."

"My great-niece is in the United States at the moment. My grandson spent the war there, and she's gone out to collect him. Mr. Lorimer will be disappointed. I shall visit him myself to explain." With the excuse that Barbary was moving around, Alexa declined to give an address, but promised to pass on the news as soon as possible.

When her visitor had left, there were decisions to be made. In the converted coach house she found Matthew in his studio with Pirry and told them what had happened.

"You'll have to tell them both the truth." Matthew spoke without hesitation, perhaps remembering the time long ago when his own life had been shattered by lies told by his elders.

"Then I make two people unhappy. Barbara discovers that she can't marry Brad without hurting Grant and Grant discovers that his wife has been unfaithful and doesn't want to return to him. Whereas if I'm prepared to lie, perhaps I could keep one of them happy, and make the other only as upset as he would be in any case." She had never liked Grant, so that it was tempting to do only what was best for Barbary. It was necessary to remember that when a man had sustained himself through great suffering with the hope of this eventual reunion, he deserved to be treated kindly. But which was the kinder—to speak the truth or conceal it?

"Perhaps Babs would be happier back with Grant," suggested Pirry. "If you tell the truth to her but not to Grant, then Brad might be the only one to suffer."

Alexa shook her head. "Barbara and Brad are right for each other. She's been so happy this past year. In a way she cut off from Grant even before that. I'm not saying that she wishes him dead, but she's no longer hoping to be told that he's alive."

"Then it's a question of being realistic." Like Matthew earlier, Pirry spoke firmly. "There's no point in lying to someone who's bound to discover the truth. You can prevent Grant learning about Brad and Ros if you choose to, and this excuse about Bernard is good enough to buy a little time. But you can't stop Babs from finding out that Grant is still alive, because she's already put in an official request for an enquiry. She's got to know. So she might as well learn from you. Then she'll have to decide what she wants to do. It's a hard decision, but no one can take it for her. All we can do is promise our support."

Alexa sighed. If only Barbary's grandmother were still alive! Margaret would would have prepared to visit Grant in hospital feeling nothing but love, and would have written to Barbary with total confidence in the rightness of honesty. Alexa felt nothing but alarm on either score.

5

Alexa's last sight of her grandson had been when he was still a young schoolboy. Welcoming him to Blaize at the end of 1945, she saw that he had grown into a man.

It was easy to recognise him, for the resemblance to Robert at the same age was as strong as ever—and there was more to it than only his red hair. Like Robert thirty years earlier, Bernard had changed from a mischievous boy with a ready grin to a serious and even studious young man who had somehow resisted the infection of an American accent. "It's a nuisance about National Service, of course," he told his grandmother. "But I want to get it over so that I can go to university here. Cambridge is the best place in the world to study science."

There were so many things to talk about: where should they start? Alexa wanted to hear all about Bernard's life in California and Bernard was full of questions about the plans for the school of music at Blaize—he had heard already that the first applicants had been auditioned. More important, they needed to discuss the future of Brinsley House. The Lorimer mansion in Bristol had been taken over by the BBC for the duration of the war. Now it was empty again and Bernard—like Pirry at Blaize—would have to consider how best to care for it until he was ready to live there himself. Before anything else, though, Alexa wanted to know about Barbary.

Barbary had not answered Alexa's letter or given any warning of her return with Bernard. Nor had she been in touch since their arrival. It had been left to Bernard himself to telephone his grandmother, and he had travelled to Blaize alone.

"She's in a bad way," he told Alexa. "The last few days in California were awful. Brad was so upset. They didn't shout at each other. There were just these terrible silences. Barbary kept on crying. Brad simply waited. I think he thought that if he waited long enough, she'd give in—that when it came to the point, she wouldn't be able to leave Ros."

"Do you mean she hasn't brought the children back with her?"

"Only Asha. Brad wouldn't let Ros go. He said he'd waited a long time to have a daughter and he wasn't going to be robbed of her now. I don't think he meant it nastily. He just wanted them all to stay. I like Brad tremendously."

"So do I," agreed Alexa. She hesitated. "You've been told all the details, then?"

"Barbary explained it. She had to make sure that I wouldn't spill the beans to Grant if I met him."

"You mean that she's going back to Grant? She's going to pretend that Brad never existed?"

"Yes. She feels that's what she ought to do. But my guess is that she doesn't *want* to do it. I expect that's why she's ill. And she's upset about Ros. Babies are a complication, aren't they?"

Yes indeed, thought Alexa—and so was Grant Lorimer's state of health. Her first sight of him had filled her with horror. Would Barbary, already upset, be able to cope with this additional strain? If Barbary was not coming to Blaize, then it was clear to Alexa that she must go to London.

Petrol was still rationed, so to justify the expedition Alexa spent a day or two arranging appointments with friends, lawyers, and banks. Bernard had left Barbary flat-hunting, and could provide no address, so Alexa telephoned the hospital in which she had visited Grant and discovered the time at which Mrs. Lorimer visited her husband each day. At three o'clock one afternoon she waited outside the hospital gates in the car, having instructed her chauffeur to open the door as soon as her great-niece was seen leaving. There was a moment of hesitation, but Barbary was not

in a fighting mood. She climbed in and gave the chauffeur the address of a flat she had found.

It was a gloomy place, dark, and inadequately heated. Alexa
kept her coat on. "Is Asha here?" she asked.

"No. She's a bright child. She started reading early, so I persuaded a school to take her before her fifth birthday. Otherwise I
should have needed someone to look after her while I'm visiting."

"You haven't taken her to the hospital?"

"Once." Barbary put on the kettle to make tea. "Grant wanted
to see her. Naturally. But he didn't want her to see him, not till
he looked normal again. He was moved out of the ward into the
nurses' section of a recovery ward for a few hours, so that he
could look through a glass wall. I didn't go in to him that day. I
took Asha and some toys into the recovery room and we played
together with him watching."

"How is he?"

"Improving, they tell me. I can't see it myself. He's still—"
Barbary broke down and began to tremble, her whole body shak-
ing as she tried to control her tears. "You've seen him, Aunt
Alexa. You know."

"Yes." Alexa waited while the tea was made and poured. "Have
you told him yet about Brad and Ros?"

"No. I can't do that. You won't tell, will you?"

"I shall do whatever you ask, dear. But surely—in the quite exceptional circumstances—Grant would understand."

"Grant would never let circumstances influence what he believes to be right. In my place he would have waited. He hasn't
much sympathy for human weakness. Or much forgiveness."

"Well then, if you don't think he can forgive, let him be angry.
Let him divorce you."

"He'd never do that. He'd say he was refusing because he was a
Christian, but really it would be to punish me."

"Then don't bother about divorce. Don't bother about marriage. Go back to Brad. Make your family whole again. I'm sure
that's the best thing for you, Barbara. If I could possibly have
kept the truth from you, I would have. It was Pirry who pointed
out that you were bound to find out. But I hoped you'd stay in
America. You could still make Brad happy, and the two little

girls. I don't believe you'll be able to make Grant happy now. You can't act a marriage. And I'm not sure that you can sustain a lie when so many people know the truth."

"I shall cut off from the friends who knew me with Brad. They think I'm in San Francisco, anyway. I've tried to muddle Asha, telling her that Brad is Ros's Daddy but I'm not Ros's Mummy— I was just helping to look after her. In a few more months, she'll forget. And you and Bernard have promised to keep quiet."

"Eleanor knows," Alexa reminded her.

"Grant has never met Eleanor, hardly knows she exists, would assume that she's still in India. She'll going back there soon, presumably. I can keep them apart."

"But is it worth it?"

"Why doesn't anyone help me?" cried Barbary in an anguished voice. "I'm trying, I really am trying, to do what I think is right. And nobody will help." She abandoned the attempt to hold back her tears, and began to pace up and down the room. "Grant is my husband. I have a duty to look after him. Whether I can make myself love him again I don't know, but he has a right to his daughter's love. He's had a terrible time, terrible, and he's only just alive. If he knew how I'd spent the years when he was suffering, it would hurt him. If I left him, it would kill him."

"Don't be dramatic, dear. People don't die of broken hearts. Or even of resentment and anger." But even as she spoke Alexa remembered Frisca, who had died because she saw no point in living. She put the thought from her mind.

"Healthy people don't, I agree. But who knows what's going on in Grant's mind? You think I'm exaggerating. Perhaps I am. But if he learned the truth and then he died—even if his death could be explained in physical, medical terms—I should have to live with that death. You think I've made the wrong choice. I don't see that I had any choice. I'd prefer not to discuss this anymore, Aunt Alexa. It's time for me to collect Asha from school. Where are you going next?"

Alexa stood up. Barbary's suddenly calm and businesslike tone of voice was unlikely to signify an equal calmness of spirit, but for the moment there seemed nothing more to be said.

"I'm sorry, Barbara dear, if I've seemed unhelpful. I do sympathise most sincerely." She kissed her great-niece on the cheek before answering her question as matter-of-factly as it had been asked. "I have to call at a bank. I put some jewels into safe deposit there years ago—my own jewels, not the Glanville ones. The receipt was one of the papers which disappeared when Glanville House was bombed, so I have an appointment to go through some procedure of describing the deposit and identifying it and signing an affidavit. All very tedious. Give my love to little Asha."

She sighed as she walked stiffly back to the car. Barbary's problems were still on her mind half an hour later when a black leather case was brought up from a vault and set before her. She unlocked it with the key she had brought from Blaize and stared in silence at its contents. A necklace of rubies, with a pendant in the form of a rose. A pair of delicate drop earrings, each a miniature version of the rose. And a tiara in which yet another rose petalled in rubies was half hidden by trembling silver leaves veined with tiny diamonds. The Lorimer rubies.

The rubies had a history of their own, stretching back almost sixty years to the collapse of the Lorimer bank in Bristol. From the moment when John Junius Lorimer had ordered the jewels to be set and had given them to Alexa's mother, they had carried misfortune with them. By now they had accumulated so many sad associations that Alexa would never again take pleasure in wearing them herself. But she was not a superstitious woman. She kept them hidden away only because she had no wish to be reminded of her own lost loves. There was no reason why the unhappiness which she associated with the jewels should continue when she passed them on. In the will she had signed many years ago they were bequeathed to her daughter. Now that Frisca was dead, she must think of someone else.

Pirry didn't need them. There were enough Glanville heirlooms to adorn his wife, should he ever acquire one. Her grandson, Bernard, would presumably have a wife one day—but Alexa wanted to choose someone she knew, not a stranger who had yet to be brought into the family. Barbary would never be able to wear them. During her radiant year of joy with Brad she had blossomed out and become beautiful: but even at her happiest she had never displayed the self-confidence and style necessary to carry off a display which by the standards of these grey days would certainly be ostentatious.

So what about Barbary's two daughters? Asha's pale skin and fair hair would one day show off the rubies to the best advantage. It should have been an easy choice—but Alexa found herself instead thinking of baby Ros. Ruby roses for a rosy child—a little girl abandoned by her mother. These jewels had played a part in the quarrel which led to the death of John Junius Lorimer and to the flight of Ros's grandfather from England. It was fitting that a child descended from both those two proud men should inherit what had once divided them.

Alexa closed the jewel case, locked it, and sent it back to the vault. She drove straight from the bank to the office of her lawyer.

1946

After her brief taste of American comfort, Barbary found the months following her return from San Francisco drab and difficult. Shortages which had been endurable while there was a war still to be won became tedious in a country which had achieved peace but not prosperity. Grant, who had so intensely longed for freedom, fretted against his confinement to a hospital bed, and it did not make life any easier when he insisted on discharging himself and returning to be nursed by his own wife in their flat.

He was still an invalid: weak and appallingly thin. One reason for his survival in captivity must have been the self-control he had shown, even before his capture, in schooling his body to survive on a starvation diet. Now he was paying the penalty, for he seemed unable to relax his mental grip on himself. Barbary had to entice him to eat with tiny and frequent meals which conformed to his medical requirements—since he was still suffering from digestive troubles and vitamin deficiencies. At a time when almost all food was on ration or on points, and when scarce items had to be tracked down to a particular shop at a particular moment, such specialised catering was a nightmare.

Asha was another problem. In spite of Grant's possessive love for his daughter, he could not tolerate the normal noise of a small child. Continually hushed, she was becoming resentful of the man—the stranger—who trembled if she cried but became irritable when she sang. Since Barbary was nervous about leaving the two of them together, in case the little girl should reveal some se-

cret from her fading memories of the past, she used Grant's edg-
iness as an excuse to send Asha to Blaize for holidays and weekends. That removed one cause of strain but, by leaving the two
adults alone, intensified others. Grant, too weak to prove to his
wife how much he loved her, grew frustrated, whilst Barbary—ir-
rationally ashamed of the healthiness of her own soft flesh—felt
guilty that she should find this weakness a relief.

Even as his strength gradually returned, Grant remained indoors. Crowds confused him and he could not cope with the
traffic on the roads. He had no friends in England, and Barbary
had cut herself off from hers. This unnatural life was not disturbed until the autumn of 1946.

The source of the eventual intrusion was a convivial reunion
held in Australia to mark the first anniversary of the Japanese surrender. Five members of the Australian 8th Division described
how they had been led through the Japanese lines in Malay to a
boat in which they were able to escape. They had never known
the name of the planter who helped them—and then went back
to look for more—but although they made it clear that they had
no use as a rule for any bloody Pom, this one, they unanimously
agreed, deserved a bloody medal.

The story was picked up from a Sydney paper by one of the
English Sundays, which enlisted the help of its readers in tracing
the unknown hero. In due course a reporter arrived at the door of
the Lorimers' flat. Grant refused to be interviewed, but Barbary
did not deny the identification, and the journalist knew how to
make two columns out of nothing.

On a snowy morning in December, Barbary took Asha to
school as usual and, also as usual, did her shopping on the way
home. Grant was back in bed when she returned. This did not
surprise her. Although he was strong enough now to walk to the
living room and spend the day in a chair, his emaciated body was
vulnerable to cold. This winter was proving severe and, even with
a doctor's certificate, Barbary could not obtain enough fuel to
keep a fire alight all day. Lacking central heating, the flat was
chilly and bed the warmest place. Grant appeared to be asleep, so
she did not disturb him. She was preparing lunch in the kitchen
two hours later when he appeared in the doorway.

"I have something to say to you, Barbara."

She looked at him in surprise. Since the day of their marriage he had called her Ba. She did not like the diminutive, but had never asked him to change it. The explanation came at once.

"Your stepmother called while you were out. She read in the paper that I was in England, and was surprised that nobody had let her know. Also, she remembered that you'd told her I was dead."

Barbary set down the knife with which she had been chopping apples and prepared for the scene which could no longer be avoided.

"I did think that. You weren't on any prisoner-of-war lists. And someone told me he'd seen you being beaten to death."

"Eleanor thought perhaps you didn't know of my return any more than she had—that you might still be living with your paramour."

If Eleanor had appeared at that moment Barbary would happily have picked up the knife and killed her. Never in her life had she felt such hatred for anyone. She could imagine how her stepmother had expressed concern for Grant's well-being when in reality she was nothing but a meddling busybody.

"Grant, I couldn't upset you when you were so ill. If I'd known you were alive—I came back as soon as I heard—I never meant—"

"I don't wish to discuss it," Grant said. "All those years—so many years, and never any sign of an ending—I thought about you. I longed for you. And all the time—"

"Not all the time," said Barbary desperately. "Grant, you must listen to me."

"No," said Grant. "I don't want to listen to you. I don't want to see you again. It makes me sick to look at you. I want you to get out. Now. I'm going to my room. I shall stay there till you've gone."

Barbary pursued him as he turned away. "Grant, you're not well. You can't look after yourself. Be reasonable. And listen—I didn't *have* to come back to you. If I did come, doesn't that show—"

He shook off her hand and limped stiffly back to the bedroom: she heard the key turn in the lock. Appalled by the suddenness of

what had happened, she went into the living room and sat down
to think.

In one sense it was a relief that the truth was out at last. She
sympathised with the shock Grant felt and did not intend to use
his reaction as an excuse to abandon what she still saw as her
duty. But the task of changing his unforgiving attitude would be
lengthy and difficult. It might be best not to fight at once but to
give his anger time to moderate. He still needed to be cared for,
but she could arrange for him to be readmitted to hospital. As
she went into Asha's room to start packing she was upset, but still
calm enough to make rational plans.

The bed was covered with her own clothes, which Grant must
have carried out of their shared bedroom so that she should have
no excuse to re-enter it. But something was missing—the row of
small stuffed animals which Asha arranged on her pillow every
morning before leaving for school. Suddenly anxious, Barbary
pulled out the drawers which should have contained Asha's
clothes. They were empty.

Not caring if she startled her husband, she pounded with her
fists on his door until it opened.

"Asha!" she cried, too disturbed to be coherent. "Asha?"

"You're not fit to be a mother." Grant's voice was cold. "Not
fit to bring up an innocent child. You'll never see her again."

"She's my daughter. You can't steal her—and you can't look
after a child. You're not well enough. My God, are you going
mad? Be sensible, Grant. Tell me what you've done."

"I've given her to Eleanor."

"You've what! You must be out of your mind. You can't do
that."

"It's done. I gave Eleanor a letter to the headmistress saying
that she had my permission to collect her granddaughter. She'll
have had time to do that by now. I recognise that I can't look
after Asha myself until I'm stronger. Until then, Eleanor will
make sure that she isn't contaminated by her mother's immorality."

"Where is she? She'll be frightened. Where has Eleanor taken
her? Asha needs me. She loves me. Grant, what have you done
with her?"

The door closed and again the key turned. Barbary's heart was pounding with panic. She tried to keep control of herself while she telephoned the retreat house in which Eleanor had stayed at the beginning of her furlough; and then the office of her missionary society. Neither was able to give her present address; but the office mentioned that Eleanor would soon be returning to India. Almost before she had put the receiver down, Barbary heard herself beginning to scream.

That was what Grant wanted, no doubt—the proof that he was successfully punishing her. Sobbing and shouting, she ran out of the flat without pausing to pack her clothes.

In the days which followed, time coiled and unwound itself in erratic fits and starts. Daylight was curtained into darkness and nighttime was illuminated with bright lights. She was always drowsy; but sometimes, in half-awake moments, she saw Alexa at her bedside. She had fled to Blaize, she remembered, sobbing throughout the train journey while the other passengers, embarrassed and worried, tried to discover the trouble. What was the trouble? Of course, Asha had been stolen. Where was Asha?

And then, at Blaize—still sobbing—she had poured out her story. Alexa had reassured her that Asha could not be taken out of the country while she was on her mother's passport and had promised to contact Eleanor. Alexa could not possibly know how implacable Grant was when he believed himself to be right. Where was Asha?

Little by little Barbary dragged herself out of the clinging quicksand of sleep. "Where is Asha?" she asked.

"Safe and well," said Alexa. "I speak to her on the telephone every day. She knows you're in hospital. She sends you lots of love and kisses and hopes you'll be better soon."

"But where is she? I want her back. Why am I in hospital? There's nothing wrong with me. What sort of hospital?"

"You've been very upset," said Alexa. "It's quite natural."

"Do you mean I went mad?"

"Of course not, dear. When someone has good reason to feel distress, then to show distress is to be sane, not mad. You've had a good rest here. You'll be able to come back to Blaize with me any day now. As soon as you're able to think about things calmly."

"How long have I been here?"

"A month."

Obeying instructions, Barbary formulated calm questions in her head before asking them. "What's been happening while I've been here?"

"It's been bitterly cold," Alexa told her. "It still is. The worst winter within living memory. The whole country is frozen up."

"That's not important." Barbary had no interest in the weather.

"Yes, it is. That flat of yours was very cold. While you were there you tried to keep a fire going. You wrapped Grant in rugs and filled hot water bottles. You made hot soup. You persuaded him to eat. I don't suppose he realised how much he depended on you to look after him."

"What are you trying to tell me?" asked Barbary.

"Eleanor is a fool," said Alexa. "Well-intentioned, perhaps, and certainly self-righteous, but a fool. She was so sure that she was doing Grant a kindness that she never stopped to think what the consequences might be, for him as well as for you. And you were ill. I should have thought, I suppose, but at first I was concerned to make sure that you were well looked after. And then—I'd promised you that I'd find Asha, and I did, but it took four days. I went to a lawyer to see how your rights could be preserved. He started proceedings to have Asha made a ward of court, so that she couldn't be taken out of the country without a formal enquiry. It all took time. And I thought Grant had treated you badly. I wasn't feeling any great urgency to call on him. But I did go in the end, to collect your clothes."

"Tell me, please." Alexa's roundabout approach was not best suited to someone just emerging from a nervous breakdown. Barbary could tell that her great-aunt was feeling guilty—but about what?

"I found him suffering from hypothermia. I didn't realise that at the time. I didn't even know what the word meant until later. Grant himself didn't seem to know that he was cold. I could tell he was ill, though. I telephoned the hospital and they readmitted him at once. But it was too late."

"You mean that he's dead?"

"Yes, dear. He's dead—and it was the Japanese who killed him.

You must be quite clear in your mind about this, Barbara dear. There's no way in which you can hold yourself responsible."

"I am responsible," Barbary said. Alexa had told her to be clear in her mind, and this was what clarity forced her to admit. "I won't get upset again, but I ought not to pretend. I am responsible." She would have liked to weep for a man who had endured so many beatings and torments during war only to fall victim to a family quarrel; but it seemed that in her earlier distraught state she had cried out all her tears. "When can I leave here? I must look after Asha."

Alexa hesitated. "There's a slight complication about Asha," she said. "Nothing really to worry about, but . . . After he sent you away, Grant wrote out a new will. I hoped it would prove not to be legal, because it wasn't drawn up by a lawyer. But Mr. Telfer—the barrister I've been consulting on your behalf—says that the courts do recognise a holograph will—that is, all in his own handwriting—as long as it's signed and witnessed and clear in its intention. And the intention was that Asha should inherit all his property and that her grandmother, Eleanor, should be her sole legal guardian."

Barbary was conscious of being watched to see how she would take this. She was surprised by the coldness of her reaction. "Thank you," she said. "That makes it easier. A moment ago I was feeling guilty because I never managed to love Grant as a husband deserves to be loved. But if Grant's bequest to me is a wish that I should hate him, I accept the legacy. I can fight for Asha, I take it?"

"Of course. She's already been made a ward in chancery. Now that you're well enough to sign the papers, you'll apply for her custody. It will be some weeks before the case comes to court. If Eleanor wants to go back to India before that, she'll have to leave Asha behind. And even if she waits, your case will be extremely strong."

"Thank you," said Barbary again. "You've been very kind, Aunt Alexa. I've caused you a lot of trouble. I do appreciate everything you've done."

"That's all right, dear." Alexa bent to kiss Barbary's forehead before standing up to go. "I'm sorry you've had such a difficult time. You'll go back to Brad as soon as this business is settled, I hope. You were so happy together, you two. And little Ros needs a mother. Anyway, get well quickly. Goodbye, dear."

Barbary had had no contact with Brad for several months. His continued pleading with her to return, and her repeated refusals, had upset them both equally. And after Grant came out of hospital she dared not receive letters at the flat. For those two reasons she had asked Brad not to write again—but her feelings for him were unchanged, and the thought of seeing him again made her so happy and excited that she was able to banish her regrets about Grant from her mind.

She must be careful not to act too openly. Eleanor would not hesitate to proclaim the immorality of Asha being returned to a household which had originally been sinful, even if it were soon to become legal. But no one could know about a letter. Barbary smiled to herself in contentment as she began to write to Brad.

1947

1

For more than two months the snow had lain undisturbed over the park and the fields of the home farm. Pirry's plans for a school to train young musicians had at last been put into effect—months after he left England for his self-imposed exile—but the bitter weather was keeping the pupils inside their part of the old house. Only on the terraces immediately surrounding Blaize was the surface of the snow scarred by the tracks of birds and small animals: without the scraps thrown out from the house they would not have survived this exceptionally harsh winter. The trees, their black branches limned in white, were beautiful in their gauntness, and the old house itself was decorated in the same way, with sills and architraves and the patterned brick of unused chimneys all pointed with thin lines of frozen snow. Winter had provided a feast for the eyes—but a series of pitfalls for feet and balance. As Alexa came cautiously down the stone steps towards her car, she was glad of the chauffeur's steadying hand beneath her elbow.

On this morning of February 1947 she had risen early to meet Barbary at the chambers of her lawyer in London. A date had been set for the hearing of the custody case. Eleanor saw it as her duty to defend the rights which Grant had given her—but Mr. Telfer had assured Alexa and Barbary that the court would start from the assumption that the best person to care for a child was her mother. A judge, moreover, might view more tolerantly than Eleanor the conduct of a woman who had believed herself to be a widow. Barbary's behaviour to her husband after his return had been beyond reproach. Her breakdown was unfortunate, in the context, but explicable. Today's meeting was to discuss what arrangements Barbary should propose for Asha's care and education and to advise her how to make a good impression. During the past nerve-racking weeks, Barbary—forbidden by Eleanor to see her daughter, and with so much at stake—had become overanxious. Alexa, though, felt confident that the matter would soon be satisfactorily settled.

She had almost reached the car when the butler caught up with her to say that there had been a call on the internal line: Would she go to the coach house? Alexa hesitated. The icy roads were dangerous and petrol was still rationed; she was using the car only to reach the station and a delay might cause her to miss the train. She wondered whether the visit could wait until she returned or whether Matthew needed something from London.

"Did Sir Matthew say what he wanted?" she asked.

"It wasn't Sir Matthew himself on the line, milady." The butler's words revealed nothing. But Alexa's ear was sensitive and his restrained tone alarmed her. She stared at him for only a second before turning away from the car and walking more rapidly than was wise down the slippery track which led to the coach house.

Matthew had two full-time attendants—a valet and a trained male nurse. As Alexa approached they were standing together in the doorway. If their master was ill, they should have been looking after him. Her fists clenched as the two men stood aside to let her go in. She walked toward Matthew's bed as slowly as though whatever had happened would not be certain until she saw it for herself.

Less than twelve hours earlier she had spent the evening with Matthew. They had played cards for an hour or so and then sat before the fire, sometimes chatting, sometimes silent—contented in each other's company. There had been no sign, nothing to prepare her for the shock of realising that it was to be their last evening together. She looked down at his peaceful face; surely he must only be sleeping.

"There wasn't a sound." The nurse, fearing to intrude but hoping to comfort, spoke softly from the doorway. "I always heard if he called in the night. But there was nothing. He just slipped away."

"You've sent for Dr. Mason, of course." But the doctor could bring nothing but an explanation. She could even guess what the explanation would be. In the thirty years since his plane was shot down, Matthew's paraplegia had made it difficult for him to take exercise. He grew heavy as a result of his immobility and his weight increased the effort required for him to propel the wheel-chair with his arms. He had been warned that he was placing an increasing strain on his heart but would not surrender the only in-dependence he retained in moving under his own power. No doubt thirty more years of life was longer than he would have been promised by the doctors who treated him after the crash. At his last birthday Matthew had been seventy-three years old. Alexa could not reasonably feel surprised by his death, but that did not lessen her shock and sorrow.

In the flurry of the doctor's arrival Alexa's chauffeur took the opportunity of enquiring whether the car would still be needed.

Alexa shook her head. "I shan't be going to London. Ask some-one to ring Mrs. Lorimer and tell her I'm sorry I can't come. And to send my apologies to Mr. Telfer." Her presence at the consul-tation was not essential. It was Barbary who needed to be coached. Alexa's was only a supporting role.

Dr. Mason came out of the bedroom. He had been Matthew's friend as well as doctor, calling once a week for an evening's bridge. "It's not much comfort for those who are left," he said. "But for Matthew himself it was a good way to go. He was paint-ing yesterday, wasn't he?"

Standing beside an easel, Alexa touched the wet paint on the canvas. She nodded, not trusting herself to speak.

There were things to be done, she supposed—all the routines of death to be performed—but she was not ready to embark on them. When Dr. Mason left she went back into the bedroom and closed the door.

Sitting at Matthew's bedside, she was not conscious of the hours passing. She was not thinking—not even feeling anything. It was as though she too were dead, a thin brittle shell enclosing only a void. A long time passed before memory began to crack the ice in her heart, flooding her body with the desolation of her loss.

For more than sixty years Matthew's life had been tangled with her own. Throughout the long period of her widowhood he had been her closest friend, consoling her with his company or the knowledge of his nearness. But long before that, at Brinsley House, he was the playmate and champion of the nine-year-old orphan rescued from the slums. He was the first love of the unsophisticated young girl who lived with her guardian in the country, and many years later he had briefly become the fiancé of the prima donna who was the toast of Paris. The late discovery that they were aunt and nephew had killed their marriage plans but not their love. Alexa had loved many other men, had slept with some of them, had been happily married to one of them: but Matthew had always held a special place in her heart. Now that he was dead, it would remain empty for the rest of her life.

As the memories flooded in she stood up stiffly and climbed the steep stairs to what had once been the loft of the old coach house. More than a hundred of Matthew's canvases were stored there in racks. With some difficulty Alexa carried one of them down to the bedroom.

This was a portrait which had never hung on any wall in the fifty-two years since Matthew painted it: the portrait of a beautiful girl whose shining red-gold hair fell to her slender waist. Her long white dress had lifted at the hem as she turned, caught in the middle of a swirling movement. One arm was raised in a gesture of youthful happiness, and her green eyes sparkled with the secret joy of a girl who for the first time knows herself to be loved.

Alexa was a realist. Each morning as she stared in the glass at her seventy-year-old face she powdered over the fine lines which had etched themselves into her complexion, but never pretended to herself that they did not exist. Nevertheless, it had not been fanciful to believe that, as long as Matthew was alive, her eighteen-year-old beauty had in a sense survived. Until this morning she had still been the same person as the girl who long ago threw up her arm and pirouetted in lighthearted gaiety. But no longer.

A chapter in her life had ended. As the hours passed and the numbness of the shock receded, exposing her at last to its pain, Alexa wished it could be the whole book which closed. If only it were possible to bring one's life to a halt by a single command:

"Now!" To lie, an elderly, ludicrous Juliet, across the bulky body of an even older Romeo.

It was not possible. She would have to learn to live with loneliness. Alexa became aware that she could no longer see the painting, nor even Matthew's face. In the darkness she kissed him tenderly and for the last time. Then, through the soft snow which had begun to fall again during the afternoon, she walked back to Blaize and spent the evening with only a decanter of whisky for company.

By the next day she was ready to deal with the necessary business. There would be a private funeral in the tiny Blaize church and a memorial service in London later. She despatched newspaper announcements and telephoned one or two of Matthew's closest friends. His sister Beatrice had died soon after her East End Mission was destroyed during the war; but Alexa wrote to Matthew's son, John, who might not care that his father was dead but had the right at least to be told. Twice during the day she tried to phone Barbary, but each time the line was engaged. Late in the afternoon she called Mr. Telfer to apologise for missing the consultation. That was when she learned that Barbary had not kept the appointment.

Earlier in the day Alexa had needed to force herself to work. Now her lethargy was abruptly banished and the whole household recognised the urgency with which she enquired who had passed on her message to Mrs. Lorimer the previous day. The line had been engaged, she was told, but no one had thought the fact important enough to warrant disturbing her vigil. Alexa tried the number once more. Then she made an emergency call to the Metropolitan police.

Three hours passed before they rang her back. After breaking into the flat they had taken Barbary to a hospital in case anything could be done for her. But it had been too late.

At the hospital the next day Alexa listened to a pathologist trying to be kind.

"She took an overdose, certainly. That doesn't mean that she did it deliberately. The tablets were prescribed quite properly by the doctor who treated her after her breakdown. Probably she took a strong dose to make sure of a good night's sleep before her appointment. She could have taken the telephone off the hook so that she wouldn't be disturbed. It's all too common for people to leave their tablets within reach and then half wake in the night and take a second dose. At the inquest I shall give it as my opinion that her death was accidental."

"Could it have been prevented?" asked Alexa. "At half-past ten, when she didn't turn up for her appointment—if someone had gone round then, would she still have been alive? Might she have been expecting that? I've read that some people who attempt suicide don't really intend to die. They're hoping to be found. Appealing for help."

"We're not talking about suicide," said the pathologist firmly. "If she had any thought of killing herself, or even of pretending to do so, she would have left a note. There was no note. Mrs. Lorimer's death was an unfortunate accident."

"Thank you." Weary but straight-backed, Alexa stood up to go. She had called at Barbary's flat on the way to the hospital, and the note was in her handbag now. It was not what a doctor meant by a suicide note, and that was why the police had failed to recognise it—for it was written not by Barbary but to her. Only Alexa could have recognised Brad's handwriting on the letter she had found in the wastepaper basket. Only Alexa could appreciate the implications of what he had to say.

It was easy to deduce that Barbary had written first. She would have told Brad that Grant was dead and that she was free to marry. Brad's answer was kind, even sad, but final. He had done his best to bring up his baby single-handed for a year after Barbary's departure, hoping all the while that she would change her mind and return. But in the end he had been forced to recognise the strength of her decision. To provide Ros with a stepmother, he had married again in December.

So a coroner's verdict of accidental death would almost certainly be incorrect. Robbed of one child by hatred and of the other by love, Barbary's desperation had made it impossible for her to look calmly ahead to a future in which Asha at least might well have been restored to her. No one would ever know if she had half hoped to be found in time. She could not have anticipated Matthew's death and its effect upon Alexa's plans.

As Alexa travelled back towards Blaize, she felt great regret at her unintended contribution to the tragedy but not guilt. The roots of her great-niece's unhappiness went too deep for any one small failure to be decisive. Like Frisca and Grant, Barbary was one of the many civilian victims of war. She had been born to a mother made distraught by the horrors of one war. In her adult life, during another war, she had made wrong decisions and regretted right ones. As Pirry would have said, the world was divided into winners and losers. Barbary had been one of the losers.

2

Daffodils forced their heads through the frozen snow, but the bitter weather showed no sign of relaxing its grip. Alexa was imprisoned at Blaize by ice and age and loneliness. The wing in which she lived alone with her servants seemed bleak and empty. The old library which had become her drawing room was still crowded with photographs, but now they peopled the room only with ghosts. She no longer had Barbary's problems to keep her busy; she could no longer look forward throughout the day to the moment when she would walk down to the coach house to sit with Matthew. Instead, her only company in the evenings was the wireless set and the whisky decanter, and each day she moved towards them a little earlier than on the day before.

Two funerals within a week had convinced her that the family itself was dying. But one day early in March the butler announced an unexpected caller.

"A Major Ryan is here, milady. From the Control Commission in Berlin, he says."

Major Ryan was younger than his rank suggested, and properly polite.

"It's good of you to see me without an appointment, Lady Glanville. I'll come straight to the point. Does the name of Dr. Kate Lorimer mean anything to you?"

"Kate? Kate! Are you telling me that Kate is still alive, Major?" Alexa's hands trembled as she poured a drink for her visitor and another for herself. Grant had already returned, as it were, from the dead, but the family had failed to keep him alive. Was there another survivor?

"I can't precisely tell you that. I'm hoping you may be able to tell me. A woman has presented herself to us in Berlin claiming that name. She appears to be Russian and has no papers—no proof of any kind—to support her statement that she's a British subject. She said that you would vouch for her."

"Of course Kate's British." Alexa frowned at the major for doubting it. "Although her father spent his working life as a missionary in Jamaica, he belonged to an old Bristol family. Certainly she's British."

"You mean that someone born as Kate Lorimer is British. We still have to establish that this woman has a right to the name. We and the Displaced Persons Commission see hundreds of refugees every day—homeless, stateless, desperate to establish a claim on some country which will take them in. This applicant could have become aware of an identity—someone else's identity—which it could be advantageous to adopt. Would you be kind enough to describe Kate Lorimer to me?"

"It's so long since I saw her. We lost touch years ago." Alexa struggled with her memory and succeeded in recalling a scene from what had now to be called the First World War. Brinsley Lorimer had just left for France, one of the thousands who would never return. His sister Kate, appalled to see wounded men lying untreated in the railway station, declared her intention of going to the front herself. "It's the fire in her eyes that I remember best. They were green eyes, like mine. And her hair was a sandy kind of auburn. The colour of a lion's mane, and just as thick. She could never get it tidy, poor girl. Her face was freckled. She was tall—like me again—but never really slim. Sturdy, you'd call her. She was a great fighter, was Kate: an idealist. It's the eyes I remember best—those shining eyes."

The major sighed. "But that was a long time age?"

"Yes. If you mean she doesn't look like that now, well, of course, she wouldn't. She was in her early twenties then. Now she must be—what?—fifty-six, fifty-seven?"

"It's not just age that may have changed her. This woman has been starving. All her hair has fallen out. She did tell us it had been reddish once, but there's nothing to prove it. And her eyes are dull. She lost her daughter. That was what brought her to us, the search for her daughter. Or rather, that was what took her halfway across Europe, trying to find where the German labour camps were, who was in them. The moment when she came to us, I suppose, was really the moment when she gave up the search." He took a notebook from his pocket and studied it. "Well, our applicant is certainly tall and green-eyed, so that's a good start."

"Did she tell you anything about her family?" asked Alexa.

"Yes. I have a good deal of information about the relationships she claims. She gave us several names, but only one address, yours. So it seemed simplest to come to you first. What relation is Kate Lorimer to you, Lady Glanville?"

"I'm her aunt. Her father was my half brother."

"She mentioned a Dr. Margaret Scott."

"Another aunt of hers. But she died almost ten years ago."

"She had two brothers, she told us, but one was killed in 1916. What about the surviving brother?"

"Grant Lorimer died a few weeks ago."

"May I ask how you came to lose touch with your niece, Lady Glanville?"

Alexa described how Kate had been sent to Serbia with one of the Women's Medical Units and caught up in the Serbian Retreat of 1916. It was a story which seemed to have its roots in a different life. "She was decorated by the Serbs for leading her patients to safety over the Albanian mountains. When they were sent to reinforce the Russians, she went with them. It's too long ago for me to remember the details. But I know she was in St. Petersburg at the time of the revolution."

"And you never heard from her again—in thirty years?"

"A year or two after the war a Russian brought us some news. He told us that she'd married a Russian and had a baby daughter. She was looking after war orphans somewhere near St. Petersburg —well, it was Petrograd then, and now it's Leningrad." Alexa shook her head over the confusion of names. "Anyway, Kate was in sympathy with the revolution, he claimed—and it could have been true. Even before she left England she used to have some very odd ideas. The orphans needed her, and she was going to stay. But because of the Intervention—I suppose you're too young to know what the Intervention was."

"You're referring to our support for the Whites against the Reds?"

"Yes. Because of the Intervention it would have been dangerous if anyone had known she was English. She was passing for a Russian and didn't dare receive letters from England. We kept hoping that a time would come when she felt safe enough to write. But she never did, and we had no address. How is she?"

"In a poor physical state. I'd say she's been living at starvation level for some time—and living rough. She must have been strong to start with. She's obsessed with the need to find her daughter, but she's having to accept that she's failed. The sad thing is that the girl is on record as surviving to the end of the war and may well be alive."

"Then she'd go home, surely. Wouldn't it have been better for Kate to wait there?"

"She told us that her orphanage was mined by the Germans. They gave the occupants time to get out and then blew the place up just as the Russian Army arrived to liberate it. It was completely demolished. And there wasn't a building left with a roof in the whole village. I don't imagine the Russian climate lends itself to sleeping under the stars. Effectively, the place has ceased to exist. This woman had to take the children away and didn't get back until six months after the war ended. If the daughter had turned up in the meantime, she'd have found nothing but a ruin and no one who could give her any information. And it seems that the girl—Ilsa, her name is—was never allowed to learn that she had any English connections. It would have been too dangerous. So there's no chance of her getting here."

Alexa sat stunned, unable to visualise a world in which people could simply be lost. In the blitz on London there had been deaths in plenty, and homes had been demolished. But the structure of society had remained uncracked. Alexa had lost one home but always had an address. She was appalled to think that across the Channel, in the devastated countries of Europe, thousands of people, torn from their families, might never be able to find them again. She poured herself another drink and invited her visitor to join her.

"No, thank you. I'm on my way home for a week's leave. Mustn't keep the family waiting any longer, but I thought I ought to see you myself. It's an unusual case." He stood up to leave. "You've been very helpful, Lady Glanville. I've only one more question. We would need a settled address for Dr. Lorimer before we could issue a temporary passport. If this woman *is* your niece —and what you've told me seems to confirm it—would you be prepared to guarantee her a home here?"

"Of course." Only after her visitor had gone did Alexa begin to wonder about sharing her house with someone whose experiences would have turned her into a stranger. They had not even been close friends in the years before the first war. Kate's social conscience had led her to consider Alexa's love of jewels and beautiful dresses frivolous. Only for the short period when they worked together to convert Blaize into a military hospital had they grown to like and respect each other.

Kate was in poor shape, the major had said. Perhaps as bad as Grant had been. And Alexa had never had any great family feeling. Her love for Matthew had nothing to do with his being a Lorimer. She had done her best to support Barbary, but her best had not been good enough. It had been no trouble for the chatelaine of Blaize to provide a home for any member of the family who needed one, but she had never felt a loving determination to help someone purely because of a family relationship. That urge had been her sister Margaret's ruling emotion. For the first time in her life, Alexa felt it now. Kate Lorimer, a defeated woman, might well prove as unlovable as her brother Grant—but Alexa was sure that she could love her.

Was it her own loneliness that made her so sure? Or the realisation that there were so few of the Lorimers left? Alexa rang for more whisky and stared at the heavy Victorian portrait of her father on the library wall. Where now were all the grandchildren of John Junius Lorimer? Matthew and Beatrice and Arthur; Kate and Brinsley and Grant; Margaret's only son, Robert; Frisca, who had loved him; and Pirry, the youngest of the cousins? All dead, all but Pirry, who had become an exile—and now, it seemed, Kate, who was about to return.

Well, the family was not finished yet. There were a few to keep it going. Asha for one—and Alexa, shocked into a sudden sobriety, realised that she had almost allowed Asha to be stolen without a fight!

The court hearing to settle her guardianship was only a few days away. Alexa—a great-great-aunt, seventy years old—was not on the face of it the ideal guardian for a child just approaching her sixth birthday. But then, no more was Eleanor, a step-grandmother with no experience of bringing up children of her own—and on the point of leaving for India, where Hindus and Moslems were busily massacring each other. Tomorrow, Alexa decided, she would telephone Eleanor and insist on taking Asha out for a day. Then she would bring the little girl to Blaize and tell her what to say.

3

Alexa unlocked the door which led from her private quarters at Blaize to the part of the old building which was occupied by the school. She was conscious of Asha's hand gripping hers tightly. Perhaps the little girl was afraid that they were trespassing. On all her previous visits she had played in the west wing, which was Alexa's home, or in the gardens. "Is this the house next door?" she asked anxiously.

"No, it's all part of Blaize."

"Does it belong to you?"

Pirry's absentee ownership was too complicated to explain to a child, so Alexa agreed that the house was hers. "I let a school use it," she said. "So I don't go in very often, because I don't want to get in the way. But they have concerts on Saturdays. I go to those. If you come to live with me, you could go the concerts as well."

"Do I know what a concert is?" asked Asha. It was a reminder that neither Barbary nor Grant had been interested in music. The gap in Asha's upbringing was something to be remedied, but not at this moment. However, the question deserved an answer. Alexa lifted Asha to look through the glass peephole of what had once been a butler's pantry and was now a practice room. A ten-year-old boy, his forehead furrowed with concentration, was working out the fingering for an exercise on his violin.

"He's practising a piece of music, and when he's got it right he'll stand up on a platform and play it to an audience. Other children will play other instruments—pianos, cellos, flutes, everything you can think of. Sometimes they'll play them alone and sometimes they'll sit together in an orchestra and play all the instruments at once. That's a concert." She opened the door of the old servants' hall and listened to a string quartet for a few moments before leading the way upstairs to continue the tour of inspection.

It didn't take long to realise that the visit was a mistake. The size of the house was out of scale with a five-year-old's imagination. Alexa had thought to offer Asha a kingdom to explore, but saw that instead it was an uncharted territory in which to become lost. The long gallery at the top of the Tudor house could wait for another day. She took the little girl back into the familiar rooms of the west wing.

"Do they have to do lessons even on Sundays, those children?" Asha asked in surprise as the communicating door closed behind them.

"No. They have classes on all the other days. But on Sundays they can do anything they like. Swim, play games, walk, anything."

"But they aren't doing those things. They're all playing music."

Alexa as a young woman had needed no bribes or threats to keep her at the piano for several hours a day, practising scales and exercises and songs. Ambition and the desire for perfection had driven her on, and her reward had been that for a time she had possessed the most beautiful voice in Europe. Fifty years had passed since that apprenticeship ended, but the memory of it helped her to take for granted the dedication shown by the young musicians at Blaize. She explained to Asha that all the children at this special school were there because they were good at music and wanted to become even better.

"They have to do ordinary lessons—reading and writing and sums—just like you. But what they like best is getting their music right. Some of them get up at six o'clock every morning to be first in the practice rooms. By the time they leave Blaize, they'll be very good—and that's what they want." They were back now in the old library which served as Alexa's drawing room. She allowed herself to drift towards the whisky decanter, pouring a generous helping to make the next part of the conversation flow more smoothly. "It's very important, Asha, to be good at something. It doesn't matter much what it is, as long as you like doing it. You need to choose something, and tell yourself that nothing but the best will do, and work hard until you can feel proud of yourself."

"Are you good at something, Aunt Alexa?"

"I was once. A long time ago." A side table was covered with photographs of Alexa in her operatic roles. She picked up one which showed her as Princess Amneris and held it out for Asha's inspection. Probably the child would not know what an opera singer was, so there was no point in boasting that she had once been a prima donna.

"That lady is very pretty." Asha made no connection between the beautiful princess and her elderly aunt. "What shall I be good at?"

"I don't know. We shall have to find out. Perhaps you'll be good at music. Then you could have lessons with the teachers here."

"I don't think I shall like music," said Asha seriously. "But I'd like to use their swimming pool, if the teachers will let me."

"You can do that anyway. It's *my* swimming pool. You can swim any time in the school holidays, and quite often in the term as well." Alexa felt no compunction about offering bribes to Asha —she merely wanted to discover what would be most acceptable.

"Granny Scott says I'm going to stay with her. She says we're going on a big boat, to live with brown boys and girls in India."

"Granny Scott doesn't really want to look after you. She doesn't know how to, because she's never had a little girl of her own, like I have. She isn't even your real granny. She married your grandfather, but that's different. She just thinks she *ought* to take care of you." The truth, like the swimming pool, was something to be concealed or produced at exactly the right moment. It could even be, Alexa thought as she refilled her glass, that she was in fact speaking the truth. She didn't know and she didn't care.

"I have to have someone to look after me." Pale-faced and straight-backed, Asha stared woodenly ahead, a child concealing distress. "When I'm grown up I shall look after myself, but I can't do it yet."

"Of course you can't, darling. *I'm* going to look after you. You'll have a lovely home here. We'll be very happy. Let me show you the bedroom which will be yours if you live here." On her holiday visits Asha had slept in a dressing room, conveniently close to Alexa's own bedroom, but too small for a permanent resident. There were two flights of stairs to be climbed now, but what caused Alexa to pause before she opened the door was more than mere breathlessness.

The nursery suite had always been in the west wing. Pirry had spent the first years of his life here, with Frisca in the schoolroom next door. But Alexa's flash of memory concerned a child who was not her own. It was to this door that Asha's mother was carried when she was only a few weeks old—her own mother dead and her father, Robert, missing and believed to have been killed in battle.

That was in the terrible period at the end of 1917 when the war appeared lost and casualty lists were driving women all over England to despair. Alexa and her husband, Piers, had offered the shelter of their home and the services of a nurse, but they were too strained and depressed to love the new arrival as they should have done. Little Pirry had been jealous and Frisca, dancing with energy, had felt no interest in a baby which could not move from the cradle. Only Grant, struggling to overcome the disabilities with which he had been born, had welcomed Barbary to Blaize.

It had been a bleak and unhappy beginning to a life which had ended, too soon, in even greater unhappiness. Alexa found herself overwhelmed by sadness and guilt at the thought of the girl who had experienced the overwhelming joy of loving and being loved for such a short time. Her voice quavered as she told Asha, "This was your mother's bedroom when she was your age."

"I want my mummy." Tears flowed down Asha's long, pale face as she stood in the middle of the room, abandoning herself to grief in a manner made more heart-rending by the fact that she did not sob or wail or make any sound except to repeat the anguished cry, "I want my mummy."

"Of course you do, my darling." Down on her knees, Alexa drew the stiff young body towards her, hugging and kissing the disconsolate child: their tears mingled with the touching of their cheeks. "Of course you do. But you know that she's dead. You know that she can't come back to you. Won't you love me instead, and let me love you? It's lonely for me here all by myself. We can look after each other. Trust me, Asha."

Sixty years earlier Alexa herself had stood by her mother's deathbed, stamping her foot and raging in a furious refusal to accept what had happened. It was this child's great-grandmother who had opened her heart and home to the young orphan then, and loved her until she died. If Alexa now could repay one-hundredth part of the care she had received then, everything would be all right.

Gulping back her sobs in an effort to control herself, Asha began to hiccup. Alexa filled a glass of water for her.

"Take seven sips from the wrong side of the glass," she commanded. "That will make the hiccups keep quiet."

Wide-eyed, Asha looked up at her. "I know that already. My mummy used to do it that way as well."

"Your mummy grew up in this house, just as you're going to." Alexa took the opportunity of wiping the tears from both their faces. "You'll learn to do everything just as she would have taught you, the way she did it herself. As long as you remember her, she'll be in this house with you." But you'll be happier, Alexa promised silently.

"Suppose Granny Scott won't let me stay here."

"She's not the one who'll decide." Alexa drew Asha towards her, gripping both hands tightly. "Listen to me carefully, Asha. Tomorrow you'll be taken to a room with a lot of people in it. Some of them will make speeches. You probably won't understand them. I shall be there, and so will Granny Scott. But one person will be more important than all the others. He's called a judge, and he'll sit in a special chair. Probably he'll wear a special white wig to show how important he is. He's going to decide who should look after you, and we shall all have to do what he says. When everyone else has finished talking, he'll ask you to go close to him—or he may take you into another room. You mustn't be frightened of him. He's a kind man and he wants to make you happy. He'll ask you what *you* would like, what you'd choose to do. He may not choose the same thing in the end, but he'll ask you. And then you must speak up as loudly as you can and say what you want. Do you understand?"

Asha nodded, her fair hair swinging over her shoulders. "I shall say I want to live at Blaize with you."

"That's a good girl." Alexa smiled into Asha's eyes. "We'll look after each other here. You and I, together."